THE MAN FROM

THE
DIOGENES
CLUB

THE MAN FROM
THE DIOGENES CLUB

MR. KIM NEWMAN, ESQ.

TITAN BOOKS

The Man from the Diogenes Club
Print edition ISBN: 9781781165744
E-book edition ISBN: 9781781165751

Published by Titan Books
A division of Titan Publishing Group Ltd
144 Southwark Street, London, SE1 0UP

First Titan edition: December 2017
2 3 4 5 6 7 8 9 10

The stories first appeared in the following venues:

'The End of the Pier Show' in *Dark of the Night* (1997)
'Moon Moon Moon' on *Subterranean Online* (2009)
'You Don't Have to Be Mad' in *White of the Moon* (1999)
'Tomorrow Town' on *SciFiction* (2000)
'Egyptian Avenue' in J. K. Potter's *Embrace the Mutation* (2002)
'Soho Golem' on *SciFiction* (2004)
'The Serial Murders' on *SciFiction* (2005)
'Cold Snap' in *The Secret Files of the Diogenes Club* (2007)
'The Man Who Got Off the Ghost Train' in *The Man From the Diogenes Club* (2006)
'Swellhead' in *Night Visions* 11 (2004)

A CIP catalogue record for this title is available from the British Library.

Printed and bound by CPI Group (UK) Ltd, Croydon, CR0 4YY

For Chris Roberson

Contents

THE END OF THE PIER SHOW

Icy winds barrelled in off the sea, lashing the front like an invisible tidal wave. Fred Regent shoved his fists deeper into the pockets of his yellow silk bomber jacket.

Apart from keeping his hands out of the cold blast, Fred was trying to prevent himself from constantly fingering the bee-fuzz on his scalp where he used to have hair like Peter Noone's. If his bonce went blue, it'd look like a copper's helmet and that'd be the end of this lark. Going undercover with the Boys now seemed a lot less like a comfortable way out of uniform than a protracted invitation to a busted mug and a cryo-dunking in the channel.

'It's April,' said Jaffa, the Führer Boy. 'Whatever happened to spring?'

'New ice age, mate,' said Oscar, the 'intellectual' of the Boys. 'Hitler's astrologers said it'd happen.'

The Boys clumped along the front, strutting in their steel-toed, cleat-soled Docs. They shivered as a razor-lash of wind cut through turn-up jeans, Fred Perry shirts and thin jackets. Only Oscar could get away with a duffel coat and Jaffa sometimes sneered 'mod' at him. The Boys were skins and hated mods; not to mention hippies, grebos, Pakis, queers, students, coons, yids, chinks, car-park attendants, and – especially – coppers.

Fred wondered if the others felt the cold on their near-exposed skulls the way he did. If so, they were too pretend-hard to mention it. Skinhead haircuts were one of the worst ideas ever. Just as the Boys were some of the worst people ever. It'd be a pleasure putting this bunch of yobs inside. If he lived that long.

The point of this seaside excursion was for Fred to get in with Jaffa. A bag of pills, supposedly nicked with aggro from a Pakistani chemist's, had bought him into the Boys. But Kevin Jaffa, so-called King Skin, didn't trust anyone until they'd helped him put the boot into a third party. It was sort of an initiation, but also made all his mates accomplices in the event of legal complications.

It had seemed a lot simpler back in London, following DI Price's briefing on King Skin and the Boys, getting into the part, learning the lingo ('Say "coon", not "nigger"') from a wheelchair-bound expert nark, picking out the wardrobe, even getting the haircut. Steel clippers snicking over his head like an insectile lawnmower. Now, barely two months out of Hendon, he was on his own, miles away from an incident room, with no one to shout for if he got on the receiving end of an unfriendly boot.

What was he supposed to do? How far was he supposed to go?

For the Boys, this was a pleasure trip, not business. And Fred was supposed to be stopping Jaffa's business.

On the train down, Jaffa had taken over a compartment, put his Docs up on the seat to defy British Rail, and encouraged everyone to pitch in ideas for entertainment. Nicking things, smashing things, getting plastered and snatching a shag were the most popular suggestions. Petty stuff, day-outing dirty deeds. Fred was supposed to let minor offences slide until he had the goods on one of Jaffa's Big Ideas, but he supposed he'd have to draw a line if it looked like some innocent was going to get hurt.

'Everything's bloody shut,' Doggo whined. 'I could do with six penn'orth of chips.'

Jaffa cuffed the smaller skin, who couldn't be older than fourteen.

2

'All you bloody think of is chips, Doggo. Set your sights higher.'

The shops along the seafront were mostly boarded up, battered by wind-blown sand and salt. Stacks of deckchairs on the beach were chained down under tarpaulins. A few hardy dog-walkers were out and about. But no one else. The whole town was shut up and stored away.

They came to the pier.

'Let's take a look-see,' Jaffa suggested, climbing over a turnstile. There was a booth nearby but it wasn't manned. The Boys trooped after their leader, clumping onto shaky boards. They fought the wind, walking towards the pagoda-like green structure at the end of the pier.

On a board in the shape of an arrow was written THIS WAY TO 'THE EMPORIUM', PALACE OF WONDERS, ARCADE OF EDUCATION, VARIETY NITELY. ADMISSION: 6d. There was no admission price in new money.

As he clambered over the turnstile, Fred noticed a poster on the side of the booth. A comical drunk in a long army greatcoat sat in a pub with a slinky blonde draped round him. Half the woman's face was covered by a wave of hair; she was smoking a cigarette in a holder, the smoke forming a skull with swastika eye-sockets. The slogan was CARELESS TALK COSTS LIVES. The poster might have been up since the War.

No, the colours were too bright, as if just from the printer's. It must be part of an exhibition.

'Come on, Fred,' said Oscar. 'Last one in's a sissy.'

Seamouth wasn't big enough to support the pleasure pier these days, but it had been a fashionable resort around the turn of the century. Seventy-odd years of decline hadn't yet dragged the attraction into the sea. The structure projected out from the beach, struts and pillars temporarily resisting the eternal push and pull of the waves. It couldn't stand up on its own much longer. Everything creaked, like a ship at sea.

Looking down, Fred saw churning foam through ill-fitting, water-warped boards. He thought he saw crabs tossed around in the water.

They reached the Emporium. It was turquoise over gunmetal, the paint coming off in swathes. Ingraham put a dent in a panel with his armoured toe. Freckles flew off.

'This shed looks about ready to collapse,' Oscar said, shaking a loose railing. 'Maybe we should give it a shove.'

Oscar hopped from one foot to another, looking like a clog-dancer, shoulders heaving.

'Everything's shut,' Doggo whined.

Jaffa sneered with pity at the kid. A three-inch orange line on the King Skin's scalp looked like a knife scar but was a birth malformation, skull-plates not knit properly. It was probably why he was a psycho nutter. With an elbow, Jaffa smashed a pane of glass and reached inside. He undid a clasp and pulled a door open, then stood aside like a doorman, indicating the way in.

Doggo straightened himself, took hold of his lapels, and strutted past. Jaffa tripped him and put a boot on his backside, shoving the kid into the dark.

Doggo whined as he hit the floor.

Jaffa went inside and the Boys followed.

Fred got out his lighter and flicked on a flame. The Emporium seemed bigger inside than it had on the outside, like Doctor Who's police box. There were posters up on free-standing boards, announcing shows and exhibitions that must have closed years ago, or attractions that were only open in the two weeks that passed for summer on the South Coast. Mysteries of the Empire, *Chu Chin Chow*, Annual Talent Contest.

'Don't think anyone's home,' Oscar said.

Fred couldn't understand why Jaffa was so interested in the pier. There was nothing here to nick, no one to put the boot into, nothing much worth smashing, certainly no bints to shag. But Jaffa had been drawn here. The King Skin was on some private excursion in his own head.

Was there something going on?

Stepping into the Emporium, Fred felt on edge, as if something just out of sight were watching. The atmosphere was heavy, between the smell of the sea and the mustiness of damp and forgotten exhibits. There was a greenish submarine glow, the last of cloudy daylight filtered through painted-over glass.

'I don't like it,' whined Doggo.

Jaffa launched a half-strength kick into the kid's gut, curling him into a foetal horseshoe around his boot. Doggo's lungs emptied and his face shut. He was determined not to cry, poor bastard.

If there wasn't a Paki or a hippie or a queer about, Jaffa was just as happy to do over one of his mates. DI Price thought there might be something political or big-time criminal about the Boys, but it was just brutishness, a small-minded need to hurt someone else.

Fred's fists knotted in his pockets. He wanted this over, and Jaffa put away.

It was getting dark outside and it couldn't be later than seven. This was a weird stretch of the coast.

Oscar was looking at the posters.

'This sounds great,' he said.

HITLER'S HORRORS: THE BEASTS OF WAR.

The illustration was crude, circus-like. A caricature storm trooper with fangs, machine gun held up like an erection, crushing a map of Europe under jackboots.

He remembered the CARELESS TALK COSTS LIVES poster.

This looked like a propaganda show left over from the War. Thirty years too late to scare the kiddies, but too bloody nasty to get nostalgic about. Fred's parents and their friends were always on about how it had been in the War, when everyone was pulling together. But Fred couldn't see it. He came along too late, and only just remembered when chocolate was rationed and half the street was bomb sites.

Ingraham clicked his heels and gave a Nazi salute. He was the pretend fascist, always reading paperbacks about the German side of WWII, ranting against Jews, wearing swastika medallions. He talked about 'actions' rather than 'aggro', and fancied himself as the Boys' master planner, the Goebbels of the gormless. Not dangerous, just stupid.

Fred's lighter was getting hot. He let the flame shrink. The storm trooper's eyes seemed to look down as the light went away.

There was a gushing trickle and a sharp smell. One of the skins was relieving himself against a wall.

'Dirty beast,' Oscar sneered.

'Don't like it here,' whined Doggo.

Fred knew what the kid meant.

'Doggo's right,' Jaffa said. 'Let's torch this shithole. Fred, you still got fluid in that lighter?'

If he helped, he'd be committing a crime, compromising any testimony he gave.

'It's out, chum,' he said.

'I got matches,' said Ingraham.

'Give the boy a prize,' said Jaffa.

Ingraham passed over the Swan Vestas. Jaffa had the others scout for newspapers or anything small that would burn. After hesitating a moment, Fred started ferreting around too. Arson, he could just about live with. At least it wasn't duffing up some shopkeeper or holding a bint down while the others shagged her.

And there was something about the pier. He wouldn't mind if it burned. By sticking out from the shore, it was inviting destruction. Fire or water, it didn't make much difference.

They split up. Though the Emporium was partitioned into various spaces, the walls only reached just above head height. Above everything was a tent-like roof of glass panels like the Crystal Palace, painted over with wavy green.

He found a row of penny-in-the-slot machines, lit up by tiny interior bulbs. He had three big dull old pennies mixed in with the shiny toy money that now passed for small change, and decided he might as well shove them into the machines.

In smeary glass cases were little puppet scenes that played out tiny dramas. The theme of the collection was execution. A French Revolution guillotining: head falling into a basket as the blade fell on the neck of a tin aristocrat. A British public hanging: felon plunging on string through a scaffold trapdoor, neck kinking with the drop. An Indian Mutiny reprisal: rebel strapped over the end of a cannon that discharged with a puff to blow away his midriff.

When he ran out of proper pennies – d. not p. – he wasn't sorry that he couldn't play the Mexican firing squad, the Spanish garrotting or the American electrocution. The little death scenes struck him as a funny sort of entertainment for kiddies. When the new money had completely taken over, penny-in-the-slot machines would all get chucked out and that would be the end of that.

Round the corner from the machines was a dark passage. He tripped over something. Someone. Scrambling up, he felt the bundle. He flicked on his lighter again. The flame-light was reflected in a bloody smear that had been a face. From the anorak, Fred recognised Oscar. He was barely alive, cheeks seeping in time with his neck-pulse. Something had torn the hood of flesh from his skull, leaving a ragged line along his chin. He wasn't a

7

skinhead any more; he was a skinned head.

Fred stood. He hadn't heard anything. Had Jaffa done this, somehow? Or was there someone else in here?

'Over here,' he called. 'It's Oscar.'

Doggo was the first there. He took one look and screamed, sounding very young. Ingraham slapped him.

Jaffa had a flick-knife out. Its blade was clean, but he could have wiped it.

'Did you do this?' Jaffa asked Fred.

Fred heard himself whimpering.

'Fuck me,' someone said. Everyone shouted, talked and moaned. Someone was sick.

'Shut up,' said Jaffa.

In the quiet, something was moving. Fred turned up the flame. The Boys huddled in the circle of light, scared cavemen imagining spirits in the dark beyond the fire. Something heavy was dragging itself, knocking things aside. And something smaller, lighter, pattered along on its own. They were circling the skinheads, getting closer.

The lighter was a hot coal in Fred's fingers. They all turned round, peering into the dark. There were partitions, covered with more posters, and glass cases full of battlefield dioramas. Nearest was a wall-sized cartoon of a bug-eyed demon Hitler scarfing down corpses, spearing a woman on his red, forked tail.

The heavy thing held back and the light thing was getting closer. Were there only two? Fred was sure he heard other movements, other footfalls. The steps didn't sound like shod feet. But there was more than an animal purpose in the movement.

Doggo was whimpering.

Even Jaffa was scared. The King Skin had imagined he was the devil in the darkness; now that was a shredded illusion. There were worse things out there than in here.

Fred's fingers were in agony but he didn't dare let the flame fall.

The Hitler poster tipped forwards, cracking down the middle. Hitler's face broke in half. And another Hitler face – angry eyes, fleck of moustache, oiled hairlick – thrust forwards into the light, teeth bared. A child-sized figure in a puffy grey Hitler mask reached out with gorilla-length arms.

Fred dropped the lighter.

Something heavy fell on them, a living net of slithering strands.

There was screaming all around.

He was hit in the face by a dead hand.

The net cut against his palm like piano-wire. Seaweed wound between the strings stung, like nettles. A welt rose across his face.

The net was pulled away.

Warm wetness splashed on his chest, soaking in. Something flailed in the dark, meatily tearing.

Someone was being killed.

He blundered backwards, slamming into a partition that hadn't been there, a leathery elephant's hide that resisted a little, and shifted out of the way. His palm was sandpapered by the moving, living wall.

There was a gunshot, a fire-flash and a loud report. Fred's eyes burned for a moment but he wasn't hit. Someone else had taken a bullet.

In the momentary light, he'd seen things he didn't believe. Uniformed creatures falling upon the Boys with human intellect and demon savagery. Doggo's head a yard from his body, stringy bone and muscle unravelling between his neck and shoulders. On his chest squatted something with green wolf-eyes and a foot of lolling tongue.

Fred bolted and collided with someone.

'Fucking hell,' said Jaffa, gripping Fred's arm.

They ran together, skinhead and copper, fleeing the other things. They made for a cold indraught of outside air.

Something came after them.

Jaffa pushed ahead and was first through the door.

None of the others was with them.

Fred stumbled out of the Emporium. They couldn't have been inside more than fifteen minutes, but night had fallen. There was no light from the town, no yellow street lamps, no electric glow from homes up on the hill. The shapes of buildings were just discernible, but it was as if no one was home.

Jaffa turned to Fred, knife raised.

An orange tendril snaked out of the Emporium at chest height and brushed Jaffa's head. It was like a squirt of living flame. The King Skin's eyes widened and mouth opened, but the fire took hold inside his skull and poured out.

He was still recognisable, still alive. Fred ran away, encumbered by the heavy boots he wasn't used to. Jaffa, a living candle, stumped after him. Fred vaulted the turnstile and looked back. Jaffa's head was a pumpkin lantern, rushing forwards in the dark.

Fred tripped and fell to his knees, not believing what he saw.

'Oi you,' someone shouted, at Jaffa.

A man in uniform stood near Fred, shaking his fist. He had a tommy's tin helmet, but wore blue cotton overalls. An armband bore the letters ARP. He was in his sixties, and had no chin to speak of, just a helmet strap under his lower lip.

Fred was near fainting.

The King Skin stopped, flame pluming six or seven feet above his head, and howled.

'Oi you,' the ARP man shouted again, 'put that bloody light out!'

'Then Jaffa was blown to one side, as if the wind had caught hold of his fire. He was pitched against the loose railings and went over the side, trailing orange and red flames. He hit the sea with a hiss. Then everything went completely black. When I woke, it was early in the morning. The bloke in the tin hat was gone. I hot-footed it for the station and got the first train back here.

'There's something not right in Seamouth.'

As he told his story, Fred concentrated on Euan Price's cold eyes. The Detective Inspector asked few questions and took no notes. He didn't interject exclamations of disbelief, or shout at him that he was a nutter or on drugs or just plain lying.

Yesterday, Constable Fred Regent had lived in a world with law and order. Now, there was only anarchy.

He sat at the desk in the interview room, feeling himself under the spotlight, cold cup of New Scotland Yard tea in front of him. Price sat opposite, listening. The strangers leaned on the sound-proofed walls, half in and half out of the light.

It disturbed him that Price could accept the horror story with such serious calm. Either his superior believed him, or the consultants were psychiatrists in disguise.

There were two of them, dressed like peacocks.

The woman was in her early twenties and could have been a model: seamless mane of red hair down to her waist; Italian mouth, painted silver; Viking cheekbones; unnaturally huge, green eyes. She wore a purple leather miniskirt and matching waistcoat with a blinding white roll-neck pullover and knee-length high-heeled white boots. Her only visible jewellery was an Egyptian-looking silver amulet with an inset emerald. A red scar-line cut through one fine eyebrow, a flaw to set off perfection.

The man was even more striking. He could have been anywhere between thirty and fifty. A coal-black mass of ringlets spilled onto his shoulders Charles II style, and he wore a pencil-line Fu Manchu moustache. His face was gaunt to the point of unhealthiness and dark enough to pass for a Sicilian or a Tuareg. Thin and tall and bony, he wore a fluorescent green velvet jacket with built-up lapels and collar, tight red Guardsman's britches with a yellow stripe up the sides and stack-heeled, elastic-sided, banana-coloured boots. A multi-coloured explosion of a scarf was knotted round his neck, and his shirt was rippling mauve silk. He had several rings on each finger, a silver belt buckle in the shape of a demon face with a curved dagger thrust through its eyes, and a single gold hoop on his right ear.

As he listened to Fred's story, he played with a wide-brimmed fedora that matched his jacket, slipping long fingers in and out of a speckled snakeskin band. He looked as if he'd be equally happy on the foredeck of a pirate ship or in a coffee bar on the King's Road.

The contrast with Euan Price in his Marks & Sparks mac was vivid. Whoever these consultants were, they were not with the police.

Though they were the sort he had been taught at Hendon to regard as suspicious, Fred had a warm feeling from these two. They might dress strangely, but did not look at him as if they thought he were a maniac. As he went through it all, starting with his undercover job but concentrating on the happenings at Seamouth Pier, the woman nodded in sympathy and understanding. The man's violet eyes seemed to glint with tiny fireflies.

Fred had expected to be dismissed as a madman.

After the story was done, Price made introductions.

'Constable Regent,' he said, 'this is Mr Richard Jeperson.'

The man fluttered a hand and curved his thin lips into a smile. As his frilly mauve cuff flapped, Fred caught sight of tiny blue marks on his wrist. Some sort of tattoo.

'I represent the Diogenes Club,' Jeperson drawled, voice

rich and deep as a BBC announcer. 'A branch of government you won't have heard of. Now you have heard of it, you'll probably be required to sign the Official Secrets Act in blood. Our speciality is affairs like this, matters in which conventional methods of policing or diplomacy or defence come up short. I gather you are still reeling from the revelation that the world is not what you once thought it was.'

Had the man read his mind?

'You can take some comfort from the fact that the Diogenes Club, which is a very old institution, has always known a little of the true state of things. There has often been someone like me on the lists of HM Government, a private individual with a public office, retained for circumstances like this.'

'This has happened before?' Fred asked.

'Not this, precisely. But things like this, certainly. Impossible obtrusions into the mundane. Vanessa and I have pursued several of these tricky bits of business to more or less satisfactory conclusions.'

The woman – Vanessa – smiled. Her teeth were dazzling.

'With your help, we shall see what we can do here,' said Jeperson.

'With my help?'

A spasm of panic gripped him.

'You're detailed to work with Mr Jeperson,' Price told him. 'Out of uniform.'

'Topping,' Jeperson said, holding out his hand.

Fred stood up and shook Jeperson's hand, feeling the smoothness of his rings and the leather of his palm. This was a man who had done hard outdoor work.

Looking down, he noticed the blue marks again. A row of numbers.

'We should probably take a spin down to the coast,' Jeperson said. 'Take a look at Seamouth.'

Fred was suddenly cold again.

'It'll be fun to go to the seaside.'

◆━◆

It didn't take detective work to deduce which of the vehicles in the New Scotland Yard car park belonged to Richard Jeperson. It was a silver-grey Rolls-Royce the size of a speed-boat, bonnet shaped like a cathedral nave, body streamlined to break land speed records.

Fred whistled.

'It's a ShadowShark, you know,' Jeperson said, running his fingers across the Rolls-Royce Spirit of Ecstasy hood ornament. 'They only made five. I have three.'

Parked among the panda cars and civilian Minis, the car was a lion in a herd of deer.

'Hop in the back, Fred,' Jeperson said with easy familiarity, opening the rear door. Fred slipped onto soft black leather and inhaled luxury. Two fresh roses were propped in sconces. Jeperson slid beside him while Vanessa got into the driver's seat. Fred was surprised the man let anyone else drive his precious car.

'Vanessa'd win Brooklands if they'd let her enter,' said Jeperson. 'She can drive anything.'

'I'm learning to fly a jump jet,' she said, over her shoulder. 'Perk of the position.'

The engine purred and she manoeuvred the ShadowShark out of the car park. Fred doubted if he'd be as blithe handling such a powerful (and expensive) car.

'Don't hurry,' Jeperson told her. 'I want to stop for a pub lunch on the way. Have a spot of rumination.'

◆━◆

Vanessa headed for the road to the South Coast, cruising through the thinning traffic. Fred found himself relaxing, enjoying the head-turns of other motorists. Jeperson obviously didn't believe in blending in with the crowd.

'A sort of uncle of mine lives in Seamouth,' Jeperson said. 'Brigadier-General Sir Giles Gallant. We'll have to look him up. He sat on the Ruling Cabal with Geoffrey Jeperson.'

'Your father?' Fred asked.

Jeperson's eyes were unreadable.

'Adoptive,' he said. 'Picked me out. In the War.'

'And this Sir Giles?'

'Also with our mob, I'm afraid. Diogenes Club. At least, he was once. Retired now. You'll find, now you know to look, that we pop up all over the board. Unless I very much miss my guess, Sir Giles will know something about your End of the Pier Show. He's too sharp to live near an incident like this jaunt without feeling tingles in the cobweb. We'll probably set up camp at his house.'

Everything since the events on the pier seemed unreal. Only now that he was on the road back to Seamouth did Fred realise quite how the usual pattern of his life had been broken. He had been handed over into the care of this odd stranger, almost palmed off on the man. What disturbed him most was that Jeperson actually seemed to know what was going on, to accept the insanity without question, without even registering shock or disbelief.

It would be easy to be afraid.

'What about the Seamouth police?' Fred asked.

'Tell you what, I don't think we'll trouble them until we have to. I like to keep my involvement with the authorities limited to a few enlightened souls like Euan Price. Too many plods have the habit of not seeing what they don't want to. No offence, Constable Regent. Your mob like to tie up neat little parcels and sometimes all we can give them is a dirty great mess.'

If he shut his eyes for a moment, Fred saw what the gun-flash had shown him on the pier. A hellish scene, impossible to understand, hideously vivid. Real, and yet…

'What was the first thing?' Jeperson asked, quickly. 'The first thing that told you things weren't in whack. Don't think, answer.'

'Careless Talk Costs Lives,' he said, just seeing it.

'And Loose Lips Sink Ships.'

'It was a poster. An old one, from the War. But it wasn't old, faded. It had been put up recently.'

'Bingo, an apport!'

'What's an apport?'

'Something which shouldn't done ought to be there but bloody well just is. Mediums often materialise the fellahs, but this isn't like that. Nothing consciously evoked. This came with the house, like wallpaper.'

'I thought there might be an exhibition.'

'There's always that possibility. Prosaic, but nonetheless not out of the question.' Jeperson seemed a little disappointed. 'Any funny smell? Ozone?'

'Just the sea.'

'The sea, my dear Fred, is not in the "just the" category. It's the oldest living thing on the planet. It abides, it shifts, it shrinks, it grows, it senses, it hints.'

They were out in the country now, bombing through winding lanes at ninety. Fred gripped the armrest on the door, reacting to the rush.

'We have a dispensation,' Jeperson explained. 'Speed limits do not apply to us. We take great risks for our country, so the least the Queen can do is exempt us from a few of the pettier regulations that bind the rest of her subjects. With Vanessa at the wheel, we needn't worry about accidents.'

They took a blind corner at speed. The road ahead was clear.

'She has second sight, poor love.'

The country pub where Jeperson had hoped to lunch was gone, knocked down and replaced by a Jolly Glutton. Fred had been in these places before; they were popping up beside motorways and A roads all over the country. Everything was brand new but already tarnished. A big cartoon Friar Tuck was the place's mascot and the struggling waitresses were dressed as monkettes, with hooded robes and miniskirts. The fare was flat pies and crinkle-shaped chips, hot enough to disguise the lack of taste, and tea worse than the stuff served at the Yard out of a machine.

Jeperson was disappointed, but decided to sample the place anyway.

As he looked at his Jolly Fare, the man from the Diogenes Club slumped in dejection. He lifted a sprig of plastic parsley from his wriggly chips and dropped it into the full tin ashtray on the Formica-topped table.

'What's the world coming to?' he asked, eyes liquid with pain.

The Jolly Glutton catered to shabby couples with extremely loud children. In the next booth, a knot of youths with Jaffa haircuts messed around with the plastic tomatoes of ketchup, and tried to get their hands up the waitresses' skirts.

'I wonder what happened to the regulars? Did they find another pub somewhere? With decent beer and proper food? Or did the fat Friar have them hanged in the forest to silence their poor plaints?'

Jeperson knitted his brows, and concentrated.

Suddenly, Fred smelled beer, heard the clink of glasses, the soft grumble of rural accents, saw the comforting smoky gloom of the snug. Then, it was all snatched away.

'What did you just do?' he asked Jeperson.

'Sorry,' Jeperson said. 'Didn't mean to impose. It's a nasty little knack sometimes. Call it wishful thinking.'

17

'I knew what you were seeing.'

Jeperson shrugged, but the tiny glints in his eyes were not apologetic. Fred had a sense of the man's power.

'I don't fancy the one with the tash,' a voice said, 'but 'er with the legs'd do for a shag.'

It was the skinheads in the next booth. They were propped up on the table and seats, leaning over the partition, looking down at Vanessa, who was sitting opposite Fred and Jeperson.

'Bloody hippie,' said the kid who had spoken. His left eye twitched. 'Hair like a girl's.'

Jeperson looked at the skin almost with pity.

'You should have seen this place the way it was,' he said. 'It was a comfort in a cold world.'

The skin didn't understand.

'What are you doing with this pouf?' Twitch asked Fred.

For a moment, he was confused. Then he remembered what his head looked like.

'I'm taking your girlfriend,' Twitch said.

Fred didn't know whether the skin meant Vanessa or Jeperson.

Twitch, who was smaller and duller than Jaffa, put his hand on Vanessa's neck, lifting aside her hair.

Jeperson nodded, almost imperceptibly, to the girl.

Vanessa reached up, swiftly, and took Twitch's ear in a firm grip. She pulled him off his perch and slammed his face into her plate of uneaten chips.

'You can look but you better not touch,' she whispered into his red ear.

Twitch's friends, an older bloke with a Rupert scarf and a wide-shouldered hulk, were astonished.

Vanessa pushed Twitch off the table and dropped him on the chessboard-tiled floor. He had maggot-shaped mashed chips all over his face.

Everyone in the Jolly Glutton was paying attention.

Twitch pulled out a sharpened screwdriver but Jeperson stepped on his wrist, bringing down a blocky yellow heel on crunching bones. The pig-sticker rolled away.

'I'll have that,' Jeperson said, picking up the homemade shank with distaste. 'Nasty thing.'

Fred was penned into the booth – these bolted-down plastic chairs and tables were traps – but Vanessa stood up and slipped out. All her movements were effortless; she wasn't just made for show.

'I'd advise you to pick up your friend and get back to your delicious fare,' Jeperson said to Rupert Scarf and Shoulders. 'My associate doesn't want to hurt you.'

The two skins looked Vanessa up and down, and made a mistake.

Shoulders clumped forward, big hands out, and was on the floor before Fred could work out what Vanessa had done to him. She seemed to have stuck her fingers into his throat and sternum, making a cattle prod of her hand. Shoulders made a lot of noise about going down and rolled over Twitch, groaning that he was crippled.

Rupert Scarf spread his hands and backed away. The message had got through.

Shoulders, still moaning, got up on his hands and knees, snarled and made another grab at Vanessa. She whirled like a ballet dancer and stuck the white point of her boot into his ear, lifting him off the floor for a moment and laying him flat out. Her hair spun round with her and fell perfectly into place. She was smiling slightly, but didn't seem to feel the strain.

Rupert Scarf pulled Twitch up, and together they picked up Shoulders.

'You're a dead dolly-mixture,' Twitch said, retreating.

Vanessa smiled, eyebrows raised.

The skins left the restaurant. All the other customers, and the waitresses, applauded. Vanessa took a bow.

'Three more friends for life,' she said.

———◆———

They continued by B roads. After the Jolly Glutton, Jeperson slumped into a fugue of despair. He said nothing, but his mood was heavy. Fred was beginning to sense that the man from the Diogenes Club was remarkably open. A changeable personality, he felt things so deeply that there was an overspill from his head, which washed onto anyone around him. Just now, Fred was lapped by the waters of Jeperson's gloom. It was the loss of his beloved country pub as much as the encounter with the yobs, maybe the loss of his beloved country.

Vanessa kept away from the main road, casually driving through smaller and smaller villages. Greenery flashed by, stretches of thickly wooded land alternating with patchwork-quilt landscapes of fields and hedgerows. Brooks and stiles and tree-canopied roads. Tiny old churches and thatched cottages. A vicar on a bicycle.

This didn't seem to be the same world as the Jolly Glutton. No Formica, no plastic tomatoes, no crinkle-cut chips.

Jeperson stirred a little and looked through the tinted window.

'Spring seems to have sprung,' he announced.

It was true. This was a fresh season.

The ShadowShark crested a hill. The road gently sloped down towards sparkling sea. Seamouth was spread out, sun shining on red tile roofs. Gulls wheeled high in the air. A small boat cut through the swell, tacking out in Seamouth Bay.

It was very different from the dull day with the Boys, when the sea had been a churning grey soup.

Fred saw the pier, a finger stretched out into the sea. He had another flash. Jeperson shivered.

'Looks like a picture postcard,' he said. 'But we know something nasty is written on the back. There are things moving under the surface.'

Fred tried to conquer his fear.

'Drive on, Vanessa love,' Jeperson said.

— ◆ —

Seamouth spread up away from the seafront onto the rolling downs, bounded to the east by the cliffs and to the west by a stretch of shivering sands. Overlooking the sea were serried ranks of whitewashed villas, at least a third of them called Sea View.

The ShadowShark attracted some friendly attention. Folks looked up from their gardening to wave and smile. A postman paused and gave a smart salute. Fred was almost touched.

'It's nearly four o'clock,' he said. 'That postie should have finished work hours ago.'

'Second afternoon post?' Jeperson suggested.

'Not in this decade.'

'I suppose not.'

Vanessa found Raleigh Avenue, where Brigadier-General Sir Giles Gallant lived. His villa was called The Laurels. Rich green bushes, planted all around, did their best to seem like trees.

The cars outside the villas were all well preserved but out of date. There wasn't a Mini Cooper or a Hillman Imp in sight, just big, elegant machines, polished to perfection, invisibly mended where they'd pranged.

They parked in the driveway of The Laurels and got out. Fred's legs had gone rubbery on the long drive and he stamped a bit on the gravel to get his circulation back.

'Good afternoon,' said a man in overalls, looking up from his spade-work. 'Here to see the Brig?'

'Yes, indeed,' said Jeperson.

'Top hole,' said the neighbour. 'I'm Marshall Michaelsmith. Two names, not three.'

Michaelsmith was a game old bird of perhaps seventy, with snow-white hair and red cheeks. He had been digging vigorously, turning over a flower bed. A stack of pulled-up rose bushes lay discarded on the lawn. There were a few plants left, tied to bamboo spears.

'I'm with the Brig on the Committee,' Michaelsmith said.

He tore up another rose bush by the roots and threw it away, momentarily sad.

'Shame to do it,' he said. 'The missus loves these blooms, worked at them for years. But one has to do one's bit. I'm putting in potatoes, cabbages, rhubarb. Dig for Victory, eh?'

The last of the roses was gone.

'The missus has taken to her bed. For the duration, probably. Still, she'll be up and about in the end.'

Michaelsmith stood on his ravaged flower bed.

'The Brig's in town, on official business. I'll see if we can scrounge you some tea in the meantime. Come into my parlour. This way, miss.'

Michaelsmith escorted Vanessa, extending a courteous arm to steady her across the rough earth. Fred and Jeperson followed.

'I hear you girls are doing your bit too,' Michaelsmith said to Vanessa. 'Before it all got too much, the missus was the same. Back to the land, girls. Jolly good show. We must all pull together, see it through. Right will prevail, my dear. Oh yes it will. Always does in the end. Never doubt it for a moment.'

Fred gathered Marshall Michaelsmith was a bit potty. Slung on the old man's back was a khaki satchel. Fred recognised the shape. His dad had kept his gas mask well past the Festival of Britain. Michaelsmith's looked to be in good order, ready to pull on in an instant.

22

Mrs MacAlister, Marshall Michaelsmith's Scottish housekeeper, brought in a silver tea-service, and Michaelsmith poured them all cups of Lipton's. He made a ritual of it, using a strainer to catch the leaves, apologising for the thinness of the brew and the condensed milk.

Michaelsmith talked about the half-brick in his cistern, to cut down on the water flushed away, and the line drawn in his bath to keep the level down to four inches. He seemed proud of his austerity measures.

Fred supposed the old man had got into the habit during the War and never let up.

Michaelsmith's reception room was cosily cluttered, with a view of the back garden through french windows. There was a black-bordered photograph of a young man in naval uniform on the piano.

'Mitch, my brother,' Michaelsmith explained. 'Went down at Jutland. In the last show.'

Jeperson sipped his tea.

Somehow, even in banana boots, he fitted in the room. Fred supposed he was such an odd sort that he'd do anywhere.

Michaelsmith was taken with Vanessa, and no wonder. He was explaining all the family photographs. There were a great many of 'the missus', following her from long-faced youth through middle-aged elegance to painful frailty.

The french windows opened and a man in uniform stepped into the room. Michaelsmith stood to attention.

'Richard,' the newcomer exclaimed. 'This is a surprise. What brings you to this backwater?'

'The usual thing, Giles.'

The man – who must be Sir Giles Gallant – was suddenly serious.

'Here? I don't believe it.'

Jeperson stood up and embraced Gallant, like a Frenchman.

'The lovely Vanessa, you know,' Jeperson said. Sir Giles clicked his heels and Vanessa demurely bobbed. 'And this is Fred Regent. He's the new bug.'

'Pleased to meet you,' Sir Giles said, inflicting a bone-crushing handshake on Fred. 'We need all the good men we can get.'

Sir Giles must have been about the same age as Michaelsmith, but his manner suggested a much younger man. He was iron where his friend was willow. His grey hair was still streaked with black and his hawk eyes were bright. He struck Fred as a very determined man.

'It's your pier we're interested in, Giles,' Jeperson said. 'Seems to be infested with apports. And other nastinesses.'

'The pier?' Sir Giles was taken aback. 'Should have blown it up years ago. Damn thing's a shipping hazard.'

'But it's not just the pier,' Jeperson said.

'No,' Sir Giles said, 'you're quite right, Richard. I should have called Diogenes myself.'

Fred remembered Richard had said Sir Giles would know what was going on.

'I thought I could cope on my own. I'm sorry.'

'No apologies, Giles.'

'Of course not.'

'We'll set up HQ at your place. I'll go over the whole thing with you. Vanessa, take the worthy Fred for a walk along the seafront, would you? I needn't tell you to stay away from the pier, but keep an eye out for oddities.'

Fred was alarmed, but at least he knew Vanessa could take care of herself. And him too, probably, though that hardly did anything for his confidence.

'It's a mild evening,' Jeperson said. 'You might go for a paddle.'

<hr>

They walked towards the seafront, zig-zagging downhill through neat, quiet roads. The sky darkened by degrees.

'Have you noticed?' Vanessa said. 'No one's turning their lights on.'

Fred looked at the windows of the villas.

'If they did, you couldn't tell,' he said. 'The houses all have those thick black curtains.'

'I knew people were conformists in these parts, but it's beyond the bounds of probability that every Sea View should have the same curtains. Whatever happened to white net?'

They looked over rows of roofs, towards the sea.

'There's something missing,' Vanessa said.

Fred saw it.

'Television aerials. There aren't any.'

'Well spotted, that man.'

'Time seems to stand still in Seamouth. I noticed it the first time I came here.' He didn't want to think further on that line. 'I feel I've come in on the last act of the panto,' he said. 'How did you get into this business?'

'Like you. I took a turn off the road, and realised things were not as they seem.'

'Meaning?'

'Have you ever heard of demonic possession?'

'I think so.'

'I don't recommend it.'

'Mr Jeperson is an exorcist?'

'Not quite. He's trickier than that. At heart, he's a sensitive.'

'He seems a funny bloke.'

'He's had a funny life.'

They were at the seafront. There were people around. The locals smiled and bade them good evening, but hurried on their way. The street lamps did not come on.

'On his wrist…' Fred began.

'The numbers? They're what you think.'

'Concentration camp?'

'Death camp, actually. His foster father and Sir Giles were with the unit that liberated the place. They pulled him out. He was just a kid then.'

'Is he Jewish?'

'Almost certainly not,' she said. 'He doesn't actually know. He has no memory of anything before the camp. I've always assumed he was born a gypsy. But he's as British as you can get.'

'And this club?'

'The Diogenes Club. They collect useful people. They've been doing it for centuries. Richard's talents were obvious, much showier then than now, if you can credit it. Probably why he was in the camp. Old Mr Jeperson – he died a few years ago – adopted the boy, sent him to his old school, brought him up. Shaped him and trained him. That wasn't easy for either of them. Richard's no one's catspaw. He's a free agent.'

'What about you?'

'I've been collected too. And now, so have you.'

A chill breeze made him hug his jacket. He still wore his skinhead outfit. He was getting used to it. The Peter Noone haircut had made him look as big a prat as… well, as Peter Noone. It was time someone reclaimed the skin look from thugs like Jaffa.

They had been ambling along the front, deliberately walking away from the pier. Now, they stopped, leaned on railings, and looked out to sea.

Waves rolled in, lapping the sands. Wreaths of kelp tangled on rocks. A man in a straw hat, barefooted with his trousers rolled up to the knee, pottered among the pools, collecting sea-shells.

'It's an idyll,' Vanessa said. 'You'd never think there was a war on.'

'What war?' Fred asked, shocked.

'There's always a war, Fred.'

***

Back at The Laurels, they found Jeperson and Sir Giles in a book-lined study, snifting brandy from glasses the size of human heads.

'How's town?' Jeperson asked.

'Quiet,' Vanessa commented.

'Always the way.'

'I've decided to bring the pier up with the Committee,' Sir Giles said. 'It's been shut down for years. Time to get rid of it altogether.'

'Let's not be too hasty,' Jeperson said. 'Our problem may not be the pier itself, but something that happens to be there at the moment. If you get rid of the structure, the problem might deem it an opportune moment to move inland.'

Sir Giles offered Fred, but not Vanessa, a drink. He thought it best not to accept.

'I'll call the Committee anyway,' Sir Giles said. 'Best to alert them all to the danger. Shan't be a sec.'

Jeperson smiled and sipped as Sir Giles left the room. Once the door was closed, his face shut down.

'We must get out of this house,' he said, serious.

Vanessa nodded, and tried the obvious exits.

The windows were fastened and barred. The study door was locked.

Vanessa handed Jeperson a hairpin. He unbent it and picked the lock of the study door. It was done in seconds. Jeperson looked pleased with himself and not in too much of a hurry to take a bow. He opened the door a crack. Sir Giles was in the hallway, on the telephone.

'We must act fast,' Sir Giles was saying. 'You don't know this man.'

Their host was between them and the front door.

Jeperson stepped silently out into the hallway.

'Giles,' he said, sharply.

Sir Giles turned, face guilty. He muttered something, and hung up.

'Richard.' He attempted a genial smile. Without much success. Brigadier-General Sir Giles Gallant was sweating and shifting.

Jeperson bent the hairpin back into shape and returned it to Vanessa.

'We should do each other the courtesy of being honest,' Jeperson said. 'You of all people know how difficult it is to deceive someone like me.'

'I would have told you,' Sir Giles said. 'I wanted you to hear it from the whole Committee.'

The door opened and uniformed men came in. Six of them. With guns. All middle-aged or older, but hard-faced, smart in khakis. Bright eyes and clipped moustaches. Proper soldier boys. Rifles were levelled.

'This is for the best, Richard.'

'Who decides?' Jeperson asked.

'We do,' Sir Giles claimed. 'We've earned that right.'

Fred was lost. He didn't know who was who and who was on whose side.

Jeperson sank to the floor, knees bowing outwards as he fitted into a lotus position. The rifle barrels followed him. Fred saw the tension in his back. He pressed his palms together, shut his eyes, and hummed almost below the threshold of hearing.

Sir Giles looked torn. For an instant, Fred thought he was about to order his men to fire. Instead, he stepped forwards, raising the telephone receiver like a club, aiming a blow at Jeperson's head.

It never connected.

Sir Giles was caught – by Jeperson's humming? – and froze, receiver held above his head, cord dangling. His face showed a struggle.

The humming was louder, machine-like, insectile.

What was Jeperson doing?

The men with guns took their directions from Sir Giles. They were spectators. Sir Giles was fighting. He wrestled the receiver, trying to bring it down. Jeperson rose as he had sunk, unbending himself. He was projecting something from inside. Static electricity crackled in his hair.

Vanessa took Fred's arm and tugged him along, in a cone of protection that emanated from the man from the Diogenes Club. As long as he could hear the humming, he felt safe.

They passed Sir Giles, whose face was scarlet. The old soldiers fell back to either side, lowering their weapons. There was a clear route out of The Laurels.

Jeperson seemed to glide across the carpet, eyes still shut, still radiating noise. The hum was wavering.

'Stop them,' shouted Sir Giles.

A rifle was raised, its barrel-end dragging up Fred's leg. Without thinking, he knocked the gun aside and shoved its owner – the chinless ARP man – backwards.

They were on the porch of The Laurels.

Vanessa was in the Rolls, turning over the engine.

Someone fired a wild shot into the air.

The humming snapped off and Jeperson stumbled. Fred caught him, and sensed that all the strength had gone out of the man. He helped him into the car.

'You don't understand,' shouted Sir Giles. 'It's for the best.'

'Drive,' breathed Jeperson.

Fred pulled the car door closed. A gun went off. He saw the muzzle-flash. He looked out of the window, and something struck the pane, making him go cross-eyed. He should have been shot in the face, but the round was stopped in a web of cracks.

'Bullet-proof glass,' Vanessa said.

'Thank God for that,' Fred said.

He was shaking.

Sir Giles's men didn't waste any more ammunition. The Rolls pulled away, down Raleigh Road.

Jeperson sprawled on the seat, exhausted. He seemed thinner, less substantial. Whatever resource he had summoned up was spent and its exercise had taken a toll.

'What was that all about?' Fred asked.

'We're on our own,' Jeperson croaked.

The ShadowShark wasn't easy to hide, so they just parked it by the road and walked away. Of course, the three of them were also pretty difficult to miss. As they walked back towards the seafront, Fred had a sense that the whole town was watching them from behind their blackout curtains, and that Sir Giles's Committee knew exactly where their three troublemakers were. More old soldiers would be despatched after them.

Jeperson had needed to be supported for a while but soon got his strength back.

'Giles couldn't have managed anything on this scale on his own,' he said. 'He must have a powerful source somewhere. But not a first-rate one. The casting isn't pure, or we'd have been absorbed at once.'

Fred understood maybe one word in three.

Vanessa didn't ask questions. He decided just to go along with it all.

'At first I thought it was your pier, but Giles's Committee hadn't reckoned on whatever you ran into. Whatever they've done here hasn't taken in the way they hoped.'

They were in the middle of the dark town.

'Fred, I'm afraid we're going to have to go to the pier.'

He had known it would come. So much else had got in the way, so much else that was impossible to follow, that he had almost put it out of his mind.

Now it hit him again.

There were monsters.

'Maybe we can get to the bottom of it all by morning.'

They were on the seafront. The pier was in sight.

———◆———

Because of the lack of street lighting, it was easy to creep up on the pier. A checkpoint was set up by the turnstile. Three men in uniform manned the point. Barbed wire was strung around the admissions booth. The soldiers were smoking cigarettes. From somewhere, Vera Lynn sang 'We'll Meet Again'.

An aeroplane whine sounded overhead.

There was a shrill whistle.

'An air raid,' Jeperson said. 'I doubt if that was part of the intended casting. It just came along with the package.'

A plane flew in from the Channel, a dark shape against black clouds, pregnant with bombs.

Jeperson signalled that they should proceed.

Fred tried to think away the painful tightness in his gut. If Jeperson and Vanessa weren't afraid, he shouldn't be. Of course, they hadn't been here before.

A column of fire rose from up among the villas. It burned his eyes. Then the sound of the explosion hit. It was strong enough to make him stagger.

They walked rapidly towards the checkpoint.

The soldiers were craning, looking up at the fire.

'Jerry blighter,' one sneered.

'Our ack-ack'll bring him down,' his mate said.

As if in reply, the crump of ground guns sounded. The earth was shaking. There were shellbursts in the sky, silhouetting the plane.

Fred was surprised by the soldiers' faces. They were not old, like the men at the villa. They were young, familiar. The three yobs from the Jolly Glutton. Rupert still had his yellow scarf tucked into the neck of his khaki jacket. Twitch was sucking on his cigarette, eye in motion. Shoulders awkwardly unslung his rifle.

'Who goes there?' he barked.

Vanessa stepped forward.

'Remember me?'

'It's a dangerous night to be out, miss,' said Rupert Scarf, politely. 'Best get down in the shelters.'

'Are you in the theatre?' Twitch asked, looking at her legs.

The three didn't remember Vanessa. Fred thought they might not remember their own names, whatever they were.

'We're with the Ministry,' Jeperson said, holding out a folded newspaper picked from a rubbish bin.

Rupert Scarf took the paper and looked at it.

Jeperson hummed again, a different pitch. Rupert Scarf looked at the paper and at their faces.

'All in order, sir,' he said, smiling, saluting.

Jeperson took back the paper and tucked it under his arm.

'Let's take a look at the problem then, shall we?' he said. 'If you could let us through.'

The three smartly dismantled the barrier.

'Shan't be a jiffy,' Jeperson said, stepping onto the pier.

Fred looked at the Emporium, dimly outlined at the end of the promenade. Its glass roof had a slight greenish glow. He had a 'Go Back Now' feeling.

'Are you coming?' Vanessa asked.

'Yes,' Fred said, resolving.

They strolled towards the Emporium.

'It feels as if we're miles from the shore,' Jeperson said.

He was right. Fred looked back. The fire up in the villas was under control. The bomber seemed to be gone. There was still a flicker from where the bomb had fallen.

'What about those skinheads?' Fred asked.

'Caught up in the casting. Weak minds are prone to that. It's like a psychic press-gang. It turns people into costume extras.'

'I can't say I miss the old versions.'

The sea sounded beneath them. An ancient susurrus.

The pier was such a fragile thing, an umbilicus connected to the shore.

Fred had to overcome an urge to bolt back.

'This is definitely it,' Jeperson said. 'The flaw in the pattern. You can feel the atoms whirling the wrong way.'

Vanessa nodded.

They were at the Emporium. There was the dent where Ingraham had kicked. And the pane Jaffa had smashed. If it were daylight, he was sure he'd see the scorch-trail Jaffa left before he went over the side.

'I don't have to tell you to be careful, do I?' Jeperson said, reaching in through the broken pane, opening the door. 'Excelsior.'

Fred looked into the darkness. He followed Jeperson and Vanessa inside.

'Someone's cleared up,' he said. 'There should be bodies all over the place.'

Vanessa had a slim torch. She played light around the space. There were scrubbed and bleached patches on the floor. And some of the exhibits were under dust-sheets.

Jeperson looked at the storm trooper poster.

'It's all to do with the War,' he said.

'Even I'd worked that out,' Fred said. 'It's been a while since anyone bombed the South Coast from the air.'

'A lot of people liked the War,' Jeperson said, scratching his wrist. 'I don't think I did, though. I can't actually remember much of it. But it wasn't anything I'd want to bring back.'

'I can understand that.'

Vanessa ran torchlight across the exhibits. She spotlit a display Fred hadn't noticed on his first visit. It was a set of caricature figures of Hitler, Goebbels and Mussolini. Hitler was child-sized and cut off at the waist, Goebbels a rat-bodied pet in Hitler's top pocket, and Mussolini a towering fat clown with an apple-sized red head and a conical Punchinello hat.

'These fellows, for instance,' Jeperson said. 'I don't miss them one bit.'

Hitler's mask crinkled in a scowl as its wearer escaped from the display. The creature walked very rapidly on its hands, detaching itself from the base. It was a legless torso.

Half-Hitler brushed past Vanessa, screeching, and slid through a panel. It had left Rat-Goebbels behind, rodent feet curled up, horrid little eyes glittering.

Man Mountain Mussolini quivered, a ton of jelly poured into a barrage-balloon uniform. His belly rumbled, and a falsetto laugh emerged from his circular lipsticky mouth.

Fred looked around. Vanessa moved the torchlight. Panels

were sliding upwards. Boots shone. Black jackboots. Then grey-uniformed knees. There were half a dozen panels. Behind them were men – mannequins? – in Nazi uniform.

Rat-Goebbels right-sided himself and scurried towards a pair of boots, nestling between them like an affectionate pet.

The panels were above leather belts. Swastikas and Iron Crosses showed on grey chests. Luger pistols and Schmeisser machine guns were pointed.

Man Mountain Mussolini, still laughing like a eunuch, rolled back and forth on his belly. His legs were normal-sized, useless with his gut-bulk, stuck out of his egg-shaped body like broken tree-branches.

Faces showed. Faces Fred knew. The Boys. Jaffa's nose was smudged with soot, his cheeks burned to the bone, his eyes dead under the rim of his storm trooper helmet. The others were similarly transformed. Ingraham in an SS uniform, Doggo a regular soldier. Oscar's face was crudely stitched back on, forehead sewn to his Afrika Corps cap, skin hanging slack like a cloth mask.

Half-Hitler advanced from between two rows of Nazi skins, using its arms like crutches, inching forwards its truncated torso. Its face was not a mask, but coated in a transparent fungus that exaggerated the familiar features. The homunculus set itself down and crossed its arms, tottering back and forth a little. The storm troopers snapped off perfect Nazi salutes.

'*Sieg Heil*,' they shouted, '*Heil* Hitler.'

'You'll excuse me if I don't respond in kind,' Jeperson said. 'But I could never stand you, you little sneak.'

He drew back his banana boot as if converting a rugby try and kicked Half-Hitler in the face. The diminished Führer tipped over backwards, outsize hands slapping the floor, and overturned completely like a chimpanzee on a trapeze, winding up face down and arms flailed out.

Safety catches clicked off. Guns fired.

———◆———

Fred grabbed Vanessa round the waist and threw himself at the floor. Together, they rolled behind the row of penny-in-the-slot machines, inches ahead of the line of bullet-pocks that raked the floorboards.

The space was too enclosed for the Nazi zombies to get much accurate use of their guns. Bullets ricocheted and spanged around. Doggo took one in his face and staggered back. Black goo leaked from the hole, but he wasn't seriously hurt.

Ingraham kicked aside the penny-in-the-slot machines.

Fred tried to put his hands up.

Ingraham raised his Luger.

The gun writhed. Its metal parts contracted as if the mechanism were about to sneeze. It was partly a gun, but infused with the life of a small rodent.

The gun-thing coughed. Fire belched. Slow enough to see, a bullet squeezed out of the barrel and sped towards them, a blob of flaming jelly.

It spattered against his chest, stinging through his shirt. He brushed the fiery glop away, feeling the flames curling around his fingers, and scraped it off on to the floor.

Ingraham's pistol growled at them.

Jaffa came over. He held Jeperson by one arm twisted playground-bully-style up behind his back. A silver-bladed dagger was held at Jeperson's throat, steel quivering with a life of its own. The zombie indicated Fred and Vanessa should surrender. Fred stood up, trying to keep his body in front of Vanessa.

Jaffa smiled. His burned lips made an expression Fred remembered from when the Nazi was King Skin.

'You're enjoying this, aren't you, Kevin?'

In the burned-out eyes anger glowed.

Half-Hitler scuttled over, and bit Jeperson's leg like a terrier. Its teeth couldn't get through the banana boot.

At a nod from the Führer, Fred was pulled away. The Nazi homunculus looked Vanessa over, little black eyes excited. She tried not to show disgust.

'Eva,' Half-Hitler breathed, besotted.

Man Mountain Mussolini rolled over to look. Other fascist freaks came out of the shadows. A pig-faced Goering, warty wings folded over his Luftwaffe tunic. Himmler-and-Hess Siamese twins, joined at the waist, *Hiel*ing with all available arms. A snake-bodied, fork-tongued Martin Bormann. An armoured Rommel, bony tank-plates coating his body, desert camouflage smearing his face. A werewolf Heydrich, cheeks and hands pierced by dozens of hooks.

They all gathered, looking at Vanessa.

Half-Hitler crawled around her legs, as if inspecting a horse. Vanessa looked down at the little creep. It retreated and barked an order.

The Nazi Boys raised their machine guns. Fred opened his mouth to protest. Guns chattered, pouring liquid fire out of hosepipe barrels. It washed against Vanessa, burning swatches of her clothing, hanging around her hair.

Where the fire burned, she was transformed. A cloak of flame enveloped her. White boots became black. Straps grew around her chest. A jewelled swastika hung at her throat. Her hair, a living thing, coiled into a braid, clinging to the back of her head like a cap. She twisted as she turned, resisting the metamorphosis, but the zombies kept pouring the changing fire at her.

Half-Hitler's eyes shone.

The light went out in Vanessa's face. The flame fell away from her. She was the same woman, but turned into a Nazi pin-up.

Jeperson was mumbling furiously, trying to call up some counter-charm.

Half-Hitler gave another order.

Eva-Vanessa uncoiled a short whip and struck Jeperson in the face, breaking his concentration. The Nazi monsters laughed. Jeperson went limp, and Jaffa dropped him.

Half-Hitler jumped up and down on its waist-stump, chortling with glee. Eva-Vanessa picked it up as if it were a child, and hugged it. They kissed. Fred felt sick.

'Today the pier,' Goebbels snickered; 'tomorrow the world.'

Jeperson got up onto his knees. As he fell, he had snatched something from Jaffa's belt. Now he opened his hand. It was a grenade. He opened his other hand. There was the pin.

Time froze.

Then everyone was scrambling out of the way.

Jeperson let the grenade roll on the floor.

Fred was kicked about by Nazi boots. He found himself behind the execution machines again.

The grenade didn't so much explode as suck light and matter in from all around. It gathered into a heavy black ball and fell through the floor.

Fred saw the dark sea frothing below. Jeperson stood over the lip of the hole and stepped into it, plunging towards the water.

Gunfire raked the room.

Fred followed Jeperson, without thinking.

He tumbled badly and hit the sea as if it were a tossing sheet of iron. Cold water slammed him in the face and tried to shove him under.

———◆———

He woke up on the beach, with water being forced out of his lungs. His mouth was full of the sick taste of too much salt. And he was as cold as he had ever been, racked with spasms of shivering.

'Welcome back,' Jeperson said. 'Thought you'd upped stumps for a minute.'

Fred rolled over on the sand and water poured out of him.

Looking out to sea, Fred saw that the Emporium at the end of the pier was lit up with fairy lights. It seemed like a jewelled palace in the darkness.

'The ARP won't like that,' Jeperson commented.

'What is going on here?' Fred asked.

'A very bad business,' Jeperson said, concerned. 'Very bad business indeed.'

People stood around, with rifles.

A man came forward wearily. Sir Giles.

'Oh dear,' he said. 'We shall have to get you two dried off.'

Fred was picked up. He recognised the ARP man he had shoved earlier. He was too weak to resist.

'A cup of tea might help,' said Sir Giles.

———◆———

They were back in the study at The Laurels. All that could be found for Fred was a naval uniform, left behind by Michaelsmith's brother. Jeperson had a change of clothes (or a dozen) in the Rolls. He now wore a tiger-striped frock coat and aquamarine knee-britches, a violet kaftan shirt, and red riding-boots. His hair was still damp.

Sir Giles sat in his favourite armchair while Marshall Michaelsmith, in an orderly's uniform, served mugs of hot tea. Fred was grateful for that. Jeperson leaned forwards, eyes blazing, fixing Sir Giles with a stern schoolmaster's gaze.

'What were you thinking of, Giles?'

The old soldier shrivelled in his chair.

Finally, feebly, he said, 'It was decimalisation.'

'What?' Jeperson shouted.

Sir Giles was embarrassed, but defiant.

'Decimal coinage, you know. The new money. I can never get it straight, all these pence and no shillings. The new coins don't mean anything. They're like counters in a child's game. That was the last straw. Not just changing the money, of course. But everything it meant. All the other changes. The Common Market coming up. Motorways. Everything plastic. High-speed inter-city trains. Racialist violence. Hot-pants. Instant soup. Hire purchase. Everything's cheapened, somehow. Since the War.'

'Regrettable, perhaps. But what about heart transplants? A man on the moon?'

'The pill?'

Jeperson sat back, and shook his head. 'Have you forgotten how you felt in 1930? That deadening weight of history, of the way things have always been. Why do you think Mr Jeperson chose me, passed on the responsibilities? Because I can still embrace the change, the chaos. I can still accommodate.'

'This is different,' Sir Giles said.

'No, it's the same. It's just that you have resources. How wide is the casting?'

'Just the town.'

'Who is the focus?'

Sir Giles hesitated. But Michaelsmith said, 'The missus.'

Jeperson looked at the man.

'She dreams of the old times,' Michaelsmith explained.

'Effective dreams? Reality-changing dreams?'

Sir Giles nodded.

'You know how dangerous that game is. And you had to pick the War.'

'Why not?' Sir Giles's defiance was growing. He needed to defend himself. 'We were all working together, all differences set aside. Everyone was prepared to sacrifice for everyone else. It was our finest hour.'

Jeperson thought for a moment.

'And what about the air raids? The pier?'

'An impurity in the casting,' Sir Giles said. 'It will be rectified.'

'No,' Jeperson said. 'Not an impurity, not a mistake. It was inevitable. You can't just have back the things you liked about the War. You want *ITMA* on the wireless and duchesses cosying up to shopgirls in the shelters, but that means you have to have the monsters. Can you really have forgotten what the War was like for most of Europe? For Britain, even.'

Jeperson rolled up his cuff to show his camp tattoo.

Sir Giles looked down at the carpet, ashamed.

Jeperson was contemptuous. 'And all because you didn't want to learn decimal coinage?'

Fred thought of Vanessa, transformed and perhaps lost.

'Couldn't we just wake his wife up?' he suggested.

Sir Giles, Michaelsmith and Jeperson looked at him, surprised that he had spoken.

'That might seem on the surface to be the best bet,' said Jeperson, 'but there are people alive in the vortex of evil at the end of the pier. We can banish the dream with a hearty breakfast, but they'll all be sucked back into whatever netherworld Giles and his Committee called the War up from.'

Fred could well do without Jaffa and the Boys.

But Vanessa?

'I'm very much afraid that we're going to have to go back to the Emporium.'

'We got hammered last time.'

'That was an exploratory mission. This time, we'll be prepared.'

Sir Giles looked up.

'We'll do what we can, Richard.'

'I should think you will,' said Jeperson, chipper but stern. 'First, you must have some young persons about town?'

Sir Giles nodded.

'Excellent. You Committee men will need to loot your sons' wardrobes. And you'll have to hook up the air-raid sirens to a gramophone. Oh, and no Vera Lynn.'

———✦———

The dawn was beginning to pink the horizon, outlining the sea beyond the pier.

'What year is it, soldier?' Jeperson asked Twitch.

The skinhead couldn't remember.

'Don't say 1941,' Jeperson prompted.

Twitch looked from Jeperson to the Committee.

The street lamps came on, two by two, lighting up the sea-front. Twitch's eyes widened.

Brigadier-General Sir Giles Gallant wore pink loon pants, a paisley tie the shape of a coat-hanger and a rainbow-knit tank top. Marshall Michaelsmith was squeezed into a pair of ripped drainpipe jeans held up by wide tartan braces, a T-shirt with Bob Marley's face on it, and an oversize flat cap with a swirl pattern.

The rest of the Committee, and their wives, were similarly kitted up. It was uncomfortably like fancy dress, a ridiculous pantomime vision of mock trendiness.

But it rang bells.

Twitch remembered, a trace of his old viciousness cutting through his artificial politeness.

'Gits,' he spat.

Ending this casting wouldn't be entirely a good thing.

'It's not then,' Twitch said. 'It's now.'

'That's right,' said Jeperson. 'The War's been over for twenty-five years.'

Twitch undid his uniform. Rupert Scarf and Shoulders looked bewildered at their posts, but caught on slowly.

'You may not like these people,' Jeperson said to the Committee. 'In fact, I can almost guarantee you won't. But you had no right to take their personalities away. Besides, a lot of tommies were more like them than you want to think. You tried to bring back the War as you remembered it, not as it was. Just imagine what would have happened if I had been your focus. Just think what the War I can't remember – which is still inside my skull – would have been like spread over your whole town. The pier wouldn't have been an impurity. It would have been the whole show.'

Sir Giles looked chastened, and not a little ridiculous. Fred guessed that was part of the idea.

'This is the future,' Jeperson announced. 'Learn to live with it. Come on, Fred.'

He started walking down the pier.

'The point is to undo the casting from the inside,' Jeperson said. 'Just think of the 1970s. Fix in your mind all the things that furnish the present.'

They stood outside the Emporium. A swastika flag flew from the summit.

'Colour television, Post Office Tower, frozen peas, Milton Keynes,' Fred chanted.

Jeperson shook his head. 'I hope we're doing the right thing.'

'Multi-storey car parks, inflatable chairs, Sunday supplements, *Top of the Pops…*'

Jeperson sighed and kicked the door open.

'Wakey-wakey, Nazis!'

They passed undisturbed through the exhibition and found the theatre. A miniature Nuremberg rally was in process. Columns of light rose from the stage. Half-Hitler was propped up on an upended dustbin, ranting in German. His monster ministers stood at attention. Eva-Vanessa stood beside her Führer, eyes blank with fanaticism. A map of Seamouth was lit up on the wall, with red swastika-marked arrows on it. An audience of Nazi zombies was arranged before the stage.

'We're just in time,' Jeperson whispered. 'They're planning an invasion.'

The zombies were rapt, intent on their leader's speech.

'They must intend to attack at dawn. How traditional.'

Half-Hitler seemed stronger than before, more substantial. It wasn't growing legs, but was secure in its perch. The more followers it had, the more power gathered in its hateful torso. The homunculus's voice was deeper, more purposeful.

The swastika arrows moved on the map, stabbing into the town.

This mob looked grotesque, but Fred had a sense of the enormity of the damage it could do. The map suggested that this 'casting' was out of the control of Sir Giles's Committee, and that these creatures would soon be able to manipulate the spell, and spread it along the coast and inland, striking towards London like the Nazi invasion that hadn't come in 1940. What was wrong here, at the end of the pier, could blanket the country, drawing strength from the millions sucked into what Jeperson had called a 'vortex of evil'.

Today the pier; tomorrow the world.

Jeperson strode into the audience, down the central aisle. He was apparently calm, but Fred caught the wiry intensity under his languid pose. This man was a warrior. The Nazis noticed the intruder, and with a liquid motion turned to look. Guns were raised.

Jeperson held up a small, shiny object.

'By this totem, I banish you,' he said.

The tiny light caught the audience's attention.

It was a seven-sided coin, one of the new fifty-pence pieces. And it shone like a star.

Half-Hitler snarled. The map shrivelled like ice on a griddle.

'All of you, turn out your pockets,' Jeperson barked. Nazis were used to obeying orders. 'If you find one of these, you'll know you've been fooled. These creatures lost their chance years ago. And a good job too. You have been sucked into someone else's nightmare.'

Goebbels chittered. Himmler-and-Hess fought over their single side-arm. Mussolini leaked jelly at his uniform neckline.

The zombies were exploring their own pockets. Fred did the same and found a fifty-pence piece. He gripped the emblem of modernity.

'Simon Dee, Edward Heath, Germaine Greer, George Best, Cilla Black,' he shouted.

More than one of the zombies had found new money in his pockets. Jaffa tore open his uniform to reveal his scorched Fred Perry. He roared.

'Rise up,' Jeperson said, 'and be free!'

Music began to play from an ancient horn Victrola. 'The Horst Wessel Song'. It quieted the zombies for a moment. The Nazi freaks stood at attention.

Half-Hitler pulled out a pistol, settled on its waist-stump, and shot at Jeperson's hand. A squirt of slow flame lashed out, and tore the fifty-pence piece away, robbing Jeperson of his totem.

Jeperson held his stinging hand. Half-Hitler managed a smug smile. With the Nazi anthem filling the room, it seemed to swell, to float above its bin on a carpet of air.

Jeperson closed his eyes, and began to hum.

Then another sound obliterated the marching band.

It was the Beatles, singing 'Let It Be'.

Half-Hitler dropped its pistol and covered its ears.

The air-raid siren PA was broadcasting at a million decibels.

The song filled the theatre.

Fred saw Vanessa's eyes register reality. The Beatles reached inside and got to her.

She kicked Half-Hitler's bin out from under it.

'Oh Lord,' Fred yelled, 'let it be...'

The zombies swayed with the all-pervasive, all-powerful sound of the 1970s. Jaffa and the Boys wouldn't have liked this music when they were alive, but it was a part of them, imprinted on their minds and on the minds of everyone who had paid attention for the last ten years.

Fred thought the Fab Four had been going downhill since *Revolver*, but for just this once conceded that there might be something in the Maharishi music-hall stuff.

The zombies began firing their guns. At the stage. The Nazi freaks exploded like ectoplasm balloons. Mussolini went off like a hydrogen bomb, fountaining gallons of green froth that washed off the stage and into the audience.

The song changed to 'Here Comes the Sun'.

Dawn broke over the sea, pouring daylight into the Emporium. Goebbels was smoking, and burst into blue flames, screeching like a dying rodent.

Vanessa, herself again, picked her way elegantly through the gunfire and the deliquescing phantoms.

Though most of the Boys were struck by the music, Jaffa was apparently immune – were his ears burned away? He reached out for Jeperson, snarling.

Fred leaped on the zombie's back, getting an armlock round his neck, and pulled him back. Jaffa's clutching hands failed to get a grip on Jeperson's hair. Fred felt the zombie's skull loosening on his neck.

Jeperson got up on the stage, borrowed rifle in his hands, and stuck a bayonet through Half-Hitler, pinning the homunculus to the boards. The creature deflated, leaking ecto-ichor through gashes in its uniform tunic.

As their Führer fell apart, the others were sucked out of the world, leaving behind only a scatter of medals and coins.

The zombie twisted in Fred's grip, eyes sparking with the last of life. Then he was gone, just a corpse dressed up in an old uniform. At the very last, Fred fancied Kevin Jaffa, King Skin, was briefly himself again, not ungrateful to be set free from the casting.

He didn't know how to feel.

The struggle was over.

Jeperson left the rifle stuck into the stage, pinning the empty jacket. He took Vanessa's hands, and kissed her. She turned her face up to the light, reborn as a sun goddess, hair loose and shining like burnished copper.

⚔

They sat on the beach. The Committee were still broadcasting, condemned to play every single in Sir Giles's eleven-year-old granddaughter's collection. Currently, Sergio Mendes was doing Joni Mitchell's 'Chelsea Morning'. Clean sunlight shone on the beach, as if it were newly sown with fresh sand.

They were still taking bodies off the pier, those who had been dead for days. All that was left of the freaks was the occasional streak of drying slime. They were phantasms, Jeperson explained, conjured up with the casting.

'They weren't real, but they would have been.'

Twitch and his cronies, themselves again with blank spots in their short-term memories, were playing football on the beach, slamming into each other, swearing loudly.

Jeperson looked down, ashamed for the skinheads.

'Welcome back to the seventies,' Fred said.

'We can't pick and choose what we accept from the present,' Jeperson admitted, tossing a pebble at the sea.

'White Horses', by Jacky, was playing.

Vanessa had taken her shoes off, and was wiggling her toes in the sand. She seemed unaffected by her brief spell with the End of the Pier Show.

'Young Fred,' Jeperson said, 'you did well when things got weird. You might have an aptitude for this line of strangeness. I've requested you be transferred off the beat. I think you might come in handy at the Diogenes Club. Interested?'

Fred thought about it.

⇜ MOON MOON MOON ⇝

'Tell you one thing,' said Major Gilbert Took-Flemyng, 'this will bloody kill science fiction stone dead.'

Richard Jeperson glanced away from the television set.

Wednesday, 16 July 1969. London: about half past two in the afternoon; Cape Kennedy: oh-nine-thirty-two hours.

The Major quaffed from a brandy balloon the size of a honeydew melon. He was an Ordinary Member, one of a necessary rump of blimps who camouflaged the Diogenes Club as a refuge for the hidebound and unsociable. OMs were selected for lack of perspicacity and absence of curiosity. If they noticed the comings and goings of Extraordinary Members, they never mentioned it. For over a century, OMs had filled capacious armchairs, as much a part of the decor as the cushions under their bottoms and the pipe-fumes above their heads. They radiated unwelcome and disapproval with such wattage the casual visitor – not that there were many – was dissuaded from wondering whether the musty, cavernous building in Pall Mall was home to Great Britain's most secret intelligence agency. Which, of course, it was.

'So this is the teleovision, eh?' muttered the Bishop of Brichester. 'Can't say I'm impressed. It's wireless with lantern slides.'

A newly purchased colour television stood in the hearth of the Informal Room, replacing the grate removed after the 1956 Clean Air Act abolished London's poisonous yellow fog. Several OMs had resigned over the appearance of 'this infernal contraption', and a vote of the full membership was necessary each time it was switched on. It would never be tuned to ITV, lest the sanctum be violated by the Devil's adverts.

The ostentatious 22-inch screen showed a Saturn V rocket rising over the coastal swamps of Florida on a column of white smoke.

The Bishop nodded off. Like the Major, he'd recently sat in silence to a heavy meal in the club's famously unpleasant restaurant room. Richard had opted to nip out to Crank's in Seven Dials for a salad.

A BBC commentator, in tones of muted enthusiasm usually heard during orchestra tuning of a mid-season proms concert, informed viewers that Apollo 11 would enter Earth orbit in twelve minutes. After a turn and a half around the world, the S-IVB third-stage engine would fire, setting Armstrong, Aldrin and Collins on course for the moon.

'It's curtains for Dan Dare and Jet Morgan,' said the Major.

Richard had heard Took-Flemyng's argument before. Robots had been there, and Apollo 8 and Apollo 10 had orbited the moon, but – until today – manned expeditions to the moon had been taken only in fancy: Lucian on a waterspout, Francis Godwin's Gonsales in a chariot pulled by geese, Cyrano de Bergerac on a firework, Baron Munchausen on a silver hatchet, Edgar Allan Poe's Hans Pfaall in a balloon, Jules Verne's Baltimore Gun Club in a capsule fired from a giant cannon, H.G. Wells' First Men in the Moon in a diving bell coated with anti-gravity paint, Hergé's Tintin in a red-and-white chequered rocket and Arthur C. Clarke's Heywood Floyd on a Pan-Am lunar shuttle. Once NASA boot-prints scarred lunar dust, would the memory of these shadow-pioneers fade? Clarke, still alive to see how close his guesses would turn out, did not seem unduly concerned he was about to be out of a job.

The city streets were empty and traffic stilled, in a way not seen since England fought Germany in the World Cup Final. Even Crank's, a vegetarian café haunted by hippies who'd rather immolate themselves than suffer the haircuts sported by the military men of the Apollo mission, had a transistor set up so customers could listen to launch coverage. US troop withdrawals from Vietnam, Rod Laver's Wimbledon win, a potential Sino-Soviet conflict and an actual El Salvador-Honduras war were relegated to the deep insides of the newspapers, squeezed in after pages of moon stories. Toyshops were filled with Airfix rockets and child-safe space helmets. People looked up at the skies and claimed they saw rocket-trails. Comedians told jokes about the cow-powered Irish moon mission.

Every magazine in W.H. Smith's had a rocket or a moon or an astronaut on the cover. The same images were silk-screened on the T-shirts sported in the summer weather by everyone under thirty. Richard's one-off tee from Stanley 'Mouse' Miller was an orange psychedelic explosion laid over a still from Georges Méliès' 1903 *Voyage dans la lune*, with a bullet-shaped spaceship lodged in the eye of an irascible man in the moon. Today, he also wore purple bell-bottoms, red-dyed Chelsea boots, a crushed velvet jacket carried over the shoulder à la Johnny Hallyday, a variety of peace sign lapel badges, a shiny-peaked Victorian band-leader's cap and wire-frame mint-green sunglasses which folded into a pocket-clip case that looked like a fat fountain pen.

Moon songs played everywhere – Frank Sinatra's 'Fly Me to the Moon', Jonathan King's 'Everyone's Gone to the Moon' (which set Richard's teeth on edge – as a 'sensitive', he knew something was badly off about Jonathan King), the Marcels' 'Blue Moon' (he couldn't get that 'moon moon moon' backing vocal out of his head), Mel Tormé's 'Swingin' on the Moon', Captain Beefheart's 'Moonlight in Vermont' (from *Trout Mask*

Replica, the double album Richard agreed with John Peel in rating higher than any Beatles LP), the Bonzo Dog Band's 'Tubas in the Moonlight'. David Bowie's 'Space Oddity' was climbing the charts. Stanley Kubrick's *2001: A Space Odyssey* was still on in the West End. The opening chords of Richard Strauss's 'Thus Spake Zarathustra', featured in the film, were heard over and over, used by the BBC as a signature tune for its moon coverage.

On television, Patrick Moore and James Burke explained what a trans-lunar injection burn was. A diagram anatomised the stages of the Saturn V already shed by the Apollo 11. The spacecraft now looked surprisingly like the bullets of Verne or Méliès, though sleek aluminium-steel-glass-phenolic rather than rivet-studded brass. 'Phenolic' and 'trans-lunar' were among the new words everyone had learned lately.

A discreet cough sounded behind Richard. Hills, the first steward in the Diogenes Club to wear his hair an inch longer than his collar, had appeared at the door of the Informal Room. Ignoring the fretful glares of Major Took-Flemyng and the few other OMs goggling the box, Richard stood.

'Miss Kaye would like to see you, sir,' said Hills, almost subaudially.

Even today, someone had to think about the Earth. Catriona Kaye, Acting Chair of the Ruling Cabal, was holding the fort. Edwin Winthrop, Richard's usual handler, was in Houston with a small party of British 'observers' at Mission Control. The Club usually had a presence at epochal events.

Richard assumed Catriona wanted his report on Brian Jones. He had spent the past fortnight investigating an instant myth. When the ex-Rolling Stone was found at the bottom of his swimming pool, a lunatic magician who called himself 'the Elder Mage of Elgin Crescent' raised a fuss in sorcerous circles, alleging that all currently successful pop groups had contracts with the

Devil which required the sacrifice of a key member to stay on top. Richard only hoped someone who was in a band with Jonathan King had the same deal. The whisper was all over the place, which did not necessarily lend it special credence. Most pop stars had contracts with EMI, Decca or Colonel Tom Parker which even the Devil's lawyers might deem excessively weighted against the talent. When it came to the Devil's music, Richard thought Hell more likely to exacerbate the torments of the damned by piping in 'Donald, Where's Yer Troosers?' or 'How Much is that Doggie in the Window? (Ruff Ruff)' than 'Paint It Black' or 'Sympathy for the Devil'.

The case had taken him from Cotchford Farm in East Sussex, former home of A. A. Milne, to Hyde Park, where Mick Jagger mangled a fragment of Shelley before the Stones played a free concert. A cloud of white butterflies was supposed to be released in a memorial tribute, but – it being a very hot day – most of them died in their boxes. Careful dowsing of the farm turned up nothing suspiciously satanic, though Richard wouldn't soon forget the inside of Brian Jones' bathroom cabinet. A casual glance at the *NME* showed the line-ups of the Who, the Doors, the Jimi Hendrix Experience and the Wurzels unaltered by recent suspicious death – though an underground magazine alleged the Beatles had ritually murdered Stuart Sutcliffe and implanted a coded confession of the magickal crime in *Rubber Soul*. Richard was prepared to close the docket, though the original complainant was noisily foretelling another significant drowning before the month was out.

This call was new business.

Catriona Kaye – born in 1900, as commemorated in the 1920s song written about her, 'Century Baby' – looked decades younger than her years. Thanks to Thoroughly Modern Millie, her modified flapper style and bobbed hair intersected with a current fashion.

Entering the Quiet Room, Richard found her sitting comfortably on the edge of Winthrop's desk, shoes dangling above the carpet. She wore a low-waisted dress the colour of her pearls and smoked a cigarette in a long, black holder. She made an appealing contrast with the Club's Victorian founder, who glowered heavily out of a monumental portrait behind her.

'Richard,' said Catriona, smiling, 'meet Special Agent Gauge.'

He turned, and had a little electric shock in the brain.

Parapsychologists called it 'psychic feedback', but Richard knew it as a kind of spark. Like him, Agent Gauge was a sensitive, a Talent. Frankly, a spook. Richard noticed that before noticing she was a she – and he knew her sex from the fragrance of Ô by Lancôme lingering in the corridor.

A tall blonde about five years younger than Richard, Agent Gauge had a figure Hugh Hefner would get excited about and a don't-mess-with-me stance which gave warning to the most octopus-handed *Playboy* subscriber. She had big grey-blue eyes and straight, mid-length hair with a pronounced widow's peak. Her only flaw was a tiny question mark scar under her right eye – easy to cover with make-up, but she chose not to. She modelled a powder-blue trouser suit over a fawn blouse. Her wide belt, worn high, matched the blouse and was fastened with a large circular buckle. Her jacket, tailored to conceal a shoulder-holster, hung oddly because she wasn't wearing a gun. That made her an American. So did the fact her title was 'Special Agent'.

She stuck out her hand to be shook, but he kissed it.

'Richard Jeperson,' he said, meeting her eyes.

That spark was now a crackle. Richard felt his hair rise as if he were touching a Van de Graaf generator.

She took her hand away.

'Special Agent Gauge,' she said. 'Whitney Gauge.'

Catriona slid elegantly off the desk and stood between them.

'Special Agent Gauge is with a Federal Bureau of Investigation.'

Richard caught the use of the indefinite article. By decades of self-serving flackery, J. Edgar Hoover made the world think there was only one FBI. Actually, Hoover was merely Director of the Bureau of Investigation of the United States Department of Justice. At least a dozen other arms of government had investigative divisions which operated across state-lines, and were thus officially Federal Bureaux of Investigation, among them the Treasury, the Alcohol and Tobacco Overseers, the Internal Revenue Service, the Commission of Major League Baseball and whatever misleading title Whitney Gauge's superiors ('the Unnameables' in spook circles) put on letterheads if they ever sent letters. Alone among overlooked investigators, the Unnameables never grumbled about Hoover's publicity-hogging.

'You're a long way off your beat, Miss Gauge. Or is it Mrs Gauge?'

'It's Special Agent Gauge,' she said.

Richard detected a tiny crack of smile.

'Something's come up,' said Catriona, 'and Assistant Director Spilsby has sent our friend to sit in. It involves the moon.'

'So does everything this week.'

Catriona arched an eyebrow. 'Indeed. All the little boys want to grow up to be spacemen now. And girls, thanks to that splendid Soviet lady…'

Whitney Gauge frowned, reddening her question mark in a manner Richard found curiously fascinating.

'When I was a lad, I wanted to be a cowboy,' he said. 'Roy Rogers was my idol.'

He mimed a fast double-draw and fired off his fingers at Whitney Gauge, blowing gunsmoke away from the tips.

'I suppose you wanted to be Eliot Ness?'

'No,' she said, 'I wanted to be a ballerina.'

She made an extraordinarily limber fast pirouette and froze, thigh and calf-muscles tight, with cerulean-painted toes – she wore open-toed sandals – hovering an inch from Richard's Adam's apple. After seconds, she broke the pose.

'But I "overdeveloped".'

To Richard's mind, Whitney Gauge had developed just fine. He knew better than to put it like that this early in their acquaintance.

'If you young people have finished flirting,' said Catriona, 'can we get on with business? I've a transatlantic call with Edwin in half an hour, and he'll need to know you're looking into the threat.'

'Threat?' said Richard and Whitney Gauge, together.

Catriona was apologetic. 'More of a niggle. A loose end, though it flaps more than it ought and deserves urgent attention. Are you sitting comfortably?'

Richard and Whitney Gauge were standing, but that wasn't the point.

'Then I'll begin. Were you aware that a group calling itself the Temple of Domina Oriens circulated a petition to pressure NASA to discontinue the Apollo programme?'

Richard looked at Whitney Gauge. They both shrugged.

'Will you stop doing that,' Catriona said, pettishly. 'It's faintly disturbing.'

'Doing what?' asked Richard and Whitney Gauge, together.

'That. You're long-lost Corsican twins. I fully understand. I nominate you, Richard, to keep quiet – indeed, to refrain from any gesture. Whitney, if you would respond, when necessary.'

Whitney Gauge said, 'Yes.' Richard suppressed an urge to nod.

'Now, if I may continue... There have, of course, been voices raised against space exploration in general and the moon mission in particular. Some argue it's an obscene waste of money, when so many problems on Earth remain unsolved. Others worry about a military/political domination of the solar system by America. The Flat Earth Society fear a precipitous decline in membership. And so on. This week, for obvious reasons, the appetite of the press for moon-related stories extends to anyone who says anything, positive or negative, about the Apollo mission. The High Priestess of the Temple of Domina Oriens – which is in Clerkenwell, by the way – holds the moon sacred, and claims setting a foot on her soil is like defiling a vestal virgin. She isn't in favour of that.'

'Who is this High Priestess and how large is her congregation?' asked Whitney Gauge.

'She is called Luna Selene Moon—'

'That's like being named Moon Moon Moon,' put in Richard.

'—which, as Richard has helpfully pointed out, is gilding the lily. She was born Bridget Gail Tully. It could have been worse. She could have called herself "June Bassoon Moon".'

'Or Luna Ticwitch?' Richard ventured.

Whitney Gauge giggled.

'Very amusing, Richard,' said Catriona. 'Now, if you'd pay attention in class, here's what we have on the silly goose.'

Catriona handed Richard a sheaf of photographs and press cuttings. After a riffle, he passed the folder to Whitney Gauge, who gave the documents a similar quick glance. The earliest pictures were sepia studies of a long-nosed thin girl in a see-through shift.

'She was an artists' model just after the War, then turned painter. You can guess her favoured subject.'

A glossy catalogue contained miniature representations of samey pictures.

'She calls them "moonscapes", but they look like fairy pictures to me,' said Catriona. 'The Diogenes Club has had several unpleasant involvements with the little folk.'

In recent press photographs, which went with 'silly season'

stories about Miss Moon's curse on NASA, the High Priestess was still thin and long-nosed, but wore more demurely opaque shifts. She had masses of white hair usually bound by a circlet with a crescent moon stuck to it.

'The Temple is fair-sized as cults go, with a few mildly influential members. They're on our List.'

Whitney Gauge raised an eyebrow, exactly the way Richard would have if he hadn't known what the List was.

'We divide Britain's home-grown occult groups into cranks, who aren't on the List, and the potentially dangerous, who are,' he explained. 'By "dangerous", we mean possessed of some sort of verifiable magic resources. You dig?'

'I grok.'

'Children,' snorted Catriona, amused. 'The Temple haven't got a record for human sacrifice or souring the milk or laming the Prime Minister, but they've registered a needle-flicker of power, especially recently. Phases of the moon, I expect. And Miss Moon Moon Moon began issuing veiled threats through the popular press. We'd let it go, except she's suddenly changed her tune. For a few weeks, any hack in Fleet Street hoping to fill a puff piece could get an ominous quote from her about how the Apollo 11 mission was a sacrilege. Terrible would be the vengeance of the ravaged goddess, woe, woe and thrice woe. She came near as spitting to claiming responsibility for the Apollo 1 launch-pad fire that nearly scuttled the lunar adventure before it was started. Two days ago, the High Priestess shut up. Pulled out of appearing on something called *The Simon Dee Show*. A big protest outside the American Embassy has been quietly called off. One of the busy bees we have combing the cuttings turned up an old associate who is extremely interesting to us. In 1948 or thereabouts, Miss Moon formed a liaison with a Magister Rex Chalfont.'

Catriona paused, as if the name might ring bells. It didn't.

'What do we know about him?' Richard asked.

'Nothing,' said Catriona. 'Not a thing. Just his name, and rank in academic sorcery. Which is wrong and impossible. I mean, we know everything...'

Catriona was referring to the secret files of the Diogenes Club.

'Whitney's Bureau know even less about Chalfont than we do,' said Catriona. 'But they're interested now. Enough to fly her over on a military aircraft and put her up at Claridge's on the sort of expenses the Royal Family can't claim. If we don't have a dossier on Chalfont, information must have been kept from us. That is very, very difficult to do.'

Richard understood that, as Chair of the Ruling Cabal of the Diogenes Club, Catriona Kaye know the birth-name of the tommy buried in the Tomb of the Unknown Soldier in Westminster Abbey, the present addresses of Ambrose Bierce and Judge Crater and why Borley Rectory burned down in 1939. Come to that, she knew where the woozle went, what songs the sirens sang and how flies landed upside down on the ceiling.

'I am perturbed more by the apparent invisibility of this Magister Rex Chalfont than the High Priestess' ominous utterances. For the sake of all our peaces of mind, it's been decided you two should look up Miss Moon and see what can be learned about her old beau. Do you think you can do that little thing for me? Good. I'm glad. Call Hills and tell him when you can make a report. Better make it before "touch-down" in the Sea of Tranquillity... "Touch-down"? Ugh, what a word...'

Richard and Whitney Gauge looked at each other.

<hr>

Whitney Gauge saw his scarlet Peel Trident parked outside the Club and laughed. The vehicle had been described as a 'flying saucer on wheels'.

'How do you expect us to fit into that?'

'If three astronauts can get into a capsule, two can ride in a bubble-car,' said Richard. 'Comfortably.'

'They said I was too tall to be an astronaut,' she declared. 'The boys in NASA didn't like being shown up.'

He unclipped the fibreglass chassis and lifted it like a cutaway diagram, disclosing comfortable red leather seats mounted on three go-kart wheels.

'I guess your Bentley is at home?'

'I drive a Rolls, actually,' he said. 'Not very manoeuvrable in Central London.'

The American woman looked up and down the empty Mall.

'It's not like this, usually,' he said. 'It's as busy as New York, with politer beeping and shouting.'

'I find that hard to believe.'

'This is a space-related anomaly, Miss America.'

'You can say that again, Carnaby Street. At least you don't have this thing painted up like a British flag.'

'I considered the option, but we're supposed to be a secret service. We try to exercise a little discretion.'

'That explains the way you dress.'

'You're not exactly unobtrusive, Agent Gauge. Six-foot Giselles are scarce in these here parts.'

She ducked and folded herself into the passenger seat, smoothed her hair and crossed her arms so they wouldn't be cut off when the dome closed. With practised ease, Richard took the driver's seat and pulled the chassis down. The Trident clicked together. The Plexiglas bubble-dome interior was scented nicely with Ô.

'Pre-launch check, Major Tom?' she said. 'All systems go for take-off?'

'Roger Charlie Chester Wilko.'

He pulled the starter. The radio came on – more commentary from Florida. Apollo 11 had left Earth orbit.

He pulled the starter again. The Zweirad motor turned over, purring like a tiger cub.

'What do you call this roadster? The "Dickmobile"?'

'She answers to "Nanny".'

'Very British.'

The Trident picked up speed, zooming through Admiralty Arch into Trafalgar Square. A plague of pigeons took off in a rapid flutter. No tourists around to feed them. The only people in sight were a gaggle of drivers at the taxi-stand and a couple of policemen – all bent around a wireless cabinet, listening to news from space. Orson Welles would have loved an audience like this. At the top of his column, Nelson was probably lifting his good eye to the stratosphere and waving on the lunar mariners.

Richard could get used to a city empty of traffic and pedestrians. Nanny was modified to his specifications, but he'd never had an opportunity to test her at top speed in an urban daytime environment. He thought he could at least double the ordinary Trident's advertised 45 mph.

'I suppose you drive something the length of a skittle alley with fins and an open top?' he ventured.

'I have a Tucker Tomorrow. Best automobile ever made.'

Turning a corner into Charing Cross Road, Nanny lurched as one of her front wheels lifted from the road, tipping his passenger against him.

'You did that deliberately,' she said.

He supposed he had.

'Don't do it again.'

He was warned. On the whole, he thought Special Agent Whitney Gauge was rather fun.

'So you abandoned promising careers as a ballet dancer and a space–woman,' he said. 'What else did you try before you signed with the Unnameables?'

'I was a Mouseketeer. They took away my ears when I told Uncle Walt I thought his pal Senator McCarthy looked like Monstro the Whale from *Pinocchio*. I appeared in the first *Beach Party* movie, but quit because they wouldn't let "the girls" surf. I can hang ten. Frankie Avalon can barely hang one–half. Do you even know what all this means?'

'I speak fluent American.'

'I passed all the NASA astronaut tests, except the one about not menstruating. Otherwise, Buzz Aldrin wouldn't be Number Two on the moon, you better believe it.'

'Are you Air Force?'

'USAAF intelligence. Officially retired. Like you, a spook. I passed the other tests they ran at NASA, the ones with the Rhine cards and the spinning needles. You know what happens when you score high psi. I got seconded to, as I said, a Federal Bureau of Investigation. Where you're famous, by the way. They teach a course about the Ghost Train you shut down in the 1950s. How old are you anyway, Mr Chips?'

'Cheek,' he said. 'And I don't know, Gidget.'

'Of course, you have no memory of your childhood. It's in the file. And nobody's been able to find out who you really are. That gives you something in common with Magister Rex.'

'I try not to think about it.'

'Liar. I can tell when people lie. That's not one of my tricks. Just a small–t talent. Comes from growing up near Hollywood agents.'

'So what are your "tricks"? Can you hard–boil an egg with your mind?'

'No, of course not. Active Talents like that are incredibly rare. I'm a Reactive Talent, like you. A psychomancer. You're an empath. That's a weird combo, they say. Not advisable.'

'You have feelings about things, I have feelings about people. Those ought to be complementary.'

They were in Holborn now, whizzing down Theobald's Road. A fish 'n' chip shop chalkboard offered 'moon' rock and 'loonar' chips.

'Catriona thinks we can work together,' he said. 'I assume Assistant Director Spilsby does too.'

A pause. 'I passed the immediate criteria for this assignment.'

'Which was…?'

'Being in the building at the time the alert came in.'

'You have a duty rota? Intrepid agents ready at all times, like the Minutemen?'

'Not exactly. I was in Spilsby's office.'

'Receiving a commendation after your latest victory over the forces of evil?'

'Submitting my resignation after an eleven-month assignment to the reception desk.'

'I see a pattern emerging.'

'You would. While I was passing all those courses in the Top Three and qualifying as a field agent, do you know who my hero was?'

Richard huffed modestly.

'No, Oh-Oh-707, not you… Her, your chief. Catriona Kaye. In the States, the Boys' Club won't let a woman into the field. Here, she gets to sit on the board. And her record makes yours look feeble.'

'Steady on. You're steaming up the Plexiglas.'

'I mean, look at it. Angel Down, the Mummy's Heart, the Blame Game, the Witch War, the Unhappy Medium… She was there, for all of them, in the thick of it.'

'She wasn't alone. A fellow named Winthrop was there too. He usually sits in Catriona's chair.'

'I'd expect you to say that. She's had to fight her whole career against people like you.'

'I'm very fond of Catriona Kaye...'

...who was, in fact, the nearest thing he had to a mother. If Whitney Gauge were cleared to know more secrets, he could tell her Catriona wasn't even the first female member of the Diogenes Club. Geneviève Dieudonné, Kate Reed, Amy Thomsett and Annette Amboise (whose memory was always a tiny stick-pin in his heart) also figured on the rolls... not to speak of Vanessa, Richard's own ward, currently orienteering in the New Forest, picking up tradecraft between A levels at Cheltenham and a Sociology degree at the LSE. Provisional membership was waiting for Vanessa when she graduated, then she'd be in Nanny's passenger seat on jaunts like this.

'But...'

'Hmmn, yes, what?'

Richard back-tracked.

'You're absolutely right. Catriona sets a mark few can hope to live up to. You couldn't choose a better heroine. And... the fact that your AD can't see past your chest just goes to show why our country is better than yours.'

Whitney Gauge's mouth formed a perfect Lancôme Ô.

'Just kidding, Minnie Mouse. Hands across the sea, and all that. This is an Anglo–American operation. Our two great nations are equal partners in the marriage.'

'Only Britain is the chick, right? You do the dishes and have America's dinner ready when it comes home?'

Richard laughed. 'Let's not continue down that path. Besides, we're where we're going. Sekforde Street, Clerkenwell. That's the Temple of Domina Oriens.'

Aside from a gilded plaster man-in-the-moon on the lintel, the building had no distinguishing features. Near-identical premises housed a socialist reading room and a community centre for Piedmontese exiles, both closed. Trades union activists and Italian mini-monarchists were at home in front of the telly.

'Ready for EVA?' he asked.

'Always.'

He released the catch, and the dome rose. They got out and he shut the car.

'Are you feeling anything?' he asked.

'Relief at being able to stand up and breathe. From the sidewalk, nada. You think I should try the door?'

'Go on, fondle the knocker.'

That came out as rather too Carry On, he felt.

'I'd rather grab the knob,' she said, and took hold. She let go again, sharply.

'A shock?'

'You think I'd know better,' she admitted, momentarily pale under her tan. 'The last hand that touched this was dipped in blood.'

He looked at her palm.

'Metaphorically, I mean,' she explained. 'If he got any on himself, I'm sure he wiped afterwards.'

'He?'

'I'm getting a man. In a hurry. And a lot of blood.'

Richard pushed the door. It opened.

'Too much of a hurry to lock up behind him.'

Whitney Gauge reached for the gun she wasn't carrying.

'Do you have a nightstick or anything? What do you call it, a truncheon?'

'I am not a policeman,' he responded, with dignity.

They stepped into the Temple. The foyer looked and smelled like the front of house of a small theatre. A tea urn and an assortment of biscuits filled a refreshments corner. A notice board behind the cashier's desk displayed type-written schedules of 'rituals, rites, oblations and obeisances'. A painting of an alien landscape was hung prominently. A lush, purplish-green jungle was inhabited by furtive creatures which might be crossbreeds of cockatoo and praying mantis. A gap in the fungoid trees showed a night-sky where the Earth shone amid a sprinkle of stars. He didn't have to be a sensitive to intuit that this was the work of Luna Selene Moon.

'Don't look like fairies to me,' said Whitney Gauge. 'More like bugs.'

'Have you ever met any fairies?'

'No.'

'How do you know what they look like?'

'Imagination.'

'Good answer.'

A set of double-doors opened into an auditorium with a raised stage. The house-lights were on. An altar-cum-lectern was set up in front of a triptych which showed three faces of the moon. The symmetrical triple-moon, repeated on the backdrop and the altar, featured a grinning full moon sandwiched between two cruelly sly crescent profiles. Folding chairs were set out for a congregation or audience. A group of the chairs were overturned or had snapped shut. A person was curled up and bleeding in the middle of the mess.

'Moon moon moon,' he muttered.

It was a middle-aged woman in a white robe with a yellow moon on the front. Luna Moon, the former Bridget Tully. Her long hair splayed around her head like an electrified crown. She had been stabbed or shot through the moon on her robe.

Richard checked for a pulse and caught a last flicker.

Then he was overwhelmed by visions. He was usually attuned simply to inchoate feelings or moods. Only in extreme circumstances did he pick up anything like an image.

This was the most extreme circumstance.

As the High Priestess departed her earthly shell for parts unknown, pictures crowded into Richard's mind.

Pictures in the style of Luna Moon.

Trees with meaty leaves, greenish spongy craters, sugary glistening webs spun by asymmetric spiders with cherry-glacé eyes. The artist's moon was edible. People in robes or jewelled diving suits frolicked – there was no other word for it – with the cockatoo-mantises or their relations, who looked like walrus-weasels or giraffe-fish. The pictures sped up, flickering like Méliès' moon-shot film.

'Richard?'

He was on his knees by the dead woman, struck by acute ice-cream headache and stabbing chest pain.

He had to let go of her, for fear that his consciousness would be pulled wherever hers had gone.

Whitney snapped fingers in front of his face.

He tried to keep the pictures in his memory. Each was crowded out by the next, like pages falling from an album into a fire.

A final image lingered a few instants longer than the others. A different subject, a different style. An Earthscape, a weathered sign in a country lane. Woods and fields. It was daytime, but the moon was out, rising above the roof of an uninviting, large house.

'Mildew Manor,' he said.

The image was gone, self-destructing in memory.

But in speaking the words on the sign aloud, he had captured them.

'Mildew Manor?' Whitney responded. 'What is that? A place? A picture? A state of mind?'

'A novel by Thomas Love Peacock? I don't know.'

'Peacock wrote *Nightmare Abbey* and *Crotchet Castle*...'

'…and *Headlong Hall* and *Gryll Grange*…'

'…but no Mildew Manor, so far as I know. He died trying to save his books from a fire.'

'You didn't learn that in the Mickey Mouse Club.'

'We have libraries in California, too.'

'Glad to hear it. I thought they'd all been torn down and turned into drive-in churches and no-tell motels…'

Whitney let go of him, and they stood up.

'In case you hadn't noticed,' she said, 'this Olde Englishe Temple is exactly the kind of ridiculous made-up religion you're stereotyping as Californian. Oh, and shouldn't we concentrate on the bleeding woman?'

'She can't help us any more, poor love.'

'She can't help you, Richard…'

Whitney knelt, and put her palm to the woman's face.

'You read people, I read things. She's not people any more…'

Whitney made contact, as with the door-knob, and juddered as if holding a live wire. She closed her eyes, pressed hard on Luna Moon's face and forced herself to maintain the touch.

Richard was concerned.

She let go, opened her eyes and breathed again.

'I hate that,' she said.

He helped her into the foyer. She sat on a saggy armchair next to a low table piled with mimeographed occult newsletters and glossy art magazines. She flipped open a powder-compact and examined her hairline minutely in the mirror.

'Shall I get you tea from the urn? You need to replenish your electrolytes. Maybe some biscuits?'

'What?'

'Cookies.'

'No, just tea… cold, if possible.'

'Is there any other kind? This'll be stewed.'

He turned a spigot and thick brownish liquid filled a mug. The Temple had their own crockery, with a smiley moon decal.

'Ah,' Whitney said, in triumph, 'there's the slut!'

She had plucked a single, silver-white hair from her head.

'Every time,' she said. 'There's always one.'

She put her compact away and took the cold tea. She drained the mug as if on a dare, trying to get it down without tasting.

He nibbled a stale custard cream.

'What did you get from her?' he asked.

'What do you think, Sherlock? A sharp, stabbing pain in the chest.'

'Fear, annoyance...?'

She shook her head. 'No, that's what you'll have felt. Empathy, remember? I just get things. Sights, sounds, processes. Pain is a thing, not an emotion. The last thing she saw was a face, fading to black.'

'Can you describe the murderer?'

She held up her mug and pointed to the decal.

'A moon-mask?'

She nodded. 'Something like that. But weirder. Yellow, hook nose, cratery skin, bulby forehead. Under curved glass, like a TV screen or a biker's visor. No, not a crash helmet, a space helmet. No NASA or CCCP logo. It was a custom spacesuit. Old-fashioned, if that's possible.'

'Did you get an idea of the weapon.'

'Oh yes,' she said. 'The bastard held it up, showed it to her. A double-edged knife. Silvery. Carvings on the blade and hilt. That triple-moon thing.'

'An athamé?' suggested Richard. He knew she'd know what an athamé was.

'Like that. Though it can't have been a ritual killing. She wasn't on the altar, or I'd have seen ceiling and the blade coming down. She was tapped on the shoulder, turned round, and was stabbed in the heart.'

'Your moon-faced astronaut murdered her?'

'Definitely,' she said. 'That's what she saw. What did she feel?'

Richard tried to remember the impressions he had taken from Luna Moon.

'What I said. Not so much fear, more annoyance. She was irritated at being murdered, as if she'd had other things to do today and was more concerned about not ticking them off her list than being killed. I got a lot of pictures from her, but not real things. Whatever you think of that –' he indicated the painting on the wall – 'she was serious about art. The images in her mind were the ones she painted. Important to her. Pregnant with personal meaning.'

'Mildew Manor?'

'That stood out,' he said. 'All the other things were mental moonscapes. The Mildew Manor picture was earthly. The English countryside, somewhere.'

'You're sure it's a real place?'

'No, but it's important. Like your "old-fashioned" astronaut.'

'Major Stabby.'

'That's his name?' he asked.

'I doubt it, but we have to call him something. You have to call out someone or something before you go after it. That's good practice in magic, isn't it?'

He agreed.

'Have you got your Girl Scout badge on you?' he asked. She nodded. 'Good. You might have to claim diplomatic immunity. Strictly speaking what we've done counts as tampering with Her Majesty's Evidence in a Murder Inquiry. The plods won't like it, but they'll lump it. Luckily, we have a friend in New Scotland Yard…'

Stumbling over a corpse within an hour of accepting a commission bordered on the vulgar. A telephone was on the front desk. He picked it up. First he would call Catriona Kaye. Then the police.

——◆——

'This isn't what I think of as a hotel bar,' Whitney said. 'Too big, too well lit, too classy.'

'I trust you didn't ring down to ask how to make the bed vibrate.'

She poked her tongue out at him.

Normally, that would have excited disapproval in Claridge's, but even here everyone was only paying attention to the moon voyage. A single barman stayed at his post, while the rest of the staff were in a back room lit by a television set.

Eight hours into its mission, Apollo 11 had shed its Saturn V rocket stages and left Earth orbit for cislunar space. *Columbia*, the command/service module, separated from the third stage and docked with the *Eagle*, the lunar excursion module. Broadcasters were already fed up with the technical chatter tossed between the Apollo crew and Mission Control ('Houston') but the public still found magic in the curt, arcane, tinny American voices. They were talking from outer space!

Whitney had changed into a hot-pink minidress with a matching Alice band and go-go boots. Even the Claridge's barman noticed her, and Richard was sure the great hotels put something in the staff tea to control natural urges insofar as lady guests were concerned.

The only other people in the bar were a table of drunk young execs in city mod uniform – paisley foulards, dayglo shirts, two pieces of three-piece Savile row suits, shaped sideburns. They were toasting a guy named Roly, who had something to do with the packaging of Sky-Ray lollies (a big seller this season). Roly took credit for the visionary spirit of the space age between sudden, rapid trips to the Gents.

None of the execs were so drunk that they didn't shoot looks over at Whitney Gauge. She noticed. Richard noticed she noticed. She noticed Richard noticing. No one was in any doubt. She had conquered Britain without really trying.

Naturally, Richard had ordered champagne and a platter of fresh strawberries. This was still a business meeting.

Richard had remained on hand at the Temple of Domina Oriens as Inspector Price, the Diogenes Club's liaison with Scotland Yard's Department of Queer Complaints, supervised a team of scene-of-crime officers and forensics men as they examined and then removed the body of Luna Moon, and searched the building. The Club and DQC had a policy of sharing information, not always observed. No bloody bootprints or daubed messages were found. Richard gave a reasonably detailed report of what he and Whitney had gathered from the deceased, but Price couldn't make much use of it. His boys were stuck with looking for witnesses, chasing up grasses and hoping for a credible confession. Embarrassingly often, even in Diogenes Club cases, boring old police-work turned up an answer before spookery. And you could take it into court, too.

'Have we been through that rigmarole,' said Whitney, biting down on a big ripe strawberry, 'where the cops warn us off the case but we stay on it anyway?'

'It's not our place to catch murderers, love,' he told her. 'Though I daresay Euan Price would be grateful if we turned over a stone and found this one. If finding out who killed Miss Moon Moon Moon leads us to understand why we don't have a Magister Rex Chalfont on the books, we should sleuth away to our hearts' content. If it's a side-issue, we drop it and try something else.

Let's face it, it would be just too bloody easy if Chalfont were our Major Stabby…'

'Magisters generally leave athamé-work to minions. Unless it's Aztec heart-ripping stuff.'

'In Aztec mythology, the moon is the severed head of the goddess Coyolxauhqui, murdered – along with four hundred siblings – by her foetal half-brother Huitzilopochtli to forestall Coyolxauhqui's attempt to force their mother Coatlicue to have an abortion. How unlike the home-life of our own dear deity! Chup-Kamui, moon goddess of the Ainu, was so disgusted at having to bear witness to the night-time naughtiness of adulterers she swapped places in the pantheon with her brother and became a sun goddess instead.'

'You've read this up, right?'

Richard admitted it. 'I took this from the Temple, and skimmed it while you were napping off jet lag.'

He tossed over a slender volume. *Moon Myths*, by Enzo Yarikh.

'If you need to tell your Basque Ilazki from your Dahomeyan Gleti, this is your I-Spy Guide… They're all moon gods and goddesses. Mostly goddesses. Selene was a Greek goddess. Well, a Titan. Luna was Roman, aka Luna Noctiluca. Humanity has been venerating our satellite since cave-days. There's a Neolithic stone circle in the Hebrides that tracks the risings of the moon in an extremely sophisticated manner. Looking up at the night sky is nothing new. And the moon is the biggest, shiniest thing in it.'

Whitney flicked through the pages.

'No pictures,' she said.

'The moon affects the tides, women's cycles, the proverbial lunatic… and some werewolves, though not as many as Lon Chaney Junior would have you believe…'

Whitney gave him back the book and stretched in her chair like a cat. On the other side of the room, she won enthusiastic reviews.

The mastermind of lolly wrapper design finally got drunk enough to do more than look sidelong at the tall blond bird. Encouraged by perhaps ill-intentioned comrades, Roly spacewalked across acres of carpet and stood over their table. He had a transparent moustache.

'Is this hippie bothering you, Pink Lady?' he asked Whitney, using the burp-speech recommended for those who have lost a larynx to throat-cancer. 'Because, if he is, I could… ah… take care of him for you.'

The other execs cheered. Roly was unsteady on his feet. Mr Sky-Ray Lolly didn't look as if he were in any position to 'take care of' a stick insect on crutches.

'That's very kind of you, hoss – but this is my grandfather. I'm seeing he doesn't get into trouble. He's uncontrollable around women.'

The young exec looked at Richard, trying to focus.

'Have a strawberry, old chap,' said Richard.

'Who are you calling a… what did you just say…?'

Roly unwisely plucked the bottle out of the ice bucket and hefted it like a club. Champagne frothed out of the neck, drenching the cuff of his salmon-coloured shirt. He swung the bottle towards Richard's head.

Whitney quick-jabbed two knuckles into Roly's side, just above the rib-cage. He froze in mid-swing, then – as Whitney innocently sipped from her flute – fell like a tree in the forest. Richard caught the bottle.

It was empty. He signalled for another.

Roly lay, face knotted, unable to move. His friends expressed concern, but none ventured to help.

'How long does that last?' Richard asked.

'About ten minutes, usually.'

The barman summoned someone to take care of the fallen exec.

If Roly were not a guest, he'd be discreetly ejected from the hotel. If he were, he'd be asked to leave as soon as his bill was settled.

Whitney shrugged, disarmingly, at the pest's friends and eggers-on.

'What can I do,' she said, raising her voice to carry across the acreage of the bar. 'I'm naturally a knockout.'

Laughter came.

'Roly's not usually that much of a prawn,' said one of his mates. 'It's moon madness.'

Richard understood.

More champagne was produced.

'We'll avoid further altercations if this is sent up to the lady's suite,' Richard told the waiter, palming him a ten-shilling note in a handshake.

'Very good, sir.'

'And more strawberries,' said Whitney. 'Many more strawberries.'

<hr />

'What are we doing outside Handel's house?' Whitney asked.

'Waiting for a bus,' he told her.

After breakfast at Claridge's, they had walked a little way down Brook Street. London was busier this morning. Most folk who had skived off to watch the launch were back at work. Tourists had emerged to wander distractedly. Richard didn't have to be especially empathic to pick up the epochal beat in the back of everyone's mind.

We're on our way to the moon…

Whitney wore a lime-green trouser suit and matching sun-hat. She had clever glasses which darkened when the sun came out – a NASA by-product, like non-stick pans and velcro. Oh, and like the orbital death rays America thought her NATO allies didn't know about. Those 'communications satellites' would blow up if activated, thanks to a tiny pre-stressed ceramic component manufactured in Milton Keynes. In trying to cut plucky little Britain out of the loop, the Pentagon underestimated Harold Wilson's capacity for sulky vengefulness.

'There's no stop here,' she said.

'It's not a regularly scheduled service. We're going to a party in a bus.'

'Very stylish. Is it a long ride?'

'As long as you want it to be. I didn't say we're going in a bus to a party, I said we're going to a party in a bus. Here it is.'

Richard pulled a psychedelic explosion out of his hankie pocket and flapped it, as if flagging a taxi. A red London bus stopped for them. The number and destination '∞ Far Out Scene'. Richard helped Whitney onto the open rear platform.

'Hold very tight please,' said a woman in a tailored black silk conductor's uniform. 'Ting ting.'

The conductress rang the bell and the bus moved on.

Both decks heaved with assorted people – fragrant hippies and flower children, pinstriped Establishment types, famous faces from fashion and sport, notable beggars and crooks, popular scientists and unpopular clergymen, a couple of exotic dancers from Soho. Something intriguing if non-sexual was happening under a pile of PVC macs between an angry Liverpool poet, an actress who'd been in a controversial Wednesday Play and a middle-aged cleaning woman who'd probably got on the wrong bus by mistake.

Upstairs, Eric Clapton and Andrés Segovia were duetting. The tune they had long left behind was 'Shine On Harvest Moon'. Downstairs, Larry Adler played harmonica while Spike Milligan made up limericks. Luckily, there were many rhymes for 'moon'. Silver-paper stars, planets, satellites and spaceships were stuck up on the windows. It was easy to guess the theme of this bash.

'Richard Jeperson,' exclaimed the conductress, kissing him full on the lips, 'how delightful! And this must be the blond Yank bird you were glimpsed with in Clerkenwell yesterday afternoon and Claridge's bar last night! Don't tell me, Whitney Gauge. With the, um, secret busybody acronym folks… you're the Girl from A.U.N.T.I.E., right?'

'I'm with a Federal Bureau of—'

'Spookery and Goblinage. How sweet.'

Whitney was surprised the conductress was in on the secret, but Richard knew her of old.

'This is Margery Device,' he said. 'Pronounced "Davis", spelled "De Vice". She's the Witch.'

Whitney noticed the definite article.

'Don't listen to Dickie,' Margery said. 'It's just a title.'

'This party is a grand tradition,' Richard said. 'It's always on somewhere in London.'

'Have a cocktail, dear,' said Margery. 'They're all just invented. Absinthe Apollo, Moon Madness, Space Shiver, Fireball XL-5, Buzz Aldrin…'

'I'll have a Rum Collins.'

'Not new, but topical – I approve,' said Margery, signalling to a Maltese bar-tender Richard had last seen on an identity parade as a near-lookalike for a trunk murderer. 'Richard…?'

'Tizer. I'm on duty.'

Margery laughed.

The hostess was Queen of London Gossip, which meant she knew everything worth knowing and was prepared to be wildly indiscreet if it amused her. The only secret she never shared was her age. She looked exactly as she had when he first went to her party – then in a sculptor's studio in Brixton – in the mid-1950s. The London Witch held up one corner of a defensive magic square which had seen the city through plague, fire, blitz and rationing.

'Is there somewhere quiet we can talk?' he asked Margery.

'No, of course not, silly boy. There's only somewhere loud.'

Richard sipped his Tizer. Whitney at least looked at her cocktail.

'You'll be here about Bridget Tully, of course. Cross-eyed, you know. Odd in a painter. Had an affair with—'

'Magister Rex Chalfont.'

'No, that's not the name I was thinking of. It was the polar explorer. Not him himself – the fellow who played him in *Scott of the Antarctic*. It'll come to me in a moment. I can see the face.'

'It's Chalfont we're interested in,' said Whitney.

'I daresay you are, my girl. An interesting sort of chap. Not a name you hear every day, either.'

'Not a name some of us have heard ever, Margery.'

The conductress gave Richard a sly smile. He hadn't believed she didn't remember the exact name of every lighting assistant and walk-on penguin in *Scott of the Antarctic*, much less one of the principal cast. And he didn't believe her casual assumption they knew as much about Chalfont as she evidently did.

Margery fairly chortled. To the point of crowing.

'Are your filing cabinets coming up short? Did you only drop in to my "happening" to quiz poor old Marge about an information gap you shouldn't ought to have? You'll hurt my feelings.'

Richard laughed with her.

'Fair enough. You win. The Diogenes Club are amateur dabblers beside you, Margery. I don't know why we even bother to get out of bed most mornings. But if you could see your way to help…'

'Quid pro quo, Dickie. Payment in kind.'

'As you've pointed out, there's an imbalance. You have all the secrets.'

She coyly chewed the corner of a roll of bus-tickets Richard guessed were impregnated with something lysergic. 'Not all…'

'All of ours. And all of Agent Gauge's too.'

''Tis true. I'm terribly well informed. Would you like to know who the first homosexual in space was?'

'Not just now.'

Margery tutted.

'Very well, but you're usually much more fun, Dickie. Now, I shall point you in a useful direction, on the condition that…'

Richard waited for it.

'…the lovely Whitney answers one single question. With gory details. Truth or dare, without the dare.'

Whitney shrugged. Richard hoped Margery wasn't going to ask something indiscreet about President Nixon. Or dredge up that old one about J. Edgar Hoover's dressmaker.

Margery leaned over, cupping her hand over her mouth, and whispered in the woman's ear. Whitney looked slightly shocked, then amused. She blushed in penny-size cheek-spots, like a cartoon character. Margery, eager, turned her own ear to receive – and Whitney whispered into it for what seemed a full five minutes. A smile spread across Margery's face, with pauses for knowing looks at Richard and mocking tuts of sham disapproval.

'I suppose I should have known…'

'All right,' said Richard, 'you've had your fun facts for the day, Margery. Now… Rex Chalfont?'

'Don't know the man,' said Margery, offhand. Richard groaned. 'But I know of him.'

Richard and Whitney listened, intently.

'In 1948, the Chalfont Group offered to conquer the moon. For Britain.'

If Chalfont had a group, Richard didn't imagine they were aiming for the pop charts.

'He was a rocket scientist?'

'No, Dickie. How many rocket scientists call themselves "magister"? He's one of those interdisciplinary fellows who mix runes and equations. You know what Artie Clarke always says about advanced technology being "indistinguishable from magic"? Chalfont responds that magic is indistinguishable from magic too. He promised he'd get to the moon before anyone relying on "Nazi fireworks".'

'So, a nut?'

'A nut we should have paid more attention to,' said Margery.

'Because he had his old girlfriend stabbed?'

'Good heavens, no. Someone would have stabbed Bridget Tully eventually. An art critic, most likely. No, we should have paid attention because he did what he said he would.'

'Conquered the moon?'

'That's the whisper. He did it in 1953. In time for the Coronation. Chalfont has always been very patriotic. I suppose Everest got all the headlines.'

'You're having us on,' said Richard.

Margery looked genuinely offended.

'Have I ever misled you?'

'Not directly.'

'Let me get this straight,' said Whitney. 'In three days' time, the *Eagle* will touch down in the Sea of Tranquillity, Neil Armstrong will clamber down his ladder with the Stars and Stripes, and come across a British flag and… what else? A tea and crumpets stand? A statue of Winston Churchill? Art students holding a "Yankee Go Home" banner?'

Margery was briefly serious. 'I don't think Sexy Rexy will let it come to that. If he's got rid of his High Priestess, who was in the moderate wing of the Chalfont Group, he'll have decided to haul down the Union Jack, fly the Jolly Roger and… well, prepare to repel boarders.'

It took seconds for that to sink in.

Whitney looked at Richard. He saw her mouth drop open exactly the way he knew his had. Space-time upended itself and turned inside out like a sock. Arthur C. Clarke would strongly disapprove.

'In the Lake District,' said Margery, 'about five miles from Scafell Pike. On the Buttermere road, you take the turn-off marked "Private Road – Trespassers Will Be Dealt With Harshly". You can't miss it.'

Richard was jolted out of his mind-expanding fugue.

'What?' he said.

'Your next question was, or should have been, "Where is Mildew Manor"?'

Richard supposed he should be grateful Margery had told them what she knew, and understood it was unreasonable to wish she'd volunteered all this some time in the last sixteen years. What happened on the moon was irrelevant to her bailiwick. She had enough on her plate looking after London, without worrying about satellites or stars. Still, a quiet heads-up wouldn't have hurt.

'Stop the bus,' he said. 'We want to get off.'

They were in Piccadilly Circus.

Margery rang her bell, and said, 'Ting ting, please take care while leaving the omnibus, and toodle-oo.'

———❖———

'How could anyone land on the moon in secret?' asked Whitney. 'In 1953?'

'I don't suppose people looked at the skies as much then,' Richard mused.

'A rocket launch is hard to keep quiet.'

'Ahem, Sputnik…'

'We knew about Sputnik,' she said. 'We just let Khrushchev

81

have his big day and pretended to be surprised. Do you know how much the covert intelligence and arcane enforcement budget went up the day after all the senators and congressmen found out a red eye in the sky could see into their swimming pools?'

They were in St James's Park, watching ducks on the lake. Defectors, spies, tramps and shady dealers congregated in twos on the benches. Wardens who picked up litter with spiked sticks here had a higher security clearance than the Secretary of State for Defence. Old government secrets, obsolete weapons plans and two-way mirror compromising filmstrips were always found in the grass – along with bloody Sky-Ray lolly wrappers, of course.

'Magister Rex Chalfont doesn't believe in rockets,' mused Richard. '"Nazi fireworks". Ergo, no rocket launch.'

'How else are you going to get to the moon? Build a stairway to Heaven?'

'A diving bell shot out of a volcano?'

She knew this game. 'The chariot drawn by geese.'

'Cavorite.'

'Dew.'

'Astral projection.'

Whitney had pause. 'That's not so lunatic.'

'Ha-ha. Neither is antigravity paint.'

'Chalfont is a magus, right? A sorcerer.'

'A flying sorcerer.'

'Not necessarily. Picture this... the great Pooh-Bah – and his circle or group or whatever – sit around omming like lamas and go into a trance. Their spirits leave their bodies, then float to the moon.'

Richard conceded that was more likely than geese or gunpowder.

It was also comforting. There were recognised procedures

for dealing with astral projectors. You found out where their entranced bodies were laid up and shouted 'wakey-wakey' in their ears. Not a few snuffed themselves by forgetting to nip home and eat, or secreted fragile flesh in places impregnable to enemies which also happened to be airtight. Most who learned the trick were just nosey parkers, anyway… Some nights, three or four at a time collided ectoplasmically in Liz Taylor's bedroom. The odd adept managed to create a semi-solid ghost body, and could use the old 'I was dozing at the theatre in full view of the whole audience when that shadowy wraith stoved in my wife's head with a brick' alibi.

A commotion of some sort was underway on Duck Island, across the lake. Birds in a tizzy. Like the Trafalgar Square pigeons, the St James's ducks had gone hungry for days while everyone was watching the telly. Perhaps there was lingering resentment at the abandonment of Francis Godwin's waterfowl-based space programme. No ducks, no *Duck Dodgers*.

'Astral projection to the moon is a new one on me,' he admitted. 'In all known cases of out-of-the-body wandering, a filament connects the projected consciousness – in whatever form it takes – back to the physical corpus. A quarter-million-mile sticky string is, to put it mildly, a stretch.'

The ducks quacked up a fuss on the water now, scrapping over floating crumbs, beating each other with tough wings. The disturbance on the island had spread.

'Didn't some turn-of-the-century mediums claim to be star voyagers?'

Richard remembered the file.

'Yes, that's why it's called astral projection. But the Club never took them seriously. If they went anywhere during their trips, it wasn't in our universe. One dotty lady claimed she'd been impregnated by an Arcturan, but the baby popped out human. We kept tabs on the lad, of course. Grew up to be a very useful bowler for Leicestershire.'

'Now you're talking mumbo–jumbo. As far as I'm concerned, cricket is a chirruping insect. Or that squeaker who bugs Pinocchio.'

'Says the girl from the he-man, steak-eating cowboy country whose rugby players need to cower inside six inches of leather armour so they don't hurt their little headsies and toesies.'

They both laughed.

'Actually, you're right about football,' she conceded.

'American football,' he corrected her.

'Those guys are sissies who can't take competition without throwing a fit.'

'They wouldn't let you play, then?'

'Uh–uh. Not after I broke my brother's leg by accident.'

'Were you playing rough while baby-sitting the little fellow?'

'Not my younger brother Brad. My older brother Trap. The Marine. He was on leave from Vietnam.'

The ducks were tearing into each other now. Feathers and blood–slicks floated on the lake.

'That's not right,' said Richard.

Whitney saw it too. In the agitated water was a rippling reflection which shouldn't be there. It looked like the moon.

Then the ducks fell silent, stopped attacking each other.

They paddled, turning in sync like a water ballet corps – and wound up looking directly at Richard and Whitney, aimed like the guns of pirate raiders.

'That's definitely not right.'

He had a flash of Sky-Ray Roly, the moment his eyes blanked and he reached for the champagne bottle.

Moon madness, again?

Richard and Whitney stood still.

Ranks of ducks advanced, sculling with wing-points. Eyes and beaks glinted in the sunlight.

'Look, Mum,' said a passing child, dripping ice-cream in his paw.

'Come away, dear, and don't bother the nice people.'

'But Mu-u-um!'

Mother and son moved on. The first ducks were off the lake, waddling on the grass. The lack of quack was disturbing.

Richard sighed inwardly. He really did not want to be seen running away from a horde of ducks in St James's Park. Margery Device would never let him hear the last of it.

'How did Tippi Hedren get out of this in *The Birds*?' Whitney asked.

'Hard to say. The film has an ambiguous ending.'

They began to back away, very slowly. More ducks made it to land.

'What about in the original story?' Whitney asked.

'That doesn't have an ambiguous ending. That has an apocalyptic ending.'

'So, no help there. Thank you, Daphne Du Maurier.'

'Dame Daphne. It was in the Queen's Birthday Honours List.'

'Swell. Remind me to send a congratulation card. Should we turn and run now?'

'Not yet.'

'You really think they might be friendly lunatic psycho ducks?'

Richard held out his hand, flat-palmed, and said, 'Stop!'

It worked, for almost a second. Then the ducks flew at them, and they ran.

──◆──

The doorman of the Diogenes Club passed no comment on the state of their apparel. Over the years, he had seen worse.

Richard and Whitney were bloodied and shredded, bruised by bills and scratched by webbed feet – who knew duck-feet had barbs? They'd only got away because the birds wouldn't leave the park.

'Really,' said Major Took-Flemyng to no one in particular, as they entered the lobby, 'it's a bloody disgrace!'

'Sorry,' said Richard to the Major. 'Bit of a difficult day.'

'Still, to bring a woman into the club…'

Richard gripped Whitney's arm. In her current ticked-off and duck-assailed state, she might serve the Major worse than her brother Trap.

'Is there a problem, Major?' asked Catriona, popping out of the Quiet Room, which was on the first-floor landing, to stood at the top of the broad stairs.

Took-Flemyng's misogyny evaporated in an instant. He revealed dentures in a would-be ingratiating grin and bowed low.

'No indeed, Miss Kaye. No problem of any kind. Might I say how charming you look this afternoon?'

'You might. Now, run along, Major.'

'Of course, Miss Kaye.'

Took-Flemyng trotted into the Informal Room, glowing like a schoolgirl awarded a gold star by 'Miss' in front of the whole form.

'If Daphne Du Maurier got damed, why not Catriona Kaye?' Whitney whispered.

'Diogenes Club tradition,' he told her. 'Turning down the K. I've only turned down the MBE. Catriona turned down a peerage once. We don't like to clutter our calling cards with letters.'

'If you say so, Galahad.'

Catriona had Hills bring them a change of clothes – a mauve tracksuit with white piping for Whitney, an orange-and-black kaftan for Richard – and personally cleaned and dressed their minor wounds. The Diogenes Club first-aid kit had a few unusual items. Besides iodine, Catriona applied sigils of something herbal to speed the healing.

'Attacked by ducks,' said Catriona, as Richard and Whitney drank tea in the Quiet Room. 'That's not the strangest item today. We've had a rash of incidents. People and animals howling at the moon. Even in daylight. There's a lot of – and I use the word carefully – lunacy about. Schoolchildren playing "spacemen and monsters" on a bomb site in Streatham managed to vaporise a builders' hut with plastic rayguns. A horticulturist in Surrey nearly choked to death on the poisonous exhalations of a greenhouse full of man-in-the-moon marigolds. Leaping fish beset an angler on the Trent.'

'Is it all connected?' Whitney asked.

'Almost certainly. Tiresome, isn't it? So, you've been to see the Witch. Any joy?'

Richard passed on what Margery Device had told them.

'She told us Luna Moon was in this Chalfont Group,' he said. 'It might be worth our while running down a membership list. Chalfont is off the books, but if we identify known intimates we ought to get a better picture.'

He expected Catriona to use the antique telephone to ring through to the Archive Room.

Instead, she said, 'I daresay the Chalfont Group found room for a science fiction writer called Mungo Zyle, an explorer named Walter Vereker and a middle-aged dropout born Lawson Hogg but known as "the Hermit of Taunton".'

She let the names lie.

'You didn't know about them yesterday,' he said. 'What brought them to your attention?'

'They were alive yesterday morning,' she admitted. 'In the afternoon and evening, in quick succession, in locations five hundred miles apart, they were stabbed to death. Probably with the same athamé used to kill Luna Moon. Zyle's wound had traces of someone else's blood in it. The assassin didn't even wipe tools between jobs.'

'Can we definitely link them to Chalfont?'

'Only by inference. We can link them to each other, though. They were of a like age, fell into the category of "crank", and have criss-crossing biographies. Luna Moon did covers for Mungo Zyle's books. Zyle and his wife Anemone co-authored the Moonmist Trilogy. It's all trilogies nowadays. I blame Johnny Tolkien. Vereker was arrested at Glastonbury Tor in 1949, taking part in a druidical erotic hullabaloo involving Hogg and a gaggle of silly women in robes. All our victims have a roundabout or direct interest in the topic of the day. Moon-worship. You'll appreciate this: Hogg's farm makes green cheese.'

'Is the Chalfont Group wiped out?' asked Whitney. 'Are there any surviving members?'

'We can take a guess at Anemone Zyle, since she's disappeared. In other circumstances, she'd be our favoured suspect. I've got research moles digging for others with connections to one or more of our dead people. They've made some suppositions. There's a publisher named Maurice Nordstrom, who isn't in his office today. I had a nice chat with his secretary. Nordstrom & Haw specialise in science fiction, so you'd think he'd be high on Apollo. In fact, he's been in a sulk for months.'

'There's a theory the moon landing is bad for science fiction.'

'I've heard it. Nordstrom publishes the Zyles, also Vereker's books on mountain-climbing. Vereker used to scale Swiss and South American peaks with a Rudolf Gosling, a nasty piece of work who leads the English Liberation Front – which is a fancy name for yet another fascist party. Their command bunker is called "the Laburnums". It's in Acacia Road, Frinton. It has net curtains. The ELF tried to get Enoch Powell to join the cause, and got an erudite earful. Gosling is another of Bridget Tully's old beaux. According to his deputy leader, he's too busy to talk with strange women. Speaking of strange women, Hogg's Farm was home to a quantity of loose young persons who helped make his cheese. I imagined hermits lived alone, but evidently this one liked the company. They've all scarpered without trace. So, that's quite a little lot of disappearees.'

'The only one I've met is Rudy Gosling,' said Richard. 'His party symbol is an *Eismond*, a moon of ice. It derives from one of Himmler's crackpot notions. We couldn't prove anything, but came away from that Handsworth Thuggee business with a strong sense that the ELF were mixed up in it. I wouldn't put it past him to stick an athamé into anyone.'

'I began one of those Moonmist novels,' said Whitney. 'It had a map on the first page, with place-names that were anagrams of brands of detergent. Then a glossary of "moon talk" that went on for pages. After that, on the first page proper, the lunar controller was described as "resting her chin on her elbows". I threw the book in the trash.'

'Margery said Luna Moon was in "the moderate wing" of the Chalfont Group,' said Richard. 'I suppose the other victims were with her. Which leaves, what? The radical wing.'

'The nasty wing,' said Whitney.

'As good a label as any. Put it on a T-shirt. Chalfont, or whoever heads the group, has had his Night of the Long Athamé and cleaned house. So, where have the nasties disappeared?'

'Everyone's gone to the moon?' suggested Whitney.

Richard tried not to hum that song.

'Initially, I think Cumberland more likely,' said Catriona. 'That's the hint Margery was dropping. The Witch is usually on the money.'

'Where the hell is Cumberland?' asked Whitney.

'Beyond the range of the Trident,' said Richard. 'We'll need the Rolls.'

Catriona picked up the phone and began dialling with the end of her cigarette holder. 'I'm concerned about Margery's "prepare to repel boarders" analogy,' she said. 'I want to make sure you don't visit Mildew Manor without proper covering fire.'

Whitney saluted. Richard could almost hear drums.

Catriona got through to the underground exchange, and played the code-word-and-response parlour game to clear a classified international line. It took her less time than it would take an ordinary telephone subscriber to reach the speaking clock.

'Houston,' she said, when connected, 'you have a problem.'

<hr>

'A pick-and-mix landscape, Cumberland,' said Whitney. 'You've got your rocks, your grass, your lakes, your mountains. And, oh, no matter how summery it is, it's wet underfoot.'

'Funnily enough, that's been noticed before.'

Richard's Rolls-Royce ShadowShark was parked in a lay-by opposite the chained-off turning. The 'Private Road – Trespassers Will Be Dealt With Harshly' sign Margery Device had described hung from the chain. The 'o' in 'Road' was a stuck-on *Eismond* decal with ELF written across it. It might as well have been a neon sign with 'Secret Lair' on it.

Richard wore baggy jungle camouflage trousers and a padded mint-green cagoule, custom-made army boots with gadgets secreted in heel and sole, a jaunty 'Che Guevara' beret and World War One aviator goggles. Whitney had kept the tracksuit and photochromatic shades from yesterday, augmented with an even jauntier 'Bonnie Parker' beret. He had turned down several offers of guns, and persuaded a reluctant Whitney not to tool up either.

She'd acquired a knobkerrie walking stick – the sort country people said they needed for walking down lanes, but mainly used for beating townies who trespassed in fields – and could twirl it like a baton.

Two army lorries were parked nearby. A platoon of squaddies was having tea around a mobile canteen, wondering why they weren't back in barracks watching the telly. Apollo 11 was only hours away from lunar orbit. A matching US Army team was due to show up to make this a joint Anglo–American operation. A diversion was in force, steering traffic away from the Mildew Manor area. Fell-walkers were being advised to fell-walk the other way. Anthrax was mentioned, though the cover story was getting whiskery. If you added up the times the British public were warned of an anthrax spill to keep them away from something that would terrify them even more, you'd assume the United Kingdom was knee-deep in the stuff. According to Whitney, the American equivalent was 'experimental nerve toxin' – though when an experimental nerve toxin actually leaked, the no-go area was blamed on foot-and-mouth.

Catriona insisted the soldiers were only there to maintain a perimeter. This was a business for specialists.

'Spectacular views all around,' said Whitney, 'except in that direction.'

A thicket of trees lined the private road and swelled to a copse.

'You'd think it'd been cultivated that way,' she said.

'A shrewd observation. Successive owners of Mildew Manor have had things to hide. In the eighteenth century, when banditti prowled the Lake District, this was the home of the wickedest man in England, Nick Goodman – yes, the irony was noticed in his lifetime – and his equally depraved wife, the dreadful Eithne Orfe. We've got two filing cabinets on them.'

'But nothing on Rex Chalfont.'

'No need to rub it in.'

Catriona had a theory that Chalfont had a government connection, and used his pull years ago to stay out of the files. In London, she was following this up – in the few moments when she wasn't suffering transatlantic phone calls from aggrieved, disbelieving and distracted American officials.

The intelligence had not been well received at NASA, even after Assistant Director Spilsby endorsed the report. He took the issue more seriously now than four days ago, when he had packed Whitney Gauge off to poke into it. Along with the global epidemic of moon madness, 'developments' in space were troubling. LM Pilot Aldrin's report that he 'saw a light moving which was not a star' was bleeped from television coverage. Anyone who used the term 'unidentified flying object' was liable to summary dismissal. Ranger 8 and Surveyor 5, unmanned probes officially dead since their publicly announced missions, had long since repurposed as weaponised robots – packed full of gizmos which guaranteed the Soviets a hot-foot if they tried to steal a march on Apollo with their Zond moon orbital vehicle. The probes had gone 'offline' after broadcasting signals that they were subject to Unusual Uncategorised Stress. Surveyor 5's last message suggested it was being 'eaten'. It was hotly debated how seriously spook stuff should be taken. A roomful of technocrats and science guys were having a hard time adjusting their worldview to take in a magic threat. Richard had suggested telling them the UUS was an anthrax outbreak.

Dusty contingency plans for engaging with 'hostiles' on the moon were hauled out of cabinets and had their seals broken. These turned out to be of no practical use: they were all contingent on either a) an unknown foreign power whose spacecraft had markings in the Cyrillic alphabet having sneakily established a covert moonbase, or b) an aggressive extra-terrestrial intelligence lurking in the craters with rayguns in its tentacles. Whoever was responsible for Plan B didn't take seriously the possibility of it ever being considered for use, and proposed drafting Flash Gordon and Captain Video. Interested parties argued over what to tell the astronauts, awaiting a decision from Senator Edward Kennedy. It turned out Kennedy chaired the Oversight Committee which effectively ran the 'Unnameables'. Even Richard was surprised to learn that. When JFK appointed Bobby Attorney General, he gave his other brother a secret job Teddy had hung on to through successive administrations.

In a lorry designated 'Forward Command Post One', Captain 'Mac' Maitland – who sported a rakish eyepatch, but had a haircut more suited to a Swinging Blue Jean than an officer in Her Majesty's Armed Forces – was on the field telephone.

'The American army took a wrong turn and are up the Old Man of Coniston,' said Mac in cut-glass Sandhurst tones – though Richard had read his file and knew he was the son of a Durham miner. 'Typical shambles. The Yanks can put a man on the moon, but get lost in a tourist attraction. No offence, miss.'

Richard and Whitney weren't supposed to venture near Mildew Manor until Anglo–American combined forces were in situ.

'Can we offer you tea?' said Mac.

Richard declined politely.

A flight of birds broke out of the copse, giving Richard harrowing duckpond flashbacks…

…then lightning struck out of a clear blue sky, three times. Close by. Flashes, no thunder. So, not ordinary lightning.

Three lithe figures appeared in the road. They wore silver body-stockings, loose but clingy enough to show female form, bulbous spherical fish-bowl helmets, thick silver boots and gauntlets, plates of shiny body-armour and gunslinger belts hung with mystery tools.

Their faces were painted bright green. Contoured chest-pieces were numbered in swirly hippie script: One, Two, Five. Richard looked around, but Three and Four weren't here. Their absences made dents in the space-women's formation.

A couple of the squaddies laughed. None reached for rifles.

The space-women all carried knives. Athamés.

'Have you noticed we've been wearing "Attack Me" buttons ever since we visited the Temple of Domina Oriens?' said Whitney.

'Yes.'

Two made the first move, tossing her athamé straight at Richard's eyes. The blade was for stabbing, not balanced for knife-throwing. Whitney swung her knobkerrie and knocked the knife off course – it stuck into the side of Maitland's lorry, inches from his head.

One came at Whitney, high. Whitney bent over as if to cartwheel, kicking out with a straight leg, catching One in her midriff, knocking her over. Her head rattled inside her fishbowl, but she got back on her feet.

The soldiers had guns at hand now, but no idea what to do with them.

Two jumped in the air, as if beginning a somersault, then popped out of space and reappeared instantly behind Richard, grabbing his arms. The country air was heavy with the smell of chemical discharge. Two had a solid hold on him, and he only hurt his head by ramming at her nose and thumping a heavy face-plate. Five advanced, lower lip sucked into her mouth, tossing her athamé from hand to hand like a Teddy girl with a flick-knife. She made teasing, stabbing motions. Now might be a good time for Maitland's men to overcome natural gallantry and fire a warning shot into Five's helmet.

Whitney and One circled each other, short knife against long stick. Both made test jabs.

Lightning struck again, cracking into the copse.

Another space-woman – Three or Four? – was stuck in the tree. Not stuck up it, like a cat – in it, trunk and limbs embedded in old wood, head kinking out like a broken branch, face rough like bark.

Two noticed and let Richard go. She grabbed her own helmet and twisted, but it wouldn't come off. Five was distracted by what had happened to the scrambled space-woman, so Richard took her athamé away.

Lightning unstruck – or so it seemed – and Whitney was blinking. One wasn't there any more, though her smoking silver boots were.

Two dropped to her knees, frantically struggling with her fishbowl.

'Help her,' Richard said to Five.

He saw concern in the space-woman's green face. After hesitation, she tried to help Two get her helmet off. Five held out her hand. Richard gave her back her knife, knowing she wanted it to cut through Two's neck-piece not stick into his chest. Another practical, everyday use for his Talent. The blade broke and Five threw the hilt away in frustration. If Two's face weren't painted, she'd have gone green of her own accord. Her eyes bulged and her mouth gaped like the little boy in the dire warning public information commercial who 'played spaceman' with a plastic bag over his head.

Though they had arrived by unorthodox means, these were Earthly beings.

Within a minute of their arrival, only Five was still standing. The ducks had been more trouble.

Mac rapped on Five's helmet with a pistol. The woman meekly put her hands up.

Two keeled over.

Soldiers looked at Three-or-Four, who was plainly dead. One of them asked if they should try to get her down.

Whitney skinned silver-foil away from Two's wrist – which was pink and had sunburn scars – and failed to find a pulse.

'Welcome to our planet,' said Richard.

Five made fists and thumped the sides of her helmet. Her faceplate popped open and she unloosed a torrent of foul language in broad West Country.

Richard deduced the space-women were the flower children from Hermit Hogg's cheese farm.

The helmet came off. Five shook out a long tangle of brown hair. The green on her face had streaked. She rubbed it with the heels of her hands.

She didn't stop swearing – not at Richard and Whitney, but at 'Magister' – for long minutes. She went around kicking things, including One's empty boots and Three-or-Four's tree.

The afterstench of bodged magic was thick. A short-term translocation spell, carelessly done.

Richard didn't think any of the space-women had struck down Luna Moon or the others. Those had been professional, vicious jobs. This had been a throwaway. A delaying tactic.

Five shook her fists at the sky. Whitney slapped her, to get her attention. Five slapped back, instantly. But calmed down.

'You,' Whitney said. 'Name?'

'Fan.'

'Fan, do you surrender?'

'Oh yerr, I gives up all roight.'

Maitland ordered his sergeant to take away Fan's tool-belt. A lot of the gadgets seemed to be toys.

'I knew we shouldn't have stepped in that morris square,' said Fan. 'So did he, Magister. Bloody posh old bastard tosser. Couldn't wait to get shot of us. It were all lies, all the time. I b'aint

96

never going to the moon. And he'm killed Jillie and Jonquil and Bertha. Hannah too, prob'ly. She never popped back. Goddess knows where her bits be spread.'

Maitland wasn't following this. Richard and Whitney were.

'Fan,' said Richard, 'we're here to stop Magister Rex Chalfont.'

''Bout bloody time, too.'

'So... take us to your leader.'

Fan led Richard and Whitney down a rutted, tree-lined path. Branches entangled above them. Sunbeams filtered down into the nearly covered way, casting shifting patches of light onto the ground.

'So that's what "sun-dappled" means,' he said. 'I'd always wondered.'

Whitney tugged his arm, to prevent an unwise step. She used her knobkerrie to snap a man-trap that had been left under a carpet of leaf litter.

'Wrong time of year for falling leaves,' she explained.

An unwholesome country smell turned out to be a dead little man splatted against a stout oak by a giant wickerwork fly-swatter studded with Viet Cong-style punji sticks.

'Magister Rex hates they poachers,' Fan explained. 'Leaves 'en up to warn off others.'

Richard got on the walkie-talkie and warned Mac to have his men be careful about following the country code. Stiles in these parts were likely to be booby-trapped and streams might well be full of mines.

From the disillusioned space-woman, they learned Magister Rex and the Inner Circle of the Temple of Domina Oriens had promised free trips to the moon for their followers. Chalfont claimed to have been there and back many times, but the happy hippie cultie side of things had become strained lately – what with the unsought-for competition from NASA. Fan wasn't in on the politics, but confirmed there'd been a little war in the group. Those left standing had fallen back to Mildew Manor, the unlikely mission control from which Chalfont promised imminent mass migration to the sacred satellite. According to Fan, the quadrilocating assassin was Gosling – who nipped about via more precise and effective spells of translocation than the Hogg Farm Space Kiddettes. It was all done by morris dancing, apparently – Moon Man's Morris, executed by the Chalfont Group with man-in-the-moon masks and belled sticks, around a square marked with yellow diagrams.

Fan was vague about how precisely Chalfont made his space voyages, but clearly believed Magister Rex had been traversing cislunar space regularly since the 1950s. Without anyone noticing. Had Chalfont perfected a long-range translocation spell? Jaunting that far was beyond the combined magical prowess of Merlin, Circe, Ali Bongo and Sooty, and Richard couldn't see Magister Rex being top of that class. Not with bloody morris dancing. If the sellotape-and-glue sorcery used to deploy Fan and her gang was an example of his prowess, Richard wouldn't trust Chalfont to pull a rabbit out of a hat without killing a volunteer from the audience. Fan only said Magister went to the moon 'through the Shimmer'.

They got out of the copse alive and came upon Mildew Manor, a big, square Gothic revival pile – complete with turrets and towers – in the middle of eighteenth-century fake ancient ruins and gardens cultivated to seem wild. Fan told them a single light was always kept burning in the East Tower window, in accordance with a tradition no one dared violate. In the driveway, a minivan with a green cheese man-in-the-moon painted on the side panels was parked next to a jeep with an ELF *Eismond* on the bonnet and a couple of bicycles. No built-in-the-garden-shed rocketship in evidence. No transdimensional police box. No Verne cannon. No antigravity trampoline. No geese.

Fan wouldn't go further.

Richard and Whitney crossed the lawn. A moondial was set on a stone table, abandoned teacups around the rim. A ceramic ashtray was full of aromatic dog-ends.

The front door hung open a crack. Whitney pushed it with her stick. No death-trap sprung.

'Anyone home?' called Richard.

'Could they have zapped themselves into oblivion?'

'We can but hope.'

In the hallway, a large Luna Selene Moon canvas hung askew. Whitney adjusted it, and had an insight. Her tactile intuition again. 'This way.'

Richard felt the thrumm – in his fillings, mostly – before he heard the churning, rumbling sound. His nerves were on edge, as if he were standing next to an invisible cataract or inside a giant disguised power station. A lot of energy in the air. He didn't need to tell Whitney to be careful.

The first room they came to was a TV lounge. BBC moon news rolled on, to empty chairs. A well-spoken announcer apologised to those tuning in for *Tich and Quackers*, usually broadcast at this time. Apollo 11 was in lunar orbit. Onscreen diagrams showed how the *Eagle* would separate from the *Columbia*, leaving Mike Collins in orbit as Armstrong and Aldrin descended to the lunar surface. The BBC didn't ask what the whole world was wondering – how pissed off was Collins at going so far, but hanging back at the last moment? Touch-down would happen tomorrow evening GMT and man would first set foot on the moon in the middle of the night. The schedule was for the convenience of American networks, but the BBC were too polite to complain. The television set was splattered with burst tomatoes, suggesting the Chalfont Group's feelings about the Apollo programme.

Richard switched off the television, and the thrumm was obvious.

Something big, nearby.

At the end of the hall, double-doors were painted with Luna Moon designs, in the same style as the décor at the Temple in Sekforde Street. The thrumm came from beyond the doors.

Whitney, wary of another shock, did not reach for the handles.

Richard pulled open the doors.

———————

The Great Hall of Mildew Manor was stripped of furniture. Tall windows were bricked over. Panelling bowed away from the walls, and had come away from bare brick in patches. Uncarpeted, polished floor strained as if the herringbone tiles were resisting universal pull.

In the middle of the room, a sphere of blue-white, crackling energy – about twenty feet from pole to pole – revolved slowly. The Shimmer. It looked like a 3D projection, the ghost of the moon. Though the Shimmer was transparent, Richard couldn't only see the far side of the room through it. Somewhere inside the shifting, semi-gaseous globe of magick hung a giant, animate Luna Moon picture.

Whitney whistled.

One other person was in the hall. A man in a red diving suit lay in a corner, clutching his right arm – which ended at the wrist, stump caulked over with blue-green sludge. Richard twisted off the man's helmet – more brassbound and Victorian than the Space Kiddettes' silver fishbowls – and recognised Maurice Nordstrom, the publisher. His comb-over flapped away from a flaky scalp. He was delirious with pain and wonder.

Nordstrom thumped himself with his stump, and muttered, 'Failure, failure, failure…'

Richard understood. Magic devices like the Shimmer depended on faith. Waver for even a second and you ended up stuck in a tree or rent apart by dwellers in the outer void. Or it just doesn't work.

Nordstrom had been cautious, tried to test the waters. The waters didn't care for the inference that they were not to be trusted.

It was no use quizzing the man. His mind was gone with his hand.

'I don't suppose there's an off switch?' said Whitney.

'Not this side.'

'That's what I was worried about,' she said. 'So, the Shimmer is a portal? A magic door to the moon. Like a Wonderland rabbit-hole or a Narnia wardrobe.'

'If Chalfont had his physics thinking cap on rather than his sorcerer's pointy hat, he'd call it a Schwarzschild wormhole or an Einstein–Rosen bridge.'

'Like I said, a magic doorway—'

'To the moon, Alice.'

The wall-panels, floor-tiles and ceiling were covered with – as Margery Device had said – runes and equations. Childish scrawls, which shone like teeth and white shirts in a discotheque when ultra-violet plays on the crowds during the chorus of 'Hi Ho Silver Lining'. Richard wondered if the spell had been touched up since 1953. It was a powerful piece of work – a masterpiece, perhaps the only one Magister Rex had in him. He'd had help, of course. Richard knew the brushstrokes of Luna Moon.

'I still don't believe you can actually get to the moon through that,' said Whitney.

'Neither did Nordstrom.'

'I'm not saying you can't get anywhere.'

Richard understood. The Shimmer was more likely a portal to another dimension than another world. Luna Moon's imagination, perhaps.

'What about Aldrin's non-star light?' he asked. 'The breakdown of Ranger 8 and Surveyor 5 on your actual moon.'

'Suggestive, not conclusive.'

He looked at her. And knew that, like him, she was more excited than terrified. But was still terrified.

Their hair was rising again, more dramatically. Whitney had a Bride of Frankenstein frizz. His scalp prickled as he sprouted a Struwwelpeter afro.

'We're putting it off, aren't we?' he said.

She agreed.

He got on the walkie-talkie, and Captain Maitland relayed him to Catriona in London. He gave a concise report about the set-up at Mildew Manor. She had dragged more secrets out of Assistant Director Spilsby.

'The good news,' she responded, 'is that someone in NASA covered their bottom by incorporating unadvertised defensive capabilities into Apollo 11. The rocket has "cold iron" and "bell, book and candle", like all British warships since Nelson fought Cagliostro. So, the – whatchumacallit – BEM ought to be shielded from sorcerous attack.'

'What's the bad news?'

'Typically, the shield can only be activated – I'm so dreadfully sorry, I'm mindlessly passing on what Americans have told me, what I mean by "activated" is "switched on" – if certain words are spoken at a certain spot by the man in charge. And he's unavailable.'

'Senator Kennedy? Don't tell me he's been shot too!'

'No, he's answering police questions after driving into a lake with a junior aide who drowned. They'd been at a party. It's not an affair from which anyone will emerge with honour. Frankly, I'm so annoyed with Teddy I could spit. Even if he's let go, we can't get him to the pentacle in the Pentagon to read the riot runes.'

'How long can the astronauts stay in orbit? Surely, Houston won't let them try a landing under these circumstances?'

'Houston's tolerance for, and I quote, "hoodoo voodoo" is at an end. They've all been intent on this since Teddy's brother said there'd be an American on the moon before the end of the decade.'

'JFK also promised to bring that American back safely.'

'Indeed. But NASA is in a risk-taking, seat-of-the-trousers mood at the moment. If they aborted the landing – hideous, term, that – they think it'd be the end of the space programme.'

'Being blasted to bits during the descent would probably put a dampener on things, too.'

'The boffins are impatient.'

'So it's down to us? Whitney and me?'

'Spilsby wants Whitney on the bench. A platoon of GIs with cruciform tattoos and holy water-pistols are on their way.'

'They're lost.'

'I know. It's a wonder they've not napalmed Grasmere. As far as I'm concerned, it really is down to you two. Richard, I don't need to tell you to come back safe. Don't try too hard to protect the girl. She'll not be grateful and can look after herself.'

'I've noticed.'

'Good. You're getting better at noticing. It bodes well. Gallantry is all very well, but it's nearly the 1970s. Lecture over. Go and save the world. And the moon.'

He told Whitney they had the go–ahead. He didn't mention Spilsby.

In an antechamber to the Great Hall, several pressure suits – not strictly diving suits, of course – hung on hooks, with helmets shelved above. It took long minutes to get properly dressed for the expedition. The gear was baggy enough to fit over their Earth clothes, though Richard had to take his boots off and transfer gadgets to flapped pouches on the thighs. Reluctantly, they left their berets behind. The suit-boots were weighted, soled with something like slate, fixed to the trouser-rims with gluey strips. The space-suit was reddish metallic oilskin, and musty inside. Somehow, the helmet did not shut off sound.

Whitney had a similar suit, but opted for silver finish and the plastic fishbowl. She struck a pin-up pose.

'Out of sight, Psychedella,' he commented.

They checked each other for straps, seals and hooks and hoped they'd followed proper procedure. The oxygen bottles were lightweight and seemed too small to be any use.

Richard peeled an *Eismond* off his chestplate.

'I'm not wearing this,' he said. 'It's the badge of an oik.'

Beside the suits was a rack of athamés. The Temple must have got a good price on a job-lot of ceremonial stabbing implements. An array of contraptions with pumps and nozzles which looked like Edwardian fly-sprays could have been moon-guns. Hung by the rack was a clipboard with printed forms and a stubby pencil on a string. Richard flipped over filled-in forms. Suits were checked out to Nordstrom, who they needn't worry about, and Rex Chalfont, Anemone Zyle and Rudy Gosling, who would likely be more problematic. Boxes were ticked, signatures appended. He and Whitney didn't bother with the paperwork.

It ought to come down to two against three. Richard knew little about Rex Chalfont or Anemone Zyle, but Rudy Gosling was a practised killer – and, whatever lay beyond the Shimmer, they were up against people who would be more familiar with the terrain.

When they returned to the Great Hall, Nordstrom was

dead. Puffy blue-green fungus was spreading across his face. It was horribly easy to imagine the poison gunk covering the whole world.

To be on the safe side, they picked him up between them, gave him a swing or two and launched him into the Shimmer with the old heave-ho.

Nordstrom flapped in the centre of the globe and disappeared, like a switched-off TV picture dwindling to a dot. Even the after-image didn't last.

'I hope he didn't just dissolve in front of our eyes,' said Richard. 'If so, what we're about to do would be cataclysmically stupid.'

Whitney shrugged.

Richard's impulse was to kiss Whitney Gauge, but he knew they would just grind helmets.

'Ready?' she asked.

They held hands, tightly enough to feel the grip through the gauntlets, and walked towards the Shimmer. After a few steps, they weren't on the floor, but above it. The phantom moon exerted gravitational pull.

Richard tried not to shut his eyes. The rushing noise increased.

He and Whitney clung to each other. Incalculable forces worked on them. He felt upside down and inside out...

———◆———

And topsy-turvy.

On the other side of the Shimmer was the moon. At least, the parti-coloured Earth, hanging bright in velvet-black night, strongly suggested they were on the satellite.

Everything else wasn't as expected.

No expanse of greyish dust plain, pitted with craters. Not even a range of green cheese. In a screamingly colourful jungle, trees had peacock feathers and birds had serpent-scales. Thick fire rivulets ran through black crystal fern. Dew-drops crawled up rock-cracks like liquid bugs. Some trees were sickly, bursting with the blue-green fungus which had tainted Mo Nordstrom. Patches of the stuff lay about. Small weird dead animals curled up in it like undigested carrots in fresh sick.

Richard's brain stopped sloshing in its pan as the trip trauma passed. But his insides still felt funny, and he was light-headed. Close to tipsy. Tipsy-topsy-turvy was not a place to be. Not with murderers about, and an official moon mission in peril.

The Shimmer was here too, but in a negative image – a globular tracery of sparks revolving in mid-air.

Whitney let go his hand and took experimental steps, making yard-long leaps between footprints. She squealed, like a kid on a fairground ride.

'Look at meeee...'

Richard bounded after her. On the moon, everyone was Peter Pan.

A Victrola gramophone, plumped down on a vegetable outcrop, played 'The Roast Beef of Old England' as if underwater.

A gloved hand had taken root in lunar muck, and grown a spindly green arm, with elbow-buds which opened as eyes. Maybe part of Nordstrom made it through the Shimmer after all. The rest of him was presumably scattered in the void.

'Far out, man,' said Whitney.

A furry balloon-bean the size of a prize-winning marrow floated towards them at shin-height, propelled by raspberries emitted from what looked like a human mouth – complete with Ringo Starr moustache – at its rear. Whitney prodded it away with her knobkerrie. It drifted placidly in another direction.

They were in the lea of a castle.

It took a moment for Richard to recognise the structure as a colossal version of Mildew Manor, grown from moon-coral. Even the light in the East Tower window was reproduced, magnified as if a white star were imprisoned in the tower. Windows migrated slowly across the castle-face, catching Earthlight like message-mirrors. One wing crumbled like a cake left out in the rain, iced with the blue-green mould. An ostentatious ELF *Eismond* banner flapped above the highest ramparts in a gentle lunar wind.

Whitney pointed at the flag with a stick.

'If there's a wind, there must be some sort of air.'

'For God's sake don't try to breathe it.'

'I wasn't considering that. It's just... there's no atmosphere on the moon.'

'There aren't any castles, either. Or gramophones. Or...'

Parked in a beaten-down driveway in front of the castle were a 1920 Type 23 Brescia Tourer, a sleek sit-astride device which might be a resting hover-scooter and a scowling orange Pon-Pon space-hopper. In a corral nearby, lizard-horses stumped on kangaroo legs, whinnying and coughing.

'Point taken. This is there, though. The moon?'

He shrugged, and wobbled in the bulky, now lightweight, suit. The weird feeling in his water was reduced gravity, he realised. His arms tended to float up in unconscious semaphore.

'I suppose...'

He was reluctant to commit. Could there be another moon, stashed in Earth orbit, so unobtrusive astronomers had never noticed? That was ridiculous – but so were the poodle zeppelins and cocktail umbrella hummingbirds and crab cowpats with human fingers.

'It's magic,' he said. 'You know how it works. It's a short cut. And short cuts don't always come out where you think.'

Whitney raised a glove to shade her eyes from the glare and scanned the lunar skies for Apollo 11.

A few minutes ago, back on Earth, the television had shown pictures taken from orbit by the astronauts. That was the moon Richard had expected from the blurry transmissions from those now-bust survey probes – less jagged than the desolate, craggy landscape seen in 70mm in the second part of *2001: A Space Odyssey*, blanketed smooth by aeons of dust, with craters of all sizes everywhere.

'This is literally wonderful,' she said.

'A rare correct usage of the word "literally". Congratulations.'

'We-all did have us prop'r schoolin' down 't the one-room shack between corn-shucking, revival meetin's and lynchin's. And at MIT.'

'Literally wonderful,' he mused. 'Full of wonders.'

A purple cow the size of the Goodyear Blimp passed over on moth-wings. It was ridden by bipedal lobsters with Maori paint on their organic armour, who stood up like water-skiers, complicated reins in their claws.

'That's not something you see every day,' she said. 'Even in our line.'

He thought about it.

'If you took every guess mankind has made about the moon, all the way back to the ancients, and mixed them together, you'd get this.'

'Maybe Luna Moon was a realist, Richard. She drew what she saw.'

'Or she saw what she drew…'

Whitney at once caught his drift.

'The Chalfont Group didn't travel to this moon. They – what? – they made it?'

'I think we all made it. This isn't the moon. Not NASA's moon, or Arthur C. Clarke's. It's a moon. It's all moons. All the imaginary moons…'

Applause sounded.

Three people in moon-suits, without helmets, popped into being around them, holding up those fly-spray gadgets. Anemone Zyle, co-authoress of *The Marquise of the Moon*, had a good seat on the back of a rearing lizard-horse, one hand on the reins, another aiming her moon-gun. A gaunt, grey-blond woman, her set expression suggested the surgical removal of her sense of humour years ago. Richard recognised the ferret-faced oik with an *Eismond* armband and a top hat as Rudy Gosling, the Frinton Führer. The fellow with the floating cloak and pop-eyes must be Magister Rex Chalfont, King of the Moon. He was the one clapping.

'Very close, very good, Mr Jeperson. But not imaginary. Nothing is truly imaginary. Potential. And imperilled. This moon is here, accessible through magic, just so long as no one comes the long way and spoils it by saying it's not so. Know what happens if one of those astronauts sets his dirty great space-boot here? Puff! All gone.'

He illustrated his point, by jabbing a finger at a passing balloon-bean. It burst and evaporated.

'At the south pole, there used to be an entrance to worlds inside the Earth. Known of for centuries. Magicians used it. Visited mole men, Atlanteans and dinosaurs. Then that boring Norwegian trudged there and the hole went away. Just like that. No yeti has been seen in the Himalayas since Hillary crawled to the top of Everest. We can't have that here, can we? You see that now.'

Richard thought it over. Many phantom moons would be lost when the real one was gained.

'Richard,' cautioned Whitney.

'Don't worry, I know he's wrong. I'm just trying to frame a way of making him see that.'

Whitney breathed again.

Richard looked at the moon people. Closed, tight, grim faces. Reluctantly, he concluded reason was probably not an option. But he had to share an insight.

'The blue-green stuff, the mould,' he said. 'It's recent, isn't it? It wasn't here before your purge?'

Only Chalfont tumbled, and tutted with irritation.

Rudy Gosling raised his fly-spray, spun slowly – he was practised in this gravity – and fired a puff of flechettes which spread and tore the Victrola to pieces. Music leaked out of the broken bell for long seconds, then died. Gosling grinned, showing ferret teeth, and brought the moon-gun to bear on Richard and Whitney.

'Hold,' said Chalfont.

'I knew you'd seen it,' said Richard. 'Why didn't you tell them?'

Gosling was furious, but didn't go against his magister.

'We need them alive,' Chalfont said. 'They're here to stop the rot.'

Richard had an answer to something that had bothered him. He knew why they were still alive when the Chalfont Group could have swatted them at any point in the last two days. Why the catspaws used against them – Sky-Ray Roly, the angry ducks, the Space Kiddettes – were non-lethal, when the Temple purge had been carried out so ruthlessly and effectively.

He and Whitney were needed.

'The dreams of nasty people are limited,' Richard told Whitney. '"Sick in the head" is the expression. This moon feeds off imagination, and is a hungry beastie. Since 1953, the Chalfont Group have preserved it – by ignoring what you could read in *New Scientist* or see through a telescope. Lately, that's taken a lot more effort. To maintain a wonderland, you need inspired loons – and this little lot killed off their big dreamers. Was it Luna Moon?

Or Mungo Zyle? Who put the most in, but wasn't noticed till you forced them out? Without them, the place has been sighing and dying. It's literally a blue moon.'

Richard knew Anemone Zyle wanted to shoot them, but understood that she couldn't without bringing down a house of cards.

'I'm imagining parasitic moon-rats with a moral compass,' Whitney told Anemone Zyle. 'Their tiny eggs lodge in the windpipes of the wicked, then hatch into furry, toothy balls which choke their hosts. So, have I thunk them into reality yet, Annie? Can you feel a tickle?'

Anemone Zyle didn't laugh. She desperately stifled a psychosomatic cough.

She was their gaoler in Moondew Manor, while Gosling and Chalfont were off upstairs about important men's business. She didn't much care for the gig.

In a lunar version of the Great Hall, Richard and Whitney were strapped to chairs bolted to the floor in the middle of a morris square.

'If you undo these tethers,' said Whitney, 'we could get down and boogie. I'll bet Mr J. has some funky moves on him.'

'Shut up, witch,' snarled Anemone Zyle.

'That's about the standard of dialogue in her books, Richard. I assume she wrote the garbage bits. Mungo was the one with the talent.'

The authoress snarled. She wore a chainmail bikini and a veil-trailing triple-moon tiara. A long, thin athamé was strapped to her thigh. She was gym-toned, with any ounce of flab scalpelled or sweated off – but her skin wasn't healthy, especially in the moonglow inside the manor.

The blue fungus spread wildly across the walls.

'Annie,' said Whitney, 'tell me something… how can you rest your chin on your elbows? Go on, demonstrate now.'

Anemone Zyle was puzzled.

'I suppose you've written so many clunker sentences you don't remember just one gaffe. I wonder which is your worst book? Some fans say *Ghyslayne, Moon-Elf of Bumph* is the absolute pits, but on consideration, I'd have to pick the wind-up of the Tomes of the Dragonwing saga. *Tome the Third: Countess of the Craters*. That one really sucks like an Electrolux! I wouldn't think anything could be more crappily drivelling than *Tome the Second: Seraphim of Satellite Sigma*, but you surprised me again. The only even passable passages are copied out of an old pulp novel by Otis Adelbert Kline. Which would you say was the worst chapter in your worst book? That scene where Blodwyn the Troll-Girl plights her troth to the Peri Prince Pyrcyvyl? Or the pie-fight which disrupts the moon-vow ceremony of the itsy-bitsy nipsies?'

Anemone strode over to Whitney's chair, hand out to clamp over the prisoner's mouth.

Whitney shut up and twisted skilfully in her chair, legs scissoring. Her entire lower body lifted and stretched, anchored by the leather straps which fastened her wrists to the armrests. Her knees hammered either side of Anemone Zyle's neck.

'This'll only take a moment.'

Anemone tried to scratch Whitney's dance-powerful legs.

'That won't help,' Whitney grunted. 'Try using your knife.'

Surprised to be getting sound advice in this situation but too pressed to wonder at its sincerity, Anemone drew her athamé and angled it to stick into Whitney's thigh. Whitney gave a squeeze and the gaoler passed out in an instant. Anemone dropped the knife, and Whitney caught its hilt between chin and chest.

Whitney let Anemone fall in a heap, and resumed sitting position, careful not to lose the knife. She manoeuvred the athamé to slide down her arm, bounce off her inner-elbow and spring into her hand. She reversed it, slipped the blade under the strap and sliced herself free.

'You should have used chains,' she said to the unconscious Anemone.

Whitney cut her other strap, but undid Richard's buckles. Between them, they hauled Anemone into Richard's chair and strapped her in. Richard took off her tiara and gave it to Whitney.

'I thought you'd only read a single page of the Zyles's books,' he said.

'As a grown-up,' she admitted. 'I was a science fiction fan in grade school. I read an enormous amount I've done my best to forget. Ever heard of Varno Zhoule? Keith Winton? Cordwainer Bird?'

'Can't say I have. I prefer mysteries myself.'

Their moon-suits had been taken off to facilitate strapping them down. The air in the mansion was breathable, if heavy with spice smells and an underscent of rot.

Anemone moaned, starting to come round.

Whitney gagged the woman with her own veil. Anemone's furious eyes sparked.

'You've had your say, hack queen.'

Whitney gave Richard the knife and fetched her knobkerrie from a corner where their stuff had been flung in a pile.

'To the battlements,' she said.

＊

Blue mould was turning grey and falling off the walls, dissipating like fluff. Richard assumed he and Whitney were responsible for that.

How many active imaginations did it take to keep this moon alive?

They climbed stairs. Twice, they stepped on morris squares which entirely negated gravity, allowing them to float up between floors. Richard gathered Chalfont and Gosling were busy up in the tall tower.

They had already hinted it wouldn't be necessary to keep their prisoners alive after their immediate Great Work was done. That had to involve the *Eagle*, now descending from lunar orbit.

How exactly did the moon prepare to repel boarders?

The answer became obvious when they came to the room with the eternal light. Approaching quietly, keeping to shadows, they peered through a doorway and saw figures clustered around a large, fat cannon aimed out at the sky through a big hole in the wall.

Chalfont and Gosling were there. Chalfont wore M&S wizard-robes, a coronet with stick-ons representing the phases of the moon, and complicated multi-lensed spectacles. He held a long taper, flame dancing slowly at its end. Gosling was in black tweed with a red sash, an *Eismond* armband, red wellington boots and a top hat – the uniform of the ELF upper echelon.

The other people in the room were phantasms. They worked on the cannon – manipulating an apparently lightweight but solid giant ball into the muzzle, attaching a fuse, making minute adjustments to an aiming device.

Some looked familiar.

'The big-schnozz guy must be Cyrano de Bergerac,' whispered Whitney.

'The one from the play, yes,' Richard agreed. 'The historical Cyrano had a normal nose. With him is Baron Munchausen. The fellow in the toga must be Lucian. The bald Frenchman is Georges Méliès, or at least his character in *Voyage to the Moon*. The bug-faced one is a Selenite, from Wells. The girls in leotards I can't place...'

'Cat-Women of the Moon. It's a film. The giant toy spider is theirs. Who's the tall silver goon with pipes in his ears?'

'A Cyberman, from *Doctor Who*. He's British.'

'The big cheerful robot with the hammer and sickle? The one who looks like a giant refrigerator?'

'It'll be from some comrades-across-the-stars socialist realist space epic.'

'The bearded drunk?'

'Captain Haddock, from the Tintin album, *Objectif Lune*.'

'The blonde in riding britches?'

'The heroine of *Frau im Mond*, the Fritz Lang film. Look who she's with…'

'Dr Floyd, from *2001*.'

'Arthur C. Clarke is a magician after all.'

A black monolith stood in the room too.

The workers were not transparent, but showed various degrees of unreality. Some were in black-and-white, or poorly tinted. Some seemed engraved rather than living.

The cannon was stamped 'Property of the Baltimore Gun Club'.

Captain Haddock looked around, rimmed eyes bulging, and pointed a fat gauntlet at Richard and Whitney.

'Bashi-bazouks!' he shouted. 'Ostrogoths! Shibboleths! Vermiform appendices! A billion blistering blue barnacles!'

Then they all turned to stare. All the lunar explorers and inhabitants, all the pioneers and colonists, the masters and the monsters. Munchausen doffed his plumed cap.

'I knew that bint was too stupid to be trusted,' fumed Gosling, reaching for a moon-gun.

Chalfont looked almost happy to see them.

After living off the books for so long, Magister Rex wanted an audience. It might be his magic needed an audience.

'You're going to blast the *Eagle* out of the sky,' Richard accused. 'Using a cannon ball painted with cavorite.'

'A defensive measure,' Chalfont admitted. 'To keep this moon alive, to keep all these moon people alive.'

'Surely, you can't want to see an end for poor Munchausen?' pleaded the Baron. 'So much would be lost.'

'Miaow,' said a Cat-Woman expressively.

Méliès mimed, impassioned. His films were silent, of course. The Soviet walking fridge saluted Permanent Revolution. The Cyberman raised a headlamp between handles. Richard recognised it as the BBC props' department's improvised Cyber-gun. Cyrano went for his deadly blade.

Whitney raised her knobkerrie, but Richard laid a hand on her arm.

Before resorting to violence, he would appeal to reason.

'Gentlemen, Selenites, Cat-Women,' he began, 'I salute you. On behalf of all mankind, you have done your job with honour. You flew ahead, on fancy, on calculation, on ambition, on a dream. Now, the rest of us must catch up. What's about to happen in the Sea of Tranquillity isn't your death, it's your glory. I implore you, in the name of the spirit which seized you all in the first place, please do not do the bidding of these mean-spirited men. It's your moon, not theirs. They made the moon sick, remember.'

One of the Selenites still had patches of fungus around its mandibles. The giant spider's legs were limp, the strings eaten away. Haddock's beard had a blueish tinge too.

'You can't hold this scrap of territory for them, you must give it up. You have other homes, where you have other shapes. There's Mars and Venus and Vulcan and Skaro. There's Metropolis and Atlantis and Freedonia and Utopia. And Narnia and Oz and Erewhon and Wonderland. The men coming in their capsule have you in their hearts, much more than these pretenders to magic. Their whole enterprise is built on your example. Dr Floyd, you must understand this. Science is indistinguishable from magic. You should welcome the *Eagle*. It's the keeping of the promise you made.'

Gosling raised his moon-gun, but was caught up short – a ghost blade stuck out of the soft part under his chin. Cyrano pulled his *epée* free, and the Frinton Führer collapsed. He was not bleeding, not even wounded, but was dead.

Chalfont raised his flaming taper.

The *Eagle* was in his sights, a multi-faceted form descending towards lunar ground, landing-pads extended. What did the astronauts see below them? Not Moondew Manor and the populated jungles. The undisturbed dust of the Sea of Tranquillity.

Chalfont touched the taper to the fuse, which began to fizz.

The ghosts swirled around the cannon. Some passed through each other.

Whitney thumped Chalfont with her stick, cracking his coronet and knocking him to the floor.

'Too late,' he murmured.

'No,' said Richard. 'It's not.'

Munchausen – who knew the worth of a good story and a grand gesture – was first. He clambered up into the barrel of the cannon, as was his habit. A Cat-Woman was next, the zip up the back of her leotard sparkling as she curled beside the Baron.

Then Floyd, letting a slide-rule float away from him.

And Haddock, bright blue hair grown past his knees. Lucian. Cyrano. The Russian robot. A two-dimensional square-jawed comic book spaceman. The Grand Lunar. Georges Méliès. Dick Tracy. The Cyberman. All of them.

A conglomeration of ghosts stopped up the cannon.

The fuse burned down, and the tower room filled with light.

The manor was falling like the House of Usher. Sublunar tremors shook its foundations. Richard and Whitney made their way down from the tower in a hurry.

'Great speech,' said Whitney. 'Off the top of your head?'

'I knew they were better than Magister Rex wanted them to be. The moon-ghosts have more in common with the astronauts than the Chalfont Group. The *Eagle* is their validation. It means we weren't wasting time dreaming them up…'

'It's all right, you can stop now. We should probably shut up and run.'

When the cannon imploded, Chalfont seemed to have been vaporised. The room was empty, even of ghosts. The *Eagle* was safe, and this dream-moon would change.

Richard believed that when the LEM touched down, this moon would pass away, or withdraw deeper into the realm of imagination, a bywater of dreams rather than a river. That meant there'd be nothing here to breathe.

They had to get back through the Shimmer.

'We should take Anemone,' said Richard.

'If we must,' responded Whitney.

Anemone was still fuming. Richard unstrapped her. Claws came for his face. Whitney stepped in and administered a right jab to the authoress' chin, putting her in a cooperative daze.

They carried Anemone Zyle out of Moondew Manor between them.

The moonscape was melting. Animals had become grey statues. A moth-cow was downed nearby, cocoon forming around her.

Richard saw the *Eagle*.

Toting Anemone, Richard and Whitney ran for the Shimmer. It still sparkled.

They reached the spot where they had arrived. Anemone came round, broke free…

'Come with us,' said Richard.

'You'll die.'

Anemone tore off her gag, and said, 'Don't care.'

'Jump, you silly woman,' said Whitney.

The Shimmer was contracting. Richard reached for Anemone, but she darted away. Whitney took his arm, and they stepped into the Shimmer…

—•—

…unscrambled again, they were back on Earth, in the Great Hall at Mildew Manor. The Shimmer, a hole in space, gave a clear view of the dying moon.

They watched as Anemone looked up. In the distance, the LEM descended.

A wireless was on somewhere nearby, loud…

'Contact light!' crackled an astronaut. 'Okay, engine stop. ACA – out of detent.'

'Out of detent,' acknowledged another astronaut.

'Mode control… both auto. Descent engine command override off. Engine arm… off. Four-thirteen is in.'

The rich jungle was gone, replaced by grey desert.

'Houston, Tranquillity Base here,' said Neil Armstrong. 'The *Eagle* has landed.'

Anemone Zyle collapsed, sank into dust.

'What happens if they find her?' Whitney asked.

'She's miles from the landing point,' he said. 'She won't be found for years. Not until the moon is covered with colony bases and cities and starship ports. Then she'll be a mystery.'

The Shimmer winked shut.

Captain Maitland came into the room, with an American officer who had finally found his way. They had been following the moon-landing on television.

119

'We cordoned off the place, sir,' said Maitland. 'Stayed well away from the big blue thing.'

'Very wise,' said Richard.

'They've landed safely on the moon,' said Maitland. 'Just thought you'd like to know.'

'Glad to hear it.'

'Any sign of the hostiles?'

'They're no longer a problem, Captain. Mission: accomplished.'

———◆———

Teams from an alphabet soup of British and American scientific, paranormal and intelligence agencies were going over Mildew Manor in minute detail, examining every rune and algorithm. Richard suspected they wouldn't work for anyone but the vanished Magister Chalfont. And that there was little use in a magic portal to a wiped-away potential realm.

He'd reported to Catriona, who was politely telling Spilsby to give Whitney Gauge a permanent promotion to fieldwork. She'd probably also be offered a congressional medal or a free ticket to Disneyland or some other honour she'd now feel obliged to turn down in the Diogenes Club tradition. Eventually, someone would pass on the news to Senator Kennedy, if he was still interested.

In Houston, arguments had continued until the last moment. The official story was a '1202 Executive Overflow Alarm' had put the landing in jeopardy, and a technician named Bales was forced to make a snap decision about whether or not to go ahead. The LEM missed its designated landing site, and Armstrong had to fly it sideways, with only a few seconds' fuel, to find a flat, safe spot between craters and a boulder field. Catriona had said everyone was impatient. Armstrong and Aldrin were supposed to take a rest period before the historic moment, but even NASA training couldn't turn people into robots who could sleep at a time like this

– so man set foot on the moon earlier than advertised, presumably to the fury of US TV networks.

Early in the morning, the garden was ghostly in cold pre-dawn light. Richard sat with Whitney on a bench by the moondial. The silver, conquered satellite was still bright.

The Man in the Moon didn't have a rocket stuck in its eye. But Richard thought the face looked like a startled, apoplectic Rex Chalfont. Perhaps that was what had happened to Magister.

'I miss the moth-cows,' said Whitney.

'They're still there, somewhere. Harder to reach. Like the monolith, and the ice-pools, and the spider on strings. We can't go there any more.'

'What would it take to find them again?'

'Time. I daresay if we left the moon alone for fifty years or so, the Selenite forests would grow back – but that's not going to happen, is it? Armstrong took his "small step". Man is on the moon now. There'll be more missions. Mines. Colonies. Probably missiles. That's the moon-dream of 1969.'

'Hooray for us,' she said, a little regretful.

'By the way, congratulations,' he said. 'You beat Armstrong. You were the first American on the moon. That's showing NASA they're wrong about girls.'

'Cool. Will my first words get in the books? What were they?' Richard laughed.

'You said, "Look at meeeee…"'

'Okay,' said Whitney, smiling wickedly. 'I'll stand by that.'

⊷⊷ YOU DON'T HAVE TO BE MAD... ⊷⊷

PROLOGUE: A GRADUATE OF THE LAUGHING ACADEMY

He arrived bright and early in the morning. At eight o'clock, the entire workforce was assembled in the open air. The managing director introduced him as an outside consultant with bad news to deliver and handed him the loud-hailer. Barely restraining giggles, Mr Joyful announced the shipyard would close down at the end of the year and they were all sacked.

Escorted off site by armed guards, ignoring the snarls and taunts of to-be-unemployed-by-1973 workmen, he was back in his bubble car, stomach knotted with hilarious agony, by eight-fifteen. He managed to drive a few miles before he was forced to pull over and give vent to the laughter that had built up inside him like painful gas. Tears coursed down his cheeks. The interior of his space-age transport vibrated with the explosions of his merriment.

At nine o'clock, chortling, he told a young mother that her son's cancer was inoperable. At ten, snickering, he personally informed the founder of a biscuit factory that he'd been unseated in a boardroom coup and would be lucky to escape prosecution over a series of mystery customer ailments. At eleven, in full view of a party of schoolboys, he wielded a length of two-by-four to execute an aged polar bear that a small zoo could no longer afford to feed. At twelve, almost unable to hold the saw steady for his shaking mirth, he cut down a seven-hundred-year-old oak tree on the village green of Little Middling by the Weir, to make way for a road-widening scheme. The chants of the protesters were especially rib-tickling.

From one until two, he had a fine lunch in a Jolly Glutton motorway restaurant. Two straight sausages and a helping of near-liquid mash. An individual apple pie with processed cream. It was a privilege to taste this, the food of the future. Each portion perfect, and identical with every other portion. That struck him as funny too.

At two-thirty, controlling himself, he murdered three old folks in a private home, with the hankie-over-the-mouth-and-nose hold. Their savings had run out and this was kinder than turning them loose to fend for themselves. His five o'clock appointment was something similar, a journalist working on a news item about hovercraft safety for the telly programme *Tomorrow's News*.

'I've got some bad news for you,' he told the surprised young woman.

'Who are you?' she demanded.

'I'm Mr Joyful. Aren't you interested in my news?'

'Why are you grinning like that? Is this a joke?'

He was about to go off again. Amused tears pricked the backs of his eyes. Laughter began to scream inside his brain, clamouring for escape.

'Your contract is cancelled,' he managed to get out.

It was too, too funny.

He produced the silenced pistol. One quick phut in the face and he could knock off for the day.

He was laughing like a drain.

What this woman didn't know – but would find out unless stopped – was that the Chairman of the Board of Directors of her employer, Greater London Television, was also responsible for Amalgamated British Hoverlines, and had personally authorised the cost-cutting scheme that resulted in the deaths of twenty-eight day-trippers.

His gun barrel shook as it pointed.

The look on the woman's face was too much. He barked laughter, like the policeman on the comedy record. His sides literally split, great tears running down from his armpits to his hips.

His shot creased the woman's shoulder.

That was funny too. People held him down, wrestling the gun out of his grip. Someone even kicked him in the tummy. It was too much to bear.

He kept on laughing, blind with tears, lances of agony stabbing into his torso. Then he stopped.

ACT 1: VANESSA IS COMMITTED

She was comfortably lotused among orange and purple scatter-cushions in the conference room of the Chelsea mansion, rainbow-socked feet tucked neatly into the kinks of her knees. Vanessa wore a scarlet leotard with a white angora cardigan. Her long red hair was in a rope-braid, knotted end gripped in a giant turquoise clothespeg. Fred Regent sat nearby, on a wire-net bucket chair, in his usual jeans and jean jacket, square head almost shaven.

Jazz harpsichord tinkled out of the sound system concealed behind eighteenth-century wood panelling. Matched Lichtenstein explosions hung over the marble mantelpiece. A bundle of joss sticks smoked in a Meissen vase on a kidney-shaped coffee table.

Richard Jeperson, silver kaftan rippling with reflected light, nested cross-legged in a white plastic chair that hung from the ceiling on an anchor chain. It was shaped like a giant egg sliced vertically, with yolk-yellow padding inside.

He showed them a photograph of a happy-looking fat man. Then another one, of the same man, lying on the floor in a pool of mess.

'Jolyon Fuller,' he announced.

Vanessa compared the shots. Fuller looked even happier in the one where he was dead.

'He made his living in an interesting way,' Richard said. 'He delivered bad news.'

'I thought that was Reginald Bosanquet's job,' put in Fred.

'Fuller doesn't look gloomy,' Vanessa ventured.

'Apparently, he wasn't,' Richard said. 'He laughed himself to death. Literally. Matters you or I would consider tragic were high comedy to him. His wires were crossed somewhere up here.'

He tapped his head.

Taking back the pictures, hawkbrows momentarily clenched, he gave them consideration. Shoulder-length black ringlets and the mandarin's moustache gave his face a soft, almost girlish cast, but the piercing eyes and sharp cheekbones were predatory. After all they'd been through together, Vanessa still hadn't got to the bottom of Richard Jeperson.

It had been weeks since the last interesting problem had come along – the business of the Satanist Scoutmaster and his scheme to fell the Post Office Tower. Richard had summoned his assistants to announce that they were to investigate a string of strangenesses. This was often the way of their affairs. At the Diogenes Club in Pall Mall, a group of clever and wise minds – under the direction of Edwin Winthrop, Grand Old Man of the Ruling Cabal – constantly sifted through court records, police reports, newspapers and statements from members of the public, ear-marking the unusual and red-flagging the impossible. If the inexplicabilities mounted up, the matter was referred to one of the Club's Valued Members. Currently, Richard was reckoned the Most Valued Member.

'Here's another pretty fizzog. Harry Egge.'

Richard showed them a glossy of a boxer, gloves up, bruises on his face.

'He was supposed to be the next 'Enery Cooper,' said Fred, who followed sport. 'He could take the Punishment for fifty rounds. Couldn't feel pain or didn't care about it. No matter how much battering he took, he kept on punching.'

'I read about him,' Vanessa said. 'Didn't he die?'

'Indeed he did,' Richard explained. 'In his home, in a fire caused by faulty wiring.'

'He was trapped,' she said. 'How horrible.'

'Actually, he wasn't trapped. He could have walked away, easily. But he fought the fire, literally. He punched it and battered it, but it caught him and burned him to the bone. Very odd. When you put your hand in flame, you take it out sharpish. It's what pain is for, to make you do things before you think about them. Nature's fire alarm. Harry Egge kept fighting the fire, as if he could win by a knock-out.'

'Was he kinky for pain?'

'A masochist, Vanessa? Not really. He just wasn't afraid of being hurt.'

'And that makes him barmy?'

'Quite so, Fred. Utterly barmy.'

Vanessa wondered what Jolyon Fuller and Harry Egge had in common, besides being mad and dead.

'There are more odd folk to consider,' Richard continued, producing more photographs and reports. 'Nicholas Mix-Elgin: head of security at a multi-national computer firm. He became so suspicious that he searched his children's pets for listening devices. Internally. Serafine Xavier: convent school teacher turned high-priced call girl, the only patient ever hospitalised on the National Health with "clinical nymphomania". We only know about her because several male patients on her ward died during visits from her. Lieutenant Commander Hilary Roehampton: a naval officer who insisted on volunteering for a series of missions so dangerous only a lunatic would consider them.'

'Like what?' asked Fred.

'Sea-testing leaky submarines.'

'Cor blimey!'

Vanessa had to agree.

'These people held more or less responsible positions. It's only by chance that their files were passed on to us. The services of the *grande horizontale* were, I believe, retained by the FO for the intimate entertainment of visiting dignitaries.'

'They all sound like loonies to me,' Fred said.

'Ah yes,' Richard agreed, extending a finger, 'but their lunacies worked for them, at least in the short-term. You are familiar with that allegedly humorous mass-produced plaque you see up in offices and other sordid places? "You Don't Have to Be Mad to Work Here" – asterisk – "But it Helps." Sometimes being mad really does help. After all, a head of security should be a bit of a paranoiac, a boxer needs to have a touch of the masochist.'

'Don't most firms and all government agencies make prospective employees take a battery of psychiatric tests these days? To weed out the maniacs?'

'Indeed they do, my dear. I have copies here.'

He indicated a thick sheaf of papers. She reached out.

'Don't bother. All our interesting friends were evaluated within the last three years as one hundred per cent sane.'

'The tests must be rigged,' Fred said. 'You don't just go bonkers overnight. This lot must have been in and out of nut-hatches all their lives.'

'As a matter of fact, they were all rated with clean certificates of mental health.'

Fred didn't believe it.

'And who gave out the certificates?' she asked.

Richard arched an eyebrow. She'd asked the right question. That was the connection.

'Strangely enough, all these persons were certified as sane by the same practitioner, one Dr Iain Menzies Ballance. He is director of the Pleasant Green Centre, near Whipplewell in Sussex.'

'Pleasant Green. Is that a private asylum?'

'Not officially,' he told her. 'It offers training courses for executives and other high-earners. Like a health farm for the mind. Sweat off those unsightly phobias, that sort of thing.'

She looked at a glossy prospectus that was in with all the case files. A Regency mansion set among rolling downs. Dr Ballance smiling with his caring staff, all beautiful young women. Testimonials from leaders of industry and government figures. A table of fees, starting at £500 a week.

'Let me get this straight,' said Fred. 'Sane people go in…'

'And mad people come out,' Richard announced.

Vanessa felt a little chill. There was something cracked in Dr Ballance's half-smile. And his staff couldn't quite not look like the dolly bird wing of the SS.

'The question which now presents itself, of course, is which of us would most benefit from a week or two under the care of the good Dr Ballance.'

Richard looked from Fred to Vanessa. Fred just looked at her.

'You're the sanest person I know, Ness,' Fred said.

'That's not saying much,' she countered.

Richard was about to give a speech about knowing how dangerous the assignment would be and not wanting her to take it unless she was absolutely sure. She cut him off. After all, she owed him too much – her sanity, at least, probably her life – to protest.

'Just tell me who I am,' she said.

Richard smiled like a shark and produced a folder.

In the garage of the Chelsea house, her white Lotus Elan looked like a Dinky Toy parked next to Richard's Rolls-Royce ShadowShark, but it could almost match the great beast for speed and had the edge for manoeuvrability. She should get down to Sussex inside an hour.

Fred was already in Whipplewell. If asked, he was a bird-watcher out after a look-see at some unprecedented avocets. Richard had given him an I-Spy *Book of Birds* to memorise. He would watch over her.

Richard had turned out to see her off. He wore an orange frock coat with matching boots and top hat, over a psychedelic waistcoat and a lime-green shirt with collar-points wider than his shoulders. He fixed her with his deep, dark eyes.

'My love, remember who you are.'

When they had met, she'd been a different person, not in command of herself. Something it was easiest to call a demon had her in a thrall it was easiest to call possession. He'd been able to reach her because he understood.

'We have less memory than most. That's why what we have, what we are, is so precious.'

Richard was an amnesiac, a foundling of the War. He had proved to her that it was possible to live without a past that could be proved with memory. Once, since the first time, she had come under the influence of another entity – she shuddered at the memory of a pier on the South Coast – but had been able to throw off the cloak dropped over her mind.

'You'll be pretending to be a new person, Vanessa Vail. That's a snakeskin you can shed at any time. While the act must be perfect, you must not give yourself up to it completely. They can do a great deal to "Vanessa Vail" without touching Vanessa the Real. You must have a core that is you alone.'

She thought she understood.

'Vanessa,' he repeated, kissing her. 'Vanessa.'

She vaulted into the driving seat of the Lotus.

'What's your name?' he asked.

She told him, and drove off.

⬩━◆━⬩

'You are an army officer?' Dr Ballance asked, looking up from the folder. He had a hard Scots accent.

Vanessa nodded. She was supposed to be a paratrooper. Looking at her long legs and big eyes, people thought she must be a fashion model, but she had the height to be a convincing warrior woman. And she could look after herself in hand-to-hand combat. It wasn't a great snakeskin but it was wearable.

'Things have changed since my day, Lieutenant Vail.'

She hated her new name. The double V sounded so cartoonish. But you couldn't be in the army without a surname.

'Were you in the services, Dr Ballance?'

He nodded and one side of his mouth smiled. The left half of his face was frozen.

She imagined him in uniform, tunic tight on his barrel chest, cap perched on his butter-coloured cloud of hair, tiger stripes on his blandly bespectacled face. She wondered which side he had been on in whichever war he had fought.

'You will be Lieutenant Veevee,' he said. 'For "vivacious". We rename all our guests. The world outside does not trouble us here in Pleasant Green. We are interested only in the world inside.'

She crossed her legs and rearranged her khaki miniskirt for decency's sake. Dr Ballance's one mobile eye followed the line of her leg down to her polished brogue. She was wearing a regimental tie tucked into a fatigue blouse, and a blazer with the proper pocket badge. Richard had suggested medal ribbons, but she thought that would be over-egging the pud.

'I'll have Miss Dove show you to your quarters,' said Dr Ballance. 'You will join us for the evening meal, and I shall work up a programme of tests and exercises for you. Nothing too strenuous at first.'

'I've passed commando training,' she said.

It was true. Yesterday, getting into character, she had humped herself through mud with an incredulous platoon of real paratroopers. At first, they gallantly tried to help her. Then, when it looked like she'd score the highest marks on the course, they did their best to drag her back and keep her down. She gave a few combat-ready squaddies some nasty surprises and came in third. The sergeant offered to have her back to keep his lads in line.

'Your body is in fine shape, Lieutenant Veevee,' said Dr Ballance, eye running back up her leg, pausing at chest-level, then twitching up to her face. 'Now we shall see what we can do about tailoring your mind to fit it.'

Dr Ballance pressed a buzzer switch. A young woman appeared in the office. She wore a thigh-length flared doctor's coat over white PVC knee-boots, a too-small T-shirt and hot-pants. Her blond hair was kept back by an Alice band.

'Miss Dove, show Lieutenant Veevee where we're putting her.'

The attendant smiled, making dimples.

Vanessa stood and was led out of the office.

—◆—

Pleasant Green manor house had been gutted, and the interior remodelled in steel and glass. Vanessa took note of various gym facilities and therapy centres. All were in use, with 'guests' exercising or playing mind games under the supervision of attendants dressed exactly like Miss Dove. They looked like Pan's People rehearsing a hospital-themed dance number. Some processes were obvious, but others involved peculiar machines and dentist's chairs with straps and restraints.

She was shown her room, which contained a four-poster bed and other genuine antique furniture. A large window looked out over the grounds. Among rolling lawns were an arrangement of pre-fab buildings and some concrete-block bunkers. Beyond the window was a discreet steel grille, 'for protection'.

'We don't get many gels at Pleasant Green, Lieutenant Veevee,' said Miss Dove. 'It's mostly fellows. High-powered executives and the like.'

'Women are more and more represented in all the professions.'

'We've one other gel here. Mrs Empty. Dr Ballance thinks she's promising. You'll have competition. I hope you'll be chums.'

'So do I.'

'I think you're going to fit in perfectly, Lieutenant.'

Miss Dove hugged her.

Vanessa tensed, as if attacked. She barely restrained herself from popping the woman one on the chin. Miss Dove air-kissed her on both cheeks and let her go. Vanessa realised she had been very subtly frisked during the spontaneous embrace. She had chosen not to bring any obvious weapons or burglar tools.

'See you at din-din,' Miss Dove said, and skipped out.

Vanessa allowed herself a long breath. She assumed the wall-size mirror was a front for a camera. She had noticed a lot of extra wiring and guessed Dr Ballance would have a closed-circuit TV set-up. She put her face close to the mirror, searching for an imaginary blackhead, and thought she heard the whirring of a lens adjustment.

There was no telephone on the bedside table.

Her bags were open, her clothes put in the wardrobe. She hoped they had taken the trouble to examine her marvellously genuine army credentials. It had taken a lot of work to get them up to scratch, and she wanted the effort appreciated.

She looked out of the window. At the far end of the lawns was a wooded area and beyond that the Sussex Downs. Fred ought to be out there somewhere with a flat cap, a thermos of tea and a pair of binoculars. He was putting up in the Coach and Horses at Whipplewell, where there were no bars on the windows and you could undress in front of the mirror without giving some crackpot a free show.

Where was Richard all this time? He must be pulling strings somehow. He was supposed to be following up on the graduates of Pleasant Green.

She felt sleepy. It was late afternoon, the gold of the sun dappling the lawn. She shouldn't be exhausted. There was a faint hissing. She darted around, scanning for ventilation grilles, holding her breath. She couldn't keep it up, and if she made an attempt the watchers would know she was a fake. She decided to go with it. Climbing onto the soft bed, she felt eiderdowns rise to embrace her. She let the tasteless, odourless gas into her lungs, and tried to arrange herself on the bed with some decorum.

She nodded off.

———◦———

Something snapped in front of her face and stung her nostrils. Her head cleared. Everything was suddenly sharp, hyper-real.

She was sitting at a long dinner table, in mixed company, wearing a yellow-and-lime-striped cocktail dress. Her hair was done up in a towering beehive. A thick layer of make-up – which she rarely used – was lacquered over her face. Even her nails were done, in stripes to match her dress. Overhead fluorescents cruelly illuminated the table and guests, but the walls were in darkness and an incalculable distance away from the long island of light. The echoey room was noisy with conversation, the clatter of cutlery and The Move's 'Fire Brigade'. She had a mouthful of food and had to chew to save herself from choking.

'You are enjoying your eyeball, Lieutenant?'

The questioner was a slight Eurasian woman in a man's tuxedo. Her hair was marcelled into a Hokusai wave. A nametag identified her as 'Miss Lark'.

Eyeball?

Chewing on jellying meat, she glanced down at her plate. A cooked pig's face looked back up at her, one eye glazed in its socket, the other a juicy red gouge. She didn't know whether to choke, swallow or spit.

The pig's stiff snout creaked into a porcine smile.

Vanessa expectorated most of the pulpy eye back at its owner.

Conversation and consumption stopped. Miss Lark tutted. Dr Ballance, a tartan sash over his red jacket, stared a wordless rebuke.

The pig snarled now, baring sharp teeth at her.

A fog ocean washed around Vanessa's brain. This time, she struggled. Flares of light that weren't there made her blink. Her own eyeballs might have been vasilined over. The room rippled and faces stretched. The guests were all one-eyed pigs.

Some eye slipped down her throat. She went away.

———◆———

This time, the smell of cooking brought her to. She was in an underground kitchen or workshop. Sizzling and screeching was in the air. Infernal red lighting gave an impression of a low ceiling, smoky red bricks arched like an old-fashioned bread-oven.

In her hands were a pair of devices which fitted like gloves. Black leather straps kept her hands around contoured grips like the handles of a skipping rope, and her thumbs were pressed down on studs inset into the apparatus. Wires led from the grips into a junction box at her feet.

She was wearing black high-heeled boots, goggles that covered half her face and a rubber fetish bikini. Oil and sweat trickled on her tight stomach, and down her smoke-rouged arms and calves. Her hair was pulled back and fanned stickily on her shoulders.

Her thumbs were jamming down the studs.

Jethro Tull was performing 'Living in the Past'.

And someone was screaming. There was an electric discharge in the air. In the gloom of the near distance, a white shape writhed. The goggles were clouded, making it impossible to get more than a vague sense of what she was looking at.

She relaxed her thumbs, instantly. The writhing and screaming halted. Cold guilt chilled her mind. She fought the fuzziness.

Someone panted and sobbed.

'I think you've shown us just what you think of the cook, Lieutenant Veevee,' said Dr Ballance.

He stood nearby, in a kilt and a black leather Gestapo cap. A pink feather boa entwined his broad, naked chest like a real snake.

'Have you expressed yourself fully?' he asked.

She could still taste the eyeball. Still see the damned pig-face making a grin.

Red anger sparked. She jammed her thumbs down.

A full-blooded scream ripped through the room, hammering against the bricks and her ears. A blue arc of electricity lit up one wall. The white shape convulsed and she kept her thumbs down, pouring her rage into the faceless victim.

No. That was what they wanted.

She flipped her thumbs erect, letting go of the studs.

The arc stopped, the shape slumped.

Half Dr Ballance's face expressed disappointment.

'Forgiveness and mercy, eh, Lieutenant? We shall have to do something about that.'

Attendants took down the shape – was it a man? a woman? an animal? – she had been shocking.

Vanessa felt a certain triumph. They hadn't turned her into a torturer.

'Now cook has the switch,' said Dr Ballance.

She looked into the darkness, following the wires.

Shock hit her in the hands and ran up her arms, a rising ratchet of voltage. It was like being lashed with pain.

Her mind was whipped out.

━◆━

She was doing push-ups. Her arms and stomach told her she had been doing push-ups for some time. A voice counted in the mid-hundreds.

Staff Sergeant Barry Sadler's 'The Ballad of the Green Berets' was playing.

She concentrated on shoving ground away from her, lifting her whole body, breathing properly, getting past pain. Her back and legs were rigid.

Glancing to one side, she saw a polished pair of boots.

Numbers were shouted at her. She upped the rate, smiling tightly. This, she could take. She was trained in dance (ballroom, modern and ballet) and oriental boxing (judo, karate and jeet kune do), her body tuned well beyond the standards of the commandos. She reached her thousand. Inside five seconds, she gave ten more for luck.

'On your feet, soldier,' she was ordered.

She sprung upright, to attention. She was wearing fatigues and combat boots.

A black woman inspected her. She had a shaved head, three parallel weals on each cheek, and 'Sergeant-Mistress Finch' stencilled on her top pocket.

Her tight fist jammed into Vanessa's stomach.

She clenched her tummy muscles a split second before hard knuckles landed. Agony still exploded in her gut, but she didn't go down like a broken doll.

Sergeant-Mistress Finch wrung out her fist.

'Good girl,' she said. 'Give Lieutenant Veevee a lollipop.'

Miss Dove, who was dressed as a soldier, produced a lollipop the size of a stop sign, with a hypnotic red and white swirl pattern. She handed it to Vanessa.

'By the numbers,' Sergeant-Mistress Finch ordered, 'lick!'

Vanessa had a taste-flash of the pig's eyeball, but overcame remembered disgust. She stuck her tongue to the surface of the lollipop and licked. A sugar rush hit her brain.

'Punishments and rewards,' commented a Scots voice.

***

She woke with the taste of sugar in her mouth and a gun in her hand. She was wearing a kilt, a tight cut-away jacket over a massively ruffled shirt, and a feathered cap. Black tartan tags stuck out of her thick grey socks and from her gilt epaulettes.

Sergeant-Mistress Finch knelt in front of her, hands clasped behind her neck, forehead resting against the barrel of Vanessa's pistol.

'Sergeant-Mistress Finch is a traitor to the unit,' said Dr Ballance. Vanessa swivelled to look at him. He wore the full dress uniform of the Black Watch.

They were out in the woods somewhere, after dark. A bonfire burned nearby. Soldiers (all girls) stood around. There was a woodsy tang in the air and a night chill settling in. A lone bagpiper mournfully played 'Knock Knock, Who's There?', a recent chart hit for Mary Hopkin.

'Do your duty, Lieutenant Veevee.'

Vanessa's finger tightened on the trigger.

This was some test. But would she pass if she shot or refused to shoot? Surely, Dr Ballance wouldn't let her really kill one of the attendants. If he ran Pleasant Green like that, he would run out of staff.

The gun must not be loaded.

She shifted the pistol four inches to the left, aiming past the Sergeant-Mistress's head, and pulled the trigger. There was an explosion out of all proportion with the size of the gun. A crescent of red ripped out of Finch's left ear. The Sergeant-Mistress clapped a hand over her spurting wound and fell sideways.

Vanessa's head rang with the impossibly loud sound.

<hr/>

She looked out through white bars. She was in a big crib, a pen floored with cushioning and surrounded by a fence of wooden bars taller than she was. She wore an outsized pinafore and inch-thick woollen knee-socks. Her head felt huge, as if jabbed all over with dental anaesthetic. When she tried to stand, the floor wobbled and she had to grab the bars for support. She was not steady on her feet at all. She had not yet learned to walk.

Veevee crawled. A rattle lay in the folds of the floor, almost too big for her grasp. She focused on her hand. It was slim, long-fingered. She could make a fist. She was a grown-up, not a baby.

A tannoy was softly broadcasting 'Jake the Peg (With the Extra Leg)' by Rolf Harris.

She picked up the rattle.

The bars sank into the floor and she crawled over the row of holes where they had been. She was in a playroom. Huge alphabet blocks were strewn around in Stonehenge arrangements, spelling words she couldn't yet pronounce. Two wooden soldiers, taller than she was, stood guard, circles of red on their cheeks, stiff

Zebedee moustaches on their round faces, shakoes on their heads, bayonet-tipped rifles in their spherical hands.

Plumped in a rocking chair was Dr Ballance, in a velvet jacket with matching knickerbockers, a tartan cravat frothing under his chin, a yard-wide tam-o'-shanter perched on his head.

'Veevee want to play-play?' he asked.

She wasn't sure any more. This game had been going on too long. She had forgotten how it started.

There were other children in the playroom. Miss Dove and Miss Lark, in identical sailor suits. And others: Miss Wren, Miss Robin and Miss Sparrow. Sergeant-Mistress Finch was home sick today, with an earache.

The friends sang 'Ring-a-ring-a-rosy' and danced around Veevee. The dance made her dizzy again. She tried to stand, but her pinafore was sewn together at the crotch and too short to allow her body to unbend.

'You're it,' Miss Dove said, slapping her.

Veevee wanted to cry. But big girls didn't blub. And she was a very big girl.

She was a grown-up. She looked at her hand to remind herself. It was an inflated, blubbery fist, knuckles sunk in baby fat.

The others were all bigger than her.

Veevee sat down and cried and cried.

ACT II: RICHARD IS RUMBLED

Alastair Garnett, the Whitehall man, had wanted to meet in a multi-storey car park, but Richard explained that nothing could be more conspicuous than his ShadowShark. Besides, two men exchanging briefcases in a car park at dead of night was always something to be suspicious about. Instead, he had set a date for two in the morning in the Pigeon-Toed Orange Peel, a discotheque in the King's Road.

He sat at the bar, sipping a tequila sunrise from a heavy glass shaped like a crystal ball. An extremely active girl in a polka-dot halterneck and matching shorts roller-skated behind the long bar, deftly balancing drinks.

Richard was wearing a floor-length green suede Edwardian motorist's coat over a tiger-striped orange-and-black silk shirt, zebra-striped white-and-black flared jeans and hand-made zig-zag-striped yellow-and-black leather moccasins. In place of a tie, he wore an amulet with the CND peace symbol inset into the eyes of a griffin rampant. In his lapel was a single white carnation, so Garnett could identify him.

He lowered his sunglasses – thin-diamond-shaped emerald-tint lenses with a gold wire frame – and looked around the cavernous room. Many girls and some boys had Egyptian eye motifs painted on bare midriffs, thighs, upper arms, throats or foreheads. The paint was luminous and, as the lights flashed on and off in five-second bursts, moments of darkness were inhabited by a hundred dancing eyes.

A band of long-haired young men played on a raised circular stage. They were called the Heat, and were in the middle of 'Non-Copyright Stock Jazz Track 2', a thirty-five-minute fugue improvised around themes from their debut album *Neutral Background Music*.

A pleasantly chubby girl in a cutaway catsuit, rhinestone-studded patch over one eye, sat next to Richard and suggested they might have been lovers in earlier incarnations. He admitted the possibility, but sadly confessed they'd have to postpone any reunion until later lives. She shrugged cheerfully and took his hand, producing an eyebrow pencil to write her telephone number on his palm. As she wrote, she noticed the other number tattooed on his wrist and looked at him again. A tear started from her own exposed eye and she kissed him.

'Peace, love,' she said, launching herself back onto the dance floor and connecting with a Viking youth in a woven waistcoat and motorcycle boots.

Across the room, he saw a thin man who wore a dark grey overcoat, a black bowler hat and a wing-collar tight over a light grey tie, and carried a tightly furled Union Jack umbrella. Richard tapped his carnation and the man from Whitehall spotted him.

'What a racket,' Garnett said, sitting at the bar. 'Call that music? You can't understand the words. Not like the proper songs they used to have.'

'"Doodly-acky-sacky, want some seafood, Mama"?'

'I beg your pardon?'

'A hit for the Andrews Sisters in the 1930s,' Richard explained.

'Harrumph,' said Garnett.

A boy dressed in tie-dyed biblical robes, with an enormous bush of beard and hair, paused at the bar while buying a drink and looked over Garnett. The Whitehall man held tight to his umbrella.

'That's a crazy look, man,' the boy said, flashing a reversed V sign.

A crimson undertone rose in Garnett's face. He ordered a gin and tonic and tried to get down to business. Though the Heat were playing loud enough to whip the dancers into a frenzy, there was a quiet-ish zone at the bar which allowed them to have a real conversation.

'I understand you're one of the spooks of the Diogenes Club,' the Whitehall man said. 'Winthrop's creature.'

Richard shrugged, allowing the truth of it. The Diogenes Club was loosely attached to the Government of the day and tied into the tangle of British intelligence agencies, but Edwin Winthrop of the Ruling Cabal had kept a certain distance from the Gnomes of Cheltenham since the War, and was given to running Diogenes more or less as a private fiefdom.

It was said of one of Winthrop's predecessors that he not only worked for the British Government but that under some circumstances he was the British Government. Winthrop did not match that, but was keen on keeping Diogenes out of the bailiwick of Whitehall, if only because its stock in trade was everything that couldn't be circumscribed by rules and regulations, whether the procedures of the Civil Service or the laws of physics. Richard was not a civil servant, not beholden to the United Kingdom for salary and pension, but did think of himself as loyal to certain ideals, even to the Crown.

'I'm afraid this is typical of Diogenes' behaviour lately,' Garnett said. 'There's been the most almighty snarl-up in the Pleasant Green affair.'

Garnett, Richard gathered, was one of the faction who thought the independence of the Diogenes Club a dangerous luxury. It was waiting patiently for Winthrop's passing so that everything could be tied down with red tape and sealing wax.

'Pleasant Green is being looked into,' Richard said.

'That's just it. You're jolly well to stop looking. Any expenses you've incurred will be met upon production of proper accounts. But all documentation, including notes or memoranda you or your associates have made, must be surrendered within forty-eight hours. It's a matter of national security.'

Richard had been expecting this curtain to lower.

'It's ours, isn't it?' he said, smiling. 'Pleasant Green?'

'You are not cleared for that information. Rest assured that the unhappy events which came to your notice will not reoccur. The matter is at an end.'

Richard kept his smile fixed and ironic, but he had a gnawing worry. It was all very well to be cut out of the case, but Vanessa was inside. If he wanted to extract her, there would be dangers.

He had been careful not to let Garnett know exactly what sort of investigation he had mounted, but it had been necessary to call in favours from the armed forces to kit the girl up with a snakeskin. Garnett might know Vanessa was undercover at Pleasant Green, and could well have blown her cover with Dr Iain M. Ballance.

Garnett finished his g and t and settled the bar bill. He asked the surprised rollergirl for a receipt. She scribbled a figure on a cigarette paper and handed it over with an apologetic shrug.

'Good night to you,' the Whitehall man said, leaving.

Richard gave Garnett five minutes to get clear of the Pigeon-Toed Orange Peel and slipped out himself.

The ShadowShark was parked round the corner. Vanessa usually drove for him, and Fred was occasionally allowed the wheel as a treat, but they were both down in darkest Sussex. He slid into the driver's seat and lowered the partition.

'You were right, Edwin,' he told the man in the back seat.

Winthrop nodded. Though he wore a clipped white moustache and had not bulked out in age, there was a certain Churchillian gravity to the Old Man. He had fought for King and Country in three world wars, only two of which the history books bothered with.

'Ghastly business,' Winthrop snorted, with disgust.

'I've been asked to cease and desist all investigation of Pleasant Green and Dr Ballance.'

'Well, my boy, that you must do. We all have our masters.'

Richard did not need to mention Vanessa. Winthrop had made the call to an old army comrade to help outfit 'Lieutenant Vail' with a believable life.

'The investigation was a formality, anyway,' Winthrop said. 'After all, we knew at once what Ballance was up to. He drives people off their heads. Now, we know who he mostly does it for. He has private sector clients but his major business is to provide tailor-made psychopaths who are placed at the disposal of certain official and semi-official forces in our society. It's funny, really. The people behind Ballance are much like us, like the Diogenes Club. Governments come and go, but they're always there. There are times when any objective observer would think them on the side of the angels and us batting for the other lot. You know what our trouble is, Richard? England's trouble? We won all our wars. At great cost, but we won. We needed a new enemy. Our American cousins might be content to clash sabres with the Soviets, but Ivan was never going to be our dragon. We made our own enemy, birthed it at home, and raised it up. Maybe it was always here and we are the sports and freaks.'

Richard understood.

'I know what Garnett wants me to do,' he said. 'What does Diogenes want?'

'Obviously, you are to stop investigating Dr Ballance's business. And start dismantling it.'

ACT III: VANESSA IS VALIANT

In the morning room, comfortable armchairs were arranged in a full circle. Group sessions were important at Pleasant Green.

In the next seat was a middle-aged man. Dr Ballance asked him to stand first.

'My name is Mr Ease,' he said.

'Hello, Mr Ease,' they all replied.

'…and I cheat and steal.'

'Good show,' murmured an approving voice, echoed by the rest of Group. She clapped and smiled with the rest of them. Dr Ballance looked on with paternal approval.

He was a businessman. It had apparently been difficult to wash away the last of his scruples. Now, after a week of Pleasant Green, Mr Ease was unencumbered by ethics or fear of the law. He had been worried about prison, but that phobia was overcome completely.

'My name is Captain Naughty,' said a hard-faced man, a uniformed airline pilot. 'And I want to punish people who do bad things. Firmly. Most of all, I want to punish people who do nothing at all.'

'Very good, Captain,' said Dr Ballance.

Next up was the patrician woman who always wore blue dresses, the star of Group.

'My name is Mrs Empty,' she announced. 'And I feel nothing for anyone.'

She got no applause or hug. She earned respect, not love. Mr Ease and Captain Naughty were clearly smitten with Mrs Empty, not in any romantic sense but in that they couldn't stay away from the sucking void of her arctic charisma. Even Dr Ballance's staff were in awe of her.

'My name is Rumour,' drawled a craggy Australian. 'And I want everything everyone thinks to come through me.'

'Good on you, sir,' Captain Naughty said, looking sideways to seek approval, not from Dr Ballance – like everyone else in Group – but from Mrs Empty.

'My name is Peace,' said a young, quiet Yorkshireman. 'I like killing women.'

Peace, as always, got only perfunctory approval. The others didn't like him. He made them think about themselves.

She was last. She stood, glancing around at the ring of encouraging faces.

Group was supportive. But this would be difficult.

'My name is Lieutenant Veevee,' she said.

'Hello, Veevee,' everyone shouted, with ragged cheer.

She took a deep breath, and said it.

'…and I will kill people.'

There. She felt stronger, now.

Mr Ease reached up, took her hand and gave a friendly squeeze. Miss Lark gave her a hug. She sat down.

'Thank you all,' said Dr Ballance. 'You are very special to Pleasant Green, as individuals and as Group. You're our first perfect people. When you leave here, which you're very nearly ready to do, you'll accomplish great things. You will take Pleasant Green with you. It won't happen soon, maybe not for years. But I have faith in you all. You are creatures of the future. You will be the Masters of the 1980s.'

Already, complex relationships had formed within Group. Mr Ease and Captain Naughty competed to be friends with Mrs Empty, but she liked Rumour best of all. Peace was drawn to Veevee, but afraid of her.

'Would anyone like to tell us anything?' Dr Ballance asked.

Captain Naughty and Mr Ease stuck hands up. Mrs Empty flashed her eyes, expecting to be preferred without having to put herself forward.

'It's always you two,' Dr Ballance said. 'Let's hear from one of the quiet ones.'

He looked at her, then passed on.

'Peace,' the doctor said. 'Have you thoughts to share?'

The youth was tongue-tied. He was unusual here. He had learned to accept who he was and what he wanted, but was nervous about speaking up in the presence of his 'betters'. Whenever Mrs Empty made speeches about eliminating laziness or what was best for people, Peace opened and closed his sweaty hands nervously but looked at the woman with something like love.

'I was wondering, like,' he said. 'What's the best way to a tart's heart. I mean, physically. Between which ribs to stab, like?'

Captain Naughty clucked in disgust.

Peace looked at her. She lifted her left arm to raise her breast, then tapped just under it with her right forefinger.

'About here,' she said.

Peace flushed red. 'Thank you, Veevee.'

The others were appalled.

'Do we have to listen to this rot?' Captain Naughty asked. 'It's just filth.'

Peace was a National Health referral, while the others were Private.

'You've just run against your last barrier, Captain,' Dr Ballance announced. 'You – all of you – have begun to realise your potential, have cut away the parts of your personae that were holding you back. But before you can leave with your Pleasant Green diploma, you must acknowledge your kinship with Peace. Whatever you say outside this place, you must have in your mind a space like Pleasant Green, where you have no hypocrisy. It will ground you, give you strength. We must all have our secret spaces. Peace will get his hands dirtier than yours, but what he does will be for Group just as what you do will be for Group.'

Mrs Empty nodded, fiercely. She understood.

'That will be all for today,' Dr Ballance said, dismissing Group. 'Veevee, if you would stay behind a moment. I'd like a word.'

The others got up and left. She sat still.

She didn't know how long she had been at Pleasant Green, but it could have been months or days. She had been taken back to the nursery and grown up all over again, this time with a direction and purpose. Dr Ballance was father and mother to her psyche, and Pleasant Green was home and school.

Dr Ballance sat next to her.

'You're ready to go, Veevee,' he said, hand on her knee.

'Thank you, Doctor.'

'But there's something you must do, first.'

'What is that, Doctor?'

'What you want to do, Veevee. What you like to do.'

She trembled a little. 'Kill people?'

'Yes, my dear. There's a "bird-watcher" on the downs. Fred Regent.'

'Fred.'

'You know Fred, of course. A man is coming down from London. He will join Fred in Whipplewell, at the Coach and Horses.'

'Richard.'

'That's right, Lieutenant Veevee. Richard Jeperson.'

Dr Ballance took a wrapped bundle out of his white coat and gave it to her. She unrolled the white flannel, and found a polished silver scalpel.

'You will go to the Coach and Horses,' he told her. 'You will find Fred and Richard. You will bring them back here. And you will kill them for us.'

'Yes, Doctor.'

'Then, when you have passed that final exam, you will seek out a man called Edwin Winthrop.'

'I've met him.'

'Good. You have been brought up for this purpose specifically, to kill Edwin Winthrop. After that, you can rest. I'm sure other jobs will come up, but Winthrop is to be your primary target. It is more important that he die than that you live. Do you understand?'

She did. Killing Winthrop meant more to her than her own life.

'Good girl. Now, go and have dinner. Extra custard for you today.'

She wrapped the scalpel up again and put it in her pocket.

'You've been in there five days, Ness,' Fred told her.

'It seems longer,' she said. 'Much longer.'

Richard nodded sagely. 'Very advanced techniques, I'll be bound.'

They were cramped together in her Elan. She drove carefully, across the downs. After dark, the road could be treacherous.

'I was close to you in the wood on the first night,' Fred said. 'For the soldier games. What was that all about?'

She shrugged.

Richard was quiet. He must understand. That would make it easier.

She parked in a lay-by.

'There's a path through here,' she said. 'To Pleasant Green.'

'Lead on,' Richard said.

They walked through the dark wood. In a clearing, she paused and looked up at the bright half-moon.

'There's something,' Fred said. 'Listen.'

It was the bag-piper, wailing 'Cinderella Rockefeller'. Dr Ballance stepped into the clearing. Lights came on. The rest of the Pleasant Green staff were there, too: Miss Lark, Miss Wren, and the others. To one side, Mrs Empty stood, wrapped up in a thick blue coat.

'It seems we're expected,' Richard drawled.

'Indeed,' said Dr Ballance.

Fred looked at her, anger in his eyes. He made fists.

'It's not her fault,' Richard told him. 'She's not quite herself.'

'Bastard,' Fred spat at Dr Ballance.

Mrs Empty cringed in distaste at the language.

Dr Ballance said, 'Veevee, if you would…'

She took her scalpel out and put it to Richard's neck, just behind the ear. She knew just how much pressure to apply, how deep to cut, how long the incision should be. He would bleed to death inside a minute. She even judged the angle so her ankle-length brown suede coat and calfskin high-heeled thigh boots would not be splattered.

'She's a treasure, you know,' Dr Ballance said to Richard. 'Thank you for sending her to us. She has enlivened the whole Group. Really. We're going to have need of her, of people like her. She's so sharp, so perfect, so pointed.'

Richard was relaxed in her embrace. She felt his heart beating, normally.

'And quite mad, surely?' Richard said.

'Mad? What does that mean, Mr Jeperson? Out of step with the rest of the world? What if the rest of the world is mad? And what if your sanity is what is holding you back, preventing you from attaining your potential? Who among us can say that they are really sane? Really normal?'

'I can,' said Mrs Empty, quietly and firmly.

'We have always needed mad people,' Dr Ballance continues. 'At Rorke's Drift, Dunkirk, the Battle of Britain, the Festival of Britain, we must have been mad to carry on as we did, and thank mercy for that madness. Times are a-changing, and we will need new types of madness. I can provide that, Mr Jeperson. These women are perfect, you know. They have no conscience at all, no feeling for others. Do you know how hard it is to expunge that from the female psyche? We teach our daughters all their lives to become mothers, to love and sacrifice. These two are my masterpieces. Lieutenant Veevee, your gift to us, will be the greatest assassin of the era. And Mrs Empty is even more special. She will take my madness and spread it over the whole world.'

'I suppose it would be redundant to call you mad?' Richard ventured.

Dr Ballance giggled.

Vanessa had Richard slightly off-balance, but was holding

him up. The line of her scalpel was impressed against his jugular, steady.

'Ness won't do it,' Fred said.

'You think not?' Dr Ballance smiled. 'Anybody would. You would, to me, right now. It's just a matter of redirecting the circuits, to apply the willingness to a worthwhile end. She feels no anger or remorse or hate or joy in what she does. She just does it. Like a tin-opener.'

'Vanessa,' Richard said.

Click.

That was her name. Not Veevee.

Just his voice and her name. It was a switch thrown inside her.

Long ago, they had agreed. When she first came to Richard, under the control of something else, she had been at that zero to which the Pleasant Green treatment was supposed to reduce her. She had escaped, with his help, then built herself up, with his love and encouragement. She was the stronger for it. Her name, which she had chosen, was the core of her strength. It was the code-word which brought her out of a trance.

Everything Pleasant Green had done to her was meaningless now. She was Vanessa.

Not Veevee.

She didn't change, didn't move.

But she was herself again.

'That's all it takes,' Richard said, straightening up. 'A name. You don't really make people, Doctor. You just fake them. Like wind-up toys, they may work for a while. Then they run down. Like Mr Joyful... Mr Achy... Mr Enemy... Miss Essex... Lieutenant-Commander Hero?'

He enunciated the names clearly. Each one was a jab at Dr Ballance. The living half of his face froze, matching the dead side.

'This Group is better than them.'

'No more crack-ups, eh? They're just mad enough, but not too broken to function?'

Mrs Empty's cold eyes were fixed on them.

'To survive in the world we are making,' Dr Ballance said, 'everybody will have to be mad.'

He reached into his coat and brought out a gun. In a blink, Vanessa tossed her scalpel. It spun over and over, catching moonlight, and embedded its point in Dr Ballance's forehead. A red tear dripped and he crashed backwards.

When he had gone for the gun, he had admitted defeat. He had doubted her. At the last, he had been proved wrong.

It all came crashing in. The programming, the torture, the disorientation – there had been drugs as well as everything else – fell apart.

With a scream, Miss Dove flew at her. She pirouetted and landed a foot in the attendant's face. The girl was knocked backwards and sprawled on the ground. She bounced back up, and came for her.

It was no match. Miss Dove was a master of disco-style roughhouse. All her movements came from her hips and her shoulders. Vanessa fell back on the all-purpose jeet kune do – the style developed by Bruce Lee which was starting to be called kung fu – and launched kicks and punches at the girl, battering her on her feet until she dropped.

The others backed away. Mrs Empty walked off, into the dark.

Fred checked Dr Ballance, and shook his head.

'Well done,' Richard said. 'I never doubted you.'

She was completely wrung out. Again, she was on the point of exploding into tears.

Richard held her and kissed her.

'I trusted you here, rather than coming myself or sending Fred, because I know your heart,' he said, kindly. 'Neither of us could have survived Pleasant Green. We're too dark to begin with. We could be made into killers. You couldn't. You can't. You're an angel of mercy, my love, not of death.'

Over his shoulder, she saw Ballance stretched out with a stick of steel in his head. She loved Richard for what he felt about her, but he was wrong. The Pleasant Green treatment might have failed to make her a malleable assassin, but Dr Ballance had turned her into a killer all the same. After his doubt, had he known a split-second of triumph?

'It was about Winthrop,' she said. 'After you and Fred, he wanted me to kill Winthrop. It was part of some plan.'

He nodded grimly, understanding.

CODA: MRS M. T.

On the croquet lawn of the Pleasant Green manor house, Richard found a Eurasian woman feeding a bonfire with an armful of file-folders. Fred took hold of her and wrestled her to the ground, but she had done her job with swift efficiency. Filing cabinets had been dragged out of the pre-fab buildings and emptied. Documents turned to ash and photographs curled in flame.

Vanessa, cloaked with her coat, was still pale. It would take a while for her to recover fully, but he had been right about her. She had steel.

The Eurasian – Miss Lark – produced a stiletto and made a few passes at Fred's stomach, forcing him back. Then, she tried to slip the blade into her own heart. Vanessa, snapping out of her daze, grabbed the woman's wrist and made her drop the knife.

'No more,' she said.

Miss Lark looked at them with loathing. Dr Ballance would never have approved of an emotion like that.

The rest of the staff had vanished into the night, melting away to wherever it was minions languished between paying jobs.

Bewildered folks in dressing gowns, among them the electric-eyed woman who had been in the wood, had drifted out to see what the fuss was all about and found themselves abandoned. The other members of the Group.

Car headlamps raked the lawns, throwing shadows against the big house. Doors opened and people got out. They were all anonymous men, except for one.

'Jeperson,' shouted Garnett.

The Whitehall man strode across the lawn, waving his umbrella like a truncheon.

Richard opened his hands and felt no guilt.

'I think you'll find Dr Ballance exceeded his authority, Mr Garnett. If you look around, you'll find serious questions raised.'

'Where is the Doctor?' demanded Garnett.

'In the wood. He seems to be dead.'

The civil servant was furious.

'He has a gun in his hand. I think he intended to kill someone or other. Very possibly me.'

Garnett obviously thought it a pity Ballance hadn't finished the job. It was a shame this would end here, Richard thought. Important folk had been sponsoring Dr Ballance, and had passed down orders to act against the Diogenes Club. Winthrop would be grimly amused to learn he was the eventual target of the plan.

'It wasn't working, though,' Richard said.

'What?' Garnett said.

'The Ballance Process or whatever he called it. He was trying to manufacture functioning psychotics, wasn't he? Well, none of them ever functioned. Didn't you notice? Look at them, poor lost souls.'

He indicated the people in dressing gowns. Ambulances had arrived, and the Pleasant Green guests were being helped into them.

'What use do you think they'll be now?'

By the ambulances was parked a car whose silhouette Richard knew all too well. There were only five Rolls-Royce ShadowSharks in existence; and he owned three of them, all silver. This was painted night black, with opaque windows to match. A junior functionary like Garnett wouldn't run to this antichrist of the road.

He would know the machine again. And the man inside it, who had ordered his death and Edwin's.

Garnett turned away and scurried across the lawn, to report to the man in the ShadowShark. The woman from the wood firmly resisted orderlies who were trying to help her into an ambulance. She asked no questions and made no protests, but wouldn't be manhandled, wouldn't be turned.

'Who is that?' he asked Vanessa.

'Mrs Empty,' she said. 'The star pupil.'

He shuddered. Mrs Empty was quite, quite mad, he intuited. Yet she was strong, mind unclouded by compassion or uncertainty, character untempered by humour or generosity. In a precognitive flash that made him momentarily weak with terror, he saw a cold blue flame burning in the future.

She was assisted finally into an ambulance, but made the action seem like that of a queen ascending a throne, surrounded by courtiers.

The ambulances left. The ShadowShark stayed behind a moment. Richard imagined cold eyes looking out at him through the one-way black glass. Then, the motor turned over and the Rolls withdrew.

He looked at Fred and Vanessa.

'Let's forget this place,' he said.

'That might not be easy,' Vanessa said.

'Then we shall have to try very hard.'

⫸ TOMORROW TOWN ⫷

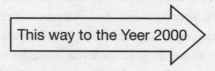

This way to the Yeer 2000 ➤

The message, in Helvetica typeface, was repeated on arrow-shaped signs.

'That'll be us, Vanessa,' said Richard Jeperson, striding along the platform in the indicated direction, toting his shoulder-slung hold-all. He tried to feel as if he were about to time-travel from 1971 to the future, though in practice he was just changing trains.

Vanessa was distracted by one of the arrow-signs, fresh face arranged into a comely frown. Richard's associate was a tall redhead in hot-pants, halter top, beret and stack-heeled go-go boots – all blinding white, as if fresh from the machine in a soap-powder advert. She drew unconcealed attention from late-morning passengers milling about the railway station. Then again, in his lime dayglo blazer edged with gold braid and salmon-pink bell-bottom trousers, so did he. Here in Preston, the fashion watchword, for the eighteenth consecutive season, was 'drab'.

'It's misspelled,' said Vanessa. 'Y Double-E R.'

'No, it's F O N E T I K,' he corrected. 'Within the next thirty years, English spelling will be rationalised.'

'You reckon?' She pouted sceptically.

'Not my theory,' he said, stroking his mandarin moustaches. 'I assume the lingo will muddle along with magical illogic as it has since "the Yeer Dot". But orthographic reform is a tenet of Tomorrow Town.'

'Alliteration. Very Century 21.'

They had travelled up from London, sharing a rattly first-class carriage and a welcome magnum of Bollinger with a liberal bishop on a lecture tour billed as 'Peace and the Pill' and a working-class playwright revisiting his slag-heap roots. To continue their journey, Richard and Vanessa had to change at Preston.

The arrows led to a guarded gate. The guard wore a British Rail uniform in shiny black plastic with silver highlights. His oversized cap had a chemical lighting element in the brim.

'You need special tickets, Ms and Mm,' said the guard.

'Mm,' said Vanessa, amused.

'Ms,' Richard buzzed at her.

He searched through his pockets, finally turning up the special tickets. They were strips of foil, like ironed-flat chocolate-bar wrappers with punched-hole patterns. The guard carefully posted the tickets into a slot in a metal box. Gears whirred and lights flashed. The gate came apart and sank into the ground. Richard let Vanessa step through first. She seemed to float off, arms out for balance.

'Best not to be left behind, Mm,' said the guard.

'Mm,' said Richard, agreeing.

He stepped onto the special platform. Beneath his rubber-soled winkle-pickers, a knitted chain-mail surface moved on large rollers. It creaked and rippled, but gave a smooth ride.

'I wonder how it manages corners,' Vanessa said.

The moving platform conveyed them towards a giant silver bullet. The train of the future hummed slightly, at rest on a single gleaming rail which was raised ten feet above the gravel railbed by chromed tubular trestles. A hatchway was open, lowered to form a ramp.

Richard and Vanessa clambered through the hatch and found themselves in a space little roomier than an Apollo capsule. They half-sat, half-lay in over-padded seats which wobbled on gyro-gimbals. Safety straps automatically snaked across them and drew tight.

'Not sure I'll ever get used to this,' said Richard. A strap across his forehead noosed his long, tangled hair, and he had to free a hand to fix it.

Vanessa wriggled to get comfortable, doing a near-horizontal dance as the straps adjusted to her.

With a hiss the ramp raised and became a hatch-cover, then sealed shut. The capsule-cum-carriage had seat-berths for eight, but today they were the only passengers.

A mechanical voice counted down from ten.

'Richard, that's a Dalek,' said Vanessa, giggling.

As if offended, the voice stuttered on five, like a record stuck in a groove, then hopped to three.

At zero, they heard a rush of rocketry and the monorail moved off. Richard tensed against the expected g-force slam, but it didn't come. Through thick-glassed slit windows, he saw green countryside passing by at about 25 miles per hour. They might have been on a leisurely cycle to the village pub rather than taking the fast train to the future.

'So this is the transport of tomorrow?' said Vanessa.

'A best-guess design,' explained Richard. 'That's the point of Tomorrow Town. To experiment with the lives we'll all be living at the turn of the century.'

'No teleportation then?'

'Don't be silly. Matter transmission is a fantasy. This is a reasonable extrapolation from present-day or in-development technology. The Foundation is rigorous about probabilities. Everything in Tomorrow Town is viable.'

The community was funded partially by government research grants and partially by private sources. It was projected that it would soon be a profitable concern, with monies pouring in from scientific wonders developed by the visioneers of the new technomeritocracy. The Foundation, which had proposed the 'Town of 2000' experiment, was a think tank, an academic-industrial coalition dedicated to applying to present-day life lessons learned from contemplating the likely future. Tomorrow Town's two-thousand-odd citizen-volunteers ('zenvols') were boffins, engineers, social visionaries, health-food cranks and science fiction fans.

Three years ago, when the town was given its charter by the Wilson government, there had been a white heat of publicity: television programmes hosted by James Burke and Raymond Baxter, picture features in all the Sunday colour supplements, a novelty single ('Take Me to Tomorrow' by Big Thinks and the BBC Radiophonic Workshop) which peaked at Number 2 (prevented from being Top of the Pops by The Crazy World of Arthur Brown's 'Fire'), a line of 'futopian fashions' from Carnaby Street, a heated debate in the letter columns of *New Scientist* between Arthur C. Clarke (pro), Auberon Waugh (anti) and J. G. Ballard (hard to tell). Then the brouhaha died down and Tomorrow Town was left to get on by itself, mostly forgotten. Until the murder of Varno Zhoule.

Richard Jeperson, agent of the Diogenes Club – least-known branch of the United Kingdom's intelligence and investigative services – was detailed to look into the supposedly open-and-shut case and report back to the current Prime Minister on the advisability of maintaining government support for Tomorrow Town.

He had given Vanessa the barest facts.

'What does the murder weapon of the future turn out to be?' she asked. 'Laser-beam? Poisoned moon–rock?'

'No, the proverbial blunt instrument. Letting the side down, really. Anyone who murders the co–founder of Tomorrow Town should have the decency to stick to the spirit of the game. I doubt if it's much comfort to the deceased, but the offending bludgeon was vaguely futurist, a stylised steel rocketship with a heavy stone base.'

'No home should be without one.'

'It was a Hugo Award, the highest honour the science fiction field can bestow. Zhoule won his murder weapon for Best Novelette of 1958, with the oft–anthologised "Court Martian".'

'Are we then to be the police of the future? Do we get to design our own uniforms?'

'We're here because Tomorrow Town has no police force as such. It is a fundamental of the social design that there will be no crime by the year 2000.'

'Ooops.'

'This is a utopian vision, Vanessa. No money to steal. No inequality to foster resentment. All disputes arbitrated with unquestionable fairness. All zenvols constantly monitored for emotional instability.'

'Maybe being "constantly monitored" leads to "emotional instability". Not to mention being called a "zenvol".'

'You'll have to mention that to Big Thinks.'

'Is he the boss–man among equals?'

Richard chuckled. 'He's an it. A computer. A very large computer.'

Vanessa snapped her fingers.

'Ah-ha. There's your culprit. In every sci-fi film I've ever seen, the computer goes power mad and starts killing people off. Big Thinks probably wants to take over the world.'

'The late Mm Zhoule would cringe to hear you say that,

Vanessa. He'd never have deigned to use such a hackneyed, unlikely premise in a story. A computer is just a heuristic abacus. Big Thinks can beat you at chess, solve logic problems, cut a pop record and make the monorail run on time, but it hasn't got sentience, a personality, a motive or, most importantly, arms. You might as well suspect the fridge-freezer or the pop-up toaster.'

'If you knew my pop-up toaster better, you'd feel differently. It sits there, shining sneakily, plotting perfidy. The jug-kettle is in on it too. There's a conspiracy of contraptions.'

'Now you're being silly.'

'Trust me, Richard, it'll be the Brain Machine. Make sure to check its alibi.'

'I'll bear that in mind.'

<hr>

They first saw Tomorrow Town from across the Yorkshire Dales, nestled in lush green and slate grey. The complex was a large-scale version of the sort of back garden space station that might have been put together by a talented child inspired by Gerry Anderson and instructed by Valerie Singleton, using egg boxes, toilet roll tubes, the innards of a broken wireless, pipe-cleaners and a lot of silver spray-paint.

Hexagonal geodesic domes clustered in the landscape, a central space covered by a giant canopy that looked like an especially aerodynamic silver circus tent. Metallised roadways wound between trees and lakes, connecting the domes. The light traffic consisted mostly of electric golfcarts and one-person hovercraft. A single hardy zenvol was struggling along on what looked like a failed flying bicycle from 1895 but was actually a moped powered by wing-like solar panels. It was raining gently, but the town seemed shielded by a half-bubble climate control barrier that shimmered in mid-air.

A pylon held up three sun-shaped globes on a triangle frame. They radiated light and, Richard suspected, heat. Where the light fell, the greenery was noticeably greener and thicker.

The monorail stopped outside the bubble, and settled a little clunkily.

'You may now change apparel,' rasped the machine voice.

A compartment opened and clothes slid out on racks. The safety straps released them from their seats.

Richard thought for a moment that the train had calculated from his long hair that he was a Ms rather than a Mm, then realised the garment on offer was unisex: a lightweight jump-suit of semi-opaque polythene, with silver epaulettes, pockets, knee- and elbow-patches and modesty strips around the chest and hips. The dangling legs ended in floppy-looking plastic boots, the sleeves in surgeon's gloves.

'Was that "may" a "must"?' asked Vanessa.

'Best to go along with native customs,' said Richard.

He turned his back like a gentleman and undressed carefully, folding and putting away his clothes. Then he took the jump-suit from the rack and stepped into it, wiggling his feet down into the boots and fingers into the gloves. A seam from crotch to neck sealed with velcro strips, but he was left with an enormous swathe of polythene sprouting from his left hip like a bridal train.

'Like this,' said Vanessa, who had worked it out.

The swathe went over the right shoulder in a toga arrangement, passing under an epaulette, clipping on in a couple of places, and falling like a waist-length cape.

She had also found a pad of controls in the left epaulette, which activated drawstrings and pleats that adjusted the garment to suit individual body type. They both had to fiddle to get the suits to cope with their above-average height, then loosen and tighten various sections as required. Even after every possible button had been twisted every possible way, Richard wore one sleeve tight as sausage skin while the other was loose and wrinkled as a burst balloon.

'Maybe it's a futopian fashion,' suggested Vanessa, who – of course – looked spectacular, shown off to advantage by the modesty strips. 'All the dashing zenvols are wearing the one-loose-one-tight look this new century.'

'Or maybe it's just aggravated crackpottery.'

She laughed.

The monorail judged they had used up their changing time, and lurched off again.

———◆———

The receiving area was as white and clean as a bathroom display at the Belgian Ideal Home Exhibition. A deputation of zenvols, all dressed alike, none with mismatched sleeves, waited on the platform. Synthesised Bach played gently and the artificial breeze was mildly perfumed.

'Mm Richard, Ms Vanessa,' said a white-haired zenvol, 'welcome to Tomorrow Town.'

A short Chinese girl repeated his words in sign-language.

'Are you Georgie Gewell?' Richard asked.

'Jor-G,' said the zenvol, then spelled it out.

'My condolences,' Richard said, shaking the man's hand. Through two squeaking layers of latex, he had the impression of sweaty palm. 'I understand you and Varno Zhoule were old friends.'

'Var-Z is a tragic loss. A great visioneer.'

The Chinese girl mimed sadness. Other zenvols hung their heads.

'Jesu, Joy of Man's Desiring' segued into the 'Dead March' from Saul. Was the muzak keyed in somehow to the emotional state of any given assembly?

'We, ah, founded the Foundation together.'

Back in the 1950s, Varno Zhoule had written many articles and stories for science fiction magazines, offering futuristic solutions to contemporary problems, preaching the gospel of better living through logic and technology. He had predicted decimal currency and the vertical take-off aeroplane. Georgie Gewell was an award-winning editor and critic. He had championed Zhoule's work, then raised finance to apply his solutions to the real world. Richard understood the seed money for the Foundation came from a patent the pair held on a kind of battery-powered circular slide rule that was faster and more accurate than any other portable calculating device.

Gewell was as tall as Richard, with milk-fair skin and close-cropped snow-white hair. He had deep smile and frown lines and a soft, girlish mouth. He was steadily leaking tears, not from grief but from thick, obvious reactalite contact lenses that were currently smudged to the darker end of their spectrum.

The other zenvols were an assorted mix, despite their identical outfits. Most of the men were short and tubby, the women lithe and fit – which was either Big Thinks's recipe for perfect population balance or some visioneer's idea of a good time for a tall, thin fellow. Everyone had hair cut short, which made both Richard and Vanessa obvious outsiders. None of the men wore facial hair except a red-faced chap who opted for the Puritan beard-without-a-moustache arrangement.

Gewell introduced the delegation. The Chinese girl was Moana, whom Gewell described as 'town speaker', though she continued to communicate only by signing. The beardie was Mal-K, the 'senior medico' who had presided over the autopsy, matched some bloody fingerprints and seemed a bit put out to be taken away from his automated clinic for this ceremonial affair. Other significant zenvols: Jess-F, 'arbitrage input tech', a hard-faced blond girl who interfaced with Big Thinks when it came to programming-dispute decisions, and thus was the nearest thing Tomorrow Town had to a human representative of the legal system – though she was more clerk of the court than investigating officer; Zootie, a fat little 'agri-terrain rearrangement tech' with a bad cold for which he kept apologising, who turned out to have discovered the body by the hydroponics vats and was oddly impressed and uncomfortable in this group as if he weren't quite on a level of equality with Gewell and the rest; and 'vocabulary administrator' Sue-2, whom Gewell introduced as 'sadly, the motive', the image of a penitent young lady who 'would never do it again'.

Richard mentally marked them all down.

'You'll want to visit the scene of the crime?' suggested Gewell. 'Interrogate the culprit? We have Buster in a secure store-room. It had to be especially prepared. There are no lockable doors in Tomorrow Town.'

'He's nailed in,' said Jess-F. 'With rations and a potty.'

'Very sensible,' commented Richard.

'We can prise the door open now you're here,' said Gewell.

Richard thought a moment.

'If you'll forgive me, Mr Jep— ah, Mm Richard,' said Mal-K, 'I'd like to get back to my work. I've a batch of anti-virus cooking.'

The medico kept his distance from Zootie. Did he think a streaming nose reflected badly on the health of the future? Or was the artificial breeze liable to spread sniffles around the whole community in minutes?

'I don't see any reason to detain you Mm Mal-K,' said Richard. 'Vanessa might pop over later. My associate is interested in the work you're doing here. New cures for new diseases. She'd love to squint into a microscope at your anti-virus.'

Vanessa nodded with convincing enthusiasm.

'Mal-K's door is always open,' said Gewell.

The medico sloped off without comment.

'Should we crack out the crowbar, then?' prompted Gewell.

The co-founder seemed keen on getting on with this: to him, murder came as an embarrassment and an interruption. It wasn't an uncommon reaction. Richard judged Gewell just wanted all this over with so he could get on with things, even though the victim was one of his oldest friends and the crime demonstrated a major flaw in the social design of Tomorrow Town. If someone battered Vanessa to death, he didn't think he'd be so intent on putting it behind him – but he was famous for being sensitive. Indeed, it was why he was so useful to the Diogenes Club.

'I think as long as our putative culprit is safely nailed away, we can afford to take our time, get a feel for the place and the set-up. It's how I like to work, Mm Gewell. To me, understanding why is much more important than knowing who or how.'

'I should think the why was obvious,' said Gewell looking at Sue-2, eyes visibly darkening.

She looked down.

'The arbitration went against Buster, and he couldn't accept it,' said Jess-F. 'Though it was in his initial contract that he abide by Big Thinks' decisions. It happens sometimes. Not often.'

'An arbitration in a matter of the heart? Interesting. Just the sort of thing that comes in a box marked "motive" and tied with pink string. Thank you so much for mentioning it early in the case. Before we continue the sleuthing, perhaps we could have lunch. Vanessa and I have travelled a long way, with no sustenance beyond British Rail sandwiches and a beverage of our own supply. Let's break bread together, and you can tell me more about your fascinating experiment.'

'Communal meals are at fixed times,' said Gewell. 'The next is not until six.'

'I make it about six o'clock,' said Richard, though his watch-face was blurred by the sleeve-glove.

'It's only f-five by our clock,' said Sue-2. 'We're on two daily cycles of ten kronons. Each kronon runs a hundred sentikronons.'

'In your time, a kronon is 72 minutes,' explained Gewell. 'Our six is your—'

Vanessa did the calculation and beat the slide-rule designer. 'Twelve minutes past seven.'

'That's about it.'

Richard waved away the objection.

'I'm sure a snack can be rustled up. Where do you take these communal meals?'

Moana signalled a direction and set off. Richard was happy to follow, and the others came too.

❦

The dining area was in the central plaza, under the pylon and the three globes, with zinc-and-chrome sheet-and-tube tables and benches. It was warm under the globes, almost Caribbean, and some zenvols wore poker-players' eyeshades. In the artificially balmy climate, plastic garments tended to get sticky inside, which made for creaky shiftings-in-seats.

An abstract ornamental fountain gushed nutrient-enriched, slightly carbonated, heavily fluoridised water. Gewell had Moana fetch a couple of jugs for the table, while the meek Sue-2 hustled off to persuade 'sustenance preparation' techs to break their schedule to feed the visitors. Vanessa cocked an eyebrow at this division of labour, and Richard remembered Zhoule and Gewell had been planning this futopia since the 1950s, well before the publication of *The Female Eunuch*. Even Jess-F, whom Richard had pegged as the toughest zenvol he had yet met, broke out the metallised glass tumblers from a dispenser by the fountain, while

Gewell and the sniffling Zootie sat at their ease at the table.

'Is that the building where Big Thinks lives?' asked Vanessa.

Gewell swivelled to look. Vanessa meant an imposing structure, rather like a giant art deco refrigerator decorated with Mondrian squares in a rough schematic of a human face. Uniformly dressed zenvols came and went through airlock doors that opened and closed with hisses of decontaminant.

Gewell grinned, impishly.

'Ms Vanessa, that building is Big Thinks.'

Richard whistled.

'BeeTee didn't used to be that size,' said Jess-F. 'Var-Z kept insisting we add units. More and more complicated questions need more and more space. Soon, we'll have to expand further.'

'It doesn't show any telltale signs of megalomania?' asked Vanessa. 'Never programs Wagner for eight straight hours and chortles over maps of the world?'

Jess-F didn't look as if she thought that was funny.

'BeeTee is a machine, Ms.'

Sue-2 came back with food. Coloured pills that looked like Smarties but tasted like chalk.

'All the nutrition you need is here,' said Gewell, 'in the water and the capsules. For us, mealtimes are mostly ceremonial, for debate and reflection. Var-Z said that some of his best ideas popped into his head while he was chatting idly after a satisfying pill.'

Richard didn't doubt it. He also still felt hungry.

'Talking of things popping into Zhoule's head,' he said. 'What's the story on Buster of the bloody fingerprints?'

Jess-F looked at Sue-2, as if expecting to be contradicted, then carried on.

'Big Thinks assessed the dispute situation, and arbitrated it best for the community if Sue-2 were to be pair-bonded with Var-Z rather than Buster.'

'Buster was your old boyfriend?' Vanessa asked Sue-2.

'He is my husband,' she said.

'On the outside, in the past,' put in Jess-F. 'Here, we don't always acknowledge arbitrary pair-bondings. Mostly, they serve a useful purpose and continue. In this instance, the dispute was more complicated.'

'Big Thinks arbitrated against the arbitrary?' mused Richard. 'I suppose no one would be surprised at that.'

He looked from face to face and fixed on Sue-2, then asked: 'Did you leave Buster for Mm Zhoule?'

Sue-2 looked for a cue, but none came.

'It was best for the town, for the experiment,' she said.

'What was it for you? For your husband?'

'Buster had been regraded. From "zenvol" to "zenpass". He couldn't vote.'

Richard looked to Jess-F for explication. He noticed Gewell had to give her a teary wink from almost-black eyes before she would say anything more.

'We have very few citizen-passengers,' she said. 'It's not a punishment category.'

'Kind of you to clarify that,' said Richard. 'I might have made a misconclusion otherwise. You say zenpasses have no vote?'

'It's not so dreadful,' said Gewell, sipping nutrient. 'On the outside, in the past, suffrage is restricted by age, sanity, residence and so on. Here, in our technomeritocracy, to register for a vote – which gives you a voice in every significant decision – you have to demonstrate your applied intelligence.'

'An IQ test?'

'Not a quotient, Mm Richard. Anyone can have that. The vital factor is application. BeeTee tests for that. There's no personality or human tangle involved. Surely, it's only fair that the most useful should have the most say?'

'I have a vote,' said Zootie, proud. 'Earned by applied intelligence.'

'Indeed he does,' said Gewell, smiling.

'And Mm Jor-G has fifteen votes. Because he applies his intelligence more often than I do.'

Everyone looked at Zootie with different types of amazement.

'It's only fair,' said Zootie, content despite a nose-trickle, washing down another purple pill.

Richard wondered whether the agri-terrain rearrangement tech was hovering near regrading as a zenpass.

Richard addressed Sue-2. 'What does your husband do?'

'He's a history teacher.'

'An educationalist. Very valuable.'

Gewell looked as if his pill was sour. 'Your present is our past, Mm Richard. Buster's discipline is surplus.'

'Doesn't the future grow out of the past? To know where you're going you must know where you've been.'

'Var-Z believes in a radical break.'

'But Var-Z is in the past too.'

'Indeed. Regrettable. But we must think of the future.'

'It's where we're going to spend the rest of our lives,' said Zootie.

'That's very clever,' said Vanessa.

Zootie wiped his nose and puffed up a bit.

'I think we should hand Buster over to you,' said Gewell. 'To be taken outside to face the justice of the past. Var-Z left work undone that we must continue.'

'Not just yet,' said Richard. 'This sad business raises questions about Tomorrow Town. I have to look beyond the simple crime before I make my report. I'm sure you understand and will extend full cooperation.'

No one said anything, but they all constructed smiles.

'You must be economically self-supporting by now,' continued Richard, 'what with the research and invention you've been applying intelligence to. If the Prime Minister withdrew government subsidies, you'd probably be better off. Free of the apron strings, as it were. Still, the extra cash must come in handy for something, even if you don't use money in this town.'

Gewell wiped his eyes and kept smiling.

Richard could really do with a steak-and-kidney pie and chips, washed down with beer. Even a Kit-Kat would have been welcome.

'Have you a guest apartment we could use?'

Gewell's smile turned real. 'Sadly, we're at maximum optimal zenvol residency. No excess space wastage in the living quarters.'

'No spare beds,' clarified Zootie.

'Then we'll have to take the one living space we know to be free.'

Gewell's brow furrowed like a rucked-up rug.

'Zhoule's quarters,' Richard explained. 'We'll set up camp there. Sue-2, you must know the way. Since there are no locks we won't need keys to get in. Zenvols, it's been fascinating. I look forward to seeing you tomorrow.'

Richard and Vanessa stood up, and Sue-2 followed suit.

Gewell and Jess-F glared. Moana waved bye-bye.

———◆———

'What are you looking for?' Vanessa asked. 'Monitoring devices?'

'No,' said Richard, unsealing another compartment, 'they're in the light fittings and the communicator screen, and seem to have been disabled. By Zhoule or his murderer, presumably.'

There was a constant hum of gadgetry in the walls and from behind white-fronted compartments. The ceiling was composed of translucent panels, above which glowed a steady light.

The communicator screen was dusty. Beneath the on–off switch, volume and brightness knobs and channel selector was a telephone dial, with the Tomorrow Town alphabet (no Q or X). Richard had tried to call London but a recorded voice over a cartoon smiley face told him that visiphones only worked within the town limits. Use of the telephone line to the outside had to be approved by vote of zenvol visioneers.

In a compartment, he found a gadget whose purpose was a mystery. It had dials, a trumpet and three black rubber nipples.

'I'm just assuming, Vanessa, that the co-founder of Tomorrow Town might allow himself to sample the forbidden past in ways denied the simple zenvol or despised zenpass.'

'You mean?'

'He might have real food stashed somewhere.'

Vanessa started opening compartments too.

It took a full hour to search the five rooms of Zhoule's bungalow. They discovered a complete run of *Town Magazeen*, a microfilm publication with all text in fonetik, and a library of 1950s science fiction magazines, lurid covers mostly promising Varno Zhoule stories as back-up to Asimov or Heinlein.

They found many compartments stuffed with ring-bound notebooks which dated back twenty years. Richard flicked through a couple, noting Zhoule had either been using fonetik since the early 1950s or was such a bad speller that his editors must have been driven to despair. Most of the entries were single sentences, story ideas, possible inventions or prophecies. *Tunel under Irish See. Rokit to Sun to harvest heet. Big lift to awbit. Stoopids not allowd to breed. Holes in heds for plugs.*

Vanessa found a display case, full of plaques and awards in the shapes of spirals or robots.

'Is this the murder weapon?' Vanessa asked, indicating a needle-shaped rocket. 'Looks too clean.'

'I believe Zhoule was a multiple Hugo-winner. See, this is Best Short Story 1957, for "Vesta Interests". The blunt instrument was…'

Vanessa picked up a chunk of ceramic and read the plaque, 'Best Novelette 1958.' It was a near-duplicate of the base of the other award. 'You can see where the rocketship was fixed. It must have broken when the award was lifted in anger.'

'Cold blood, Vanessa. The body and the Hugo were found elsewhere. No blood traces in these quarters. Let's keep looking for a pork pie.'

Vanessa opened a floor-level compartment and out crawled a matt-black robot spider the size of an armoured go-kart. The fearsome thing brandished death-implements that, upon closer examination, turned out to be a vacuum cleaner proboscis and limbs tipped with chamois, damp squeegee and a brush.

'Oh, how useful,' said Vanessa.

Then the spider squirted hot water at her and crackled. Electrical circuits burned out behind its photo-eyes. The proboscis coughed black soot.

'Or maybe not.'

'"I have seen the future, and it works,"' quoted Richard. 'Lincoln Steffens, on the Soviet Union, 1919.'

'"What's to become of my bit of washing when there's no washing to do?"' quoted Vanessa. 'The old woman in *The Man in the White Suit*, on technological progress, 1951.'

'You suspect the diabolical Big Thinks sent this cleaning robot to murder Varno Zhoule? A Frankensteinian rebellion against the Master-Creator?'

'If BeeTee is so clever, I doubt it'd use this arachnoid doodad as an assassin. The thing can't even beat as it sweeps as it cleans, let alone carry out a devilish murder plan. Besides, to use the blunt instrument, it would have to climb a wall and I reckon this can't even manage stairs.'

Richard poked the carapace of the machine, which wriggled and lost a couple of limbs.

'Are you still hungry?'

'Famished.'

'Yet we've had enough nourishment to keep body and spirit together for the ten long kronons that remain until breakfast time.'

'I'll ask medico Mal-K if he sees many cases of rickets and scurvy in futopia.'

'You do that.'

Richard tried to feel sorry for the spider, but it was just a gadget. It was impossible to invest it with a personality.

Vanessa was thinking.

'Wasn't the idea that Tomorrow Town would pour forth twenty-first-century solutions to our drab old 1970s problems?'

Richard answered her. 'That's what Mr Wilson thought he was signing up for.'

'So why aren't Mrs Mopp Spiders on sale in the Charing Cross Road?'

'It doesn't seem to work all that well.'

'Lot of that about, Mm Richard. A monorail that would lose a race with Stephenson's Rocket. Technomeritocratic *droit de seigneur*. Concentrated foods astronauts wouldn't eat. Robots less functional than the wind-up ones Fred's nephew Paulie uses to conquer the playground. And I've seen the odd hovercraft up on blocks with "Owt of Awder" signs. Not to mention Buster the Basher, living incarnation of a society out of joint.'

'Good points all,' he said. 'And I'll answer them as soon as I solve another mystery.'

'What's that?'

'What are we supposed to sleep on?'

Around the rooms were large soft white cubes which distantly resembled furniture but could as easily be tofu chunks for the giants who would evolve by the turn of the millennium. By collecting enough cubes into a windowless room where the lighting panels were more subdued, Richard and Vanessa were able to put together a bed-shape. However, when Richard took an experimental lie-down on the jigsaw-puzzle affair, an odd cube squirted out of place and fell through the gap. The floor was covered with a warm fleshy plastic substance that was peculiarly unpleasant to the touch.

None of the many compartment-cupboards in the bungalow contained anything resembling twentieth-century pillows or bedding. Heating elements in the floor turned up as the evening wore on, adjusting the internal temperature of the room to the point where their all-over condoms were extremely uncomfortable. Escaping from the Tomorrow Town costumes was much harder than getting into them.

It occurred to Richard and Vanessa at the same time that these spacesuits would make going to the lavatory awkward, though they reasoned an all-pill diet would minimise the wasteful toilet breaks required in the past. Eventually, with some cooperation, they got free and placed the suits on hangers in a glass-fronted cupboard which, when closed, filled with coloured steam. 'Dekontaminashun Kompleet,' flashed a sign as the cabinet cracked open and spilled liquid residue. The floor was discoloured where this had happened before.

Having more or less puzzled out how the bedroom worked, they set about tackling the bathroom, which seemed to be equipped with a dental torture chamber and a wide variety of exotic marital aids. By the time they were done playing with it all, incidentally washing and cleaning their teeth, it was past ten midnight and the lights turned off automatically.

'Nighty-night,' said Richard.

'Don't let the robot bugs bite,' said Vanessa.

He woke up, alert. She woke with him.

'What's the matter? A noise?'

'No,' he said. 'No noise.'

'Ah.'

The Tomorrow Town hum, gadgets in the walls, was silenced. The bungalow was technologically dead. He reached out and touched the floor. It was cooling.

Silently, they got off the bed.

The room was dark, but they knew where the door – a sliding screen – was and took up positions either side of it.

The door had opened by touching a pad. Now the power was off, they were shut in (a flaw in the no-locks policy), though Richard heard a winding creak as the door lurched open an inch. There was some sort of clockwork back-up system.

A gloved hand reached into the room. It held an implement consisting of a plastic handle, two long thin metal rods, and a battery pack. A blue arc buzzed between the rods, suggesting lethal charge.

Vanessa took the wrist, careful not to touch the rods, and gave a good yank. The killing-prod, or whatever it was, was dropped and discharged against the floor, leaving a blackened patch and a nasty smell.

Surprised, the intruder stumbled against the door.

As far as Richard could make out in the minimal light, the figure wore the usual Tomorrow Town suit. An addition was an opaque black egg-shaped helmet with a silver strip around the eyes which he took to be a one-way mirror. A faint red radiance suggested some sort of infra-red see-in-the-dark device.

Vanessa, who had put on a floral bikini as sleepwear, kicked the egghead in the chest, which clanged. She hopped back.

'It's armoured,' she said.

'All who defy Buster must die,' rasped a speaker in the helmet.

Vanessa kicked again, at the shins, cutting the egghead down.

'All who defy Buster must die,' squeaked the speaker, sped-up. 'All who de– de– de– de—'

The recorded message was stuck.

The egghead clambered upright.

'Is there a person in there?' Vanessa asked.

'One way to find out,' said Richard.

He hammered the egghead with a bed-cube, but it was too soft to dent the helmet. The intruder lunged and caught him in a plastic-and-metal grasp.

'Get him off me,' Richard said, kicking. Unarmoured, he was at a disadvantage.

Vanessa nipped into the en-suite bathroom and came back with a gadget on a length of metal hose. They had decided it was probably a water-pick for those hard-to-clean crannies. She stabbed the end of the device at the egghead's neck, puncturing the plastic seal just below the chin-rim of the helmet, and turned the nozzle on. The tappet-key snapped off in her fingers and a high-pressure stream that could have drilled through cheddar cheese spurted into the suit.

Gallons of water inflated the egghead's garment. The suit self-sealed around the puncture and expanded, arms and legs forced out in an X. Richard felt the water-pressure swelling his captor's chest and arms. He wriggled and got free.

'All who defy Buster…'

Circuits burned out, and leaks sprouted at all the seams. Even through the silver strip, Richard made out the water rising.

There was a commotion in the next room.

Lights came on. The hum was back.

It occurred to Richard that he had opted to sleep in the buff and might not be in a decorous state to receive visitors. Then again, in the future taboos against social nudity were likely to evaporate.

Georgie Gewell, Moana and Jess-F, who had another of the zapper-prod devices, stood just inside the doorway.

There was a long pause. This was not what anyone had expected.

'Buster has escaped,' said Gewell. 'We thought you might be in danger. He's beyond all reason.'

'If he was a danger to us, he isn't any longer,' said Vanessa.

'If this is him,' Richard said. 'He was invoking the name.'

The egghead was on the floor, spouting torrents, super-inflated like the Michelin Man after a three-day egg-eating contest.

Vanessa kicked the helmet. It obligingly repeated 'All who defy Buster must die.'

The egghead waved hands like fat starfish, thumbing towards the helmet, which was sturdier than the rest of the suit and not leaking.

'Anybody know how to get this thing off?' asked Richard.

The egghead writhed and was still.

'Might be a bit on the late side.'

Gewell and Jess-F looked at each other. Moana took action and pushed into the room. She knelt and worked a few buttons around the chinrim of the helmet. The egghead cracked along a hitherto-unsuspected crooked seam and came apart in a gush of water.

'That's not Buster,' said Vanessa. 'It's Mal-K, the medico.'

'And he's drowned,' concluded Richard.

—◆—

'A useful rule of thumb in open-and-shut cases,' announced Richard, 'is that when someone tries to murder any investigating officers, the case isn't as open-and-shut as it might at first have seemed.'

He had put on a quilted double-breasted floor-length jade-green dressing gown with a Blakeian red dragon picked out on the chest in sequins.

'When the would-be murderer is one of the major proponents of the open-and-shut theory,' he continued, 'it's a dead cert that an injustice is in the process of being perpetrated. Ergo, the errant Buster is innocent and someone else murdered Mm Zhoule with a Hugo award.'

'Perhaps there was a misunderstanding,' said Gewell.

Richard and Vanessa looked at him.

'How so?' Richard asked.

Wheels worked behind Gewell's eyes, which were amber now.

'Mm Mal-K might have heard of Buster's escape and come here to protect you from him. In the dark and confusion, you mistook his attempted rescue as an attack.'

'And tragedy followed,' completed Jess-F.

Moana weighed invisible balls and looked noncommittal.

It was sixty-eight past six o'kronon. The body had been removed and they were in Zhoule's front room. Since all the cubes were in the bedroom and wet through, everyone had to sit on the body-temperature floor. Vanessa perched decorously, see-through peignoir over her bikini, on the dead robot spider. Richard stood, as if lecturing.

'Mm Jor-G, you were an editor once,' he said. 'If a story were submitted in which a hero wanted to protect innocent parties from a rampaging killer, would you have allowed the author to have the hero get into a disguise, turn off all the lights and creep into the bedroom with a lethal weapon?'

'Um, I might. I edited science fiction magazines. Science fiction is about ideas. No matter what those New Wavers say. In sf, characters might do anything.'

'What about "All who defy Buster must die"?' said Vanessa.

'A warning?' Gewell ventured, feebly.

'Oh, give up,' said Jess–F. 'Mal–K was a bad 'un. It's been obvious for desiyears. All those speeches about "expanding the remit of the social experiment" and "assuming pole position in the larger technomeritocracy". He was in a position to doctor his own records, to cover up instability. He was also the one who matched Buster's fingerprints to the murder weapon. Mm and Ms, congratulations, you've caught the killer.'

'Open–and–shut–and–open–and–shut?' suggested Richard.

Moana gave the thumbs–up.

'I'm going to need help to convince myself of this,' said Richard. 'I've decided to call on mighty deductive brainpower to get to the bottom of the mystery.'

'More yesterday men?' said Jess–F, appalled.

'Interesting term. You've been careful not to use it before now. Is that what you call us? No, I don't intend to summon any more plods from the outside.'

Gewell couldn't suppress his surge of relief.

'I've decided to apply the techniques of tomorrow to these crimes of the future. Jess–F, I'll need your help. Let's take this puzzle to Big Thinks, and see how your mighty computer does.'

Shutters came down behind Jess–F's eyes.

'Computer time is precious,' said Gewell.

'So is human life,' answered Richard.

The inside of the building, the insides of Big Thinks, was the messiest area Richard had seen in Tomorrow Town. Banks of metal cabinets fronted with reels of tape were connected by a spaghetti tangle of wires that wound throughout the building like coloured plastic ivy. Some cabinets had their fronts off, showing masses of circuit-boards, valves and transistors. Surprisingly, the workings of the master brain seemed held together with a great deal of sellotape, string and Blu-tack. Richard recognised some components well in advance of any on the market, and others that might date back to Marconi or Babbage.

'We've been making adjustments,' said Jess-F.

She shifted a cardboard box full of plastic shapes from a swivel chair and let him sit at a desk piled with wired-together television sets. To one side was a paper-towel dispenser which coughed out a steady roll of graph-paper with lines squiggled on it.

He didn't know which knobs to twiddle.

'Ms Jess-F, could you show me how a typical dispute arbitration is made? Say, the triangle of Zhoule, Buster and Sue-2.'

'That documentation might be hard to find.'

'In this futopia of efficiency? I doubt it.'

Jess-F nodded to Moana, who scurried off to root through large bins full of scrunched and torn paper.

Vanessa was with Gewell and Zootie, taking a tour of the hydroponics zone, which was where the body of Varno Zhoule had been found. The official story was that Buster (now, Mal-K) had gone to Zhoule's bungalow to kill him but found him not at home. He had taken the Hugo from its display case and searched out the victim-to-be, found him contemplating the green gunk that was made into his favourite pills, and did the deed then and there. It didn't take a computer to decide it was more likely that Zhoule had been killed where the weapon was handy for an annoyed impulse-assassin to reach for, then hovercrafted along with the murder weapon to a public place so some uninvolved zenvol clot could find him. But why ferry the body all that way, with the added risk of being caught?

'Tell you what, Ms Jess-F, let's try BeeTee out on a hypothetical dispute. Put in the set-up of *Hamlet*, and see what the computer thinks would be best for Denmark.'

'Big Thinks is not a toy, Mm.'

Moana came back waving some sheaves of paper.

Richard looked over it. Jess-F ground her teeth.

Though the top sheet was headed 'Input tek: Buster Munro', this was not the triangle dispute documentation. Richard scrolled through the linked print-out. He saw maps of Northern Europe, lists of names and dates, depositions in non-phonetic English, German and Danish, and enough footnotes for a good-sized doctoral thesis. In fact, that was exactly what this was.

'I'm not the first to think of running a hypothetical dispute past the mighty computer,' said Richard. 'The much-maligned Buster got there before me.'

'And wound up recategorised as a zenpass,' said Jess-F.

'He tried to get an answer to the Schleswig-Holstein Question, didn't he? Lord Palmerston said only three men in Europe got to the bottom of it – one who forgot, one who died and one who went mad. It was an insanely complicated argument between Denmark and Germany, over the governance of a couple of border provinces. Buster put the question to Big Thinks as if it were a contemporary dispute, just to see how the computer would have resolved it. What did it suggest, nuclear attack? Is that why all the redecoration? Buster's puzzle blew all the fuses.'

Richard found the last page.

The words 'forgot died mad' were repeated over and over, in very faint ink. Then some mathematical formulae. Then the printer equivalent of scribble.

'This makes no sense.'

He showed it to Jess-F, hoping she could interpret it. He really would have liked Big Thinks to have got to the bottom of the tussle that defeated Bismarck and Metternich and spat out a blindingly simple answer everyone should have seen all along.

'No,' she admitted. 'It makes no sense at all.'

Moana shrugged.

Richard felt a rush of sympathy for Jess-F. This was painful for her.

'BeeTee can't do it,' said Richard. 'The machine can do sums very fast, but nothing else?'

Jess-F was almost at the point of tears.

'That's not true,' she said, with tattered pride. 'Big Thinks is the most advanced computer in the world. It can solve any logic problem. Give it the data, and it can deliver accurate weather forecasts, arrange schedules to optimise efficiency of any number of tasks—'

'But throw the illogical at it, and BeeTee just has a good cry.'

'It's a machine. It can't cry.'

'Or arbitrate love affairs.'

Jess-F was in a corner.

'It's not fair,' she said, quietly. 'It's not BeeTee's fault. It's not my fault. They knew the operational parameters. They just kept insisting it tackle areas outside its remit, extending, tampering, overburdening. My techs have been working all the hours of the day—'

'Kronons, surely?'

'...all the bloody kronons of the day, just trying to get Big Thinks working again. Even after all this, the ridiculous demands keep coming through. Big Thinks, Big Thinks, will I be pretty, will I be rich? Big Thinks, Big Thinks, is there life on other planets?'

Jess-F put her hands over her face.

'"They"? Who are "they"?'

'All of them,' Jess-F sobbed. 'Across all disciplines.'

'Who especially?'

'Who else? Varno Zhoule.'

'Not any more?'

'No.'

She looked out from behind her hands, horrified.

'It wasn't me,' she said.

'I know. You're left-handed. Wrong wound pattern. One more question: what did the late Mm Mal-K want from Big Thinks?'

Jess-F gave out an appalled sigh.

'Now, he was cracked. He kept putting in these convoluted specific questions. In the end, they were all about taking over the country. He wanted to run the whole of the United Kingdom like Tomorrow Town.'

'The day after tomorrow, the world?'

'He kept putting in plans and strategies for infiltrating vital industries and dedicating them to the cause. He didn't have an army, but he believed Big Thinks could get all the computers in the country on his side. Most of the zenvols thought he was a dreamer, spinning out a best-case scenario at the meetings. But he meant it. He wanted to found a large-scale technomeritocracy.'

'With himself as Beloved Leader?'

'No, that's how mad he was. He wanted Big Thinks to run everything. He was hoping to put BeeTee in charge and let the future happen.'

'That's why he wanted Vanessa and me out of the story. We were a threat to his funding. Without the subsidies, the plug is pulled.'

'One thing BeeTee can do is keep track of figures. As a community, Tomorrow Town is in the red. Enormously.'

'There's no money here, though.'

'Of course not. We've spent it. And spent money we don't have. The next monorail from Preston is liable to be crowded with dunning bailiffs.'

Richard thought about it. He was rather saddened by the truth. It would have been nice if the future worked. He wondered if Lincoln Steffens would have had second thoughts during the Moscow purge trials?

'What threat was Zhoule to Mal-K?' he asked.

Jess-F frowned. 'That's the oddest thing. Zhoule was the one who really encouraged Mal-K to work on his coup plans. He did see himself as, what did you call it, "Beloved Leader". All his stories were about intellectual supermen taking charge of the world and sorting things out. If anything, he was the visioneer of the tomorrow take-over. And he'd have jumped anything in skirts if femzens wore skirts here.'

Richard remembered the quivering Sue-2.

'So we're back to Buster in the conservatory with the Hugo award?'

'I've always said it was him,' said Jess-F. 'You can't blame him, but he did it.'

'We shall see.'

Sirens sounded. Moana put her fingers in her ears. Jess-F looked even more stricken.

'That's not a good sign, is it?'

❖

The communal meal area outside Big Thinks swarmed with plastic-caped zenvols, looking up and pointing, panicking and screaming. The three light-heat globes, Tomorrow Town's suns, shone whiter and radiated hotter. Richard looked at the backs of his hands. They were tanning almost as quickly as an instant photograph develops.

'The fool,' said Jess-F. 'He's tampered with the master controls. Buster will kill us all. It's the only thing he has left.'

Zenvols piled into the communally owned electric carts parked in a rank to one side of the square. When they proved too heavy for the vehicles, they started throwing each other off. Holes melted in the canopy above the globes. Sizzling drips of molten plastic fell onto screaming tomorrow townies.

The sirens shrilled, urging everyone to panic.

Richard saw Vanessa through the throng.

She was with Zootie. No Gewell.

A one-man hovercraft, burdened with six clinging zenvols, chugged past inch by inch, outpaced by someone on an old-fashioned, non-solar-powered bicycle.

'If the elements reach critical,' said Jess-F, 'Tomorrow Town will blow up.'

A bannerlike strip of paper curled out of a slit in the front of Big Thinks.

'Your computer wants to say goodbye,' said Richard.

SURKIT BRAKER No. 15.

'Not much of a farewell.'

Zootie walked between falling drips to the central column, which supported the three globes. He opened a hatch and pulled a switch. The artificial suns went out. Real sunlight came through the holes in the canopy.

'Now that's what computers can do,' said Jess-F, elated. 'Execute protocols. If this happens, then that order must be given.'

The zenvol seemed happier about her computer now.

Richard was grateful for a ditch-digger who could read.

——◆——

'This is where the body was?' he asked Zootie. They were by swimming-pool-sized tanks of green gunk, dotted with yellow and brown patches since the interruption of the light-source. 'Bit of a haul from Zhoule's place.'

'The body was carried here?' asked Vanessa.

'Not just the body. The murder weapon too. Who lives in that bungalow?'

On a small hill was a bungalow not quite as spacious as Zhoule's, one of the mass of hutches placed between the silver pathways, with a crown of solar panels on the flat roof, and a dish antenna.

'Mm Jor-G,' said Moana.

'So you do speak?'

She nodded her head and smiled.

<hr>

Gewell sat on an off-white cube in the gloom. The stored power was running down. Only filtered sunlight got through to his main room. He looked as if his backbone had been removed. All the substance of his face had fallen to his jowls.

Richard looked at him.

'Nice try with the globes. Should have remembered the circuit-breaker, though. Only diabolical masterminds construct their private estates with in-built self-destruct systems. In the future, as in the past, it's unlikely that town halls will have bombs in the basement ready to go off in the event that the outgoing mayor wants to take the whole community with him rather than hand over the chain of office.'

Gewell didn't say anything.

Vanessa went straight to a shelf and picked up the only award in the display. It was another Hugo.

'Best Fan Editor 1958,' she read from the plaque.

The rocketship came away from its base.

'You killed him here,' said Richard, 'broke your own Hugo, left the bloody rocketship with the body outside. Then, when you'd calmed down a bit, you remembered Zhoule had won the same award. Several, in fact. You sneaked over to his bungalow – no locks, how convenient – and broke one of his Hugos, taking the rocket to complete yours. You made it look as if he were killed with his own award, and you were out of the loop. If only you'd got round to developing the glue of the future and fixed the thing properly, it wouldn't be so obvious. It's plain that though you've devoted your life to planning out the details of the future, your one essay in the fine art of murder was a rushed botch-up job done on the spur of the moment. You haven't really improved on Cain. At least Mm Mal-K made an effort with the space-suit and the zapper-prod.'

'Mm Jor-G,' said Jess-F, 'why?'

Good question, Richard thought.

After a long pause, Gewell gathered himself and said, 'Varno was destroying Tomorrow Town. He had so many... so many ideas. Every morning, before breakfast, he had four or five. All the time, constantly. Radio transmitters the size of a pinhead. Cheap infinite energy from tapping the planet's core. Solar-powered personal flying machines. Robots to do everything. Robots to make robots to do everything. An operation to extend human lifespan threefold. Rules and regulations about who was fit to have and raise children, with gonad-block implants to enforce them. Hats that collect the electrical energy of the brain and use it to power a personal headlamp. Non-stop, unrelenting, unstoppable. Ideas, ideas, ideas...'

Richard was frankly astonished by the man's vehemence. 'Isn't that what you wanted?'

'But Varno did the easy bit. Once he'd tossed out an idea, it was up to me to make it work. Me or Big Thinks or some other plodding zenvol. And nine out of ten of the ideas didn't work, couldn't ever work. And it was always our fault for not making them work, never his for foisting them off on us. This town would be perfect if it hadn't been for his ideas. And his bloody dreadful spelling. Back in the fifties, who do you think tidied all his stories up so they were publishable? Muggins Gewell. He couldn't write a sentence that scanned, and rather than learn how he decreed the language should be changed. Not just the spelling, he had a plan to go through the dictionary crossing out all the words that were no longer needed, then make it a crime to teach them to children. It was something to do with his old public school. He said he wanted to make gerunds extinct within a generation. But he had these wonderful, wonderful, ghastly, terrible ideas. It'd have made you sick.'

'And the medico who wanted to rule the world?'

'Him too. He had ideas.'

Gewell was pleading now, hands fists around imaginary bludgeons.

'If only I could have had ideas,' he said. 'They'd have been good ones.'

Richard wondered how they were going to lock Gewell up until the police came.

—•—

The monorail was out of commission. Most things wcrc. Some zenvols, like Jess-F, were relieved not to have to pretend that everything worked perfectly. They had desiyears – months, dammit! – of complaining bottled up inside, and were pouring it all out to each other in one big whine-in under the dead light-heat globes.

Richard and Vanessa looked across the Dales. A small vehicle was puttering along a winding, illogical lane that had been laid out not by a computer but by wandering sheep. It wasn't the police, though they were on the way.

'Who do you think this is?' asked Vanessa.

'It'll be Buster. He's bringing the outside to Tomorrow Town. He always was a yesterday man at heart.'

A car-horn honked.

Zenvols, some already changed out of their plastic suits, paid attention. Sue-2 was excited, hopeful, fearful. She clung to Moana, who smiled and waved.

Someone cheered. Others joined.

'What is he driving?' asked Vanessa 'It looks like a relic from the past.'

'For these people, it's deliverance,' said Richard. 'It's a fish 'n' chip van.'

⊶⊷ EGYPTIAN AVENUE ⊶⊷

'This tomb's leaking sand,' said Fred Regent. 'And beetles.'

Fine white stuff, hourglass quality not bucket-and-spade material, seeped from a vertical crack, fanning out around and between clumps of lush, long green grass. Black bugs glittered in morning sunlight, hornlike protrusions rooting through the overgrowth, sand-specks stuck to their carapaces. Fred looked up at the face of the tomb, which was framed by faux-Egyptian columns. The name BUNNING was cut deep into the stone, hemmed around by weather-beaten hieroglyphs.

It was the summer of 197—. Fred Regent, late of the Metropolitan Constabulary, was again adventuring with the supernatural. As before, his guide off life's beaten track was Richard Jeperson, the most resourceful agent of the Diogenes Club, which remained the least-known branch of Britain's intelligence and police services. All the anomalies came down to Jeperson. Last month, it had been glam rock-ghouls gutting groupies at the Glastonbury Festival and an obeah curse on Prime Minister Edward Heath hatched somewhere inside his own Cabinet; this morning, it was ghosts in Kingstead Cemetery.

Jeperson, something of an anomaly himself, scooped up a handful of sand and looked down his hawk nose at a couple of fat bugs.

'Were we on the banks of the great River Nile rather than

on a pleasant hill overlooking the greater city of London,' said Jeperson, 'I shouldn't be surprised to come across these little fellows. As it is, I'm flummoxed. These, Fred, are *scarabus* beetles.'

'I saw *Curse of the Mummy's Tomb* at the Rialto, Richard. I know what a scarab is.'

Jeperson laughed, deepening creases in his tanned forehead and cheeks. His smile lifted black moustaches and showed sharp teeth-points. The man from the Diogenes Club sounded as English as James Mason, but when suntanned he looked more like an Arab, or a Romany disguised as Charles II. His mass of black ringlets was not a wig, though. And no gypsy would dress as gaudily as Richard Jeperson.

'Of course you do, Fred. I elucidate for the benefit of exposition. Thinking out loud. That is Sahara sand and these are North African beasties.'

'Absolutely, guv'nor. And that bloody big dead one there is a scorpion.'

Jeperson looked down with amused distaste. The scorpion twitched, scuttled and was squashed under Jeperson's foot.

'Not so dead, Fred.'

'Is now.'

'Let us hope so.'

Jeperson considered his sole, then scraped the evil crushed thing off on a chunk of old headstone.

For this expedition to darkest N6, he wore a generously bloused, leopard-pattern safari jacket and tight white, high-waisted britches tucked into sturdy fell-walker's boots. His ensemble included a turquoise Sam Browne belt (with pouches full of useful implements and substances), a tiger's-fang amulet that was supposed to protect against evil, and an Australian bush hat with three corks dangling from the rim. Champagne corks, each marked with a date in felt-tip pen.

'The term for a thing so out of place is, as we all know, an "apport",' said Jeperson. 'Unless some peculiar person has for reasons unknown placed sand, scarabs and scorps in our path for the purpose of puzzlement, we must conclude that they have materialised for some supernatural reason. Mr Lillywhite, this is your belief, is it not? This is yet another manifestation of the spookery you have reported?'

Lillywhite nodded. He was a milk-skinned, fair-haired middle-aged man with burning red cheeks and a peacock's-tail-pattern smock. His complaint had been passed from the police to the Diogenes Club, and then fielded to Jeperson.

'What is all this doing here?' asked Vanessa, Jeperson's other assistant – the one everyone noticed before realising Fred was in the room. The tall, model-beautiful redhead wore huge sunglasses with swirly mint-and-yellow patterns on the lenses and frames, a sari-like arrangement of silk scarves that exposed a ruby winking in her navel, and stack-heeled cream leather go-go boots. Beside the other two, Fred felt a bit underdressed in his Fred Perry and Doc Martens.

'Appearing supernaturally, I should say, Vanessa,' said Jeperson. 'That's generally what apports do.'

'Not just the apports,' she went on. 'All the obelisks and sphinxes. Oughtn't this to be in the Valley of the Kings, not buried under greenery in London North Six?'

Jeperson dropped the sand and let the scarabs scuttle where they might. He brushed his palms together.

Vanessa was right. Everything in this section of Kingstead Cemetery was tricked out with Ancient Egyptian statuary and design features. The Bunning tomb was guarded by two human-headed stone lions in pharaonic headdresses. Their faces had weathered as badly in a century as the original sphinx in millennia. All around were miniature sandstone pyramids and temples, animal-headed deities, faded blue-and-gold hieroglyphs and ankh-shaped gravestones.

'I can explain that, Miss... ah?' said Lillywhite.

'Vanessa. Just Vanessa.'

'Vanessa, fine,' said the scholarly caretaker, segueing into a tour-guide speech. 'The motif dates back to the establishment of the cemetery in 1839. Stephen Geary, the original architect, had a passion for Egyptiana which was shared by the general public of his day. From the first, the cemetery was planned not just as a place for burying the dead but a species of a morbid tourist attraction. Victorians were rather more given to visiting dead relatives than we are. It was expected that whole families would come to picnic by grandmama's grave.'

'If my gran were dead, we'd certainly have a picnic,' said Fred. Lillywhite looked a little shocked. 'Well, you don't know my gran,' Fred explained.

'They held black-crêpe birthday parties for the many children who died in infancy,' the caretaker continued, 'with solemn games and floral presents. Siblings annually gathered around marble babies well into their own old age. It's not easy to start a graveyard from scratch, especially at what you might call the top end of the market. Cemeteries are supposed to be old. For a Victorian to be laid to rest in a new one would be like you or me being bundled into a plastic bag and ploughed under a motorway extension.'

'That's more or less what Fred has planned,' said Jeperson.

'I can't say I'm surprised. To circumvent the prejudice, Geary decided to trade on associations with ancient civilisations. If his cemetery couldn't be instantly old, then at least it would look old. This area is Egyptian Avenue. Geary himself is buried here. Originally, there were three such sections, with a Roman Avenue and a Grecian Avenue completing the set. But the fashionable had a craze for Egypt. The Roman and Grecian Avenues were abandoned and overtaken. It was no real scholarly interest in Egyptology, by the way, just an enthusiasm for the styles. Some of the gods you see represented aren't even real, just made up to fit in with the pantheon. A historian might draw a parallel between Ancient Egyptian obsession with funerary rites and the Victorian fascination with the aesthetics of death.'

Fred thought anyone who chose to spend his life looking after a disused cemetery must nurture some of that obsession himself. Lillywhite was an unsalaried amateur, a local resident who was a booster for this forgotten corner of the capital.

'It's certainly ancient now,' said Fred. 'Falling to pieces.'

'Regrettably so. Victorian craftsmen were good on surface, but skimped everything else. Artisans knew the customers would all be too dead to complain and cut a lot of corners. Impressive stone fronts, but crumbling at the back. Statues that dissolve to lumps after fifty years in the rain. Tombs with strong corners but weak roofs. By the 1920s, when the original site was full and children and grandchildren of the first tenants were in their own grave-plots, everything had fallen into disrepair. When the United Cemetery Company went bust in the early 1960s, Kingstead was more or less abandoned. Our historical society has been trying to raise money for restoration and repair work. With not much luck, as yet.'

'Put me down for fifty quid,' said Jeperson.

Fred wasn't sure if restoration and repair would improve the place. The tombs had been laid out to a classical plan like miniature pyramids or cathedrals, and serpentine pathways wound between them. Uncontrolled shrubbery and ivy swarmed everywhere, clogging the paths, practically burying the stonework. A broken-winged angel soared from a nearby rhododendron, face scraped eyeless. It was the dead city of a lost civilisation, like something from Rider Haggard. Nature had crept back, green tendrils undermining thrones and palaces, and was slowly taking the impertinent erections of a passing humanity back into her leafy bosom.

'This is the source of your haunting?' asked Jeperson, nodding at the Bunning tomb.

Fred had forgotten for a moment why they were there.

'It seems to be.'

There had been a great deal of ghostly activity. Yesterday, Fred had gone to the newspaper library in Colindale and looked over a hundred and twenty years of wails in the night and alarmed courting couples. As burial grounds went, Kingstead Cemetery was rather sporadically haunted. Until the last three months, when spooks had been running riot with bells and whistles on. A newsagent's across the road had been pelted with a rain of lightning–charged pebbles. A physical–culture enthusiast had been knocked off his bicycle by ectoplasmic tentacles. And there had been a lot of sightings.

Jeperson considered the Bunning tomb. Fred saw he was letting down his guard, trying to sense what was disturbed in the vicinity. Jeperson was a sensitive.

'According to your report, Lillywhite, our spectral visitors have run the whole gamut. Disembodied sounds...'

'Like jackals,' said Lillywhite. 'I was in Suez in '56. I know what a jackal sounds like.'

'...Phantom figures...'

'Mummies, with bandages. Hawk–headed humans. Ghostly barges. Crawling severed hands.'

'And now, physical presences. To whit: the scarabs and other nasties. Even the sand. It's still warm, by the way. Does anyone else detect a theme here?'

'Spirits of Ancient Egypt,' suggested Vanessa.

Jeperson shot her a finger-gun. 'You have it.'

Fred would have shivered, only…

'Richard, isn't there something funny here?' he said. 'A themed haunting? It's a bit Hammer Horror, isn't it? I mean, this place may be done up with Egyptian tat but it's still North London. You can see the Post Office Tower from here. Whoever is buried in this tomb—'

'Members of the Bunning Family,' put in Lillywhite. 'The publishing house. Bunning and Company, Pyramid Press. You can see their offices from here. That black building, the one that looks like the monolith in *2001: A Space Odyssey*. It's called the Horus Tower.'

Fred knew the skyscraper, but had never realised who owned it.

'Yes, them. The Bunnings. They were just Victorians who liked the idea of a few hieroglyphs and cat-headed birds in the way they might have liked striped wallpaper or a particular cut of waistcoat. You said it was a fashion, a craze. So why have we got authentic Egyptian ghosts, just as if there were some evil high priest or mad pharaoh in there?'

'George Oldrid Bunning was supposedly buried in a proper Egyptian sarcophagus,' said Lillywhite. 'It was even said that he went through the mummification process.'

'Brains through the nose, liver and lights in canopic jars?'

'Yes, Mr Jeperson. Indeed.'

'That would have been irregular?'

'In 1897? Yes.'

'I withdraw my objection,' said Fred. 'Old Bunning was clearly a loon. You might expect loon ghosts.'

Jeperson was on his knees, looking at the sand. The scarabs were gone now, scuttling across London in advance of a nasty surprise come the first frost.

'I've been trying to get in touch with the descendants for a while,' said Lillywhite. 'Even before all this fuss. I was hoping they might sponsor restoration of the Bunning tomb. The current head of the family is George Rameses Bunning. He must maintain the family interest in Egypt, or at least his parents did. It appears George Rameses has his own troubles.'

'So I'd heard,' said Jeperson. 'All dynasties must fail, I suppose.'

Fred had vaguely heard of the Bunnings but couldn't remember where.

'Pyramid Press are magazine publishers,' said Jeperson, answering the unspoken query. 'You've heard of *Stunna*.'

Vanessa made a face.

Stunna was supposedly a blokes' answer to *Cosmopolitan*, with features about fast cars and sport and (especially) sex. It ran glossy pictures of girls not naked enough to get into *Playboy* but nevertheless unclad enough for you not to want your mum knowing you looked at them. The magazine had launched last year with a lot of publicity, then been attacked with a couple of libel suits from a rival publisher they had made nasty jokes about, Derek Leech of the *Daily Comet*. *Stunna* had just ceased publication, probably taking the company down with it. Fred realised he had heard of George Rameses Bunning after all. He was doomed to be dragged into bankruptcy and ruin, throwing a lot of people out of work. The scraps of his company would probably be gobbled up by the litigious Leech, which may well have been the point of the legal action.

'Bunning and Company once put out *British Pluck* and *The Halfpenny Marvel*,' said Jeperson. 'Boy's papers. At their height of popularity between the wars. And dozens of other titles over the years. Mostly sensation stuff. Generations of lads were raised on the adventures of Jack Dauntless, RN, and the scientific vigilante, Dr Shade. I think the masthead of *Stunna* bears the sad legend "incorporating *British Pluck*".'

'You think there's a tie-in,' said Fred. 'With all the pluck business. It's a penny-dreadful curse.'

Jeperson's brow furrowed. He was having one of his 'feelings', which usually meant bad news for anyone within hailing distance.

'More than that, Fred. I sense something very nasty here. An old cruelty that lingers. Also, this is one of those "hey, look at me" hauntings. It's as if our phantoms were trying to tell us something, to issue a warning.'

'Then why start making a fuss in the last month? Any ghosts around here must have been planted...'

'Discorporated, Fred.'

'Yes, that. They must have been dead for eighty years. Why sit quietly all that time but kick up a row this summer?'

'Maybe they object to something topical,' suggested Vanessa. 'Like what's Top of the Pops?'

'It's not dreadful enough to be after the Bay City Rollers, luv,' said Fred.

'Good point.'

Jeperson considered the Bunning tomb, and stroked his tash.

Fred looked around. The cemetery afforded a pleasant green dappling of shadow, and swathes of sunstruck grass. But Jeperson was right. Something very nasty was here.

'Vanessa,' said Jeperson. 'Pass the crowbar. I think we should unseal this tomb.'

'But...' put in the startled Lillywhite.

Jeperson tapped his tiger-fang. 'Have no fear of curses, man. This will shield us all.'

'It's not that. This is private property.'

'I won't tell if you don't. Besides, you've already established that George Rameses Bunning has less than no interest in the last resting place of his ancestors. Who else could possibly object?'

'I'm supposed to be a guardian of this place.'

'Come on. Haven't you ever wanted to open one of these tombs up and poke around inside?'

'The original Mr Bunning is supposed to have had an authentic Egyptian funeral. He might be surrounded by his treasures.'

'A bicycle to pedal into the afterlife? Golden cigar cuspidors? Ornamental funerary gas lamps?'

'Very likely.'

'Then we shall be Howard Carter and Lord Carnarvon.'

Fred thought that wasn't a happy parallel. Hadn't there been an effective curse on the tomb of King Tutankhamun?

Vanessa produced a crowbar from her BOAC hold-all. She was always prepared for any eventuality.

Fred thought he should volunteer, but Jeperson took the tool and slipped it into a crack. He strained and the stone didn't shift.

'Superior workmanship, Lillywhite. No skimping here.'

Jeperson heaved again. The stone advanced an inch, and more sand cascaded. Something chittered inside.

Vanessa had a trowel. She cleared some of the sand and picked out dried-up mortar.

'Good girl,' said Jeperson.

He heaved again. The bottom half of the stone cracked through completely, then fell out of the doorway. The top half slid down in grooves and broke in two pieces. A lot more sand avalanched.

Fred tugged Lillywhite out of the way. Jeperson and Vanessa had already stepped aside.

A scarecrow-thin human figure stood in the shifting sands, hands raised as if to thump, teeth bared in a gruesome grin. It pitched forward on its face and broke apart like a poorly made dummy. If it were a Guy, it would not earn a penny from the most intimidated or kindly passer-by.

'That's not George Oldrid Bunning,' gasped Lillywhite.

'No,' said Jeperson. 'I rather fear that it's his butler.'

<hr />

There were five of them, strewn around the stone sarcophagus, bundles of bones in browned wrappings.

'A butler, a footman, a cook, a house-keeper and a maid,' said Jeperson. Under his tan, he was pale. He held himself rigidly, so that he wouldn't shake with rage and despair. He understood this sort of horror all too well – having lost the memory of a boyhood torn away in a Nazi camp – but never got used to it.

The servants' bodies wore the remains of uniforms.

Lillywhite was upset. He was sitting on the grass, with his head between his knees.

Vanessa, less sensitive than Jeperson, was looking about the tomb with a torch.

'It's a good size,' she called out. 'Extensive foundations.'

'They were alive,' bleated Lillywhite.

'For a while,' said Jeperson.

'What a bastard,' said Fred. 'Old George Oldrid Bunning. He got his pharaoh's funeral, all right, with all his servants buried alive to shine his boots and tug their forelocks through all eternity. How did he do it?'

'Careful planning,' said Jeperson. 'And a total lack of scruples.'

Lillywhite looked up. He concentrated, falling back on expertise to damp down the shock.

'It was a special design. When he was dying, George Oldrid contracted a master-mason to create his tomb. It's the only one here that's survived substantially intact. The mason died before Bunning. Suspiciously.'

'Pharaohs had their architects killed, to preserve the secrets of their tombs from grave-robbers. There were all kind of traps in the pyramids, to discourage looters.'

A loud noise came from inside the tomb. Something snapping shut with a clang.

Jeperson's cool vanished.

'Vanessa?' he shouted.

Vanessa came out of the tomb, hair awry and pinned back by her raised sunglasses. She had a nasty graze on her knee.

'I'm fine,' she said. 'Nothing a tot won't cure.'

She found a silver flask in her hold-all and took a swallow, then passed it round. Fred took a jolting shot of brandy.

'Who'd leave a man-trap in a tomb? Coiled steel, with enough tensile strength after a century to bisect a poor girl, or at least take her leg off, if she didn't have a dancer's reflexes.'

'George Oldrid Bunning,' said Jeperson.

'Bastard General,' clarified Fred.

'Just so. He must have been the *bastardo di tutti bastardi*. It would have been in the will that he be laid personally to rest by his servants, with no other witnesses, at dead of night. They were probably expecting healthy bequests. The sad, greedy lot. When closed, the sarcophagus lid triggered a mechanism and the stone door slammed down. For ever, or at least until Vanessa and her crowbar. The tomb is sound-proof. Weather-proof. Escape-proof.'

'There's treasure,' said Vanessa. 'Gold and silver. Some Egyptian things. Genuine, I think. Ushabti figures, a death-mask. A lot of it is broken. The downstairs mob must have tried to improvise tools. Not that it did them any good.'

The now-shattered stone door showed signs of ancient scratching. But the breaks were new, and clean.

'How long did they…?'

'Best not to think of it, Lillywhite,' said Jeperson.

'In death, they got strong,' said Vanessa. 'They finally cracked the door, or we'd never have been able to shift it.'

The sight of the little maid, tiny skull in a mob-cap, was especially disturbing. She couldn't have been more than fourteen.

'No wonder the ghosts have been making a racket,' said Fred. 'If someone did that to me, I'd give nobody any rest until it was made right.'

Jeperson tapped his front tooth, thinking.

'But why wait until now? As you said, they've had a hundred years in which to manifest their understandable ire. And why the Egyptian thing? Shouldn't they be Victorian servant ghosts? I should think an experience like being buried alive by a crackpot with a King Tut complex would sour one on ancient cultures in general and Egypt in particular.'

'They're trying to tell us something,' said Vanessa.

'Sharp girl. Indeed they are.'

Fred looked away from the tomb. Across the city.

The Horus Tower caught the light. It was a black glass block, surmounted by a gold pyramid.

'George Rameses Bunning is dying,' said Lillywhite. 'A recurrence of some tropical disease. News got out just after Derek Leech International started suing Pyramid Press. It's had a disastrous effect on the company stock. He's liable to die broke.'

'If he's anything like his great-great, then he deserves it,' said Vanessa.

Jeperson snapped his fingers.

'I think he's a lot like his great-great. And I know what the ghosts have been trying to tell us. Quick, Fred, get the Rolls. Vanessa, ring Inspector Price at New Scotland Yard, and have him meet us at the Horus Tower immediately. He might want to bring a lot of hearty fellows with him. Some with guns. This is going to make a big noise.'

———◆———

Fred didn't care to set foot inside the Horus Tower. Just thinking about what had been done in the building made him sick to his stomach. He was on the forecourt as the coughing, shrunken, handcuffed George Rameses Bunning was led out by Inspector Euan Price. Jeperson had accompanied the police up to the pyramid on top of the tower, to be there at the arrest.

Employees gathered at their windows, looking down as the boss was hauled off to pokey. Rumours of what he had intended for them – for two hundred and thirty-eight men and women, from senior editors to junior copy-boys – would already be circulating, though Fred guessed many wouldn't believe them. Derek Leech's paper would carry the story, but few people put any credence in those loony crime stories in the *Comet*.

'He'll be dead before he comes to trial,' said Jeperson. 'Unless they find a cure.'

'I hope they do, Richard,' said Fred. 'And he spends a good few years buried alive himself, in a concrete cell.'

'His Board of Directors were wondering why, with the company on the verge of liquidation, Bunning had authorised such extensive remodelling of his corporate HQ. It was done, you know. He could have thrown the switch tomorrow, or next week. Whenever all was lost.'

Now Fred shivered. Cemeteries didn't bother him, but places like this – concrete, glass and steel traps for the enslavement and destruction of living human beings – did.

'What did he tell what's-his-name, the architect? Drache?'

'It was supposed to be about security, locking down the Tower against armed insurrection. Rioting investors wanting their dividends, perhaps. The spray nozzles that were to flood the building with nerve-gas were a new kind of fire-prevention system.'

'And Drache believed him?'

'He believed the money.'

'Another bastard, then.'

'Culpable, but not indictable.'

The Horus Tower was equipped with shutters that would seal every window, door and ventilation duct. When the master-switch was thrown, they would all come down and lock tight. Then deadly gas would fill every office space, instantly preserving in death the entire workforce. Had George Rameses Bunning intended to keep publishing magazines in the afterlife? Did he really think his personal tomb would be left inviolate in perpetuity with all the corpses at their desks, a monument to himself for all eternity? Of course, George Oldrid Bunning had got away with it for a century.

'George Rameses knew?'

'About George Oldrid's funerary arrangements? Yes.'

'Bastard bastard.'

'Quite.'

People began to file out of the skyscraper. The work-day was over early.

There was a commotion.

A policeman was on the concrete, writhing around his kneed groin. Still handcuffed, George Rameses sprinted back towards his tower, shouldering through his employees.

Jeperson shouted to Price. 'Get everyone out, now!'

Fred's old boss understood at once. He got a bullhorn and ordered everyone away from the building.

'He'll take the stairs,' said Jeperson. 'He won't chance us stopping the lifts. That'll give everyone time to make it out.'

Alarm-bells sounded. The flood of people leaving the Horus Tower grew to exodus proportions.

'Should I send someone in to catch him?' asked Price. 'It should be easy to snag him on the stairs. He'll be out of puff by the fifth floor, let alone the thirtieth.'

Jeperson shook his head.

'Too much of a risk, Inspector. Just make sure everyone else is out. This should be interesting.'

'Interesting?' spat Fred.

'Come on. Don't you want to see if it works? The big clockwork trap. The plans I saw were ingenious. A real economy of construction. No electricals. Just levers, sand and water. Drache kept to Egyptian technology. Modern materials, though.'

'And nerve gas?' said Fred.

'Yes, there is that.'

'You'd better hope Drache's shutters are damn good, or half London is going to drop dead.'

'It won't come to that.'

Vanessa crossed the forecourt. She was with the still-bewildered Lillywhite.

'What's happening?' she asked.

'George Rameses is back inside, racing towards his master-switch.'

'Good grief.'

'Never fear, Vanessa. Inspector, it might be an idea to find some managerial bods in the crowd. Read the class register, as it were. Just make sure everyone's out of the tower.'

'Good idea, Jeperson.'

The policeman hurried off.

Jeperson looked up at the building. The afternoon sun was reflected in black.

Then the reflection was gone.

Matt shutters closed like eyelids over every window. Black grilles came down behind the glass walls of the lobby, jaws meshing around floor-holes. The pyramid atop the tower twisted on a stem and lowered, locking into place. It was all done before the noise registered, a great mechanical wheezing and clanking. Torrents of water gushed from drains around the building, squirting up fifty feet in the air from the ornamental fountain.

'He's escaped,' said Fred. 'A quick, easy death from the gas and it'll take twenty years to break through all that engineering.'

'Oh, I don't think so,' said Jeperson. 'Fifteen at the most. Modern methods, you know.'

'The ghosts won't rest,' said Lillywhite. 'Not without revenge or restitution.'

'I think they might,' said Jeperson. 'You see, George Rameses is still alive in his tomb. Alone, ill and, after his struggle up all those stairs, severely out of breath. Though I left the bulk of his self-burial mechanism alone, I took the precaution of disabling the nerve gas.'

'Is that a scream I hear?' said Vanessa.

'I doubt it,' said Jeperson. 'If nothing else, George Rameses has just sound-proofed his tomb.'

⤟⟹ SOHO GOLEM ⟸⤞

Of all quarters in the queer adventurous amalgam called
London, Soho is perhaps least suited to the Forsyte spirit...
Untidy, full of Greeks, Ishmaelites, cats, Italians, tomatoes,
restaurants, organs, coloured stuffs, queer names, people
looking out of upper windows, it dwells remote from the
British Body Politic.

John Galsworthy

I. SPOILING THE BARREL

On a fine May day in 197—, Fred Regent and Richard Jeperson
stood in Old Compton Street, London W1. The pavement
underfoot was warm and slightly tacky, as if it might retain the
prints of Fred's scruffy but sturdy Doc Martens and Richard's
elastic-sided claret-coloured thigh-high boots.

Slightly to the north of but parallel to the theatrical parade
of Shaftesbury Avenue, Old Compton Street was among Soho's
main thoroughfares. Blitzed in the War, the square-mile patch had
regenerated patchwork fashion to satisfy or exploit the desires of a
constant flux of passers-through. People came here for every kind
of 'lift'. Italian coffee-houses had opened on this street a century
ago; now, you could buy a thousand varieties of frothy heart-attack
in a cup. This was where waves of 'dangerous' music broke, from
bebop to glitter rock. Within sight, careers had begun and ended:

Tommy Steele strumming in an espresso skiffle trio, Jimi Hendrix choking in an alley beside the Intrepid Fox.

Also, famously and blatantly, Soho was a red-light district, home to the city's vice rackets for two hundred years. Above window displays were neon and plastic come-ons: GIRLS GIRLS GIRLS – LIVE NUDE BED REVUE – GOLDILOXXX AND THE THREE BARES. Above door-bells were hand-printed cards: 'French Model One Flight Up', 'Busty Brunette, Bell Two', 'House of Thwacks: Discipline Enforced'.

Fred checked the address against his scribbled note.

'The scene of the crime,' he told Richard.

Richard took off and folded his slim, side-panelled sunglasses. They slid into a tube that clipped to his top pocket like a thick fountain-pen.

'Just the one crime?' he said.

'Couldn't say, guv,' replied Fred. 'One big one, so far this week.'

Richard shrugged – which, in today's peacock-pattern watered silk safari jacket, was dangerously close to flouncing. Even in the cosmopolitan freak show of Soho, Richard's Carnabetian ensemble attracted attention from all sexes. Currently, he wore scarlet buccaneer britches fitted tighter than a surgical glove, a black-and-white spiral-pattern beret pinned to his frizzy length of coal-black hair, a frill-fronted mauve shirt with a collar-points wider than his shoulders, and a filmy ascot whose colours shifted with the light.

'I certainly feel a measure of recent turmoil,' said Richard, who called himself 'sensitive' rather than 'spooky'. He flexed long fingers, as if taking a Braille reading from the air. 'It certainly could be a death unnatural and occult. Still, in this parish, it'd be unusual not to find a soupçon of eldritch atmos, eh? This is east of Piccadilly, *mon ami*. Vibes swirl like a walnut whip. If London has a psychic storm centre, it's on this page of the *A to Z*. Look about, pal – most punters here are dowsing with their dickybirds. It's not hard to find water.'

A skinny blonde in hot-pants, platforms and a paisley halter-top sidled out of Crawford Street. She cast a lazy look at them, eyes hoisting pennyweights of pancake and false lash. Richard bowed to her with a cavalier flourish, smile lifting his Fu Manchu. The girl's own psychic powers cut in.

'Fuzz,' she sniffed, and scarpered.

'Everyone's a detective,' Richard observed, straightening.

'Or a tart,' said Fred.

The girl fled. Heart-shaped windows cut out of the seat of her shorts showed pale skin and a sliver of Marks and Sparks knicker. Four-inch stack-soles made for a tottering, Thunderbirds-puppet gait which was funny rather than sexy.

'That said, shouldn't this place be veritably swarming with the filth?' commented Richard. 'One of their own down, and all that. Uniforms, sirens, yellow tape across the door, Black Marias hauling in the usual susses, grasses shaken down? All holidays cancelled, whole shift working overtime to nick the toerag who snuffed a copper while he was about his duty? And where's the wreath? There should be one on the street, with some junior Hawkshaw posted in that alcove there, in case the crim revisits the scene to gloat and lingers long enough to get nabbed.'

Richard had put his finger on something which had bothered Fred. One of the man's talents was noticing things unusual by their absence. The proverbial dog that didn't bark in the night.

'This isn't Dock Green, Richard. And DI Brian "Boot Boy" Booth isn't – wasn't – George Dixon.'

Now he thought about it, Fred wondered if Busy had even told the Yard about Booth. He might have thought giving Fred the shout was all duty, and a sense of self-preservation, required. In which case, there would be a load of forms to fill in before bedtime.

Usually, Fred got involved in cases thanks to Richard. They were both assets of the Diogenes Club, an institution which quietly existed to cope with matters beyond the purview of regular police and intelligence services. Last month, it had been flower children plucked from Glastonbury Tor by 'bright lights in the sky' which the boffins reckoned were extra-dimensional rather than extra-terrestrial; before that, a Brixton papaloi whose racket was giving out tetrodotoxin-cut ganja at a street festival and enslaving a cadre of zombies through the voodoo beat of a reggae number Fred still couldn't get out of his head.

This time, the call came directly to Fred from Harry 'Busy' Boddey. Fred's secondment to work with Richard had been extended so long he sometimes forgot he was still a sergeant in the Metropolitan Police, with space in the boot-rack at New Scotland Yard. He hadn't seen Busy since Hendon College, which was deliberate. DC Boddey was a trimmer, a taker-of-shortcuts; the cheery cheeky chappie chatter and carved-into-his-cheeks smirk didn't distract from ice-chips in his eyes. Through rozzer gossip, Fred heard Busy had landed his dream job.

On the phone, Busy hadn't sounded as if he were still smirking.

'It's my guv'nor, Freddo,' he had explained. 'DI Booth is dead. Killed. It's one of yours, pal. One of the weird ones, y'know. Off the books. So far off the books it's not even on the bloody shelf. The horror shows that bring out that long-haired pouf with the tash and the clothes. Booth was smashed. While sittin' in his office. Looks like he was hit by a bleedin' express train. Five blokes with sledge-hammers couldn't do that much damage.'

Fred's first reaction was to assume five blokes with sledge-hammers had outdone themselves and the regular plods could track them easily by the blood-drip trail. Gruesome, admittedly,

211

but hardly in the same docket as time-warping Nazi demons, extra-dimensional hippie harvesting, spirits of ancient Egypt, dreadlocked Rasta zombies or brainbending seminars in Sussex. Still, the Diogenes Club had nothing on at the moment and it was sunny out. No point lazing around the flat on an inflatable chair with a slow leak, with the snooker commentator on the BBC continually rubbing it in that he hadn't sprung for a colour telly ('for those of you watching in black and white, Reardon's coming up on the pink'). Once Busy was off the line, Fred had given Richard a bell and arranged to meet him here, outside Booth's Soho HQ.

Richard arched an elegant eyebrow. "'Skinderella's"?'

The name was up in glittery purple letters, surrounded by silver-paper suns whose points curled like two-days-dead starfish. The light of this constellation was reaching Earth well after the stars had burned out. In the star-hearts were photographs of female faces, with hairstyles and smiles from ten years before. Once colour, the snaps were bleached to a peculiar aquamarine that made the girls look drowned. The door was wedged open, but glittery streamers curtained the way in.

Somewhere, tinny music played through maladjusted speakers. It could have been Melanie's 'Brand New Key' or John Fred and His Playboy Band's 'Judy in Disguise (With Glasses)' or anything with that rinky-dink, teeth-scraping rhythm.

Fred checked his note again. He guessed why Busy had given him a street address rather than just named the place.

A board propped on an easel on the street promised 'Tonite's tasties – Helena Trois, the Mysterious Zarana and Freak-Out Frankie'. Black-and-white head-shots were pinned around the names, all of women looking back over naked shoulders. In the window stood life-size cardboard cut-outs of girls who wore only sparkly G-strings and high-heels, leaning in unnatural and/ or uncomfortable positions. As a token of respect to passers-by, coloured paper circles were stuck like grocer's price-tags over nipples. One or two had fallen off, leaving the girls stuck with blobby glue-pasties.

A book rack, just like the ones in a newsagent's or bus station, was chained to a Victorian boot-scraper to prevent theft. Paperback shapes in the wire-slots were wrapped in brown paper like a surrealist installation. The wrapping was partially torn off one, disclosing a title which caught Fred's eye, *Confessions of a Psychic Investigator*. He plucked out the book, skinned it and looked at the cover. A thirtyish blonde in a school-cap and navy-blue knickers, braids conveniently arranged over her breasts, did a shocked comedy double-take as a 'ghost' in a long sheet ripped off her gymslip with warty rubber horror-hands. The author was a Lesley Behan.

'Nice to see the field getting serious attention,' drawled Richard. 'You should buy that. I'm not aware of Miss Behan's contribution to the literature of the occult.'

Also on offer were 'films – continuous', at a ticket price well above that charged by self-respecting Odeons or Classics; this afternoon's 'XXX' triple-bill was *Sixth Form Girls in Chains*, *Chocolate Sandwich* and *Sexier Than Sex*.

'Now, that's just ridiculous,' exclaimed Fred. 'How can anything be, well, sexier than sex? It's like saying wetter than water.'

'Perhaps a philosophical point is intended. After all, is not reality sometimes a disappointment, set against its imagined or anticipated version?'

'One thing I guarantee is that what won't be sexier than sex will be these films.'

'You sound like a connoisseur.'

'I once spent two weeks in the back row of one of these pokey little cinemas on an undercover job. We were after some nutter

213

who liked to throw ammonia in the faces of the usherettes. In the end, they nabbed him somewhere else. All I got out of it was eyestrain. I didn't even want to think about chatting up a bird for six months. I've actually seen *Chocolate Sandwich*. It's about this West Indian bloke, a plumber, and these housewives...'

Richard made a face, indicating he didn't want to know any more.

Locating a panel of buttons by the streamers, Richard pressed one. A buzzer sounded inside.

'Frederick,' Richard began, 'this might seem naïve to someone au fait with the ins and outs of policing the capital, but isn't it something of a conflict of interests that the policeman in charge of the Obscene Publications Squad should work above – not to put too fine a point on it – a strip club?'

Fred coughed a little. The OPS was one of those embarrassments the average copper tried not to bring up if he had any intention of becoming an above-average copper.

'Don't hem and haw, man,' snapped Richard.

'Have you ever heard the expression "one bad apple"?'

'"Spoils the barrel"? Indeed.'

Fred found himself whispering. 'You know we don't have police corruption in this country?'

'That's the impression given by the patriotic press.'

'Well, it might not be one hundred per cent true.'

Before he could further disenchant Richard, the streamers parted. White, beringed hands reached out and fastened on Fred's shoulders. He was pulled into warm, fragrant darkness.

II. QUEEN OF THE NILE

When his eyes got used to the gloom, Fred found he was being held close by a tiny woman in a Cleopatra outfit. She had Egyptian eye make-up and a sprinkling of glitter on her bare shoulders. A rearing tin cobra stuck to the front of her stiff black wig prodded his chin.

'Steady on, luv,' he said.

'You've made a conquest, Fred,' commented Richard, slyly.

Fred took the girl's fingers off his shoulders and gave them back to her. She waved them about in the region of her brass bra, then put them behind her. He had an idea she was a bit embarrassed by her hands, which were large for her size.

'You're the ghost-exterminators,' she said, in broad Sarf Lahndahn tones. 'Thank Gawd you're here.'

Richard reached behind her, took one of her hands, turned it over and kissed her palm dead-centre.

'And you must be the Mysterious Zarana, Queen of the Nile.'

Her eyes widened, cracking a black bar of eyeshadow.

'Lumme, you really are psychic.'

Richard smiled. 'Your picture is outside,' he said.

She was a bit disappointed. 'It's Zarana Roberts, really. Dad was out in Egypt during the War.'

'Pleased to meet you. I'm Richard Jeperson, and the fellow you've enraptured is Fred Regent.'

Fred wondered if he was blushing. It'd be too dim in here to tell.

Zarana did something like a curtsey, with a little eyelash-fluttering smile like the one in her mug-shot.

Then she was serious.

'Busy Boddey's goin' spare,' she said. 'Ever since the thing happened. He's been on the blower to half the town…'

Which meant there should be more police here.

'Now he's up outside Boot Boy's office, keepin' guard. None of the girls wanted to go up there. Not even before the thing. I mean, taking your knickers off in public for a livin' is one thing, but Boot Boy Booth is another, if you know what I mean.'

Fred had heard a few things about DI Booth.

'We should take a look-see,' said Fred, trying to sound more casual than he felt.

'Rather you than me, ducks,' said Zarana. 'Fancy a cuppa? Typhoo's two pound to the customers, but I can get you sorted complements of the management.'

'That would be most welcome, Miss Roberts,' said Richard.

'Zarana, please. No need to be formal.'

'Thank you, Zarana.'

'You too, Freddy Friday,' she said, prodding him in the ribs with a knuckle-ring, finding a soft spot close to his heart and grinding it. 'Come on.'

'Zarana,' he said.

'Not so difficult, is it?'

It wasn't, but he thought she'd left her mark on him.

She bustled off, 'backstage' – which might have been called a cupboard anywhere else. The walls, floor and ceiling were covered with brown shagpile. At the end of the corridor was a bar-theatre space, where a Chinese girl, spotlit on a dais, peeled a cheongsam off her shoulders. A sparse audience kept to the shadows. Fred wondered who these folk were – it was half past three in the afternoon, didn't they have jobs to go to? Mechanical moaning and oom-pah muzak seeped from an alcove under the stairs. The basement screening room was probably a fire-trap. Booth should at least have made sure the place was up to public safety specifications.

A proper staircase led upwards. Serried beside it were framed posters of strippers.

'There's your ghosts,' said Zarana, returning with tea-bag teas in an 'I'm Backing Britain' mug and a breast-shaped tankard. She gave Richard the Union Jack and Fred the pewter tit.

The posters were in different styles, going back through the years – Sunday supplement full-colour and psychedelic design giving way to black-and-white and blocky red lettering. It was like a reverse strip: the older the picture, the more clothed the girls. Over the years, standards had changed – at least insofar as what could be shown on the street.

'Tiger Sharkey, also known as Theresa D'Arbanvilliers-Holmes,' said Zarana, in gossipy museum-guide tones, indicating a wild-haired blonde in a Jungle Jillian leather bikini. 'Married a Tory MP, she did, and pays Boot Boy a fair slice of cake every month not to have the "glamour films" she used to make sent to the *News of the World*. I hope you don't count that as a motive, since she's a love, honestly. Felicity Mane, the Flickering Flayme. On the game in Huddersfield, poor dear. Trixie Truelove. Her proper name's Mavis Jones and she's still here, doin' make-up and costumes. She knitted my snake-wig. Put on a bit of weight since that photo was taken.'

Zarana had accompanied them to a landing, where she paused.

'And here's our founder, bleedin' Royalty with tassels. If I'd half a crown for every cove who comes in here and says birds today ain't fit to tie her G-string, I'd have a villa on Capri and be payin' muscle boys to shake their bums at me.'

The poster showed a slim-hipped blonde posing coyly, Venus-style. Even in faded black-and-white, she was a startler. A platinum rope of hair wound around her neck, across her breasts, about her waist and fanned out to serve as a loincloth. She had huge, sad eyes and a dimple in one cheek.

'Pony-Tail,' said Zarana.

Fred knew. Trev Bailey, who sat two desks along from him at school, once had a 'photography' magazine with Pony-Tail's picture on the cover confiscated by a maths master. Later, the offending article was found in the rubbish bin by the bike sheds, crumpled and suspiciously stained. The teacher was called 'Wanker' Lewis for the rest of his career.

Zarana considered the poster.

'You'd think she invented nudity from the way they rabbit on about her.'

During that two-week stint in a porn cinema, the only film that had jolted Fred awake – and even slightly stirred his interest – was *Views of Nudes*. A scratchy black-and-white 1950s antique about well-spoken naked persons playing volleyball at a Torquay naturist camp, with strategically placed shrubs to save their embarrassment, it was out of place amid the bloodily colourful socks-on couplings of randily joyless Scandinavians as Glenn Miller at the Frug a-Go-Go. *Views of Nudes* was booed by raincoats, until they were stunned to a hush by Pony-Tail. In a blatantly spliced-in, gloriously faded-to-pink colour sequence, she stripped in a stable, getting out of riding habit and jodhpurs (editing tricks were necessary to manage the boots) and whipping her hair about. She frightened the horses but excited the audience; the tally-ho soundtrack was soon augmented by the chink of spare change in active pockets. Fred had to admit Pony-Tail, who could look young as twelve or old as sin, had something.

'Where is she now?' asked Richard.

Zarana made mystic gestures. 'That's the ghosty part. Nobody knows. Or is sayin', if they do. She vanished. She could write her own paycheques if she came out of retirement. Of course, she'll be a crone now. Bleedin' Pony-Tail. I bet it wasn't even her own hair. Nice mince pies, though. I heard she might have been got out of the way, so she could really be a ghost. I think that's why you're here. It's what Busy Boddey's afraid of.'

They looked upwards, where the stairway narrowed. Bulbs were burned out or broken. The next landing was in deep shadow.

'I'll stay here, if you don't mind,' said Zarana.

'Come on, Fred, let's get on with it,' said Richard.

Zarana's fingers touched the lapel of his Crombie jacket, felt the fabric and let him go.

'Be careful, Freddy,' she said.

'Certainly will, Queenie.'

Richard was halfway up, into the dark. Fred left the girl and followed.

III. MR SLUDGE

Fred saw DC Harry 'Busy' Boddey was in a right state. When Fred and Richard entered the ante-chamber, Busy jumped off his stool.

The inner door was smashed off its hinges.

The 'six blokes with sledge-hammers' theory looked better and better.

Neither Fred nor Richard had so much as sipped their tea, but the stench made them raise cups to their mouths, not so much for the swallow but the strong smell.

'See,' said Boddey, nodding at the empty doorway.

Fred got a look into the office beyond. Something limp sat at and over a broken desk. Red splashes Jackson Pollocked over strewn papers, abused glossies, demolished furniture and pulled-down posters.

'Stone the crows,' said Fred.

Busy whimpered. Fred would have marked him down as one of those joke-over-dismembered-body-parts coppers, but this took things to extremes.

Richard had his feelers out – he called them 'mentacles'. He stood straight and calm, eyes fluttered shut, nose raised like a wine-taster doing a blind test, fingers waving like fronds.

'What's the looney up to?' asked Busy bitterly.

Fred slapped him.

'Trying to help,' he told the shocked policeman. 'Now shut up, Busy Lizzie!'

Richard snapped out of it.

'No need for additional ultra-violence,' he said. 'There's been quite enough of that. You, Constable Boddey, give me the court report.'

Busy looked up at Richard. Fred nodded at him.

'This morning, something came here and did... that... to Booth.'

'Very concise. Did you find the corpus?'

Busy shook his head. 'No, it was Brie. One of the girls. Massive knockers. Does secretarial stuff too. She's scarpered. You won't see her Bristols round here again in a hurry.'

'Was anything seen of the assailant or assailants?'

Busy shut up.

'Now, now, come, come. You called Fred for a reason. The Diogenes Club has a reputation. We don't involve ourselves in gangland feuds or routine police-work. We're here for more arcane matters.'

Busy tried hard to stop shaking. 'I saw it,' he said.

'The murder?' prompted Richard.

'The murderer.'

'It?'

'Him, I suppose. When Brie screamed, I came upstairs. It was still here, standing in that doorway. It had done its business, just like that, in seconds, I reckon. Thump thump thump and the show's over, folks, haven't you got homes to go to? It had a big coat, like a flasher, a dirty mac, and a hat, old-fashioned...'

'Tricorn, shako, topper...'

'No, one of those movie-gangster jobs. Trilby.'

'So, we have his clothes described. What about the rest? Size?'

Busy held his hands apart, like a fisherman telling a whopper.

'Huge, giant, wide, thick...'

'Face?'

'No.'

220

'No, you can't bear to remember? Or no, no face?'

Busy shook his head.

'What you said second. Just greyey white, sludge-features. With eyes, though – like poached eggs.'

'A mask,' suggested Fred.

'Don't think so. Masks can't change expressions. Can't smile. It did. It saw me and Brie, and it smiled. How can something with no mouth to speak of smile? Well, it was bloody managing, that's all I can say. God, that smile!'

Busy covered his face again.

Richard looked about the ante-chamber. Spots of blood and something like mud dotted about the doorway, but this room was clean. Floor-to-ceiling shelves held box-files with faded ink dates on their spines. A coffee-table by Busy's stool had a neatly arranged fan of girlie magazines – *Knight*, *Whoops!*, *Big and Bouncy*, *Strict*, *Cherry*, *Exclusive*. An undisturbed coat-tree bore a mohair topcoat, a bowler hat and an umbrella. Savile Row, definitely. Better quality than anyone on a Scotland Yard wage could afford without going into debt.

There was a clear demarcation line. The devastation was confined to the inner office.

'Your Mr Sludge made quite an entrance,' said Richard. 'Splashy, in fact. But the exit was more discreet.'

Busy nodded.

Fred took the constable's chin and forced him to look at Richard.

Busy swallowed.

'It emptied out somehow,' he said, making a swirling gesture, 'as if going down a plughole, then it was just gone, coat and hat and all.'

'Intriguing.' Richard took another gulp of tea, and put his mug down on the cover of *Knight*, blotting the chest of a girl

221

wearing parts of a suit of armour. 'So we have something here substantial enough to wreak considerable damage but capable of, as it were, evaporating. You were quite right to call us, Constable Boddey. If there's a phantasm, golem or afrit in the case, it falls under our purview.'

Fred let Busy go.

He was surprised to find he felt a sympathy twinge for Busy. He wasn't a chancer any more, just a shell-shocked survivor who'd have to live with bad dreams.

Richard produced a scraper from a flapped side-pocket. He ventured gingerly into the office, careful not to brush against anything dripping. He took a sample of something congealed and sticky.

'Sludge, indeed,' he said. 'Plasm of some specie. Ecto-, perhaps. Or psycho-, eroto- or haemo-. Then again, it could just be gunk.'

He scraped it back onto the door-jamb.

'I just need to know one more thing,' said Richard, addressing Busy. 'Who else have you told?'

Busy looked up, a sparkle of the old cunning reminding Fred he was still the same flash git he'd known at Hendon.

'Um,' began Busy.

There was a commotion downstairs. People arriving.

'Not the police,' Richard observed, instantly.

His hawkish brows narrowed. Busy shrank, trying to slip back into shivering wreck status to avoid answering for his actions.

A yelping and ouching indicated someone was being dragged upstairs.

Zarana was pushed into the room. This time Fred caught hold of her. She put her face to his chest so as not to look into Booth's office.

A beef-faced, big-bellied man in a dark suit that had fitted him better in 1965 was at the top of the stairs, wheezing. Charging up two flights was something he hadn't done in a while. Someone (almost certainly a young woman) had persuaded him that a paisley scarf worn under an open violet shirt would make him look less behind-the-times – the sweaty foulard flopped on his sternum like a dead (but with-it) herring.

A pair of heavy lads backed him up.

The newcomer was so used to being a hard man he hadn't bothered to keep in shape. People were still afraid of him for things he'd done years ago. If half what Fred had heard about Mickey 'Burly' Gates were true, people were right. Gates had apprenticed as a meat-cutter at Smithfield's before joining the firm. Throughout his career, Gates had been in meat of one sort or another.

Allegedly, he kept his hand in with his old chopper.

Gates took in Richard, from pointed boot-toes to tumble of long hair.

'Who the bloody hell are you?' he demanded, 'and what the bleeding hell do you think you look like?'

Richard shrugged his eyebrows and commented, 'Charming.'

Then the meat-cutter saw Boot Boy Booth.

'Jesus wept!' he said, involuntarily crossing himself.

'Friend of yours?' asked Richard, casually.

Gates tore his gaze away from the red ruin in the inner office and looked again at Richard, squinting.

'This is them, Mickey,' said Busy Boddey – it didn't surprise Fred that a DC in the OPS was on first-name terms with Burly Gates. 'Specialists in ghosties and ghoulies. The Odd Squad.'

Richard cocked an eyebrow. 'I haven't heard that one before. Not so sure I care for it.'

'I understand about specialists,' said Gates, making an effort to calm down. 'I use them a lot. Like plumbers. If they do a diamond job, I'm a happy chappie and the packet of notes is nice and thick. If they don't… well, they forfeit my custom and, as it happens, tend to retire early. Clear?'

'Crystalline,' drawled Richard, not really listening.

A framed photograph had caught his attention. Pony-Tail, again – in St Trinian's uniform, with hockey-stick and straw boater. Ten years gone, and the girl was still all over Soho.

'Diamond,' said Gates. 'So, get on and specialise. I don't really care what happened, just so long as it don't happen again on my patch. Track down who—'

'What, most likely.'

'…or what did this, and make sure they get put out of business.'

Richard looked at Gates and did something shocking. He giggled.

Gates's red face shaded towards crimson. Sweat steamed off his forehead.

Richard's giggle became a full-throated King Laugh. He made gun-fingers and shot off all twelve chambers at Gates. Fred had to swallow a smirk.

Gates searched his waistband for a chopper. Mercifully, he had left it at home.

Richard shut off his laugh. 'You've made a fundamental error in assessing this situation,' he told Gates. 'I am not a plumber or a cabbie. I am, as it were, not for hire. I cannot be suborned into serving your interests – or, indeed, any but my own. Call me a dilettante if you wish, but there it is. I am here as a favour to my good friend, Sergeant Regent, and because the matter has features of uncommon interest.'

Gates goggled in amazement.

'You evidently consider yourself a power in this district,' observed Richard.

'I could have Eric and Colin snap you like a twig, sunshine.'

Gates's heavy lads pricked up their ears. They cracked hairy knuckles.

'You could have them try,' said Richard, amused. 'It wouldn't advance your cause one whit, but if you feel the need, go ahead. Powerlessness must be a new, disorienting condition for you. I understand your need to attempt to reaffirm yourself. However, if upon second thought you'd rather not annoy me further and leave me to continue my investigations, kindly quit my crime scene. This isn't your fiefdom any more. This is where the wild things are. Is that, ah, diamond?'

Gates's mouth opened and closed like a beached fish's.

He grunted and left. Eric and Colin directed the full frighteners at the room, but only Busy cringed. Richard waved at them, a flutter of farewell and dismissal.

'Toodle-oo, fellows.'

Eric and Colin vanished.

Fred breathed again. He hoped Zarana hadn't noticed him trembling.

IV. LOCAL HISTORY

'Let's see if I have this straight,' began Richard, setting his thimble-cup down on the red Formica table, '"Skinderella's" is owned by that irritable gent Gates, but was managed by a serving police officer? Setting aside that puzzle, I understand that Mr Gates is a big fellow around these parts?'

Zarana nodded. 'He has a ton of clubs. Chi-Chi's, the Hot-Lite in Dean Street, Dirty Gertie's (at Number Thirty), the Prefects' Hut, the National Girlery...'

She had taken off her *Carry On Cleo* gear (on stage, not that Fred had caught her turn), and now wore a lime-green mini with matching knit waistcoat, Donovan hat and shaggy boots. She had nondescript, shortish brown hair – pinned so she could get the wig back on quickly for her 5.30.

They sat in Froff, a Greek Street café. Gleaming, steam-puffing espresso machinery was held over from when it was called Mama Guglielmi's. A new vibe was signalled by deep purple tactile wallpaper, paper flowers stuck to mirrors and sitar muzak. Waiters wore tie-dye T-shirts and multi-coloured jeans wider at the ankles than Fred's sta-presses were at the waist. The staff were wary of Fred. His grown-out skinhead haircut (a 'suedehead') made him look like the natural enemy of all things hippie, but he sussed that they had Soho antennae that twitched if there was a non-bent policeman about. He had pointedly been asked if he'd like a bacon sarnie. As it happened, the one that turned up was excellent, even if he had to make a conscious effort to blank out the memory of Boot Boy Booth's death-site to face his nosh.

Two tables over, a rat-faced herbert in a fringed Shane jacket two sizes too big for his thin shoulders sold silver-foil slivers to fresh-from-the-country kids who were going to be disappointed when they tried to smoke the contents.

'Mr Gates strikes me as somewhat traditional for these environs,' said Richard.

Zarana drew four corners in the air and sniggered.

'Indeed,' said Richard. 'The original Soho Square.'

'Burly Gates started out as meat-cutter,' said Fred. 'Then was a bouncer, for Schluderpacheru.'

'Yeah, for Popeye,' said Zarana. 'Now there's a real creep.'

'Fred, you are familiar with this foreign-sounding person.'

'Konstantin Schluderpacheru. Vice Lord back when we had rationing. Soho was overrun by demobbed blokes with money in their pockets and bad habits picked up in the War. No one's sure where he comes from, but he claims to be Czech. Besides the striptease places, he was – probably still is – landlord for a lot of first- and second-floor properties with single female tenants.'

'Knockin' shops,' said Zarana, with distaste. 'Don't gawp, Freddy. I show it, I don't sell it.'

Richard patted a hand over Zarana's large fist.

'I'm amazed you have such a command of local history,' Richard told Fred.

'It's what Every Young Copper Should Know. Faces and statistics. At the Yard, they print them on cigarette cards.'

Fred was pleased that for once he was filling in Richard on arcana. Usually, it was the other way around.

'Pray continue, Frederick.'

'Come the late fifties, Mickey Gates is a jumped-up Teddy boy rousting drunks at Schluderpacheru's places. He was a double act with a cove by the name of Grek Cohen, who used to be a wrestler. One of those man-mountain types. The story went that you could stick a flick-knife into Grek over and over for five minutes and he wouldn't even notice. Burly and Grek worked up a nice little protection racket, originally targeting Schluderpacheru's competition. Also, they started smut-peddling – brown-paper-wrapped little mags and pics. Gates calls himself a "publisher" now, which means the same stuff on glossier paper. You saw his stuff in Booth's reception area. *Knight*, *Whoops!*, *Cherry*. Those are the "respectable" ones.'

'You're well up on this.'

'Where do you think all the stuff confiscated in raids winds up? Night shifts at police stations get very boring.'

'I was in *Knight* once,' said Zarana. 'A Roarin' Twenties set, shimmerin' fringes, long beads.'

'Schluderpacheru thought porn was peanuts, and let Burly and Grek scurry around picking up grubby pennies. Big mistake. Pennies add up to a grubby pile. They acquired leases to half the district. They were the new Vice Lords.'

'How did their erstwhile employer take that?' asked Richard.

'That's the funny part. Schluderpacheru was in the Variety Club of Great Britain by then. He got into the film business, as an agent and then a producer. He leased his "talent" to quota quickies. Pony-Tail played the victim in a murder mystery, *Soho Girl*. After she got killed and before Zachary Scott found out Sid James did it, audiences lost interest. But when she was on the screen, they sat up to attention. Schluderpacheru reckoned he had the next Diana Dors under exclusive contract. Well, maybe the next Shirley Anne Field. Blond and British, you know. This made him feel like the unpronounceable answer to Lew Grade. He planned to build a whole film around her—'

'*Brighton Belle*,' said Zarana. 'Mavis was goin' to be in it.'

'He was going to give her a proper name. Gladys Glamour, or something. But it didn't happen. Schluderpacheru became a producer, but not with Pony-Tail as his star. She disappeared about that time – presumably wriggling out of the lifetime contract, and making things easier for Shirley Anne Field. Burly and Grek were taking over the clubs and Schluderpacheru had to put up some sort of fight or lose face. If people weren't respectful, which is to say terrified, of him, his empire would tumble. But he also knew he needed to ditch girlie shows if he wanted to be invited to the Royal Film Performance. So, in 1963 or thereabouts, Soho had a not very convincing gang war. In the end, Schluderpacheru divested himself of the clubs – retaining enough of an interest to claim a stipend from Gates.'

'And Grek Cohen?'

'When the dust settled, Grek was nowhere to be seen. His missing persons file at the Yard is still open. In order to make friends again, Schluderpacheru and Gates had to agree neither were to blame for their disagreement. But someone had to be, to satisfy pimps' honour or whatever. Grek was handy, stupid and expendable. That said, God knows how they got rid of him. Not with a flick-knife, obviously.'

'Mavis says it was her,' blurted Zarana.

Richard and Fred looked at the girl. There was a long pause.

'I'm not goin' to be a grass,' she said. 'Life expectancy is short enough in this place.'

'I'm not a policeman,' said Richard. 'And Fred barely counts as a plod. Look at the crimes he's ignoring just by sitting here.'

The rat-faced bogus dealer pricked up his ears, took a good look at Fred and headed for the hills.

'This is all gossip. Mavis tells it different every time. She gets it mixed up with Samson and Delilah. The big thing is that Grek Cohen was besotted with Pony-Tail, devoted like a kid to a kitten, the whole King Kong scene.'

'"It wasn't the airplanes,"' quoted Richard, '"it was Beauty killed the Beast."'

Zarana nodded. 'How else could Popeye and Gates get to Grek? They took Pony-Tail away, threatened to carve her face up unless Grek turned himself over to them, lay down for whatever was comin' – an express train, most likely. Then, the bastards probably did her in anyway, no matter what they say about her now.'

'So, at the bottom of it all, there's an unwilling femme fatale, a lure and a sacrifice.'

'It makes sense,' said Fred, 'two mystery disappearances about the same time. Bound to be a connection.'

Richard clicked a spoon against his teeth.

'It seems singular to me that this Pony-Tail person is so frequently mentioned. As if she were a presiding spirit, patron saint of stripteaserie, the Florence Nightingale of ecdysiasts.'

Fred remembered the girl in the stables. He slowed the film down in memory. Pony-Tail was looking beyond the camera, fixing her eye on one face in the darkness, undressing just for him.

'She can't have been that good,' said Zarana. 'She just took her clobber off to music. It's not astrophysics.'

Richard and Fred were still thinking about her.

'Men,' said Zarana. 'What a shower!'

Something exploded against the window like a catapulted octopus, splattering black tentacles across the glass.

'Interesting,' said Richard.

V. THE FESTIVAL

The girl Fred had scared earlier staggered into Froff, one heel broken, halterneck torn, hair dripping. Tarry black stuff streaked her face and arms.

Outside the star-splattered window, a black-uniformed army marched down Greek Street, lobbing paint-grenades. Advance scouts whirled plastic bull-roarers. Voiceless screaming and sticky missiles generally cleared the way.

A waiter tried to shove the tom back onto the street, but she wasn't shifting. A runnel of blood mixed in with black on her face.

'Assault with a deadly weapon, miss,' said Fred, raising his voice. 'Could you identify the culprit?'

She shook her lopsided head, and said, 'I don't want to get involved. It's not healthy.'

'Nothing you do seems healthy. Have you considered going home to Mum?'

'Who do you think put me out in the first place, PC Plod?'

She sat down at a table and asked for tea, spilling odd coins from a tiny, long-handled purse to prove she could pay for it. She fished out some safety-pins and made emergency repairs to her top. Then, she picked at her hair. The drying, setting goo made unusual spikes. If she kept at it, she might set a new fashion.

A second wave of marchers passed, waving banners. It was less like a parade of protest than a show of force.

'They do this once a bleedin' week,' groaned Zarana.

Fred saw slogans – 'Down with Sin!', 'Heed the Wrath', 'Harlots Out', 'Smite the Flesh-Peddlers'.

'Booth went spare about that little lot,' said Zarana.

'The late, lamented?' prompted Richard.

'Someone must lament, though you'd be hard-pressed to find anyone to own up to it.'

'We never did establish why the Obscene Publications Squad was headquartered in "Skinderella's". If you remember, I did ask.'

Zarana looked to Fred for the nod. He gave it.

'It was a payoff to Boot Boy from Mickey Gates. Booth took a fat profit out of the place. In Soho, the coppers are full partners in the smut rackets. They get all the perks. Law's in the way of folk who want to sell and other folk who want to buy, so who's to complain if the law ducks aside? Then sticks out its greedy hand?'

Richard looked disappointed. His battles took place beyond the ken of the rest of the world, and he hadn't kept up on tediously everyday crime.

'She's right, guv'nor,' said Fred. 'It's an open secret. Every new broom at the Yard promises to sweep clean, then lifts the rock in Soho, takes a look at what's squirming, and decides to do something else. More parking meters.'

'You're telling me that the squad charged with regulating obscenity is actually responsible for disseminating it?'

'More or less.'

'Good grief,' said Richard. 'I assume our friends in black take objection to this laissez-faire situation?'

Zarana nodded. 'When this mob showed up, Gates bent Booth's ear off. He was payin' for protection, so he thought he was entitled to it.'

The marchers wore plain unisex boiler-suits, and had wound black scarves around their heads and lower faces. It must get steamy in those outfits on a hot day, but they were also indistinguishable from each other come an identity parade. They were well-drilled – placard-wavers, bull-roarers and paint grenadiers all in place and working with brisk, brutal efficiency.

'You can't buy them off,' said Zarana. 'Booth tried that straight away. They're god-bothered loonies.'

'There's no explicit mention of God in their various slogans,' mused Richard.

'They call themselves the Festival of Morality,' said Zarana.

Richard looked at the protesters. He steepled his fingers and closed his eyes, reaching out to get a deeper impression of them. Then he snapped to.

'Frederick, are you up-to-date on this movement?'

'Only what I read in the papers. You can imagine why they're here – to take a stand against immorality and licentiousness. They're a reaction to the "permissive society". When blokes like Booth get too blatant, and stop keeping seamy stuff out of sight, someone else will step in and call for a bonfire of the bleedin' vanities.'

'Lord Leaves,' said Zarana.

'Of course,' said Richard. 'Algernon Arbuthnot Leaves, Lord Leaves of Leng. Him, I know of.'

'That's the bloke,' she said, pointing. 'High Lord Muckety-Muck of Killjoy.'

An open-top black limousine decorated with white symbols crawled along at the centre of the procession. Sat on a raised throne-like affair in the back was an old, old man in long black robes and an ear-flapped skullcap. It struck Fred that he really had copied his look from Savonarola. His hands were liver-spotted and gnarled, but he could hold up a megaphone and bellow with the best of them.

'Is he singing?' asked Fred.

'Not exactly Gilbert O'Sullivan, is he?' sniped Zarana.

'You have to applaud the effort,' said Richard. 'He's not afraid of seeming ridiculous.'

Zarana, who obviously took the Festival personally, kept quiet.

Lord Leaves continued to give vent. In the front passenger seat, next to a uniformed chauffeur, sat a twelve-year-old blond boy with a black blindfold over his eyes – presumably to save him from sights that might warp his little mind. The lad strummed an amplified acoustic guitar, accompanying the Father of the Festival. Looking up beside His Lordship was an adoring young woman dressed like some sort of nun, hair completely covered by a wimple, blue eyes blazing with groupie-like adoration.

Fred made out the words.

'Sin and sodomy, lust and lechery... bring about man's fall,

'Filth and blasphemy, porn and obloquy... I despise them all!'

The woman rattled a black tambourine. It struck Fred that she was the most genuinely aroused person he'd seen all day – certainly more turned on than the tarts and punters on the streets.

The insight gave him a weird thrill, which Zarana noticed. She tugged his sleeve, drawing attention to herself with a cattish little frown.

'Not often one hears the word "obloquy" used in a lyric,' said Richard. 'I shall consider writing a letter to *The Times*.'

The tambourine woman's electric gaze passed over the street, as if scouting (quite sensibly) for assassins, and hit on Froff. Fred thought for a moment she was looking exciting hatred directly into his bowels, but then sensed the attention was for Zarana.

He put an arm round her (again).

'Don't let them bother you, luv,' he said.

'Easy for you to say,' she sniffed. 'It takes a week to get that gunk off, and you can't work. In my line, there ain't exactly paid sick days or invalidity benefits.'

'Is that Leaves's granddaughter looking daggers?' Fred asked Zarana. 'High Priestess in charge of ripping out hearts.'

'You should glance at the society pages when flipping through the paper to the racing results,' said Richard. 'That is Lady Celia Asquith-Leaves. His Lordship's wife.'

'Dirty old sod,' breathed Zarana.

'One mustn't rush to judgement,' said Richard, which was quite comical in the circumstances.

An image of His Lordship's wedding night sprang up in Fred's mind. He did his best to try to expunge it completely.

'I bet they read the magazines before throwin' them into the fire,' said Zarana, not helping at all. 'Then get worked up into a lather and...'

'You're making our Fred uncomfortable, Queen of the Nile,' said Richard.

'Sorry, I'm sure,' said Zarana, wriggling close to him.

Fred wished he were somewhere else. Say, sinking knee-deep into freezing mire on Dartmoor with hooded slime-cultists puffing poison thorns at him through blowpipes and ichorous elder things summoned from the bog-bottom padding after him on yard-long, mossy feet.

The parade came to a halt. Uniformed police constables moved in. Their path was blocked by serried ranks of bull-roarers and placard-wavers. The Festival had a solid grasp of demo tactics.

Lord Leaves finished his song and tossed his megaphone to a minion.

He flung back his robes like the Man With No Name tossing his poncho over his shoulder. He wore what looked like a black body stocking, circled with the white symbols that were also marked on his car. He picked up something that looked a lot like a sten gun fed by a thick hosepipe.

Zarana darted under the table.

Fred realised the girl knew more than he did and was probably being sensible, but couldn't resist the street theatre.

Soho residents – 'denizens', really – were mounting some sort of counter-attack, ponces linking arms with toms, bruisers emerging from sex shops and strip clubs to put up a stout defence. They jostled the foot soldiers of the Festival.

Lord Leaves of Leng twisted a nozzle on his gun.

A high-pressure stream of black liquid squirted in an arc, splashing down on the counter-protesters – who scattered.

A disciplined, scripted cheer rose from the black-clad ranks.

'I defy,' yelled His Lordship, unamplified but booming. 'I shall smite.'

He played the jet-spray against windows and hoardings.

Wheeling around, back and forth, Lord Leaves scrawled thick, dripping lines across signage and come-on posters, upping the flow whenever an image of an unclad woman got in the way. The black liquid was thinner than paint but lumpy and staining. Neon tubes fizzed and burst. He aimed his jet at a porn-broker's window, pushing in the glass and smashing down racks of 8mm film loops, Swedish magazines, plastic novelties and brown-paper-bagged glossies. An angry manager lost his footing as he tried to protect his merchandise. He scrabbled around in the wet mess, falling heavily.

The cheers became more genuine. Harsh, mocking laughter.

Zarana peeped up again. 'Tell me when it's over,' she said.

'His Lordship enjoys taking the fight to the fallen,' observed Richard. 'He is something of a showman.'

'You know what these Jesus freaks are like, guv'nor.'

'Those white symbols on his suit and car have nothing to do with Christianity, Frederick. Which is interesting, don't you think? Lord Leaves is a man of great faith, evidently. An inspiration to followers. A black beacon of morality in an age he might deem is going to the dogs. Yet his faith isn't one hitherto associated with morality in the limited sense expressed here. The only thing I've seen in Soho that really goes with those symbols was your dead policeman. Lord Leaves is a great one for smiting and the late DI Booth was certainly smitten.'

Fred looked again at Lord Leaves exulting as liquid filth poured down upon harlots and whoremongers. He considered the blue-eyed priestess, the blindfolded minstrel, the well-drilled troops. The Nazis had been against decadence, too.

'That, my dears,' said Richard, pointing at Lord Leaves of Leng, 'is a Suspect.'

VI. REPEAT OFFENDER

By nightfall, the street looked as if the Luftwaffe were blitzing again. Lights came on by fits and starts, many broken or sparking. The pavement was shiny, as black goo congealed into plasticky, pungent shellac.

Fred tried to avoid getting any on his Docs.

The march turned into a torchlight rally in Soho Square. Lord Leaves sang more songs – 'Cast the First Stone' was surprisingly catchy – between other 'turns'. 'Concerned parents' made halting speeches, and 'fallen souls' recanted previous harlotry at great length and in explicit detail.

Zarana had popped back to 'Skindy's', to see if she needed to go on again. The management might dim the lights this evening, if not in tribute to the late DI Booth then to avoid attracting an angry mob of torch-wielding zealots. She had invited Fred to come watch her Queen of the Nile routine some time when all hell wasn't breaking loose. A snake was involved, apparently.

Richard pottered around ruins, trying to pick up 'impressions'. Fred gathered it wasn't easy. At the calmest of times, Soho was awash with emotional discharge. Now, it was a maelstrom of mixed feelings. If all this energy could be piped to power stations, the United Kingdom wouldn't need North Sea oil.

Fred showed his warrant card to a stray constable and asked for a report. The copper had a splurge of black across his uniform and was looking for his lost helmet. He was in a state of high pissed–offness.

'If this had been a student demo at the Yank Embassy,' complained the constable, 'the Special Patrol Group would be out in body–armour, with CS gas and riot–shields. A hundred arrests before supper–time, commendations all round. Because it's bloody prudes, it was just me and poor old Baxter trying "move along nicely now" on an army of roaring dervishes. Bastards said they'd march tomorrow, then switched schedules. That Lord Leaves is a menace. I'd rather have Hell's Angels any day.'

Fred remembered he still hadn't called New Scotland Yard to share the sad news about DI Booth. At this rate, they would read about it in the morning papers. Richard said a forensics team would only get in the way. It was nice having such pull in high places that he could conduct his own private murder investigation.

Among those who came out to peep at the mess was Mickey Gates.

Through the rolled–down window of an I've–got–money Rolls–Royce, Gates watched, a hard–faced dolly bird in each armpit, foot–long cigar in his gob. Eric and Colin, his monkeys, supervised damage control at a couple of Gates enterprises – a private cinema club and a 'sex arcade'. They chased off scavengers.

'Mr Gates is having a bad day,' said Fred.

The PC cheered up a bit.

'Isn't his Roller illegally parked?' said Fred. 'See if you can rustle up a traffic warden. Get him ticketed.'

The constable laughed. 'Wouldn't I like to see that.'

Gates caught sight of Richard and frowned, even more

furiously. He was on the point of shouting something.

Suddenly, with an almighty *whump!*, a giant invisible boot came down on the Rolls. The roof caved and windows burst. Side-doors buckled, ejecting the matched set of dollies. They crab-walked away, awkward in hot-pants and fishnets, scraping knees and elbows, hairdos loose. At least they were well out of it.

Fred saw Mickey bite off a chunk of cigar and swallow it.

Then metal folded around him. The car lifted off the street, and bent. Metal crumpled with dinosaur screams. Dents appeared in the bodywork. The car's boot ruptured, vomiting a stream of bright, shiny paper – torn girlie magazines.

Richard was nearer than Fred. He considered the sight with cool interest. Sometimes, the guv'nor just plain forgot to be sensibly scared – that was one of the talents Fred brought to the team.

Eric and Colin just stood and gaped, like dozens of others. None of them tried to get too close.

Whatever was crushing the Roller wasn't quite invisible after all.

Greyish stuff swirled up, from the street and the rubble, lacing out of thin air, forming a giant, squat man-shape. Mr Sludge had a domed lump of head but no neck. The bubble body, thick and smeary, distorted light. Power flexed in trunk-like limbs.

Red dripped from the car, which buckled and compacted as if in a press at a wrecking yard. As the Rolls was abused, the giant became more solid. Fred had no doubt this was the phantasm, golem or afrit that had killed Booth. The MO was unmistakable. Mr Sludge glistened, glowing, almost. Blood-squirts shot into its body, lighting up a nerve-network of red traces. Girlie pictures clung to its torso, plastered like papier-mâché layers, smoothing over an enormous musculature. Bright smiles and air-brushed curves, pink tits and bums, faded to grey leatheriness. Dozens of nipples stood out like scabs for a few seconds, then healed.

Like a Herculean weight-lifter, Mr Sludge hoisted high a rough cube that had been a car and its occupant.

Richard tried gestures and incantations, which got the thing's attention but little else.

The grey giant looked down at the man from the Diogenes Club.

Fred remembered what Busy Boddey had said about its mouthless smile. Here it was again. Eyelights shone.

The car-lump was bowled at Richard.

Fred ran and jumped, shoving his guv'nor out of the way. They sprawled on the pavement as the heavy cube tore into the road. The Spirit of Ecstasy bonnet-ornament stuck up from the mess, undamaged, wings shining. Solid workmanship, that. Gates had known enough to buy British.

Mr Sludge bellowed triumph, an unearthly sound produced by leather lungs and Aeolian-harp vocal cords. The roar rose into the skies. Fred's eardrums hurt, and the noise invaded his skull, sprouting pain-blossoms behind his eyes. The giant's substance flowed into sound, and departed with the dying echo. The killer flew up, up and away, passing from this plane of existence. Detritus showered from the space it had occupied. Stiff, faded fold-outs fell like autumn leaves.

Richard sat up, fastidiously flicking bits of filth from his clothes.

'So, it's a repeat offender,' he said. 'Naughty, naughty.'

VII. GO-GO GOLEM

'What was that?' Fred asked.

'As I said, a phantasm, golem, afrit, revenant, whatever. An energy presence.'

'It came out of nothing.'

Richard raised a finger. 'No, Frederick, not nothing. It accumulated matter, stuff. It displaced air. It had a physical effect on this world.'

Fred looked at the metal lump in the road. Workmen with acetylene-torches were trying to crack it open.

'I'll say it was physical.'

An ambulance was on the scene. No one had hopes for the 'patient'. Ordinary police took witness statements, then quietly tore pages from their note-books. Reports of the day's business had been made to Euan Price, Fred's guv'nor at New Scotland Yard, and the Ruling Cabal of the Diogenes Club, Richard's notional superiors. Assistance had been grudgingly offered, but there was a sense that since Fred and Richard had got into the case by themselves – thank you very much, Busy Boddey! – it would be as well if they did the heavy lifting and got it tidied away as quietly as possible.

'It came from nothing, though,' said Fred. 'Empty air.'

'There's no such thing as nothing,' said Richard. 'All sort of stuff washes about. And it can change form, just as water solidifies into ice. Our Mr Sludge gets punching weight from what comes to hand. Very neat and efficient. It's probably tethered to the district. You heard Lord Leaves: "Sin and sodomy, lust and lechery." Potent stuff, that. Especially if you stir in the frustration. Tantalising come-ons whip up the imagination. Then, there's the let-down of finding out that what's on offer can't match what was hoped for. That's what's really wrong with porn, by the way – not that it's against morality, but that it always delivers short measure.'

Fred wasn't so sure. Richard had never seen Pony-Tail.

He thought of Zarana's snake dance – and had an inkling that her reality might live up to what he could imagine. At least he had something to look forward to.

'There's so much surplus emotion around here,' said Richard, 'strewn like used paper tissues. It's a wonder these things don't spontaneously generate all the time.'

The cube cracked. Someone swore.

'It'll be closed casket,' said Fred.

Dark, silent figures joined the crowds, members of the Festival. They watched the cutting-crew extricate the former meat-man from his car. The rally in Soho Square was over. To the faithful, it must seem as if Lord Leaves's prayers produced impressive instant results.

A banner unfurled, proclaiming the wages of sin as death.

'The most interesting thing about our go-go golem,' said Richard, 'is that there's someone inside.'

'A dog-handler, setting the beast on its prey?'

'There is such a person, undoubtedly. A summoner. We'll get to him or her later. But what interests me just now is that some personality persists inside our Mr Sludge. An earthbound spirit, doing the summoner's bidding. It's not easy to get a ghost to follow orders. There has to be some sort of shared purpose. You can't just invoke, say, Henry V, dress him in ectoplasmic armour, and send him out to murder the Bay City Rollers for offences against humanity.'

'But you could get him to fight the French?'

'Precisely. You're learning.'

'It rubs off after a while. So, you've got His Bloody Lordship, who hates the porn barons...'

'And dresses like a high initiate in the sort of religion with a solid track record in revenant-raising.'

Fred remembered Lord Leaves's stern, aged features as he sang or hosed. And his wife's ecstatic excitement. These people loved smiting more than they hated sin.

'So who's he raised up? Some old-time Puritan book-burner?'

'That's a thought. Mrs Grundy or Dr Bowdler? I think

not, though. No point going to all the trouble of ensouling an amorphous mass of power if all it's going to do is sing hymns or write complaining letters.'

Fred thought about the crimes. He set aside the method – the weird stuff – and tried to concentrate on the motive. Maybe thinking of the golem as a plain old crim would help.

'What about a nutter? Someone "down on whores" like that nutcase who threw ammonia in porn cinemas. He hated it that the films turned him on, but couldn't stop himself being in the front row every night. He was looking to blame someone else for his own "urges".'

They were outside the Dog and Duck pub now. There was a buzz about an 'accident' in Greek Street earlier, and a grumbling persisted regarding the Festival's hosepipe habits. But things were getting back to Soho normal – shrill laughs, loud music (Mott the Hoople's 'All the Way From Memphis' from the Dog versus Roxy Music's 'Virginia Plain' from the Crown and Two Chairmen up the road), busy fillies getting close to sozzled blokes, shills from the strip-joints inviting passers-by, plods looking the other way.

Richard considered Fred's Ripper theory and decided it wouldn't do. 'Our victims have both been men. The higher-ups. The inadequates you're talking about go after women – strippers, models, prostitutes, usherettes. Our killer has been precise about who gets hurt. The girls in Gates's car got away with damage only to their dignity.'

'So, we're scouting the afterlife for someone who hates bent coppers and cockney ponces?'

Richard spread his hands.

'Neither of the dead men had fan clubs, mate,' said Fred.

'I can think of two Soho disappearees who might have motive for doing away with Mickey Gates. We can rule out Pony-Tail, the patron saint of strip-tease. Our golem is definitely a feller. Shaped like a former wrestler, bouncer and strong-arm man. "One of those man-mountain types", you said. Droppeth the penny?'

'Grek Cohen?'

Richard snapped his fingers.

'Of course, it would be peachier if Cohen had some grudge against Booth.'

Fred bit his lip.

'Very sharp,' he said. 'In '63, Booth was a rising DC, already knee-deep in Soho rackets. They say he brokered the deal between Schluderpacheru and Gates. It's what set him up for... well, for life. I wouldn't be surprised if he was the one who snatched the girl, to lure Grek. Then, afterwards, he... *thwick!*'

He cut his throat with a thumb.

Richard's brows narrowed. 'It occurs to me that Mr Schluderpacheru might, at present, be a worried man.'

'Couldn't happen to a nicer bloke.'

'Come, come, now, now. We frown on killing people with the dark arts, no matter their character defects. There are often unhappy consequences. It's proverbially difficult to get the genie back in the bottle.'

That was not a comforting thought.

VIII. LORD SOHO

Back at Skinderella's, Fred learned Zarana had done her snake dance to an audience of precisely two paying punters, plus malingerers from a clean-up crew the Yard sent round to remove Booth's body and seal his files. The ghost at the feast was Inspector Roger 'No Mates' Macendale, who had annoyed someone once and been cursed with the job of investigating police corruption cases. Macendale had avoided the OPS mess for years; now, in Booth's office, he was literally treading in it.

Boddey was trying to make himself helpful, hopping from

one foot to the other like a playground semi-outcast trying to get in cosy with bullies by directing their attention to even more marginalised kids. Busy hoped to cast himself as a heroic whistle-blower, soldiering on in an impossible job, never taking so much as a penny from the Vice Lords who'd suborned his guv'nor. It was going to be hard to explain away the Jaguar in the garage of his family villa in Surbiton, and the equally high-maintenance, luxury model girlfriends in rented flats from Belgravia to Hampstead.

With the corpse removed from the premises, Richard had commandeered the phone and was making calls. The Ruling Cabal had pull from the House of Lords to the councils of gangland. Richard used it to solicit backstory on the Festival of Morality, the Big Soho Carve-Up of 1963, the box-office records of Imperial Anglo-British/John Bull Films, Ltd (Graf Konstantin Hermann Rezetsky Bolakov ze Schluderpacheru, prop.), golem-raising rituals, the presumably late Immanuel Cohen ('Grek' was from his wrestling style, 'Graeco-Roman') and the legal tangle of the Obscene Publications Act.

Fred sat in the bar, skim-reading *Confessions of a Psychic Investigator*. He had slipped the book into his pocket earlier and, what with the excitement, forgotten it until now. Chapter One, 'The Ghost Gets Laid', introduced medallion-wearing open-frilly-shirt magician 'Robert Jasperson' and his cheeky cockney wide-boy sidekick 'Bert Royale', who ran a cleaning service to get rid of unwanted spooks. Their first big case was a summons to a posh school where a succubus was molesting older girls and younger teachers with 'midnight gropings and tonguings'. Fred was miffed to discover that the gormless Bert spent all his time peeping through keyholes, getting 'hot and bothered' as the apparently irresistible Jasperson enjoyed 'rampaging rumpy-pumpy' with the French and Biology mistresses, the girls' netball team, his 'tantric sex magickian' assistant Clitoria, and a passing district nurse. At the climax, the randy git solved the case by converting the 'heavily knockered' ghost girlie (a nun walled up centuries earlier for instructing the novitiates in 'Mysteries of the Orgasm') to 'proper hetero shaggery' with vigorous application of his 'mighty shaft'. Lesley Behan (which Fred suspected wasn't her birth name) made Jasperson out to be the sort of psychic detective who couldn't so much as take out an anemometer to read a cold spot in a haunted house without being pounced upon by suburban housewives, high society nymphomaniacs, teenage virgins, Dutch au pair girls, or two-way bike chicks.

'Losin' yourself in a good book?'

Fred looked up from a scene involving an 'Orgy of Bubastis' and saw Zarana, in her civvies.

'Not exactly,' he said, folding the book and hiding it in his back pocket. 'You heard about Gates?'

Zarana cringed. 'Some of the girls from Dirty Gertie's were in after it happened. We're all worried about bein' out of jobs. A lot of us are considerin' other lines of work. Actin', mostly.'

'Including you?'

She looked glum. 'John Bull Films has a company to compete with Hammer, Gruesome Pictures. I've done three-day bits for them – wenches chewed by werewolves, maids bitten on the nipple by vampire queens, dollymops gutted by Reg the Ripper. They couldn't afford Jack, apparently. I don't much fancy gettin' killed over and over again. And those are Popeye's "respectable" pictures. He also makes the Sexploits films... you know, *Sexploits of a Long-Distance Lorry Driver*, *Sexploits of a Merseyside Meter Maid*, *Sexploits of a Quantity Surveyor*. You don't get in those unless you turn up at his palace for bun-fights they call "trade shows" and go upstairs with fat, baldin' men who own provincial cinemas and stink of stale Kia-Ora. I'd rather work in a biscuit factory in Barnet.'

'There are other film companies.'

'Not if you've got a John Bull brand on your bum. Popeye can get you blacklisted. So I ain't goin' to be a Bond girl or a wife of Henry VIII. It'll be back to modellin'.'

Zarana held up her hands, made gestures in the air, turned her wrists.

'Glamour modelling?'

'Hand modellin'. Close-ups of washin'-up liquid bottles bein' squeezed. Fingers brushin' a freshly shaved manly chin.'

She brushed his chin, reminding him that he wasn't freshly shaved.

'Don't you think I have delectable digits?'

'Absolutely, Queenie.'

'You're a love, Freddy Friday. The mitts are too big for the rest of me, but in close-up no one notices.'

She stuck a kiss on the side of his head, tiny tongue slipping into his ear.

Fred realised he was doing better on this case than poor old Bert Royale. Still, Zarana wasn't like the paper-cut-out birds in the book. And, after two appalling crime scenes in one day, he doubted whether he'd be able to raise the enthusiasm for 'rampaging rumpy-pumpy'.

'I'll get by,' said Zarana. 'I'm gettin' too old and tired for strippin'. It's murder on the plates.'

Fred thought she might be about twenty-four.

Richard slid out of the darkness and took a stool next to them, squeezing Zarana's hand in greeting. Fred, for once, was sensitive – Zarana liked Richard, but fancied Fred. One in the eye for Robert Jasperson, Mighty Shaftsman.

'Here's a funny thing,' said Richard. 'Where do you think Lord Leaves of Leng hangs his hat?'

'Some Georgian pile with half Hampshire around it?' ventured Fred.

'And a dinky pied-à-terre in Knightsbridge,' added Zarana, 'handy for Harrods so his wife can shop her little heart out?'

Richard smiled in triumph.

'That's what I thought, but – no – Algernon Arbuthnot Leaves resides right here, in Soho. It's a Georgian, all right. A town house in Golden Square, about five minutes away from this fleshpot. You notice he didn't have his rally outside his own front door and tick off the neighbours. Konstantin Schluderpacheru is one of those, two doors down. According to *Screen International*, John Bull Films have a more or less permanent party going on there. Top folk from showbiz getting zonked, dollies draped around the furniture, hospitality free-flowing, cut-throat deals signed in blood in the bathrooms.'

Fred noticed Zarana shudder. He remembered what she'd said about 'trade shows'.

'Gates lived on three floors above the Hot-Lite, in Dean Street. DI Booth had a split-level mews flat off D'Arblay Street for which he didn't pay rent. Fred's old classmate Harry Boddey makes do with five spacious rooms and a rooftop garden in Ramillies Street. Soho is the place to live, it seems.'

'I share with two other girls in Falconberg Court, off Soho Square,' said Zarana, unashamed. 'Handy for the clubs.'

'Undoubtedly. But it's His Lordship who stands out, as it were.'

'That explains why he's so worked up about smut,' said Fred. 'What with him being local. Probably worried about his wife getting a shock every time she pops out for a pinta. The place fills up with blokes out looking for… well, you know. A decent woman isn't safe.'

'I doubt Lady Celia does her own popping, Frederick. Folk like the Leaves have people to do that for them.'

Fred felt a full-bore glare aimed at him. Zarana was furious.

He hadn't thought through that 'decent woman' remark and had dug a hole it would take a lot of fancy footwork to get out of.

'No woman is safe,' he amended, which actually didn't make things better.

Those model's hands made knuckly fists.

'You know what I mean,' he said, exasperated, fending her off. 'You must get as much unwanted aggro out there as anyone.'

Zarana cooled and decided to let him off with a vicious pinch.

'Fair point. When I walk home, if I can't get a bouncer to see me to my door, I wrap up in an old coat that makes me look like someone's grandmother. Even then, idiots give me stick. They see you naked and think they know about you.'

'Besides, there's something weird about Leaves's wife,' said Fred. 'Did you see her face? She might be against filth and fun, but she's charged-up about something.'

'Yeah, I know,' admitted Zarana. 'Among his other earners, Gates puts out – used to put out – a spankin' mag. You know, "It's six of the best 'pon your quiverin' buttocks, Fiona!" Lady Leaves looks like a *Strict* model. One of the thrashers.'

Fred liked the idea of Lord Leaves flicking through a porn mag before writing his next morality song and seeing wifey's bright little eyes staring up from a fladge lay-out. Under her wimple and robe, Lady Celia could easily be wearing black leather and straps. He tried to stop thinking of that. It was all Lesley Behan's fault, for warping his mind.

'I've looked over some of Lord Leaves's recent speeches,' said Richard. 'He continually harps on the theme of himself as the last moral man in Soho, surrounded by a rising tide of obscenity, crying *halt!* to the advance of corruption. He sounds like someone who wants something back. This whole square mile.'

IX. PRIVATE FILES

Boddey was in handcuffs, being eased firmly towards the door and a waiting Black Maria. *About time too,* thought Fred.

'What are you doing him for, sir?' he asked DI Macendale.

'Tampering with evidence, for a start.'

'Freddo, it weren't me,' pleaded Busy.

'Files upstairs have been filleted,' said Macendale. 'We've got enough to hang Booth and a whole lot more, but choice items have been spirited away…'

Richard was interested. 'What, specifically, is missing?'

Macendale looked glum. 'Hard to say. But gaps are obvious.'

'Constable Boddey,' said Richard, 'have you any ideas what ought to be there but isn't?'

'I didn't touch it!'

'I didn't say you did,' said Richard. 'I asked you if you knew what it was.'

'Will it help me?' Busy asked, a tiny spark of cunning twitching the corners of his mouth. It was the ghost of his smirk.

'It will help us,' said Richard, gesturing to keep Busy's attention.

Macendale shook his head. He wanted to get home to his cocoa and be up early tomorrow to swoop on high-ranking bent coppers. He would already have Busy down as grass-in-training, ready to cut a deal to get the higher-ups named. The people who'd let Booth get away with it all these years.

Busy swallowed. He had got more tear-streaked throughout the day.

'I'd have to look.'

'Under no circumstances…' began Macendale.

Richard unfolded a document and presented it to the inspector. Macendale's lips moved and his eyes swivelled from side to side as he read. Richard kindly pointed out official seals and signatures.

'Uh, carry on, Mr Jeperson,' said Macendale, fuming.

Richard took back the precious document, and slipped it into an inside pocket.

'Let's take Constable Boddey upstairs,' he said.

Busy shrank with terror. Macendale at least got enjoyment from that, and manhandled his prisoner up to Booth's office.

A door that looked like a broom cupboard led to a tiny space lined with metal filing cabinets. Locks were smashed. Richard took an interest in the damage, which could have been done with a sledge-hammer. He scraped dried scum from a shiny dent in the dull metal and showed it to Fred.

Only two people at a time could get in the room, and they found it cramped if any drawers were pulled out. Richard withdrew and let Macendale supervise Busy as he went through the files. The inspector kept a close eye on the miscreant – as if expecting him to grab and swallow something incriminating. At that, Fred wouldn't have put it past him.

Richard took Fred aside.

'Our Mr Sludge has subtler habits than we thought,' he said. 'Smash-kill-grind-crunch is one thing, but filching evidence from locked cabinets in a hidden room suggests a lighter touch. That's where our summoner comes in.'

'Still think it's Leaves?'

Richard considered. 'Booth's files would interest a moral crusader. In addition to protesting against the mere existence of licentiousness, I assume Lord Leaves agitates against folk who profit from immorality, encouraging their prosecution on criminal grounds. I imagine that's why Booth was first on the to-kill list – it should have been his job to pursue Gates and the like for what I assume were many, many infractions of the letter of the law.'

'Campaigners have tried private prosecutions,' admitted Fred. 'Stooges fronting the sex shops or porn cinemas get slapped with huge fines, which are paid promptly in big bundles of cash. Confiscated stock is replaced by closing time, and some new face is behind the counter the next day. Burly Gates rarely even gets mentioned in court.'

Macendale brought Busy out of the file-room.

'So?' asked Richard.

'He's shamming,' said Macendale.

'I'm not,' whined Busy. 'Honest. All that's missing is old stuff. Records from the sixties. Memorabilia.'

'Memorabilia?' asked Richard, intrigued.

'Publicity eight-by-tens, brochures, mags. Too tame for today's market, but nostalgia is booming. Private collectors pay high prices for vintage smut. Anything with Pony-Tail is worth a packet.'

Fred and Richard exchanged a look. Pony-Tail, again. Was Grek still trying to rescue his tasselled princess?

'Booth had it salted away. Came with the place. Called it his school-fees fund. He had kids.'

'That's all that's gone?' asked Richard.

Busy wriggled, which was what a shrug looked like with handcuffs.

'There's something else,' said Richard.

Busy couldn't look away from Richard's eyes.

'It's other... investments,' admitted Busy. 'Eight millimetre films of tarts who've got new lives and want to keep old ones forgotten. Explicit photos of girls, and some lads as well, with prominent people – film and TV stars, business magnates, politicians, policemen, judges, pop singers. You can imagine the kinkiness, and how eager they are to keep it hush-hush. Some were paying off like rigged slot-machines.'

'Blackmail,' said Richard.

Busy wriggled again. 'That's it. That's all of it.'

Fred remembered Zarana had mentioned Booth was milking

a former stripper to keep her stag films out of the Sunday papers. Evidently, it was a cottage industry. That bulked out the suspect list, though – with the goods flown – it'd be hard to add actual names.

'It's no surprise Booth and Gates were in the blackmail racket,' said Fred.

'Not Gates,' said Busy, surprised. 'The other one, Schluderpacheru.'

X. THE PARTY SCENE

Golden Square, London W1. Handy for Wardour Street, where all the film companies – major and (very) minor – keep offices. A semi-secluded haven of dignified mansions off Brewer Street, the (even) sleazier continuation of Old Compton Street.

A hop south was the Windmill Theatre, where nude girls had been appearing nightly since the War. The Windmill boasted 'We never closed,' despite air raids and police sweeps, working within the law of the day by presenting bare lovelies in posed tableaux. Vice squad officers kept reserved seats, allegedly prepared to haul the curtain down if a gooseflesh girl so much as blinked. Fred assumed the predecessors of Boot Boy Booth just enjoyed the ogling opportunities, and the thick envelopes of ten-bob notes mysteriously slipped into their programmes. The Windmill was now a dad's idea of naughty – patriotic songs and patter comedians, and mere glimpses of skin. It was rendered outmoded by flickering X-certificate fare on offer in Piccadilly Circus at the Moulin and Eros sex cinemas (the latter opposite the statue of Eros), let alone the clubs, 'revues' and in-all-but-name brothels clustered at the lower end of Berwick Street. Plus *Oh, Calcutta!*, settled in for a long run at the Royalty Theatre: a Windmill-style show with sarky sketches and nudes that moved, suitable for trendy poseur and carriage trade alike.

Konstantin Schluderpacheru's town house might as well

have sported a huge neon sign with 'Bad Scene' written on it. The windows were open but curtained. Shifting, multi-coloured lights gave the building a flashy, disco come-on look. Live music poured out, heavy on the bongos and the fuzz-pedal. Glittery people came and went, in states of disrepair. A Eurovision Song Contest runner-up clung to the square's railings, bird-thin shoulders exposed by her backless dress, heaving liquid vomit into the bushes. A working-class novelist swigged from a pint-mug of vodka, and berated the pop princess. He blamed her for his inability to write anything worthwhile since moving from Liverpool to Hampstead and Ibiza.

'No wonder Lord Leaves hates these people,' said Richard.

Two doors down, His Lordship's house was dark and shut up tight. At ten-thirty in the evening, all good moral crusaders should be tucked into their twin beds, eyes screwed shut, ears plugged against the seepage of party noise. Or else peering with night-vision scopes at the comings and goings two doors away, keeping careful note of the names and faces.

Schluderpacheru might be the King of Blackmail, but Fred had no doubt that the Festival would use the same tactics. Lord Leaves needed a flock of politicians and newspaper people in his pocket. No one made a better, more vocal supporter of decency than a dignitary with something to hide.

As expected, Schluderpacheru's front door was guarded like a *Führerbunker*. With the soaring death rate among the host's known associates, extra muscle was packed in. Skin-headed ex-boxers in tuxedos stood by. Fred spotted a couple of off-duty plods stationed about the square, moonlighting to cover their hire-purchase payments.

'Come on, lads,' said Zarana, linking arms with Fred and Richard, and steering them towards the door. 'Teeth and smiles.'

There were flashbulb photographers in wait.

After Richard had theorised that it would be difficult to secure an entrée into the Schluderpacheru house, Zarana pointed out that it was one of the many places in London to which entrance was impossible unless you were, or were with, a stunningly beautiful girl. She then dug out her standing invitation, initialled K.S. in green ink. When not working her Queen of the Nile routine, Zarana did a high-society act as 'Contessa de Undressa'. With different make-up and costume, she looked like a different person. In full Contessa drag, she wore a floor-length red silk evening dress secured by four tiny-but-sturdy clasps, an upswept blond wig (complete with tiara) and a boxful of impressive paste jewels. Thanks to spike-heels and the towering wig, she was a foot taller. She looked down her patrician nose like someone who would snub the Royal Family as middle-class German parvenus. If she kept her mahf shut, the illusion was perfect.

To Richard, this was a stroke of luck. He had no qualms about letting an 's.b.g.' join the fun. A semi-official amateur himself, he would take help from whoever offered, assuming they were capable of taking care of themselves. Even with multiple deaths and supernatural maniacs in the case, Richard saw it as a bit of a lark that would be jollier with a pretty face along. Fred was less cavalier: from their earlier chat, he knew Zarana would put herself in an uncomfortable position by taking up the green-initialled invitation. She assured him that Schluderpacheru's guests could hardly be a bigger shower than the Skindy's clientele and besides she could rely on him to protect her. That was a joke, but he took it seriously. She covered doubt well – she was a skilled performer, after all – but Fred picked it up. Again, it struck Fred funny that where Zarana was concerned, he was more in tune with the vibes than the supposed 'sensitive'.

Zarana presented the invitation to a squat, thick man who wore sunglasses after dark and turned on a full-wattage smile.

'This is Happenin' Herbert, the pop artist,' she said, indicating Richard, who flashed the peace sign. 'And this is the famous Fred, who you must have read about in the Sunday supplements.'

The goon clocked the 'K.S.', returned the gilt-edged card to Zarana, and stood aside. The door opened.

The mirror-lined reception hall multiplied their images to infinity. Fred wore a white dinner jacket appropriated from the Skinderella's costume store (what act was it part of?) and now saw it didn't really go with his jeans and Docs. He tried to be the sort of Fred who made sure he got written up as fashionable, then wore something else equally stupid when people copied him.

One of the mirrors had a tell-tale grey-veil tint. There would be two-way glass all over the house, especially in the upstairs bedrooms, and cine-cameras grinding away, adding to the Blackmail King's investment portfolio. Fred resolved not to use the toilet while he was there.

Zarana made a kiss-mouth at the mirror.

They proceeded into a large, half-sunken room full of chattery people and flashing lights. On a stage, a combo performed 'She's Not There', trying not to mind that nobody was paying attention. In the centre of the ballroom was a bath of light – a swimming pool the size of a family plot, with a lighting array inset into the walls. A very drunk, very white girl wearing only a bikini bottom sat on the edge, splashing with her little legs, making waves that broke against the chest of a fully dressed, white-haired man who floated with a dreamy smile stuck on his face, puffing happily on a pipe of tobacco and hash, the wings of his Ganex raincoat spread out like lily-pads.

'That's—' began Fred.

'Yes,' said Richard.

'And with him is—'

'Yes, her,' said Zarana. 'She's in all the Sexploits films, and

Stow It, Sandra. Not much of an actress, but she does this trick with her mouth and two golf balls that turns strong men to custard. I worked with her once. She's a right cow.'

'Blimey,' said Fred. 'You wouldn't have thought it. I'd have expected him to be with Lord Leaves's crowd, protesting. He couldn't exactly show up at his party conference with her on his arm and expect to get re-elected.'

'Don't be so sure, Freddy,' said Zarana.

'I'd say something about "strange bedfellows",' said Richard, 'but I suspect that the beds here have seen a lot stranger.'

A small, round man in a skin-tight moiré kaftan approached Zarana, pupils contracted to pinpricks, sweating profusely. He stuck out his tongue, which had a half-dissolved pill balanced on its end, and reached for Zarana with chubby, wriggly hands. Fred slapped him away and wagged a finger. He looked as if he was about to cry, then latched onto a passing black girl with a silver wig and matching lipstick and paddled along in her wake.

'Business as bleedin' usual,' she said.

'*Ou se trouve* mine host?' asked Richard.

She scanned the room. 'Not here. There's a room upstairs, for his inner circle. Wood panels, ghastly pictures of satyrs and fat bints, hundred-year-old brandy, private screenin' room. Popeye holds court there. Though most of his cronies are here. You can tell them because they look bloody worried.'

Dotted throughout the senseless crowd were furrowed faces.

Richard hummed. 'The oases of desperation do stand out somewhat. Or, at least, sobriety.'

'Ever seen that Vincent Price film about the fancy-dress ball?'

Fred knew what Zarana meant. '*The Masque of the Red Death*?'

'This is that, isn't it? Rich people makin' animals of themselves tryin' to have a good time, with the plague outside, ravagin' the countryside.'

'And the Red Death approaches the castle doors,' said Richard.

'It's time Death knocked here like bleedin' Avon callin',' said Zarana.

'Let's slide upstairs and try to see Prince Prospero,' said Richard.

Fred turned to Zarana to tell her to find a loitering spot in the crowd and wait for them.

'No fear, Freddy,' she said. 'You're not leavin' me behind. It's not safe here.'

A couple of football players with enormous bouffant perms and mutton chops shaped like Roman helmet cheek-pieces caught sight of Zarana and began dribbling towards the goal area. They wore suits that flapped like flags.

'Point taken,' said Fred.

XI. COMING IN AT THE END

Without Zarana, they would never have found the inner sanctum. Schluderpacheru's house was like a funfair maze: zigzag corridors that cheated perspective, flock wallpaper with an optical-illusion theme, floor-to-ceiling joke paintings of doors, set decoration left over from Gruesome Pictures, actual doors chameleoned into walls, burning bowls of heady incense. There were chalk-marks on the floor, recently scrawled runes.

'Schluderpacheru has taken precautions,' said Richard, toeing a symbol. 'I suppose he learned in the old country.'

Zarana led them round a corner and they found themselves looking up at a nine-foot-tall man, with a distinguished rising wave of grey hair and a superbly cut, wide-lapelled suit. He was sleek, with shining, somehow wicked eyes, and wore a medieval armoured glove.

It was a lifelike portrait, painted directly onto a wood panel.

'That's Popeye,' said Zarana. 'Larger than life and twice as creepy.'

One of his eyes was brown and lazy-lidded, the other green and staring.

Voices came from behind the picture, raised but indistinct, arguing in a language Fred didn't recognise.

'There's a trick to this,' said Zarana, patting the portrait. She found studs on the metal glove, and twiddled them. 'Boys and their bleedin' toys.'

With a click and a whoosh, the painting split diagonally and disappeared into recesses.

Beyond was a room illuminated by a blazing fire in an open grate – in contravention of the Clean Air Act, Fred noted – and burning oil-lamps. Two men were outlined by flame-light, both wearing symbol-marked dressing gowns, locked in struggle, their argument turned physical. One was Schluderpacheru, under-sized in person, hair awry. Half his face was wrinkled with effort, but the left side was plastic surgery-smooth, with a fixed, glaring green eye. He had the upper hand, but Lord Leaves – for all his years – fought fiercely; his fingers sank deep into Schluderpacheru's windpipe, incantations rattled in the back of his throat. In one corner shrank Lady Celia, holding a fold of habit over her face like an Arab wife, eyes startlingly bright and excited.

Swirling in the air before the fire were scraps of matter in the shape of a big man, struggling to cohere but tearing apart as much as he came together. Mr Sludge – Grek Cohen – had an invitation to the party, but wasn't here yet.

Everyone froze to look at them. Even the phantasm.

'We seem to have come in at the end of the story,' said Richard.

Schluderpacheru and Lord Leaves spared them barely a glance, then got back to their grappling. The artificial side of the host's face bulged. His eyeball popped, escaping its wet red socket. The egg-sized glass eye fell heavily, thumping Lord Leaves on the forehead. His Lordship, stunned, lost his grip and

Schluderpacheru – who presumably couldn't pull that trick twice – dropped him. The King of Blackmail passed a hand over his hair, prissily fixing its dove-grey wave in place, but didn't seem concerned about his empty eye-socket.

'I know who you are, magician,' Schluderpacheru told Richard. 'And I don't need help. This war of witchery is about to end. To my satisfaction.'

He took a metal triangle from a stand, holding it like a trowel. It gleamed, two sides sharpened to razor-edges. Schluderpacheru dropped to one knee, raising the triangle high, then brought the killing point down heavily. Lord Leaves's breast-bone snapped.

Lady Celia yelped, but her husband said nothing.

The wedge-knife was embedded in His Lordship's chest. He kicked, leaked a little, and was still.

'There,' said Schluderpacheru. 'That's done. No more Festival. No more bother.'

Smug and suave, he considered the man-shaped cloud.

'Go away, Grek,' he said. 'Your summoner's dead. You've no place here, no toehold in this world. You should have stayed where you were.'

Matter swarmed thickly, lacing together. Embers from the fire were sucked up and clustered into a burning heart. Stuff came from somewhere, from all around, and knitted. Greyish liquid seeped out of the air, running into and around the big shape, slicking over. A big-browed face formed out of the darkness. It looked down on the one-eyed man.

For a moment, Schluderpacheru was puzzled. He glanced at Lord Leaves, to make sure he was dead, then – panic sparking in his remaining eye – around the room, fixing on each face in turn.

'You—' he blurted.

Grek Cohen was solid now, a colossal statue of sludge, boiling with ghost-life. He gave off a spent-match stink.

Huge hands clapped, catching Schluderpacheru's head. The top of his skull popped and his one eye leaked blood as his face was ground to paste between rough, new-made palms.

Zarana shoved her face into Fred's jacket, again. Richard whistled. Cohen lifted Schluderpacheru – his arms and legs flopped limp, his shoes dangled inches above the carpet. Cohen tossed the corpse into the fireplace. The robe flared at once, then fire began to eat into the flesh. Foul cooking smell filled the room.

'That's the last of them,' Richard addressed the colossus. 'The three who betrayed you, Mr Cohen. The three who did away with the girl you died for. And Lord Leaves, too. You have no master here. Your purpose is achieved. Yet you remain. Why, I wonder?'

Richard walked up to the golem, examining him as if he were thinking of buying. Grue dripped from its spade-sized hands. Fred held Zarana, and looked around the room.

Lady Celia was mad, poor love, tearing at her habit.

Richard made some experimental gestures. Cohen stood solid.

'Hmmn, interesting. By all rights, you should evaporate. This is a rum do.'

Lady Celia's wimple came apart, leaving her pale face framed by an Alice band. Her unconfined hair poured out – impossible lengths of it, blinding white-blond, shining in firelight.

In a flash, Fred put it together. It was dizzying, sickening.

'Pony-Tail,' he said.

Zarana dared to peep.

'So it bleedin' is,' she exclaimed. 'Wonders never cease!'

Richard also directed his attention to Lord Leaves's young widow.

Lady Celia stood up, shedding the remains of her habit as elegantly as she had ever undressed, slipping the band off her crown, shaking out her hair.

'Now I see what they were talking about,' said Richard.

The woman was nude, Godiva-curtained by her hair. It seemed alive, like Medusa-tendrils. She gathered the mane in her hands, and held it at the back of her neck, winding her band about it. She had her pony-tail again.

She couldn't have been thirty yet; how young had she been when she was a striptease star? She hadn't been legal, for certain.

'Grek Cohen had no master, just a mistress.'

Lady Celia nodded to Richard. She formed a sly smile.

Fred felt it again, the warmth this woman projected. An icy warmth, to be sure, but persuasive. He saw the guile working on Richard too, on the thing that had been Grek Cohen. This was a woman a man wanted to shield – he would put himself between her and any horror, and think the prick of a blade-point in his spine was the first touch of a caress.

Pony-Tail stood over Lord Leaves.

'Goodbye, Daddy,' she said. She had a finishing-school accent, clear and sharp as crystal. She raised her bare foot to his face, stroked his slack cheek with her toes, then deftly scraped his eyes shut. 'You were always my first.'

'Clouds of mystery part,' said Richard.

Pony-Tail giggled, and looked fifteen again. 'Have I been naughty?'

'Does he know what you did?' Fred asked.

She looked at him, teasing and quizzical. Fred indicated Cohen.

'Does he know it was you? Booth, Schluderpacheru and Gates didn't kidnap you in 1963. I'll bet it was your idea. His original body is under a foundation stone somewhere, isn't it? Did you do it yourself, or just watch? Was he happy anyway, just that you smiled at him as the concrete poured in? What a mug! Ten years on, and he's still your pet, isn't he? This has all been cleaning house. Had they started blackmailing you – those idiots! – threatening to expose Lady Celia Leaves as the notorious Pony-Tail? That would be one for the *News of the World*. Scupper His Lordship's Festival of Morality once and for all. Or was it just money they wanted?'

She smiled, enigmatically.

'You know what they really wanted?' she said, tilting her head to one side. 'More than money, more than business as usual, more than power? They wanted me. They wanted me back.'

She did a few steps, hair alive around her shoulders.

'Pony-Tail… returns,' she said, presenting herself. 'Pony-Tail… rides again!'

Fred fancied Cohen was smiling, appreciating her act. He had never really been fooled, but her act was just so damned good that it was impossible not to play along. Fred guessed Lord Leaves had been the same, opening his big book of spells just for a wink and a smile and a peek.

'I suppose this is your final performance,' said Richard.

'Maybe not. What with everything, I'm Queen of Soho. No one in the way. The Festival will follow my lead. Can you imagine what I can make them do? It'll be a twenty-four-hour riot. And I can buy or run everything else in sight. Maybe I will come back, do the shows and the films and the telly. Only this time, I'll do it for me, not them, not men, not you.'

She laid her head against Cohen's pebbled side, a girl petting her horse.

'It's the dancing, isn't it?' asked Richard, fascinated.

'Very clever, Mr Magician,' she said. She bent over double from a full-stand and touched her toes, then sprang back upright, hands on hips, perfectly balanced, perfectly supple. 'Yes, it's the dancing. Daddy started me off. He brought me up to be an initiate of Erzuli, Baphomet and Nyarlathotep. Ritual dance, steps along the paths of power. I had to go out into the world, break away from the Festival, find my own dance. Then I had to go back, for a while. It was part of the pattern. Now, I have new steps, new paths, new dances. I don't need any of them any more.'

She was always in motion, dancing to the rhythm of her heartbeat. She was a white flame, endlessly mesmerising, lovely but deadly.

'What about him?' asked Fred.

Pony-Tail looked up at Cohen's caricature of a face, almost fondly.

'He's my masterpiece,' she said. 'How many other strippers really can dance to raise the dead?'

'You know a lot of dead people,' Richard observed.

'I'm afraid I shall know some more, soon.'

Zarana flashed anger at the woman.

'You ain't that special, you know.'

'My friend would argue with you,' said Pony-Tail, concentrating.

Cohen reacted to her change of mood, swelling into a more menacing aspect.

Richard muttered magics, which the dancing priestess dispelled with blown kisses.

'She's not your friend, Grekko,' said Zarana. 'She killed you, for a start.'

'He knows, he doesn't care. None of them would care. Because it was me. Next to me, you're nothing, missy.'

Zarana faced up to Pony-Tail.

Cohen's arm rose, ratcheting like a guillotine blade. Fred stepped forward, to pull Zarana out of the way.

The girl eluded him and bore down on Lady Celia. The Queen of the Nile versus the Queen of Soho. Pony-Tail meets Contessa de Undressa. No holds barred. One fatal fall for the crown.

Zarana punched Pony-Tail in the stomach. Cohen roared.

Lady Celia doubled, hair tenting around her, then recovered in an instant and flicked out with contemptuous fingers. She twisted a clasp off Zarana's shoulder, and the dress came apart. Zarana held the scraps to her body, hobbled.

'I can't believe that rag is still kicking around. It was made for me.'

Fred helped Zarana stay on her feet. He looked from the cockney Egyptian, awkward in the too-loose gown, to the white goddess, sinuous and unashamed in the firelight. Like everyone else, he dreamed of Pony-Tail; the difference was he knew she wasn't real.

'After this, I suppose the big fella's finished,' said Fred. 'All work done.'

Pony-Tail cocked her head, considering.

'I might bring him out for special occasions. Summoning is an effort, but he's worth it, don't you think?'

'You hear that, Immanuel?' said Fred. 'After this, you're going back in the attic.'

Cohen was a statue, arm up.

'Good work, Frederick,' said Richard. 'Keep at it.'

'You did all this to be with her, and she's shafted you. Again. Are you really as dim as they say? The cleverclogs – Burly Gates, Boot Boy Booth, Popeye Schluderpacheru – they all laughed at you, Grek. Know what I mean? The big ape doolally over the princess. Like King Sodding Kong, they said. When they decided to dump you, she leaped at the chance to help. It was how she bought her way out, got back into His Lordship's house. Couldn't get into the Royal Enclosure with a lovesick gorilla mooning about, could she?'

'None of this matters,' said Pony-Tail, bored. 'Really.'

'And now you've done for them all, and you still don't get

the girl! Mate, you have been fitted up for a proper set of cap and bells. You must be the biggest mug punter in Soho.'

The huge arm came down. The hand closed, on Pony-Tail's rope of hair.

'Ouch,' she said, irritated.

Cohen held her by a leash.

Fred saw a glint of annoyance in her eye, an unattractive, petty expression. Then a sense of what was suddenly lost, a bulb of panic sprouting.

Thick arms hoisted Lady Celia Asquith-Leaves, the incomparable Pony-Tail, off the floor and hugged her to Cohen's chest, her struggling body shoved into the muck and mud of its trunk. Her arms and feet stuck out, flapping and kicking. Her face sank under the surface. Grey mass surged around the screaming O of her mouth, then filled it, staunching her noise.

'Finally,' said Richard.

Now Grek Cohen had Pony-Tail, rather than the other way round, Richard's gestures and incantations had an effect. The colossus, growing insubstantial, rose like a hot-air balloon, bumping the ceiling. On its excuse for a face was a last smile.

'I think a withdrawal is in order,' said Richard.

Fred and Zarana backed out of the inner sanctum. Richard followed, keeping up a stream of reverse conjurations.

'Where's his wand?' asked Zarana.

'It's in the fingers,' said Richard.

'Magic.'

The colossus shrank to the size of a floating man, Grek Cohen superimposed upon Pony-Tail, her limbs encased in his, her face shrieking soundlessly through his battered mask, her electric eyes staring madness through his dull, dead lamps.

The carpet pulled up and spiralled around the phantasm, spilling flaming oil and rolling Leaves away. Cohen contracted to a dozen flaming points and whooshed into darkness.

The girl was gone with him, leaving only her hair. It drifted to the floor, strands crackling as they brushed flame. Swathes fell about like cast-off string.

The gorilla got the girl, which should count as a happy ending. Fred hoped never to see either again.

'The socially conscious thing would be to put out that fire,' said Richard, 'before the house burns down around the guests.'

Zarana shifted a vase and disclosed a fire-extinguisher.

'Just the ticket.'

As she tossed the extinguisher to Richard, her dress finally fell off.

Fred couldn't look away. She noticed.

'That's better,' she said. 'I was worried. I thought that cow had you under her bloody spell, like she had all the other idiots.'

After long, brazen seconds, she gathered up the gown and fastened it.

Weirdly, the little fiddle she did to reassemble her costume and cover herself struck Fred as sexier than Pony-Tail getting her kit off.

'There's no comparison, luv,' said Fred.

Richard unloosed a surge of white foam at the flames.

XII. SEXPLOITS OF A PSYCHIC INVESTIGATOR'S ASSISTANT

Near dawn, in the big bed in her tiny room in Falconberg Court, Fred finally drifted towards sleep.

As far as he was concerned, Zarana was the real Queen of the Nile.

A warm, dry, intimate touch slid across his belly.

'Luv, I'm not sure I could manage again…'

She pressed her fingers to his face and he realised he had

spoken too soon. She planted a tongue-twisting kiss on him. He pulled her closer, as they negotiated the tangle of sheets.

The sliding touch across his stomach was still there.

Zarana broke the kiss and stroked his chest, fingertips moving towards the slithering touch.

'Freddy, meet Ramsbottom.'

He was fully awake now, and – as Lesley Behan might have it – 'raring for rumpy-pumpy'. But there was a new player in the game.

'Ramsbottom?' he demanded.

'The other bloke in my life,' said Zarana.

In the pre-dawn light, Fred discovered he and Zarana were wound together in the coils of a contented snake.

'Love me, love my python,' said Zarana.

'Fair enough,' said Fred.

~≈ THE SERIAL MURDERS ≈~

I.

'Surely, this is common-or-garden crime,' said Richard Jeperson, knuckle-tapping one-way glass, getting no reaction from the woman in the interrogation room. 'The Diogenes Club doesn't do ordinary murders.'

'Don't watch ordinary television either, do you?'

Inspector Euan Price had a strong Welsh accent: 'you' came out with extra vowels, 'yiouew'.

'The odd nature documentary on BBC Two,' he admitted, wondering what the goggle-box had to do with the price of tea in China.

'And *Doctor Who*, sir,' put in Fred Regent, Richard's liaison with Scotland Yard.

'Professional interest,' explained Richard. 'If you had Daleks, we'd do Daleks. Or Autons. That would be Diogenes Club material. We are the boys – and occasional girl – who cope with the extra-normal. This is so... so *News of the World*.'

'"Jockey Ridden to Death by Top Model",' said Vanessa, the 'occasional girl' Richard had thought of. 'Sport, crime, smut... just needs a randy vicar to tinkle all the bells.'

Richard looked again at the murderess beyond the mirror. She wore jodhpurs and a scarlet huntswoman's jacket. Her hard riding hat was on the table, but her blond hair was still bunned up. He might assume the only creature Della Devyne wanted to see killed had a brushy tail, pointed ears and a folkloric reputation for cunning. This was not a description of the corpse in the case. Della had calmed down and was waiting patiently for what came next – whether another cup of Ealing Police Station tea or a twenty-five-year stretch in Holloway.

Though the mirroring was on the other side of the glass, Richard saw the tinted ghost of his reflection superimposed over Della. He looked like a crash-dieting Charles II. His moustache alone required more barbering than a glam-rock pop star's hair. Today, he wore a tight white-and-pink striped-waistcoat over a loose scarlet ruffle shirt, black matador britches tucked into oxblood buckle-boots, and a crimson cravat noosed through a scrimshaw ring representing the Worm Ourobouros. He did not match the olive-and-tobacco institutional décor.

Keenly attuned to unvoiced feelings, he could sense mental turmoil whenever a policeman saw him. Your basic bluebottle constantly had to fight a primal urge to yell 'Get yer hair cut!' at him. When a policeman saw Richard Jeperson, it was usually because his particular, peculiar services were urgently needed. A measure of tact – not to say begging and pleading – was required to secure his assistance.

'Which of you is going to tell him?' said Price, to Fred and/ or Vanessa.

Tact – indeed, begging and pleading – seemed not to be on offer today.

Richard had the unfamiliar impression that everyone else in the room knew more than he did. He was supposed to be the sensitive, who told people things they hadn't picked up on, then basked – just a little – in the glow of admiration.

Fred and Vanessa looked at each other, furtively. His sensitivities prickled again. Neither wanted to own up... but to what? They had alibis, and this wasn't even a whodunit. Price had evidence and a confession. He should be turning Miss Guilty over to briefs, quacks and the Old Bailey.

'Where have you heard this before?' began Price. 'Discovering that her famous, Grand National-winning jockey boyfriend secretly hates horses and takes every chance to maim, injure or abuse one of the blessed beasts, our lovely lass feels compelled – by a gold-maned nag which speaks to her in dreams – to saddle him up and gallop him around the practice track, with liberal applications of the whip and spurs, until he drops frothing dead?'

'Unique in the annals of crime and lunacy, I'll be bound,' said Richard. 'But still not a matter for us. Miss Della Devyne—'

'Née Gladys Gooch,' put in Vanessa.

'...the former Miss Gladys Gooch is out of her tree, Inspector. That's why she rode Jamie Hepplethwaites to death. And don't try to say the dream horse nonsense makes this a paraphenomenon. Pack her off to Broadmoor and get on with your proper mysteries, like the Ministerial Disappearances or the City Throat-Cuttings.'

'Unique, you say?'

'In my experience, which – as you know – is extensive, yes.'

'It's not unique, though, look you. DS Regent, tell him.'

Richard arched an eyebrow at Fred, who looked distinctly sheepish. Vanessa found something absorbing to examine in her paper cup, which couldn't be tea-leaves.

'Zarana, my girlfriend,' began Fred, 'she follows it, and... you know... you watch a couple, and you need to keep on watching, just to find out what happens next. It's rubbish, of course. Real rubbish. But...'

He fell silent, as if he'd just delivered a speech which began, 'My name is Frederick and I'm an alcoholic,' to a circle of inadequates on primary-school chairs.

'Miss Vanessa,' prompted Price. 'Could you enlighten our Mr Jeperson?'

Vanessa crushed the cup and dropped it in a bin.

'We're talking about *The Northern Barstows*, Richard,' she said. 'A television programme. A soap opera.'

'I've never heard of it.'

'It's on the channel with adverts.'

'Ah.' Richard made a point of limiting his select viewing to the BBC. So far as he knew, the channel-changer on the front of his set only went up to '2'.

'Richard believes commercial television was invented by Satan,' Vanessa explained to Price.

Actually, Richard didn't believe that – he knew it for a fact.

'What about this "soap opera"?' he asked.

'Last night, on the *Barstows*,' said Vanessa, '"Delia Delyght" killed "Jockie Gigglewhites" with exactly the same MO. Whips, spurs, saddle, the lot. I didn't see that coming, and the storyline's been running for months.'

Yesterday evening, Vanessa had cried off a visit to a reputedly haunted Tube station, disused since the Blitz and blighted by spectral ARP wardens. Her story was that an unexpected old school friend was in town and needed looking after. It seemed improbable to Richard that he hadn't sensed the dissembling, but Vanessa was too close. He didn't suspect his associates of leading secret, shameful lives. The 'haunting' turned out to be down to rumbling drains and a rack of forgotten gas-masks.

'Highest viewing figures since that documentary about the Queen eating cornflakes,' said Fred. 'Pubs empty when the show is on. People everywhere rabbitting nine to the dozen about Delia and Jockie. And you didn't notice.'

'I imagine I was too busy re-reading Proust in the original,' said Richard.

'I don't doubt it, guv,' said Fred. Richard picked up his glum resentment. Now the secret was out, Fred would be in for some ribbing. Except ribbing usually came from Vanessa's direction, and she evidently shared his shameful addiction.

Richard raised an eyebrow at Price, who was lighting his pipe.

'Oh yes,' he said, 'me too. Never miss the *Barstows*. At the Yard, see, the lads have a portable set. If you want to rob the Bank of England, do it on Tuesday or Thursday between eight and eight-thirty. No one will show up to nick you till you're well away from Threadneedle Street with the loot and Max Bygraves is on.'

'I didn't think it was possible to learn anything new at my age,' said Richard, 'but you've all surprised me. Congratulations.'

Clearly, he was the only one whose brain wasn't fogged with "soap". He needed to deliver an incisive explanation, then go back to *Albertine disparue*. The rest of the populace could happily gorge their minds on rubbish twice a week without bothering him.

'This woman is another sad addict,' he declared, pointing at Della-née-Gladys, 'and has become a "copycat". Struck by the coincidences of names and professions in the fiction, she felt compelled to enact the television story in real life. An argument for severe regulation of such programming, no doubt. The answer to crimes like these is more nature documentaries. But this is a psychological curiosity, not a supernatural event.'

'It's not so simple, Jeperson,' said Price. '*The Northern Barstows* guard their future scripts better than MI5 guard our military secrets.'

'Lots better,' said Vanessa, from bitter experience.

'The point is to be surprising, see. The whole country had to wait to find out what Golden told Delia to do to Jockie. But last night, this woman, Della, did exactly the same thing to the real-life Jamie, at the same time as the programme was going out.'

Richard thought about this.

'It's happened before, Jeperson. This case is the Ministerial Disappearances.'

'On the *Barstows*, "Sir Josiah Shelley" and "Falmingworth" vanished from a locked cabinet room,' said Vanessa. 'Just as, in real life, Sir Joseph Keats and his secretary Farringwell disappeared, scuppering passage of the Factories Regulation Bill.'

'And the City Throat-Cuttings,' said Fred. 'Prince Ali Hassan was assaulted by that fanatic on the floor of the Stock Exchange just when the same thing happened on telly to "Prince Abu Khazzim".'

Despite himself, Richard became interested.

II.

'The horse told me to do it,' said Della Devyne.

'In your dreams?' prompted Richard.

'No, that was the horse on the telly. It wasn't exactly like that. Nothing was exactly the same. They changed it just enough to be different. "Just enough not to be sued," Jamie always says. Used to say. Oh dear, I'm sorry. That programme used to drive him mad.'

'*The Northern Barstows?*'

Della nodded. She was being cooperative, going over the whole thing with Richard. He'd interviewed murderers before and knew the types. The professionals didn't talk at all, just shut up and took their medicine. The enthusiastic amateurs liked to brag, and wanted to see their pictures in the papers. Della fell into a third category, the escapists. Before the big event, they'd been nagged and nagged about something, either by other people (not infrequently their victims-to-be), brute circumstances or a persuasive inner voice. Ultimately, the only way to make the irritation go away was to reach for a blunt instrument or a bottle of pills. Such cases were as likely to kill themselves as anyone else: self-murder was an escape, too.

Della was in a kind of did-I-really-do-that-oh-I-suppose-I-must-have daze. To Richard's certain knowledge, inner voices did occasionally turn out to be external entities, human or otherwise.

'You also watch this television series?'

Della shook her head. 'Lately, Jamie stopped me, said it would upset me to see what they'd made us out to be. I always used to follow it, though, used to love it, but when they brought in those characters... "Jockie" and "Delia"? Well, anyone could tell they were supposed to be us.'

'You think the characters were based on you and Jamie?'

'No doubt, is there? They say "any resemblance with persons, living or dead is unintentional" but they have to, don't they? By law. Jamie looked into having them up for libel... or is it slander? Slander's when it's said out loud and libel's written down.'

'A tricky point,' Richard conceded. 'It would be written down in the script but said out loud by the cast. Who to sue, the writer or the actors?'

'It also has to be not true.'

Della stopped. She had owned up to killing, but now wanted to hold back.

Richard took her hands and squeezed. He had the sense that in some way this woman was innocent and he needed to help her.

Price's instincts were good. This was a Diogenes Club case.

'Was it true?' he asked gently, fixing his gaze on her.

'You have lovely eyes,' she said, which was nice but not really where he wanted this interview to go. He faintly heard Fred stifling laughter beyond the mirror.

'Yes,' she went on, 'it was all true. So far as I could make out, from what Jamie said and the questions people kept asking me. As I said, I haven't seen the *Barstows* in three months. With Jamie gone, I suppose I can watch again. That's something. They have telly in prison, now, don't they? Anyway, when Jockie and Delia came on, Jamie shut me out of the front room and watched on his own. He always came out furious. If you ask me, he was angrier after episodes when Jockie and Delia weren't in the story than when they were.'

'Did he take any action? Against the programme?'

'He sacked a couple of grooms, some secretaries and his manager. Swore up and down that someone must be talking. "Leaking" he called it, like secrets. It was Watergate to him, you see. They were getting inside his circle, ferreting things out, then putting them on telly. One of the grooms was supposed to have sold some of our old clothes to the people who make the show, for the actors to wear. And not just clothes, but other things, personal things. Jamie kept being asked if he hated horses like Jockie. Every time he denied it, it seemed more like the truth. I know it didn't used to be true, but somehow it came true. I don't know how they did it. There were things only he knew about – things I didn't know – which went out on telly.'

'For example?'

'Do you remember Bright Boy, the horse that threw Jamie at Goodwood, that was kidnapped and never found? On the programme, a horse called "Lively Lad" injured Jamie... I mean, Jockie. They showed him beating it to death with a cricket bat, then faking the kidnapping. Jamie would never come out and say so, but I think the telly had it right and his story to the papers was a lie. He showed me the ransom note, and the ears and tail the kidnappers were supposed to have posted to him. The police took it seriously. They never caught the crooks, though. Jamie got rid of his golf clubs about the same time. Not in the rubbish – in the furnace. You don't burn your clubs if you give up golf, do you? And he didn't give up. He bought a new set. No, Jamie killed Bright Boy, just like Jockie killed Lively Lad. They knew, those clever telly people, they knew.'

'Just like they knew about you? About what you did?'

Della's brow creased. Now, she was gripping his hand. He felt strength in her – as well as modelling, she was a show-jumper. She knew how to hold the reins, apply the whip. The spurs were excessive, but they had come from Jamie's private tack-room.

'I can remember it,' she said. 'I remember having the idea. I'm not mad. I know a horse doesn't speak inside my head. I know that I'm the horse really. It's just… it really does seem like someone else was there. Someone who's not here any more. Does that make sense?'

'Almost nothing makes sense, Della.'

He leaned in close and whispered, so Price couldn't overhear. 'Say that Jamie forced you to ride him, begged you not to stop. It was a sexy game that went too far.'

'But—'

'It wasn't exactly like that, I know. But it was something like that, and you should not suffer for this. Understand?'

There was a rattle at the door. Price coming in. Richard let Della's hands go, and sat back.

'Inspector Price, how nice to see you. We've got to the bottom of this, I think. Has Miss Devyne been charged?'

Price's face fell. He saw his closed case opening like a parachute.

'The inquest will rule misadventure in embarrassing circumstances. We should let this young lady go. She's had a gruelling experience and needs to be with her friends and family.'

Vanessa slipped in, past the Inspector.

'Come along with me, Della,' she said. 'We'll get you out the back. There are reporters out front.'

'No,' said Della. 'I'd like to see reporters. I have to some time. And I have something to say they'll want to hear. Before I go, I want to fix my face. May I?'

'Of course,' purred Richard.

Price glared at him in a you've-created-a-monster manner.

Vanessa led Della away, to be presented to her public.

'She bloody did it, Jeperson,' said Price, when Della was out of earshot. 'You know she bloody did it!'

'Yes, but she didn't bloody mean it.'

'What about the throat-cutter? Do we let him go too? He killed five people to get at the Prince.'

'Leave him be, for now.'

'For now?'

Price would have to do a deal of fancy footwork to explain the handling of this case. In the end, it would be all right. If viewers felt the martyred Delia was more than justified in treating the odious Jockie the way she did, they would feel the same about Della. Besides, *The Northern Barstows* was officially fiction. If it couldn't be proved that what they showed on television had happened in real life, then Della was off the hook.

'Look at it this way, Price – what with the TV tie-in, you'd never be able to get an unprejudiced jury. It'd be a show trial, run longer than the series, and we'd all end up looking like right plonkers. This way, she gets her own spin-off, and we can go after the real source of the problem.'

'Which is?'

'*The Northern Barstows*. I want to know more about how the programme is made and the people who make it. Don't worry, I've not forgotten your ordinary murder. It's just something extraordinary is mixed in.'

Price shrugged. Richard saw through his gloom to dour Celtic triumph. The Inspector had been right to call the Diogenes Club. Now he could let them make the running.

Vanessa returned.

'How did she do?' Fred asked.

'Stunning… marvellous… saucy,' said Vanessa.

'So much for the *Grauniad*,' said Fred. 'What would the *News of the Screws* say?'

'"My Kinky Sex Hell With Jammy Jamie: Top Model Tells

All – Exclusive!" She called her agent, and had him pass on a message to her lawyer. She knew just how much slap to put on for that tearful, yet glamorous look.'

'Bless,' said Richard.

'Now what, guv?' asked Fred.

'You're going to follow up the police cases. Go over the Disappearances, the Throat-Cuttings and Hepplethwaites. Plus anything else that turns up – my gut tells me there'll be more. Vanessa, doll yourself down to mere gorgeousness so you can pass for a struggling actress and have Della's agent get you an audition for this *Barstows* effort. Seems like they could do with a touch of metropolitan glamour. I will get up to speed on this apparently significant cultural phenomenon that has somehow managed to pass me by. It seems likely the programme is at least haunted and at worst cursed, so it behoves someone like us to investigate. Oh, wait a mo, I've just remembered, there isn't anyone like us. We're the only hope for a happy outcome. Any questions?'

Price, Fred and Vanessa were all about to speak.

'No, I thought not,' Richard said, hurriedly. 'Let's get cracking. Mysteries don't solve themselves, chaps and chapesse.'

III.

'When I were a lass, Brenda-girl,' said Mavis Barstow, ever-accusing finger jabbing at her long-suffering daughter's eye, frosted perm shaking with indignant fury, 'times were 'ard... bloody 'ard.'

It was a familiar speech, delivered in an accent thick as a Yorkshire coal-seam or a Lancashire pie-crust without feeling bound to the specific vocal traits of any geographical county. The Barstows lived in Bleeds, an industrial stain on the misty moors of Northshire, a region impossible to locate on Ordnance Survey maps. In black-and-white, Mavis was resplendent in a sparkling jet-beaded ensemble over a blinding silver blouse. Her diamonds kept flashing under the studio lights. Richard assumed the idea was a low-budget, North of England Joan Crawford. The frankly frumpy Brenda, victim of many a cutting remark, wore a grey swirly minidress, and was self-conscious about her chubby knees.

'We 'ad none o' yer fancy edyecashun,' continued Mavis, warming to a favourite subject, 'an' only a tart'd wear a frock like tha', but we 'ad respect, Brenda-girl... bloody respect! I'll hear no more o' this tripe an' onions about you gettin' engaged to a sooty, cause ye're no' too grown-up to bare yer rump an' get a stripin' from yer da's old miner's belt.'

'But, Mam,' whined Brenda, who strangely had a Birmingham accent, 'I'm with child!'

Mavis's face set in the gargoyle snarl which always meant someone would suffer serious emotional or physical damage in the next episode. The theme tune cut in, an unacknowledged collaboration between the Brighouse and Rastrick Brass Band and the Pink Floyd. Credits slid across still photographs of slag-heaps, urchins and strikers from the 1930s. The Barstows had come a long way since then, though you'd not know it from listening to Mavis the Matriarch.

Richard was once held captive for three weeks by a scorpion cult who were practised in Black Acupuncture, the science of inflicting non-lethal but excruciating pain by applying venom-tipped needles to the nerve-endings. On another occasion, he had found it necessary to crawl through three miles of clogged-up Victorian sewer filth in order to throw off a determined shapeshifter who was on his scent. Not to mention a childhood spell in a Nazi extermination camp, traumatic enough to blank out any memory of whoever he had been before Captain Geoffrey Jeperson found him in the ruins of Europe and adopted him. But nothing in his experience was quite as agonising as a fortnight in the basement screening room of Amalgamated Rediffusion

Television's West London offices, watching episode after episode of *The Northern Barstows*. He would never hear that infernally memorable theme tune again without wincing.

Lady Damaris Gideon, MP, was on the ART board of directors, and owed a favour to the Diogenes Club. In 1928, Edwin Winthrop – Richard's predecessor as Most Valued Member and sometime mentor – supervised a gruesome pest-control exercise at Gideon Towers, ridding caverns underneath the estate of a branch of the family who had practised obscene rites in the sixteenth century and degenerated into nastily toothy mole-folk. Thirty-five years on, no longer the ingénue who'd required rescuing from her many-times-removed cousins' appalling larder, Lady Dee wore long sleeves to cover bite-marks and tinted contacts to conceal the pink, distinctive Gideon Eye. A tough-minded survivor of far more terrifying battles in business and politics, she was well up on the trouble in Northshire and was only too happy to dump the problem in someone else's lap.

'O'Dell-Squiers have their own fiefdom with that wretched programme,' she had said, 'and the Board would not be unhappy to see them taken down a peg, just so long as the unwashed keep watching the adverts.'

Having now seen their O'D-S logo over two hundred times, Richard knew O'Dell-Squiers made *The Northern Barstows* on behalf of ART, who syndicated it through the Independent Television network. The production company was owned by June O'Dell, the actress who played Mavis Barstow, and her ex-husband, Marcus Squiers, the writer who had 'created' the show.

Lady Dee was the only person Richard had run into on this case who wasn't a *Northern Barstows* fan. In fact, the MP refused even to cast a cold, contemptuous Gideon Eye at anything broadcast by the company which paid her a fat salary plus dividends simply for gracing an annual meeting with her presence and a letterhead with her esteemed name. In what sounded like an uppercrust Mavis Barstow rant, she told him she loathed the wireless ('especially those ghastly transistors'), despised television on principle ('it's for being interviewed on, not watching'), was iffy about talking pictures and none too sure if music halls should be allowed.

The most useful thing to come out of the meeting was that Lady Dee had put Richard in touch with Professor Barbara Corri, 'this batty spinster from one of those plate-glass pretend-universities'. The Professor was infamous for pestering ART with questions about *The Northern Barstows*. The programme was her field of study, and she taught a course around it at the University of Brighton.

'In my salad days at Shrewsbury,' said Lady Dee, coming over Mavis again, 'it was Greek and Latin, with a bare minimum of Shakespeare to satisfy the "moderns". None of this rot you read in the Sundays about degrees in plays full of swearing or pop records by the Bootles. But she knows her onions, this Barbara Corri. If you absolutely have to find out about this dreadful thing, she's your best bet. ART could scrape up a consultancy fee if needs be. We've an interest in settling this curse. Sir Joseph Keats was on the Board too. Is still, if he ever turns up alive.'

Among Professor Corri's works was a paper in *Television Monograph* entitled '"Women of A Certain Age": The Stereotyping of the Independent, Powerful Woman in British Television Serial Drama: *Crossroads*, *The Northern Barstows*, *Coronation Street*'. Richard tracked it down and did his best to understand the argument before phoning her and offering to spring for train tickets and accommodation over an unspecified period if she would pitch in on what he vaguely defined as 'a research project'. The students were on vac, so she was available and had enthusiastically agreed to meet Richard at the ART offices.

He arrived first and waited in the company's reception area, under a bank of photo-portraits of the company's in-favour stars.

Pride of place was given to a positively Queen Motherly, four-times-the-size-of-the-rest June O'Dell. A workman was replacing a scowling young man with a grinning, quiffed comedian. Richard considered the discarded picture.

'That's Donald Shale,' said a woman who'd come in while he was pondering the brevity of fame in an age of mass communications. '"Jockie Gigglewhites". Written out and gone from our screens. Typecast as a sadistic shrimp. Not good for long-term career prospects.'

Richard turned to meet Professor Corri, then mentally rebuked himself for subscribing to a stereotype of 'women of a certain age' just as set in stone as anyone else's in 'the dominant culture'. Lady Dee called Barbara Corri a 'spinster', which might technically be true in that she was past forty and unmarried. It wasn't the label Richard would have applied. He would have inclined to something like 'stunner'.

The Professor's well-fitted mustard-and-cream trouser suit emphasised her womanly shape. A double rope of pearls circled her admirably swanlike neck. Her face was sculptured and cool, with symmetrical smile lines. She raised Queen Bee sunglasses, using them as an Alice band in her upswept auburn hair, and showed amused, sparkling light-hazel eyes. Male students with little interest in 'Approaches to British Television Serial Drama' must sign up for her course just to sit at the front and watch her suit stretch tighter as she stood on tiptoes to chalk up a reading list.

'I really must thank you, Mr Jeperson,' she said, shaking his hand with a good grip. She wore violet chamois gloves. 'I've been trying to get in here for ages. You obviously know the magic words which open up the vaults.'

She offered him her arm, a curiously old-fashioned gesture, and proposed, 'Shall we delve?'

Having spent two weeks in a darkened room steeped with Barbara Corri's fragrance, Richard wished the flickering twaddle on the screen hadn't been a distraction. However, without the waft of ylang-ylang and the delicate susurrus of the Professor's rapider breath during 'high-emotion' moments, he'd have been driven to gnaw off his own arm by June O'Dell's relentlessly strident Mavis, let alone the provincial stooges who came and went as the fortunes of the family rose and fell and rose and fell again.

Bleeds seemed bereft of a middle class. The characters – most related by blood, marriage or liaison – were either disgustingly rich and vulgar or appallingly poor and noble, sometimes shifting from one end of the socio-economic spectrum to the other within a few episodes. The show featured a strange meld of cartoonish social stratification and fractured time-space continuum. The haves lived in the highly coloured present, where floating walls were adorned with pop-art prints and dolly birds strutted in hot-from-Carnaby-Street fashions. The have-nots were stuck in a black-and-white Depression of an earlier decade or even – in the cobbles, fog and gaslight district – a bygone century.

After each episode, the lights came up and Professor Corri added footnotes while the desk-sized videotape-player cooled down and an archivist rewound the magnetic tape and stowed the fanbelt-sized spool.

'"Brenda's Black Baby" is the big plotline of 1969 to 1970,' said the Professor. 'It divided the country, played out over two whole years. It's something only a soap can do, tackle story in real time. We see Brenda's affair with Kenny Boko, a jazz musician who works in one of Cousin Dodgy Morrie's nightclubs. She has to deal with a voodoo curse placed by Mama Cartouche, Kenny's former girlfriend...'

For a moment, Richard was interested. Voodoo curses were in his usual line.

'...then Mavis finds out, and is set against the relationship, as in the episode we've just seen. For a short time, Mavis becomes a pin-up for the National Front. They fight a Birmingham by-election using a Mavis quote, "No Daughter of Mine Would Marry a Bloody Darky". Their vote share goes up, and for the first time in that constituency they don't lose their deposit. But, over the months, Mavis comes to accept the situation, and delivers Baby Drum herself on Guy Fawkes Night, with fireworks in the background. The "Birth of Drum" episode was the first *Barstows* in colour. Sales of colour sets tripled in the weeks before the event.'

'What happened to the baby? He's not in the recent shows we've seen.'

'Lost in an Andean plane crash with Brenda, when Karen Finch, the actress, was written out overnight. She had a salary dispute with O'Dell-Squiers and got unceremoniously dumped. Aside from O'Dell, Finch was the longest-lasting member of the original cast. And she doesn't have a piece of the show. Rather a sad story, actually, Finch. Had a breakdown and went around saying she was "Brenda Barstow", soliciting donations for a mission to rescue Baby Drum from South American cannibals. There's a cruel instance of inter-textuality on *Barstows* as Mavis is strung along by a con-woman who claims to be Brenda, her face different thanks to plastic surgery, also running a bogus charity scam. Of course, this is where we came in. The vexed relationship between reality and fiction. *Romans-à-clef* are nothing new in serial drama, back to Dickens and Eugène Sue. People have been bringing suit or making complaint that this or that fictional character is a libellous version of themselves at least since Whistler forced George Du Maurier to rewrite *Trilby* to take out some digs at him. Sometimes, it seems our reality is a disguised version of *The Northern Barstows* rather than the other way round. The bogus Brenda is arrested and imprisoned before Karen Finch is taken to a secure hospital.'

'Just like Delia and Della?'

'That seems to be near-simultaneous, which goes beyond my idea of credible. Still, Marcus Squiers says every time he dreams up a storyline the rest of the writing staff pooh-pooh as beyond belief, he reads in the newspapers that the exact same thing is happening somewhere.'

'An assassin in full Omar Sharif gear riding a camel into the Stock Exchange and slashing about himself with a scimitar?'

'That's one of the more extreme incidents.'

'But there are more?'

'Dozens. In the early days, when *Barstows* is squarely in the British realist tradition, it doesn't happen much or at all. Mavis and the rest are metaphorically, and occasionally literally, incestuous. Storylines concentrate on the family and their dependants. Then, Barstow & Company become a power corporation and Mavis goes high society and mixes with government ministers, pop stars, sports celebrities and gangsters. Slightly disguised caricatures of well-known people are a major ingredient in the formula. Clive James says you're not really famous until you've been misrepresented on *The Northern Barstows*, but of course they've never done him so that might be sour grapes. Then, as we know, Bleeds bleeds. Things happen on *Barstows* which then happen in real life. It's a problem for me. My interest is in soap as representation, but it seems *Barstows* has stopped representing and started being. I'm not sure what discipline covers the situation now. Yours, probably.'

'Mine, definitely.'

Barbara Corri had looked him up too, and had a fair idea of his discipline. The University of Brighton had its own two-man School of Parapsychology, where student volunteers took carefully measured doses of hallucinogen to open their third eyes and played with Rhine cards or tried to make hamster-wheels spin with the power of their minds. She had asked about Richard there, and her colleagues were impressed – not to mention murderously envious as only underfunded academics could be – that she was being seconded by the legendary Diogenes Club.

'Shall we press on and look at the next episode?'

Two weeks ago, they had started with the original six-part drama from 1964, in which self-made rag trade millionairess Mavis Barstow coped with the sudden loss of her husband ('Da') and recriminations around the funeral led to an irreversible break-up of her extended family. The serial proved so popular that ART commissioned an ongoing series from O'Dell-Squiers, which meant the irreversible break-up turned out to be reversible after all. Richard had sampled episodes from different periods of the show. After looking at the recent storylines which paralleled the Hepplethwaites, Keats and Hassan cases, they had dipped back into the archive to view representative or significant episodes selected by Professor Corri to give a sense of the 'evolving totality of *Barstows*'.

He put his hand on the Professor's warm knee and shook his head.

'I think I've seen enough. My eyes have gone square and I can't get Mavis's voice out of my head when I try to sleep. This phase of the project is concluded.'

'Where do you want to go from here, Richard?'

It was the first time she had used his first name. He had an impulse to take things from here in a direction entirely unconnected with the mystery. He recalled his duty and took back his hand, hoping he could sense in the Professor a response that should be filed away and dealt with later.

'Barbara,' he said, savouring the syllables, 'I believe there is only one logical place to go. Bleeds, in Northshire.'

Her eyes were startled a moment, then she smiled, shocked to giggles.

'Can I come too?'

'I insist on it.'

'What fun. I'm on sabbatical, so I'm yours for as long as you need me.'

He could not resist putting his hand back on Barbara's knee.

'Excellent,' he said. 'I'm sure you'll come in handy. You can be my native guide in the jungles of... television.'

V.

'Northshire' was confined to Haslemere Studios, deep in the Home Counties. As a boy, Richard had assumed there was a connection between the Home Counties and the BBC's Home Service. The cut-glass accent he had grown up speaking issued from both.

'Semiologically, Surrey is more "Southern" than Brighton,' observed Barbara as they drove past a road-sign indicating the turn-off for the studios. 'The South Coast is southerly in a mere geographic sense. Haslemere is what Northerners mean when they talk about "the South".'

Professor Corri was from Leicester, originally – which was neither up nor down. Like Richard, she spoke with an accent learned from the wireless and films with Celia Johnson. It struck him that in thirty years' time everyone in the United Kingdom might speak like *The Northern Barstows*. He felt a chill in his bones.

'To a world of bad faith and inauthenticity,' he pronounced.

His gloomy toast sounded odd in the leather-upholstered interior of the Rolls-Royce ShadowShark. After all, his own, 'natural' voice was a legacy of listening to the clipped, posh urgency of *Dick Barton, Special Agent* and *Journey Into Space*. Still, he dreaded the idea of newsreaders, cabinet ministers and Harley Street specialists who sounded like Mavis Barstow.

The car slid down a narrow lane, with tall hedgerows to either side, and a tree canopy that gave the road ahead a jungle dappling.

He remembered Barbara was supposed to be his 'native guide'.

They were waved past a barrier by a uniformed guard who didn't check the authorisation Lady Damaris had provided. Anyone in a Rolls was entitled to enter the lot. After they had passed, the boom came down before a carpenter's van, and the guard executed a thorough inspection of a load of lumber some production designer was probably fretting about.

A young man with hair past the coat-hanger-shaped collar of his tight-waisted lemon-and-orange shirt was waiting in the car park. He carried a clipboard and a shoulder-slung hold-all that could only be called a handbag.

'Lionel Dilkes,' said the Professor. 'PR. An old enemy.'

For an old enemy, Lionel was demonstratively huggy and kissy when Barbara got out of the ShadowShark. He looked at everything sidelong, tilting his head one way or the other and peering through or over aviator shades. Richard estimated that he was envious of Barbara's plunging crêpe de Chine blouse and pearl choker.

'This is Richard Jeperson,' she said.

Lionel tried looking at him with and without the tint, and from several angles.

'The ghost-hunter?'

'Think of me as a plumber. You have a funny smell coming from somewhere and damp patches all over the living-room ceiling. I'm here to find out what the trouble is and put a stop to it.'

Lionel shrugged, flouncing his collar-points.

'Make my job easier, luv,' he said. 'All the rags want to write up is the bloody curse. Can't give away pics of Ben Barstow's new bit on the side. And she's a lovely girl. She'll show her tits. She says she won't now, that she's an "actress", but a flash of green and it'll wear off. No worries at all on that score. You'd think she was a natural for the *Comet* or *Knight*. But no, all the pissy reptiles care about is the sodding curse. They're all running girlie shots of that horsey cow Della Devyne! All she's ever done is kill someone, and not in an original way. I voted to sue her for plagiarism. It's getting to be a complete embarrassment. And guess who Mavis Upstairs blames?' Lionel thumbed at his own chest.

'Mavis Upstairs?'

'June O'Dell, luv. Round here, she's Mavis Upstairs. You can't get near her, I should warn you now. She's leading artiste and is always in her own head-space. When she's not on set, she's in her "trailer" – that's a bloody caravan to you, luv – surrounded by joss sticks, chocolate assortments and botty totty.'

'I will need to "access all areas" if I'm to do any good.'

'You can need all you want, sunshine. I'm just telling you Mavis Upstairs isn't covered by the law of the land. She's a National Institution, though some round here who say she ought to be in one. Ooops, pardon, slip of the tongue, naughty me.' Lionel extended a wrist, limp enough to count as a stereotype all of its own, and slapped himself. 'Lionel mustn't let his tongue flap like that. Slappy slap slap!'

Richard raised an eyebrow.

'You'll get used to it, luv,' said Lionel. 'We're all indiscreet round here. You don't get appointed to a job on *The Northern Barstards*, you get sentenced to one. No time off for good behaviour, so don't expect to find any.'

Lionel turned and walked away. His dayglo green velvet trousers were too taut at the hip to allow circulation to the legs, but flared so widely at the ankle that he could only progress with a peculiar wading motion.

'Come on,' he said, looking back over his shoulder, lowering his shades, 'meet the Barstards…'

VI.

Lionel took Richard and Barbara up to what looked like a Zeppelin hangar and touched a black plastic lozenge to a pad beside a regular-sized door, which sprang open for thirty seconds to let them in, then slammed shut and refastened like an airlock. The PR led them up a rickety staircase to an ill-lit nest of desks and couches, where people were shouting at each other while talking on telephones to (presumably) other people elsewhere.

'Welcome to the Bad Vibes Zone,' said Lionel.

'Interesting expression,' commented Richard.

'Came up with it on my own, luv. Now, don't take this wrong, but walk this way.'

He flounced – deliberately – into a labyrinth of partitions, leading Richard and Barbara along a twisting path, hurrying them past perhaps-interesting individuals in their own cubicles.

'We need more space,' admitted Lionel. 'ART like to keep O'D-S in a tiny box. Stops us getting too big for our boots. In theory. Guess what? Theory don't work. They don't make boots ginormous enough for how big this lot think they are.'

They came to an area where a small, bald, damp-cheeked, middle-aged man in a cheesecloth sarong sat cross-legged on a giant mauve cushion with appliqué sunflowers. The Buddha-like figure was surrounded by long-haired youths of both sexes who were waving long strips of yellow paper like Taoist prayers. On the strips were scrawled arcane symbols in biro.

'This is a script conference,' whispered Lionel. 'Hush hush, genius at work. That's Mucus Squiers. It's his fault.'

'For creating the programme?' asked Richard.

'For not throttling Mavis Upstairs in her sleep when he had the chance. They used to be married, though that's not a picture anyone should have in their head, luv.'

Richard looked again at Squiers. The writer-producer would

be happier in a bowler hat, collar and tie, carrying a rolled-up umbrella. The guru look was the only way he could get respect from his staff writers. For a moment, Richard thought the man was holding a blue security blanket – but it was a large handkerchief which he was using to mop his freely perspiring brow.

Two girls with beehive hairdos, whose general look was ten years out of date rather than the normal-round-here five, took shorthand dictation on big pads, like courtroom stenographers. Squiers was assembling a script by taking suggestions from the circle, rejecting a dozen for every one he took. Whenever he let a line or a bit of business through, the originator glowed with momentary pride and the rest of the pack looked at him or her with undisguised hatred even as they agreed that the contribution was a work of genius. The genius in question belonged to Marcus Squiers for making the selection, not to any of the acolytes for chattering forth stream-of-consciousness material, tossing out notions to burn and die in the sunlight, in the hope that one or two might grow up to be concepts, then get a thick enough carapace to become actual ideas.

'Next, after the ad-break…?' asked Squiers.

'We've not seen Cousin Dodgy Morrie for two weeks,' put in a girl with glasses that covered four-fifths of her face. 'His plots are still dangling.'

'Uh-uh, Mavis won't have it. She's in a sulk with Morrie since he got that good notice in the *Financial Times*.'

'He could have an "accident",' pressed someone, seeing an opportunity.

Squiers shook his head. 'We still need CDM. It's poor bloody Sydney who got the review.'

'Sydney Liddle plays Cousin Dodgy Morrie,' whispered Barbara.

'Could we "Darrin"?' asked a smart-suited Pakistani man.

Squiers blotted droplets from his temples. 'We've used up our "Darrin" this year, with the Bogus Brenda.'

'To "Darrin" is the practice of replacing an actor in a continuing role with another,' said Barbara. 'It comes from the American sitcom *Bewitched*.'

'The BB wasn't a full "Darrin",' said the girl with the glasses. 'That was a "Who".'

'A "Who" is a modified "Darrin",' said Barbara, 'from—'

'*Doctor Who*?'

Barbara patted him on the shoulder. 'You're learning to speak TV, good. A "Who" is when you do a "Darrin", but have an excuse, like the Doctor regenerating from one star to another, or plastic surgery, which is what they did with the Bogus Brenda, who—'

'...returned, having had the face-change she had previously only claimed to have had, intent on getting revenge on Mavis Barstow for cutting her inside man, Mavis's nephew Ben, out of the family business.'

'You're a fan!'

'No, I just paid attention in the last two weeks.'

Squiers looked up and fixed them with watery eyes.

'Who are these people, Lionel, and do we pay them to mutter during script time?'

'This is the... um, plumber.'

Lionel made all sorts of eye-rolls and contortions. Squiers squinted, blankly.

'He's come about the... you know... thing we do not mention... the c-word?'

The penny dropped. At least with Squiers, who took another look at Richard. The writer-producer was in the loop on the investigation, but the rest of the pack were best kept in the dark. If this was where the ideas came from, this was the likely source of the problem.

'Fair enough,' said Squiers. 'Sit comfortably at the back, and don't speak up unless you've got a better idea than any of these serfs. Which, on their recent record, isn't unlikely.'

There were only large scatter-cushions available. Richard settled on one, achieving perfect lotus. Barbara managed side-saddle. Lionel leant against a wrought-iron lamp-post that happened to have sprouted in the middle of the office, and cocked his hip as if the fleet were in.

'Now, CDM is out until the Moo cools down...'

Barbara mouthed the words, so Richard could lip-read. 'M.U. Mavis Upstairs. The Moo.'

'Besides, we've got other patches to water.'

'D-Delia D-Delyght is about to go to t-trial,' stuttered a fat fellow who wore a school cap with a prefect's tassel.

'Last month's story, Porko,' sneered Squiers. 'You lose the cap.' He snatched it away.

'B-b-but...' began Porko.

Squiers waved the cap about by its tassel.

'Who wants the thinking cap this week? Come on, you fellows. Pitch in. There's all to play for. Yaroo. What about Ben's new bit?'

'Lovely Legs,' said someone, approving.

'That's right. The lovely Lovely Legs. The bogus Brenda, of whom we just spoke, people! More formally, Miss Priscilla Hopkins. Grand-daughter of... come on, anyone, it wasn't that long ago? I know you were all in nappies when the series started. Come on...'

Blank looks all around.

'Barnaby Hopkins,' said Barbara. 'Da Barstow's original partner, whom Mavis cheated out of his share of the business.'

Squiers nodded approval.

'Thank you, whoever you are. It goes to show we do better with strangers off the street – I beg your pardon, madam, but I'm making a point – than with you bright new graduates and ashram dropouts. With my producer's hat on, I have to wonder why we pay you all so much.'

Faces fell in shame.

'Yes, Priscilla Hot-pins,' emphasised Squiers, 'away being Eliza Doolittled to extreme poshness, not to mention tending and caring for her remarkably glamorous gams, and now back for... what?'

'Revenge,' suggested Glasses Girl, tentative.

'One of your basic plot motors, yes. But what else? Is she cracking a bit? Learning to love the enemy? Has Ben's crooked smile and sans-gorm charm worked a spell on her? Who knows? I don't. But let's get them together a bit more and find out, eh?'

The business of putting a scene together seemed a lot like Cluedo – Colonel Mustard in the Library with the Candlestick. This was Priscilla in the Barstow Boardroom with the Suspender Belt. About the first thing Richard had noticed about *The Northern Barstows* was that every other scene involved sex. The writing pack got excited as they frothed up the seduction of Mavis's nephew. With the Bogus Brenda back as a new face, a whole spiral of story possibilities fell into place. It was another *Barstows* standard procedure: over the years, especially since the Bona Fide Brenda was written out, several other women had been brought in as antagonists for Mavis, built up either as villains or martyrs, and eventually ejected in some cataclysmic plot event, such as the murder which had just removed Delia Delyght from the screen. Richard wondered if these women tended to depart soon after the actresses started to get as much fan-mail or column inches as June O'Dell.

He tuned out what was being said and tried to get a feel for the room, for the way the meeting worked. Squiers was in control, but barely. He tossed the prefect's cap to whoever was in favour at the moment, and other rituals established a tribal pecking order, and ways to jostle for position, claim or forfeit advantage or be expelled from the light. At times, Squiers was like a preacher, at others like an orchestra conductor. The stenos kept taking it down in shorthand and yellow strips were waved, spindled or shredded in the writers' fingers.

'The Moo tells Ben that Priscilla is the Bogus Brenda, that she has always known this, that – in fact – she was responsible for getting her out of jail and bringing her to Bleeds with a new face,' said Squiers. 'Ben stunned, as usual. Close on Junie's Number Two Expression: Smug Triumph. In with the oompah-and-custard music, and we're done till next Tuesday. And God bless us every one. Now scatter and make babies.'

He waved and the writers moved away. Porko's face was wet with tears. Glasses Girl, who had proposed Mavis be behind the Bogus Brenda's return, looked flushed under the prefect's cap, as if experiencing the aftershocks of the best orgasm of her life.

Squiers discarded the now-soaked handkerchief in a receptacle and slumped on his raised couch. Then, he noticed Richard and Barbara were still in the circle.

'Not writers, luv,' explained Lionel. 'They don't vanish when you clap your hands.'

Squiers looked at them again, as if this was all new to him. Richard realised the writer-producer's brain had to contain all 'the evolving totality' of *The Northern Barstows*. He was like a medium, a conduit for all the voices of Bleeds. Whatever was going on here was transmitted through the mind of Marcus Squiers. Unlike some people Richard had dealt with, he did not have invisible, evil entities perched on his shoulder. He might well be mad, but it seemed that most folks in his business were.

'Just so long as they don't rattle the Moo cage.'

VII.

After lunch – Richard had taken the precaution of bringing a Fortnum's hamper for Barbara and himself, thus avoiding the

O'D–S 'hostilities' table – Lionel took them onto the studio floor, where the seduction scene discussed at the script meeting was already being rehearsed in front of bulky television cameras. Lionel told them the pages had been typed over the break. If a stenogs couldn't read her own shorthand she was empowered to make up whatever she thought would fit. It usually wasn't any worse than what came out of the writing pack.

There was quite a bit of excitement at the entrance of Lovely Legs. Stagehands, camera assistants, make-up people and cast members not in this scene all crowded around to get a look.

'See,' said Lionel. 'Star is born.'

Lovely Legs wore only a shortie bathrobe and stockings. She did indeed have lovely legs.

'Odd stage-name,' Lionel admitted. 'She's really called Victoria Plant.'

The alias had been Fred's idea. Vanessa was a plant, so she might as well be called one.

'That girl knows you,' Barbara said to Richard, perceptively. 'She looked over here, then away. Really fast.'

'What's that, ducks?' asked Lionel.

'Nothing that matters,' said Richard. 'She's a very pretty girl.'

'Just watch what happens when Mavis Upstairs clocks her. She'll be out of that nightie and into floor-length winceyette with mud on her face and her hair in curlers for the next scene. It's always the way. Still, enjoy the view while it lasts, eh?'

Richard had an insight. 'You're not even slightly homosexual are you, Lionel?'

'Shush, luv, think of my position if talk like that gets out. For shame. You can't get a job in telly PR unless you're bent as a twelve-bob note. 'Sides, I like the frocks.'

He pantomimed another wrist-slap.

Richard shook his head.

'Look, this really is how I talk, dearie. Can't help that. Blame *Round the Horne.*'

Another victim of the media. When he'd first seen Barbara, Lionel hadn't been envying her blouse but trying to peer down it.

'If you need a proper poof for some reason, apply to Dudley Finn over there, aka Beefy Ben Barstow. Forget all those stories about him in nightclubs with models and pin-up girls. I planted them all personally. When those long legs wrap round his middle, he's not going to enjoy this scene one bit. Dud the Dud and Geordie the Security Guard make a lovely couple. Oh, slap my wrist and call me Mabel, I've done it again. Talking out of school.'

Richard had learned a valuable lesson. No one around here was who they pretended to be, and most of them weren't even the people they seemed to be behind the obvious pretence at being someone else again. The onion layers peeled off, and there were sour little cores in the middle.

As it turned out, watching *The Northern Barstows* being made was even duller than watching it on television. Even the rapid pace of twice-a-week production meant an enormous amount of waiting around for things to happen, while tedious tasks were repeated ad infinitum. Barbara, of course, was rapt – like a historian with a personal time machine rubbernecking at the first read-through of *Hamlet* at the Globe or the huddle of commanders around Alexander as he scratched out battle plans in Assyrian dirt.

He found a quiet space behind some flats – painted backdrops of Bleeds which hung outside windows on several different sets as if every home and workplace in the city had the same view – and let down his guard, extending mental feelers, opening himself to the ebb and flow of immeasurable energies. This could be dangerous, but he had to do a full psychic recce. It wasn't an exact science. The emotional turmoil around regular humans at the studio was complicated enough to blot obvious traces of the supernatural.

Many paraphenomena were overspill from ordinary people's heads, anyway. No ghosts, demons or extra-dimensional entities were required to whip up a mindstorm of maelstrom proportions. Maybe a little ritual, conscious or unconscious, to unlock the potential, but it could just be a crack in the skull, allowing boiling steam to jet into the aether.

Of course, Haslemere Studios were haunted. If you knew how to look, everywhere was haunted. Richard had already noticed three separate discarnates on the premises. Tattered flags planted long ago, incapable of doing harm in the immediate vicinity, let alone reaching across distances and forcing others to do their bidding. In an arclight pool, he came across a faded wraith who had been a film actress in the 1920s, almost a star when talking pictures came in and her mangle-worzel accent disqualified her from costume siren roles. Pulled from a historical film begun silent but revamped as a talkie, losing the role of Lady Hamilton to a posher actress, she'd drowned herself in the studio tank, waterlogged crinolines floating like a giant lily among miniature vessels ready to refight the Battle of Trafalgar. All this he gathered from letting her flutter against his face, but the only name he could pick up for her was 'Emma', and he didn't know if it was hers or Lady Hamilton's.

He tried to ask about the *Barstows* curse, but Emma was too caught up in her own long-ago troubles to care. Typical suicide. She chattered in his skull, Mummerset still thick enough to render her wailing barely comprehensible. The only spectral revenge Emma might have wreaked would be on Al Jolson – and he had never shot a film at Haslemere. Richard asked if any other presences were here, recent and ambitiously malevolent. It was often a profitable line of questioning, like a copper squeezing underworld informants. No joy. If anything floated around capable of hurt on that scale, Emma would have known at once what he was asking about. Communing with the ghost left his face damp and slightly oily. When he moved on, she scarcely noticed and went back to exaggerated gestures no one else there could see. She wrung her hands like a caricature spook, but he guessed that was just silent-picture acting style.

On set, Vanessa was giving the hot-and-cold treatment to Dudley Finn. It was textbook slap-and-kiss, come-here-but-go-away wrapping-around-the-little-finger business. Richard saw Vanessa was enjoying herself as Lovely Legs, not so much the acting but the pretending. As she made faces, she let the whirring wheels show, daring anyone to call her a fake. Barbara was watching, critically. Having picked up the connection between Richard and Vanessa, she was looking for more clues. He should let the two clever women know they were on the same side or else they'd waste time suspecting each other.

He looked at the faces watching from darker corners. Squiers stood between the director Gerard Loss, a toothbrush-moustached military type, and the floor-manager Jeanne Treece, an untidy blond woman with a folder full of script pages and notes. Squiers wore a stained flat cap that failed to match his guru threads. At the script conference, Squiers had several times used the expression 'with my producer's hat on', and now – swallowing a bark of laughter – Richard realised there really was such a garment, and it served an actual purpose in demarcating his functions on the show.

A great many other people watched, most with reasons to be there, none with a mark of Cain obvious on their foreheads. Richard picked up many emotions, all within the usual range. Jealousy from Geordie the Security Guard as 'Ben' clinched with 'Lovely Legs'. Boredom from seen-it-all grips and minders. Frustration from a cameraman with ambitions to art, shackled to an outdated camera with three lenses that could be revolved with all the ease and grace of rusty nineteenth-century agricultural equipment. Severe cramps from Jeanne Treece. Concern from a wardrobe assistant who knew there was only one dupe of Vanessa's top and that if what she was wearing got torn in the tussle, she'd have to match the rip on the back-up. Quite a few people in the room idly thought of killing quite a few of the rest, but that too wasn't exactly unusual.

So, how did the *Barstows* reach out and possess people?

It was possible that someone here at the studio was a human lens, a focus for energies summoned in script conferences and unleashed during production, who could channel malignancies into the actual broadcast. A talent like that might slip by without disturbing a ghost, like a light that isn't switched on – but would flare as bright as a studio filament when in use, probably burning out quickly. Raw psychic ability, perhaps not even recognised by its possessor, amplified and sent out to every switched-on television set in the land. Even if people weren't dying, Richard would have been troubled by the concept. If there was a person behind this, they needed to be shut down. Richard dreaded to consider what might happen if the advertising industry discovered this possible psychic anomaly and tried to replicate the process of affecting reality via cathode rays.

There was a slap, a rip, and a clinch. Richard felt the wardrobe assistant's inner groan and the security guard's spasm of hate.

There was no shortage of suspects.

'That's a wrap for the day,' said Loss, though not before getting a nod of the producer's hat from Squiers. 'The talent are released. The rest of you strike the boardroom and throw up...' (Squiers whispered in the director's ear) '...Mavis's lounge, for tomorrow.'

Squiers clapped, and the orders were followed. Television was not a director's medium.

Vanessa threw Richard a look, then slipped out with the other dismissed persons. Her co-star had a quiet, hissy row with

Geordie. Lionel shrugged and angled his head, tossing off a 'told you so' flounce, sneaking a gander under his shades at Vanessa's departing legs. Richard was amused but not yet ready to write off the PR as comedy relief. In this soap, anyone could be anything. No rule said killers couldn't be amusing.

He stood by Barbara.

'Is it all you expected? Or are you faintly disappointed?'

She smiled. 'You're sharp, but try not to be too clever. I'm interested in *The Northern Barstows* and what it means, in why it's popular, why so many people find it important. Whether it's, in objective terms, "any good" is beside the point.'

'So these people aren't the new Dickens or Shakespeare.'

'No, though Dickens and Shakespeare might have been the old "these people". Come back in a century and we'll decide whether the Marcus Squiers method counts as art or not.'

'Method?'

'Crowd control is a method, Richard.'

'Is he in control?'

'Not completely. He knows that, you can tell. June O'Dell – who, you'll note, hasn't been around all day – has more say, if only negatively, in what goes out on the show. In the end, the audience has the conductor's baton. If they switch off a storyline, it gets dropped. If they tune in, it's extended. This is all about showing people what they want to see and telling them what they want to hear.'

'Wonderful. Fifteen million suspects.'

Barbara laughed, pretty lines taut around her mouth and eyes. 'If it were an easy puzzle, it wouldn't be a Diogenes Club case.'

'You pick up a lot.'

'So do you. Tell me, is this place really haunted?'

'Of course. Want to meet a ghost?'

She laughed again, then realised he meant it.

'There's a ghost?'

'Several.'

He led her to Emma's arc-light patch. The lamp was off but she was still tethered to her spot.

'I don't see anything.'

'I'm not surprised. Hold out your hand.'

He took her wrist, easing back filigree bracelets and her sleeve, enjoying the warmth of her skin, and puppeteered her arm. She stretched her fingers, which slid into the ghost's wet dress.

'Feel that?' he asked.

'Cold... damp?'

She took her hand back, shivering, somewhere between fear and delight.

'A frisson. I've always wondered what that meant. It really was a frisson. Tell me, what should I see?'

'You don't have to see anything. I can't see anything, though I have an image in my mind.'

'Like a recording?'

Richard realised Emma was in black-and-white. She had been around before films were in colour.

'That's one type of ghost,' he said. 'Empty, but going through the motions. A record stuck in a groove. This is a presence, with the trace of a personality. Very faint. She probably won't last much longer.'

'Then where will she go?'

'Good question. Search me for an answer though. We have to let some Eternal Mysteries stand.'

'You know more than you're letting on.'

He really didn't want to answer that. But he had reasons other than shutting off this line of questioning for kissing Barbara Corri.

She had reasons for kissing him back, but he didn't feel the need to pry.

'You two, watch out, or the fire marshal will bung a bucket of sand over you,' shrilled Lionel. 'Come away and exeunt studio left. Pardon me for mentioning it, but you're an unprofessional pair of ghost-hunters. It's a wonder you can find so much as a tipsy pixie the way you carry on.'

Richard and Barbara held hands, fingers winding together.

The studio was dark now, floor treacherous with cables and layers of sticky tape. Lionel led them towards the open door to the car park.

As they stepped outside, Richard felt a crackle nearby, like a lightning strike. He flinched, and Barbara felt his involuntary clutch. She squeezed his hand, and touched his lapel.

'Nothing serious,' he said.

She lifted aside his hair and whispered, 'You are such a poor liar,' into his ear.

VIII.

They had two rooms at a guest house near the studio. As it happens, they only had use for one room.

Richard decided the unnecessary expense wouldn't trouble the accountants of the Diogenes Club. After an 'it's not just the precious metal, it's the workmanship' argument over a bill for silver bullets, his chits tended to get rubber-stamped without query.

He let Barbara sleep on, primping a little at her early-morning smile, and went down for his full English. Framed pictures of supporting players who'd stayed here while making forgotten films were stuck up on the dining-room wall. The landlady fussed a little, but lost interest when he told her he wasn't an actor.

The third pot of tea was on the table and he was well into toast and jam when Fred arrived. He had come down from London on his old Norton and wore a leather jacket over his Fred Perry. The landlady frowned at his heavy boots, but became more indulgent when Richard introduced him as a stuntman who had worked on *Where Eagles Dare*. More toast arrived.

Fred had new information. He was fairly hopping with it.

'Guv, this is so far off your beat that it has got to be a false trail,' he said, 'but I've tripped over it more times than is likely, and in so many places I'd usually rule out coincidence.'

Barbara appeared, light-blue chiffon scarf matching her top, tiny row of sequin buttons down the side of her navy skirt. Her hair was up again, fashioned into the shape of a sea-shell. She joined them at the breakfast-table.

Fred, quietly impressed, waited for an introduction.

'This is Professor Corri, Fred. Barbara, this is Fred Regent. He's a policeman, but don't hold it against him. Continue with your input, Fred. We keep no secrets from the Professor.'

Fred hesitated. Barbara signalled for the 'continental breakfast': grapefruit juice, croissants, black coffee.

'I'm all ears,' she announced, nipping at a croissant with white, even, freshly brushed teeth whose imprint Richard suspected was still apparent on his shoulder. 'Input away.'

Fred cleared his throat with tea and talked.

'I've been calling in favours on the force and the crook grapevine, asking about, as requested. I started with Jamie the Jockey, since he's our most recent case. Then I looked into Sir Joseph and Prince Ali. Plus a few we didn't think about, Queenie Tolliver and Buck D. Garrison.'

Richard furrowed his brow.

'Queenie Tolliver ran nightclubs in Manchester,' put in Barbara.

'That's one way of putting it,' said Fred.

'Very well. She was, what would you call her, a gang boss? The Godmother, the press said in her obits. Choked on a fishbone at her sixtieth birthday party. Just when—'

'I can guess,' said Richard. 'The same thing happened on *The Northern Barstows* to a character based on her.'

'"Lady Gulliver", Cousin Dodgy Morrie's backer, and Mavis Barstow's deadly enemy last year,' said Barbara. 'Garrison I've never heard of. But there was a Texas tycoon called "Chuck J. Gatling" on the *Barstows*. Drowned in a grain elevator just after he tried to buy up a controlling interest in Barstow and Company.'

Fred flipped his note-book. 'I was iffy about listing Garrison as a curse victim. He died just like Gatling, but on his own spread in Texas. He'd never visited Britain. He'd probably never heard there was a character like him on some English TV show. But he's where I first tripped over the Thing.'

'The Thing?' prompted Richard.

'The Strange Thing. Actually, the Non-Strange Thing. Professor, we don't do regular police-work. We look for the unbelievable. What happened to Buck D. is all too believable. He annoyed some business rivals, and the FBI say he was hit.'

'Hit? I really must frown upon this Yankee slang, Frederick.'

'Sorry, guv. You know what I mean. Hit. Assassinated. Killed. By a professional. High-priced, smooth, hard to catch. In, out and dead.'

'He was rubbed out by a torpedo?' blurted Barbara. 'Don't look so aghast, Richard. I teach a course on Hollywood Gangster Cinema.'

Richard shrugged.

'I like her,' said Fred. 'Can we keep her?'

'Entirely her decision,' said Richard. 'After much more of this, she may not want to keep us.'

Barbara sipped coffee, enigmatic but adorable.

'I put Garrison to one side and came back at the others. The Thing is… whisper has it that they were hit too.'

This was not what Richard expected.

'Jamie Hepplethwaites was in hot water with almost everyone he ever met,' said Fred. 'He was under investigation for race-fixing and rumour was that he was on the point of telling all. Which would have been inconvenient for certain followers of the turf. The sort of enthusiasts who'd have no scruple about laying out cold cash to put Jamie in a morgue drawer.'

'Della Devyne is not a "tarpaulin",' said Richard.

'A torpedo, guv. No, I'm not saying she is. I'm just saying some big crims are puffing cigars and bragging that they did for Jamie. Ditto Prince Ali, Queenie and Sir Joe. The Prince can't talk any more with his vocal cords slashed, which is dead convenient for his uncle the King, who was not a big fan of Ali's international playboy act. Queenie's Mancunian empire is being carved up by her old competition, which mostly consists of her daughters.'

'How *Lear*.'

'Manchester CID say they hope the war of succession thins out the herd a bit. Unofficially.'

'What about Keats? He's the only one of the victims who had any prior connection with the people who make the show. He was on the board of Amalgamated Rediffusion.'

'The more that comes up, the more the show looks like a complete blind alley. It's not just Sir Joe who went missing but his secretary. Between them, they had ten months' worth of work on the Factories Regulation Bill in their heads which is all out the window and back to the drawing board now. That means very happy proprietors of unregulated factories. Guess what's being said about them?'

'That they paid to get the job done?'

Fred snapped his fingers. 'Got it in one.'

Richard whistled and sat back to think.

'I reckon it's a smokescreen,' said Fred. 'Our Mystery Murder-to-Order Limited is twisting the *Barstows* to put a spin on their business, keeping the fuzz off their case while advertising a service to potential clients. Jobs like Prince Ali, Queenie and Sir Joe do not come cheap. This is not an envelope full of fivers to a couple of washed-up boxers to do over a builder who put the bathroom taps in the wrong way. This is serious money for a serious business.'

Richard waved his friend quiet.

'It won't do,' he said. 'It's still too… weird.'

'You don't want to let it go, guv. But if it's just killers with a gimmick, then this goes back to Inspector Price. We're surplus to requirements.'

'I mean weird in the strictest sense, Fred. Not merely bizarre and freakish, but occult – concealed and supernatural. I'm tingling with an awareness of it.'

'Don't you reckon the Professor might have something to do with that?'

'Cheek,' said Barbara, smiling and sloshing Fred with a napkin.

'Very well,' said Richard. 'Fred, hie thee back to town and share this with Euan Price. Start the Yard moving on this from the other end. Go after the putative clients of your phantom assassination bureau. See if the urge to boast about getting away with it leads to indiscretion.'

'What about you two? You'll continue the canoodling holiday?'

'We'll stay here, with the *Barstows*. There's something or someone we've not seen yet. Some big piece which will fill in the jigsaw.'

Richard's tea was cold.

IX.

June O'Dell knew how to make an entrance.

The company made an early start. Dudley Finn was pressed up against a wallpapered backdrop by a single camera. He held a phone to his ear, though the dangling cord didn't attach to anything. Jeanne Treece hoisted a large sheet of card ('an idiot board') on which one side of a phone conversation was written in magic marker. Ben Barstow was getting news about Delia Delyght.

'We're tying off plot ends,' Lionel whispered to Richard as Finn took one of many breaks – the actor wasn't as good at reading off the card as he had been yesterday at instantly memorising his lines. 'Viewers have written in asking what happened after the murder so Mucus whipped up this bit overnight to reveal all. It's how this show always goes. Big build-up, over months and months, nation on the edges of their three-piece suites, a shattering sensational climax... then we drop the whole thing and move on. Once your plot is over, there's no hanging around. No trial scene with an expensive courtroom set and guest actors in those ducky wigs, no twelve extras on the jury. Just one side of a call. "So, she's copped an insanity plea, eh... fancy that... well, never mind... you're telling me she's going to be locked up in a looney bin for t' rest of her natural life? Fancy that. We'll remember Delia Delyght for a long time in Bleeds." Like fork, we will. That's all over, and we're onto something else. Makes your head spin.'

Finally, Finn got the speech down. As Lionel indicated, the actor had to repeat what had supposedly been said to him by the non-person on the line, with interjected expressions of astonishment.

'It's the famous Phantom Phoner,' said Barbara.

Richard knew the show had a habit of cutting into the middle of telephone conversations, without identifying the unseen party, to get over plot developments while avoiding potentially costly scenes ('Morrie's Boom–Boom Room Hot Spot has burned down to t' ground? In a mysterious fire t' police say might well be arson? Eeh, I'm right astonished!') or repeat the last week's bombshell for viewers who might have missed an episode ('Brenda's up t' duff?

By that coloured bloke who plays t' drums? Well, I'll be blowed!').
At the end of the call, Finn had to hang the phone up out of frame.
Since there was no cradle for the receiver, a stagehand stood by
with a weird little gadget that made the click sound (and was surely
more expensive and harder to come by than an actual phone).

Gerard Loss insisted Finn hasten over pauses where, logically,
the Phantom Phoner should be speaking. Finn had an actory spat
about believability, but was reminded which show this was and
agreed just to read the board. His last line, crammed close to the
bottom of the card, was a cipher scrawl, 't'll be H to P w/ M
h a't t – BH!' Richard was worried that he knew instantly what
that was about. Every Phantom Phoner scene in the episodes he
had watched concluded with Ben Barstow looking straight into
the camera, shaking his head and musing, 'There'll be hell to pay
when Mavis hears about this! Bloody hell!'

Loss called for quiet. Finn took a deep breath, and began.

Three sentences in, the big studio door slid noisily open,
admitting blinding light and a cloud of Lalique.

Outside the stage building was a red box which lit up the
word 'Recording'. June O'Dell must have waited for it to go on
before commanding her entourage to open the door and make way
for the Queen of Northshire.

Finn grimly carried on with the 'take'. Loss chewed his
moustache. Jeanne Treece hit herself over the head with the
idiot board.

Marcus Squiers hopped to and danced attendance on his ex-
wife. He had to negotiate a way past two tall young men who flanked
the star. They had mullet haircuts, sideburns like flat-ironed
hedgehogs, and had overdone their daily splash of Früt aftershave.
Their knitted rainbow tank-tops showed off muscular arms.

In person, June O'Dell was tiny – though enormous hair took
her height a little over five feet. She had hard, sharp, glittering eyes

and her skin was shinily tight across the cheekbones and under her chin. Richard had heard her described as 'a cross between Miss Piggy and Charles Manson', but she was more frail than he expected. The Tank-Top Twins might well be there to rush in and prop her up if a stiff wind blew.

Ignored by everyone, including a dead camera, Dudley Finn finished his scene. Without the board, he was word-perfect.

'There'll be hell to pay when Mavis hears about this,' he said, flatly. 'Bloody hell.'

Jeanne Treece whipped the crew into shifting the cameras to the lounge set and getting it lit properly.

'Madame Moo is prepared to work today,' said Lionel. 'Lesser morts have to strike while the icon is hot.'

'What about the Phantom Phoner?' asked Barbara.

Lionel shrugged. 'Scene's scrubberood. Not that many people wrote in. Delia Delyght is in TV limbo now. Make up your own ending, luv.'

'Delia escapes from Broadmoor and comes back chained to an axe-murderer? Then they chop up as many Barstows as they can get to?'

'Pitch it to Mucus, luv. In a year or two, he'll do it. Folk are always coming back to Northshire to get their own back. I shouldn't be surprised if British Rail do a Revenge Special Awayday fare to Bleeds.'

One of the Twins handed Squiers a thin script, heavily scrawled on in what looked like pink neon. June pointed a long fingernail at a particular passage and tapped the paper.

'I see the star writes her own lines?' observed Richard.

'Never touches 'em. The pack know how to write Mavis the way Junie likes her. No, she always scribbles over everyone else's sides. Loves to give the supporting artistes a hard time. She'd force them to run their lines backwards and on their heads if she could. Eventually she will. Knows all the tricks, that one. How to cut the heart out of someone else's scene. How to take it all away with a single nasty look. What to wear to blind the other actors. Of course, Mavis on the show is an evil domineering cow, so Junie's approach might be method acting.'

Squiers looked over June's suggested changes, agreeing with every one out of his mouth, appalled fury spitting out of his eyes.

Loss had to chivvy Finn onto the lounge set, while jamming June's line-changes into him. The actor didn't complain. Squiers, who literally took off his producer's hat when talking with June, diplomatically made a few suggestions.

The lights came up on Mavis Barstow's Lounge, the most-used *Barstows* set. Its two walls had shaggy purple paper that matched the carpet. At least once an episode, the camera would overshoot while panning to follow the action and afford glimpses of studio blackness and the odd crew member where the other walls ought to be. Inflatable plastic chairs leaked slowly around a glass-and-chrome coffee table loaded with mocked-up fictional glossy magazines. A drinks trolley held rattling bottles of cold tea and dyed water. On *The Northern Barstows*, no actual products were shown (that was saved for the commercial breaks); everyone drank 'Funzino', 'Bopsi-Coolah' and 'Griddles Ale'. Mavis's mother's old mangle stood in a corner like an industrial art piece, to remind her where she came from: she would often tell relatives at length about the way her mam flattened her hands in a washing accident that threw the whole family into the poorhouse when she were a lass.

An idealised portrait of the very late Da Barstow, in dayglo on velvet, cap on his head and miner's pick over his shoulder, had pride of place above a shaped fibreglass marble mantelpiece where his ashes supposedly sat in a silver urn to which many of Mavis's most vehement or nostalgic speeches were addressed. The cremains had once been 'kidnapped' by Cousin Dodgy

Morrie and held to ransom. Since their return, Mavis often got close to the polished urn to talk to the departed, usually after one too many Funzinos, and the camera had to focus on her distorted, wobbly reflection as she reminisced about how much happier everyone was when they were dirt poor. Jeanne Treece stalked the set, putting odd little folded cards like place-markers in ash-trays, on the magazines, hanging out of Finn's blazer pocket, around the mantel and under light fittings.

When the floor manager had finished distributing the cards, she gave Dudley Finn a once-over as if checking for dandruff and nodded to Squiers, who signalled to Loss, who made a gun-gesture at the Twins, who lifted June O'Dell up by her arms as if she were part of their circus acrobatic act. The actress was propped on two eight-inch blocks with wheels. One Twin steadied her while the other knelt and fixed clamps from the blocks to her calves.

'The Mavis Glide,' exclaimed Barbara. 'That's how she does it. Platform roller-skates.'

While her undercarriage was checked and fiddled with, a make-up girl made last-minute adjustments to June's white mask. Then, her pit crew stood back. Suddenly, with a girlish giggle, she set off at a wheeled stride and did a figure eight around the set, skirts billowing. Applause was mandatory, but Richard conceded that it was a good act. She lifted one heavy skate off the floor and rolled on elegantly, leg out like a ballerina, then twirled and came to a dead stop.

She was next to Dudley Finn. Thanks to the platforms, June O'Dell was now taller than him.

'If a word of the risers leaks out, you'll be killed,' Lionel told them. 'No question about it.'

The recording light went on again, and June and Finn – Mavis and Ben – went through a scene which had evolved from yesterday's script meeting. June floated about the set as she spoke, picking up phrases or single-word cues from the tiny cards Jeanne Treece had distributed, skating through speeches with the aid of these prompts. The scene built up to the revelation that Mavis knew all along that Priscilla was the Bogus Brenda returned. Richard accepted the sad inevitability that he was now a follower of *The Northern Barstows* like everybody else in the country. He knew who all these people were and how they related to each other, and suffered a nagging itchy need to know what they would get up to next. This must be what it was like to be a newly body-snatched vegetable duplicate and click in sync with the collective consciousness of the pod people.

'She's an old ghost, Ben,' said June, in a line Richard hadn't heard yesterday. 'There've bin too many bloody old ghosts round hereabouts lately. Spectre horses, headless spooks, all manner o' witchcraft and bogeyness. I'm beginning to think this family's bloody haunted. An' somethin' should be done about it or my name's not Mavis Barstow.'

Ben weakly put in a line about what was to be done.

'Get me a bloody ghost-hunter,' said Mavis. 'Someone to put a stop to t' haunting. Or else someone t' haunting will put a stop to.'

June's face froze. Richard had assumed the effect was a camera trick, but she really did just stop still and stare at the lens for long seconds.

Loss called 'cut' and June was applauded again.

'What was that about?' Barbara asked Richard. 'The ghost-hunter bit?'

'I wouldn't say it came out of nowhere,' he replied. 'I'm rather afraid we've been noticed.'

June, who had perspired through her pancake, was wheeled off the set by the Tank-Top Twins and repaired by the make-up girl, who applied what looked like number-two gloss from a bucket with a brush. Then, June was trundled towards Richard and Barbara, with Squiers hopping along in her wake. From her artificial height, June O'Dell looked Richard in the eye.

'So, you've come about the mystery?'

Her natural voice would have suited her to play Lady Bracknell if she could ever be persuaded to admit she was old enough. It was nasal, aristocratic, reedy with that Anglo-Irish affectation known as 'West Brit'. Richard wondered if she had ever met Lady Damaris Gideon. If so, Lady Dee would probably have come second in a peering-down-the-nose-with-disdain contest. Richard had previously reckoned the MP a likely British champion in the event.

'The haunting?' he prompted. 'Very topical.'

June tittered, a tiny hand over her mouth. She fluttered long, feathery eyelashes.

'Must remain abreast of current events. It's part of the format. Keeps us all on our toes. Or, in my case, wheels.'

'Am I to have a writer tagging along as I work? Taking notes on my ghost-hunting activities?'

'Not one of our writers, I trust. You wouldn't want any of those oiks about. I don't understand why we have to have them. Some of us are quite capable of making it up as we go along.'

'June has the utmost respect for our writing staff,' put in Squiers. 'She is being amusing. The poltergeist plot has been thoroughly worked out by trained professionals.'

June flicked a glance at her ex-husband and he withered. Then, she noticed Barbara.

'Professor Corri, how nice to see you again. Peachy.'

Barbara had not mentioned that she'd met June O'Dell. She nodded in acknowledgement of peachiness, but did not attempt a curtsey.

'This curse has become infinitely tiresome and makes our blessed calling far more difficult than it need be. We have a duty to our viewers. They depend on us to take them out of their drab, wretched lives for two brief half-hours a week. Half-hours of entertainment, of education, of magic. It's a terrible responsibility. Many say that *the Northern Barstows* are more real to them than their wives, husbands and children. And for some who live alone, the elderly and the loveless, we are the only family they have. It's for them that we do this, undertake the endless struggle of the business we call show. I trust you will bring your investigation to a swift and happy conclusion. Rid us of all ghosts, ghoulies and ghastliness. You are, I understand, supported by tax-payers' money.'

'To an extent.'

'Excellent. You are accountable, then. You will come to me tomorrow at tea-time, and give a report of your progress.'

Richard kissed June's hand. 'Of course.'

'Alone,' she said, eyes swivelling to Barbara.

He felt again the crackle he had experienced yesterday. This was a very powerful woman, perhaps a conduit for a higher, greedier power. He tried to let June's hand go, but she pinched his fingers for a moment, hanging on, then released him when she decided to.

'Now, I must rest. It's fearfully exhausting, you know. Being Mavis.'

June pushed off and skated away, independent of the Twins, making Squiers cringe. She did a circuit of the studio, whooshing through the shadowed areas away from the brightly lit lounge.

Richard watched her brush past Emma's cold, damp spot.

There was a sound in his head like a bubble being popped and June sped back, puffed out a little like a cat with a mouthful of feathers. She zoomed across the set towards the door, which the Twins got open in time, and whizzed out onto the car park.

Richard walked towards Emma's spot.

'What happened?' Barbara asked.

Richard opened himself up, trying to find yesterday's

presence. Emma was gone, completely. Her psychic substance had been consumed.

'That woman's a sponge,' he told Barbara. 'She just ate a ghost.'

X.

The *Daily Comet*, Britain's best-selling tabloid, led with the headline 'TERROR STALKS BARSTOWS' – bumping England's failure to qualify for the World Cup and another oil crisis to the inside pages. The popular press had been filling their middles with trivial showbiz stories since the days of Marie Lloyd sitting among the cabbages and peas and Lillie Langtry snaring the Prince of Wales, but now ephemera like this made page one. Richard sensed another trend in the making, another step downstairs. From now on, *Coronation Street* would get more newspaper coverage than coronations, Harold Steptoe would be more newsworthy than Harold Wilson, and the doings of Barstow and company would be followed more intently than those of Barclay's Bank. Eventually, there would only be television. More and more of it, expanding to fill the unused spaces in the general consciousness.

The *Barstows* weren't taping this afternoon, so before-cameras talent had time off. Squiers and the writing pack were conjuring up the next script. June was in her caravan with a nervous ghost writer, one of a string employed on her much-delayed autobiography; it seems she ate them up, just as she consumed real ghosts. Finn, suitably equipped with a dolly bird as 'arm ornament', was opening a supermarket in Bradford; 'Victoria Plant' had turned down an offer of £15 to play the lucky girl, diminishing her chances of getting ahead in the business. Lionel was working on a futile press release to deny all these silly curse rumours.

Richard and Barbara met Vanessa in the Grand Old Duke of North.

Vanessa was perched on a bar-stool not designed with modern female fashions in mind. Unless she fixed her tangerine-and-lemon minidress firmly over her hips, it rode up and turned into a vest. She looked down, with an unjustly critical eye, at her officially lovely legs.

Richard sipped Earl Grey from one of the silver Thermos cups in today's Fortnum's hamper, and took a psychic temperature reading. Vanessa and Barbara had hit it off at once, which was a positive. Otherwise, the Grand Old Duke was a chilly place.

The pub, another *Barstows* standing set, was in the studio's smallest stage. Here, many a 'pint of Griddles' had been called for and swallowed by a Barstow who needed a drink before spitting out the latest news, usually some bombshell lobbed just before the adverts to keep viewers transfixed as they were mind-controlled to hire-purchase fridge-freezers, terrorised by the catastrophe of hard-to-shift understains, warned of things their best friends wouldn't tell them and urged to buy the world a Coke. Here, Ben Barstow had enjoyed (or perhaps not) a liaison with Blodwyn, the Welsh barmaid who broke up his third marriage and then died in a plane crash two episodes before his fourth wedding. Here, for weeks and weeks, Da's kidnapped urn had been hidden in plain sight, in the display case along with clog-dancing, whippet-racing and brass band trophies. There had been a nationwide contest to 'spot the ashes', with viewers writing in to suggest where they might be and newspapers running stories about urns seen in surprising real-life locales from the Jewel House in the Tower of London to an Olde Junke Shoppe in Margate. Some even sent in ashes of their own, in home-made or shop-bought urns: most were just from the grates of open fires, but some contained authentic human bone fragments. It was no wonder the show wound up cursed.

'I think the culprit is the Phantom Phoner,' said Vanessa, breaking into his prophetic gloom.

'You think there's a culprit?' asked Barbara.

Vanessa deferred to Richard.

'Sometimes, a curse – by which I mean an infestation of malign extranormal phenomena – is like weather or a bad cold. No one's fault, but hard to do anything about except wait for it to blow over. This happens in more cases than you hear of. Sometimes, it really is a ghost or a spirit – a discarnate, spiteful entity, making mischief or bearing a grudge, acting on its own accord or directed by a houngan who has summoned or tapped into a power and is using it for his or her own ends.'

'A houngan?' quizzed Barbara.

'Voodoo sorcerer,' shuddered Vanessa. 'Like Mama Cartouche, remember?'

'It doesn't have to be voodoo,' said Richard. 'That's an Afro-Caribbean tradition. Europe has more than enough witchery to go round. Australasia and the Americas too. Everywhere except Antarctica, and that's only because the Sphinx of the Ice won't allow it. In this case, however, I think we are dealing with something vaguely voodoo.'

'So there is a culprit?'

'I definitely suspect a suspect,' said Richard. 'Someone is deliberately shaping events, channelling a force, and, as it happens, charging money for it. What we have here is a hit-man, as Fred suggested, but one with an unusual MO. Working with *The Northern Barstows*, through the psychic energy generated by the machinery of the show, and directing it, essentially, to kill people. To order, for cash. So, yes, there's a culprit. One who either needs or wants money for their services. In my experience, that tends to rule out ghosts and demons. Some miserly spirits cling to the idea of worldly goods even when they're beyond a plane in which they'd be any good to them. You've heard of the ghost who collects bright trinkets – coins and jewels – like a magpie. A nuisance, but not serious, especially since you usually get the pleasant surprise of finding the hoard of goodies at the end of the day. This isn't like that. This is large sums transferred to Swiss bank accounts. This is organised crime.'

Barbara, intent on what he was saying, put down her salmon sandwich.

'But how is it done? How can something that happens on a television programme, which boils down to actors pretending, lead to something happening to real people out there in the real world? When Delia rode Jockie to death, what happened to make Della do the same thing to Jamie? Or am I getting the order wrong?'

'I have ideas about that. Vanessa, what was the most significant thing Della told us about the case?'

Vanessa shrugged.

'Think "Penny for the Guy".'

'Old clothes,' said Vanessa, tumbling to it at once. 'We were told that Jamie fired a groom who was supposed to have stolen some of their clothes. Jamie thought the actors' costumes included items filched from him and Della.'

'"And not just clothes, but other things, personal things."'

Vanessa snapped her fingers. 'It's pins! Pins in dolls!'

Barbara shook her head. She hadn't caught up.

'What do you think the personal things were?' Vanessa asked. 'We can find out from Della, but what do you think—'

'Anything really. Combs, with hair. Make-up. Cigarette-ends. Rings. Things impregnated with sweat, skin, hair. Clothes should do it alone, but the rest would put the pink bow on it.'

'Voodoo dolls,' said Barbara, catching on. 'On the *Barstows*, Mama Cartouche made a doll of Brenda, with nail-clippings and hair pressed in, and stuck pins through it. Brenda had twinges.'

'Probably where our culprit got the idea,' said Richard.

'You have to admit this is a new one,' said Vanessa. 'Fashioning characters on a television programme into voodoo dolls, then torturing or killing them in front of fifteen million people…'

'Some of whom believe in the characters. June said the *Barstows* were more real to viewers than their own families. All that belief has to mean something, has to do something, has to go somewhere!'

'God, there's a paper in this,' said Barbara.

Richard and Vanessa looked at her.

'But there is,' she said. 'This is what I've been saying all along. TV soaps matter. They shape reality. I'm not saying it's a good thing, I'm saying it's a thing thing.'

Richard slipped an arm around the Professor and kissed her ear.

'Hold off on publication for a while, Barbara. Let's at least nab the killer first.'

'I have a name,' said Fred.

They looked at the stage door. Fred had come in, motorcycle helmet under his arm. Richard knew he had heard enough to be up to speed.

'I went after the gambling syndicate, the ones who hired Jamie's murderer,' said Fred. 'Price hauled in some minor faces, put the squeeze on… and someone coughed up a name. Our hit-man.'

Fred let the pause run.

'Do tell,' prompted Richard.

'Stop faffing about, Regent,' said Vanessa. 'This isn't the end of an episode that we can pick up on Thursday.'

'"Darius",' said Fred. 'That's the name he uses. "Darius Barstow".'

Richard was sure he had turned to where the camera would be and frozen his face long enough for the credits to start rolling.

He shivered as he heard the *Barstows* theme in his head.

XI.

Head of Wardrobe at O'Dell-Squiers was Madame Louise Ésperance d'Ailly-Guin ('Mama-Lou'), a tall, slender woman, graphite-black, with large, lively eyes and a bewitching islands accent. Her office ensemble ran to a red mushroom-shaped turban, white silk strapless evening dress with artfully ragged hems and matching PVC go-go boots. Behind her desk was an altar to Erzulie Freda and a framed snapshot of a younger Mama-Lou frozen in the middle of a snake-waving dance under a Haitian waterfall.

Richard, inclined by instinct to look gift horses in the mouth, felt the same way about a gift houngan.

Tara, the wardrobe assistant Richard had seen on set, was showing Mama-Lou a range of designs for Priscilla's future dresses. Mama-Lou pencilled crosses on the rejects, flicking away hours of work.

Richard did not insist on being attended to. It was more useful to observe.

Last night, in the TV room at the guest house, Richard had for the first time watched *The Northern Barstows* as it went out to the nation, even though there was an interesting-sounding programme about cane toads on BBC Two. Barbara, Vanessa and Fred helped him through it. He turned the sound down during the adverts and covered the screen with a sheet of grease-proof paper to shield his senses from mind-altering subliminals in the baked bean and gravy commercials. It was the episode he had followed from script to shooting, so there shouldn't have been surprises. Vanessa thought they hadn't used her best 'takes' and detected the hand of June O'Dell in the editing suite. A few interesting bits and pieces were slipped in that hadn't come up at the script meeting, which must have been shot when he wasn't looking – a shadow stalking through the fogs of Bleeds, hobnail boots clumping on the cobbles; a mysterious wind blowing through the Grand Old

Duke, giving Bev the new barmaid horrors; objects wobbling slowly (on visible strings) around the boardroom, indicating a poltergeist problem. The curse was being worked into the show, which set up Mavis's speech about calling a ghost-hunter.

'In trut', nix to ahll these,' Mama-Lou said to Tara, returning the last design.

The girl was exasperated, dreading the work of going back to the beginning.

'They won' be needed,' said the head of Wardrobe. 'Word come from on high.'

Mama-Lou thumbed upwards, at the ceiling. The Wardrobe Department was a windowless bunker beneath the writers' den. Multiples of costumes hung in cellophane shrouds, continuity notes pinned to them, indicating when they had last been worn on air. Shoes, hats, coats, gloves, scarfs and belts had their own racks. Principal characters had niches, where their two or three outfits were looked after. There was a separate room, temperature-controlled and with a combination lock, for June O'Dell's wardrobe, which was twice the size of the rest of the cast's put together.

'We can't keep Lovely Legs in that fruit punch frock,' said Tara. 'It goes fuzzy in transmission and looks like she's wearing a swarm of bees. Technical have sent several memos about it. Sound on vision. And the poor cow at least needs a new pair of tights.'

Mama-Lou drew a finger across her throat.

Tara was sobered. Mama-Lou put the finger up to her mouth.

'Hush-hush, chile,' she said. 'Don't nobody know outside of you, me and the loas.'

Mama-Lou's eyes flashed at Richard.

Whatever it was nobody knew, he didn't know it either. Unless he did.

'Now, run off and see to Dudley's latest split trews, while I converse wit' this gentlemahn.'

Tara's head bobbed and she withdrew.

'Now, Mist' Jeperson…'

'Richard.'

'Reechar'.'

Mama–Lou reached out and touched his chest, appreciatively feeling the nap of his velvet collar.

'I like a mahn who knows how to dress.'

She left his jacket alone.

'Now, what can I do for you?'

'I'm interested in how you costume some of your characters. You can guess the ones I mean.'

'Jockie and Della. Prince Abu. Sir Josiah and Falmingworth. Lady Gulliver. Masterman and Dr Laurinz. Mr Gatling. Pieter Bierack.'

She had obviously been waiting for someone to ask.

'You have a few more on your list than I do.'

'I've been workin' here long-time, Reechar'. I'm firs' to know who's comin' and who's goin'. When word comes down from on-high, I have to dress the word, send it out decent to the studio floor. You dig?'

'I think so.'

'A costume is more than jus' clothes. It's the t'ings in the pockets, the pins under the lapels, the dirt in the soles of the shoes, weathering and ageing…'

She led him to the 'Ben' rack, raised cellophane from a jacket, showed the fray of the sleeve-cuffs, a loose button, a stitched-over stab-mark. From the pocket, like a stage magician, she pulled out a stream of items: a bus ticket, a paper bag of lemon-drops, an item of female underwear, a tied fishing-fly in the form of a water-boatman.

She smiled, showing sharp, very white teeth.

He laughed as she flourished an artificial flower.

'I'm not so interested in Ben Barstow,' said Richard.

'Wouldn't surprise me if he be interested in you,' said Mama-Lou.

Richard wondered if he was exuding psychic pheromones. Since he and Barbara had happened, people treated him differently. Mama-Lou was closer to him than decorum would advise. And she was right – Dudley Finn had been giving him glances. And so had June O'Dell.

'Very flattering,' he said, 'but not the field I wish to explore. Where are the racks for Jockie and Della?'

Mama-Lou made a fist, then opened it suddenly.

'Gone. To the 'cinerator. No room roun' here. New come, so old gotta go. Policy directive.'

She looked to the ceiling.

'And all the others. Gone too?'

She made an up-in-smoke gesture.

'I'd have been interested to know how you costumed them.'

'Carefully,' she said. 'We go to great lengths to procure the… suitable items, to give them the proper… treatment.'

'You don't make the costumes yourselves? You buy them in.'

'Some t'ings we run up here. Got an award for it. Mavis Barstow wears only original Mama-Lou designs. She insists. Not'ing June O'Dell puts on has been roun' a human body before. Some of the other women's t'ings we do the same. Had a Carnaby Street designer under contract for this new girl's clothes. He'll be gone, now. Change of policy. For the ones you'll be interested in, we procure. We copy sometimes, but we make the copy good. You understand what I'm tellin'?'

'Indeed.'

'Good. You put a stop to it?'

She stood back and folded her arms. He didn't try to pretend he didn't know what she meant.

'I'll certainly try.'

Mama-Lou nodded, once. 'Good. A sacrilege is no good to anyone. If a blessing is put to an evil end, evil comes to everyone, even the mos' blessed. Maybe the idea comes from my island, but none of the conjuring comes from me. Dig?'

'Dug.'

'I follow Erzulie Freda, loa of love. This be the path of the Saturday Man. Know him?'

'Baron Samedi?'

'Hush-hush, Reechar',' she said, laying a finger on his lips. 'Say not his name, lest he come to your house. Caution agains' the Saturday Man. And come this way.'

With beckoning finger, Mama-Lou lured him deeper into the bunker, past more and more racks. Finally, she came to two new racks, which held only hangers and cellophane. No clothes yet.

'I said I know firs' when new people come. They get a rack, even before the role is cast. These are the ghost-hunters' racks.'

Character names were stuck to the racks. An invisible fist thumped against Richard's chest.

ROGET MASTERMAN. DR CANBERRA LAURINZ.

'Sound familiar?' asked Mama-Lou.

While Richard was calming, Mama-Lou placed something soft on his head. She looked at him sideways.

'Not your style, but you'll need it.'

He took off the headwear and looked at it. It was an old flat cap.

Mama-Lou stroked his coat again, more wistful than flirtatious.

'Now you go think what has to be done. Then come back to Mama-Lou, give blessings to Erzulie Freda, and we make a conjuring. Dig?'

'The most.'

XII.

'Did Mama–Lou dispense any useful wisdom?' Vanessa asked him.

'Yes, dear. You're being written out.'

She swore, elegantly. 'You got this from the wardrobe mistress?'

'No more dresses for Lovely Legs, ergo... no more Lovely Legs.'

Richard was holding council of war in the boarding house sitting room. Fred had used his best 'intimidating skinhead' glower to scare off a commercial traveller who had been settling down to ogle Vanessa and Barbara through slits cut in the *Evening Mail*. Now, they had privacy.

'Have they tumbled that she's a plant?' asked Fred.

Richard wondered about that.

'I think not,' he concluded. 'They want shot of Lovely Legs to make room for new developments.'

'The poltergeist plot?' prompted Barbara, who had sat in with the writing pack all day. 'It's come out of nowhere and isn't really the *Barstows* style. No matter how unlikely things have got before, with plastic surgery or unknown twins coming back from Australia, they've stayed within the bounds of possibility. No ghosts or UFOs.'

Realising the others were giving her hard looks, Barbara wondered what she had said wrong, then caught up with herself.

'Sorry,' she said. 'It's not easy to get used to. This is new ground for me. Of course, there are ghosts and UFOs. That's what you're here for.'

'No UFOs,' said Fred. 'That's rubbish. There aren't any little green men from outer space.'

'Yet,' said Richard.

'There are ghosts,' said Vanessa. 'And other things.'

'Vampires?'

'Yes,' said Richard and Vanessa.

'Werewolves?'

'More than you'd think,' said Richard. 'And all manner of shapeshifters. There are were-amoebae, which need to be strictly regulated.'

'Possession, like in *The Exorcist*?'

'God, yes,' shuddered Vanessa. 'Not a favourite.'

Barbara shook her head and sighed.

'Welcome to the club, Prof,' said Fred. 'I know how you feel. This isn't natural for me either.'

'The poltergeist plot?' prompted Richard.

'Yes, that,' said Barbara, drawn back to her original thought train. 'For most normal people, which – strangely – includes the O'Dell-Squiers writing staff, there's a line between barely plausible and outright unbelievable. With the Bleeds Bogey – that's what they're calling the poltergeist – the line has been crossed. At today's conference, the girl with the big glasses was summarily sacked for questioning whether the programme should go down that street.'

Richard wasn't surprised by that. It suggested their quarry knew how close they were to catching up.

'The rest of the pack are frothing,' continued Barbara. 'It's Hallowe'en come early. With his producer's hat on, Marcus Squiers wants to retain you as technical advisor.'

'That means they'll make up what they want anyway but pay you to put your name in the end credits,' said Fred.

'My understanding is that they want to give me more than a name-check. Barbara, did Squiers mention the ghost-hunters who're showing up on the programme?'

'There's a buzz about them, though the pack got secretive when the subject came up. They suddenly remembered I was in the circle.'

'The character names have been decided,' Richard told them. 'I've seen their racks in Wardrobe. Masterman and Dr Laurinz. Roget Masterman and Dr Canberra Laurinz.'

'Canberra!' blurted Barbara, appalled. 'I must say this crosses the line. I'm supposed to engage critically with the subject, not be swallowed by it.'

Richard had a pang about involving an outside party in the investigation. It did not do to get civilians turned into frogs.

'Who's playing you, guv?'

'I assume someone called Peter Wyngarde has been approached,' said Richard. 'The supposed resemblance keeps being mentioned.'

Vanessa looked at him, thought about it, then ventured, 'I wonder how Peter Cushing would look in a multi-coloured Nehru jacket and moon boots?'

'It'll be someone from provincial rep or Früt adverts,' said Fred. 'No one you've ever heard of gets on the *Barstows*. No offence, Ness.'

'None taken. It's true. The Moo is reigning star, and doesn't like pretenders to the throne. "Victoria Plant" found that out in about two minutes.'

'In some instances, they cast for physical likeness, not talent,' said Richard. 'They'll be poring over *Spotlight* for lookalikes. A wig and a tash will do for me, but I imagine Barbara will be harder to match.'

'Don't you believe it,' said Professor Corri, trying not to be frightened. 'I'm always being mistaken for some woman who wears fangs in Hammer films.'

'Will you get script approval?' asked Fred. 'They could make you look a proper nana if they wanted. Like they did Jamie Hepplethwaites. We work in the shadows, guv. If you get famous for being lampooned on telly, the Ruling Cabal will Not Be Best Pleased.'

'That had occurred to me.'

Richard reached across the sofa and held Barbara's hand. She returned his grip, firmly.

'Something occurs to me,' said Vanessa. 'You should be careful about giving away old clothes to War on Want.'

'A little late for that,' Richard admitted.

They all looked at him.

'Today, while we were out, our rooms here were broken into. Not so you'd notice, but I take precautions and I can tell.'

'Don't tell me, your closets are empty?'

'No, Fred, they're full. Exactly as they were this morning.'

'I don't get it.'

'Barbara and I have brand new clothes. The same styles as the old ones, but different. I'm not sure, technically, what crime has been committed.'

'They can't think you wouldn't notice,' said Fred.

'The new outfits have been aged to match the old. By Tara, the wardrobe assistant, if the faint trace of Coty's Imprevu I whiffed around the counterfeit of my Emilio Pucci shirt is a significant clue. I understand Tara's specialty is scrounging up dupes for established costumes. Mama-Lou will not be pleased by the girl's involvement.'

'They're after you, guv. You and the Prof.'

'Yes, Fred. They are.'

'Barstards!'

The landlady came in, like a hurry-the-plot-along bit player, and told Vanessa she had a call.

'The Phantom Phoner,' she said, and left the room.

Richard pulled Barbara towards him. The Professor was not used to being in supernatural cross-hairs, and her mind was racing to keep up. A few weeks ago, she hadn't even known there were such things as curses, and now she was at the sharp end of one.

'I should have specialised in nineteenth-century woman novelists,' she said. 'My postgraduate thesis was on George Eliot. But the field was so crowded. The bloody structuralists were moving in, throwing their weight about. No one was thinking hard about television. So, here I am. I suppose I brought this on myself. You might have mentioned this was dangerous, though. If I'd stayed on campus, the worst that could happen was... well, getting burned at the stake during the next student demo... but being cursed is fairly bloody drastic.'

Vanessa came back.

'That was my agent,' she said. 'The one Della set us up with. Your scoop was on the money. Priscilla of the Lovely Legs is off to Nepal to find her missing father in a lamasery. She's left a note for Ben, which will make matters worse. I don't even get an exit scene. My pay packet is waiting at the studio and I can swap my entry lozenge for it any time in the next two days. My digs are no longer being paid for by O'Dell-Squiers. She tells me, if it's any consolation, that "Victoria Plant" has had a ton of fan mail, plus a film offer.'

'Exciting?' asked Fred.

'Not really. *Sexploits of a Suburban Housewife*. More in your lady friend's line than mine.'

Zarana, Fred's girlfriend, was an 'exotic dancer' who cheerfully admitted to being a stripper and did occasional modelling and actress jobs. She had been gruesomely murdered in several movies.

Vanessa looked glum at the sudden end of her brief television career.

'Knock knock?' said Fred.

'Who's there?' asked Barbara, trying to cheer up.

'Victoria.'

'Victoria who?'

Fred spread his hands. 'That's showbiz!'

Vanessa laughed, but chucked a newspaper at him too. Which made him concentrate on business again.

'If the assistant's working against us, is this wardrobe woman behind the scam?' he asked. 'The voodoo princess?'

'No,' said Richard, 'Mama-Lou is sympathetic to our cause. She knows or at least suspects what's going on, and sees it as a transgression of her religion. She gave me a hat.'

Fred whistled.

'Not a very nice hat,' Richard admitted. 'But a significant hat. We've seen its like about the place.'

He pulled the flat cap out of his pocket and set it on his head.

"Ey oop, there's trooble at t'mill,' said Fred, in a Londoner's impression of a Northshire accent. 'What do you look like?'

'Anyone?' asked Richard.

'You've got a producer's hat on,' said Barbara. 'Now I remember where Squiers got it. There's one exactly like it on the set. It's been on a hook since the programme started. Mavis left it there where her husband hung it just before his fatal stroke.'

'Da Barstow,' said Fred. 'Our hit-man.'

'Da Barstow used to be married to Mavis,' said Richard.

'And Marcus Squiers used to be married to June,' said Vanessa. 'He's put himself right in the frame.'

'Literally,' said Richard, taking off the cap. 'Da's wearing this in his portrait.'

'So this little bald git is diabolical mastermind of the month?' said Fred, who only knew Squiers from press cuttings. 'Can't say I'm surprised. He's a dead ringer for Donald Pleasence.'

'Is that a dupe?' asked Vanessa.

Richard looked at the stained lining-band. He had noticed how much Squiers sweated. He fingered the cap.

'It may be a dupe of the cap on the set, but it's the original

331

"producer's hat". I imagine Mama-Lou's slipped Squiers another dupe, which he's been wearing without noticing. Are you following this, Frederick?'

'The *Barstards* have got your clothes and you've got his cap.'

'Very good, Fred.'

'But what help is that to us?' asked Barbara.

'Level playing field, Prof,' said Fred.

'Two can do voodoo,' said Vanessa.

'Ah,' said Barbara, catching up.

Richard was thrilled. He recognised this was the most dangerous phase of the case. When he became excited by the problem and had a solution in mind, he was tempted to let down his guard and take silly risks. With a volunteer along for the ride, he needed to remember that when black magic got out of hand people tended to get horribly hurt.

'I will not let you be harmed,' he told Barbara.

She smiled, showing grit. He was pleased with her.

'We'll need to call in favours,' he told them, 'and work fast. Squiers is ahead on points and is setting us up for a knock-out before the end of the round.'

Fred shivered. 'It gives me chills when you talk like Frank Bough. It only happens when we're on a sticky wicket, up against the ropes, down to the last man, and facing a penalty in injury time.'

'How many episodes does a hit take?' asked Vanessa.

'I defer to Barbara's expertise,' said Richard.

'Typically,' she began, 'it's been done over six to ten weeks, twelve to twenty shows. To get the audience involved, I suspect. You said emotional investment in the characters was a key ingredient. I imagine it's important to get all fifteen million viewers on the hook. Of course, Squiers can usually afford to take the time to build slowly, work the relevant plot into the other things going on. None of the earlier, ah, commissions have taken over the programme completely. There've always been other stories running, about Mavis, Ben and the rest. Now, since we're close to exposing him, there's urgency. The ghost-hunters – us! – were set up on last night's episode, and will be introduced at the end of next Tuesday's show. They're due to turn up for the cliffhanger, as all hell breaks loose in the lounge. In the programme, by the way, the Bleeds Bogey is Da Barstow's angry ghost. He reckons Mavis killed him all those years ago. I estimate next Thursday's *Barstows* will be the crucial episode, when "Roget" and "Canberra" are established as characters.'

'That's when the voodoo is done,' said Richard. 'When our "dolls" are fixed in the public mind.'

Barbara shivered. 'The way things are going,' she said, 'I suspect we'll be horribly killed the week after. Does that sound right?'

'Just about,' said Richard.

'They really are Barstards,' spat Barbara. Good. She had progressed from fear to anger.

'We've a week and a half to defy the Saturday Man,' said Richard. 'A challenge. I enjoy a challenge.'

'And I enjoy breathing,' said Barbara, 'so rise to it, Richard.'

XIII.

First thing Monday morning, after a weekend spent mostly on the phone, Richard and Barbara turned up at Haslemere Studios to meet their newly costumed doppelgangers outside the sound-stage. Lionel had arranged for publicity photographs. Marcus Squiers, wearing what he fondly thought was his producer's hat, beetled around sweatily in the background, presumably to keep an eye on the doll-making spell.

Actors named Leslie Veneer and Gaye Brough were freshly

cast as "Roget Masterman" and "Canberra Laurinz". Veneer had not been in any films or done any television Richard had ever heard of. Having all but given up on acting in favour of work as an insurance adjuster, he no longer had an agent. His head-shot was still in *Spotlight* just so he could say he was an actor rather than an insurance man when talking to girls at keys-in-a-bowl parties. Gaye's curriculum vitae was more impressive, listing page after page of seemingly everything made in the United Kingdom from *A Man for All Seasons* to *Devil Bride of Dracula* – though she admitted you'd need to run prints frame by frame through a Steenbeck to catch her face. In twenty-five years in the profession, Gaye Brough had never played a part with a character name. Essentially, she was an extra. He assumed both players had been cast purely for physical resemblance, which was considerable. When they were posed, Barbara instinctively cosied up to Veneer, and Richard had to reclaim her – prompting blushes, which Gaye instantly matched.

Veneer, obviously shrieking inside with ambitious glee, projected an exaggerated disdain that would come across on screen as woodenness. Gaye bubbled delight and enthusiasm, and kept bumping into things – either because the sudden career jump undid her spatial sense or she usually wore thick glasses that were left at home so she could dazzle with her Barbara-like eyes.

The quartet of interchangeables posed together. Veneer and Gaye wore Richard and Barbara's original clothes. Richard and Barbara made do with Tara's dupes.

'With my producer's hat on, I have to say these are perfect.'

Squiers looked from the originals to the copies, meek but smug. From him, Richard sensed a species of hurt resentment that his racket had been tumbled, but also a belief that Marcus Squiers was the aggrieved and persecuted party, that he had every right to call on the Saturday Man for aid against those who would thwart his killing business. This was interesting, but beside the point – Richard was curious about the conjurer's motives, but knew they weren't important. Squiers thought he was home safe and the interlopers doomed. He was arrogant enough to play the I-know-you-know-that-I-know-you-know game and loiter to enjoy the show as his enemies were supposedly drawn deeper into his trap. Richard hoped that was a mistake.

Richard pinched his wrist and saw Veneer rub what he thought was a gnat-bite.

The writing pack had also turned out and were circling, admiring the casting. As several photographers took thousands of exposures, writers tossed questions at Richard and Barbara, which often bounced off onto Veneer and Gaye, who were bewildered but kept up the mysterioso brooding and glossy smiling that were their single-note performances.

'Richard, do you get enough exorcise?'

'Barbara, what crept into the crypt and crapped?'

'Richard, have you ever laid a ghost?'

'Barbara, what's the best recipe for ectoplasm omelette?'

Mama-Lou watched, from a distance. Richard caught her eye, and she winked. Blessings of Erzulie Freda. That was a comfort.

After an age, it was over. Lionel shooed away the photographers, and Veneer and Gaye were ushered off to the make-up department.

'They have to get head-casts made,' said Lionel.

That was a significant clue as to what Squiers had in mind for Roget and Canberra. A brace of severed heads should be ready for the episode to be broadcast tomorrow week.

Richard's neck itched. It was the wrong collar.

The props department were calling in axes from the warehouse, to give Gerard Loss a selection to choose from.

Next, Richard had an important interview. In June O'Dell's trailer.

XIV.

Tuesday's episode climaxed with the Bleeds Bogey manifesting a full-on telekinetic storm in Mavis Barstow's lounge. Objects were hurled through the air on dozens of fishing lines and Ben sank to his knees pleading for mercy as invisible forces lashed his face.

For a brief shot that took longer to set up than the rest of the episode, Dudley Finn had make-up scars applied, with flesh-coloured sticking plasters fixed over them – when the plasters were torn away by fishing lines, Ben had claw-marks on his face. Then, as Mavis shouted defiance at her late husband, the doors were torn off their hinges, a flood of dry ice fog-smoke-mist-ectoplasm poured onto the set and cleared to show Leslie Veneer and Gaye Brough posed in the doorway as if hoping for a spin-off series. Loss needed a dozen takes before he was browbeaten by Marcus Squiers – with his producer's hat on, tapping his watch as the shoot edged ever-nearer the dreaded and never-embraced 'Golden Time' when union rules insisted the crew's wages tripled – into accepting Veneer's reading of Roget Masterman's introductory line, 'Avaunt, Spirit of Evil! We've come about your bogeys, Mrs Barstow, and not a moment too soon!'

Having been on set during the taping, and even smarmily consulted on the finer points of psychokinesis by an unctuous Squiers, Richard felt he could skip the transmission. His associates were back at the guest house, watching the programme for him.

Inspector Price had said it would be easy to break into the Bank of England while *The Northern Barstows* was on the air. It was certainly easy to slip into the studio where the show was made. Almost everyone connected with the programme was at home in front of the telly, fuming about the way June O'Dell stepped on their lines or taking notes for the 7 a.m. post-mortem in the writers' pit the next morning.

Wearing Marcus Squiers's producer's hat and a long drab

coat, Richard felt like a walking manifestation of the Bleeds Bogey. He stalked through the car park and approached the stage door, which should have been accidentally left unlocked. No lozenge-filching had been required.

When the door gave at his push, he was relieved. Mama-Lou was off her fence. The revelation about Tara, who was after the top job in Wardrobe, fully committed the woman to their cause.

She was a believer, not a priestess – but belief was what this was all about.

Barbara reported that the writers had been forthcoming in discussing Thursday's episode, asking her parapsychology questions she had to invent answers for, but reticent when it came to next Tuesday's, confirming to Richard's satisfaction that Roget and Canberra were due for the chop then. Leslie Veneer, who now had an agent again, and Gaye Brough, who was hoping for the cover of the *TV Times*, didn't yet know how short-lived their stardom was due to be.

So, it all came down to next Tuesday's episode – which had already been written, in semi-secret, by Marcus Squiers independent of the pack. Barbara had asked around tactfully and discovered this was standard procedure for shows with major plot developments – and, also, obviously, when Squiers was using his video voodoo to kill people. The floor taping was due on Friday, with special effects pick-up shots (decapitations?) scheduled for Monday morning.

That gave Richard a weekend to counter the spell. He trusted making television was as easy as it looked. After a few days hanging round the production team, he thought he could wear all their hats. But he still needed help from inside the enemy camp.

It was dark on the stage. His night-senses took moments to adjust.

Someone clapped and lights came up.

He was in the middle of Mavis Barstow's lounge. Prop objects were strewn everywhere, tossed by the Bogey. Cards stuck to them warned against violating continuity by moving anything.

'Mama-Lou,' he called out.

His voice came back to him.

He sensed something wrong. Other people were here, who he had not expected, who weren't part of his deal.

Strong hands gripped his arms. Two sets.

He bent over and threw one of the men over his shoulder with an aikido move, then sank a nasty knee into the other's goolies. Thanks to Bruce Lee and David Carradine, everyone accepted what British schoolboys used to call 'dirty fighting' as an ancient, noble and religious art form. Richard realised he had just floored the Tank-Top Twins. They rolled and fell and groaned and hopped, but had enough presence of mind – or fear of the consequences – not to disturb any labelled props. They got over their initial hurt and came at him, more seriously. Richard brought up his fists, and thought through six ways of semi-permanently disabling two larger, younger, stupider opponents within the next minute and a half.

'Leave them alone,' said a woman. 'They're expensive.'

The instruction was for him but it made the Twins stand down and back away. Richard opened his fists and made a monster-clutch gesture while doing a ghost-moan. They flinched.

'Was that necessary?' he asked the woman.

'Now I know you can take care of yourself,' said the woman. 'Good.'

June O'Dell, Mavis Barstow, stood on the set as if it were really her home. In slippers, she barely came up to the mantelpiece, but still seemed to fill any spare space. Richard fancied she looked younger tonight, with a little colour in her cheeks that might come from digesting Emma. Ghost-eaters could do that, often without even knowing how they retained their youthful blush. She wore a filmy muu-muu with mandarin sleeves, diamonds at her ears and around her throat. Mama-Lou was with June, wearing a white bikini bottom augmented by a mass of necklaces, armlets, anklets, bracelets and a three-pointed tiara surmounted with the skulls of a shrew, a crow and a pike. Maybe she was more than just a believer.

The Twins faded into the shadows.

'I've been thinking about what you suggested to me the other day about Marcus's sideline, Mr Jeperson,' said June. 'It was hard to believe.'

'Was?'

'It answers so many questions. I knew Marcus was up to something sneaky. I just didn't imagine it could be so unusual. Such a betrayal of the sacred trust between creative artist and the audience.'

'It's dangerous to use the Saturday Man,' said Mama-Lou. 'Betimes, the Saturday Man wind up usin' you.'

'Don't make excuses for the wretched clot, Louise. He was always a worm!'

Richard took off the cap Mama-Lou had given him.

'Ugh. Ghastly thing,' said June.

Mama-Lou took the cap back, reverentially. It had become a sacred object.

Richard went to the mantelpiece. All the framed photographs and trinkets had been distributed across the set by the poltergeist, save for Da Barstow's urn – which issued green smoke when it became obvious who the Bogey was. The eyes of the portrait had burned like hot coals. Richard saw where red bulbs had been set into the picture.

He took the urn and twisted off the top.

Screwed up inside were dozens of used cue cards.

'Marcus's words,' said June. 'This is where he gets to choke on them.'

339

The Twins came back, stepping cautiously. They had fetched a rusty barbeque from the props vault. It usually sat on the obviously indoor set of Ben Barstow's back garden.

Richard lifted the grille and poured the cue cards into the pan.

'You bring what I tol' you,' Mama-Lou said to June.

June snapped her fingers and a Twin handed over a brown paper bag.

Mama-Lou looked inside and smiled.

She emptied the bag onto the crumpled cards. Nail-clippings, a still-damp handkerchief, bristles shaved off a toothbrush, blood-dotted Kleenex.

'Obviously, you can't get hair from a bald man,' said June. 'But Marcus never learned to shave. I think his mummy did it until he married me, and he expected I would take over. No wonder it didn't last. Blood is better than hair, you said?'

'Blood is good, Miss June,' said Mama-Lou.

'Will you do the honours, Mama-Lou?' said Richard, bowing.

'Indeed I will. This is my religion, an' I despise what's been done wit' it.'

She had a box of Swan Vesta matches caught between her thigh and the tie of her bikini-bottom. She took the box and rattled the matches.

'Erzulie Freda, we call you to the flame,' she said, looking up.

Mama-Lou was dancing to unheard music. Her necklaces – which were strung with beads, feathers, items of power, bones and tiny carvings – rattled and bounced against her dark, lithe torso.

The set lights went down – it wasn't magic, one of the Twins was at the dimmer switch. June snapped her fingers, banishing her familiars – who had orders to stand guard outside. In the darkness, Mama-Lou struck a match. The single flame grew, swelling around the matchhead, burning down the matchstick, almost to her enamelled nails. She dropped the match onto the pile of combustibles, humming to herself. The flame caught.

'Hocus pocus mucus Marcus,' improvised June.

Mama-Lou slapped her shoulders, breasts, hips and thighs, with gestures Richard had seen performed by warlocks, witches and morris dancers. She added certain herbs to the fire, filling the studio with a rich, pungent, not-unpleasant musk. Mama-Lou shook herself into a trance, channelling her patron, Erzulie Freda. She invoked others of her island pantheon, reciting the 'Litanie des Saints'. Damballah Wedo, Lord Shango, Papa Legba.

And Baron Samedi. The Saturday Man.

When the barbeque was fully alight, Richard laid the producer's hat into the bed of flames.

They watched until everything was burned down to ashes.

Then they filled the urn.

Richard fastened the lid.

'Now, the seal of Erzulie Freda,' announced Mama-Lou. She surprised June O'Dell with a deep, open-mouthed kiss and then applied herself to Richard with nips and an agile tongue. The wardrobe mistress's personal loa was the Haitian goddess of love and sensuality. He would have to admit he knew how ceremonies performed under the patronage of Erzulie Freda were traditionally concluded.

Mama-Lou pulled him and June towards Mavis Barstow's enormous Friesian cowhide three-piece suite, elbows crooked around their necks, lips active against their faces. She had a lot of strength in her arms. This development came as something of a shock to June, but Mama-Lou whispered something to her in French which made reservations evaporate. The actress became as light on her feet as she was on her platform-skates and slipped busy fingers inside Richard's shirt.

He remembered the star's hunger, and the consequences

for unwary ghosts. He must be careful not to let her leech away too much of him. She had used up the best part of her husband, literally. But Mama-Lou was strong too, with a different kind of hunger, a different kind of need.

Two bodies, one very pale, one very black, wound around him and each other. And two spirits, burning inside the bodies, pulled at him.

When he told Barbara about the evening, he would tactfully omit this next stage of the ritual.

He checked the cameras with quick glances. They were hooded. The red recording lights were off.

Which was a mercy.

June and Mama-Lou impatiently helped him off with his trousers. Richard thought of England, then remembered he wasn't actually English.

XV.

Vanessa, of course, saw what had happened in an instant, and held it over him all week, exacting numerous favours. She obviously told Fred, and he went around looking at his 'guv'nor' with envious awe. Richard was not entirely comfortable with his own behaviour, and took care to be exceptionally solicitous to Barbara, which – later on the night in question – involved a fairly heroic effort in their shared bedroom. He put his evident success down to the lingering effect of Mama-Lou's voodoo herbs rather than the strength of his own amative constitution. Now he was glad, not only that he had not been found out by the Professor, but that a night spent with her had followed his hour or so under the spell of Erzulie Freda.

Being open to the feelings of others often led him into choppy waters, and he was not about to excuse himself on the grounds of diminished responsibility. He accepted the less admirable, very male, elements of his make-up, and determined to rein them in more effectively. The Swinging Sixties were over, and this ought to be the Sensible (or at least, the Sober) Seventies. Besides, he could self-diagnose the symptoms and knew he was falling in love with Barbara Corri.

It was his gift to know how other people felt. All the time. Without fail. But with one exception. He could tell when a woman was attracted to him. He could tell when she was infuriated with him and performing a supernatural feat by concealing it from the world. But he could not tell if a woman he loved even liked him. If Barbara were in love with him, she'd have to come straight out and say so. Even then, he was no more able to tell if she meant it than anyone else in the world could. It struck him that this blind spot was probably the one thing, along with his unique upbringing under the aegis of the Diogenes Club, that prevented him from becoming a monster.

Too many people with talents went bad.

Look at Marcus Squiers. Obviously, the fellow had some raw abilities, or he'd never have been able to co-opt the arcana to a criminal venture. He could have used the influence of *The Northern Barstows* over the viewing public for good. Or he could have left well enough alone and concentrated on making better TV programmes.

'I wonder if he hit on this by accident,' Barbara said, on Monday morning, as they sat on the studio lawn. They watched Leslie and Gaye, who had grown close over the last fortnight, console each other before the taping of the worst-concealed surprise twist in *Barstows* history – their deaths. 'I keep thinking of Brenda's black baby. The way apparently the whole audience changed opinion when Mavis did. That might have been when it started.'

'There was Karen Finch,' said Richard.

'She must have been the first victim. The Bogus Brenda was

her doll. What happened to BB on the programme happened to her in life. Not killed, but certainly her options were limited.'

'Barbara?' he held her hand.

'Yes?'

'I won't let him murder us. What we did this weekend will work. In the end, Squiers is an amateur and I am a professional.'

From the corner of his eye, he saw Leslie and Gaye embracing, in tears.

He kissed Barbara and thought, for a moment, he knew how she felt.

Then it was gone again, and he found himself looking at her face and wondering.

'You know,' she said, 'I can never tell what you're thinking.'

'Good. I'd hate to spoil any more surprises.'

She laughed, like the sun coming out.

'So, do you want to watch our heads getting chopped off?'

'Why not?'

He took her arm and they walked across the lawn, towards the stage. As they passed, Leslie and Gaye were brushing grass-strands off their costumes and getting it together to undergo their career-ending ordeal.

'Cheer up,' Richard told them, 'it might never happen.'

'Easy for you to say,' snarled Leslie Veneer, with more feeling than any of his line-readings. 'You're not the bloody God of Bleeds.'

They arrived on the stage before Leslie and Gaye, and – as had become tediously predictable – an assistant director was hustling them onto the set when the real actors arrived. Everyone's identities got sorted out.

Gerard Loss was nowhere to be seen. Marcus Squiers was directing this scene himself, wearing his rarely seen director's hat – a baseball cap. He sat on a high-chair like a tennis umpire and wielded the sort of megaphone Cecil B. DeMille had been fond of until talking pictures came in.

Squiers was surprised to see Richard and Barbara, but nodded at them with the kind of magnanimous admiration only someone who thought he'd long since won could show for an already mortally wounded foe he was about to decapitate. Richard waved cheerily back.

Almost all of the episode had been taped on Friday. Roget and Canberra were shown up as yet more confidence tricksters (a habitual *Barstows* plot tic). It turned out they were in with Ben Barstow and had been faking the haunting in order to extort a fortune from Mavis – but this had raised the real angry spirit of Da Barstow, who was about to get his revenge.

Clarence 'Gore' Gurney, a special effects man who usually worked on cinema films about Satanic accidents, was hired in at great expense – and with resentful grumbling from the O'D-S make-up people – to supervise the Decapitation of Roget Masterman and, to vary things, the Exploding Head of Canberra Laurinz. Realistic dummies, faces contorted in frozen screams, were held in waiting, tubes and wires fed into slit holes in the backs of their clothes. Richard assumed the dummies now wore the clothes filched from his and Barbara's closets. At last, here were proper voodoo dolls, with hairs stolen from brushes applied to the heads. Tara, exceeding her wardrobe job, was helping Gurney set up the effects.

Barbara kept looking at the dummies, struck by the terror on her own faked face.

Leslie and Gaye only had to flounder screaming around the set, while Dudley-as-Ben begged Da for forgiveness and fire spurted out of the portrait's eyes. Then the actors were hauled off – and essentially kicked out the studio door, final pay packets exchanged for entry lozenges – and the dummies were set up. This took an age.

Lionel dropped by to say hello.

'They'll never get away with this, luv,' he said. 'Mucus is mental. Grannies in Hartlepool will have heart attacks. Folk tune in to the *Barstards* to see Mavis being a cow and Northshire idiots whining about the old days over pints of Griddles, not blood and guts all over the shop. It's like the worst bits of James Herbert spewed into front parlours and the audience won't like it. The duty officer will log a record number of complaints when this airs. Once it's out, ART will come down like a ton of angry bricks. Mark my words.'

'We only have one shot at this,' announced Squiers through his megaphone. 'All three cameras, make sure you can't see each other or the edge of the set.'

Three cameramen gave thumbs-up.

'Gore?'

Gurney crouched over a wooden control-box studded with lights and switches, and plungers like the ones used to detonate cartoon dynamite. He checked all the leads and saluted Squiers.

'Supernatural smoke, please.'

Odorous clouds were puffed onto the set by stagehands wielding gadgets like industrial vacuum cleaners on reverse. Finn coughed and the smoke settled like a grey ground-mist.

'Light the picture.'

Da's eyes shone. It struck Richard that Marcus Squiers must have posed for the portrait.

'Dudley?'

Finn went down on his knees, warily ready.

'And action!'

Gurney flicked switches and the dummies flailed with alarming realism. Finn, nervous to be on set with so much explosive, picked up his ranted lines.

'Dr Laurinz!' shouted Squiers.

Gurney depressed a plunger. The Canberra dummy's head burst, flinging watermelon-bits and cottage cheese across the set. Barbara pressed her face against Richard's collar, unable to watch.

Richard did not miss Squiers's nasty little smile.

The last splatters of the head's contents rained down. Red syrup spurted from the neck as if it were a sugary drinking fountain. The headless dummy toppled over, mechanics inside sparking dangerously.

'And Masterman!'

Gurney depressed the other plunger.

A rubber axe flew across the set. Richard watched his own head come off, tumble through the air and fall, still-blinking, at the feet of a screaming Ben Barstow.

'Cut! Thank you all very much. You've made TV history.'

There was a smattering of applause, mostly from the writing pack who had been let off school especially to watch the deaths.

'The *Ti*-bloody-*tanic* made history,' said Lionel, who was annoyed to get gluey red cornstarch on his Clarks tracker shoes.

'What do you think, Mr Jeperson?' asked Squiers through his megaphone. 'How did it look from down there?'

Richard made an equivocal gesture.

'I'll have to see it go out to be sure.'

'Indeed you will. Would you and Professor Corri care to be my guests tomorrow? Because it's a "special" episode, we're having a select celebration here at the studio. We can watch you die and then have canapés and wine. It'll be a treat. Are you up for it?'

Barbara was white-lipped with fury and terror, but rigidly self-possessed, refusing to let Squiers see. Richard's blood was up too, but he was calm. He'd seen the worst and it wasn't so bad.

'We wouldn't miss it for the world,' he said.

XVI.

'You're early,' said Squiers.

'I thought we might not get the chance to chat later.'

Squiers was surprised, calculated a moment, then chose to laugh.

Coolly, Richard sauntered down the aisle of the small, luxurious screening room, fingers brushing the leatherette of the upholstered seats. Squiers stood in front of a wall of colour television sets, turned on and tuned to ITV but with the sound off, images repeated as if through insect-eyes. A quiz programme was on, the grinning host in a silver tuxedo dropping contestants into vats of gunk when they failed to answer correctly, showgirls in spangly tights posed by washer-dryers and Triumph TR7s, mutant puppets popping up between the rounds to do silent slapstick. No wonder Richard preferred reading.

Squiers wore a different hat tonight, a large purple Stetson, with bootlace tie, orange ruffle shirt, faux-buckskin tuxedo and rawhide cowboy boots with stack heels and spurs. Richard intuited that the ten-gallon titfer was the writer-producer's 'party hat'. Marcus Squiers saw himself as a gunslinger.

'Nice threads, Squiers.'

'Thank you, Mr Masterman.'

'Jeperson. Masterman is your fellow. The one on TV.'

'I was forgetting. It's easy to get mixed up.'

'I suppose it is.'

Richard was not what Squiers expected. In the producer's mind, Richard (and Barbara) ought to be getting sweaty, nervous, close to panic, sensing the trap closing, feeling a frightful fiend's breath warming their backs. They should be jitterishly trying to evade the inescapable, pass mrjamesian runes on to some other mug, get out of the way of safes and grand pianos fated to fall from the skies.

348

Disappointment roiled off Squiers, who – as ever – was the sweaty one.

For him, this should have been a new pleasure. All his previous marks had been unaware of the gunsights fixed on their foreheads. Richard knew what was happening and was powerless to dodge the bullet. This was the first time Squiers could afford to let anyone know how clever he had been.

'It was Junie's fault,' said Squiers. 'That first serial, just six weeks of it, was damn good telly. Damn good writing. Better than your Dennis Potter or Alan Plater any night of the week. Junie was good in it. She's always been able to play Mavis. She was the one who pushed for the series. I wanted to go on to other things. Plays, films, novels. I could have, you know. I had ideas, ready to go. But Junie tied me to the *Barstards*. The things she did. You wouldn't believe. The first few years, I kept trying to quit and she'd wrestle me back. There was never much money. Muggins here got stuck with his nineteen-sixty-flaming-four salary, while the Moo's fees climbed to the sky. Read the bloody small print – first rule of showbiz. There were other ways to keep me on the hook. Even when we weren't married any more, she'd find means. "No one else can produce the show," she says. "No one." Who would want to? I mean, have you watched it?'

Richard nodded.

'I have to live with it. So there might as well be some use in it.'

'Your discovery?'

'Yes.' The bitterness turned sly. A petulant smile crept in, barely covering his teeth. 'That's a good way of putting it. The discovery.'

'It must be galling to waste shots on Roget and Canberra. I mean, who's to pay for us?'

Squiers chuckled.

'Oh, there's a purpose to you. Nothing goes to waste in

television. I have a select company joining us for this party. But you and Professor Corri are my guests of honour. Where is she, by the way?'

'Present,' said Barbara.

She wore a bias-cut tangerine evening gown, with matching blooms in her hair and on her shoulder. She stood a moment in the doorway, then glided down. Squiers applauded. Richard kissed her.

'You make a lovely couple,' said Squiers. 'But you'll be lovelier without heads.'

Richard felt an itch around the neck. It was becoming quite persistent.

Barbara was wound tight. Her arm around his waist was nearly rigid with suppressed terror.

'If you haven't learned something by the end of the evening,' said Squiers. 'I'll eat my hat.'

'And what a fine hat it is,' said Richard.

The room filled up. The theatre seats took up barely a quarter of the screening room, which was otherwise available for general milling and swilling. Minions in black-and-white livery weaved among the guests with trays of food: little cubes of cheese and pineapple on sticks; champagne glasses stuffed with prawns, lettuce and pink mayonnaise; quartered individual pork pies, with dollops of Branston Pickle; fans of After Eight mints; ashtrays of foil-wrapped Roses chocolates. A barman served wine (Mateus rosé, Blue Nun, Black Tower) and beer (Watney's Red Barrel, Whitbread Trophy Bitter, Double Diamond). There had been an attempt to market a real Griddles Ale, but it had not been successful – beer connoisseurs reckoned the cold tea they drank on telly had a better flavour.

Not everyone from O'D-S was there. Richard and Barbara kept score. Anyone on this guest list was almost certainly in it with Squiers; the rest were on the outside and innocent. So far, the guilties ran to Tara (no surprise), Dudley Finn (but not his boyfriend), Jeanne Treece and a good three-quarters of the writing pack. Lionel was evidently guiltless, and so was Gerard Loss. Some people surprised you.

Squiers whizzed about, ten-gallon hat bobbing among a sea of heads, pressing the flesh, meeting and greeting. Richard saw three people come in who were his own invitees. Squiers had pause when he recognised Vanessa, but clearly had no idea who Fred was and was puzzled to see the third added guest, whom he must be dimly aware of but couldn't put a name to. That was another black mark against Evil on the score-board.

Richard was about to make introductions when a fresh knot of outside guests appeared and Squiers barged through the crowd to welcome them, sweatily unctuous and eager.

Now Richard understood Squiers's crack about nothing going to waste in television.

'Good grief,' he said, 'we're starring in a sales pitch!'

Squiers led his VIP guests down the aisle, towards Richard and company. Richard sensed Vanessa and Fred, dapper book-ends in white matador-cut tuxedos, taking flanking defensive positions. Good move.

As Squiers grinned and got closer, Richard saw Mama-Lou and June O'Dell – as near to disguised as they could manage – slip in, and take seats hunched down in the back row, huge hat-brims over their faces.

'Mr Jeperson, Professor Corri,' said Squiers. 'I'd like you to meet some people. Prospective sponsors. This is Adam Onions.'

'O-nye-ons,' corrected a youngish man in a blazer and polo-neck. 'Not like the vegetable.'

He stuck out a hand, which Richard opted not to shake.

'Hello, Barb,' said Onions, shyly fluttering his fingers.

The Professor was furious at Onions's presence, which she took as a personal betrayal.

Richard guessed how Onions fit in. He was from the Brighton University Department of Parapsychology. Barbara had talked to him before getting involved with the Diogenes Club. His ambition must have been piqued, along with his curiosity. He had made connections and ridden the hobby-horse.

'I'm with a government think tank now,' he said. 'The Institute of Psi Technology. Pronounced "Eyesight". We're getting in a position to be competitive, Mr Jeperson. Your gentlemen's club has had the field to itself for too long. Your record is astounding, but your horizons have been limited. Effort has been wasted smashing what should be measured. There are applications. Profitable, socially valuable, cutting edge.'

Richard could guess what Onions's political masters would want to cut with their edge.

'Heather Wilding,' continued Squiers, indicating a woman with a ring-of-confidence smile, slightly ovoid pupils like cat's eyes, feathery waves of honey-blond Farrah hair and a tailored red velour suit with maxi-skirt and shoulder pads. 'She represents—'

'I know what Miss Wilding represents.'

'Ms,' said the woman, who was American.

'Private enterprise,' commented Richard. 'Very enterprising enterprise.'

Heather Wilding was a name Richard had come across before. She fronted for Derek Leech, the newspaper proprietor (of the *Comet*, among other organs) who sat at the top of a pyramid of interlinked corporations and was just becoming a major dark presence in the world. Leech was taking an ever-greater interest in television, so his representation here should not be a surprise. This woman sat on the Devil's left hand and fed him fondue.

'And this is General Skinner. He's with NATO.'

The General was in uniform, with a chest-spread of medal-ribbons and a pearl-handled side-arm. Over classically handsome bone structure was stretched the skin of a white lizard, making his whole face an expressionless, long-healed scar. He was the single most terrifying individual Richard had ever met. How long had this man-shaped creature walked among humanity? Some of his medals were from wars not fought in this century. Not a lot of people must notice that.

'Mr Jeperson,' said Skinner. 'You. Have. Been. Noticed.'

No response was required. A restraining order had been served. Richard was eager to look away from the shark to consider the trailing minnows.

'Mr Topazio and Mr Maltese are—'

'Olive-oil importers?' Richard suggested.

The little old men with scarred knuckles and gold rings caught the joke at once – it was a reference to the legitimate business of the Corleones in *The Godfather* – but it went over Squiers's head. These must be his longest-standing clients, the fellows who had interests in seeing Jamie Hepplethwaites and Queenie Tolliver out of the picture. Did they feel uneasy at the ever more high-flying company? How could their poor little organised-crime business compete with government departments out to declare psychic war, a monster with the resources of the military-industrial master-planners at his disposal or the tentacles of a hellfire-fed multimedia empire? Richard wondered if old-fashioned crims would even get bones thrown to them when Squiers took *The Northern Barstows* up in the world.

He had been worried about ad-men getting hold of Squiers's voodoo. Now – though Derek Leech had his claws deep into that business too – he saw there were worse things waiting. He had a bubble of amusement at the thought of what would have to be written into *The Northern Barstows* if these powers took over –

earthquakes in countries a long way from Northshire, economic upheavals on a global scale, mass suicides among unfriendly governments. The poor old Barstows would have to expand their field of operations, spreading misery and devastation wherever they went.

If Richard knew who Squiers's guests were and what they represented, Squiers was still puzzling over Richard's third extra guest.

'Have we met?' Squiers asked.

'Good heavens, no,' said Lady Damaris Gideon, casting a pink eye over the fellow. 'Why ever should we have? On the Amalgamated Rediffusion Television board, we don't care to deal with tradesmen.'

Maybe Squiers saw what was coming. His grin almost froze.

Lights went down and sound came up on the televisions. There was a hustle to get into seats. Richard found himself between Barbara, who held his hand fiercely, and Onions, who settled back with a prawn cocktail in one hand and a tiny fork in the other. The *Barstows* theme came out of all the speakers.

'This is going out to an estimated audience of nineteen million nation-wide,' said Squiers, over the music. 'Five OAPs and a dog are watching the *Dad's Army* repeat on BBC One. If BBC Two are putting out the test card instead of the classical music quiz literally no one will notice. Our poltergeist plot has pulled in new viewers. Under other circumstances, we'd keep Roget and Canberra on board. They've proved popular. However, you know what they say in writing class, "Kill your darlings."'

In the first scene, Ben Barstow was down the Grand Old Duke, sinking pints of Griddles and blathering about the horrific events up at the Barstow house. All the extras were impressed. Bev the barmaid crossed herself.

Then, Roget and Canberra were on screen, setting up mystical equipment in the lounge – an electric pentagram, bells on strings, black-out sheets scrawled with white symbols.

Onions snorted at this arcane nonsense.

'There's no science in that.'

The academic was shushed from all around the room. Mavis had a 'when I were a lass' speech coming up.

At the end of the scene as scripted was a moment when the fraudsters let their guards slip after Mavis has left the room and chuckle over their scam. In the programme as broadcast, the end-of-part-one card came up early and the network cut to adverts.

Squiers saw at once that this wasn't the show he had written, produced, directed, edited and handed over to ART for transmission. With VIPs in the room, he couldn't make a fuss, but he did hurry out to try to make an urgent call. He came back ghost-faced and shaking. Fred had disabled the studio's external telephone lines. Even the Phantom Phoner could not get out.

During the ad break, Richard looked away from the screens and was amused to notice Heather Wilding shielding her eyes, too. A wrestler known for his thick pelt plastered on the Früt and got a grip on a girl in a bathing suit – without ever having seen the advert, it had seeped into Richard's consciousness, which ticked him off. Skinner's strange face reflected the highly coloured images sliding across the wall of screens. Topazio was asleep and snoring gently, as Maltese tossed peanuts like George Raft spinning a coin and caught them with his mouth.

On the way back to his seat, Squiers saw June in the audience. She bent up her hat-brim and blew him a kiss. Her presence was a blow to his heart. He was unsteady on his feet the rest of the way. When he sat down, he slipped off his Stetson and unconsciously began to chew the leather.

After the adverts, the new material took over. Though she had studied *The Northern Barstows* from the beginning, Barbara had found it surprisingly difficult to pastiche even a few scenes of script. After hours of effort, she had come up with six typewritten pages, which June scrawled all over with her magic marker – some sort of seal of approval Richard frankly didn't understand, but which the Professor did. Considering she was writing on and appearing in her specialist subject, she had crossed an academic line which might be hard to hop back over. They had taped their alternate scene over the weekend, using technicians bound to a vow of secrecy by Super-Golden Time wages. June, who authorised the expense in her capacity as a controlling interest in O'Dell-Squiers, participated as if it were a regular episode, while Mama-Lou fussed over the costumes. Richard had worried that sparks might combust between the three women, with unfortunate revelations to follow – but he had defused several potential mines.

On screen, Roget and Canberra began a ritual of exorcism.

Fred laughed out loud, realising he was now watching Richard and Barbara, not Leslie and Gaye. Few others in the room noticed the switch, which was a tribute to the casting. Some of the pack knew this wasn't what they expected, but they were used to Squiers's 'last-minute' changes and accepted what was being broadcast as the authentic *Barstows*. Squiers had a chunk of leather in his mouth and was chewing steadily. He was indeed eating his hat. His shirt was sweated through.

The ritual was nonsense, of course. If it hadn't been, the characters wouldn't have been Roget and Canberra as established on the programme. It was important to keep consistent, not to break the audience's compact with unlikeliness.

The pentagram crackled and Da Barstow's urn levitated off the mantel.

Squiers clutched his chest, choking on his hat. Apart from Richard, nobody noticed.

'You… barstards,' Squiers croaked.

The chanting rose, whipping up a supernatural wind in Mavis's lounge. Mavis blundered in, eliciting a round of applause from the audience, and held hands with the ghost-hunters. June had insisted on being in the scene. It was her show, after all.

'Chant after me,' said Richard-as-Roget.

June-as-Mavis nodded.

'Spectre of Evil, Spectre of Pain,' said Richard-as-Roget.

'Spectre of Evil, Spectre of Pain,' echoed Barbara-as-Canberra and June-as-Mavis.

'Begone from this house, begone from this plane!'

'Begone from this house, begone from this plane!'

The urn wobbled a bit, but winds continued to buffet the exorcising trio, and flash-powder went off around the lounge.

'Spirit of Darkness, Spirit of Gloom...'

'Spirit of Darkness, Spirit of Gloom...'

'Return to thy graveyard, return to thy tomb!'

'Return to thy graveyard, return to thy tomb!'

The lid came off the urn and flaming ashes sprinkled.

Squiers was severely affected now, jerking and gasping in seizure, ragged-brimmed hat bucking up and down on his lap. The people sitting around him noticed. Tara ripped open his shirt, scattering buttons, and pressed his heaving chest.

On the screens, the ashes of Da Barstow – the 'doll' of Marcus Squiers – spewed out of the urn in a human-shaped cloud, with trailing limbs and a thickness around the head that was unmistakably a flat cap.

It wasn't even special effects, it was an illusion, a lighting trick.

June-as-Mavis held up a silver crucifix, forged by melting down Da's shove ha'penny champion sovereign. Richard-as-Roget raised a fetish of Erzulie Freda, on loan from Mama-Lou. And Barbara-as-Canberra pulled an old-fashioned toy gun which shot out a flag bearing the word 'bang!'

'You were always bloody useless, Darius Barstow,' said Mavis, at full blast. 'Now clear off out of it and leave decent people alone.'

'Dispel,' said Richard, underplaying.

The cloud of ash exploded, pelting the entire set – it had taken longer to clean up than to shoot the scene – and then vanished.

Dawnlight filtered in on a dimmer-switch. Tweeting bird sound effects laid over the settling dust.

The camera rolled towards Mavis, who gave a speech about how the nightmare was over and life in Bleeds could get back to 'normal'.

There was a commotion around Squiers's seat. Squiers wasn't in it any more. He wasn't in anything any more. All that was left was a hat on the floor, a fine scattering of grey ash and an after-the-firework-display smell.

Tara's hands, which had been against Squiers's chest, were withered, like an arthritic eighty-year-old's. One of her fingers snapped off, but she was too shocked to scream.

The end titles scrolled and the screening room lights came up.

Richard thanked Lady Dee, without whom the substitution of master tapes could not have been managed. The board was pleased that the proper order of things had been restored – little companies like O'Dell-Squiers (soon to be O'Dell Holdings) might make television, but networks like Amalgamated Rediffusion owned the air-waves and decided what was fed into the boxes. Squiers had focused on working magic in the making of the show, and taken transmission for granted, but Richard had understood the pins didn't skewer the doll until the episode in question was watched by the believing millions.

Wilding and Skinner were gone. Not like Squiers, and leaving fewer traces behind. This hadn't worked out, but they had other irons in the fire – which Richard, or someone like him, would have to deal with eventually.

Adam Onions wasn't in that class yet. He was a nuisance, not a danger. The man from I–Psi–T bubbled around excitedly, scratching at everything, diagnosing a new, unknown form of spontaneous combustion. Richard was more than willing to cede the investigation to him. As he was scooping ash into a bag, Barbara stuck her tongue out at his back. She successfully overcame the temptation to boot his rump, mostly because she was wearing toeless spiked court shoes over sheer black silk stockings and reckoned permanent damage to her wardrobe not worth the passing pleasure of denting Onions's negligible dignity.

Maltese and Topazio made themselves scarce, but Inspector Price would know where they lived.

'Well done, guv,' said Fred.

'Tricky thing, voodoo,' said Vanessa. 'Not to be trifled with.'

On the way out, Richard nodded to June O'Dell. She and Mama-Lou sat in their seats, ignoring the fuss around Squiers's sudden exit from this world. Richard did not doubt that the show would go on. With June wearing the producer's hat.

Richard walked with Barbara. Fred and Vanessa flanked them. Their way to the door was barred. By the writers' pack.

They really looked like a pack now, fangs bared, hunched over, angry at the loss of their alpha, fingers curled into claws. After all this hocus-pocus, Squiers's followers might opt for good old-fashioned violence and rip their enemies to shreds.

Fred and Vanessa tensed, ready for a scrap.

'Heel,' said June, firmly.

As one, the pack looked to her.

'You lot, there's work to do. I'll be taking more of an interest in the writing from now on. Porko, tomorrow you will sign Leslie Veneer and Gaye Brough on six-month contracts. Roget and

Canberra will be staying in Bleeds to mop up after the Bogey. No decapitations necessary.'

The chubby writer checked his colleagues' faces and nodded vigorously. The rest agreed with him. June O'Dell was in charge.

'Professor Corri,' she said, 'we've had our differences, but I'd like to offer you a job as head writer. This is yours for the taking.'

She snatched the school cap from one of the writers' pockets and offered it to Barbara.

'I'll think about it,' said the Professor.

Beside June, Mama-Lou smiled, eyes glittering.

The Moo and Mistress Voodoo exerted a tug on Barbara, which Richard knew would have an effect. He was more worried about how the Professor would fare in the television jungle than he had been when she was only under a deadly curse. But she could take care of herself.

Richard acknowledged these women of power, trusting – against prior experience – they would wield it only for good. He might have to keep watching the blasted programme to make sure they avoided the shadow of the Saturday Man.

He helped the Professor, now steady on her feet, out of the room.

The Rolls awaited.

He turned to look into Barbara's eyes, and kissed her. Her terror had passed, and new, exciting feelings were creeping in.

'Did we win?' she asked.

'Handsomely,' said Richard.

⇒ COLD SNAP ⇐

I.

'Nice motor,' said Richard Jeperson, casting an appreciative eye over Derek Leech's Rolls-Royce ShadowShark.

'I could say the same of yours,' responded Leech, gloved fingertips lightly polishing his red-eyed Spirit of Ecstasy. Richard's car was almost identical, though his bonnet ornament didn't have the inset rubies.

'I've kept the old girl in good nick,' said Richard.

'Mine has a horn which plays the theme from *Jaws*,' said Leech.

'Mine, I'm glad to say, doesn't.'

That was the pleasantries over.

It was the longest, hottest, driest summer of the 1970s. Thanks to a strict hosepipe ban, lawns had turned to desert. Neighbours informed on each other over suspiciously verdant patches. Bored regional television crews shot filler about eggs frying on dustbin lids and sunburn specialists earning consultancy fees in naturist colonies. If they'd been allowed anywhere near it, a considerably more unusual summer weather story was to be had. A news blackout was in effect, and discreet roadblocks limited traffic onto this stretch of the Somerset Levels.

The near-twin cars were parked in a lay-by equidistant from the seemingly Mediterranean beaches of Burnham-on-Sea and Lyme Regis. While the nation sweltered in bermuda shorts and flip-flops, Richard and Leech shivered in arctic survival gear. Richard wore layers of bearskin, furry knee-length boots with claw-toes, and a lime-green balaclava surmounted by a scarlet Andean bobble hat with chinchilla earmuffs – plus the wraparound anti-glare visor recommended by Jean-Claude Killy. Leech wore a snow-white, fur-hooded parka and baggy leggings, ready to lead an Alpine covert assault troop. If not for his black Foster Grants, he could stand against a whitewashed wall and impersonate the Invisible Man.

Around them was a landscape from a malicious Christmas card. They stood in a Cold Spot. Technically, a patch of permafrost, four miles across. From the air, it looked like a rough circle of white stitched onto a brown quilt. Earth stood hard as iron, water like a stone... snow had fallen, snow on snow, snow on snow. The epicentre was Sutton Mallet, a hamlet consisting of a few farmhouses, New Chapel (which replaced the old one in 1829) and Derek Leech International's weather research facility.

Leech professed innocence, but this was his fault. Most bad things were.

Bernard Levin said on *Late Night Line-Up* that Leech papers had turned Fleet Street into a Circle of Hell by boasting fewer words and more semi-naked girls than anything else on the newsstands. Charles Shaar Murray insisted in *IT* that the multi-media tycoon was revealed as the Devil incarnate when he invented the 'folk-rock cantata' triple LP. The Diogenes Club had seen Derek Leech coming for a long time, and Richard knew exactly what he was dealing with.

Their wonderful cars could go no further, so they had to walk.

After several inconclusive, remote engagements, this was their first face-to-face (or visor-to-sunglasses) meeting. The Most Valued Member of the Diogenes Club and the Great Enchanter were expected to be the antagonists of the age, but the titles meant less than they had in the days of Mycroft Holmes, Charles Beauregard and Edwin Winthrop or Leo Dare, Isidore Persano and Colonel Zenf. Lately, both camps had other things to worry about.

From two official world wars, great nations had learned to conduct their vast duels without all-out armed conflict. Similarly, the Weird Wars of 1903 and 1932 had changed the shadow strategies of the Diogenes Club and its opponents. In the Worm War, there had almost been battle-lines. It had only been won when a significant number of Persano's allies and acolytes switched sides, appalled at the scope of the crime ('the murder of time and space') planned by the wriggling mastermind ('a worm unknown to science') the Great Enchanter kept in a match-box in his waistcoat pocket. The Wizard War, when Beauregard faced Zenf, was a more traditional game of good and evil, though nipped in the bud by stealth, leaving the Club to cope with the ab-human threat of the Deep Ones ('the Water War') and the mundane business of 'licking Hitler'. Now, in what secret historians were already calling the Winter War, no one knew who to fight.

So, strangely, this was a truce.

As a sensitive – a Talent, as the parapsychology bods had it – Richard was used to trusting his impressions of people and places. He knew in his water when things or folks were out of true. If he squinted, he saw their real faces. If he cocked an ear, he heard what they were thinking. Derek Leech seemed perfectly sincere, and elaborately blameless. No matter how furiously Richard blinked behind his visor, he saw no red horns, no forked beard, no extra mouths. Only a tightness in the man's jaw gave away the effort it took to present himself like this. Leech had to be mindful of a tendency to grind his teeth.

They had driven west – windows rolled down in the futile hope of a cool breeze – through parched, sunbaked countryside.

Now, despite thermals and furs, they shivered. Richard saw Leech's breath frosting.

'Snow in July,' said Leech. 'Worse. Snow in this July.'

'It's not snow, it's rime. Snow is frozen rain. Precipitation. Rime is frozen dew. The moisture in the air, in the ground.'

'Don't be such an arse, Jeperson.'

'As a newspaperman, you appreciate accuracy.'

'As a newspaper publisher, I know elitist vocabulary alienates readers. If it looks like snow, tastes like snow and gives you a white Christmas, then...'

Leech had devised *So What Do You Know?*, an ITV quiz show where prizes were awarded not for correct answers, but for matching whatever was decided – right or wrong – by the majority vote of a 'randomly selected panel of ordinary Britons'. Contestants had taken home fridge-freezers and fondue sets by identifying Sydney as the capital of Australia or categorising whales as fish. Richard could imagine what Bernard Levin and Charles Shaar Murray thought of that.

Richard opened the boot of his Rolls and hefted out a hold-all which contained stout wicker snowshoes, extensible aluminium ski-poles and packs of survival rations. Leech had similar equipment, though his boot-attachments were spiked black metal and his rucksack could have contained a jet propulsion unit.

'I'd have thought DLI could supply a Sno-Cat.'

'Have you any idea how hard it is to come by one in July?'

'As it happens, yes.'

They both laughed, bitterly. Fred Regent, one of the Club's best men, had spent most of yesterday learning that the few places in Great Britain which leased or sold snow-ploughs, caterpillar tractor bikes or jet-skis had either sent their equipment out to be serviced, shut up shop for the summer or gone out of business in despair at unending sunshine. Heather Wilding, Leech's executive assistant, had been on the same fruitless mission – she and Fred kept running into each other outside lock-ups with 'come back in November' posted on them.

Beyond this point, the road to Sutton Mallet – a tricky proposition at the best of times – was impassable. The hamlet was just visible a mile off, black roofs stuck out of white drifts. The fields were usually low-lying, marshy and divided by shallow ditches called rhynes. In the last months, the marsh had set like concrete. The rhynes had turned into stinking runnels, with the barest threads of mud where water usually ran. Now, almost overnight, everything was deep-frozen and heavily frosted. The sun still shone, making a thousand glints, twinkles and refractions. But there was no heat.

Trees, already dead from Dutch elm disease or roots loosened from the dry dirt, had fallen under the weight of what only Richard wasn't calling snow, and lay like giant blackened corpses on field-sized shrouds. Telephone poles were down too. No word had been heard from Sutton Mallet in two days. A hardy postman had tried to get through on his bicycle, but had not come back. A farmer who had set off to milk his cows had also been swallowed in the whiteness. A helicopter had flown over, but the rotor blades slowed as heavy ice-sheaths grew on them. The pilot had barely made it back to Yeovilton Airfield.

Word had spread through 'channels'. Unnatural phenomena were Diogenes Club business, but Leech had to take an interest too – if only to prove that he wasn't behind the cold snap. Heather Wilding had made a call to Pall Mall, and officially requested the Club's assistance. That didn't happen often or – come to think of it – ever.

Leech looked across the white fields towards Sutton Mallet.

'So we walk,' he said.

'It's safest to follow the ditches,' advised Richard.

Neither bothered to lock their cars.

They clambered – as bulky and awkward as astronauts going EVA – over a stile to get into the field. The white carpet was virginal. As they tramped on, in the slight trough that marked the rime-filled rhyne, Richard kept looking sidewise at Leech. The man was breathing heavily inside his polar gear. Being incarnate involved certain frailties. But it would not do to underestimate a Great Enchanter.

Derek Leech had popped up apparently out of nowhere in 1961. A day after Colonel Zenf finally died in custody, he first appeared on the radar, making a freak run of successful long-shot bets at a dog track. Since then, he had made several interlocking empires. He was a close friend of Harold Wilson, Brian Epstein, Lord Leaves of Leng, Enoch Powell, Roman Polanski, Mary Millington and Jimmy Saville. He was into everything – newspapers (the downmarket tabloid *Daily Comet* and the reactionary broadsheet *Sunday Facet*), pop records, telly, a film studio, book-publishing, frozen foods, football, road-building, anti-depressants, famine relief, contraception, cross-channel hovercraft, draught lager, touring opera productions, market research, low-cost fashions, educational playthings. He had poked his head out of a trapdoor on *Batman* and expected to be recognised by Adam West – 'It's not the Clock King, Robin, it's the English Pop King, Derek Leech.' He appeared in his own adverts, varying his catch-phrase – 'If I didn't love it, I wouldn't…' eat it, drink it, watch it, groove it, use it, wear it, bare it, shop it, stop it, make it, take it, kiss it, miss it, phone it, own it. He employed 'radical visionary architect' Constant Drache to create 'ultra-moderne work-place environments' for DLI premises and the ranks upon ranks of 'affordable homes for hard-working families' cropping up at the edges of conurbations throughout the land. It was whispered there were private graveyards under many a 'Derek Leech Close' or 'Derek Leech Drive'. Few had tangled with Derek Leech and managed better than a draw. Richard counted himself among the few, but also suspected their occasional path–crossings hadn't been serious.

They made fresh, ragged footprints across the empty fields. They were the only moving things in sight. It was quiet, too. Richard saw birds frozen mid-tweet on boughs, trapped in globules of ice. No smoke rose from the chimneys of Sutton Mallet. Of course, what with the heat wave, even the canniest country folk might have put off getting in a store of fuel for next winter.

'Refresh my memory,' said Richard. 'How many people are at your weather research station?'

'Five. The director, two junior meteorologists, one general dogsbody and a public relations–security consultant.'

Richard had gone over what little the Club could dig up on them. Oddly, a DLI press release provided details of only four of the staff.

'Who's the director again?' he asked.

'We've kept that quiet, as you know,' said Leech. 'It's Professor Cleaver. Another Dick, which is to say a Richard.'

'Might have been useful to be told that,' said Richard, testily.

'I'm telling you now.'

Professor Richard Cleaver, a former time-server at the Meteorological Office, had authored *The Coming Ice Age*, an alarmist paperback propounding the terrifying theory of World Cooling. According to Cleaver, natural thickening of the ozone layer in the high atmosphere would, if unchecked, lead to the expansion of the polar icecaps and a global climate much like the one currently obtaining in Sutton Mallet. Now, the man was in the middle of his own prediction, which was troubling. There were recorded cases of individuals who worried so much about things that they made them happen. The Professor could be such a Talent.

They huffed into Sutton Mallet, past the chapel, and went

through a small copse. On the other side was the research station, a low-lying cinderblock building with temporary cabins attached. There were sentinels in the front yard.

'Are you in the habit of employing frivolous people, Mr Leech?'

'Only in my frivolous endeavours. I take the weather very seriously.'

'I thought as much. Then who made those snowmen?'

They emerged from the rhyne and stood on hard-packed ice over the gravel forecourt of the DLI weather research facility. Outside the main doors stood four classic snowmen: three spheres piled one upon another as legs, torso and head, with twigs for arms, carrots for noses and coals for eyes, buttons and mouths. They were individualised by scarves and headgear – top hat, tam-o'-shanter, pith helmet and two toy bumblebees on springs attached to an Alice band.

Leech looked at the row. 'Rime-men, surely?' he said, pointedly. 'As a busybody, you appreciate accuracy.'

There were no footprints around the snowmen. No scraped-bare patches or scooped-out drifts. As if they had been grown rather than made.

'A frosty welcoming committee?' suggested Leech.

Before anything happened, Richard knew. It was one of the annoyances of his sensitivity – premonitions which come just too late to do anything about.

Top Hat's headball shifted: it spat out a coal, which cracked against Richard's visor. He threw himself down, to avoid further missiles. Top Hat's head was packed with coals, which it could sick up and aim with deadly force.

Leech was as frozen in one spot as the snowmen weren't. This sort of thing happened to others, but not to him.

Pith Helmet, who had a cardboard handlebar moustache like

Zebedee from *The Magic Roundabout*, rose on ice-column legs and stalked towards Leech, burly white arms sprouting to displace feeble sticks, wicked icicles extruding from powdery fists.

Tam and Bee-Alice circled round, making as if to trap Richard and Leech in the line of fire.

Richard got up, grabbed Leech's arm, and pulled him away from Pith Helmet. It was hard to run in polar gear, but they stumped past Tam and Bee-Alice before the circle closed, and legged it around the main building.

Another snowman loomed up in front of them. In a postman's cap, with a mail-bag slung over its shoulder. It was larger and looser thing than the others, more hastily made, with no face coals or carrot. They barrelled into the shape, which came apart, and sprawled in a tangle on the cold, cold ground – Richard felt the bite of black ice through his gauntlets as the heel of his hand jammed against grit. Under him was a dead but loose-limbed postman, grey-blue in the face, crackly frost in his hair. He had been inside the snowman.

The others were marching around the corner. Were there people inside them too? Somehow, they were frowning – perhaps it was in the angle of their headgear, as if brows were narrowed – and malice burned cold in their eye-coals.

Leech was on his feet first, hauling Richard upright.

Snow crawled around the postman again, forming a thick carapace. The corpse stood like a puppet, dutifully taking up its bag and cap, insistent on retaining its identity.

They were trapped between the snowmen. The five walking, hat-topped heaps had them penned.

Richard was tense, expecting ice-daggers to rip through his furs and into his heart. Leech reached into his snowsuit as if searching for his wallet – in this situation, money wasn't going to be a help. A proper devil would have some hellfire about his person. Or at least a blowtorch. Leech – who had recorded a series of anti-smoking adverts – managed to produce a flip-top cigarette lighter. He made a flame, which didn't seem to faze the snowmen, and wheeled around, looking for the one to negotiate with. Leech was big on making deals.

'Try Top Hat,' suggested Richard. 'In cartoon terms, he's obviously the leader.'

Leech held the flame near Top Hat's face. Water trickled, but froze again, giving Top Hat a tear-streaked, semi-transparent appearance. A slack face showed inside the ice.

'Who's in there?' asked Leech. 'Cleaver?'

Top Hat made no motion.

A door opened, and a small, elderly man leaned out of the research station. He wore a striped scarf and a blue knit cap.

'No, Mr Leech,' said Professor Richard Cleaver, 'I'm in here. You lot, let them in, now. You've had your fun. For the moment.'

The snowmen stood back, leaving a path to the back door. Cleaver beckoned, impatient.

'Do come on,' he said. 'It's fweezing out.'

Richard looked at Leech and shrugged. The gesture was matched. They walked towards the back door.

The last snowman was Bee-Alice. As they passed, it reared up like a kid pretending to be a monster, and stuck out yard-long pseudopods of gleaming ice, barbed with jagged claws. Then it retracted its arms and silently chortled at the shivering humans.

'That one's a comedian,' said Cleaver. 'You have to watch out.'

Leech squeezed past the Professor, into the building. Richard looked at the five snowmen, now immobile and innocent-seeming.

'Come on, whoever you are,' urged Cleaver. 'What are you waiting for? Chwistmas?'

Richard slipped off his sun-visor, then followed Leech.

II.

'You in the van, wakey-wakey,' shouted someone, who was also hammering on the rear doors. 'The world needs saving...'

'Again?' mumbled Jamie Chambers, waking up with another heat-headache and no idea of the time. Blackout shields on the windows kept out the daylight. Living in gloom was part of the Shade Legacy. He didn't even need Dad's night-vision goggles – which were around here somewhere – to see well enough in the dark.

He sorted through stiff black T-shirts for the freshest, then lay on his back and stuck his legs in the air to wriggle into skinny jeans. Getting dressed in the back of the van without doing himself an injury was a challenge. Sharp metal flanges underlay the carpet of sleeping bags, and any number of dangerous items were haphazardly hung on hooks or stuffed into cardboard boxes. When Bongo Foxe, the drummer in Transhumance, miraculously gained a girlfriend, he'd tactfully kicked Jamie out of the squat in Portobello Road. The keys and codes to Dad's old lair inside Big Ben were around somewhere, but Jamie could never get used to the constant ticking. Mum hated that too. Between addresses, the Black Van was his best option.

'Ground Control to Major Shade,' called the hammerer, insistent and bored at the same time. Must be a copper.

'Hang on a mo,' said Jamie, 'I'm not decent.'

'Hear that, Ness?' said the hammerer to a (female?) colleague. 'Shall I pop the lock and give you a cheap thrill?'

One of the few pluses of van living, supposedly, was that gits like this couldn't find you. Jamie guessed he was being rousted by gits who could find anybody. For the second time this week. He'd already listened to Leech's twist, Heather Wilding. This'd be the other shower, the Diogenes Club. One of the things Jamie agreed with his father about was that it made sense to stay out of either camp and make your own way in the night.

Even parked in eternal shadow under railway arches, the van was like a bread oven with central heating. The punishing summer continued. After seconds, his T-shirt was damp. Within minutes, it'd be soaked and dried. This last six weeks, he'd sweated off pounds. Vron was freaked by how much his skeleton was showing.

He ran fingers through his crispy shock of raven hair (natural), checked a shaving mirror for blackheads (absent), undid special locks the hammerer oughtn't have been able to pop, and threw open the doors.

A warrant card was held in his face. Frederick Regent, New Scotland Yard (Detached). He was in plainclothes – blue jeans, red Fred Perry (with crimson sweat-patches), short hair, surly look. He couldn't have been more like a pig if he'd been oinking and had a curly tail. The girlfriend was a surprise – a red-haired bird with a *Vogue* face and a *Men Only* figure. She wore tennis gear – white plimsolls, knee-socks, shorts cut to look like a skirt, bikini top, Cardin cardigan – with matching floppy hat, milk-blank sunglasses (could she see through those?) and white lipstick.

'I'm Fred, this is Vanessa,' said the Detached man. 'You are James Christopher Chambers?'

'Jamie,' he said.

Vanessa nodded, taking in his preference. She was the sympathetic one. Fred went for brusque. It was an approach, if tired.

'Jamie,' said Fred, 'we understand you've come into a doctorate?'

'Don't use it,' he said, shaking his head. 'It was my old man's game.'

'But you have the gear,' said Vanessa. She reached into the van and took Dad's slouch hat off a hook. 'This is a vintage "Dr Shade" item.'

'Give that back,' said Jamie, annoyed.

Vanessa handed it over meekly. He stroked the hat as if it were a kitten, and hung it up again. There was family history in the old titfer.

'At his age, he can't really be a doctor,' said Fred. 'Has there ever been an Intern Shade?'

'I'm not a student,' he protested.

'No, you're one of those dropouts. Had a place at Manchester University, but left after a term. Couldn't hack the accents oop North?'

'The band was taking off. All our gigs are in London.'

'Don't have to justify your life-choices to us, mate. Except one.'

Fred wasn't being quite so jokey.

'I think you should listen,' said Vanessa, close to his ear. 'The world really does need saving.'

Jamie knew as much from Heather Wilding. She'd been more businesslike than this pair, drenched in Charlie, cream suit almost-invisibly damp under the arms, two blouse buttons deliberately left unfastened to show an armoured white-lace foundation garment.

'The other lot offered a retainer,' he said. 'Enough for a new amp.'

'We heard you'd been approached,' said Vanessa. 'And were reluctant. Very wise.'

Wilding hinted Transhumance might be signed to a Derek Leech label. They didn't only put out moaning hippie box sets and collected bubblegum hits.

'You won't need an amp in the ice age,' said Fred. 'They'll be burning pop groups to keep going for a few more days.'

'Yeah, I'm already shivering,' said Jamie, unpicking wet cotton from his breastbone. 'Chills up my spine.'

'All this heat is a sign of the cold, they say.'

'You what?'

Fred cracked a laugh. 'Trust us, there could be a cold spell coming.'

'Roll on winter, mate.'

'Careful what you wish for, Jamie,' said Vanessa.

She found his dad's goggles in a box of eight-track tapes, and slipped them over his head. He saw clearly through the old, tinted glass.

'Saddle up and ride, cowboy,' she said. 'We're putting together a posse. Just for this round-up. No long-term contract involved.'

'Why do you need me?' he asked.

'We need everybody,' said Fred, laying a palm on the van and wincing – it was like touching a griddle. 'Especially you, shadow-boy. You've got a license to drive and your own transport. Besides standing on the front lines for democracy and decent grub, you can give some of your new comrades a lift to the front. And I don't mean Brighton.'

Jamie didn't like the sound of this. 'What?' he protested.

'Congratulations, Junior Shade. You've got a new backing group. Are you ready to rock and – indeed – roll?'

Jamie felt that a trap had snapped around him. He was going into the family business after all.

He was going to be a doctor.

III.

Inside the research station, crystals crunched underfoot and granulated on every surface. White stalactites hung from door-frames and the ceiling. Windows were iced over and stunted pot-plants frostbitten solid. Even lightbulbs had petals of ice.

Powdery banks of frost (indoor rime? snow, even?) drifted against cabinets of computers. Trudged pathways of clear, deep footprints ran close to the walls, and they kept to them – leaving most of the soft, white, glistening carpet untouched. Richard saw little trails had been blazed into the rooms, keeping mainly to the edges and corners with rare, nimbler tracks to desks or work-benches. The prints had been used over again, as if their maker (Professor Cleaver?) were leery of trampling virgin white and trod carefully on the paths he had made when the cold first set in.

The Professor led them through the cafeteria, where trestle tables and chairs were folded and stacked away to clear the greatest space possible. Here, someone had been playing – making snow-angels, by lying down on the thick frost and moving their arms to make wing-shapes. Richard admired the care that had been taken. The silhouettes – three of them, with different wings, as if writing something in semaphore – matched Cleaver's tubby frame, but Richard couldn't imagine why he had worked so hard on something so childish. Leech had said he didn't employ frivolous people.

If anything, it was colder indoors than out. Richard felt sharp little chest-pains when he inhaled as if he were flash-freezing his alveoli. His exposed face was numb. He worried that if he were to touch his moustache, half would snap off.

They were admitted to the main laboratory. A coffee percolator was frosted up, its jug full of frothy brown solid. On a shelf stood a goldfish bowl, ice bulging over the rim. A startled fish was trapped in the miniature arctic. Richard wondered if it were still alive – like those dinosaurs they found in the 1950s. Here, the floor had been walked over many times, turned to orange slush and frozen again, giving it a rough moon-surface texture. Evidently, this was where the Professor lived.

Richard idly fumbled open a ring-binder that lay on a desk, and pressed his mitten to brittle blue paper.

'Paws off,' snapped Cleaver, snatching the file away and hugging it. 'That's tip-top secwet.'

'Not from me,' insisted Leech, holding out his hand. 'I sign the cheques, remember. You work for me.'

If Derek Leech signed his own cheques, Richard would be surprised.

'My letter of wesignation is in the post,' said Cleaver. He blinked furiously when he spoke, as if simultaneously translating in Morse. Rhotacism made him sound childish. How cruel was it to give a speech impediment a technical name sufferers couldn't properly pronounce? 'I handed it to the postman personally. I think he twied to deliver it to you outside. Vewy dedicated, the Post Office. Not snow, nor hail, and so on and so forth.'

Leech looked sternly at the babbling little man.

'In that case, you'd better hand over all your materials and leave this facility. Under the circumstances, the severance package will not be generous.'

Cleaver wagged a shaking hand at his former employer, not looking him in the eye. His blinks and twitches shook his whole body. He was laughing.

'In my letter,' he continued, 'I explain fully that this facility has declared independence from your organisation. Indeed, fwom all Earthly authowity. There are pwecedents. I've also witten to the Pwime Minister and the Met Office.'

Leech wasn't used to this sort of talk from minions. Normally, Richard would have relished the Great Enchanter's discomfort. But it wasn't clear where his own – or, indeed, anybody's – best interests were in Ice Station Sutton Mallet.

'Mr Leech, I know,' said Cleaver, 'not that we've ever met. I imagine you thought you had more important things to be bothewing with than poor old Clever Dick Cleaver's weather wesearch. Jive music and porn and so forth. I hear you've started a holiday company. Fun in the sun and all that. Jolly good show. Soon you'll be able to open bobsled runs on the Costa Bwava.

I'm not surprised you've shown your face now. I expected it and I'm glad you're here. You, I had planned for. No, the face I don't know... don't know at all... is yours.'

Cleaver turned to Richard.

'Richard Jeperson,' he introduced himself. 'I'm from—'

'The Diogenes Club!' said Cleaver, viciously. 'Yes, yes, yes, of course. I see the gleam. The wighteous gleam. Know it of old. The insuffewability. Is that fwightful Miss Cathewina Kaye still alive?'

'Catriona,' corrected Richard. 'Yes.'

Currently, Catriona Kaye was Acting Chairman of the Ruling Cabal of the Diogenes Club. She had not sought the position. After the death of Edwin Winthrop, her partner in many things, no one else had been qualified. Richard was not yet ready to leave active service, and had a nagging feeling he wouldn't be suited to the Ruling Cabal anyway. There was talk of reorganising – 'modernising' – the Club and some of their rivals in Whitehall were bleating about 'accountability' and 'payment by results'. If it weren't arcanely self-financing, the Club would have been dissolved or absorbed long ago.

'If it weren't for Cathewina Kaye, and a disservice she did me many many years ago, I might have taken a diffewent path. You know about this, Mr Jeperson?'

A penny, long-teetering at the lip of a precipice, dropped – in slow motion, setting memory mechanisms ticking with each turn.

'Richard Cleaver? Clever Dick. You called yourself Clever Dick. That's who you are!'

'That's who I was... until that w-woman came along. She hates people like me... like both of you, pwobably... she only likes people who are n-normal. People who can't do anything. You know what I mean. Normal.'

He drew out the word, with contempt. Richard remembered a time – at school, as a young man – when he might have given the word such a knife-twist. Like Dick Cleaver, he had manifested a Talent early. While Cleaver demonstrated excess brain capacity, Richard showed excess feeling. Insights did not always make him happy. Ironically, it was Catriona – not his father or Edwin Winthrop – who most helped him cope with his Talent, to connect with people rather than become estranged. Without her, he might be a maniac.

'It was never about who you were, Cleaver,' said Richard, trying to be kind. 'It was about what you did.'

Fury boiled behind Cleaver's eyes.

'I didn't do anything! We were the Splendid Six, and she took us apart, one by one, working in secwet with your dwatted Diogenes Club. We were hewoes – Blackfist, Lord Piltdown, the Blue Stweak – and sh-she made us small, twied to make us normal. I'm the last of us, you know. The Splendid One. The Bwightest Boy in the World. The others are all dead.'

Cleaver was coming up to pensionable age, but he was as frozen inside as his goldfish – still eleven, and poisonous.

'If I suffered a speech impediment like yours, I'd avoid words like "dratted",' commented Leech. 'All this ancient history is fascinating, I'm sure. I know who you used to be, Professor. I don't hire anyone without knowing everything about them first. But I don't see what it has to do with all this... this cold business.'

A sly look crept into Cleaver's eye. An I-know-a-secret-you're-not-going-to-like look.

'I wather think I've pwoved my point, Mr Leech. You've wead my book, *The Coming Ice Age*?'

'I had someone read it and summarise the findings for me,' said Leech, off-handedly. 'Very convincing, very alarming. It's why you were headhunted – at a salary three times what you got at the Met – to head my weather research programme.'

What exactly had Derek Leech been doing here? Scientific

weather control? For reasons which were now all too plain, Richard did not like the notion of a Great Enchanter with command over the elements.

'I employ the best, and you were the best man for this job. What you did as a schoolboy was irrelevant. I didn't even care that you were mad.'

Clever Dick Cleaver sputtered.

'Sorry to be blunt, pal, but you are. I can show you the psych reports. Your insanity should not have hindered your ability to fulfil your contract. Quite the contrary. Derek Leech International has a policy of easing the lot of the mentally ill by finding them suitable positions. We consider it our social service remit, repaying a community that has given us so much.'

Richard knew all about that. Myra Lark, acknowledged leader in the field of shaping minds to suit the requirements of government and industry, was on Leech's staff. Some jobs you really had to be mad to take. Dr Lark's, for instance.

'Your book convinced me it could happen. World Cooling. And only drastic action can forestall the catastrophe. With the full resources of DLI at your disposal, I was expecting happier results. Not this... this big fridge.'

Cleaver smiled again.

'If you'd actually wead my book, you wouldn't be so surpwised. Tell him, Jeperson.'

Leech looked at Richard, awaiting enlightenment.

'Professor Cleaver writes that an imminent ice age will lead to worldwide societal collapse and, in all probability, the extinction of the human race.'

'Yes, and...?'

'He does not write that this would be a bad thing.'

Realisation dawned in Leech's eyes. Cleaver grinned broadly, showing white dentures with odd, cheap blue settings.

Derek Leech had given his weather control project to someone who wanted winter to come and freeze everything solid. Isidore Persano and his worm would be proud.

'What about the snowmen?' Leech asked.

'I was wondewing when you'd get to them. The snowmen. Yes. I'm not alone in this. I have fwiends. One fwiend, mainly. One big fwiend. I call her the Cold. You can call her the End.'

IV.

He was supposed to park outside the Post Office Tower and wait for the other recruits. One of the group would have further instructions and, he was promised, petrol money. Jamie was off to the Winter War.

Now he'd (provisionally) taken the Queen's Shilling, he wondered whether the Diogenes Club just wanted him as a handy, unpaid chauffeur, ferrying cannon fodder about. Dad wouldn't have thought a lot of that. Still, Jamie only wanted to dip a toe in the waters. He was leery about the shadow life. The Shade Legacy hadn't always been happy, as Mum would tell him at the drop of a black fedora with razors in the brim. At the moment, he was more interested in Transhumance – especially if they could find a better, preferably celibate drummer… and a new bass–player, a decent PA and enough songs to bump up their set to an hour without reprises. Vron had been promising new lyrics for weeks, but said the bloody heat made it hard to get into the proper mood. Perhaps he should scrub Transhumance and look for a new band.

The GPO Tower, a needle bristling with dish–arrays, looked like a leftover design from Stingray. The revolving restaurant at the summit, opened by Wedgy Benn and Billy Butlin, stopped turning in 1971, after an explosion the public thought was down to the Angry Brigade. Jamie knew the truth. His father's last 'exploit' before enforced retirement had been the final defeat of his long-time enemies, the Dynamite Boys. The Tower was taken over by the now-octogenarian Boys, who planned to use the transmitters to send a coded signal to activate the lizard stems of every human brain in the Greater London area and turn folks into enraged animals. Dad stopped them by setting off their own bombs.

Jamie found a parking space in the thin shadow of the tower, which shifted within minutes. Inside the van, stale air began to boil again. Even with the windows down, there was no relief.

'Gather, darkness,' he muttered. He hadn't Dad's knack with shadows, but he could at least whip up some healthy gloom. The sky was cloudless, but a meagre cloud-shadow formed around the van. It was too much effort to maintain, and he let it go. In revenge, the sun got hotter.

'Jamie Chambers,' said a girl.

He looked out at her. She was dressed for veldt or desert: leather open-toe sandals, fawn culottes, baggy safari jacket, utility belt with pouches, burnt orange sunglasses the size of saucers, leopard-pattern headscarf, Australian bush hat. In a summer when Zenith the Albino sported a nut-brown suntan, her exposed lower face, forearms and calves were pale to the point of colourlessness. People always said Jamie – as instinctively nocturnal as his father – should get out in the sun more, but this girl made him look like an advert for Air Malta. He would have guessed she was about his own age.

'Call me Gené,' she said. 'I know your aunt Jenny. And your mother, a bit. We worked together a long time ago, when she was Kentish Glory.'

Mum had stopped wearing a moth-mask and film-winged leotards decades before Jamie was born. Gené was much older than nineteen.

He got out of the van, and found he was several inches taller than her.

'I'm from the Diogenes Club,' she said, holding up an envelope. 'You're our ride to Somerset. I've got maps and money here. And the rest of the new bugs.'

Three assorted types, all less noticeable than Gené, were loitering.

'Keith, Susan and… Sewell, isn't it?'

A middle-aged, bald-headed man stepped forward and nodded. He wore an old, multi-stained overcoat, fingerless Albert Steptoe gloves and a tightly wound woolly scarf as if he expected a sudden winter. His face was unlined, as if he rarely used it, but sticky marks around his mouth marked him as a sweet-addict. He held a paper bag, and was chain-chewing liquorice allsorts.

'Sewell Head,' said Gené, tapping her temple. 'He's one of the clever ones. And one of theirs. Derek Leech fetched him out of a sweet shop. Ask him anything, and he'll know.'

'What's Transhumance?' asked Jamie.

'A form vertical livestock rotation, practised especially in Switzerland,' said Sewell Head, popping a pink coconut wheel into his mouth. 'Also a London-based popular music group which has never released a record or played to an audience of more than fifty people.'

'Fifty is a record for some venues, pal.'

'I told you he'd know,' said Gené. 'Does he look evil to you? Or is Hannah Arendt right about banality? He's behaved himself so far. No decapitated kittens. The others are undecideds, not ours, not theirs. Wavering.'

'I'm not wavering,' said the other girl, Susan. 'I'm neutral.'

She wore jeans and a purple T-shirt, and hid behind her long brown hair. She tanned like most other people and had pinkish sunburn scabs on her arms. Jamie wondered if he'd seen her before. She must be a year or two older than him, but gave off a studenty vibe.

'Susan Rodway,' explained Gené. 'You might remember her from a few years ago. She was on television, and there was a book about her. She was a spoon-bender. Until she stopped.'

'It wore off,' said the girl, shrugging.

'That's her story, and she's sticking to it. According to tests, she's off the ESP charts. Psychokinesis, pyrokinesis, psychometry, telepathy, levitation, clairvoyance, clairaudience. She has senses they don't even have Latin names for yet. Can hard-boil an egg with a nasty look.'

Susan waved her hands comically, and nothing happened.

'She's pretending to be normal,' said Gené. 'Probably reading your mind right now.'

Irritated, Susan snapped. 'One mind I can't read, Gené, is yours. So we'll have to fall back on the fount of all factoids. Mr Head, what can you tell us about Geneviève Dieudonné?'

Sewell Head paused in mid-chew, as if collecting a ledger from a shelf in his mental attic, took a deep breath, and began, 'Born in 1416, in the Duchy of Burgundy, Geneviève Dieudonné is mentioned in—'

'That's quite enough of that,' said Gené, shutting him off.

Jamie couldn't help noticing how sharp the woman's teeth were. Did she have the ghost of a French accent?

'I'm Keith Marion,' said the kid in the group, smiling nervously. It didn't take ESP to see he was trying to smooth over an awkward moment. 'Undecided.'

He stuck out his hand, which Jamie shook. He had a plastic tag around his wrist. Even looking straight at Keith, Jamie couldn't fix a face in his mind. The tag was the only thing about him he could remember.

'We have Keith on day-release,' said Gené, proudly. 'He has a condition. It's named after him. Keith Marion Syndrome.'

Jamie let go of the boy's hand.

'I don't mind being out,' said Keith. 'I was sitting around waiting for my O-level results. Or CSEs. Or call-up papers. Or…'

He shrugged, and shut up.

'We make decisions all the time, which send us on varying paths,' said Gené. 'Keith can see his other paths. The ones he might have taken. Apparently, it's like being haunted by ghosts of yourself. All those doppelgangers.'

'If I concentrate, I can anchor myself here,' said Keith. 'Assuming this is the real here. It might not be. Other heres feel just as real. And they bleed through more than I'd like.'

Sewell Head was interested for a moment, as if filing some fact nugget away for a future *Brain of Britain* quiz. Then he was chewing Bertie Bassett's liquorice cud again.

'He's seen two other entirely different lives for me,' said Gené.

'I'm having enough trouble with just this one,' commented Susan.

'So's everybody,' said the pale girl. 'That's why we've been called – the good, the bad and the undecided.'

She opened her envelope and gave Jamie a map.

'We're heading west. Keith knows the territory. He was born in Somerset.'

Jamie opened the rear doors of the van. He had tidied up a bit, and distributed cushions to make the space marginally more comfortable.

Susan borrowed 50p from him and the foursome tossed to see who got to sit up front with the driver. Keith called, 'Owl,' then admitted to Gené his mind had slipped into a reality with different coins. Head droned statistics and probabilities but couldn't decide what to call, and lost to Susan by default. In the final, Gené called tails. The seven-edged coin spun surprisingly high – and slower than usual – then landed heads-up in Susan's palm.

'Should have known not to toss up with a telekinetic,' said

Gené, in good humour. 'It's into the back of the van with the boys for me.'

She clambered in and pulled the door shut. There was some kicking and complaining as they got sorted out.

Susan gave the coin back to Jamie. It was bent at a right-angle.

'Oops,' she said, arching her thick eyebrows attractively.

'You said it wore off.'

'It did. Mostly.'

They got into the front of the van. Jamie gave Susan the map and appointed her navigator.

'She can do it with her eyes closed,' said Gené, poking her head through between the high-backed front seats.

'Just follow the Roman road,' said Keith.

Susan held the map up the wrong way, and chewed a strand of her hair. 'I hate to break it to you, but I'm not that good at orienteering. I can tell you about the three people – no, four – who have owned this map since it was printed. Including some interesting details about Little Miss Burgundy. But I don't know if we're best off with the A303.'

Gené took the map away and playfully swatted Susan with it.

'Mr Head,' she began, 'what's the best route from the Post Office Tower, in London, to Alder, in Somerset?'

'Shortest or quickest?'

'Quickest.'

Sewell Head swallowed an allsort and recited directions off the top of his head.

'I hope someone's writing this down.'

'No need, Jamie,' said Gené. 'Tell him, Susan.'

'It's called eidetic memory,' said Susan. 'Like photographic, but for sounds and the spoken word. I can replay what he said in snippets over the next few hours. I don't even need to understand what he means. Now, "turn left into New Cavendish Street, and drive towards Marylebone High Street…"'

Relaying Sewell Head's directions, Susan imitated his monotone. She sounded like a machine.

'One day all cars will have gadgets that do this,' said Keith.

Jamie doubted that, but started driving anyway.

V.

An hour or so into Professor Cleaver's rhotacist monologue, Richard began tuning out. Was hypothermia setting in? Despite thermals and furs, he was freezing. His upper arms ached as if they'd been hit with hammers. His jaws hurt from clenching to prevent teeth-chattering. He no longer had feeling in his fingers and toes. Frozen exhalation made ice droplets in his moustache.

Cold didn't bother Clever Dick. He was one of those mad geniuses who never outgrew a need for an audience. Being clever didn't count unless the people he was cleverer than knew it. The Professor walked around the room, excited, impassioned, frankly barking. He touched ice-coated surfaces with bare hands Richard assumed were freezer-burned to nervelessness. He puffed out clouds of frost and delighted in tiny falls of indoor hail. He constantly fiddled with his specs – taking them off to scrape away thin film of iced condensation with bitten-to-the-quick thumbnails, putting them back on until they misted up and froze over again. And he kept talking. Talking, talking, talking.

As a child, Dick Cleaver had been indulged – and listened to – far too often. He'd been an adventurer, in the company of immature grown-ups who didn't take the trouble to teach him how to be a real boy. When that career ended, it had been a mind-breaking shock for Clever Dick. Richard had read Catriona Kaye's notes on the Case of the Splendid Six. Her pity for the little boy was plain as purple ink, though she also loathed him. An addendum (initialled by Edwin Winthrop) wickedly noted that Clever Dick suffered such extreme adolescent acne that he become known as 'Spotted Dick'. Angry pockmarks still marred the Professor's chubby cheeks. As an adult, he had become a champion among bores and deliberately entered a profession which required talking at length about the most tedious (yet inescapable) subject in Great British conversation – the weather. Turned out nice again, eh what? Lovely weather for ducks. Bit nippy round the allotments. Cleaver's best-selling book was impossible to read to the end, which was why many took *The Coming Ice Age* for a warning. It was actually a threat, a plan of action, a promise. To Professor Cleaver, the grip of glaciation was a consummation devoutly to be wished for.

Behind his glasses, Cleaver's eyes gleamed. He might as well have traced hearts on frozen glass with a fingertip. He was a man in love. Perhaps for the first time. A late, great, literally all-consuming love.

Derek Leech, who rarely made the mistake of explaining his evil plans at length, had missed the point when he funded Cleaver's research. That alarmed Richard – Leech might be many things, but he was not easily fooled. Cleaver came across as a ranting, immature idiot with a freak IQ, but had serious connections. If anything could trump a Great Enchanter, it was the Cold.

'The Cold was here first,' continued Cleaver. 'Before the dawn of man, she weigned over evewything. She was the planet's first evolved intelligence, a giant bwain consisting of a near-infinite number of ice cwystals. A gweat white blanket, sewene and undying. When the glaciers weceded, she went to her west. She hid in a place out of weach until now. Humanity is just a blip. She'd have come back eventually, even without me. She was not dead, but only sleeping.'

'Lot of that about,' said Leech. 'King Arthur, Barbarossa, Great Cthulhu, the terra-cotta warriors, Gary Glitter. They'll all be back.'

Cleaver sputtered with anger. He didn't like being interrupted when he was rhapsodising.

'You won't laugh when blood fweezes in your veins, Mr Leech. When your eyes pop out on ice-stalks.'

Leech flapped his arms and contorted his face in mock panic.

'How many apocalypses have come and gone and fizzled in this century, Jeperson?' Leech asked, airily. 'Four? Five? Worm War, Wizard War, Water War, Weird War, World War... and that's not counting Princess Cuckoo of Faerie, Little Rosie Farrar as the Whore of Babylon, the Scotch Streak and the Go-Codes, the Seamouth Warp, six alien invasions counting two the Diogenes Club doesn't think I know about, two of my youthful indiscretions you don't think I know you know about, and the ongoing Duel of the Seven Stars.'

'Don't the Water War, the Scotch Streak and the Egyptian Stars count as alien invasions?' asked Richard. 'I mean, technically, the Deep Ones are terrestrial, but your Great Squidhead Person is from outer outer space. And the other two bothers were down to unwelcome meteorites.'

'You've a point. Make that eight alien invasions. The Water War was a local skirmish, though. Extra-dimensional, rather than extra-terrestrial...'

Cleaver hopped from one foot to the other. The little boy in him was furious that grown-ups were talking over his head. If he hadn't been chucked off his course in life – by Catriona, as he saw it – he might have been in on the secret history. The Mystic Maharajah, oldest of the Splendid Six, had carried a spear (well, an athamé) in the Worm War. Captain Rattray (Blackfist), another Splendid, emerged from disgrace to play a minor role in the Wizard War. Teenage Clever Dick was too busy squeezing pus-filled blemishes to get involved in that set-to. Child sleuths, like child actors, seldom grew up to be stars. Richard was named after Richard Riddle, the famous boy detective of the turn of the century (so was Cleaver, probably). Few knew what, if anything, happened to Riddle in later life.

'You won't listen, you won't listen!'

'Have you considered that the Cold might be extra-dimensional rather than antediluvian?' asked Leech, offhandedly. 'Seems to me a bright young man of my acquaintance reported something similar in a continuum several path-forks away from our own. It cropped up there in 1963 or so, during the Big Freeze. Didn't do much harm.'

'You can't say anything about her,' insisted Cleaver, almost squeaking.

'Interesting that you see the Cold as a her,' continued Leech. 'Then again, I suppose women have been "cold" to you all your life. You made a poor impression on Miss Kaye, from all accounts. And she's always been generous in her feelings.'

Cleaver's face tried to burn. Blood rose in his blueing cheeks, forming purplish patches. He might break out again.

'I know what you're twying to do, you wotter!'

Leech laughed out loud. Richard couldn't help but join in.

'I'm a "wotter", am I? A wotten wetched wight woyal wascally wotter, perhaps?'

'You're twying to get me angwy!'

'Angwy? Are you succumbing to woawing wed wage?'

Cleaver couldn't help sounding like a toffee-nosed Elmer Fudd. It was cruel of Leech to taunt him, Fourth Form fashion. Richard remembered bullies at his schools. With him, it had been his darker skin, his literal lack of background, the numbers tattooed on his wrist, his longer-than-regulation hair, his eyelashes, for heaven's sake. He had learned early on to control his temper. If he didn't, people got hurt.

'You missed one off your list of apocalypses,' said Cleaver, trying to be sly again. 'Perfidious Albion. That was an extwa-dimensional thweat. An entire weality out to oblitewate the world. And we stopped it. In 1926! Not your Diogenes Club or those Undertaker fellows, but us! The Splendid Six! Clever Dick, yes. They first called me that to poke fun, but I pwoved it was a wightful name. I stood with the gwown-ups. Blackfist and Lord Piltdown and the Blue Stweak...'

'...and Aviatrix and the Mystic Maharajah,' footnoted Richard.

'Should never have let girls and foweigners in,' muttered Cleaver. 'That's where the wot started.'

'Chandra Nguyen Seth turned out to be Sid Ramsbottom, from Stepney,' said Richard. 'As British as corned-beef fritters and London fog. Used boot polish on his face for years. He might have been mystic, but he was no maharajah.'

Cleaver didn't take this in – he was a ranter, not a listener. 'Seth and the girl helped,' he admitted. 'The Splendids saved the day. Beat back the Knights of Perfidious Albion. Saved evewyone and evewything. Without us, you'd all be cwawling subjects of Queen Morgaine. I was given a medal, by the pwoper King. I was witten up in *Bwitish Pluck*, for months and months. I had an arch-nemesis. Wicked William, my own cousin. I bested the bounder time after time. Made him cwy and cwy and cwy. There was a Clever Dick Club, and ten thousand boys were members. No g-girls allowed! I was in the Lord Mayor's Show and invited to tea at the palace twice. I could have been in your wotten old wars. Won them, even. In half the time. Dark Ones, Deep Ones, Wet Ones, Weird Ones. I could have thwashed the lot of 'em and been home before bedtime. But you couldn't leave me alone, could you? No woom in the Gwown-Ups' Club for Clever Dick. Not for any of the Splendids. That w-w-woman had to bwing us down to her level.'

'He means your club now,' said Leech. 'In some circumstances, I'd agree with him.'

'You'd both have to climb a mountain to be on a level with Catriona Kaye.'

'Touché,' said Leech.

'You're both just twying to change the subject.'

'Oh dearie me,' said Leech. 'Let's talk about the weather again, shall we? It's an endless topic of fascination. I was getting bored with writing heatwave headlines...'

Leech's *Daily Comet* had been censured for running the headline 'Sweaty Betty' over a paparazzo shot of Queen Elizabeth II perspiring (in ladylike manner) at an official engagement.

'How do you think he's done it, Jeperson? Science or magic?'

'No such thing as magic,' said Cleaver, quickly.

'Says the boy whose best friend used a magic diamond to become hard as nails. What was his name again, Captain—?'

'Wattway!' shouted the Professor, duped into using a double-r name. When he wasn't angry, he spoke carefully, avoiding the letter r if possible. Sadly, Cleaver was angry most of the time. 'Dennis Wattway! Blackfist!'

'Not a magic person, then?'

'The Fang of Night was imbued with an unknown form of wadioactivity. It altered Captain Wattway's physiology.'

'I could pull a hat out of the air and a rabbit out of the hat, and you'd say I accessed a pocket universe.'

'A tessewact, yes.'

'There's no "weasoning" with you. So, Jeperson, what do you think?'

Richard wondered whether he should follow Leech's tactic, getting the Professor more and more flustered in the hope of breaking him down and finding a way to roll back the Cold. It was all very well unless Clever Dick decided to stop trying to impress his visitors and just had the snowmen stick icicles through their heads.

'I assume the phenomenon is localised,' said Richard. 'Deep under the levels. There must have been a pocket of the Cold. Once it was all over the world, a giant organism – a symbiote, drawing nourishment from the rock, from what vegetation it let live. When the Great Ice Age ended, it shrank, shedding most of its bulk into the seas or ordinary ice, but somewhere – maybe in several spots around the world – it left parcels of itself.'

'No, you're wong, wong, wong,' said Cleaver, nastily.

'Is that a Chinese laundry?' said Leech. 'Wong, Wong and Wong.'

'Wwong,' insisted Cleaver. 'Ewwoneous. Incowwect. Not wight.'

He spluttered, frustrated not to find an r-free synonym for 'wrong'.

'The Cold didn't hide below the gwound, but beyond the spectwum of tempewature. Until I weached out for her.'

'I see,' continued Richard. 'With the equipment generously supplied by your former employer, you made contact with the Cold. You woke up Sleeping Beauty... with what? A kiss. No, a signal. An alarm-call. No, you had instructions. What common language could you have? Music, Movement and Mime? Doubtful. Mathematics? No, the Cold hasn't got that sort of a mind. A being on her scale has no use for any number other than "one".'

Richard looked about the room, at the thickening ice which coated everything, at the white dusting over the ice. Tiny, tiny jewels glittered in the powder. He made a leap – perhaps by himself, perhaps snatching from Cleaver's buzzing mind.

'Crystals,' he mused. '"A near-infinite number," you said. Each unique and distinctive. An endless alphabet of characters. Chinese cubed.'

Cleaver clapped his hands, delighted.

'Yes, snowflakes! I can wead them. It cost a gweat deal of Mr Leech's money to learn how. First, to wead them. Then to make them.'

'Your bird must think you're a right mug,' said Leech, sourly. 'She must have seen you coming for a million years.'

'Eighteen million years, at my best guess,' said Cleaver, smugness crumpling. He didn't like it when his goddess was disrespected.

'How do you make snowflakes?' Richard asked. 'I mean, snow is frozen rain...'

Cleaver was disgusted, as Richard knew he would be. 'You don't know anything! Fwozen wain is sleet!'

Leech laughed bitterly as Richard was paid back for his pedantry.

'Snow forms when clouds are fwozen,' said Cleaver, lecturing. 'You need humidity and cold. It's vapour to ice, not water to ice. Synthetic snow cwystals have been made in vapour diffusion chambers since 1963. But no one else has got beyond dendwitic stars. Janet and John cwystallogwaphy! The colder you get inside the box, the more complex the cwystals – hollow plates, columns on plates, multiply capped columns, skeletal forms, isolated bullets, awwowhead twins, multiple cups, skeletal forms. Then combinations of forms. I can sculpt them, shape them, carve them. *Finnegans Wake* cwystallogwaphy! You need extwemes of tempewature, and a gweat deal of electwicity. We dwained the national gwid. There was a black–out, wemember?'

A week or so ago, a massive power–cut had paralysed an already–sluggish nation. Officially, it was down to too many fans plugged in and fridge–doors left open.

'You knew about that?' Richard asked Leech.

The Great Enchanter shrugged.

'He authowised it!' crowed the Professor, in triumph. 'He had no idea what he was doing. None of the others did, either. Kellett and Bakhtinin. McKendwick. And certainly not your spy, Mr Pouncey!'

Leech had listed the other staff: 'two junior meteorologists, one general dogsbody and a public relations-security consultant'.

'McKendwick had an inkling. He knew I was welaying instwuctions. He made the Box – the vapour diffusion chamber – to my specifications. He kept asking, why all the extwa conductors? Why the designs? But he cawwied out orders like a good little wesearch assistant.'

Cleaver stood by an odd apparatus which Richard had taken for a generator. It consisted of a lot of blackened electrical coils, bright copper slashes showing through shredded rubber. There was a cracked bakelite instrument panel, and – in the heart of the coils – a metal box the size of a cigarette packet, ripped open at one edge. It had exploded outward. The metal was covered with intricate, etched symbols. Line after line of branching, hexagonally symmetrical star-shapes. Representational snowflakes, but also symbols of power. Here, science shaded into magic. This was not only an experimental apparatus, but an incantation in copper-wire and steel-plate, a conjuring machine.

'It's burned out now,' he said, slapping it, 'but it did the twick. In the Box, I took the tempewature down to minus four hundwed and fifty-nine point seven thwee degwees Fahwenheit!'

Richard felt a chill wafting from the ice-slopes of Hell.

'We're supposed to be impressed?' said Leech.

'You can't get colder than absolute zero,' said Richard. 'That's minus four hundred and fifty-nine point six seven Fahrenheit.'

'I have bwoken the Cold Bawwier,' announced Cleaver, proudly.

'Not using physics, you haven't.'

'So what was it, magic?'

Richard wasn't going to argue the point. There weren't instruments capable of measuring theoretically impossible temperatures, but Richard suspected the Professor wasn't making an idle boast. Within his Box, reality had broken down. Quantum mechanics gave up, packed its bags and went to Marbella, and the supernatural house-sat for a while.

'It's where I found the Cold. Minus point zewo six. She was sleeping there. A basic hexagon. I almost missed her. Bweaking so-called absolute zewo was so much of an achievement. McKendwick saw her first. The little lab assistant took her for pwoof we had failed. There shouldn't be ordinawy cwystals at minus point zewo six. And she wasn't ordinawy. McKendwick found that out.'

Richard assumed McKendrick was the snowman with the tam-o'-shanter. The others must be the rest of Cleaver's staff. Kellett, Bakhtinin, Pouncey. And whoever the postman was. What about the few other residents of Sutton Mallet? Frozen in their homes? Ready to join the snow army?

'Fwom a hexagon, she gwew, into a dendwitic star, with more stars on each bwanch. A hexagon squared. A hexagon cubed.'

'Six to the power of six to the power of six?'

'That's wight, Mr Leech. Amusing, eh what? Then, she became a cluster of cwystals. A snowflake. Then… whoosh. The Box burst. The power went out. But she was fwee. She came fwom beyond the zewo bawwier. A pinpoint speck. Woom tempewature plummeted. The walls iced over, and the fweeze spwead out of the building. She took the village in hours. She took McKendwick and the others. Soon, she'll be evewywhere.'

'What about you?' asked Leech. 'Will you be the Snow Queen's "Pwime Minister"?'

'Oh no, I'm going to die. Just like you. When the Cold spweads, over the whole planet, I'll be happy to die with the west of the failed expewiment, humanity. It's quite inevitable. Hadn't you noticed – when you were coming here – hadn't you noticed she's gwowing? I think we'll be done in thwee months or so, give or take an afternoon.'

Richard whistled.

'At least now we know the deadline,' he told Leech, slipping the hypodermic out of his hairy sleeve.

Cleaver frowned, wondering if he should have given so much away. It was too late to consider the advisability of ranting.

Leech took hold of the Professor and slammed his forehead against the older man's, smashing his spectacles. A coconut-shy crack resounded. Cleaver staggered, smearing his flowing moustache of blood.

"Yhou bwoke mhy nhose!'

Richard slid the needle into Cleaver's neck. He tensed and went limp.

'One down,' said Leech. 'One to go.'

'Yes, but she's a big girl. What are the snowmen doing?'

Leech looked out of the window, and said, 'Most have wandered off, but the postman's still there, behaving himself.'

'While Cleaver's out, they shouldn't move,' Richard said, unsure of himself. 'Unless the Cold gets angry.'

Richard plopped the Professor in a swivel chair and wheeled him into a corner, out of the way. Leech unslung his giant backpack and undid white canvas flaps to reveal a metal box studded with dials and switches like an old-time wireless receiver. He unwound an electrical cord and plugged it into a socket that wasn't iced over. His bulky gadget lit up and began to hum. He opened a hatch and pulled out a Trimphone handset, then cranked a handle and asked for an operator.

'Who else would want a telephone you have to carry around?' asked Richard.

Leech gave a feral, humourless smile and muttered, 'Wouldn't you like to know?' before getting through.

'This is DL 001,' he said. 'Yes, yes, Angela, it's Derek. I'd like to speak with Miss Catriona Kaye, at the manor house, Alder.'

Leech held the Trimphone against his chest while he was connected.

'Let's see if Madam Chairman has gathered her Talents,' he said.

Richard certainly hoped she had.

VI.

They were on the road to Mangle Wurzel Country because some paranormal crisis was out of hand. Jamie had a fair idea what that meant.

Growing up as the son of the current Dr Shade and the former Kentish Glory, it had taken several playground spats and uncomfortable parent–teacher meetings to realise that other kids (and grown-ups) didn't know these things happened regularly and – what's more – really didn't want to know. After getting kicked out of a third school, he learned to answer the question 'What does your Daddy do?' with 'He's a doctor,' rather than 'He fights diabolical masterminds.' Since leaving home, he'd seen how surreally out-of-the-ordinary his childhood had been. No one ever said he was expected to take over his father's practice, but Dad taught him about the Shade Legacy: how to summon shadows and travel the night-paths, how to touch people inside with tendrils of velvet black, how to use the get-up and the gadgets. Jamie was the only pupil in his class who botched his mock O levels because he'd spent most of his revision time on the basics of flying an autogyro.

Jamie thought Mum was pleased he was using the darkness in the band rather than on the streets. He was carrying on the Shade line, but in a different way. His father could drop through a skylight and make terror blossom in a dozen wicked souls; Jamie could float onto a tiny stage in a pokey venue and fill a dark room with a deeper shadow that enveloped audiences and seeped into their hearts. When Jamie sang about long, dreadful nights, a certain type of teenager knew he was singing about them. Because of Transhumance, they knew – if only for the forty-five minutes of the set – that they weren't alone, that they had friends and lovers in the dark, that tiny pinpoints of starlight were worth striving for. They were kids who only liked purple lollipops because of the colour they stained their lips, wore swathes of black even in this baking summer, would drink vinegar and lie in a bath of ice cubes to be as pale as Gené, lit their squats with black candles bought in head shops, and read thick paperback novels 'from the vampire's point of view'. Teenagers like Vron – who, come to think of it, he was supposed to be seeing this evening. If the world survived the week, she'd make him pay for standing her up.

Gené had found Vron's dog-eared *Interview With the Vampire* under a cushion in the back of the van, and was performing dramatic passages. Read out with a trace of (sexy) French accent, it sounded sillier than it did when Vron quoted bits of Anne Rice's 'philosophy' at him. Vron wrote Transhumance's lyrics, and everyone said – not to her face – the lyrics needed more work. Bongo said, 'You can't rhyme "caverns of despair" with "kicking o'er a chair" and expect folk not to laugh their kecks off.' About the only thing the band could agree on was that they didn't want to be funny.

So what was he doing on the road? In a van with four weird strangers – weird, even by his standards.

Gatherings of disparate Talents like this little lot were unusual. Fred had said they needed 'everybody'. Jamie wondered how far down the list the likes of Sewell Head came – though he knew enough not to underestimate anyone. According to Gené, the

Diogenes Club were calling this particular brouhaha 'the Winter War'. That didn't sound so bad. After the last few months, a little winter in July would be welcome.

Beyond Yeovil, they came to a road-block manned by squaddies who were turning other drivers away from a 'military exercise' barrier. The van was waved out of the queue by an NCO and – with no explanation needed – the barrier lifted for them. A riot of envious hooting came from motorists who shut up as soon as a rifle or two was accidentally pointed in their direction. Even Gené kept mum once they were in bandit country – where they were the only moving thing.

As they drove along eerily empty roads, Susan continued to relay Head's directions. 'Follow Tapmoor Road for two and a half miles, and turn right, drive half a mile, go through Sutton Mallet, then three miles on, to Alder – and we're there.'

Jamie spotted the signpost, which was almost smothered by the lower branches of a dying tree, and took the Sutton Mallet turn-off. It should have been a short cut to Alder, the village where they were supposed to rendezvous with the rest of the draftees in the Winter War. The van ploughed to a halt in a four-foot-deep snowdrift.

The temperature plunged – an oven became a fridge in seconds. Gooseflesh raised on Jamie's bare arms. Keith and Sewell Head wrapped themselves in sleeping bags. Susan's teeth chattered, interrupting her travel directions – which were academic anyway. The road was impassable.

Only Gené didn't instantly and obviously feel the cold.

Jamie shifted gears, and reversed. Wheels spun, making a hideous grinding noise for half a minute or so, then the van freed itself from the grip of ice and backed out of the drift. A few yards away, and the temperature climbed again. They were all shocked quiet for a moment, then started talking at once.

'Hush,' said Gené, who was elected Head Girl, 'look.'

The cold front was advancing, visibly – a frozen river. Hedges, half-dead from lack of rain, were swallowed by swells of ice and snow.

They all got out of the van. It was as hot as it had been, though Jamie's skin didn't readjust. He still had gooseflesh.

'It'll be here soon and swallow us again,' said Keith.

'At the current rate, in sixteen minutes forty-five seconds,' said Sewell Head.

It wasn't just a glacier creeping down a country lane, it was an entire wave advancing across the countryside. Jamie had no doubt Head knew his sums – in just over a quarter of an hour, an arctic climate would reach the road, and sweep around the van, stranding them.

'We have to go ahead on foot,' said Gené. 'It's only a couple of miles down that lane.'

'Three and a half,' corrected Head.

'A walk in the park,' said Gené.

'Thank you, Captain Scott,' said Susan. 'We're not exactly equipped.'

'You were told to bring warm clothes.'

'Naturally, I didn't believe it,' said Susan. 'We should have been shouted at.'

Jamie hadn't been told. He'd take that up with Fred and Vanessa.

'Fifteen minutes,' said Head, unconcerned.

'There's gear in the back of the van,' said Jamie. 'It'll have to do.'

'I'm fine as I am,' said Gené. 'Happy in all weathers.'

Jamie dug out one of his father's black greatcoats for Susan. It hung long on her, edges trailing on the ground. Head kept the sleeping bag wrapped around him, and looked even more like a tramp. He must be glad he came out with his scarf and gloves. Keith found a black opera cloak with red-silk lining, and settled it around his shoulders.

'Careful with that, Keith,' Jamie cautioned. 'It was the Great Edmondo's. There are hidden pockets. You might find a dead canary or two.'

Jamie pulled on a ragged black-dyed pullover and gauntlets. He fetched out a hold-all with some useful items from the Legacy, and – as an afterthought – slung the Shade goggles around his neck and put on one of his dad's wide-brimmed black slouch hats.

'Natty,' commented Gené. 'It's the Return of Dr Shade!'

'Sod off, Frenchy,' he said, smiling.

'Burgundian, remember?'

The cold front was nearly at the mouth of the lane, crawling up around the signpost. He rolled up the van windows, and locked the doors.

Gené climbed onto the snowdrift, and stamped on the powder. It was packed enough to support her. Bare-legged and -armed, she still looked comfortable amid the frozen wastes. She held out a hand and helped haul Susan up beside her. Even in the coat, Susan began shivering. Her nose reddened. She hugged herself, sliding hands into loose sleeves like a mandarin.

'Come on up, lads, the water's l-lovely,' she said.

Jamie, Keith and Head managed, with helping hands and a certain amount of swearing, to clamber up beside the girls.

Ahead was a snowscape – thickly carpeted white, trees weighed down by ice, a few roofs poking up where cottages were trapped. Snow wasn't falling, but was whipped up from the ground by cold winds and swirled viciously. Jamie put on his goggles, protecting his eyes from the spits of snow. The flakes were like a million tiny fragments of ice shrapnel.

Gené pointed across the frozen moor, at a tower.

'That's Sutton Mallet chapel. And, see, beyond that, where the hill rises... that's Alder.'

It ought to have been an hour's stroll. Very pleasant, if you liked walking in the country. Which Jamie didn't, much. Now, it seemed horribly like a death march.

Susan, he noticed, stopped shivering and chattering. She was padding, carefully across the powder, leaving deep footprints.

Gené applauded. 'Now that's thinking,' she said.

Jamie didn't know what she meant.

'She's a pyrokinetic, remember?' explained Gené. 'That's not just setting fire to things with your mind. It's control over temperature. She's made her own cocoon of warmth, inside her coat. Look, she's steaming.'

Susan turned, smiling wide. Hot fog rose from her shoulders, and snowflakes hissed when they got near her as if falling onto a griddle.

'Are my ears burning?' she asked.

'Never mind your ears,' said Keith. 'What about everything else?'

Susan's footprints were shallow puddles, which froze a few seconds after she had made them.

'I'm not a proper pyro,' she said. 'I don't set fires. I just have a thing with warmth. Saves on coins for the meter. Otherwise, it's useless – like wiggling your ears. It takes me an hour to boil enough water for a cup of tea, and by then I'm so fagged out I have to lie down and it's cold again when I wake up. That's the trouble with most of my so-called Talents. Party pieces, but little else. I mean, who needs a drawer full of bent spoons?'

'I think it's amazing,' commented Keith. 'Mind over matter. You could be on the telly. Or fight crime.'

'I'll leave that to the professionals, like Jamie's dad. You're not seeing me in a Union Jack bikini and one of those eye-masks which aren't really disguises.'

'You'd be surprised how well those masks work,' said Jamie. 'When she was Kentish Glory, Mum wore this moth-wing domino. Even people she knew really well didn't clock it was her.'

'I like a quiet life,' said Susan. 'So, enough about me being a freak. Gené, what's your secret?'

The blonde shrugged, teasing. 'Diet and lots of sleep.'

'Come on, slowcoaches,' said Susan, who was getting the hang of it. 'Last one there's a rotten—'

The snow collapsed under her and she sank waist-deep, coat-skirts spreading out around her.

'Shit,' she said. 'Pardon my Burgundian.'

'Didn't Gené say you could levitate?' said Keith, going to help her.

'She's not the one who knows everything,' said Susan. 'That was only once, and I was six. I've put on weight since then.'

Keith took her hands – 'She's all warm!' – and hauled her out of her hole.

'Abracadabra,' he said, flapping the cloak.

'It doesn't do to get overconfident,' cautioned Gené.

Susan made a rude gesture behind the other girl's back.

Jamie felt something. Deeper than the cold. He looked around. The whirling blizzard was thickening. And something was different.

'Hey, gang,' he said. 'Who made the snowmen?'

VII.

'I know the Cold is spreading,' Catriona Kaye told Derek Leech. 'It's here, in Alder. We're three miles from you. Now put Richard on, would you?'

In the manor house, the telephone was on a stand near the front door. She had to leave her guests in the drawing room to

403

take Leech's call. The hallway was still cluttered from Edwin's days as lord of this manor: hats and umbrellas (and Charles Beauregard's old swordstick) in a hideous Victorian stand, coats on hooks (she liked to use Edwin's flying jacket – still smelling of tobacco and motor-oil – for gardening), framed playbills from the 1920s, shotguns (and less commonplace armaments) in a locked case. Since Edwin's death, she'd tidied away or passed on most of his things, but here she let his ghost linger. Upstairs, on the landing, his shadow was etched permanently into the floorboards. After a lifetime in service to the Diogenes Club, it was all he had for a grave. She supposed she should throw a carpet over it or something.

As she waited for Leech to pass the phone to Richard, Catriona caught sight of herself in the tall, thin art deco mirror from the Bloomsbury flat she had shared with Edwin. At a glance, she was the girl she recognised – she had the same silhouette as she had in her, and the century's, twenties. If she looked for more than a few seconds, she saw her bobbed hair was ash-grey, and even that was dyed. Her wrists and neck were unmistakably a seventy-six-year-old's. Once, certain Valued Members had been grumpily set against even admitting her to the building in Pall Mall, never mind putting her on the rolls. Now, she was practically all that was left of the Diogenes Club as Mycroft Holmes would have recognised it. Even in the Secret World, things were changing.

'Catriona,' said Richard, tinny and distorted as if bounced off a relay station in the rings of Saturn. 'How are you? Is the Cold—?'

'In the village? Yes. A bother? No. We've enough lively minds in the house to hold it back. Indeed, the cool is misleadingly pleasant. What little of the garden survived the heatwave has been killed by snow, though – which is really rather tiresome.'

Richard succinctly explained the situation.

'"The planet's first evolved intelligence"?' she queried. 'That has a familiar ring to it. I shall put the problem to our little council of war.'

'Watch out for snowmen.'

'I shall take care to.'

She hung up and had a moment's thought, ticking off her long string of black pearls as if it were a rosary. The general assumption was that they had been dealing with an unnatural phenomenon, perhaps a bleed-through from some parallel wintery world. Now, it seemed there was an entity in the picture. Something to be coped with, accommodated or eliminated.

The drawing room was crowded. Extra chairs had been brought in.

Constant Drache, the visionary architect, wanted news of Derek Leech. Catriona assured him that his patron was perfectly well. Drache wasn't a Talent, just a high-ranking minion. He was here with the watchful Dr Lark, corralling the persons Leech had contributed to the council and making mental notes on the others for use after the truce was ended. That showed a certain optimism, which Catriona found mildly cheering. She had told Richard's team not to call Leech's people 'the villains', but the label was hard to avoid. Fred and Vanessa were still in London, liaising with the Minister.

Anthony Jago, wearing a dog-collar the Church of England said he was no longer entitled to, was Leech's prime specimen – an untapped Talent, reputed to be able to overwrite reality on a large scale. The former clergyman said he was looking for property in the West Country and had taken a covetous liking to the manor house. The man had an understandable streak of self-regarding megalomania, and Lark was evidently trying to keep him unaware of the full extent of his abilities. Catriona would have been terrified of Jago if he weren't completely trumped by Ariadne ('just Ariadne'). The white-haired, utterly beautiful creature had made her way unbidden to the Club and offered her services in the present emergency. She was an Elder of the Kind. Even the Secret Files had almost nothing on them. The Elders hadn't taken an interest in anything in Geneviève Dieudonné's lifetime, though some of their young – the Kith – had occasionally been problematic.

Apart from Jago, none of Leech's soldiers were in the world-changing (or -threatening) class. The unnaturally thin, bald, haggard Nigel Karabatsos – along with his unnaturally small, plump, clinging wife, Joan – represented a pompous Neo-Satanic sect called the Thirteen. Typically, there weren't thirteen of them. Maureen Mountmain was heiress to a dynasty of Irish mystics who'd been skirmishing with the Club for over eighty years. Catriona would gladly not have seen the red-headed, big-hipped, big-busted Amazon in this house again (she'd been there when the shadows took Edwin). Maureen and Richard had one of those complicated young persons' things, which neither cared to talk of and – Catriona hoped – would not be resumed. There were enough 'undercurrents' in this council for several West End plays as it was. Jago and Maureen, comparatively youthful and obnoxiously vital, pumped out more pheromones than a beehive. They took an interest in each other which Dr Lark did her best to frustrate by interposing her body. Leech obviously had separate plans for those two.

The mysterious Mr Sewell Head, the other side's last recruit for the Winter War Effort, was out in a snowfield somewhere with Geneviève's party. Catriona suspected they'd have a hard time getting through. Fair enough. If this council failed, someone needed to be left alive to regroup and try a second wave. Geneviève had young Dr Shade and the interesting Rodway girl with her – they had the potential to become Valued Talents, and the Cold crisis should bring them on. Still, it didn't do to think too far ahead. In the long run, there was always an unhappy outcome – except, just possibly, for Ariadne.

Watching Jago and Maureen flex and flutter, attracting like magnets, Catriona worried that the Club's Talents were relics. Swami Anand Gitamo, formerly Harry Cutley, was only here for moral support. He had been Most Valued Member once, but had lately taken a more spiritual role. Still, it was good to see Harry again. His chanted mantras irritated Jago, a point in his favour. Paulette Michaelsmith had even more obviously been hauled out of retirement. She could only use her Talent (under the direction of others) when asleep and dreaming, and was permanently huddled in a bath-chair. Catriona noted Dr Lark wasn't too busy playing gooseberry to take an interest in poor, dozy Paulette. Dr Cross, the old woman's minder, was instructed to ward the witch off if she made any sudden moves. Louise Magellan Teazle, one of Catriona's oldest friends, always brought the sunshine with her – a somewhat undervalued Talent this summer, though currently more useful than all Karabatsos's dark summonings or Jago's reality-warping. It was thanks to Louise that the Cold was shut out of the manor house. She was an author of children's books, and a near neighbour. In her house out on the moor, she'd been first to notice a change in the weather.

While Catriona relayed what Leech and Richard had told her, Louise served high tea. Paulette woke up for fruitcake and was fully alert for whole minutes at a time.

'This Cold,' Drache declared. 'Can it be killed?'

'Anything can be killed,' said Karabatsos.

'Yes, dear, anything,' echoed his wife.

'We know very little about the creature,' admitted Catriona. 'The world's leading expert is Professor Cleaver, and his perceptive is – shall we say – distorted.'

'All life is sacred,' said Anand Gitamo.

'Especially ours,' said Maureen. 'I'm a mum. I don't want my girl growing up to freeze in an apocalypse of ice and frost.'

Catriona had a minor twinge of concern at the prospect of more Mountmains.

'How can all life be sacrosanct when some life forms are inimical, hein?' said Drache. 'Snake and mongoose. Lion and gazelle. Humanity and the Cold.'

'Tom and Jerry,' said Paulette, out of nowhere.

'I did not say "sacrosanct",' pointed out Anand Gitamo.

'The Cold can die,' said Ariadne. Everyone listened to her, even Jago. 'But it should not be killed. It can kill you and live, as you would shrug off a virus. You cannot kill it and expect to survive, as you cannot murder the seas, the soil or the great forests. The crime would be too great. You could not abide the consequences.'

'But we do not matter?' asked Drache.

'I should miss you,' admitted Ariadne, gently. 'As you cannot do without the trees, who make the air breathable, the Kind cannot do without you, without your dreams. If the Cold spreads, we would outlive you – but eventually, starved, we would fade. The Cold has mind, but no memory. It would retain nothing of you.'

'The world doesn't end in ice, but fire,' said Jago. 'This, I have seen.'

'The Old Ones will return,' said Karabatsos.

'Yes, dear, Old,' echoed his wife.

It seemed to Catriona that everyone in this business expected a personal, tailor-made apocalypse. They had enlisted in the Winter War out of jealousy – a pettish wish to forestall every other prophet's vision, to keep the stage clear for their own variety of Doom. The Cold was Professor Cleaver's End of the World, and the others wanted to shut him down. Derek Leech, at least, needed the planet to stay open for business – which was why Catriona had listened when he called a truce with the Diogenes Club.

The doorbell rang. Catriona would have hurried back to the hall, but David Cross gallantly went for her. Louise poured more tea.

It was not Geneviève and her party, but Mr Zed, last of the Undertakers. He brought another old acquaintance from the Mausoleum, their collection of oddities (frankly, a prison).

Mr Zed, eyes permanently hidden behind dark glasses, stood in the drawing room doorway. Everyone looked at him. The brim of his top hat and the shoulders of his black frock coat were lightly powdered with snow. Many of the council – and not only those on Derek Leech's side of the room – might once have had cause to fear immurement in the Mausoleum, but the Undertaking was not what it had been. Mr Zed politely took off his hat and stood aside.

Behind him was a little girl who could have stepped out of an illustration from one of Louise's earliest books. She had an Indian braid tied with a silver ribbon, and wore a neat pinafore with a kangaroo pouch pocket. She looked like Rose Farrar, who disappeared from a field in Sussex in 1872, 'taken by the fairies'. This creature had turned up on the same spot in 1925, and come close to delivering an apocalypse that might have suited Jago's biblical tastes. At least she wasn't playing Harlot of Babylon any more.

'Good afternoon, Rose.'

Catriona had not seen the girl-shaped creature since the Undertaking took her off. She still had a smooth, pale patch on her hand – where Rose had spat venom at her.

The creature curtseyed. When she looked up, she wore another face – Catriona's, as it had been fifty years ago. She used the face to smile, and aged rapidly – presenting Catriona with what she looked like now. Then, she laughed innocently and was Rose Farrar again.

The procedure was like a slap.

The thing that looked like Rose was on their side, for the moment. But, unlike everyone else in the room – good, bad or undecided – she didn't come from here. If the Cold won, Rose wouldn't necessarily lose a home, or a life, or anything she put value on.

Catriona wasn't sure what Rose could contribute, even if she was of a mind to help. Ariadne, Louise and, perhaps, the Rodway girl were Talents – they could alter reality through sheer willpower. Jago and Paulette were 'effective dreamers' – they could alter reality on an even larger scale, but at the whim of their unconscious minds. Rose was a living mirror – she could only change herself, by plucking notions from the heads of anyone within reach. She resembled the original Rose because that's who the people who found her in Angel Field expected her to be. She had been kept captive all these years by confining her with people (wardens and convicts) who believed the Mausoleum to be an inescapable prison – which wasn't strictly true.

'What a dear little thing,' said Ariadne. 'Come here and have some of Miss Teazle's delicious cake.'

Rose meekly trotted over to the Elder's side and presented her head to be stroked. Jago turned away from Maureen, and was fascinated. Until today, he hadn't known there were other Talents in the world. Paulette perked up again, momentarily – the most powerful dreamer on record, now in a room with at least two creatures who fed on dreams.

End of the world or not, Catriona wondered whether bringing all these big beasts together was entirely a bright idea.

'More tea, Cat,' suggested Louise, who had just given a steaming cup to the Undertaker.

Catriona nodded.

VIII.

Jamie wasn't surprised when the snowmen attacked. It wouldn't be a war if there weren't an enemy.

The frosties waited until the five had tramped a hundred difficult yards or so past them, committing to the path ahead and an uncertain footing. They were in Sutton Mallet. It wasn't much of a place. Two Rolls-Royces were parked by the path, almost buried, icicles dripping from the bonnet ornaments. Nice machines. His dad drove one like them.

'What's that thing called again?' he muttered, nodding at the dancers.

'The Spirit of Ecstasy,' said Sewell Head. 'Originally, the Spirit of Speed. Designed by Charles Sykes for the Rolls-Royce Company in 1911. The model is Eleanor Velasco Thornton.'

'Eleanor. That explains it. Dad always called the little figure "Nellie in Her Nightie". I used to think she had wings, but it's supposed to be her dress, streaming in the wind.'

Everyone had fallen over more than once. It stopped being remotely funny. Each step was an uncertain adventure which only Gené was nimble enough to enjoy. Then, even she skidded on a frozen puddle and took a tumble into a drift.

She looked up, and saw the four snowy sentinels.

'What are you laughing at?' she shouted.

At that, the snowmen upped stumps and came in a rush. When they moved, they were localised, roughly human-shaped blizzards. They had no problem with their footing, and charged like touchy rhinos whose mothers had just been insulted by howler monkeys.

'There are people inside,' yelled Keith. 'I think they're dead.'

'They better hope they're dead,' said Gené, flipping herself upright and standing her ground, adopting a fighting stance.

The first and biggest of the frosties – who wore a top hat –

barrelled towards the Burgundian girl, growing into a creature that seemed all shoulders. She met it with an ear-piercing 'ki-yaaa' and a Bruce Lee-approved power-kick to the midriff. The topper fell off and the frosty stopped in its tracks, shedding great chunks of packed ice to reveal a well-dressed gent with a deeply cut throat and a slack mouth. He had bled out before freezing. The snow crawled back up around the corpse, cocooning it with white powder, building layers of icy muscle, growing icicle spines and teeth. It reached down with an extensible arm, picked up its hat, and set it back on its head at a jaunty angle. The coals of its mouth rearranged themselves into a fierce grin.

And the other three – who wore a tartan cap, a jungle hat and two bugs on springs – caught up with their leader. They were swollen to the size of big bruisers.

Jamie looked down at his hands. His gauntlets were mittened with black clouds, containing violet electrical arcs. Out in the open, with snow all around and cold sunlight, there was too little shade. Night was far off. He cast darkstuff at the Scotch Snowman, who was nearest, and sheared away a couple of icicles. They instantly grew back.

He would have to do better.

Fred Astaire Snowman patted its healed-over tummy, and shot out a big fist which clenched around Gené's throat. Astaire lifted Gené off the ground. She kicked, but floundered with nothing to brace against. Jamie saw she had longer, sharper nails than normal – but any tears she made in the snow–hand were healed over instantly. She gurgled, unable to talk.

Comical Bugs Snowman and Jungle Explorer Snowman shifted, in opposite directions. They were forming a circle. A killing circle.

Astaire grew a yard-long javelin of solid ice from its shoulder, and snapped it off to make a stake. It pressed the ice-spear against Gené's ribs, ready to hoist her up like a victim of Frosty the Impaler.

Susan had her eyes shut, and radiated warmth – but not heat. Sewell Head was chattering about snowmen in fact and fiction, citing pagan precedents, Christmas cake decorations and the Ronettes. Keith wrapped himself in his magician's cape, and rolled his eyes up so that only the whites showed. Jamie supposed he was having a fit.

Gené squeaked a scream out through her crushed throat. Scarlet blood showed on her safari jacket.

He tried to gather more darkness, from inside.

Suddenly, Keith's eyes snapped back – but they were different.

'Don't waste your energy, Shade,' he said, in a commanding tone. 'Use this.'

From the depths of the cloak, Keith produced a thin, diamond-shaped, black object. It was Dennis Rattray's Fang of Night. Jamie had wondered where Dad had put it after taking it from Blackfist. Keith tossed the jewel to Jamie, who caught it and staggered back. The Fang was the size of a gobstopper, but weighed as much as a cannonball. He held it in both hands. It was like sticking his fingers into a live electric socket.

'Sue,' Keith said, 'cover Shade's – Jamie's – back. Imagine a wall of heat, and concentrate. Swellhead, give me some dark refraction indices, considering available light, the Blackfist gem and whatever these snow-things are. Today would be a help.'

Astonished, Head scrawled sums in the snow with his forefinger.

'Gené, hang on,' said Keith. Gené even tried to nod, though her face was screwed up in agony and spatters of her blood stained the snow under her kicking feet.

'Can you feel it, Shade?'

Jamie was seeing a different Keith Marion. And the jewel

didn't seem so heavy once he'd worked out how to hold it. Rattray had tapped into its energy by making a fist around it, but Dad said that was what had killed him in the end. There were other ways of using the Fang of Night.

Head put his hand up, and pointed to a formula he had traced.

'Well played, Swellhead,' said Keith, patting Head's bald bonce. 'Shade, hold the Fang up to your forehead and focus. Aim for the hat!'

Behind him, Susan grunted, and he heard slushing, melting sounds.

'Ugh, disgusting,' she said.

Jamie fought an urge to turn and find out what had happened.

'Concentrate, man,' insisted Keith. 'Gené can't hold out much longer.'

Head began to give a figure in seconds, but Keith shut him up.

Jamie held the stone to his forehead. It seemed to fit into the V above his goggles. The dark matter was sucked in through the gauntlets, thrilling into his palms, surging through his veins and nerves, and gathered in his forebrain, giving him a sudden ice-cream migraine. Then, it was set free.

He saw a flash of dark purple. Astaire's top hat exploded in flames that burned black, and the snowman fell apart. Gené was dropped, and pulled out the ice-shard in her chest before she sprawled in the snow. She crabwalked away from the well-dressed, still-standing corpse that had been inside Astaire. Its knees kinked, and it pitched forward.

'Now, turn,' ordered Keith. 'The others.'

Jamie wheeled about. Susan was on her knees, with her arms held out, fingers wide. Scotch Snowman and Explorer Snowman loomed over her, meltwater raining from their arms and chests and faces – the trapped corpses showing through. Susan was running out of charge, though. A slug of blood crawled out of her nose. Angry weals rose around her fingernails.

This time, it was like blinking. He zapped the tartan cap and the sola topi to fragments, and the snowmen were downed. Susan swooned, and Keith was there to catch her, wrapping her in his cloak, wiping away the blood, squeezing her fingers. She woke up, and he kissed her like someone who'd known her longer and better than few hours.

'Excuse me,' said Gené, 'but I nearly had an icicle through my heart.'

Keith looked at her and asked brusquely, 'You all right?'

Gené eased her bloody jacket out of the way. Her scrape was already healing.

'Seem to be,' she admitted.

'Good. Now help Shade with the last of them. It's the most dangerous.'

Gené saluted.

'Sue,' whispered Keith.

'Do I know you?' she asked, frankly irritated. He let her go, and stood up, stiffly. In his cloak, he looked like the commander of a victorious Roman legion. Jamie didn't know where the kid had got it from.

Bugs had either legged it or melted into the ground.

Jamie had purple vision. It was like night-sight, but in the daytime. With the Fang of Night, he could think faster. He didn't feel the cold. He could take anyone, any day of the week. He could only imagine what he would sound like if he used this onstage.

Keith plucked the jewel from his grasp, holding it between thumb and forefinger as if it were radioactive, then magicked it away with a conjurer's flourish.

'You of all people should know to treat those things carefully,' said Keith.

For an instant, Jamie wanted to batter the kid's face and take back the jewel. Then, he understood. Use it, but don't let it get its hooks in you. Dad had said that all the time.

'So, which Keith is this?' said Gené, tugging on the kid's wrist-tag. 'What school do you go to?'

'School? There hasn't been any school since the Spiders came. Good job too. They don't teach you anything useful. You have to learn survival, and resistance, on the job.'

This Keith had a firmer jaw, healed-over scars, and a steady, manly, confident gaze. People snapped in line when he spoke and threw themselves under trains if there was a tactical advantage in it.

'He told us about this before we met you,' Gené explained. 'Some other Keith lives on an Earth overrun by arachnoid aliens. He's a guerrilla leader. He also plays opening bat for Somerset and has three girlfriends. Opinion is split as to whether it's a viable alternate timeline or some sort of Dungeons and Dragons wish-fulfilment fantasy. At the moment, I don't really care.'

She kissed Keith on the mouth. He took it as if it were his right, and then started struggling.

'What happened?' he asked, shaking free of Gené. 'Who was here?'

Gené let the familiar – the original? – Keith go, and edged away from him. He still looked confused. The other Keith had been useful in a pinch, but Jamie couldn't say he missed him.

IX.

Putting Professor Cleaver to sleep hadn't brought back the summer, but did shut him up – which was a relief.

Richard looked through the heavily frosted window. There was proper snow, now. Precipitation. It dropeth-ed like the gentle rain from Heaven, fluttering down picturesquely before being caught in erratic, spiralling winds and dashed hither and yon. The Cold's sphere of influence scraped the upper atmosphere, where it found clouds to freeze.

According to Catriona, the white blanket was gaining pace, spreading across the moors and fields. Soon, the perimeter of exclusion would be breached. So far, three villages had been evacuated on a flimsy cover story. When the Cold gripped fair-sized towns like Yeovil and Sedgwater, the domesticated feline would be well and truly liberated from the portable container.

Cleaver snorted in his sleep, honking through his broken nose. Not content with tying the Professor to a swivel chair, Leech had shoved a sock in his mouth and bound a scarf around his jaws. Richard loosened the gag, so he wouldn't asphyxiate on bri-nylon and his own false teeth.

Leech shot him a pitiful look. He was picking through Clever Dick's papers.

'The man couldn't maintain an orderly file if his soul depended on it,' he said in exasperation. 'From now on, every scientist or researcher who works for me gets shadowed by two form-fillers and a pen-pusher. What's the use of results if you can't find them?'

'He wasn't working for you,' said Richard.

'Oh yes he was,' insisted Leech. 'He drew his pay-packet and he signed his contract. Derek Leech International owns his results. If this Cold creature is real, then we own her. The *Comet* has exclusive rights to her story. I could put her in a zoo, hunt her for sport, license her image for T-shirts, or dissect her crystal by crystal to advance the progress of science and be entirely within my legal rights.'

'Tell her that.'

Leech turned a page and found something. 'I just might,' he said.

He tore out a sheaf of papers covered in neat little diagrams. Richard thought it might be some form of cipher, then recognised the hexagonal designs as snow crystals. Under each was a scrawl – mirror-written words, not in English.

'Backwards in Latin,' mused Leech. 'Paranoid little boffin, wouldn't you say? This is Cleaver's Rosetta stone. Not many words, no subtleties, no syntax at all. But he received instructions. He made and used his Box. He broke the Zero Barrier, and violated the laws of physics.'

'All because he could grow snowflakes?'

'Yes, and now I own the process. There might not be applications yet, but things get smaller. Transistorisation won't stop at the visible. Imagine: trademarked weather, logos on bacteria, microscopic art, micro-miniaturised assassins…'

'Let's ensure the future of mankind on the planet before you start pestering the patent office, shall we?'

Leech bit down, grinding his teeth hard. Richard thought something had snapped in his mouth.

'You should watch that,' he advised.

Leech smiled, showing even, white, perfect gnashers. Richard suspected he had rows of them, eternally renewed – like a shark.

All rooms have ghosts. Acts and feelings and ideas all have residue, sometimes with a half-life of centuries. Richard took his gauntlets off and began to touch things, feeling for the most recent impressions. His fingertips were so numb that the cold shocks were welcome. His sensitivity was more attuned to living people than dead objects, but he could usually read something if he focused. He scraped a brown stain on the wall, and had a hideous flash: Cleaver, with a knife, smiling; a red-haired man in a white coat, gouting from an open throat.

'What is it?' Leech asked.

Richard forced himself to disconnect from the murder. 'The

staff,' he said. 'I saw what happened before they were snowmen.'

'Where are they, by the way?' asked Leech.

'Wandered off. Didn't seem to be the sorts to listen to reason. I doubt if you can negotiate with them.'

The memory flashes floated in his mind, like neon after-images. He blinked, and they began to dispel. Cleaver had made four sacrifices to the Cold. McKendrick, Kellett, Bakhtinin, Pouncey.

'Were the staff dead before or after they got snow-coated?' asked Leech.

'Does it matter?'

'If the Professor killed them to give the Cold raw material to make catspaws, they were just unused machines when she got them. If they were alive when the Cold wrapped them up, she might have interfaced with minds other than Clever Dick's.'

Richard didn't approve of Leech's use of 'interfaced' as a verb-form, but saw where he was going.

'He killed them first,' he confirmed. Leech didn't ask him how he knew. 'They aren't even zombies. The dead people are more like armatures. The only traces of personality they have—'

'The hats.'

'…were imposed by Professor Cleaver. I think he was trying to be funny. He's not very good at humour. Few solipsists are.'

Richard proceeded to the remains of the Box. The Cold had come through this doorway. He doubted it could be used to send her back, even if it were repaired. Banishing was never as easy as conjuring. Sometimes performing a ritual backwards worked, but not in a language with six planes of symmetry. You would always get hexagonal palindromes.

Pressing his palm to a frost patch on the surface of a work-bench, he felt the slight bite of the crystals, the pull on skin as he took his hand away. He didn't sense an entity, not even the life he would feel if he put his naked hand against the bark of a giant redwood. Yet the Cold was here.

'When the Cold broke through the Zero Barrier,' said Leech, 'the Professor's Box blew up. After that, he couldn't make his little tiny ice sculptures, but they still talked. She turned the others into snowmen, but spared him. How could he make her understand he was a sympathiser?'

Richard thought about that. 'He persuaded the Cold he was her high priest,' he said. 'And she let him live... for a while.'

'Cleaver said the Cold was an intelligent form of life,' said Leech. 'He did not say she was clever. Imagine: you're utterly unique, near-omnipotent and have endured millennia upon millennia. You wake up and the only person who talks to you – the only person you have ever talked to – is Clever Dick Cleaver. What does that give you?'

'A grossly distorted picture of the world?'

'Exactly. Perhaps it's time our Cold Lady heard another voice.'

'Voices,' said Richard, firmly.

'Yes, of course,' said Leech, not meaning it.

Derek Leech was excited, fathoming possibilities, figuring out angles. Letting the Great Enchanter cut a separate deal with the Cold would be a terrible idea. He was entirely too good at negotiating contracts.

'Now,' Leech thought out loud, 'how did he talk with her?'

Richard remembered the snow angels. He wandered out of the laboratory. Not caring to maintain Cleaver's obsessive little paths, he waded through snow. It drifted over his ankles. From the cafeteria doorway, he looked again at the three angels. They had reminded him of semaphore signals.

'This is how,' he said.

Leech had tagged along with him. He saw it at once too.

'See the feet,' said Leech. 'Not heel-marks, but toe-marks. When kids make snow angels, they lie on their backs. Cleaver lies on his front. You can see where his face fits, like a mould for a mask.'

A muffled screech sounded. Back in the laboratory, the Professor was awake.

Richard stepped into the room and knelt by an angel, touching the negative impression of Cleaver's face. He felt nothing. If this had been the connection, it was dead now. The Cold had moved on.

He would have to try outside.

'Leech,' he said, 'get on your backpack blower and ring Catriona again. We have to tell her what we're doing, in case it doesn't work. No sense the next lot making the same mistakes…'

A chill rolled down the corridor.

The doorway was empty. Richard saw a white tangle on the floor. Leech's parka. And another further away. His leggings.

Richard's stomach turned over. He was feeling things now.

'Leech!' he shouted.

Only the Professor responded, rattling his chair and yelling around his gag.

Richard jogged down the corridor, past more of Leech's discarded arctic gear. He turned a corner. The main doors were open. One flapped in the blizzard.

He made it to the doors and took the full force of the wind in his face.

Leech – in a lightweight salmon suit – had walked a few yards away from the building. He stood in the middle of whirling snow, casually undoing his wide orange knit tie.

One of the snowmen was back. It was Bee-Alice, swollen to mammoth size, twelve or fourteen feet tall, body-bulbs bulging as if pregnant with a litter of snow-babies. Queen Bee-Alice stood over Leech like a Hollywood pagan idol, greedy for human sacrifice.

It should be a summer evening. Daylight lasting past ten o'clock. Plagues of midges and supper in the garden. A welcome cool after another punishingly blazing drought day. Any sunlight was blocked by the Cold, and premature gloom – not even honest night – had fallen.

Leech popped his cat's-eye cufflinks and began unbuttoning his chocolate-brown ruffle shirt. He exposed his almost-hairless chest, clenching his jaws firmly to keep from chattering. He wasn't quite human, but Richard had known that.

This was not going to happen on Richard's watch. Bad enough that the Cold's wake-up call had come from an embittered lunatic whose emotional age was arrested at eleven. If her next suitor were Derek Leech, the death by freezing of all life on Earth might seem a happier outcome.

Richard tried to stride towards Leech, but wind held him back. He forced himself, inch by inch, out into the open, struggling against pellets of ice to take the few crucial steps.

Queen Bee-Alice creaked, head turning like the world before the BBC TV news. The novelty bumblebees bounced over her, a crown or a halo. She had giant, wrecking-ball fists. Sharon Kellett, junior meteorologist. Two years out of a polytechnic, with a boyfriend in the Navy and a plan to be national weather girl on the television station Derek Leech wanted to start up. She was among the first casualties of the Winter War. Dead, but not yet fallen. Richard ached at the life lost.

Leech shucked his snug-at-the-crotch, flappy-at-the-ankles trousers. He wore mint-green Y-fronts with electric blue piping.

Richard got to the Great Enchanter and crooked an arm around his neck.

'I won't let you do this,' he shouted in his ear.

'You don't understand, Jeperson,' he shouted back. At this volume, attempted sincerity sounded just like whining. 'I have to. For the greater good. I'm willing to sacrifice my – or anyone's – life to end this.'

Richard was taken aback, then laughed.

'Nice try, Derek,' he said. 'But it won't wash.'

'It won't, will it?' replied Leech, laughing too.

'Not on your nellie.'

'I still have to go through with this, though. You understand, Jeperson? I can't pass up the opportunity!'

Leech twisted as if greased in Richard's grip, and shot a tight, knuckly fist into his stomach. Even through layers of protective gear, Richard felt the piledriver blow. He lost his hold on Leech and the Great Enchanter followed the sucker-punch with a solid right to the jaw, a kick to the knee, and another to the goolies. Richard went down, and took an extra kick – for luck – in his side.

'"You rearn now, Grasshopper,"' said Leech, fingers pulling the corners of his eyes, '"not to charrenge master of ancient and noble art of dirty fighting!"'

Leech couldn't help gloating. Stripped to his underpants, whipped by sleet, skin scaled by gooseflesh, his expression was a mask of ugly victory. His exultant, grin showed at least a hundred and sixty-eight teeth. Was this the Great Enchanter's true face?

'Really think you can make a deal with the Cold?'

Leech wagged his finger. 'You're not getting me like that, Grasshopper. I'm no Clever Dick. I'm not going to explain my wicked plan and give you a chance to get in the way. I'm just going to do what I'm going to do.'

Richard had a lump in his fist, an ice-chunk embedded with frozen gravel. His eyes held Leech's gaze, but his hand was busy with the chunk, which he rolled in the snow.

'You didn't go to public school, did you, Derek?'

'No, why?'

'You might have missed a trick.'

Richard sat up and, with practised accuracy, threw the heavy-cored snowball at Leech's forehead. The collision made a satisfying sound. Richard's heart surged with immature glee and he recalled earlier victories: as an untried Third Form bowler, smashing the centre-stump and putting out the astonished captain of the first XI; on an autumn playground, wielding a horse chestnut fresh from the branch to split the vinegar-hardened champion conker of the odious Weems-Deverell II.

A third eye of blood opened above Leech's raised brows. His regular eyes showed white and he collapsed, stunned. He lay, twitching, on the snow.

Queen Bee-Alice made no move. Richard hoped she was impartial.

Unable to leave even Derek Leech to freeze, Richard picked him up in a fireman's lift and tossed him inside the building – slamming the doors after him. He didn't know how much time he had before Leech's wits crept back.

He took off his furs. Cold bit, deeper with each layer removed. He went further than Leech, and eventually stood naked in the blizzard. Everything that could shrivel, turn blue or catch frost did so. When the shivering stopped, when sub-zero (if not sub-absolute zero) wind-blast seemed slightly warm, he recognised the beginnings of hypothermia. There was no more pain, just a faint pricking all over his body. Snow packed his ears and deafened him. He was calm, light-headed. Flashes popped in his vision, as the cold did something to his optic nerves he didn't want to think about. He shut his eyes, not needing the distraction. There were still flashes, but easier to ignore.

He knelt before Queen Bee-Alice. Some feeling came from his shins as they sank into the snow – like mild acid, burning gently to the bone. His extremities were far distant countries, sending only the occasional report, always bad news. Cleaver had lain face down, but indoors – with no snowfall. Richard lay back, face up, flakes landing on his cheeks and forehead, knowing his whole body was gradually being covered by layer after layer. His hands were swollen and useless. With his arms he shovelled snow over himself. Snow didn't melt on his skin – any body warmth was gone. He fought the urge to sit up and struggle free, and he fought the disorienting effects that came with a lowering of the temperature of his brain. He was buried quickly, as the Cold made a special effort to clump around him, form a drift, smooth over the bump, swallow him.

As his body temperature lowered, he had to avoid surrendering to the sleep that presaged clinical death. His blood slowed, and his heartbeats became less and less frequent. He was using a meagre repertoire of yogic techniques, but couldn't be distracted by the business of keeping the meat machine running.

He opened up, physically, mentally, spiritually.

In the darkness, he was not alone.

Richard felt the Cold. It was hugely alive, and more alien than the few extra-terrestrials he'd come across. Newly awake, it stretched out, irritated by moving things and tiny obstructions. It could barely distinguish between piles of stone and people. Both were against the nature it had known. It had an impulse to clean itself by covering these imperfections. It preferred people wrapped in snow, not moving by themselves. But was this its genuine preference, or something learned from Clever Dick Cleaver?

'Hello,' shouted Richard, with his mind. 'Permit me to introduce myself. I am Richard, and I speak for mankind.'

Snow pressed around his face, like ice-fingers on his eyes.

He felt tiny crystals forming inside his brain – not a killing flash-freeze, but the barest pinheads. The Cold was inside him.

'You are not Man.'

It wasn't a voice. It wasn't even words. Just snowflake hexagons in the dark of his skull, accompanied by a whisper of arctic winds. But he understood. Meaning was imprinted directly into his brain.

To talk with the Cold, it had to become part of him. This was an interior monologue.

'I am Richard,' he tried to reply. It was awkward. He was losing his sense of self, of the concept of Richard. 'I am not Man.' Man was what the Cold called Cleaver. 'I am another Man.'

To the Cold, the idea of 'other' was still fresh, a shock which had come with its awakening. It had only just got used to Man/Cleaver. It was not yet ready for the independent existence of three billion more unique and individual intelligences. As Richard had guessed, it hadn't previously had use for numbers beyond One/Self. The corpse-cores of its snowmen weren't like Man/Cleaver. They were tools, empty of consciousness. Had Cleaver killed his staff because he knew more voices would confuse his ice mistress? Probably.

What would Leech have said to the Cold? He would try to make a deal, to his own best advantage. Richard couldn't even blame him. It was what he did. In this position, the Great Enchanter might become a senior partner, stifle the Cold's rudimentary mind and colonise it, use it. Leech/Cold would grip the world, in a different, ultimately crueller way. He wanted slaves, not corpses; a treadmill to the inferno, not peace and quiet.

What should Richard say?

'Please,' he projected. 'Please don't k— us.'

There were no snowflakes for 'kill' or 'death' or 'dead'. He shuffled through the tiny vocabulary, and tried again. 'Please don't stop/cover/freeze us.'

The Cold's mind was changing: not in the sense of altering its intention, but of restructuring its internal architecture. So far, in millennia, it had only needed to make declarative statements, and – until the last few days – only to itself. It had been like a goldfish, memory wiped every few seconds, constantly reaffirming, 'This is me, this is my bowl, this is water, this is me, this is my bowl, this is water.' Now, the Cold needed to keep track, to impose its will on others. It needed a more complicated thought process. It was on the point of inventing a crucial mode of address, of communication. It was about to ask its first question.

Richard had got his point over. The Cold now understood that its actions would lead to the ending of Man/Richard. It had a sense Man/Richard was merely one among unimagined and unimaginable numbers of others. For it, 'three' was already equivalent to a schoolboy's 'gajillion-quajillion-infinitillion to the power of for ever'. The Cold understood Man/Richard was asking to be allowed to continue. The life of others was in the Cold's gift.

'Please don't kill us,' Richard repeated. There was a hexagram for 'kill/end' now. 'Please don't.'

The Cold paused, and asked, 'Why not?'

X.

It was getting dark, which didn't bother Jamie. He lifted his goggles and saw in more detail. He also felt the cold less. Most of his team-mates were more spooked as shadows spread, but Gené was another night-bird. You'd never know she'd come close to having a dirty great icicle shoved all the way through her chest. Perhaps she had a little of the Shade in her. She'd said she knew Auntie Jenny.

Regular Keith was bewildered about what had happened while he was away, and Susan was trying to fill him in. Sewell

Head was quoting weather statistics since before records began. It was snowing even harder, and the slog to Alder wasn't going to be possible without losing one or more of the happy little band. Finding shelter was a high priority. They were in the lee of Sutton Mallet chapel – which was small, but had a tower. The place was securely chained.

'Can't you break these?' Jamie asked Gené.

'Normal chains, yes. Chapel chains, I have a bit of a mental block about. Try the spoon-bender.'

Susan stepped up and laid hands on the metal. She frowned, and links began to buckle.

'Where's Head?' asked Keith.

Captain Cleverclogs wasn't with them. Jamie couldn't understand why anyone would wander off. Had the last snowman got him?

'Here are his tracks,' said Gené.

'I can't see any,' said Keith.

'Trust me.'

Jamie saw them too. Sewell Head had gone into a thicket of trees, just beyond what passed for the centre of Sutton Mallet. There were buildings on the other side.

'I'll fetch him back,' he said.

'We're not being that stupid, Jamie,' said Susan, dropping mangled but unbroken chains. 'You go, we all go. No sense splitting up and getting picked off one by one.'

She had a point. He was thinking like Dad, who preferred to work alone.

Beyond the trees were ugly buildings. A concrete shed, temporary cabins.

'This is Derek Leech's weather research station,' said Gené. 'Almost certainly where all the trouble started.'

Derek Leech was in the public eye as a smiling businessman,

but Jamie's dad called him 'a human void'. Jamie had thought Dad a bit cracked on the subject of Derek Leech – like everyone else's parents were cracked about long hair or short hair or the Common Market or some other bloody thing. He was coming round to thinking more of what his old man said.

'Shouldn't we stay away from here?' cautioned Keith. 'Aren't we supposed to join up with folks more qualified than us?'

'You mean grown-ups?' asked Jamie.

'Well, yes.'

'Poor old Swellhead'll be an ice lolly by the time you fetch a teacher.'

Beside the building was a towering snowman. Bugs, grown to Kitten Kong proportions. The front doors were blown inward and jammed open by snowdrifts. It was a fair guess Head had gone inside. If he could get past the snow-giant, they had a good chance.

'Susan,' he said. 'Can you concentrate on the snowman? At the first sign of hassle, melt the big bastard.'

The woman snapped off a salute. 'Since you ask so nicely,' she said, 'I'll give it a whirl.'

'Okay, gang,' he said. 'Let's go inside.'

They sprinted from the thicket to the doors. Bugs didn't make a move, but Keith tripped and Gené had to help him up and drag him.

Inside the building, which was an ice-palace, the wind was less of a problem, and they were protected from the worst of the snow. Overhead lights buzzed and flickered, bothering Jamie's eyes. He slipped his goggles back on.

They found Sewell Head in a room which might have been a mess hall. He was acting as a valet, helping a man dress in arctic gear. Jamie recognised the bloke from the telly. He was the one who said, 'If I didn't love it, I wouldn't own it.' He must love lots

429

of things, because he owned a shedload of them.

'Hi,' he said. 'I'm Derek. You must be the new Dr Shade.'

Yes, Jamie realised. He must be.

Leech's smile jangled his shadow-senses. The dark in him was something more than night.

'I'm a big fan of your father's,' said Leech. 'I learned to read from tear-sheets of the newspaper strip they ran about his adventures. Ahh, "the Whooping Horror", "the Piccadilly Gestapo". How I longed for my own autogyro! I have a car just like Dr Shade's. A ShadowShark.'

Jamie remembered that there had been two Rollses in the snow. Whose was the other one?

'Leech,' said Gené, acknowledging him.

'Geneviève Dieudonné,' said Leech, cordially. 'I thought you'd aged hundreds of years and died.'

'I got better.'

'Well done. Though live through the night before you pat yourself on the back too much. Where's the rest of the army? The heavy mob. Ariadne, Jago, Mrs Michaelsmith, Little Rose? The Cold's already got Jeperson. We need to go all-out on the attack if we're to have a chance of stopping it.'

'We're it, right now,' said Jamie.

'You'll have to do, then.'

Jamie boiled inside at that. He didn't even know the people Leech had listed. Whoever they might be, he doubted they'd have done as well against the snowmen.

'Who might you be, my dear?' Leech said to Susan.

'I might be Susan Rodway. Or Susan Ames. Mum got remarried, and I have a choice.'

'I know exactly who you are,' said Leech. 'Shade, why didn't you say you had her? She's not Rose Farrar or an Elder of the Kind, but she's a bloody good start.'

Susan began primping a bit at the attention. Jamie couldn't believe she'd let this hand-kissing creep smarm her up like that. He'd never understand birds.

'Now, Sewell,' said Leech, addressing his instant orderly. 'Get on the blower and tell Miss Kaye to pull her finger out. The telephone kit is in the laboratory down the hall. The room with the tied-up-and-gagged idiot in it. It's simple to use. You'll have the specs for it in your head somewhere.'

Head meekly trotted out of the room. He was taking orders without question.

Leech looked over the four of them – Jamie, Gené, Susan, Keith.

'Susan,' he said, 'can you do something about the room temperature?'

Susan, bizarrely, seemed smitten. 'I can try,' she said, and shut her eyes.

A little warmth radiated from her. Some icicles started dripping. Jamie felt his face pricking, as feeling returned.

'Good girl,' said Leech. 'You, young fellow-me-lad. Any chance of getting some tea going?'

'Give it a try, sir,' said Keith, hunting a kettle.

Jamie already resented Derek Leech. For a start, he had released all those triple LPs of moaning woodwind hippies which got played over and over in student common rooms. Even if he weren't the literal Devil, that alone made him a man not to be trusted. But he was magnetic in person, and Jamie felt a terrible tug – it would be easier to go along with Leech, to take orders, to not be responsible for the others. Dad could be like that too, but he always drummed it into Jamie that he should become his own man. Dad didn't even disapprove of him being in a band rather than joining the night-wars – though he realised he'd done that anyway, as well. If he was the new Dr

Shade, he was also a different Shade.

It was Leech's world too. If this big freeze was spreading, it was in his interest to side with the angels. If everyone was dead, no one would make a deal with him. No one would buy his crappy music or read his raggy papers.

Jamie saw that Gené was sceptical of anything Leech-related, but Susan and Keith were already sucked in. Keith had found his grown-up, his teacher. Susan had found something she needed too. Jamie had been revising his impression of her all day. Leech saw at once that she was the most useful Talent in their crowd. Jamie hadn't even noticed her at first, and he had been around Talents all his life. Susan Rodway was not only Shade-level or better in her abilities, but extremely good at keeping it to herself. She kept talking about the things she couldn't do, or making light of the things she could.

Leech had been briefly interested in Jamie, in Dr Shade – but he had instantly passed over him, and latched onto Susan.

He realised – with a tiny shock – that he was jealous. But of whom? Susan, for going to the head of the class? Or Leech, for getting the girl's attention? There wasn't time for this.

'What did you say about Richard Jeperson?' Gené asked Leech.

Jamie knew Jeperson was Fred and Vanessa's guv'nor at the Diogenes Club. He tied in with Gené too.

'Mad, definitely,' said Leech, with just a hint of pleasure. 'Dead, probably. The Cold took him – it's a thinking thing, not just bad weather – and he went outside, naked. He lay down and let himself be buried. I tried to stop him, but he fought like a tiger, knocked me out... gave me this.'

Leech indicated a fresh wound on his forehead.

'Stone in a snowball,' he said. 'Playground trick.'

Gené thought a few moments and said, 'We've got to go out

and find him. He might still be alive. He's not helpless. He's a Talent too. If he's buried, we can dig him up.'

'I think that's a good idea,' said Leech.

Anything Leech thought was a good idea was almost certainly good mostly or only for him. But Jamie couldn't see any alternative. That Fred would give him a right belting if he let Jeperson die.

'Okay, I'll go,' he said. 'Gené, Susan, stay here. Give Mr Leech any help he needs.'

i.e. Keep a bloody eye on him! Gené, though worried for her friend, picked that up.

Leech was bland, mild, innocent.

'Keith,' said Jamie, at last. 'Find a shovel or something, and come with me.'

Keith, infuriatingly, looked to Leech – who gave him the nod.

'Come on, find someone useful inside you. Let's get this rescue party on the road!'

Keith gulped and said, 'O-okay, Jamie.'

XI.

Derek Leech was on the telephone again. Really, the man had the most terrible manners. He had some minion bother Catriona, then brushed her aside because he wanted to talk with Maureen Mountmain, of all people. Catriona passed the receiver to the woman, who listened – to her master's voice? – and clucked. Yes, Mr Leech, no Mr Leech, three bags bloody full, Mr Leech... Catriona caught herself: this was no time to be a cranky old woman.

The Cold was getting into the manor house, overwhelming Louise Teazle's bubble of summer. Frost grew on the insides of the windows. Sleet and snow rattled against the panes.

In the gloom of the gardens, drifts and banks shifted like beasts.

Catriona had pain in her joints, and was irritated. She could list other age-related aches and infirmities, exacerbated by the Cold.

Only Rose Farrar and Ariadne were immune. Rose skipped around the drawing room, exhaling white clouds. Ariadne stood by the fireplace – where the wood wouldn't light, and shivers of snow fell on tidy ashes – and smoked a cigarette in a long, elegant holder.

Paulette Michaelsmith shivered in her sleep, and Louise rearranged her day-blanket without any effect. Karabatsos and his wife huddled together. Mr Zed was white. Swami Anand Gitamo chanted mantras, but his nose was blue. Lark and Cross, the white-coats, passed the china teapot between them, pressing their hands against the last of its warmth. Even Anthony Jago, who feared not the ice and fire of Hell, had his hands in his armpits. The house itself creaked more than usual.

'Richard?' exclaimed Maureen. 'Are you sure?'

Catriona, who had been trying not to listen, had a spasm of concern. Maureen had blurted out the name in shock. She and Richard had—

Maureen hung up, cutting off Catriona's train of thought. The room looked to Maureen for a report.

'Derek needs us all,' she said. 'He needs us to hurt the Cold.'

A lot of people talked at once, then shut up.

'Catriona,' said Maureen, fists pressed together under her impressive bosom, 'your man Richard Jeperson is lost.'

'Lost?'

'Probably dead. I'm sorry, truly. Derek says he tried to reach the Cold, and it took him. It's a monster, and wants to kill us all. We have to hit it with all we've got, now. All our big guns, he says. Maybe it can't be killed, but can be hurt. Driven back to its hole.' A tear dribbled from Maureen's eye. 'Reverend Jago, Lady Elder, Rose… you're our biggest guns. Just tear into the Cold. Miss Teazle, work on Mrs Michaelsmith – direct her. Think of the heat-wave. Karabatsos, clear a circle and make a summoning. A fire elemental. The rest of you, pray. That's not a figure of speech. The only way we can beat this thing is with an enormous spiritual attack.'

The news about Richard was a terrible blow. Catriona let Maureen go on with her 'to arms' speech, trying to take it in. She was not a sensitive in the way any of these Talents were, but she was not a closed mind. And Maureen had said Richard was only probably dead.

Mr and Mrs Karabatsos were the first to act. They rolled aside a carpet and began chalking a circle on the living-room floor.

'Excuse me,' said Catriona. 'Is this your house?'

Karabatsos glared at her, nastily triumphant. Catriona would not be looked at like that in her home.

'No need to bother with that,' said Anand Gitamo.

'Summoning a fire elemental requires a circle, and a ritual,' said Karabatsos. 'Blood must be spilled and burned.'

'Yes dear, spilled and burned,' echoed his wife.

'In normal company, maybe,' said the Swami, sounding more like plain old Harry Cutley. 'But we've got extraordinary guests. We can take short cuts. Now, you two sorcerers shut your eyes and think about your blessed fire elemental. Extra-hot and flaming from the Pits of Abaddon and Erebus and all that. Think hard, now think harder. Imagine more flames, more heat, more burning. Take your basic fire elemental, add the Japanese pikadon, the Norse Surtur, Graeco-Roman Haephaestus or Vulcan, the phoenix, the big bonfire at the end of *The Wicker Man*, that skyscraper from *The Towering Inferno*, the Great Fire of London in 1666, enough napalm to deforest the Republic of Vietnam and the eternal blue flame of the lost city of Kôr...'

Nigel Karabatsos and his wife shut their eyes and thought of fire.

'Rose, dear,' said Gitamo, 'peek into those tiny minds.'

Rose Farrar caught fire and expanded. She grew into a nine-foot-tall column of living flame, with long limbs and a blazing skull-face. Though she was hard to look at and her radiant heat filled the room, she didn't burn the ceiling or the carpet. She was Fire.

'Reverend Jago,' said Gitamo, 'would you open the doors. Rose needs to go outside.'

The man in the dog-collar was astonished by what the apparent little girl had become. Anthony Jago didn't know whether to bow down before a fiery angel of the Lord or cast out a demon from Hell. His already peculiar belief system was horribly battered by this experience. Catriona feared no good would come of that.

But, if anything could hurt the Cold, it would be Fire Rose.

Louise Teazle reported that the snow outside was melting. Fire Rose was radiating, beyond the walls.

'No,' said Ariadne, snapping her fingers. 'I think not.'

Fire Rose went out. Spent-match stink filled the room. The little girl, unburned and unburning, sat on the floor exactly as she had been. She was bewildered. No one had ever switched her off like a light before.

Jago was enraged. All the cups, saucers and cutlery on the table near him and all the books on the shelves behind him leaped at once into the air, and hovered like projectiles about to be slung. Catriona had known he was a telekinetic, but this was off the scale. In any other drawing room, parapsychologists like Cross and Lark would be thinking of the book deals and the lecture tours – though, after Fire Rose, this little display scarcely made the needle tick. Jago's eyes smouldered.

Ariadne shook her head, and everything went neatly back to its place. Not a drop of tea spilled or a dust-jacket torn. Jago knitted his brows, blood vessels pulsing, but not so much as a teaspoon responded.

Mr Zed took out a gun, caught Ariadne's gaze, then pointed it at his own head. He stood still as a statue.

'If we're not going off half-cocked,' said the Elder of the Kind, 'let us review our plan of action. In dealing with the Cold, do we really want to do what Derek Leech says?'

Exactly. Ariadne had said what Catriona felt.

'You can't win a Winter War with fire,' she said. 'Fire consumes, leaves only ashes.'

'Then what?' said Maureen, frustrated, red-eyed. 'If not Derek's plan, what? I'd really like to know, ladies. I'm freezing my tits off here.'

'There, there,' said Catriona, touching Maureen's shoulder. 'Have faith. He'll be all right.'

Maureen didn't ask who she meant.

'He'll see us through,' Catriona said.

Richard.

XII.

On some other path in life, an expert outdoorsman Keith had loads of survival training in extreme weather conditions. Probably, Keith had to weed out a couple of dozen plonkers who didn't know how to tie their own shoe-laces, but he'd found the useful life in seconds. Not a bad trick. While Jamie scanned for tracks or a human-shaped bump in the snow, Keith barked instructions – keep moving, breathe through your nose, turn your shoulder to the wind.

One good thing: in all this mucky weather, Richard Jeperson couldn't have gone far.

Any footprints were filled by new snow. The marks they had made coming from the thicket to the buildings were already gone.

Jamie looked for dark traces, the shadows of shadows. It was Dad's game, and he wasn't expert in it yet – but he could usually see shadow-ghosts, if he caught them in time.

He found a discarded fur-boot. And another.

A shaggy clump a little past the boots turned out not to be the missing man, but an abandoned coat. A fold of dayglo green poking up from the snow was a cast-off balaclava. Leech had said Jeperson went out naked. That was not true. Jeperson had gone outside, then taken his clothes off. Leech wouldn't have got that wrong unless he were deliberately lying. If Jeperson knocked Leech out and left him inside, Leech would not have known what Jeperson did next – but he had said Jeperson took his clothes off, went out and lay down in the show. Had Leech attacked Jeperson, stripped him, and left him to freeze to death, cooking up a story to exonerate himself? Jamie should have checked at once – tried to replay the shadows in the building. He had an inkling it wouldn't have worked. There was something wrong with Leech's shadow.

He hoped Gené and Susan could take care of themselves. Derek Leech was dangerous.

They were near Bugs, the mammoth snowman. It had lost human shape and become a mountain. Novelty insects still bobbed on its summit like the Union Jack on top of Everest.

Jamie saw the shadow lying at the foot of Mount Bugs. A man, stretched out. Jeperson was under there.

He pointed to the spot and told Keith, 'Dig there, mate. There.'

'Where?'

Keith didn't have the Shade-sight. Jamie knelt and began scooping snow away with gloved hands. Keith used a tray from the cafeteria as a spade, digging deep.

A face emerged, in a nest of long, frozen hair. Thin, blue,

hollow-cheeked, jagged-moustached and open-eyed.

'Hello,' said Jeperson, smiling broadly. 'You must be the new boys.'

XIII.

Suddenly, Richard felt the cold. Not the Cold – he was disconnected, now. The little crystals were out of his brain. He hoped he had given the Cold something to think about.

'Would you happen to have seen some clothes in your travels?' he asked the two young men. One wore a long dark greatcoat and goggles, the other a red-lined magician's cloak.

They dragged his fur coat along and tried to wrap him in it. What he could see of his skin was sky-blue.

'It's stopped snowing,' he observed.

The wind was down too. And sun shone through, low in the west. It was late evening. Long shadows were red-edged.

The Cold was responding to his plea, drawing in its chill. It could live on in perpetuity as a sub-microscopic speck inside a rock, or confine itself to the poles, or go back to the void below absolute zero. Without Cleaver telling it what it wanted, it had its own choices. Richard hoped he had persuaded the Cold that other life on Earth was entertaining enough to be put up with.

Now, he would probably die.

He hoped he had done the right thing. He was sorry he'd never found out who his real parents had been. He wished he'd spent more time with Barbara, but – obviously – he'd been busy lately. His personal life hadn't been a priority, and that was a regret. He could trust Fred and Vanessa to keep on, at least for a while. And, if these lads were anything to judge by, the Diogenes Club, or something like it, would continue to stand against Great Enchanters present and future, and all manner of other inexplicable threats to the public safety.

The boy in the goggles tried rubbing Richard's hands, but his friend – who knew something about hypothermia treatment – told him not to. Friction just damages more blood vessels. Gradual, all-round warmth was needed. Not that there was an easy supply around here.

He tried to think of quotable last words.

Some people came out of the building. Leech, and two women. One flew to him. Geneviève. Good for her. They'd not worked together much, but the old girl was a long-standing Valued Member.

'Richard, you won't die,' she said.

'I think I'll need a second opinion,' he muttered. 'A less optimistic one.'

'No, really,' she insisted.

Leech hung back, shiftily. Richard expected no more. Geneviève pulled the other woman – a brown-haired girl who kept herself to herself – to help, and got her to press her hands on Richard's chest.

Warmth radiated from her touch.

'That's very… nice,' he said. 'Who are you?'

'This is Susan,' said Geneviève. 'She's a friend.'

Richard had heard of her. Susan Rodway. She was on Catriona's list of possibles.

He felt as if he were sinking into a hot, perfumed bath. Feeling returned to his limbs. He heard hissing and tinkling, as snow and ice melted around them. A bubble of heat was forming. Susan took it slowly, not heating him too fast. His temperature came up like a diver hauled to the surface in stages to avoid the bends.

He tactfully rearranged a flap of fur to cover his loins. Susan's magic warmth had reached there, with an unshrivelling effect he rarely cared to share on such brief acquaintance.

'What did you do?' asked Geneviève. 'Are we saved?'

Richard tried to shrug. 'I did what I could. I think the Cold is getting a sense of who we are, what we're about and why we shouldn't just be killed out of hand. Who knows what something like that can really feel, think or do? You have to call off the blitzkrieg, though. Any smiting with fire and sword is liable to undo the work of diplomacy and land us back in the big fridge.'

Leech was expressionless. Richard wondered how things would be if he'd had his way.

Geneviève looked back and said, 'Make the call, Derek.'

He made no move. Geneviève stood. Leech nodded, once, and walked back to the building.

'I see you've met Dr Shade and Conjurer Keith,' said Geneviève. 'They've done all right too.'

Susan took her hands away. Richard regretted it, but knew her touch couldn't last. Everyone looked at the huge, liquefying snow-giant as he stood up and got dressed as best he could. Sharon Kellett would be inside that glacier. The others would be strewn around the fields.

This patch of Somerset would be better-irrigated than the rest of Britain – for a few days.

'Who else turned up for the ice age?' Richard asked.

'There's a knowledgeable little fellow you don't need to meet just now,' said Geneviève. 'He didn't even waver, like some folks. Went straight to Leech. He's inside the weather station. At the manor house, Catriona has a whole tea-party. Old friends and new. Including a strong contingent from the Other Side.'

'I can imagine.'

'Maureen Mountmain's here,' she said, pointedly.

Richard was glad to be warned of that potential complication. Geneviève let the point stick with a needling glance.

'It was a ritual,' said Richard, knowing how weak the excuse was.

'It was still…' She mouthed the word 'sex'.

Richard knew he was being ribbed. Now they were less doomed, they could start squabbling, gossiping and teasing again.

Leech came back.

'We're invited to supper at the manor house,' he said. 'It's only nine o'clock, would you believe it? You'll have to make my excuses, I'm afraid. I have to get back to London. Things to do, people to buy. Give my best to Miss Kaye. Oh, Cleaver's dead. Choked on his false teeth. Pity.'

The blotch on his forehead was already gone. Leech recovered quickly.

'See you soon,' he said, and walked away.

Richard knew an autopsy wouldn't show anything conclusive. Professor Cleaver would be listed as another incidental casualty.

'I feel much warmer now he's gone,' said Geneviève. 'Didn't he say something about supper?'

XIV.

Most of the company had scurried back to their holes. Catriona was relieved to have them out of the house.

She sat in her drawing room. Paulette Michaelsmith was upstairs, tucked up and dreaming safely. Louise Teazle had walked home to the Hollow, her house on the moor. Geneviève was outside in the garden, with the young people. She was the last of the old ladies.

Ariadne had taken Rose with her. Mr Zed, round weal on his temple, didn't even complain. The Undertakers were a spent force, but even in their prime they couldn't have stood against an Elder of the Kind. Rose would be safe with Ariadne, and – more to the point – the world would be safe from her. Catriona assumed that Ariadne could pack Rose off to where she came from, just as – eighty years ago – Charles Beauregard sent Princess Cuckoo home. However, the Elder might choose to raise the creature who usually looked like a little girl as her own. At this stage of her life, Catriona doubted she'd live to find out. Charles wasn't here. Edwin wasn't here. At times, Catriona wondered if she were really here. She knew more ghosts than living people, and regretted the rasher statements made about spirits of the unquiet dead in books she had published in her long-ago youth. Occasionally, she welcomed the odd clanking chain or floating bedsheet.

Maureen Mountmain, clearly torn, had wanted to stay and see Richard – she babbled a bit about having something to tell him – but Leech had ordered her to rally a party – Mr and Mrs Karabatsos, Myra Lark, Jago – and leave. Jago, well on the way to replacing Rose as Catriona's idea of the most frightening person on the planet, took a last look around the manor house, as if thinking of moving in, and slid off into the evening with Maureen's group. They wouldn't be able to keep him for long. Jago had his own plans. Leech had picked up Sewell Head, too – though Catriona had looked over his file, and concluded it would take a lot to lure him out of his sweet shop and away from his books of quiz questions.

On the plus side, the Club had tentative gains. Susan Rodway and Jamie Chambers – the new Dr Shade! – were hardly clubbable in the old-fashioned sense, but Mycroft Holmes had founded the Diogenes Club as a club for the unclubbable. Even Keith Marion, in a reasonable percentage of his might-have-been selves, was inclined to the good – though finding a place for him was even more of a challenge. Geneviève reported that the Chambers boy showed his father's dark spark, tempered with a little more sympathy than habitually displayed by Jonathan Chambers. Derek Leech must want to sign up Dr Shade. The Shades wavered, leaning towards one side or the other according to circumstance or their various personalities. The boy could not be forced or wooed too strongly, for fear of driving him to the bad. Leech would not give up on such a potent Talent. There might even be a percentage in letting Jamie get close to Leech, putting the lad in the other camp for a while. Susan was reluctant to become a laboratory rat for David Cross or Myra Lark, but was too prodigious to let slip. Without her warm hands, Richard would not have lived through this cold spell. Susan needed help coping with her Talent, and had taken Catriona's card. If Jamie could be a counter for Leech, Susan was possibly their best hope of matching Jago. It chilled Catriona that she could even consider sending a girl barely in her twenties up against an Effective Talent like Anthony Jago, but no one else was left to make the decisions.

She was thinking like Edwin now, or even Mycroft. The Diogenes Club, or whatever stood in its stead, had to play a long game. She had been a girl younger than Susan or Jamie when this started for her. The rector's daughter, not the lady of the manor. At eighteen, with Edwin away at the front, she had been escorted by Charles to Mycroft's funeral. That had been a changing of the guard. Some of the famous names and faces of generations before her own seemed like dinosaurs and relics in her eyes. Even Mycroft's famous brother was a bright-eyed old gaffer with a beaky nose, fingers bandaged from bee-stings and yellow teeth from decades of three-pipe problems. Richard Riddle had been there, with his uncle and aunt. In his RFC uniform and jaunty eye-patch, the former boy detective was impossibly glamorous to her. She had a better idea than most where he had flown to in 1934, and still expected him to turn up again, with his chums Vi and Ernie.

Charles had pointed out Inspector Henry Mist, Thomas Carnacki, Sir Henry Merrivale, Winston Churchill, General Hector Tarr, John Silence, Sir Michael Calme, Mansfield Smith-Cumming, Margery Device, the Keeper of the Ravens, and others. Now, Catriona knew Geneviève had been there too, spying through blue lenses from the edge of the crowd – Mycroft's most secret secret agent and, contrary to the public record, the first Lady Member of the Diogenes Club. After all the fuss, Catriona turned out not to be the first of her sex to be admitted to the Inner Rooms – though she was the first woman to chair the Ruling Cabal.

It had been a busy sixty years. Angel Down, Irene Dobson, the Murder Mandarin, the Seven Stars, the last flight of the Demon Ace, Spring-Heel'd Jack, Dien Ch'ing, the Splendid Six, Weezie's Hauntings, the Rat Among the Ravens, the Crazy Gang, Parsifal le Gallois, the Water War, Adolf Hitler, Swastika Girl, the Malvern Mystery, the Scotch Streak, the Trouble with Titan, Castle De'ath, the Drache Development, Paulette's dream, the Soho Golem, the Ghoul Crisis, the Missing Mythwrhn, and so many others. And now the Cold. There was more to come, she knew. Richard Jeperson's work wasn't done. Her work wasn't done. The Secret Files of the Diogenes Club remained open.

She felt a whisper against her cheek.

XV.

The garden was Disneyfied: white pools of melting ice, night-birds singing. Light spilled onto the lawns from the upstairs windows of the manor house. Glints reflected in dwindling icicles. Jamie saw activity streaks in the shadows. With the Cold drawn in, the land was healing.

No one had to worry about World Cooling any more.

Richard Jeperson, the man from the Diogenes Club, tried to explain what he had done. It boiled down to getting the attention of a vast, unknowable creature and asking it very nicely not to wipe out all life-forms which needed a temperature above freezing to survive. Jamie realised how lucky they had been. Only someone who could ask very politely and tactfully would have gotten a result. A few bumps the other way, along one of Keith's paths, and it could have been Derek Leech under the snow...

Leech had left Jamie his card, and he hadn't thrown it away.

Many of the people drawn to the Winter War had melted away like the ice. Some were sleeping over in the house. Jamie's van was parked next to Richard's ShadowShark in the drive.

He sat on a white filigree lawn-chair, drinking black coffee served from an electric pot. The hostess, an elderly lady who had not joined them outside, provided a pretty fair scratch supper for the survivors and their hangers-on. Now, there were wafer-thin mints. Gené was in a lawn-swing, drinking something red and steaming which wasn't tomato soup. Richard, still glowing with whatever Susan had fed into him, smoked a fat, hand-rolled cigarette that wasn't a joint but wasn't tobacco either. Considering what he'd done, Jamie reckoned he could demand that the Archbishop of Canterbury and the Prime Minister hand-deliver an ounce of Jamaican, the Crown Jewels and Princess Margaret dressed up in a St Trinian's uniform to his room within the next half-hour and expect an answer of 'right away, sir'.

'How was your first day on the job?' Gené asked him.

'Job?'

'Your dad called it a practice. Being Dr Shade.'

'Not sure about the handle. I thought I'd just go with "Shade" for a bit. "Jamie Shade", maybe? I'd use it for the band, but it sounds too much like Slade.'

'I quite like Slade,' said Richard.

'You would,' said Jamie. 'What a year, eh?'

'It has had its meteorological anomalies.'

'No, I mean the charts. Telly Savalas, Real Thing, the Brotherhood of Man, Abba, the Wurzels, J. J. Barrie, Demis Roussos... "Brand New Combine Harvester", "Save Your Kisses for Me", bloody "No Charge"... It has to be the low-point in music since for ever. It's like some great evil entity was sucking the guts out of our sounds. Some other great evil entity. You can't blame Leech for all of it. Even he wouldn't touch the Wurzels. Something's got to change. Maybe I'll stick with the band, leave monsters and magic to other folk. Kids are fed up, you know. They want to hear something new. And you lot are getting on.'

'Do you feel "long in the tooth?", Geneviève?' Richard asked.

Gené bared teeth which Jamie could have sworn were longer than they had been earlier.

'It's not about how old you are,' said Susan, who had been quietly sipping a drink with fruit in it. 'It's about what you do.'

'Here's to that,' said Richard, clinking his glass to hers.

Keith was sitting quietly, not letting on which of his selves was home. The primary Keith had reluctantly given Jamie back the Great Edmondo's cloak and its hidden tricks. He had asked if Dr Shade needed an assistant, and started shuttling through selves when Jamie told him he really needed a new drummer. Now, despite what he'd said, he wasn't sure. Being Dr Shade meant something, and came with a lot of baggage. He half-thought Vron was only with him because of who his dad was. These people kept calling him 'Junior Shade', 'Young Dr Shade' or 'the New Dr Shade'. Perhaps he should take them seriously. He was already a veteran of the Winter War, if something over inside two days counted as a war.

Like Dad, he wasn't much of a joiner. He couldn't see himself putting a tie on to get into some fusty old club. But he played well with others. How randomly had his vanload of raw recruits been assembled? Even Sewell Head, now lost to Leech, had come in handy. Maybe, he'd found his new band. Susan, Gené and Keith all had Talents. Perhaps the old hippie with the ringlets and the tash could take the odd guest guitar solo. One thing was for certain, they wouldn't sign with a Derek Leech label.

In the house, the lights went off, and the garden was dark.

Jamie didn't mind the dark. From now on, he owned it.

'Catriona's gone to bed,' said Richard.

Gené, another night person, stretched out on the grass, as if sunning herself in shadows.

'Some of us never sleep,' she said. 'Someone has to watch out for the world. Or we might lose it.'

'We're not going to let that happen,' said Richard.

THE MAN WHO GOT OFF THE GHOST TRAIN

PROLOGUE: CULLER'S HALT

'Ten hours, guv'nor,' said Fred Regent. 'That's what the timetable says. Way this half-holiday is going, next train mightn't come for ten months.'

Richard Jeperson shrugged. A cheek-muscle twitched.

Pink-and-grey-streaked autumn skies hung over wet fields. Fred had scouted around. No one home. Typical British Rail. He only knew Culler's Halt was in use because of the uncollected rubbish. Lumpy plastic sacks were piled on the station forecourt like wartime sandbags. The bin-men's strike was long-since settled, but maybe word hadn't reached these parts. A signpost claimed 'Culler 3m'. If there were a village at the end of the lane, it showed no lamps at the fag-end of this drab afternoon.

Fred wasn't even sure which country Culler was in.

On the platform, Richard stood by their luggage, peering at the dying sunlight through green-tinted granny glasses. He wore a floor-length mauve travel coat with brocade frogging, shiny PVC bondage trousers (a concession to the new decade) and a curly brimmed purple top hat.

Fred knew the man from the Diogenes Club was worried about Vanessa. When a sensitive worried about someone who could famously take care of herself, it was probably time to panic.

At dawn, they'd been far south, after a nasty night's work

in Cornwall. They had been saddled with Alastair Garnett, a civil servant carrying out a time-and-motion study. In a funk, the man from the ministry had the bad habit of giving orders. If the local cops had listened to Richard rather than the 'advisor', there'd have been fewer deaths. The hacked-off body parts found inside a stone circle had to be sorted into two piles – goats and teenagers. An isolated family, twisted by decades of servitude to breakfast food corporations, had invented their own dark religion. Ceremonially masked in cornflakes packets with cut-out eyeholes, the Penrithwick Clan made hideous sacrifice to the goblins Snap, Crackle and Pop. Bloody wastage like that put Richard in one of his moods, and no wonder. Fred would happily have booted Garnett up his pin-striped arse, but saw the way things were going in the eighties.

Trudging back to seaside lodgings in Mevagissey, hardly up for cooked breakfast and sworn off cereal for life, they were met by the landlady and handed Vanessa's telegram, an urgent summons to Scotland.

Abandoning the Penrithwick shambles to Garnett, Richard and Fred took a fast train to Paddington. They crossed London by taxi without even stopping off at their respective homes in Chelsea and Soho for a change of clothes or a hello to the girlfriends – who would, of course, be ticked off by that familiar development – and rattled out of Euston in a slam-door diesel.

The train stank of decades' worth of Benson & Hedges. Since giving up, Fred couldn't be in a fuggy train or pub without feeling queasily envious. At first, they shared their first-class compartment with a clear-complexioned girl whose T-shirt (sporting the word 'GASH', with an Anarchy symbol for the A) was safety-pinned together like a disassembled torso stitched up after autopsy. She quietly leafed through *Bunty* and *The Lady*, chain-smoking with a casual pleasure that made Fred wish a cartoon anvil would fall from the luggage rack onto her pink punk hairdo. At Peterborough, she was collected by a middle-aged gent with a Range Rover. Fred and Richard had the compartment to themselves.

Outside Lincoln, something mechanical got thrown. The train slowed to a snail's pace, overtaken by ancient cyclists, jeered at by small boys ('get off and milk it!'), inching through miles-long tunnels. This went on for agonising hours. Scheduled connections were missed. The only alternative route the conductor could offer involved getting off at York, a stopping train to Culler's Halt, then a service to Inverdeith, changing there for Portnacreirann. In theory, it was doable. In practice, they were marooned. The conductor had been working from a timetable good only until 1 September of last year. No one else had got off at Culler's Halt.

Beyond the rail-bed was a panoramic advertising hoarding. A once-glossy, now-weatherworn poster showed a lengthy dole queue and the slogan 'Labour isn't working – Vote Conservative'. Over this was daubed 'No Future'. A mimeographed sheet, wrinkled in the fly-posting, showed the Queen with a pin through her nose.

'There's something wrong, Frederick,' said Richard.

'The country's going down the drain, and everyone's pulling the flush.'

'Not just that. Think about it: "God Save the Queen" came out for the Silver Jubilee, two years before the election. So why are ads for the single pasted over the Tory poster?'

'This is the wilds, guv. Can't expect them to be up with pop charts.'

Richard shrugged again. The mystery wasn't significant enough to be worth considered thought.

They had more pressing troubles. Chiefly, Vanessa.

Their friend and colleague wasn't a panicky soul. She wouldn't have sent the telegram unless things were serious. A night's delay, and they might be too late.

'I'm not happy with this, Frederick,' said Richard.

'Me neither, guv.'

Richard chewed his moustache and looked at the timetable Fred had already checked. Always gaunt, he was starting to look haggard. Deep shadow gathered in the seams under his eyes.

'As you say, ten hours,' said Richard. 'If the train's on time.'

'Might as well kip in the waiting room,' suggested Fred. 'Take shifts.'

There were hard benches and a couple of chairs chained to pipes. A table was piled with magazines and comics from years ago: Patrick Mower grinned on the cover of *Tit-Bits*; Robot Archie was in the jungle in *Lion*. A tiny bookshelf was stocked with paperbacks: *Jaws*, *Mandingo*, *Sexploits of a Milk Monitor*, *Zen and the Art of Motorcycle Maintenance*, Guy N. Smith's *The Sucking Pit*. Richard toggled a light-switch and nothing happened. Fred found a two-bar electric fire in working order and turned it on, raising the whiff of singed dust. As night set in, the contraption provided an orange glow but no appreciable heat.

Fred huddled in his pea-coat and scarf. Richard stretched out on a bench like a fakir on a bed of nails.

The new government wasn't mad keen on the Diogenes Club. Commissions of Inquiry empowered the likes of Alastair Garnett to take a watching brief. Number Ten was asking for 'blue skies suggestions' as to what, if anything, might replace this 'hold-over from an era when British intelligence was run by enthusiastic amateurs'. Richard said the 1980s 'would not be a comfortable decade for a feeling person'. His chief asset was sensitivity, but when his nerves frayed he looked like a cuckoo with peacock feathers. Called up before a Select Committee, he made a bad impression.

Fred knew Richard was right to be paranoid. Wheels were grinding and the team was being broken up. He had been strongly advised to report back to New Scotland Yard, take a promotion to detective inspector and get on with 'real police work'. Rioters, terrorists and scroungers needed clouting. Task Forces and Patrol Groups were up and running. If he played along with the boot boys, he could have his own command, be a Professional. The decision couldn't be put off much longer.

He'd assumed Vanessa would stay with the Club, though. Richard could chair the Ruling Cabal, planning and feeling. She would handle fieldwork, training up new folk to tackle whatever crept from the lengthening shadows.

Now, he wasn't sure. If they didn't get to Vanessa in time...

'There used to be a through train to Portnacreirann,' mused Richard. 'The Scotch Streak. A sleeper. Steam until 1962, then diesel, then... well, helicopters took over.'

'Helicopter?' queried Fred, distracted. 'Who commutes by helicopter?'

'NATO. Defence considerations kept the Scotch Streak running long after its natural lifetime. Then they didn't. March of bloody progress.'

Richard sat up. He took off and folded his glasses, then tucked them in his top pocket behind an emerald explosion of display handkerchief.

'It's where I started, Frederick,' he said. 'On the Scotch Streak. Everyone has a first time...'

'Not 'arf,' Fred smiled.

Richard smiled too, perhaps ruefully. 'As you so eloquently put it, "not 'arf". For you, it was that bad business at the end of the pier, in Seamouth. For your lovely Zarana, it was the Soho Golem. For Professor Corri it was the Curse of *The Northern Barstows*. For me, it was the Scotch Streak... the Ghost Train.'

Fred's interest pricked. He'd worked with Richard Jeperson for more than ten years, but knew only scattered pieces about the man's earlier years. Richard himself didn't know about a swathe of his childhood. A foundling of war, he'd been pulled out of a death camp by Captain Jeperson, a British officer who saw his sensitivity. Richard had been raised as much by the Diogenes Club as his adoptive father. He had no memory of any life before the camps. Even the tattoo on his arm was a mystery. The Nazis were appallingly meticulous about record-keeping, but Richard's serial number didn't match any name on lists of the interned or to-be-exterminated. The numbers weren't even in a configuration like those of other holocaust survivors or known victims. Suspicion was that the Germans had seen the boy's qualities too and tried to make use of him in a facility destroyed, along with its records and presumably other inmates, before it could fall into Allied hands. The lad had slipped through the clean-up operation, scathed but alive. Geoffrey Jeperson named him Richard, after Richard Riddle – a boy detective who was his own childhood hero.

Of Richard's doings between the War and the Seamouth Case, Fred knew not much. After Geoffrey's death in 1954, Richard's sponsors at the Club had been Edwin Winthrop, now dead but well remembered, and Sir Giles Gallant, now retired and semi-disgraced. Vanessa came into the picture well before the Seamouth Case. She had Richard's habit of being evasive without making a fuss about it. All Fred knew was that her first meeting with their patron was another horror story. Whenever it came up, she'd touch the almost-invisible scar through her eyebrow and change the subject with a shudder.

'Now we're near the end of the line,' said Richard, 'perhaps you should hear the tale.'

They were here for the night. Time enough for a ghost story.

'Frederick,' said Richard, 'it was 195—, and I was down from Oxford...'

ACT I: LONDON EUSTON
I.

It was 195— and Richard Jeperson was down from Oxford. And the LSE. And Cambridge. And Manchester Poly. And RADA. And Harrow School of Art. And... well, suffice to say, many fine institutions, none of which felt obliged to award him any formal qualification.

Geoffrey Jeperson had sent him to St Cuthbert's, his old school. Richard hadn't lasted at 'St Custard's', setting an unhappy precedent insofar as not lasting at schools went. After the Captain's death, Edwin Winthrop took over in loco parentis. He encouraged Richard to regard schooling as a cold buffet, picking at whatever took his fancy. Winthrop called himself a graduate of Flanders and the Somme, though as it happened he had a double first in Classics and Natural Philosophy from All Souls. Since Richard was known for his instincts – his sensitivities, everyone said – he was allowed to follow his nose. He became a 'New Elizabethan renaissance man', though teachers tended to tut-tut as he acquired unsystematic tranches of unrelated expertise then got on with something else before he was properly finished.

Though the Diogenes Club supported him with a generous allowance, he took on jobs of work. He assisted with digs and explorations. He sleuthed through Europe in search of his past, and drew suspicious blanks – which persuaded him to pay more attention to his present. He spent a summer in a biscuit factory in Barnsley, making tea and enduring harassment from the female staff. He was a film extra in Italy, climbing out of the horse in *Helen of Troy*. He couriered documents between British embassies in South America. He studied magic – stage magic, not yet the other stuff – with a veteran illusionist in Baltimore. He dug ditches, modelled for catalogues, worked fishing boats, wrote articles for manly magazines, and the like.

Between education and honest toil, he did his National Service. He was in the RAF but never saw an aeroplane. The Club placed him in a system of bunkers under the New Forest. He fetched and carried for boffins working on an oscillating wave device. After eighteen months, a coded message instructed him to sabotage an apparently routine experiment. Though he liked the backroom boys and had worked up enthusiasm for the project, he followed orders. The procedure failed and – he was later given to understand – an invasion of our plane of existence by malign extra-dimensional entities was prevented. That was how the Club worked under Edwin Winthrop: pre-emptive, unilateral, cutting out weeds before they sprouted, habitually secretive, pragmatically ruthless. A lid was kept on, though who knew whether the pot really had been boiling over?

After the RAF, Richard spear-carried for a season at the Old Vic, and played saxophone with the Frigidaires. The doo-wop group was on the point of signing with promoter Larry Parnes – of 'parnes, shillings and pence' fame – when the girl singer married a quantity surveyor for the security. Though her rendition of 'Lipstick On Your Collar', lately a hit for Connie Francis, was acceptable, Richard couldn't really argue with her. Frankly, the Frigidaires were never very good.

Richard only knew within a year or so how old he actually was, but he must be out of his teens. Edwin felt it was time the boy knuckled down and got on with the work for which he had been prepared. Richard moved into a Georgian house in Chelsea which was in the gift of the Club, occasionally looked after by an Irish housekeeper who kept going home to have more children. He meditated, never missed *Hancock's Half Hour* on the wireless and read William Morris and Hank Jansen. Edwin told him to wait for a summons to action.

Richard dressed in the 'Edwardian' or 'Teddy boy' manner:

scarlet velvet frock coat with midnight black lapels (straight razor slipped into a special compartment in the sleeve), crepe-soled suede zip-up boots with winkle-picker toe-points, a conjurer's waistcoat with seventeen secret pockets, his father's watch and chain, bootlace tie with silver tips, navy-blue drainpipe jeans tighter than paint on his skinny legs. His thin moustache was only just established enough not to need augmentation with eyebrow pencil. A Brylcreem pompadour rose above his pale forehead like a constructivist sculpture in black candyfloss.

If he took his life to have begun when his memory did, his experience was limited. He had never seen a woman naked, except in *Health & Efficiency* magazine. He could not drive a car, though he intended to take lessons. He had never killed anything important. He had never had a broken bone. He had never eaten an avocado.

Within a year, all that would change.

One morning, a special messenger arrived on a motorbike, with instructions that he give himself over to a side-car and be conveyed to the Diogenes Club. This, he knew, was to be his debut.

The retired Royal Marines sergeant who kept door in Pall Mall went beet-coloured as Richard waltzed past his post. Outlandish folk must come and go from the Diogenes Club, but Richard's clothes and hair were red rag to a bull for anyone over twenty-five – especially a uniformed middle-aged man with short back and sides and medal ribbons. There was talk about playwrights and poets who were 'angry young men', but the older generation would not easily yield a monopoly on sputtering indignation.

Richard rather admired himself in the polished black marble of the hallway pillars. The whole look took hours to achieve. His face no longer erupted as it had done a few years earlier, but the odd plague-rose blemish surfaced, requiring attention.

Escorted by a silk-jacketed servant beyond the famously

noiseless public rooms of the Club, he puffed with pride. Ordinary Members mimed harrumphs, seconding the doorman's opinion of him. The servant opened an inner door, and stood aside to let Richard pass. He had not been this deep into the building since childhood. Then, he had almost been a possession, shown off by his father. Now, he was entitled to pass on his own merit. He could walk the corridors, consult the archives, visit the private collections, accept commissions. He was not merely a Life Member, inheriting that status from Captain Jeperson, but an asset, whose Talent suited him to act for the Club in Certain Circumstances.

He was treading in the footsteps of giants. Mycroft Holmes, the mid-Victorian civil servant who was instrumental in founding what was ostensibly a 'club for the unclubbable' but actually an auxiliary extraordinary to British intelligence and the police. Charles Beauregard, the first Most Valued Member – the great puzzle-chaser of the 1880s and 1890s and visionary chairman of the Ruling Cabal through the middle-years of the current century. Carnacki, the Ghost-Finder. Several terrifying individuals who operated covertly under the goggles of 'Dr Shade'. Adam Llewellyn de Vere Adamant, the adventurer whose disappearance in 1903 remained listed on the books as an active, unsolved case. Catriona Kaye, Winthrop's lifelong companion, the first woman to accept full membership in the Club. Flaxman Low. Sir Henry Merrivale. Robert Baldick. Cursitor Doom.

He was ushered upstairs. In an underlit ante-room, his coat was taken by a turbaned orderly. He had a moment before a two-way mirror to be awed by the great tradition, the honour to which he would ascend in the presence of the Ruling Cabal. He patted his pockets, checked his fly and adjusted his tie. The weight of the razor was gone from his sleeve. Somewhere between the street and the ante-room, he had been frisked and defanged.

A baize door opened, and a tiny shove from the silent Sikh was necessary to propel him along a short dark corridor. One door shut behind him and another opened in front. Richard stepped into the windowless Star Chamber of the Ruling Cabal.

'Good gravy, Edwin,' said someone sour, 'is this what it's come to? A bloody Teddy boy!'

Some of Richard's puff leaked out.

'I think he's sweeet,' purred a woman with a whisky-and-cigarettes voice, like Joan Greenwood or Fenella Fielding. 'Winner of the Fourth Form fancy dress.'

The last of his self-esteem pooled on the floor.

'Cool, man,' said another commentator, snapping his fingers. 'Straight from the fridge.'

He didn't feel any better.

Edwin Winthrop sat at the big table that had been Mycroft's desk, occupying one of three places. He had slightly hooded eyes and an iron-grey moustache. Even if Richard weren't attuned to 'vibrations', he'd have had no doubt who was in charge. Next to him was Catriona Kaye, a compact, pretty woman as old as the century. She wore a dove-grey dress and pearls. The only one of the Inner Circle who had treated him as a little boy, she was now the only one who treated him as a grown-up. She was the heart and conscience of the Diogenes Club. Edwin recognised his own tendency to high-handedness, and kept Catriona close – she was the reason why he wasn't a monster. To Edwin's right was an empty chair. Sir Giles Gallant, make-weight on the Ruling Cabal, was absent.

'If we've finished twitting the new boy,' said Edwin, impatiently, 'perhaps we can get on. Richard, welcome and all that. This is the group…'

Edwin introduced everyone. Richard put faces to names and resumés he already knew.

Dr Harry Cutley, the pipe-smoking, tweed-jacketed scowler,

held a chair of Physics at a provincial redbrick university. He had unexpectedly come under the Club's remit, as quantum mechanics led him to parapsychology. When Edwin vacated the post of Most Valued Member to run the Ruling Cabal, Sir Giles recruited Cutley to fill his roomy shoes. The academic finally had funds and resources to mount the research programme of his dreams, but was sworn not to share findings with his peers, turning his papers over instead to the Cabal. They then had to root out others capable of understanding Cutley's work and determining what should leak onto the intellectual open market and what the world was not yet ready to know. In practice, Cutley had exchanged one set of grumbling resentments for another. He knew things no one else on the planet did, but colleagues in the real world wrote him off as a dead-ended time-server whose students didn't like him and whose ex-wife slept with other faculty members. Cutley had a boozer's red-veined eyes, hair at all angles and a pulsing, hostile aura – the plainest Richard had ever sensed, as if his inner thoughts were written on comic-strip bubbles.

The husky-voiced blonde in the black leotard and pink chiffon scarf was Annette Amboise, of Fitzrovia and the Left Bank. She wore no lipstick but a lot of eye make-up and had hair cropped like Jean Seberg as Joan of Arc. She smoked Gauloises in a long, enamel holder. Of Anglo-French parentage, she'd spent her mid-teens in Vichy France, running messages for the Resistance and Allied intelligence. She came to the Club's notice after an unprecedented run of good fortune, which is to say she outlived all other agents in her district several times over. Catriona diagnosed an inbuilt ability to intuit random factors and predict immediate danger. Annette thought in knight moves – two hops forward, then a kink to the side. Since the War, she'd been doing other things. A retired interpretive dancer, past thirty with too many pulled muscles, she was authoress of a slim volume, *Ectoplasm and*

Existentialism. Knowing what would probably happen next gave her a peculiarly cheerful fatalism. She had no accent, but showed an extremely French side in occasional *ça va* shrugs.

The tall, thin hipster was Danny Myles, whom Richard recognised as Magic Fingers Myles, piano-player in a modern jazz combo famous for making 'I Can't Get Started With You' last an entire set at Ronnie Scott's. He wore a green polo-neck and chinos, and had a neatly trimmed goatee. His fingers continually moved as if on an infinite keyboard or reading a racy novel in Braille. Born blind, Myles developed extra senses as a child. Gaining sight in his teens, Myles found himself in a new visual world but retained other sharpnesses. Besides his acute ear, he had 'the Touch'. Richard and Annette took the psychic temperature of a room with invisible antennae (Catriona called them 'mentacles'), but Myles had to lay hands on something to intuit its history, associations or true nature. The Magic Fingers Touch worked best on inanimate objects.

'This is Geoffrey's boy,' explained Edwin. 'We expect great things from him.'

From Magic Fingers, Richard gathered non-verbal information: he understood how everyone related to each other, where the frictions were, who he could trust to come through, when he'd be on his own. Cutley was like a football manager required to play a board member's nephew in goal. He hated 'spook stuff' and wanted to haul paraphenomena back to measurable realities. Annette was emotionally off on another plane, but mildly amused. She had vague, not-related-by-blood auntie feelings for Richard and a nagging concern about his short-term future which did little for his confidence. Richard thanked Myles with a nod no one else noticed.

This is what it was like: Richard knew things most people had to guess at. A problem growing up, which he was not quite done with, was that he rarely appreciated few others felt and understood as he did. His first thought was that English people were too polite to mention things which were glaringly obvious to him. That had not gone down well at St Custard's. If he hadn't been able to a chuck a cricket ball with a degree of devious accuracy, he'd likely have been burned at the stake behind the Prefects' Hut.

'Now we're acquainted,' said Edwin, 'let's get to why you've been brought together. Who's heard of the Scotch Streak?'

'It's a train, man,' said Myles. 'Euston to Edinburgh, overnight.'

'Yes,' said Edwin. 'In point of fact, the service, which leaves London at seven o'clock every other evening, does not terminate in Edinburgh. It continues to Portnacreirann, on Loch Linnhe.'

'Is this one of those railway mysteries?' asked Annette, squeezing her palms together. 'I adore those.'

Edwin nodded, and passed the conch to Catriona.

II.

'In 1923, Locomotive Number 3473-S rolled out of foundry sheds in Egham,' began Catriona Kaye, the Club's collector of ghost stories. 'It was an A1 Atlantic Class engine. To the non-trainspotters among us, that means a shiny new chuff-chuff with all the bells and whistles. It was bred for speed, among the first British trains to break the hundred-mile-an-hour barrier. The London, Scotland and Isles Railway Company presented the debutante at the British Empire Exhibition in 1924, and christened it "the Scotch Streak". A bottle of champagne was wasted on the cow-catcher by the odious Lady Lucinda Tregellis-d'Aulney. She mercifully passes out of the narrative. The LSIR got wind of a scheme by a rival to run a non-stop from London to Edinburgh, and added a further leg to their express, across Scotland to Portnacreirann. This sort of one-upmanship happened often before the railways were taken into public ownership. The Streak's original colours were royal purple and gold. Even in an era of ostentation in high-speed transport, it was considered show-offy.

'The Scotch Streak was quickly popular with drones who wanted to get sozzled in Piccadilly, have a wee small-hours dram in Edinburgh, then walk off the hangover in Glen Wherever while shooting at something feathery or antlered. All very jolly, no doubt. Until the disaster of 1931.

'There are stories about Inverdeith. In the eighteenth century, fishermen on Loch Gaer often netted human bones. After some decades, this led to the capture of the cannibal crofter famed in song as "Graysome Jock McGaer". He was torn apart by a mob on his way to the scaffold. During the interregnum, the Scots God-botherer Samuel Druchan, fed up because he would never be as famous as England's Matthew Hopkins, presided over a mass witch-drowning. As you know, proper witches float when "swum", so Druchan took the trouble to sew iron weights to his beldames' skirts. In 1601, a local diarist recorded that a "stoon o' fire spat out frae hell" plopped into the waters with a mighty hiss. However, the railway bridge disaster really put Inverdeith on the tragedy map.

'What exactly happened remains a mystery, but... early one foggy morning in November 1931, the Scotch Streak was crossing Inverdeith Bridge when – through human agency, gremlins, faulty iron or sheer ill-chance – 3473-S was decoupled from the rest of the train. The locomotive pulled away and steamed safely to the far side. The bridge collapsed, taking eight passenger carriages and a mail car with it. The rolling stock sank to the bottom of Loch Gaer with the loss of all hands, except one lucky little girl who floated.

'A board of inquiry exonerated Donald McRidley, the engine driver, though many thought he'd committed the unforgivable sin of cutting his passengers loose to save his own hide. Only Nicholas Bowler, the fireman, knew for sure. Rather than give testimony, Bowler lay on the tracks and was beheaded by an ordinary suburban service. McRidley was finished as an engineer. Some say that, like T. E. Lawrence re-enlisting as Aircraftman Ross, McRidley changed his name and became a navvy, working all weathers on a maintenance gang, looking over his shoulder at dusk, dreading the reproachful tread of the Headless Fireman.

'Whatever he might or might not have done, McRidley couldn't be blamed for the "In-for-Death Bridge". All manner of Scots legal inquiries boiled down to an unlovely squabble between Inverdeith Council and the LSIR. One set of lawyers claimed the sound structure wouldn't have collapsed were it not for the Scotch Streak rattling over it at speeds in excess of the recommended. Another pack counter-claimed eighty-nine people wouldn't be dead if the bridge wasn't a rickety structure liable to be knocked down by a stiff breeze. This dragged on. A newspaperman dug up a local legend that one of Druchan's witches cursed her weights as she drowned, swearing no iron would ever safely span the loch. "Local legend" is a Fleet Street synonym for "something I've just made up". The Streak ran only from London to Edinburgh until 1934, when a new bridge was erected and safety-tested. A fuss was made about the amount of steel used in the construction. Witches have nothing against steel, apparently. Then, full service to Portnacreirann resumed.

'Memories being what they were, folks who didn't have a financial interest in the venture were reluctant to board the "In-for-Death Express". Only grimly smiling directors and their perspiring wives and children were aboard for the accident-free re-inaugural run. You can imagine the sighs of relief when Inverdeith Bridge was safely behind them. Controlling interest in the LSIR was held by Douglas Gilclyde of Kilpartinger, who horsewhipped a secretary he thought misreferred to him as "Lord Killpassengers". It was a point of pride for His Lordship, a parvenu ennobled by Lloyd George, to make the Scotch Streak a roaring success again. He tarted 3473 up with a fresh coat of purple and replaced the gold trim with his own newly minted tartan – which the unkind said made the engine look like a novelty box of oatcakes.

'Kilpartinger lured back the hunting set by trading speed records for social cachet. From 1934, the Scotch Streak became famously, indeed appallingly, luxurious. Padding on padding, Carrara marble sinks, minions in Gilclyde kilts servicing every whim. The train gained a reputation as a social event on rails. 3473 pulled a ballroom carriage, a bar to rival the Criterion and sleeping cars with compartments like rooms at the Savoy. In addition to tweedy fowl-blasters, the Streak gained a following among the "fast" crowd. Debutantes on the prowl booked up-and-down services for months on end, in the hope of snaring a suitable fiancé. One or two even got married before they were raped. When his disgusted pater kicked him out of the family pile, Viscount St John "Buzzy" Maltrincham took a permanent lease on a compartment and made the Scotch Streak his address – until a pregnant Windmill Girl cut his throat somewhere between the Trossachs and Clianlarich.

'He wasn't the only casualty. The Streak's Incident Book ran to several spine-tingling volumes. People threw themselves under the train, got up on top and were swept off in tunnels, were decapitated when they disregarded "do not lean out of the window" notices, opened doors and flung themselves across the landscape. Naturally, a number of fatalities occurred around Inverdeith. There was a craze for booking the up service on the Streak, naturally not bothering with the return. The procedure was to put a particular record on the wind-up Victrola as the train crossed the bridge, then take a graceful suicide leap as Bing Crosby crooned "a golden goodbye". Mistime it, and you smashed into a strut and rained down in pieces.

'Kilpartinger played up the Streak's glamour by engaging the likes of Noël Coward, Elsie and Doris Waters, Jessie Matthews and Gracie Fields to entertain through the night. A discreet doctor prescribed pick-me-ups to keep the audience, and not a few performers, awake and sparkling. Houdini's less-famous brother escaped from a locked trunk in the mail van and popped out of the coal tender. The Palladium-on-Rails business soured when a popular ventriloquist was institutionalised after an argument with his dummy. His act started off with the usual banter, then the dummy began making passes at women in the carriage. The vent was besieged. His dummy jeered him as he was beaten up by angry escorts. He snatched a hatchet and chopped at the dummy's mocking head, taking off three of his own fingers.

'Of course, there were whispers. Among railwaymen, the Streak picked up a new nickname, "the Ghost Train". In 1938, I drafted a pamphlet for inclusion in my series, *Haunted High-Ways*. I got a look at the Incident Book. I conducted tactful interviews with passengers. They expressed a vague, unformed sense of wrongness. They saw things, felt things. Anecdotes piled up. The dirty dummy and the throat-cut bounder were the least of it. Several regulars dreaded trips on the Streak, but were unable to resist making them – as if afraid of what 3473 would do if they abandoned it. Real addicts use the serial number, never the name. Lord Kilpartinger issued writs and threats, then invited me to tea at Fortnum & Mason. With some justification, he pointed out that any train which carried as many passengers over as many years must collect horror stories and that I might as well investigate tragedies associated with the five-twelve from Paddington to Swindon. Besides, he had just bought a controlling interest in my publisher and wondered if I wouldn't rather write books on flower-arrangement or how to host a dinner party.

'As I left, in something approaching high dudgeon, His Lordship tried to reassure me about the train. After all, he said, he'd travelled more miles on the Streak than anyone else with no obvious ill-effects. A month later, for some anniversary run or other, he boarded at Euston, posing cheerfully in his tartan cummerbund for the newspapers, clouds of steam billowing all around. After retiring to his compartment, he disappeared and did not pop out of the coal tender. He didn't get off at Edinburgh or Portnacreirann. The general consensus was that he had contrived a fabulous exit to avoid the bankruptcy proceedings which, it turned out, were about to bring down the LSIR. Maybe Kilpartinger became another anonymous navvy on his beloved line, swinging a hammer next to the disgraced McRidley. Or perhaps he dissolved into a Scotch mist and seeped into the upholstery. If you run across him, give him my best.

'With the LSIR in ruins, it seemed likely the Streak had made its last run. It was saved by the War. Luxury took a backseat to pulling-together, but the Streak was classified an essential service, supporting the Royal Navy Special Contingencies School at Portnacreirann. The Diogenes Club was busy on other fronts, but spared a young parapsychologist with a plum-bob and an anemometer to make a routine inspection. He ruled the train, the tracks and Inverdeith Bridge were perhaps slightly haunted. Had the Ruling Cabal listened to me rather than that bright lad, we would perhaps not be in this current pickle, but there's no use squalling about it now.

'Soon, there was another strange story about: take the Streak to your Special Contingencies course, and you'd win a medal. I went over the records last week – an enormously tedious job – and can confirm this was, in fact, true. "Special Contingencies", as you might guess, is a euphemism for "Dirty Fighting", which goes a long way towards explaining things. Nevertheless, a high proportion of the Streak's sailors proved aggressive, valiant and effective in battle. A high proportion of that high proportion got their gongs posthumously. The more often a man rode the Scotch Streak, the more extreme his conduct. We don't publicise the British servicemen tried for war crimes, but out of fewer than a dozen bad apples in the Second World War, five were Streak regulars. Americans rode the Ghost Train too. We don't have official access to their records, but they have Alexanders and Caligulas too.

'After the War, the railways were nationalised. In *Thomas the Tank Engine*, the Fat Director became the Fat Controller. The LSIR was swallowed by British Rail. 3473-S steams still, purple faded to the colour of a weak Ribena, tartan trim buried under a coat of dull dun. No Noël, no Gert and Daisy, no Archie Andrews. Providing you don't mind changing trains at Edinburgh, there are cheaper, faster ways of getting to Loch Linnhe. But the Scotch Streak clings to its "essential service" classification. Which saves it from the unsentimental axe taken to unprofitable branch-lines and quaint countryside stations.

'The haunting never stopped.'

III.

'We've reams of anecdotal evidence for ab-natural activity,' said Edwin, taking over from Catriona. 'Apparitions, apports, bilocation, sourceless sound, poltergeist nuisance, echoes from deep time, fits of precognition, possession, spontaneous combustion, disembodied clutching hands, phantoms, phantasms, pixies, nipsies, revelations, revenants, Old Uncle Tom Cobley and all. Few sleep well on the sleeper. A typical toff thinks he's slightly train-sick and decides to spend his next day out murdering English foxes rather than Scottish grouse. A percentage have much nastier turns. Outcomes range from severe ill-health and mental breakdown to disappearance and, well, death.'

'What about the staff, Ed?' asked Cutley, who had been taking notes.

Richard saw Edwin calculate how to keep aces in his hole while seeming to lay his cards on the table. It was habitual in these circles.

'BR have trouble keeping guards, waiters and porters,' Edwin admitted. 'Even then, one see-no-evil conductor who's been on the Streak for yonks swears the shudder stories are all hogwash. Presumably, he's the opposite of sensitive.'

'Why now?' asked Annette, pluming smoke. She drew a question mark in the air with her burning cigarette-end.

'That's the thing, Annie,' said Edwin. 'With fewer souls riding the Streak, the haunting isn't as noticeable as when Cat was on the case. But the Americans have expressed a concern. HM Government is under diplomatic pressure to sort things out, and you know where Ministers of the Crown call when ghoulies and ghosties rattle chains without permission.'

Edwin opened his hands, indicating the whole room.

Richard had paid close attention to Catriona Kaye's story. Something in it jogged his mind.

'We've Miss Kaye's manuscript and the wartime report,' said Harry Cutley, as if giving a tutorial. 'Everyone is to read them by Thursday, then we'll start fresh. Those of you who were with me on the Edgley Vale Puma Cult know how I like things done. Those of you who weren't will find out soon enough. Annette, visit the newspaper library and go over all the cuttings on the Scotch Streak since the boiler was cast. Magic Fingers, get out in the yards, talk to railwaymen, choo-choo bores... pick up any more stories for the collection. You... ah, sorry... the Jeperson boy...'

Cutley knew very well what his name was, but waited for the prompt.

'Richard.'

The Most Valued Member flashed a joyless smile.

'Thank you. I will remember. Not Greasy Herbert, but Richard. Richard Jeperson. Dick the Lad. Rickie the Roll-and-Rocker. Fixed in the mind's file, now. Anyway, Richard, you get your haircut down to Euston, trying not to slash cinema seats or terrorise old ladies en route, and book us on Thursday's Streak. Get me and Annette first-class sleeping compartments, a berth in second for Magic Fingers, and the railway equivalent of steerage for you. We have to cover the whole train.'

'I'll ride the mail car if you think it's a good idea.'

Cutley considered it.

'The Club can spring for four compartments,' put in Edwin, airily. 'If you're all in first class, no one will mind if you wander. With any other tickets, Richard and Danny wouldn't be allowed where interesting business might be going on.'

'Whatever you think best,' said Cutley. 'If money's no object, we might as well all get the gold toilet seats and mints on the pillows. Dickie will qualify for a half-fare anyway.'

The academic was used to working on the cheap, in fear of a redbrick budget review. He also wasn't happy to be given command of a group and then undercut in front of them. Edwin had made Cutley Most Valued Member, but was prone to step out from behind the desk and upstage his successor. Catriona laid a hand on Edwin's elbow, chiding with a gesture only the recipient, though Richard noticed.

'Keep all the chits,' said Cutley. 'Bus tickets, and so forth. My procedure is big on chits, *comprenons-oui*?'

Now, Cutley was needling Richard because he couldn't afford to prick back at Edwin. Richard was getting a headache with the politics.

'This is a haunted house on wheels,' Cutley told them. 'There are boring procedures for haunted houses, which will be followed. Background check, on-the-spot investigation, listing of observable phenomena and effects. Once that's over, I will assess findings and make recommendations. If the haunting can be dispelled through scientific or spiritual efforts, no one will complain. Annette, I'd appreciate a run-down of possible rituals of exorcism or dispellment. Bell, book and railwayman's lamp? Of course, we can always advise the train be taken out of service and the line abandoned. If there are no passengers to be haunted, it doesn't matter if spectres drag their sorry shrouds along the rails.'

Richard put his hand up, as if in class.

Cutley, annoyed, noticed. 'What is it, boy?'

'A thought, sir. If the train could be put out of service, it already would have been. There must be a reason to keep it running.'

Richard looked at Edwin. So did everyone else. Catriona massaged his arm.

At length, Edwin responded. 'No use trying to keep secrets in a roomful of Talents, obviously.'

Danny Myles whistled.

'What is it?' asked Cutley, catching up.

'The Scotch Streak must stay in service. The Special Contingencies School is now a submarine base. A vital component in our national deterrent.'

'The gun we have to their heads while theirs is stuck into our tummy,' put in Catriona.

'Cat goes on Aldermaston marches and wants to ban the Bomb,' Edwin explained. 'As a private individual, it is within her rights to hold such a position. In this Club, we do not decide government policy and can only advise.'

Annette almost snorted. She obviously knew Edwin Winthrop better.

'Every forty-eight hours,' Edwin continued, 'mathematicians

convene in Washington, DC, and use a computer to generate number-strings which are fed into an electronic communications network accessible only from secure locations at the Pentagon and our own Ministry of War. There's another terminal in Paris, but it's a dummy – the French can fiddle all they want, but can't alter the workings of the big machine. We wouldn't want them getting offended by the creeping use of terms like "le week-end" and kicking off World War Three in a fit of haughty pique. Annie, the French half of you didn't hear that. Once the numbers are in the net, they have to be conveyed to the President of the United States, the Prime Minister of Great Britain and selected officers on the front-lines of the Western Alliance. We don't use telephone, telegraph, telegram or messenger pigeon – we send couriers. The number-strings are known as the "Go-Codes". Unless they are keyed properly on special typewriters, orders cannot be given to arm a warhead, launch a missile or drop a bomb. Without the Go-Codes, we have no nuclear weapons.'

'And with them, we can end the world,' put in Catriona.

'So,' said Myles, waving his hands for emphasis, 'we've B-52s zooming over the Arctic, nuclear subs cruising the seven seas, ranks of computers the size of the Royal Pavilion, and brave soldier boys in the trenches ready to respond to any dire threat from the godless commie horde... but it all depends on some git catching a seven o'clock steam train from Euston every other evening?'

'That's it, exactly,' said Edwin.

'Crazy, man,' said Myles, snapping his fingers.

'As I said, matters of defence policy are beyond our remit. You understand now why governments are in a lather. If the Streak isn't secure, NATO wobbles. Quite apart from the haunting, they're worried about spies. One reason the Go-Codes are still carried by train is that our fiendish intelligence friends think the Russkies don't believe we'd really entrust so vital a duty to a couple of junior ratings on an overnight puff-puff.'

'I hope I meet a spy,' said Annette, posing languidly. 'I always saw myself as Mata Hari. Can I lure young lieutenants to their doom?'

'Leave them alone, Annie,' said Edwin. 'They've enough on their plates, what with World Peace in their pockets. There's been a high turnover on that detail. One nervous collapse, one self-inflicted gunshot wound, one sudden convert off in a monastery somewhere. Do not let it be known outside this room, but in the past year there have been four separate blocks of up to eighteen hours when our defences were compromised because the Go-Codes didn't arrive without incident. Consider the poor general whose burdensome duty it is to inform the President of this situation, let alone the possibility the Other Side might get wind of a first-strike opportunity. If we do hold a gun to their head, they'd best not find out the firing pin is wonky.'

Richard felt sickness in the pit of his stomach, as if he had washed down a half-pint of salted cockles with a strawberry milkshake. Despite Cutley's 'boring procedures for haunted houses', this was a bigger deal than pottering around Borley Rectory feeling out cold spots. The nausea passed and, to his embarrassment, he found he was physically in a state of high excitement. He gathered this was common in the corridors of power – though, since his voice broke, it seemed the minutes of the day when he wasn't sporting a raging erection were more noteworthy. Tight trousers did not make him any more comfortable. He blushed as Annette, perhaps peeping indelicately into his immediate future, smiled at him.

'Will the Yanks know we're aboard?' asked Cutley.

'In theory, at the highest level. The boys on the train don't know anything. They've been encouraged to believe they're a decoy, and that their envelopes are to do with an inter-services gambling ring organised by a motor-pool sergeant in Fort Baxter, Kansas. Spot the couriers, if you must, but don't get too close. Come back with concrete intelligence about whatever threats are gathering in the dark. I've always wanted to end a briefing by saying "this mission could shorten the War by six months". The next best thing is "the fate of the free world depends on you", which, I am sorry to say, it does. I'm sure you'll do us proud, Harry.'

The lecturer shot glances at his group. Richard knew what Cutley thought of Annette, Magic Fingers and him. Two beatniks and a Ted, not an elbow-patch between them, just the sorts Hard-Luck Harry hoped to get away from, bloody students!

'We'll make the best of it, Ed,' said Cutley.

IV.

Richard walked under the Doric arches of Euston Station at five o'clock, two hours before the Scotch Streak was due to depart. He was among crowds streaming from city offices to commuter trains.

'*Star*, *News* and *Standard*,' shouted competing sixty-year-old 'boys', hawking the evening papers. Khrushchev was in the headlines, sabre-rattling. The Premier wouldn't be such a growling bear if he knew Uncle Sam's pants were down for up to eighteen hours at a time. If his Sputnik spied a gap in the curtain, Old Nikita might well lob a couple of experimental hot ones just to see what happened.

'Don't even think about it, kiddo,' said a voice close to his ear. 'World's safe till midnight, at least. After that, it gets blurry… but Madame Amboise sees all. Worry not your pretty little head.'

He recognised Annette from her perfume, Givenchy mingled with Gauloises, before he heard or saw her. She spun him round and kissed both his cheeks, not formally. Her wet little tongue dabbed the corners of his mouth.

For the trip, she had turned out in a black cocktail dress,

elbow-length evening gloves, a shiny black hat with a folded-aside veil and a white fox-fur wrap with sewn-shut eyes. This evening, she wore lipstick – thin lines of severe scarlet. She posed like Audrey Hepburn, soliciting his approval, which was certainly forthcoming.

'That's the spirit,' she said, patting his cheek.

He had a mental image of Annette in her underclothes – black, French and elaborate. It flustered him, and she giggled.

'I'm doing that,' she said. 'It's a trick.'

She slipped off her shoulder strap to show black lace.

'And it's accurate,' she added. 'Sorry, I mustn't tease. You're so easy to get a rise out of. I don't get to play with anyone in the know very often.'

She tapped the side of her head and made spooky conjuring gestures.

Under her brittle flirtatiousness, she ran a few degrees high, trying to shake off a case of the scareds. That, in turn, worried him. Annette Amboise might come on like the Other Woman in a West End farce, but in the Diogenes Club's trade – not to mention actual war – she was a battle-proved veteran. All he'd ever done was switch some wires. If she knew enough to be frightened, he ought to be terrified.

'Aren't the arches magnificent?' she said. 'They'll be knocked down in a year or two. By idiots and philistines.'

'You're seeing the future?'

'I'm reading the papers, darling. But I do see the future sometimes. The possible future.'

'What, about...?'

She puffed and opened a fist as if blowing a dandelion clock. 'Boom? Not this week, I think. Not if we have anything to do with it. Of course, that'd bring down the arches too.'

She touched the stone with a gloved hand, and shrugged.

'Nada, my love,' she said. 'Of course, that's Magic Fingers' specialty, not mine. Laying on of hands. The Touch That Means So Much.'

Annette took him by the arm and steered him into the station. A porter followed, shoving a trolley laden with a brassbound trunk, matching pink suitcases, a vanity case and a hat-box. Richard had one item of luggage, a Gladstone bag he'd found in a cupboard.

'There's our leader,' said Annette, pointing.

Harry Cutley sat at a pie-stall, drinking tea. His own personal cloud hung overhead. Richard wondered whether Edwin would show up to see them off, then thought he probably wouldn't.

Annette stopped and held Richard back.

'Darling, promise me you'll be kind to Harry,' she said, pouting, adjusting his tie as if he were a present done up with a bow.

Richard shrugged. 'I didn't have other plans.'

'You don't need plans to be unkind. You're like me, a feeler. Try to be a thinker too. Heaven knows, I won't be. You and Harry aren't a match, but a mix. Don't be so quick to write him off. Now, let's go and be nice.'

Harry looked up and saw them coming. He waved his folded newspaper.

'Where's Myles?' he asked.

Neither Richard nor Annette knew. Harry tutted, 'Probably puffing "tea" in some jive dive.'

'Tea would be lovely, thanks,' said Annette.

Harry looked at the mug in his hand.

'Not this muck,' he said, sourly. The woman behind the counter heard but didn't care.

'Supper on the train, then?' said Annette. 'Sample that famous Scotch Streak luxury?'

'Just make sure to keep the chits,' cautioned Harry.

'Don't be such a grumpy goose,' said Annette, leaning

close and kissing the lecturer, who didn't flinch. 'This will be a great adventure.'

'Like last time?'

'Well, let's hope not that great an adventure.'

Harry pulled back the sleeve of his tweed jacket and showed a line of red weals leading into his cuff.

'Puma Cults,' commented Annette, 'miaow.'

Richard gathered Harry and Annette had both come off the Edgley Vale case with scars. The Most Valued Member had put that successfully to bed. An away win for the Diogenes Club. No points for the forces of evil. Harry even smiled for a fraction of a second as Annette purred and stretched satirically.

At once, Richard understood the difference between his Talent and Annette's. He received, she sent. He picked up what others were feeling; she could make them feel what she felt. A useful knack, if she was in an 'up' moment. Otherwise, she was a canary in a mineshaft.

Suddenly, Myles was there.

'Hey, cats,' he said, raising an eyebrow as that set Annette off on more miaows. 'Ready to locomote?'

'If we must,' said Harry.

Magic Fingers dressed like a cartoon burglar – black jeans, tight jersey, beret, capacious carpet-bag. All he needed was a mask.

Passengers travelling first class on the Scotch Streak had their own waiting room, adjacent to the platform where the train was readied. On presenting tickets, the party were admitted by a small, cherubic, bald, uniformed Scotsman.

'Good evening, lady and gentlemen,' he said, like a head-waiter. 'I'm Arnold, the conductor. If there is any way I can be of service, please summon me at once.'

'Arnold, the conductor,' said Harry, fixing the name in his mind.

Annette made arrangements to have her extensive luggage, and their three underweight bags, stowed on the train.

No extra-normal energies poured off Arnold, just polite deference. Considering his age and Richard's style, that was unusual. In the conductor's view, purchase of a first-class sleeping compartment ensured admission to the ranks of the elect. The passenger was always right, no matter what gaudy finery he wore or what gunk was slathered on his hair. Richard realised Arnold was the see-no-evil fellow Edwin had mentioned. The man who was not haunted. The conductor might be immune to ghosts, the way some people didn't catch colds. Or he could be a very, very good dissembler.

The waiting room wanted a thorough clean, but a residue of former glory remained. While second- and third-class passengers made do with benches on the platform, first-class oiks could plump posteriors on divans upholstered in the Streak's 'weeping bruise' purple. Complimentary tea was served from a hissing urn – which made Cutley mutter about wasting threepence (and collecting a chit) at the pie-stall. Framed photographs hung like family portraits, commemorating the naming ceremony (there was that Lady Lucinda Catriona disliked), the inaugural runs of 1928 and 1934 (Lord Kilpartinger in an engineer's hat) and broken speed records. Nothing about Inverdeith Bridge, of course.

Other passengers arrived. Two young men might as well have had 'Secret Courier' stitched to their hankie pockets. They had adult-approved US Navy crewcuts and wore well-fitted civilian suits which didn't yet bend with their bodies. Matching leather briefcases must contain the vital envelopes. Annette cast a critical eye over the talent; one nudged the other, who cracked a toothy smile which dimpled in his cornfed American cheek.

'So, where's the spy?' whispered Annette.

'We're the spies,' said Richard. 'Remember? Mata Hari.'

Three sailors in whites looked like refugees from a road company of *On the Town*; one very drunk, his mates alert for the shore patrol. They'd be through for Portnacreirann too, though it would be a surprise if they really were travelling first class. An allied uniform counted with Arnold. Mrs Sweet, an elderly lady in a checked ulster, was particular about her gun-cases. She issued Arnold with lengthy instructions for their storage. A clergyman swept in and Richard's first thought was that he was a disguised Chicago gangster. His ravaged cheeks and slicked-down widow's peak irresistibly suggested a rod in his armpit and brass knucks up his sleeve. However, he radiated saintly benevolence. Richard ought to know not to judge by appearances.

A fuss erupted at the door. Arnold and a guard were overwhelmed by a large, middle-aged woman. She wore a floral-print dress and a hat rimmed with wax grapes and dry, dead roses.

'I've got me ticket somewhere, ducks,' she said. 'Give us a mo. Here we are. Me ticket, and me card.'

The woman had a Bow Bells accent and one of those voices which could crack crystal. Something about her alerted Richard. Annette and Myles had the same reaction. Psychic alarm bells.

'What is it?' asked Harry, noticing his group's ears all pricked up at once.

'Calm,' said Annette.

Richard realised his heart was racing. He breathed deliberately and it slowed. Myles let out a whistle.

'Me card,' repeated the woman. 'Elsa Nickles, Missus, Psychic Medium. I'm here to 'elp the spirits. The ones tevvered to this plane. The ones who cannot find the rest they need. The ones trapped on your Ghost Train.'

Arnold was less interested in the woman's card than her ticket, which turned out to be third class. Not a sleeping compartment, but a seat in the carriage next to the baggage car. A trained contortionist with no feeling at all in her back or lower limbs might stretch out and snooze.

The conductor told her this waiting room was first class only. She wasn't offended.

'I don't want to go in, ducks. Just wants a butchers. The vibrations are strong in the room. No wonder your train's got so many presences.'

The 'psychic medium' craned over Arnold's head and scanned the room, more obviously than Richard had done. She frankly stared at everyone in turn.

'Evenin', vicar,' she said to the saturnine clergyman, who smiled, showing rotten teeth. 'Should have those fixed,' she advised. 'Pull 'em all on the National Health and get porcelain choppers, like me.'

She grinned widely, showing a black hollow rim around her plates.

The vicar wasn't offended, though he looked even more terrifying when assembling a smile.

Mrs Nickles didn't give Harry, Richard or the US Navy a second glance, but fluttered around Annette – 'Cor, wish I had the figure for that frock, girl' – and was taken with Magic Fingers.

'You've got the Gift, laddie. I can always tell. You see beyond the Visible Sphere.'

Myles didn't contradict her.

'I sense a troubled soul 'ere, or soon to be 'ere,' she announced. 'Never mind, I can make it well. It's all we can do, ducks, make things well.'

Mrs Sweet hid behind her *Times* and rigidly ignored everything.

Harry muttered, unnoticed by Mrs Nickles.

The woman was a complication, not accounted for in Harry's 'boring procedures'. Richard sensed the Most Valued Member wonder idly if Mrs Nickles might step under rather than onto the train.

The first time he'd 'eavesdropped' on a musing like that, he'd picked up a clear vision from the Latin master; the Third Form mowed down by a machine gun barrage. He'd been horrified and torn: keep quiet and share in the guilt, speak out and be reckoned a maniac. Even if he prevented slaughter, no one would ever know. For two days, he'd wrestled the problem, close to losing bowel control whenever he saw the master round the quad with an apparently distracted smile and mass murder in mind. Then, Richard picked up a similar stray thought, as the captain of the second XI contemplated the violent bludgeoning of a persistent catch-dropper. With nervy relief, he realised everyone plotted atrocities on a daily basis. So far, he hadn't come across anyone who really meant it. Indeed, imagined violence seemed to take an edge off the homicidal urge – folks who didn't think about murder were more likely to commit one.

'Ahh, bless,' said Mrs Nickles, standing aside so someone with a proper ticket could be let into the room.

A solemn child, very sleepy, had been entrusted by a guardian into the care of the Scotch Streak. She wore a blue, hooded coat and must be eight or nine. Richard, who had little experience with infants, hoped the girl wouldn't be too near on the long trip. Children were like time bombs, set to go off.

'What's your name?' asked Annette, bending over.

The girl said something inaudible and hid deeper in her hood.

'Don't know? That's nothing to be ashamed of.'

Mrs Nickles and Annette were both smitten. Richard intuited neither woman had living children. If Mrs Nickles really was a medium, that was no surprise. Kids were attention sponges and sucked it all up – a lot of Talents faded when there was a pram in the house.

Annette found a large label, stiff brown paper, fastened around the girl's neck.

'"Property of Lieutenant-Commander Alexander Coates, RN",' she read. 'Is this your daddy?'

The little girl shook her head. Only her freckled nose could be seen. In the hooded coat, she looked more like a dwarf than a child.

'Are you a parcel, then?'

The hooded head nodded. Annette smiled.

'But you aren't for the baggage car?'

Another shake.

Arnold announced that the train was ready for boarding.

The Americans jammed around the door as the British passengers formed an orderly queue. Annette took the little girl's hand.

The Coates Parcel looked up and Richard saw the child's face. She had striking eyes – huge, emerald-green, ageless. The rest of her face hadn't fully grown around her eyes yet. A bar of freckles crossed her nose like Apache war paint. Two red braids snaked out of her hood and hung on her chest like bell-pulls.

'My name is Vanessa,' she said, directly to him. 'What's yours?'

The child was strange. He couldn't read her at all.

'This is Richard,' said Annette. 'Don't mind the way he looks. I'm sure you'll be chums.'

Vanessa stuck out her little paw, which Richard found himself shaking.

'Good evening, Richard,' she said. 'I can say that in French. *Bon soir*, Rishar'. And German. *Guten Abend*, Richard.'

'Good evening to you, Vanessa.'

She curtseyed, then hugged his waist, pressing her head against his middle. It was disconcerting – she was hugging him like a pony, a pillow or a tree rather than a person.

'You've got a fan, man,' said Magic Fingers. 'Congrats.'

Vanessa held onto him, for comfort. He still didn't know what to make of her.

Annette rescued him, detaching the girl.

'Try not to pick up waifs and strays, lad,' said Harry.

Richard watched Annette lead Vanessa out of the waiting room. As the little girl held up her ticket to be clipped by Arnold, she looked back.

Those eyes!

V.

Richard was last to get his ticket clipped. Everyone found their proper carriages. Mrs Nickles strode down the platform to third class, trailed by sailors.

He took in 3473-S. At a first impression, the engine was a powerful, massive presence. A huge contraption of working iron. Then, he saw it was weathered, once-proud purple marred and blotched, brass trim blackened and pitted. The great funnel belched mushroom clouds. He smelled coal, fire, grease, oil. Pressure built up in the boiler and heat radiated. A gush of steam was expelled, wet-blasting the platform.

'Bad beast, man,' said Myles, fingertips to metal.

As Annette said, his talent was to read inanimate, or supposedly inanimate, objects. He was qualified to evaluate the locomotive.

'Got a jones in it, like a circus cat that's tasted blood, digs it, wants more.'

'That's a comfort.'

Myles clapped his shoulder, magic fingers lingering a moment. Briefly, Richard felt a chill. Myles took his hand away, carefully.

'Don't fret, man. I've known Number 73 buses go kill-crazy. Most machines are just two steps from the jungle. No wonder witches don't dig iron. Come on, Rich. "All aboard for the Atchison, Topeka and the Santa Fe."'

Arnold blew his whistle, a shrill night-bird screech. It was answered by a dinosaurian bellow from the locomotive. The steam-whoop rattled teeth and scattered a flock of pigeons roosting in the Euston arches.

'The train now standing at Platform 14,' said an announcer over the tannoy, sounding like a BBC newsreader fresh from an elocution lesson, 'is the Scotch Streak, for Edinburgh, and Portnacreirann. It is due to depart at seven o'clock precisely.'

Richard and Myles stepped up into their carriage. The wide, plush-carpeted corridor afforded access to a row of sleeping compartments.

'You're next to me, Richard,' said Annette, who had been installing Vanessa nearby. 'How cosy.'

He looked at Magic Fingers, who shrugged in sympathy – with a twinge of envy – and went to find his place.

Richard checked out his compartment. It was like a constricted hotel room, with built-in single bed, fixed desk (with complimentary stationery and inkwell) and chair, a cocktail cabinet with bottles cradled in metal clasps, wardrobe-sized en-suite 'bathroom' with a sink (yes, marble) and toilet (no gold seat). A second bed could be pulled down from an upper shelf, but was presently stowed. From murder mysteries set on trains, he knew the upper berth was mostly used for hiding bodies. Richard's Gladstone bag rested at the foot of the bed like a faithful dog. His towel and toiletries were stowed in the bathroom.

At first look, everything in first class was first class, then the starched white sheets showed a little fray, and that greyish, too-often-washed tinge; the blue-veined sink had orange, rusty splotches in the basin and a broken plug-chain; cigarette-burns pocked the cistern. 'Kindly refrain from using the water closet while the train is standing in the station,' said a framed card positioned above the toilet. In an elegant hand, someone had added, 'Trespassers will be shot.'

Richard thought he saw something in the mirror above the sink, and had to fight an instinct to turn and look behind him. He knew there would be nothing there. He looked deeper into the mirror, peering past his pushed-out face, ignoring a fresh-ish blotch on his forehead, searching for patches where the silvering was thin. He exhaled, misting the mirror. Rune-like letters, written in reverse, stood out briefly. He deciphered 'danger', 'warning' and 'fell spirit', then a heart, several Xs and a sigil with two As hooked together.

'Made you look,' said Annette, from the corridor. She giggled.

He couldn't help grinning. She was hatless now, languidly arranged against the door-frame, dress riding up a few inches to show a black stocking-top, shoulders back to display her fall of silky hair. She drew her AA in the air with her cigarette end, and puffed a perfect smoke ring.

She drew him along the corridor. They joined Harry and Myles in the next carriage. The ballroom in Lord Kilpartinger's day, it was now designated the first-class lounge.

Magic Fingers found a piano, and extemporised on 'The Runaway Train', which Annette found hilarious. She curled up in a scuttle-like leather seat.

At the far end of the carriage sat the vicar – probably working on a sermon, though his expression suggested he was writing death threats to be posted through the letter-boxes of nervous elderly ladies.

Arnold passed through the carriage, and informed them the bar would be open as soon as they were underway.

'Hoo-ray,' said Annette. 'Mine's a gimlet.'

She screwed a fresh cigarette into her holder.

Arnold smiled indulgently and didn't tell Myles not to tinkle the ivories. They were in first class and could swing from the chandeliers – which were missing a few bulbs, but still glinted glamorously – if they wanted.

'Impressions?' asked Harry, who had a fresh folder open and a ballpoint pen in his hand.

'All clear here,' said Annette. 'We'll live past Peterborough.'

'This box has had its guts battered,' said Magic Fingers, stuttering through a phrase, forcing the notes out, 'but we're making friends, and I think he'll tell me the stories. "The runaway train came over the hill, and she ble-e-ew…"'

Harry looked at Richard and prompted, 'Jeperson? Anything to add?'

Richard thought about the little girl's ageless eyes.

'No, Harry. Nothing.'

Harry bit the top of his pen. The plastic cap was already chewed.

'I hope this isn't a wasted journey,' said the Most Valued Member. 'Just smoke and mirror stories.'

'It won't be that,' said Annette. 'I can tell.'

The whistle gave out another long shriek, a Johnny Weissmuller Tarzan yell from the throat of a castrated giant.

'…and she ble-ew-ew-ew-ew…'

Without even a lurch, as smooth as slipping into a stream, the Scotch Streak moved out of the station. The train rapidly picking up speed. Richard sensed pistons working, big wheels turning, couplings stretching, the irresistible pull…

He had a thrill of anticipation. All boys loved trains. Every great mystery, romance or adventure must have a train in it.

'…the engineer said the train must halt, he said it was all the fireman's—!'

Myles's piano-playing was shut off by a crash. The lid had snapped shut like a bear-trap.

The jazzman swore and pulled back his hands. His knuckles

were scraped. He flapped them about.

'Pain city, man,' he yelped.

'First blood,' said Annette.

'The beast's impatient,' said Myles. 'Antsy, itchy-pantsy. Out to get us, out to show who's top hand. Means to kill.'

Harry examined the piano, lifting and dropping the lid. A catch should have held it open.

'Catch was caught, Haroldo,' said Magic Fingers, pre-empting the accusing question. 'No doubt about it.'

Harry said the lid could easily have been jarred loose by the train in motion. Which was true. He did not make an entry in his folder.

Annette thought it was an attack.

'It knows we're here,' she said. 'It knows who we are.'

They were on their way. Outside the window, dark shapes rushed by, lights in the distance. The train flashed through a suburban station, affording a glimpse of envious, pale-faced crowds. They were only waiting for a diesel to haul them home to 'villas' in Hitchin or Haslemere and an evening with the wireless, but all must wish they were aboard the brightly lit, fast-running, steam-puffing Streak. Bound for Scotland – mystery, romance and adventure!

Richard found he was shaking.

ACT II: ON THE SCOTCH STREAK
I.

Over the train-rattle, Annette Amboise heard herself scream.

She was in the corridor. The lights were out. One of her heels was broken, and her ankle turned.

The train was being searched, papers demanded, faces slapped, children made to cry, bags opened, possessions strewn. She'd soon be caught and questioned. Then, hours of agony culminating in shameful release. She'd hold off as long as she could. But, in the end, she'd break.

She knew she'd talk.

Fingers slithered around her neck. A barbed thumb pressed into the soft flesh under her jaw.

Her scream shut off. She couldn't swallow her own spit. Air couldn't reach her lungs.

The grip lifted her off her feet. Her back pressed against a window which felt like an ice-sheet. She was wrung out, couldn't even kick.

She smelled foul breath, but saw only dark.

The train passed a searchlight. Bleaching light filled the corridor. Uniform highlights flashed: twin lightning-strike insignia, broken cross armband, jewel-eyed skull-badge, polished cap-peak like the bill of a carrion bird. No face under the cap, not even eyes. A featureless bone-white curve.

The *boche* had her!

She tried to forget things carried in her head. Names, code phrases, responses, locations, times, number-strings. But everything she knew glowed red, ready for the plucking.

Her captor held up his free hand, showing her a black, wet Luger. The barrel, cold as a scalpel, pressed to her cheek.

The light passed.

The pistol was pushed into her face. The gunsight tore her skin. Her cheek burst open like a peach. The barrel wormed between her teeth. Bitter metal filled her mouth.

The grip around her throat relaxed, a contemptuous signal.

She drew in breath and began to talk.

—◆—

'Annie,' said Harry Cutley, open hand cupped by her stinging cheek, 'come back.'

She had been slapped.

She was talking, giving up old names, old codes. 'Dr Lachasse, Mady Holm, Moulin Vielle, La Vache, H–360…'

She choked on her words.

Harry was bent over her. She was on a divan in the lounge carriage. Myles and Richard crowded around. Arnold the conductor attended, white towel over his arm, bearing cocktails. Hers, she remembered, was a gimlet.

'Where were you?' asked Harry. 'The War?'

She admitted it. Harry had been holding her down, as if she were throwing a fit. Suddenly self-conscious, he let her go and stood away. Annette sat up and tugged at her dress, fitting it properly. Nothing was torn, which was a mercy. She wondered about her face.

Her heart thumped. She could still feel the icy hand, taste oily gunmetal. When she blinked, SS scratches danced in the dark.

'Can we get you anything?' asked Harry. 'Water? Tea?'

'I believe that's mine,' she said, reaching out for her cocktail. She tossed it back at a single draught. Her head cleared at once. She replaced the empty glass on Arnold's tray. 'Another would be greatly appreciated.'

Arnold nodded. Everyone else had to take their drinks from the tray before he could see to her request. They sorted it out – a screwdriver for Myles, whisky and water for Harry, a Virgin Mary for Richard. Arnold, passing no comment on her funny turn, withdrew to mix a fresh gimlet.

'Case of the horrors?' diagnosed Myles.

She held her forehead. 'In spades.'

'A bad dream,' said Harry, disappointed. His pen hovered over a blank sheet in his folder. 'Hardly a manifestation.'

'To dream, wouldn't she have to be asleep?' put in Richard. 'She went into it standing up.'

'A fugue, then. A fit.'

Harry erred on the side of rational explanation. Normally, Annette admired that. Harry kept an investigation in balance, stopped her – and the rest of the spooks – from running off with themselves. Usually, ghosts were only smugglers in glow-in-the-dark skeleton masks. Flying saucers were weather balloons. Reanimated mummies were rag week medical students swathed in mouldy bandages. Now, his thinking was just blinkered. There were angry spirits on the Scotch Streak. And, for all she knew, little green Martians and leg-dragging Ancient Egyptians.

'Have you had fits before?' asked Richard.

'No, Richard,' she said patiently, 'I have not.'

'But you do get, ah, "visions"?'

'Not like this,' she said. 'This was a new experience. Not a nice one. Trust me. It reached out and hit me.'

'"It"?' said Harry, frowning. 'Please try to be more scientific, Annie! You must specify. What "it"? Why an "it" and not a "them"?'

Her heartbeat was normal now. She knew what Harry – irritating man! – meant. She tried to be helpful.

'Just because it's an "it" doesn't mean there's no "them". An army is an "it", but has many soldiers, a "them".'

Harry angry, at something Richard called him.

'What came for me wasn't one of my usuals,' she continued. 'I see what might happen. And not in "visions", as Richard put it. I don't hear "voices" either. I just know what's coming, or might be coming. As if I've skipped ahead a few pages and skim-read what happens next.'

Harry, Richard and Myles backing away from her. No, they were still close – they wouldn't back away for a few minutes.

'I see round corners. Into the future. This was from somewhere else.'

'The past?' prompted Richard. 'A ghost?'

490

'The past? Yes. A ghost? Not in the traditional sense. More like an incarnation, an embodiment. Not a personality. My idea of the Worst Thing. It reached into me, found out what my Worst Thing was, and played on it. But there was still the train. I was on the train. It lives here. The Worst Thing. The Worst Thing Ever. The Worst Thing in the World.'

'Dramatic, Annie, but not terribly helpful.'

Harry put the top back on his biro.

'Listen to her,' said Richard, slipping an arm around her shoulder – a mature gesture for such a youth. 'She's not hysterical. She's not imagining. She is giving you a report. Write down what she's said.'

Harry was not inclined to pay attention to the Jeperson boy.

'I can't,' he said. 'It's static. It'll cloud the issue. We need observable phenomena. Incidents that can be measured. Traced back to a source. I'll get the instruments.'

'We have instruments,' said Richard. 'Better attuned than your doodads, Daddy-O. We have Annette and Magic Fingers.'

He didn't include himself, but should have.

A burst of indignant fury belched from Harry as Richard called him 'Daddy-O'. She flinched at the psychic outpouring, but less than she would have done if she hadn't known it was coming.

The lad was pushing with Harry. He couldn't help himself.

Myles laid a hand on her forehead, nodded.

'Something's been at her,' he said. She didn't like the sound of that. 'Left claw marks.'

'Will everybody please stop talking as if this were my autopsy,' she said. 'I have been attacked, affronted, shaken. But I am not a fragile flower you need to protect. I can take care of myself.'

Like she did in the War.

The curve under the SS cap came back to her. If questioned, she would have talked. Everyone did, eventually. It had never come to it, because of her trick, her way of putting her feet right, of avoiding situations. Others – the names that had come back to her – had been less fortunate. As far as she knew, they were dead or damaged beyond repair. Most had been caught – talking made no difference in the end, they were still killed.

Ever since, she had been putting her feet right. Walking near peril, not into it. Here, she was on a train – a row of linked boxes on wheels. There might be no right steps here. There might only be danger. Her gift was often knowing where not to be. Here, knowing where not to be did not mean she could avoid being there.

She trusted her instincts. Now, they were shouting: pull the communication cord! She could afford the fine for misusing the emergency stop signal. One swift tug, and brakes would be thrown. The Scotch Streak would scream to a halt. She could jump onto the tracks, head off over the fields.

Harry, Richard and Myles backed away from her. Just as she'd known they would. She ticked off the moment, grateful there wasn't anything more to it.

She was pulling the communication cord.

She suppressed the instincts. The red cord – a chain, actually – still hung, above a window, unbothered in its recess. She would ignore it.

Would she pull the cord in the future or was she imagining what it would be like? No way to tell. She saw herself in the dock, being lectured, then paying five one-pound notes to a clerk of the court – but the clerk had no face. That usually meant she was imagining. If this was going to happen, she would see a face, and recognise it later.

Then, her brain buzzed. She couldn't mistake this for wandering imagination. Before the War, a child psychiatrist labelled Annette's puzzling malaise as 'acute *déjà vu*'. Catriona Kaye modified the diagnosis and coined the term '*jamais vu*'.

Annette did not have I-have-been-here-before memories of the present, but I-will-be-here-soon memories of the future.

An open exterior door, night-time countryside rushing past. Someone falling from the train, breaking against a gravel verge. And someone coming for her, from behind.

If that was a few pages ahead, she'd rather fold the corner at the end of this chapter, put the book on her bedside table and never open it again. But that wasn't how the world worked.

Arnold came with her second gimlet. This one she sipped.

'Perfect,' she told the conductor, suppressing shivers.

II.

Annette's recovery impressed Richard. Two gimlets and a nip to her compartment to fix her face, and she was set. Her strings were notches too tight, but so were everyone else's. She flirted, presumably on instinct, flitting among her colleagues, seeming to offer equal time. Only Richard noticed he was getting marginally more serious attention than Harry Cutley or Danny Myles. She already knew them but needed to puzzle out the new boy, fix him in her mind the way Harry fixed names, by rolling him around, pinching and fluffing, testing reactions. Which, as ever, were warm and, he thought, horribly obvious.

Harry sourly made shorthand notes in his folder.

The frightening vicar gently enquired as to the lady's condition. Annette said she was fine, and he retreated, satisfied. Richard still wondered if the man was faking his aura. His killer's hands seemed made to be gloved in someone else's blood.

Standing nearby, Annette was carefully not looking at the communication cord. Of course. Anyone who travelled by train knew that imp of the perverse which popped up at the sight of a 'Penalty for improper use – £5' notice – pull the chain, see what happens, go on, you know you want to. On the Scotch Streak, the imp was a bullying, nagging elemental.

Annette felt Richard's lapel between thumb and forefinger.

'Real,' she said. 'Sometimes I can't tell any more.'

He didn't know where to put his hands.

'Put the boy down, Annie,' said Harry. 'Come fill in this Incident Form. Since you're convinced you were assaulted, we must have a first-person account before memories fade.'

She shuddered and joined Harry. He gave her a sheet of paper and a pencil, which she proceeded to use as if sitting an exam, producing neat, concise notations in the spaces provided.

Danny Myles sat at the piano, fingers tapping the closed lid. His bruises were rising. He smiled, did a little two-finger Gene Krupa solo on the polished wood.

'Me next, you think?' Richard asked.

Myles lifted his shoulders.

'Watch your back, Jack.'

The carriage windows were ebony mirrors. If Richard got close to the glass and strained, he could make out the rushing countryside. A late supper would soon be served in the dining carriage. The train didn't stop until Edinburgh, at half past one; then, after a twenty-minute layover, it would continue to Portnacreirann, arriving with the dawn.

The overnight express felt more like an ocean liner than a train. Safe harbour was left behind and they were alone on the vast, deep sea.

Though they had compartments, none of them would sleep.

Richard took out his father's watch, checked it against the clock above the connecting door. He had ten past nine, the train clock had ten to. He'd wound the watch at Euston, setting the time against the big station clock.

Myles saw what he was doing, rolled his sleeve back and felt a glassless watch – a holdover from his blind days. 'Stopped, man,' he said. 'Dead on the vine. Seven seven and seven seconds. That's a panic and a half.'

'I won't have one of those things,' said Annette, looking up from her form. 'Little ticking tyrants.'

'Prof?' Myles prompted Harry.

Harry pulled a travel clock out of a baggy pocket and held it next to his wrist-watch.

'Eight thirty-two. Ten oh six.'

'Want to take a stab at which is the real deal?' asked Magic Fingers.

They all looked at the train clock, ticking towards supper time.

'What I thought,' said the jazzman.

Harry Cutley riffled through his folder and dug out more forms. He handed them out. Myles got on with it, turning out a polished paragraph. Richard simply wrote down 'watch fast'.

'Perhaps now you'll stay away from mechanical instruments and rely on people,' said Annette. 'You know clocks run irregularly in haunted places, so why do you trust thermometers, barometers, wire-recorders and cameras?'

'People run irregularly too,' said Harry, reasonably. 'Even – no, especially – Talents.'

Richard was piqued. His watch was no ordinary timepiece. His father had inherited it from his grandfather, who had sat with Mycroft Holmes on the first Ruling Cabal. Geoffrey Jeperson had carried the watch all through the War. The Captain, having supervised arrests in a death camp, had been checking the time when he and a large-eyed, hollow-bellied child noticed one another. The watch brought them together. The boy who would become Richard Jeperson reached for the bauble, taking it reverentially when the Captain, on instinct, trusted it to him. He had solemnly felt its weight, listened to its quiet tick, admired its

Victorian intricacy through a panel in the face. Inside gears and wheels were tiny fragments of unknown crystal, which sparkled green or blue in certain light. The roman numerals were lost in tiny engravings of bearded satyrs and chubby nymphs.

Those first ticks were where Richard's memory began. Before now, the watch had never betrayed him.

If Jeperson's watch wasn't to be trusted, what else in the life furnished for him by the Diogenes Club was left? The watch wound with a tiny key, which was fixed to the chain – it could also stop the mechanism, and Richard did so. If the watch could not run true, it should not run at all. He felt as if a pet had died, and he'd never had pets. He unhooked the chain and wondered if he'd ever wear it again. He slipped watch and chain into a pocket and handed back the incident form.

Arnold, who obviously had no trouble with his watch – a railway watch, as much a part of the Scotch Streak as the wheels or the windows – announced that supper was served. According to the train clock, it was nine o'clock precisely.

Harry reset his watch and clock against the train time. He made a note in his folder.

'I foresee you'll be at that all night,' said Annette. 'Without using a flicker of Talent. It's Sod's Law.'

Harry smiled without humour, not giving her an argument.

It hit Richard that something had gone on between Harry Cutley and Annette Amboise, not just an investigation into a Puma Cult. Harry took teasing from her he wouldn't from anyone else. He sulked like a boy when she paid attention elsewhere. She'd told Richard not to underestimate the Most Valued Member.

Now, in a way that annoyed him, he was jealous.

'Should we sample the Scotch Streak fare?' said Annette. 'In Kilpartinger's day, the cuisine was on a par with the finest continental restaurants.'

'I doubt British Rail have kept up,' said Harry. 'It'll be beef and two veg, pie and chips or prehistoric bacon sarnies.'

'Yum,' said Magic Fingers. 'My favourite.'

'Come on, boys. Be brave. We can face angry spirits, fire demons, Druid curses and homicidal lunatics. A British Rail sandwich should hold no horrors for us. Besides, I've seen the menu. I rather fancy the quail's eggs.'

Annette led them to the dining carriage. Wood-panel and frosted-glass partitions made booths. Tables were laid for two or four.

As he passed under the lounge clock, Richard looked up. For a definite moment, he saw a face behind the glass, studded with bleeding numbers, clock-hands nailed to a flattened nose, cheeks distended, eyes wide, clockmaker's name tattooed on stretched lips.

'That's where you've got to,' he mused, recognising Douglas Gilclyde. 'Lord Killpassengers himself.'

The face was gone. Richard thought he should mention the apparition, then realised he'd only have to fill in another form and opted to keep stumm. There'd be plenty more where that came from.

III.

They were all laughing at him, the bastards!

Harold Cutley tasted ash, bile and British Rail pork pie. He wanted to tell the bastards to shut up. The only noise he produced was a huffing bark which made the bastards laugh all the more.

'Gone down the wrong tube,' said the insufferable Jeperson boy.

The French tart slapped him on the back, not to clear the blockage – taking an excuse to give him a nasty thump.

'Get Prof a form to fill in,' snarked the beatnik. 'See how he likes it.'

Cutley stood and staggered away from the table. He honked and breathed again. He could talk if so inclined. As it happened, he bloody well wasn't.

He knew they'd all gang up on him!

That was how it always was. At Brichester, no one understood his work and he was written off as 'the Looney'. Muriel hadn't helped, betraying him with all of them. Even Head of Physics, Cox-Foxe. Even bloody students! He was with the Diogenes Club toffs on the sufferance of Ed Winthrop, who habitually overruled and sidelined and superseded. Ed had saddled Harry with this shower so he couldn't get anywhere, would never have any findings to call his own.

No one was coming after him. He shot a glance back at the booth, where Annette was canoodling with the Teddy boy. The bitch, the bastard! Magic Fingers was tapping the table, probably hopped up on 'sneaky pete'. If there were results to be had, he'd have to find them on his own.

He would show them. He would have to.

The conductor – what was his name? Why hadn't he fixed it? – was in his way, blocking the narrow aisle. Cutley got past the man, shrinking to avoid touching him, and strode towards the dark at the end of the carriage.

'Well, really,' said the frumpy bat who was the only other diner, the old girl with the guns. She'd spilled claret on her gammon and pineapple and was going to blame Harold Cutley. 'I must say. I never did.'

Cutley thought of something devastating to snap back at the pinch-faced trout, but words got mixed up between his brain and his pie-and-bile-snarled tongue and came out as spittle and grunts.

The woman ignored him and forked a thin slice of reddened meat into her mouth.

He looked back. The carriage had stretched. The rest of his so-called group were dozens of booths away, in a pool of light, smiling and fondling, relieved he was gone, already forgetting he'd ever been there. The bastarding bastards! They had the only bright light. The rest of the carriage was dim.

Now there were other diners, in black-and-white and silent. One or two to every fifth or sixth booth. Shadows on frosted-glass partitions. Starched collars and blurry faces. Some were missing eyes or mouths, some had too many.

Muriel was here somewhere, having her usual high old time while someone else brought home the bacon.

Bitch!

'May I see your ticket?'

It was the conductor. Or was it another official? This one looked the same, but the tone of voice was not so unctuous. He sounded deeper, stronger, potentially brutal. More like a prison warder than a servant.

What was the name again? Albert? Alfred? Angus? Ronald? Donald?

Arnold – like Matthew Arnold, Thomas Arnold, Arnie, Arnoldo, Arnold. That was it. Arnold.

'What is it, Arnold?' he snapped.

'Your ticket,' he insisted. His collar insignia, like a police constable's, was a metal badge. LSIR. That was wrong, out of date. 'You must have your ticket with you at all times and be prepared to surrender it for inspection.'

'You clipped mine at Euston,' said Cutley, patting his pockets.

Cutley searched himself. He found his bus ticket from Essex Road to Euston, a cinema stub (1s 9d, *Naked as Nature Intended*, the Essoldo), a slip pinned inside his jacket since it was last dry-cleaned three years ago, a sheaf of shorthand notes for a lecture he'd never given, an invitation to Cox-Foxe's thirty-years-service sit-down dinner, a page torn out of the Book of Common Prayer with theorems pencilled in the margin, a linked chain of magician's handkerchiefs some bastard must have planted on him as a funny, a Hanged Man tarot card that had been slipped to him as a warning by that blasted Puma Cult, his primary-school report card ('Fair Only'), an expired ration book, a French postcard Muriel had once sent him, his divorce papers, a signed photograph of Sabrina, a Turkish bank-note, a card with spare buttons sewn onto it, a leaf torn out of a desk calendar for next week, and a first edition of Thomas Love Peacock's *Headlong Hall* he had once taken out of Brichester University Library and not gotten round to returning but which he could've sworn he'd left behind in the house Muriel had somehow wound up keeping when she walked out on him. But no ticket.

'Would this be yours?' said Arnold, holding up a strip of card.

Cutley was more annoyed. This was ridiculous.

'If you had it all the time, why didn't you say so, man?'

'We have to be sure of these things.'

Cutley noticed that the conductor wasn't 'sirring' him any more. Before he could take the proffered ticket, he had to return his various discoveries to his pockets. Even if he piled up the things he could afford to throw away, it was a devil of a job to fit everything back into his jacket, which was baggier and heavier by the minute.

Arnold watched, still holding out the ticket.

Beyond the conductor, the dining car was nearly empty again. Jeperson, Annette and Magic Fingers were in the far distance, merrily tucking into knickerbocker glory or some other elaborate, sickly-sweet pud. None of that on his old ration book, he remembered with a bitter twinge.

He was sorted out. Except he had put the Peacock with the used bus and cinema tickets. He slid the book into his side-pocket, tearing a seam with a loud rip. He had a paper of buttons but no needle and thread. Muriel always had a needle, ready threaded, pinned about her in case of emergencies. She wasn't in the dining carriage now – probably off in some fellow's compartment, on her knees, gagging for it, the cow, the harlot!

'Why are you still here?' he asked Arnold, snatching his ticket.

'To make sure,' said the conductor. 'This isn't your place. This is for first-class passengers only.'

Bloody typical! These jumped-up little Hitlers put on a blue serge uniform that looked a bit like a policeman's and thought they could order everyone else about, put them all in their proper and bloody places. One look at Harry Cutley was enough to tell them he didn't belong with silver cutlery and long-stemmed roses at every table. All the knickerbocker glory a fat girl could eat conveyed with the complements of the chef to the table in crawling, grovelling deference! Only, just this once, Harry Cutley did belong. Baggy, torn, patched jacket and all, Cutley was in first class. He had a first-class ticket, not bought with his own money, but his all the same. With angry pride, he brandished it at the conductor's nose.

'What does this say, my good man?'

'I beg your pardon,' responded Arnold, with a tone Cutley didn't like at all. 'What does what say?'

'This ticket, you bastard. What does this ticket say?'

'Third class,' said the conductor. 'Which is where you should be, if you don't mind my saying. This is not the place for you. You would not be comfortable here. You would be conscious of your, ah, shortcomings.'

Cutley looked at his ticket. It must be some sort of funny.

'This isn't mine,' he said.

'You said it was. You recognised it. You would not want to make a scene in the first-class dining carriage.'

'First class! I don't call a stale pork pie first-class dining!'

'The fare in third class might be more suited to your palate. More your taste. Rolls are available. Hard-tack biscuits. Powdered eggs, *snoek*, spam. Now, move along, there's a good fellow.'

Arnold, seeming bigger, stood between him and the booth where the others were downing champagne cocktails. Cutley tried to get their attention but Arnold swayed and swelled to block him from their sight. Cutley tried to barge past. The conductor laid hands on him.

'I must ask you to go back to your place.'

'Bastard,' spat Cutley into the man's bland face.

Arnold had a two-handed grip on Cutley's lapels. So where did the fist that sank into Cutley's stomach come from?

Cutley reeled, hearing another long rip as a lapel tore in the conductor's hand. His gut clenched around pain. He knew when he was beaten. He slunk off, towards the connecting door. Beyond was second class, not his place either. He was supposed to be at the back of the train, with the baggage and the mail, probably with live chickens and families of untouchables sat on suitcases tied with string, lost in the crowd, one of the masses, trodden under by bastards and bitches. In his place.

There were things back there which he could use. He knew where they were. He had overheard, at Euston. He remembered the long cases.

Guns!

He limped out of the dining carriage, into the dark.

IV.

'What's up with Harry?' Richard asked.

'Gyppy tummy?' suggested Magic Fingers.

'I should go after him,' said Annette, folding her napkin. 'We shouldn't be separated.'

Richard touched her arm. His instincts tingled. So, he knew at once, did hers.

Harry had stumbled past Arnold, who briefly appeared bewildered, and charged out of the carriage.

'You stay here,' said Richard. 'I'll go.'

He stood. Annette was supposed to admire his manly resolve. She radiated a certain mumsy pride as if he were a schoolboy striding to the crease to face the demon bowler of the Upper Sixth. Not quite what he intended.

Harry Cutley had been seized in the middle of a mouthful of pie. Not necessarily a phenomenon worth an Incident Form. Something in his eyes as he veered off, trying to staunch coughing, suggested he wasn't seeing what Richard was. The man had been touched. Attacked, even.

'Your friend, sir,' said Arnold, with concern. 'He seems taken poorly.'

'What did he say?'

'Nothing repeatable, sir.'

'I'll see to him, thank you, Arnold.'

'Very good, sir.'

Every time he spoke with Arnold, Richard had to quash an impulse to tip him. At the end of the journey, was it the done thing to palm a ten-bob note and pass it over with a handshake?

He walked the length of the carriage, rolling with the movement of the train. He had become accustomed to the Scotch Streak. He had to concentrate to hear the rattle of wheels, the chuff-chuff of the engine, the small clinkings of cutlery and crockery. Almost comforting. Catriona Kaye said the most dangerous haunted houses always feel like home.

Harry had barged past Mrs Sweet. Richard thought of talking with her, but she glared as he walked towards her. He was a duck's-arse-quiffed affront to everything she believed in. Real killers wore respectable suits from Burton's and had faces like trustworthy babies. That was how they got close. Richard had a pang of worry that Mrs Sweet might have an extra gun about her – a hold-out derringer in her stocking-top or a pepper pot in her reticule – in case a wounded grouse flapped close enough to need its head dissolving with a single, deadly accurate shot. This train gave people funny ideas. She might easily pot him on the off chance.

He got by Mrs Sweet unshot, looked over his shoulder at Annette and Myles, and stepped through the connecting door into the second-class carriage. He checked the lavatory and didn't find Harry – though he caught sight of a cracked mirror and started, shocked at a glimpse of an antlered, fox-faced quarry with a target marked on his forehead in dribbling blood. *How others see us.*

The carriage was empty. The corridor was unlit. Second class did not have sleeping berths, but there were regular compartments, suitable comfortably for six, which could take ten in a pinch. The dark made it easier to see out of the windows. This stretch of track ran though ancient forest. Branches twisted close, leaves reaching for the passing express.

Richard made his way down the carriage, checking each compartment. None of the privacy blinds were down. One seat supported a huddle of old clothes that might have been a sleeping second-class passenger – though it was early to turn in for the night. On a second look, no one was there. He knew better than be caught out that way, and looked again. Whatever had been huddled was gone back to its hole. He trusted it would stay there.

It couldn't be the throat-cut spectre of 'Buzzy' Maltrincham. The vicious viscount wouldn't have been caught dead in second class. 3473 had many more ghosts than him. Would Lord Kilpartinger show up again? Disgraced old Donald McRidley – assuming he was dead? The Headless Fireman? The passengers of '31? The waterlogged witches of Loch Gaer?

It got darker as he proceeded. Turning back, he saw the glass of the connecting door was now opaque – had someone drawn a blind? – and the dining carriage cut off from view.

'Harry?' he called out, feeling foolish.

Something pattered, near the toilet cubicle. Fast and light. Not clumsy Harry Cutley. It might be a large cat. They had railway cats, didn't they? There was one in Old Possum's. But usually on stations, not on trains.

Another of Catriona Kaye's sayings was that sometimes observers brought their own ghosts and the haunted place merely fleshed them out. Was there a puma person still after Harry? Hadn't Annette been bothered by something from the War? Her 'it', her Worst Thing? Some entities fished out your worst nightmare – your worst memory, your darkest secret – and threw it at you. But nothing dug for your happiest moments, your fondest wishes, your most thrilling dreams and wrapped them up as a present. What had Magic Fingers called it, Sod's Law?

Richard remembered his father's advice about how to see off a tiger if you were unarmed. Knock sharply on its snout, as if rapping on a front door. Just the once. Serve notice you are not to be bothered. The big cat would bolt like a doused kitten, leaving rending, clawing and devouring for another day. Pumas are just weedy imitation tigers, so the Captain Jeperson treatment should send one chasing its tail. Of course, his father never claimed to have used his tiger-defying technique in the wild. It was wisdom passed down in the family – untested, but comforting.

'Harry?'

Now, Richard felt like an idiot. Plainly, lightfeet wasn't Harry Cutley.

He walked back, past the compartments – that huddle was still absent, thank you very much – towards the toilet and the connecting door. He moved with casual ease, controlling an urge to scream and run. The puma was Harry's Worst Thing. Not Richard Jeperson's.

The area between cubicle and door was untenanted. He thought. He held the door-handle, torn. He couldn't return to Annette and Myles with no news of Harry, but didn't want to venture further into the train without reporting back, even if he raised a fuss. Harry, technically, was in charge. He should have left instructions – not that Richard would have felt obliged to follow them. If it had been Edwin Winthrop, maybe. Catriona Kaye, certainly – though she never instructed. She provided useful information and a delicate nudge towards the wisest course.

The nagging imp came again – he was just a kid; he wasn't ready for this; he wasn't sure what this was. None of that nonsense, he told himself, sternly, trying to sound like Edwin or his father. You're a Diogenes Club man. Inner Sanctum material. Most Valued Member potential. Bred to it, sensitive, a Talent.

Click. He'd tell Annette Harry had gone far afield, then co-opt Arnold and make a thorough search. This was a train, it was impossible to go missing (Lord Kilpartinger did) and Harry was simply puking his pie, not held by the Headless Fireman and clawed by a Phantom Puma.

He opened the connecting door.

And wasn't in the dining carriage, but the first-class sleeping corridor. Discreet overhead lights flickered.

At the end of the corridor, by an open compartment-door, stood a small figure in blue pyjamas decorated with space-rockets, satellites, moons and stars. Her label was tied loosely around her neck. Her unbound red hair fell to her waist, almost covering her face. Her single exposed eye fixed on him.

What was the girl's name? He was as bad as Harry.

'Vanessa?' It came to him. 'Why are you up?'

Setting aside the Mystery of the Vanishing Carriage, he went to the child, and knelt, sweeping hair away from her face. She wasn't crying, but something was wrong. He recognised emptiness in her, an absence he knew well – for he had it himself. He made a smile-face and she didn't cringe. At least she didn't see him as a werebeast whose head would fit the space over the mantelpiece. She also didn't laugh, no matter how he twisted his mouth and rolled his eyes.

'What's wrong?'

'Dreams,' she said, hugging him around the neck, surprisingly heavy, lips close to his ear. 'Bad dreams.'

V.

'…and then, chicklet, there were two.'

Magic Fingers wished the Scotch Streak's famous facilities stretched to an espresso machine. He could use a Java jolt to electrify the old grey sponge, get his extra-senses acting extra-sensible. Like most night-birds, he ran on coffee.

Annie pursed her lips at him and looked at the doorway through which Hard Luck Harry and now the Kid had disappeared.

'You said we shouldn't split the band and you were on the button,' he told her. 'We should have drawn the wagons in a circle.'

'You're not helping,' she said.

Was he picking up jitters from her? When Annie was discombobulated, everyone in the house came down with the sweats. It was a downside of her Talent.

'Chill, tomato, chill,' he said. 'Put some ice on it.'

She nodded, knowing what he meant, and tried hard. There was a switch in her brain, which turned off the receptors in her fright centre. Otherwise she'd never have made it through the War.

Danny Myles had been blind during the War, evacuated

from the East End to the wilds of Wales. He had learned his way around the sound-smell-touch-tastescape of Streatham in his first twelve years, but found the different environment – all cold wind-blasts, tongue-twisting language and lava bread – of Bedgellert a disorienting nightmare. He had run away from Mr and Mrs Jones the farmers on his own, and felt his way back across two countries, turning up in his street to find it wasn't there any more and Mum was with Auntie Brid in Brixton. Lots of cockney kids ran away from yokels they were packed off to during the Blitz – some from exploitation or abuse far beyond lava bread every evening and tuneless chapel most of the weekend – but they weren't usually blind. It was a nine days' wonder. Mum wasn't sure whether to send him back to the Joneses, with a label round his neck like that chick who took a shine to the Kid, or keep him in London, sheltering in the Underground during the raids.

Born without sight, it was hard for Danny to get his head round the idea of blindness or realise his extra-senses were out of the ordinary. Then, the switch in his brain was thrown. No miracle operation, no bump on the bonce, no faith healer – it was just like a door suddenly swinging open. There was a black-out, so there wasn't even much to see – until the sun came up. He didn't stop whooping for a week. At first, the bright new world in his eyes blotted out the patterns of sound and touch he had made do with, but when things settled, his ears were sharper than ever. Soon, he could channel music through anything with eighty-eight keys, really earning his 'Magic Fingers' handle. Then Edwin Winthrop came into the scene and the Diogenes Club took an interest, labelling him a Talent.

He'd been doing these gigs for years. In '53, he'd unmasked the Phantom of the Festival of Britain. Then, he'd busted the Insane Gang. Defused the last of Goebbels' Psychic Propaganda Bombs. Rid London Zoo of the Ghost Gorilla and his Ape Armada. It was a sideline. Also, he knew, an addiction. Some jazzmen popped pills, mainlined horse, bombed out on booze, chased skirts – he went after spooks. Not just any old sheet-wearers, but haints which could turn about and bite. Heart-eaters. Like 3473-S. This was a bad one, worse than the Phantom, worse than the Ghost Gorilla. He knew it. Annie and the Kid knew it too, but they hadn't his extra-senses. They didn't know enough to be properly wary. Hell, not wary – terrified.

'You're doing it again,' Annie chided him.

He realised he'd been drumming his fingers. 'Stella By Starlight'. A song about a ghost. He stopped.

His hands hurt. That snap from the piano-lid was coolly calculated to show him who was boss. The sides of his thumbs were numb. His knuckles were purple and blobby. He spread his fingers on the tablecloth.

'Like, ouch, man,' he said.

Annie giggled.

'It hurts, y'know. How'd you like it if your face fell off?'

She was shocked for a moment.

'Not a lot,' she said.

'These hands are my fortune, ought to be wrapped in cotton wool every night. If I could spring for payments, I'd insure them for lotsa lettuce. This… this train went for them, like a bird goes for the eyes. Dig?'

'The Worst Thing in the World.'

'On the button, Mama.'

'Less of the "Mama". I'm not that much older than you.'

The Kid ought to be back by now. But he was a no-show. And Harry Cutley was far out there, drowning.

Magic Fingers cast his peepers over the dining car. There'd been an elderly frail strapping on the feed-bag down the way. She'd skedaddled, though he didn't recall her getting up. Arnold

– the conductor-waiter-majordomo-high priest – was gonesville also. He and Annie were alone.

Man, the rattle and shake of the train was fraying his nerves with bring-down city jazz! It was syncopation without representation! All bum notes and missed melodies.

At first, movement had been smooth, like skimming over a glassy lake. Now, the waters were choppy. Knives and forks hopped on the tables. Windows thrummed in their frames. The cloth slid by fractions of an inch and had to be held down, lest it drag plates over the edge and into the aisle.

He felt it in his teeth, in his water, in his guts, in the back of his throat.

Speed, reckless speed. This beast could come off the rails at any time.

The windows were deep dark, as if the outsides were painted – or black-out curtains hung over them. Even if he got close to the cold glass, all he saw was a fish-eye-distorted, darked-up reflection.

They weren't in a tunnel. They could have been on a trestle stretched through a void, steaming on full-ahead, rails silently coming to pieces behind them. Alone in the night.

He raised his hand and fingertipped the glass, getting five distinct icy shocks. He'd been leery of using his touching, but now was the time.

'Anything?' asked Annie.

He provisionally shook his head, but felt into the glass. It was thick, like crystal, and veined. He felt the judder of pane in frame, and caught the train's music, a bebop with high notes, warning whistles and a thump of dangerous bass. 3473 had a heartbeat, a pulse.

A shock sparked into his fingers, pain outlining his hand-bones.

He was stuck to the window, palm flat against the glass,

fingers splayed. Waves of hurt pulsed into him, jarring his wrist, his arm… up to the elbow, up to the shoulder.

Annie sat, mouth open, not moving. Frozen.

No, he felt her gloved fingers on his wrist, pulling. He scented her perfume, close. The brush of her hair, the warmth of her, near him.

But he saw her sat still, across the table.

It was as if his eyes had taken a photograph and kept showing it to him, while his extra-senses kept up with what was really happening. He moved his head: the picture in front of him didn't change.

Annie was speaking to him, but he couldn't make it out. Was she talking French? Or Welsh? He had the vile taste of lava bread in his mouth. He heard the train rattle, the music of 3473, louder and louder.

The picture changed. For another still image.

Annie was trying to help, one knee up on the table, both hands round his wrist, face twisted in concentration as she pulled.

But he couldn't feel her hands any more, couldn't smell her.

In his eyes, she was with him. But every other sense told him she'd left off.

His vision showed him still images, like slides in a church hall. It was as if he were in a cinema where the projector selected and held random frames every few seconds while the soundtrack ran normally.

A scream joined train noise.

Annie was in the aisle, arms by her sides, hands little fists, mouth open. Dark flurries in the air around her. Birds or bats, moving too fast to be captured by a single exposure.

The scream shut off, but Annie was still posed in her yell. Something broke.

In the next image, she was strewn among place-settings a

few booths down, limbs twisted, dress awry. The frosted glass partition was cracked across.

The window let go of him. His hand felt skinless, wet.

Someone, not Annie, was talking, burbling words, scat-singing. No tune he could follow.

He waited for the next picture, to find out who was there. Instead the frame held, fixed and unmoving no matter how he shook his head. He stood and painfully caught his hip on the table-edge. He felt his way into the aisle, still seeing from his sat-by-the-window position. He tried to work out where he was in the picture before him, reaching out for chair-backs to make his way hand-over-hand to Annie, or to where Annie was in his frozen vision.

A heavy thump, and a hissing along with the gabble.

He stood still in the aisle, bobbing with the movement of the train, like the hipsters who didn't dance but nodded heads to the bop, shoulders and hands in movement, carried by jazz. He guesstimated he was three booths away from his original viewpoint.

Then the lights flared and faded.

The picture turned to sepia, as if there were an even flame behind the paper, and the brown darkened to blackness.

He shut and opened his sightless eyes.

His hands were on chair-backs and he had a better sense of things than when treacherous eyes were letting him down. He heard as acutely as before. The gabbling was a distraction. Just noise, sourceless. There was no body to it – nothing displacing air, raising or lowering temperature, smelling of cologne or ciggies. There was one breathing person in the carriage – Annette Amboise, asleep or unconscious. Otherwise, he was alone, inside the beast.

This was different; blindness, with the memory of sight. It was as if there had been white chalk marks around everything, just-erased but held in his mind as guide-lines.

It wasn't like seeing, but he knew what was where.

Tables, chairs, roses in sconces, windows, connecting doors, the aisle. Under him was carpet. Under that was the floor of the carriage. Under that hungry wheels and old, old rails.

Now there were shapes in the dark. Sitting at the tables. White clouds like human-sized eggs or beans, bent in the middle, limbless, faceless.

He heard the clatter of cutlery, grunts and smacks of swinish eating. In the next carriage, the piano was assaulted. Someone wearing mittens plunked through 'Green Grow the Rushes-Oh', accompanied by a drunken chorus. This wasn't now. This was before the War.

This was the Scotch Streak of Lord Killpassengers.

How far off was the In-for-Death Bridge?

He couldn't smell anything. It was worse than being struck blind. He knew he could cope without eyes. He'd made it from Wales to London, once. He had the magic fingers.

Someone called him, from a long way away.

All he could taste was dry, unbuttered lava bread. Butter wasn't to be had in London, what with rationing – his mum used some sort of grease that had to be mixed up in a bowl. In Wales, with farms all about, there was all the butter in the world and no questions asked, but Mr and Mrs Jones didn't believe in it. Like they didn't believe in hot water. Or sheets – thin blankets of horsehair that scratched like a net of tiny hooks would do. Or music, except the wheezing chapel organ. When Danny drummed his fingers, he'd get a slap across the hand to cure him of the habit. He was not to get up from the table, even if he needed to take the ten steps across the garden to the privy, until he'd cleared his plate and thanked the Good Lord for His bounty. Most nights, he'd sit, fighting his bladder and his tongue, struggling to swallow, trying not to have acute taste-buds, ignoring the hurt in his mouth until the lump was solid in his stomach. 'There's lovely,' Mrs Jones would say. 'Bless the bread and bless the child.'

In the dining carriage, there was lava bread on every table.

The communicating door opened. The racket rose by decibels, pouring in from the canvas-link between carriages where the din was loudest. A cold draught dashed into his face. Someone entered the dining car, someone who shifted a lot of air. The newcomer moved carefully, like a fat man who knows he's drunk but has to impress the Lord Mayor. A grey-white shape appeared in the dark and floated towards Danny, scraps of chalk-mark and neon squiggles like those sighted people have inside their eyelids coalescing into a huge belly constrained by vertically striped overalls, an outsize trainman's hat, a pitted moon-face. Danny saw the wide man as if he were spotlit on a shadowed stage, or cut out of a photograph and pasted on a black background.

He recognised the face.

A huge paw, grimy with engine dirt, stuck out.

'Gilclyde,' boomed the voice, filling his skull. 'Lord Kilpartinger.'

Not knowing what else to do, Magic Fingers offered his hand to be shaken. Lord Killpassengers enveloped it with his banana-fingered ape-paws and squeezed with nerve-crushing, bone-crushing force.

Agony blotted out all else – he was in the dark again, feeling the vice-grip but not seeing His Lordship dressed up as Casey Jones. Burning pain smothered his hand.

It was a bad break. At the end of his wrist hung a limp, tangled dustrag.

Then he felt nothing – no pain. No sound. No smell. No taste. No feeling.

For the first time in his life, he was completely cut off.

VI.

Even beyond the usual assumption that quiet English children were aliens, there was something about Vanessa.

She made Richard feel the way grown-ups, even those inside the Diogenes Club, felt around him when he was a boy, the way a lot of people still felt when he was in the room. At first, they were on their guard because he dressed like the sort of youth the *Daily Mail* reckoned would smash your face in – though, in his experience, Teds were as sweet or sour as anyone else, and the worst beatings he'd personally taken came from impeccably uniformed school prefects. Once past that, people just got spooked – because he felt things, saw things, knew things.

Now he knew about Vanessa.

He was almost afraid of her. And this from someone who accepted the impossible without question.

Sherlock Holmes, brother of the Club's founder, said, 'When you have eliminated the impossible whatever remains, however improbable, must be the truth.' Less frequently quoted was Mycroft's addendum, 'And when you cannot eliminate the impossible, refer the matter to the Diogenes Club.' It was recorded in the Club's archives, though not in the writings of John Watson, that the Great Detective several times found himself stumped, and fielded the case to his contemporary Carnacki the Ghost-Finder.

It was barely possible that a gigantic conjuring trick could rearrange, or seem to rearrange, the carriages while the train was steaming through the darkened countryside. The archives weren't short of locked-room mysteries and like conundra. For some reason, especially from the 1920s and early 1930s. The Scotch Streak dated from then, so it could have been built to allow baffling disappearances. However, an uncanny explanation required less of a stretch of belief. Richard couldn't see a point to the carriage substitution, and pointlessness was a frequent symptom of the supernatural.

Haunted houses often had 'treacherous' doors, opening to different rooms at different times. It should have been expected, by know-it-all Harry Cutley, for instance, that a haunted train would have something along these lines. However, the switcheroo wasn't on the train's list of previously recorded phenomena.

Where was everybody? Harry was downwind, last seen heading towards second and third class. Annette and Myles were in the misplaced dining car. Arnold the conductor, omnipresent earlier, was nowhere to be seen.

Were the other passengers where they should be? Though it was easy to get distracted by fireworks, this investigation was supposed to be about protecting the American couriers.

Three compartments had blinds drawn and 'Do Not Disturb' signs hung. One was Annette's, and she wasn't there. Another was Vanessa's, and she was with him.

That was a puzzle. Besides the couriers, Mrs Sweet and the sinister vicar (one of whom must be a spy) should be here. They couldn't all be crammed into one compartment playing whist with nuclear missiles. In theory, the British Government had other agents to deal with that sort of mess, kitted out with exploding cufflinks and licences to kill. In a pinch, Richard could muddle in. The Club had been dabbling in 'ordinary' espionage since the Great Game of Victoria's reign. Edwin had served as an intelligence officer in the RFC during the First World War ('no, I didn't shoot down the Bloody Red Baron; what I shot was a lot of photographs from the back of a two-seater – if it matters, each exposure got more Huns killed than all the so-called flying aces put together') before taking over Carnacki's ghost-finding practice.

'Have you seen any Americans?' he asked the child.

She solemnly shook her head and stuck out her lower lip. She wanted more attention paid to her.

He looked again at her label.

'Who is Lieutenant-Commander Coates?'

She gave a 'don't know' shrug.

'Not your dad, you said. Where are your parents?'

Another shrug.

'Lot of that about,' he said, feeling it deeply. 'Where do you live, usually?'

A small sound, inaudible – as if the girl weren't used to speech, like a well–bred, upper–middle–class Kaspar Hauser in spaceman pyjamas.

'Come again, love?'

'Can't remember,' she said.

Richard had a chill, born of kinship. But he was also wary. This was too close to where he came from. If the train could come up with Worst Things to get under Annette's or Harry's skin, it could sidle up close to him and bite too.

'Vanessa What?'

Another 'Can't remember.'

'It must be Vanessa Something. Not Coates, but Something.'

She shook her head, braids whipping.

'Just Vanessa, then. It'll have to do. Nothing wrong with "Vanessa". Not a saint's name, so far. Not forged in antiquity and refined through passage from language to language like mine. Richard, from the Germanic for "Rule-Hard", also "Ricardo", "Rickard", "Dick", "Dickie", "Dickon", "Rich", "Richie", "Clever Dick", "Dick-Be-Quick", "Crookback Dick". Your name – like "Pamela", "Wendy" and "Una" – was invented within recorded history. By Jonathan Swift, as it happens. Do you know who he was?'

'He wrote *Gulliver's Travels*.'

So she remembered some things.

'Yes. He coined the name "Vanessa" as a contraction – like "Dick" for "Richard" – for an Irish girl called "Esther Vanhomrigh".'

'Who was she?'

'Ah, she was a fan of Dean Swift, you know, like girls today might be fans of Tommy Steele.'

'Don't like Tommy Steele.'

'Elvis Presley?'

Vanessa was keener on Elvis.

'Miss Vanhomrigh was Swift's biggest fan, so he invented a name for her. He preferred another woman called Esther, Esther Johnson, whom he called "Stella". I expect he made up the names so as not to get them mixed up. Stella and Vanessa didn't like each other.'

'Did they fight?'

'In a way. They competed for Swift's attention.'

'Did Vanessa win?'

'Not really, love. Both died before they could settle who got him, and he wasn't entirely in the business of being got.'

Best not to mention the author might have married Stella.

How did they get into this? He didn't set out to be a lecturer, but he was recounting things he didn't think he remembered to this inquisitive, reticent child. Talking to her calmed him.

'Are we being got?' she asked.

'I'm afraid we might be.'

'Please don't let me be got.'

'Not if I can help it.'

'Promise?'

'Promise.'

Vanessa smiled up at him. Richard worried he had just given his word in the middle of a great unknown. He might not be in a position to keep his promise.

But he knew it was important.

Vanessa must not be got.

They were by the compartment with the 'Do Not Disturb'

sign. He saw a 'Through to Portnacreirann' notation. The blind wasn't pulled all the way down, and a spill of light wavered on the compartment floor. In that, Richard saw a pale hand dangling from the lower berth, thin chain fixed to the handle of a briefcase on the floor. It was one of the couriers.

At least they were safe.

Vanessa put her eye up to the gap and looked in, for a long while.

'Come away,' he said. 'Let the nice Americans sleep.'

She turned and looked up at him. 'Are you sure they're nice?'

'No, but they're important. And it's best to leave them alone. There are other people I want to find first.'

'Your friends? The pretty lady. The scowly man. The blind person.'

'Danny's not blind. Well, not now. How did you know he'd been blind?'

She shrugged.

'Just sensitive, I suppose,' he prompted. 'And, yes, them. I left them in the restaurant but I, ah, seem to have mislaid the carriage. It used to be there' – pointing at the connecting door – 'but now it isn't.'

'Silly,' she said. 'A restaurant can't get lost.'

'You've got a lot to learn.'

'No I haven't,' she declared, sticking up her freckled nose. 'I've learned quite enough already.'

Richard was slightly irked by her tone. He might have said Vanessa's education could hardly be considered complete since she'd omitted to learn her own full name. But that would be cruel. He understood too well how these situations came about.

'The supper carriage is through that door,' she said. 'I peeked, earlier.'

She led him by the hand, back towards the connecting door.

'We should be careful,' he said.

'Silly silly,' she said. 'Come on, Mr Richard, don't be scared...'

When anyone – even a little girl – told him not to be scared, his natural instinct was to wonder what there was not to be scared of, then whether the person giving the advice was as well up on the potential scariness or otherwise of the situation or entity in question as they might be.

The subdued lamps in the train corridor had dimmed to the point when everything seemed moonlit. The glass in the connecting door was black – he had a nasty thought that the carriages could have shifted about again, and there might be cold night air and a nasty fall to the tracks beyond.

He let Vanessa's hand go, and looked – trying to show more confidence than he felt – towards the door. He was over twice the girl's age, and should take the lead; then again, twice a single figure wasn't that much. He didn't really know how old he was, let alone how old he should act.

He hesitated. She gave him a little push.

The train noise was louder near the door, the floor shakier.

Richard told himself he was opening the door. Then he found he actually was.

Beyond was...

VII.

Something had given her an almighty thump. And had got to Danny Myles.

Annette came to on a table. Forks were driven through her shoulder-straps, pinning her to Formica. She couldn't sit without ruining her Coco Chanel. Obviously, this was the work of a fiend from Hell. Or a jealous wife.

The table rattled. Was the Scotch Streak shaking to pieces?

A length of something spiny, like overboiled stringy asparagus with teeth, stretched across her mouth. She clamped down, tasted bitter sap, and spat it away. It was the long-stemmed rose from the place-setting.

She carefully detached the forks, trying to inflict no more damage to her dress, and sat up. Wet, sticky blood pooled on the tablecloth. Then she noticed a paring-knife sticking out of her right thigh. Her stocking was torn. She gripped the handle, surprised not to feel anything but slight stiffness. Upon pulling out the knife, a gush of jagged pain came. She ignored it, and improvised a battlefield dressing – another useful trade learned in the War – with a napkin and cocktail sticks.

Sliding off the table, she looked up and down the dining carriage.

Danny Myles was backed into a space between the last booth and the door to the galley, hugging his knees, face hidden. He trembled, but she couldn't tell if it was with silent sobbing or the movement of the train.

She saw no one else, which didn't mean no one else was there.

Someone had forked and knifed her. The skewering had been too deliberate, too mocking, to be the result of a directionless phenomenon like the common-or-garden poltergeist. Something with a personality had attacked her. Something that thought itself a comedian. The worst kind of spook, in her opinion. Or maybe she'd been pinned by a mean person who wasn't here any more. Never neglect human agency. People could be wretched enough on their own, without calling in ghosts.

There were ghosts here, though.

'Danny,' she said.

He didn't hear her. That tinkled a warning – Danny heard everything, even when you didn't want him to. He could probably smell or taste what was whispered in the next building in a room with taps running.

'Danny,' she said, louder.

She went to him, feeling stabbed again with every step.

He wasn't dead, she saw, but in shock, crawled back into his shell. He looked up and around, seeing nothing.

Danny 'Magic Fingers' Myles held up useless hands.

'Busted,' he said. 'Gone.'

She knelt by him and examined his hands. No bones were broken. She found no wound of any kind. But they were dead, like sand-filled gloves.

'*Salauds boches*,' she swore. Nazi bastards!

She knew what the Worst Thing was for Danny Myles.

His head jerked and he flinched, as if he were being flapped at by a cloud of bats. He knew someone was near, but not that it was her. All his senses were gone. He was locked in his skull.

She took his arms and stood him up. He didn't fight her. She tried to reach him – not by talking or even touching, but with her inside self. She projected past the bony shields around his mind, to reassure, to promise help...

She didn't know if the damage was permanent – but she squashed the thought, screwing it into a tiny speck. He mustn't get that, mustn't catch despair from her, to compound his own.

It's Annie...

Because it was her way, she tried kissing him, but just smeared her lipstick. She held him tight, her forehead against his.

He wriggled, escaping from her. The napkin bandage came loose and her leg gave out. For support, she grabbed a tall trolley with shelves of dessert. It rolled down the aisle, dragging her. She bumped her head against the silvered frame. Cream and jam smeared the side of her face, matting in her hair. The trolley got away, and she was left, tottering, reaching out for something fixed...

Danny walked like a puppet, jerked past the galley, pulled

522

towards the end of the carriage. Annette had seen people like that before, in shock or under the influence.

'Danny!' she called out, frustrated. Nothing reached him.

She repaired her bandage. How much blood had she lost? Her foot was a mass of needles and pins. She wasn't sure her knee was working properly. Her fingers weren't managing too well knotting the napkin.

Danny was at the end of the carriage. The door slid open, not through his agency – the train had tilted to slam it aside. He vanished into shadow beyond, and fell down. She saw his trouser-cuffs and shoes slither into darkness as he pulled himself – or was pulled – out of the dining car.

This had gone far enough.

She reached out, slipped her hand into the alcove, and took a firm hold on the communication cord.

She had felt this coming. Now, here it was.

'"Penalty for improper use – five pounds,"' she read aloud. 'Cheap at half the price.'

She pulled, with her whole body. There was no resistance. She sprawled on the carpet. The red-painted metal chain was loose. Lengths rattled out of the alcove, yards falling in coils around her.

No whistle, no grinding of breaks, no sudden halt.

Nothing. The cord hadn't been fixed to anything. It was a con, like pictures of lifebelts painted on the side of a ship.

The Scotch Streak streaked on.

If anything, the din was more terrific. Cold wind blew, riffling Annette's sticky hair.

Between the carriages, one of the exterior doors was open.

Another earlier flash-forward came back to her. An open door. Someone falling. Breaking.

'Danny,' she yelled.

She scrabbled, tripping over the bloody useless chain, got to her feet, one heel snapped. That had been in her Worst Thing vision. Slipping free of her pumps, she ran towards the end of the carriage, as light flared in the passage beyond. She saw the open door, had an impression of hedgerows flashing by, greenery turned grey in the scatter of light from the train. Danny Myles hung in the doorway, wrists against the frame, body flapping like a flag.

She grabbed for him. Her fingers brushed his jersey.

Then he was gone. She leaned out of the train, wind hammering her eyes, and saw him collide with a gravel incline. He bounced several times, then tangled with a fencepost, wrapping around it like a discarded scarecrow.

The train curved the wrong way and she couldn't see him. Magic Fingers was left behind.

Tears forced from her, she wrenched herself back into the train, pulling closed the door. It was as if she had taken several sudden punches in the gut, the prelude to questioning, to loosen up the prisoner.

She found herself sitting down, crying her heart out. For a long time.

'Why is your friend bawling?' asked a small voice.

Smearing tears out of her eyes with her wrist, Annette looked up.

Richard was back – from the wrong direction, she realised – with Vanessa. The little girl held out a handkerchief with an embroidered V. Annette took it, wiped her eyes, and found she needed to blow her nose. Vanessa didn't mind.

'Danny's gone,' she told Richard. 'It got him.'

She looked up at her colleague, the boy Edwin Winthrop had confidence in, the youth she'd entertained fantasies about. Recruited at an early age, educated and trained and brought up to become a Most Valued Member. Richard Jeperson was supposed to take care of things like this. Harry Cutley led this group, but insiders tipped Richard as the man to take over, to defy the worst the dark had to offer.

She saw Richard had no idea what to do next. She saw only a black barrier in the future. And she swooned.

ACT III: INVERDEITH
I.

He had nothing.

Annette was out cold. Harry was missing in action. Danny was finished. He was no use to them, they were no help to him.

Richard was at the sharp end, with no more to give.

Vanessa tugged his sleeve, insistent. She needed him, needed comfort, needed saving.

Nearby, in one of these shifting carriages, the NATO couriers slept. And others – Arnold the conductor, the scary vicar, Mrs Sweet, that cockney medium, more passengers, the driver and fireman sealed off from the rest of the train in the cabin of the locomotive. Even if they didn't know it, they all counted on him. With the Go-Codes up for grabs, the whole world was on the table and the big dice rattled for the last throw.

The Diogenes Club expected him to do his duty.

He had the girl fetch chilled water in a jug from the galley, and sprinkled it on Annette's brow. The woman murmured, but stayed under. He looked at Vanessa, who shrugged and made a pouring motion. Richard resisted the notion – it seemed disrespectful to treat a grown-up lady like a comedy sidekick. Vanessa urged him, smiling as any child would at the idea of an adult getting a slosh in the face. With some delicacy, Richard tipped the jug, dripping fat bullets of water onto Annette's forehead. Her eyes fluttered and he tipped further. Ice-cubes bounced. Annette sat up, drenched and sputtering.

'Welcome back.'

She looked at him as if she were about to faint again, but didn't. He shook her shoulders, to keep her attention.

'Yes, I understand,' she said, 'Now don't overdo it. And get me a napkin.'

Like the perfect waiter – and where was Arnold? – he had one to hand. She dabbed her face dry and ran fingers through her short hair. She'd like to spend fifteen minutes on her make-up, but was willing to sacrifice for the Cause.

'You're lovely as you are,' he said.

She shrugged it off, secretly pleased. She let him help her to her feet and slid into one of the booths. Vanessa monkeyed up and sat opposite. The child began to play, tracing scratch-lines on the tablecloth with a long-tined fork.

'I tried the communication cord,' she said. 'No joy.'

He got up, found the loose loop of cord, examined it, sought out the next alcove, pulled experimentally. No effect whatsoever.

'Told you so,' she said.

'Independent confirmation. Harry Cutley would approve. It counts as a finding if we fill in the forms properly.'

Richard sat next to the little girl and looked at Annette, reaching out to catch a drip she had missed.

'Harry's gone?' she asked.

Richard thought about it. He calmed, reaching into his centre, and tried to feel out, along the length of the train.

'Not like Danny's gone,' he concluded. 'Harry's on board.'

'What's he doing when he goes quiet like that?' Vanessa asked, interested. 'Saying his prayers?'

'Being sensitive,' said Annette.

'Is that like being polite, minding his Ps and Qs?'

Richard broke off and paid attention to the people immediately around him.

'Something missing,' he said. 'Something's been taken.'

'Time, for a start,' said Annette. 'How long have we been aboard?'

Richard reached for his watch-pocket, then remembered he'd retired the timepiece. There was a clock above the connecting door. The one in the ballroom carriage seemed to keep the right time when all others failed. The face of this clock was black – not painted over, but opaque glass. It still ticked.

'I won't carry a watch,' said Annette, 'but I've an excellent sense of time. And I've lost it. How long was I unconscious?'

'Ages,' said Vanessa. 'We thought you'd died.'

'A few seconds,' said Richard.

'See,' said Annette. 'No sense of time at all.'

Richard looked at the nearest window. It was black glass, like the clock – a mirror in which he looked shockingly worn-out. Even when the overhead lights flickered, which they did more and more, he couldn't see out. He didn't know if they were rushing through England, Scotland or some other dark country. He felt the rattle-rhythm of the train – that, he knew, came from rolling over slight joins between lengths of rail, every ten or twenty feet. The Scotch Streak was still on tracks.

'Have we passed Edinburgh?' said Annette.

Edinburgh! That was a way out, a way off the Ghost Train!

From the station, he could phone Edwin, have the Club use its pull to cancel the rest of the journey, get everyone else out safely. Danny's death was justification for calling off the whole jaunt, shutting down the line. The couriers could be sent across Scotland in a taxi. It would take longer, but they'd be surer to arrive intact. If anyone wanted to start World War Three, they'd have to wait until after lunch.

Then, he could think of something else to do with his life. What life?

'I have a picture of the station in my mind,' said Annette, concentrating. 'Passengers get off, coal is taken on. They try to do it quietly, so as not to wake the sleepers, but you can't pour tons of anything quietly. I can't tell if I'm seeing ahead or remembering. My Talent seems to be on the blink at the moment. "Normal transmission will be resumed as soon as possible." There's a black wall...'

'We've already stopped once,' said Vanessa, in a small, scared voice. 'In Scotland.'

This was news. Richard couldn't imagine not noticing.

'Quite right, miss,' said Arnold the conductor, coming back from where the first-class carriages should be. 'I've clipped the ticket of the Edinburgh-to-Portnacreirann passenger. Just the one. Not what it used to be. Ah, someone's made a bit of a mess here. Don't worry. We'll get it cleaned up in a jiffy. Madame, might I bring you more water? This jug seems to be empty.'

Richard, suddenly cool inside, saw Arnold was either mad or with the other side. Not the other side as in the Soviets (though that was possible) but the other side as in beyond the veil, the Great Old Whatevers. Maybe he'd been normal when he first boarded the Scotch Streak, who knows how many nights ago – now he was one of Them, aligned with Annette's It. The conductor wore an old-fashioned uniform, a crimson cutaway jacket and high-waisted flyless matador trousers. His tiepin was the crest of the long-gone London, Scotland and Isles Railway Company. His cap was oversize, a child's idea of railwayman's headgear.

He resisted an impulse to take Arnold by his antique lapels, smash him through a partition, throw a proper Teddy boy scare into him, get the razor against his jugular, demand straight answers.

'Thank you,' he told the conductor. 'A refill would be appreciated.'

Arnold took the jug and walked off. Annette, greatly upset, was about to speak, but Richard made a gesture and she bit her lip instead. She was up to speed. It wasn't just the train and the spooks. It was the people aboard, some of them at least.

'What is it?' said Vanessa, picking up on the wordless communication between grown-ups. 'A secret? Tell me at once. You're not to have secrets. I say so.'

Annette laughed indulgently, at the girl's directness. The corners of her eyes crinkled in a way she hated and tried to avoid, but which Richard saw was utterly adorable. She was far more beautiful as herself than the made-up mask she showed the world.

'No secrets from you, little thing,' she said, pinching Vanessa's nose.

The little girl looked affronted by the impudence and stuck her fork into Annette's throat.

'Don't call me "little thing",' she said, in a grown man's voice. 'You French cow!'

II.

Richard scythed a white china dinner-plate edge-first into the little girl's face. The plate broke, gashing Vanessa's eyebrow – it would leave a scar. Blood fountained out of the child-shaped thing.

She gave out a deep, roaring howl and held her face, kicking the underside of the table, twisting and writhing as if on fire.

Richard looked across the table at Annette.

She held her hand to her throat, fork stuck out between her fingers, blood dribbling down her arm. Her eyes were wide.

'Didn't see... that coming,' she said, and slumped.

The light went out in her eyes.

Vanessa's hooked little fingers scrabbled at Richard's face, and he fell out of his seat. The child hopped onto his chest, pummelling, scratching and kicking. He slithered backwards, working his shoulders and feet, trying to throw the miniature dervish off him. Her blood poured into his face.

He caught hold of one of her braids and pulled.

A little-girl yell came out of her, a Mummy-he's-hurting-meee scream. Was that the real Vanessa? Something else was in there with her, whoever she was, whatever it was.

The girl was possessed.

It had been hiding, deep in the blanks of her mind, but had peeped out once or twice. Richard hadn't paid enough attention.

And now another of the group was gone.

Annette Amboise. He'd only known her a few days, but they'd become close. It was as if they knew they would be close, had seen a future now cruelly revoked, had been rushing past this long night, speeding to get to a next leg of their journey, which they would take together.

All that was left of that was this monster.

As Vanessa shrieked, Richard hurled her off. He got to his feet, unsteady. He looked to Annette, hoping she was unconscious but knowing better. Slack-mouthed, like a fish, she toppled sideways, towards the window, slapping cheek-to-cheek with her equally dead reflection.

Arnold was back – not from the direction he had left. He carried a full jug.

'The lady won't be needing this now,' he said.

The conductor ignored the frothing child-thing, who was crawling down the aisle, back seemingly triple-jointed, tongue extending six pink-and-blue inches, braids stood on end as if pulled by wires. It was like a giant gecko wearing a little girl suit, loose in some places and too tight in others. As its limbs moved, the suit almost tore.

One eye was blotted shut with blood. The other fixed on Richard.

The girl hissed.

Then the Gecko became bipedal. The spine curved upwards, straining like a drawn bow. Forelegs lifted and became floppy arms, hands limp like paddles. The belly came unstuck from the aisle carpet. Snake-hips kinking, it hopped upright. It stood with feet apart and shoulders down, as if balancing an invisible tail.

'Vanessa,' said Richard, 'can you hear me? It's Richard.'

Hot, obscene anger burst from whatever it was. He flinched. Annette might have been able to reach the girl inside, help her. That was her Talent. His left him open to emotional attack.

He stood his ground.

The label around the Gecko's neck was soggy with blood, words washed away, black shapes emerging.

He reached out and tore the label away. It left an angry weal around Vanessa's neck.

'Mine,' she said, in her own voice. 'Give it me back, you bastarrrd,' in the thing's masculine, somehow Scots voice. 'Mine,' both voices together, blasting from her chest and mouth.

He rubbed his thumb over the bloody card. Scrapes came away. The label was actually an envelope, with a celluloid inner sleeve sealing strips of paper. He clawed with a nail, and saw number strings.

The couriers were decoys, after all.

'Give me those,' said the Gecko.

Richard knew what he held. Not numbers, but a numerical key. Put in a slot, they could bring about Armageddon.

'Is that what you want?' he asked, talking to the thing.

The smile became cunning, wide. The unblotted eye winked.

'Give me back my numbers,' it said, mimicking the girl's voice.

He could tell now when it was trying to fool him. Could tell how much she was Vanessa and how much the Gecko.

'Conductor,' she said. 'That man's got my ticket. Make him give it back to me.'

'Sir,' said Arnold. 'This is a serious matter. May I see that ticket?'

Richard clutched the celluloid in his fist. He wouldn't let Arnold take the Go-Codes. He was with the Gecko.

Vanessa's eye closed and she crumpled. He had a stab of concern for the girl. If she fell badly, hit her head…

Arnold's gaze had a new firmness.

'Sir,' he said, holding up his ticket-clippers. 'The ticket.'

By jumping from the girl to the conductor, the Gecko had got closer to him. But it wore a shape he was less concerned about damaging.

He stuck the Go-Codes into his top pocket, and launched a right cross at Arnold, connecting solidly with his chin, staggering him back a few steps. He'd perfectly hit the knock-out button, but the thing in Arnold didn't pay attention. It lashed out, clipper-jaws open, aiming for an ear or a lip, intent on squeezing out a chunk of face.

Richard ducked and the clippers closed on his sleeve, slicing through scarlet velvet, meeting in the fold. He hit Arnold a few more times, hearing school boxing instructors tell him he shouldn't get angry. In his bouts, he always lost on points or was disqualified, even if he pummelled his opponent insensible. What he did in a fight wasn't elegant or sporting, or remotely allowable under the Queensberry rules. He had learned something in the blanked portion of his childhood.

From a crouch, he launched an uppercut, smashing Arnold's face, feeling cartilage go in the conductor's nose. The clippers hung from Richard's underarm. They opened and fell to the juddering floor, leaving neat holes in his sleeve.

Not above booting a man while he was down, he put all his

frustration into a hefty kick, reinforced toe sinking into Arnold's side, forcing out a Gecko-groan. The conductor emptied.

Then an arm was around Richard's neck. He was dragged to the floor.

Annette's elbow nut-crackered around his throat and her dead face flopped next to his, one eye rolling.

He felt a wave of disgust, not at physical contact with a corpse, but at the abuse of Annette's body. He couldn't fight her as he had Arnold, or even as he had Vanessa (he'd broken a plate on a child's face!) because of what had hung between them until moments ago.

The thing working Annette took the fork out of her throat and held it to Richard's eye.

'The codes,' it said, voice rattling through her ruptured windpipe. 'Now.'

He pressed his hand over his top pocket. He blinked furiously as the fork got close. One jab, and there would be metal in his brain.

This trip was nearly over.

III.

The Gecko inside Annette held Richard in a death-grip, fork-tines hugely out of focus against his eye. Beyond the blur, he saw Arnold watching with his habitual air of quizzical deference. Anything between the passengers was their own business.

Someone shouldered Arnold aside and levelled two double-barrelled shotguns at Richard and Annette.

It was Harry Cutley. Hard-Luck Harry to the Rescue!

'Ah-hah,' declared Harry, a melodrama husband finding his wife in a clinch with her lover, 'ah-bleedin'-hah! I knew Dickie-Boy was a wrong 'un from the first. Hold him steady, Annie and I'll save you!'

It wasn't easy to aim two shotguns at the same time, what with the swaying of the train. Harry couldn't keep them level.

'Annette's not home,' Richard said. 'Look at her eyes.'

Harry ignored him.

He must have broken into the baggage car and requisitioned Mrs Sweet's guns. His pockets were lumpy with cartridges. He had a lifetime of resentments to work off, in addition to being under the influence of the Scotch Streak. Harry still couldn't hold the guns properly, but was close enough to Richard that aiming wouldn't make much difference.

At least the fork had gone away.

The Gecko relaxed a little, holding Richard up as a shield and a target.

Harry saw Vanessa, half her face bruised and bloody.

'I see you can't be trusted on your own,' he said. 'There's a reason I'm Most Valued Member, Clever Dick. I observe at a glance, take in all the clues, puzzle out what has happened, make a snap decision, and act on it, promptly and severely.'

He managed with an effort to get one gun half-cocked, but his left-hand gun twisted up and thumped his face. He flinched as if someone else had attacked him, and pointed the gun he had a better grip on.

Richard shrugged off Annette's dead fingers and stood.

The gun-barrel raised with him.

'Look at Annette, Harry,' he said. 'It got her. It got Danny. It had Vanessa. It's tried to have me. It is trying to get you. You can hear it, can't you? It's talking to you now.'

Richard stood aside, to let Harry see Annette.

The Gecko couldn't get the corpse to stand properly. Her bloodied neck was a congealed ruin. Her bloodless face was slack, empty – only her eye mobile, twitching with alien intellect.

'Annie,' said Harry, shocked, grieving.

'You see,' said Richard, stepping forward. 'We've got to fight it.'

Both guns swung. The barrels jabbed against Richard's chest.

'Stay where you are, young feller-me-lad,' said Harry, fury sparking again. 'I know you're behind this. You may have Ed Winthrop fooled, but not Harry Cutley, oh no. Too clever by half, that's your bloody trouble. Went to a public school, didn't you?'

'Several,' Richard admitted.

'Yes, I can tell. They're all like you, bright boys with no depth, no backbone. Had it too easy, all your lives. Silver spoons up your bums from day one. Never had to work, never had to think. Reckon you can put one over on us all. Smarm out the posh accent and walk away from it.'

Harry was off on his own. With the guns steady, he got all the cocks back.

Annette had pulled herself upright, assisted by Arnold. She puppet-walked towards them.

'Look behind you,' whispered Richard, like a kid at a pantomime.

Harry showed a toothy grin. 'Won't fool me with that one, boy.'

Annette's hands were out, thumbs barbed, nearing Harry's neck. When she gripped, his hands would clench – and four barrels-worth of whatever Mrs Sweet liked to load would discharge through Richard's torso.

'Just this once, do me a favour, Harry, and listen,' said Richard.

The barrels jammed deeper. Richard shut up – he couldn't do anything about his educated accent, which set off Harry's class hatred.

Annette's hands landed, not around Harry's neck, but on his shoulders. He shivered, in instinctive pleasure. He was enjoying himself. He had everyone where he wanted them. He angled his head and rubbed his cheek, like a cat's, on Annette's dead hand.

The Gecko used Annette's face to make a smile and kissed Harry's ear.

It was a miracle the guns didn't go off.

'See, just this once, bright boy, you lose.'

The light in Annette's eyes went out and she was a corpseweight against Harry's back. Harry was bothered, his eyes flickering.

'Don't do that,' he said.

While Harry was distracted, Richard took hold of the barrels and tried to shift them. No dice. Harry shook his head as if trying to see off a buzzing wasp.

Annette fell away, collapsing on the floor.

Harry stepped backwards, his upper body jerking as if the wasps were now pestering in force. The guns slipped away from Richard's chest. He took the opportunity to get out of the way. Harry tripped over Annette's legs and went arse over teakettle.

One of the guns finally went off, blasting a plate-sized hole in the ceiling.

Night air rushed through. Up there somewhere were stars.

Harry, without even knowing what he was doing, resisted the Gecko. So it couldn't take anyone – only unformed minds, long-time Streak freaks, or the newly dead. It could whisper, influence, mislead, work on weaknesses, but couldn't just move in and take over.

Richard sensed the thing's formless anger.

Then Vanessa, standing quietly a dozen feet away, was tagged and was 'it' again. She ran, hopping past Annette, leap-frogging Harry, and soared at Richard, in defiance of gravity, a living missile.

Vanessa's head collided with Richard's stomach, and he was knocked over.

She snatched the celluloid from his pocket, and – with a girlish whoop of nasty triumph – was out of the carriage.

He heard her laugh dwindle as she got further away.

Harry stood, brushing a blood-smear on his jacket. He'd

dropped one of the guns, but had the other under his arm. He flapped his wrung-out hand, still jarred from the discharge. The thumb, broken or dislocated, kinked stiffly.

Another person lumbered into the dining carriage, bulky in shawls, thick-ankled. Richard thought for a moment it was Mrs Sweet come to complain about the ill-treatment of her precious guns, but it was the old dear last seen at Euston. 'Elsa Nickles, Missus, Psychic Medium.'

Mrs Nickles eased past Arnold, who didn't tell her she was out of her class. She looked at the bloody ruins, the dead woman, the mad people.

'I knew no good would come of this,' she said. 'Them spirits is angered, furious. You can't be doin' anythin' wiv 'em when they're stirred up. Might just as well poke an umbrella into a nest of snakes. Or stick your dickybird in a mincer.'

Mentally, Richard told Harry not to shoot the woman.

He could tell the Most Valued Member was thinking of it. Firing guns was addictive. The first time, you were afraid, worried about the noise, the danger, the mess. Then, you wanted to do it again. You wanted to do it better.

Didn't matter if your finger was on the trigger of a .22 bird-blaster or the launch button of an Intercontinental Ballistic Missile, the principle was the same. Didn't even matter what you were aiming at. Pull... point and press! Ka-pow!

'Listen to her, Harry,' he said.

Harry didn't know what Richard meant. Why should he pay attention to some unscientific loon? In Harry Cutley's parapsychology, cranks like Elsa Nickles were the enemy, dragging the field into disreputability, filler for the Sunday papers.

'Listen to her accent,' Richard insisted.

'Oi don't know what 'e means,' said Mrs Nickles, indignant.

Class solidarity in Harry. If Richard's manner got his back up,

Elsie's plain talk – even when spouting nonsense – should soothe him. Of course, she was from London and he was a Northerner. He might hate her just for being Southern, in which case Richard would give up and let the world hang itself.

Harry put the gun down and held up his wonky thumb.

'Cor, that's shockin',' said Mrs Nickles. 'Let me 'ave a butchers. Been a school nurse for twenty years an' never seen a kiddie do that to hisself.'

Harry let the woman examine his hand. She thought for a moment, then took a firm grip on the twisted digit and tugged it into place. Harry yelped, swore, but then flexed his thumb and blurted gratitude.

'That's better,' said Mrs Nickles.

The pain had cleared Harry's mind, Richard hoped.

'We've met the thing behind the haunting,' he told the Most Valued Member. 'It was hiding in the little girl. It tried to possess you, but you fought it off. Do you remember?'

Harry nodded, grimly.

'Continue with the report, Jeperson,' he said.

'It's some sort of discarnate entity…'

'A wicked spirit,' said Mrs Nickles. 'A frightful fiend.'

'Not a ghost. Not the remnant of a human personality. Something bigger, nastier, more primal. But clever. It plucks things from inside you. It understands who we are, how we can be got at. It's simple, though. It does violence. That's its business. Feeds off pain, I think. Call it "the Gecko". When it's in people, they move in a lizardy way. Maybe it nestles in that reptile part of the brain, pulls nerve-strings from there. Or maybe it knows we don't like creepy-crawlies and puts on a horror show.'

'The Gecko,' said Harry, trying out the name. 'I'll make a note of that. You found it, Jeperson. You're entitled to name it.'

'Thank you.'

538

'Now we know what we're up against, we should be better able to cage it. I'll write up the findings and, after a decent interval, we can come back with a larger, more specialist group. We can get your Gecko off the Ghost Train into a spirit box. In captivity, it can be properly studied.'

Richard knew a spirit box wasn't necessarily of wood or metal. If 'sealed' properly, a little girl could be a spirit box.

Looking at Annette, who'd rolled under a table, Richard said, 'If it's all the same, Harry, I'd rather kill it than catch it.'

'We can still learn, Jeperson. How to deal with the next Gecko.'

'Let's cope with this one first.'

Richard's attention was called by the train's rattle. Something had changed.

A whistle–blast sounded. Had there been another ellipsis in time?

'Are we there yet?' asked Harry. 'Portnacreirann?'

'Oh no, sir,' said Arnold, who still didn't acknowledge anything unusual. 'We're slowing to cross Inverdeith Bridge.'

Richard felt the pace of the rattle.

'We're not slowing,' he said. 'We're speeding up.'

IV.

'It was on a night like this, in 1931,' said Mrs Nickles, 'Inverdeith Bridge fell.'

Richard understood why the Gecko had killed Annette. She'd have seen what was coming next.

'We're in no position to make a report and act later,' he told Harry. 'The Gecko's going to kill us now. It has what it wants.'

Harry and Mrs Nickles both looked puzzled.

Richard had a familiar sensation, of knowing more than others, of the power that came with intuition. It was warm, seductive, pleasant – he had the urge to flirt with revelation, to hint that he was privy to mysteries beyond normal comprehension, to crow over his elders. No, that was a temptation – had it been left there to dangle by the Gecko, or some other 'wicked spirit'? Or was it nestled in the reptile remnant of his own brain, a character trait he should keep in check?

'The Go–Codes,' he said. 'It has the number–strings.'

Mrs Nickles nodded, as if she understood – Richard knew she was faking, just to stay in the game. Harry was white, genuinely understanding.

'It was lunacy to send the damned things by train,' said Harry. 'Ed advised against it, but the Club was overruled. By the Americans. Bloody Yanks.'

'Bloody us too, though,' said Richard. 'This might have happened eventually, but it happened tonight because we were aboard. We pushed the Gecko. Which is what it wants. Us extraordinary people. We notice things, but things notice us too. We give it more fuel. If regular folks are lumps of coal, we're gallons of jet fuel. Annette, Danny, you, me.'

'Not me,' said Harry.

Richard shrugged. 'Maybe not.'

'But her?'

Harry looked at Elsa Nickles.

Richard did too, for the first time really. Psychic Medium. A Talent. But she had something else. Knowledge.

'Why are you on the Streak, Mrs Nickles?' he asked.

'I told you. To 'elp the good spirits and chase off the wicked.'

'Fair enough. But there are many haunted places. Ruins you don't have to buy a ticket for. Why the Scotch Streak?'

She didn't want to explain. Harry helped her sit down in a booth. Arnold was eager to fetch her something.

'Gin and tonic, luv,' she said.

The conductor busied himself. Richard hoped the Gecko hadn't left something in Arnold, to spy on them.

The whole carriage shook, from the speed. Crockery, cutlery, roses, anything not held down, bounced, slid, shifted. Air streamed through the hole in the roof, blasting tablecloths into screwed-up shrouds.

Arnold returned, dignified as a silent-movie comedian before a pratfall, drink balanced on a tray balanced on his hand. Mrs Nickles drained the g and t.

'Hits the spot,' she said.

'Why… this… train?' Richard asked.

'Because they're 'ere, still. Both of 'em. They're not what you call "the Gecko", but they made it grow. What they did, what they didn't do, what they felt. That, and all the passengers who drownded. And all who come after, who were took by the train, bled their spirits into it. That's your blessed Gecko, all them spirits mixed up together and shook. It weren't born in 'Ell. It were made. On the night when the bridge fell. Somethin' in the loch woke up, latched onto 'em.'

'Them? Who do you mean?'

'Nick and Don,' she said, a tear dribbling. 'Me 'usband and… well, not me 'usband.'

'Nick… Nickles?'

'Nickles is what you call me pseudernym, ducks. It's Elsa Bowler, really. I was married to Nick Bowler.'

'The Headless Fireman,' said Harry, snapping his fingers.

Mrs Nickles grimaced as about to collapse in sobs. The reminder of her husband's suicide was hardly tactful.

'Don would be the driver, Donald McRidley?' he prompted.

Arnold almost crossed himself at that disgraced name. The conductor fitted into this story somewhere. He looked at Mrs Nickles as if he were a human being with real feelings, rather than an emotionless, efficient messenger of the railway gods.

'Donald,' spat Mrs Nickles. 'Yes, blast 'is 'ide. The Shaggin' Scot, they used to call him. The girls in the canteen. We were all on the railways, on the LSIR. I was there when they named the Scotch Streak, serving drinks. I was Assistant Manager of the staff canteen in '31. Up the end of the line, in Portnacreirann. Don and Nick weren't usually on shift together, but someone was off sick. They were both speedin' towards me that night. I think it came out, while they were togevver in the cabin. About me. The bridge was comin' down, no matter what. But somethin' was goin' on in between Don and Nick. Afterwards, Don scarpered and Nick... well, Nick did what he did, poor lamb. So we'll never know. Don was a right basket. Don't know how I got in with him, though I was a stupid tart in them days and no mistake. Don weren't the only bloke who wasn't me 'usband. Even after all the mess. If you want to call anyone the Gecko's mum, it's me.'

'The driver and the fireman were arguing? Over you?'

Mrs Nickles nodded. Her false teeth jounced, distorting her mouth. Richard's fillings shook. Harry's face rippled. It was as if the Streak were breaking the sound barrier.

The train was going too fast!

'What about the uncoupling?'

'That! No human hand did that. It was your Gecko, come out of the loch and the fires in the 'earts of Don and Nick, reachin' out, like a baby after a first suck of milk. It killed all them passengers, let the carriages loose to go down with the bridge. That was a big meal for it, best it's ever had, gave it strength to live through its first hours. I've lost three kiddies, in hospital. That happened in them days. All the bloody time. One was Don's, I reckon. That little mite's in the Gecko too. It sucked in all the bad feelin', all the spirits, and it's still suckin'.'

Richard understood.

But he saw where Mrs Nickles was lying. 'No human hand.' Maybe the Gecko was partly poltergeist. Using the shake, rattle and rock of the train to nudge inanimate objects. The piano-lid snapping at Danny was classic polter-pestering. But for the big things, the fork-stabbings and grabbing the Go-Codes, it needed human hands, a host, a body or bodies.

'It was both of them,' he said. 'It took them both. It made them do it, made them uncouple the train.'

He saw it, vividly. Two men, in vintage LSIR uniform, crawling past the coal-tender, leaving the cabin unmanned, gripping like lizards, inhumanly tenacious. Four hands on the coupling, tugging the stiff lever which ought not be thrown while the train was in motion, disabling the inhibitor devices that should prevent this very act. Hands bleeding and nails torn, the hosts' pain receptors shut off by the new-made, already cunning, already murderous Gecko.

The coupling unlatched. A gap growing. Between engine and carriages. The awful noise of the bridge giving way. The train screaming as it plunged. Carriages coming apart among clanging girders and rails. Bursts of instantly extinguished flame. Sparks falling to black waters. Breaking waves on the loch shores.

An outpouring of shock and agony. Gecko food.

'Jeperson,' said Harry, snapping his fingers in front of his nose.

'I know what it did,' he told the Most Valued Member. 'What it wants to do. How it plans to do it. Another Inverdeith disaster, all of our deaths, and it can get off the train. Free of the iron of the Scotch Streak, it'll be strong enough to possess living, grown-up bodies. It can piggyback, get to the base, play pass the parcel between hosts, handing the Go-Codes on to itself. It can sit at a modified typewriter keyboard and use the numbers. It's a hophead, needing bigger and bigger fixes. The deaths of dozens don't cut it any more, so it needs to shoot up World War Three!'

Harry swore.

'We've got to stop the little girl,' said Richard. 'Pass me that shotgun.'

V.

At the connecting door, ready to barge after the Gecko, Richard caught himself.

'Fooled me once, shame on you, fooled me twice, shame on me.'

He turned and walked deliberately to the other end of the dining carriage, past Harry, Mrs Nickles and Arnold.

'That's the wrong way, Jeperson.'

'Is it?'

'I came from that way. Back there is, ah, second and third class. And the baggage car.'

Harry held up the other shotgun, left-handed.

'Things change. Haven't you noticed?'

Harry wasn't stupid or inexperienced. 'Dislocation phenomena? Escher space?'

'Topsy-turvy,' Richard said.

'How do you know the configuration won't switch back? The Gecko could keep us off balance, charging back and forth, always the wrong way? At Wroxley Parsonage in '52, there was a corridor like that, a man-trap. The MVM before me lost two of his group in it.'

Jeperson was given pause.

He looked up through the hole in the ceiling, at telephone wires, clouds, the sky. He could tell which way the train was travelling but lost that certainty if he stepped too far away from the hole. The windows were no help. They might have been painted over or gooed on. A rifle-stock blow rattled but did not break the glass.

'There's a spirit 'ere 'oo wants to speak,' said Mrs Nickles.

Harry was impatient. 'There are too many spirits here.'

'This is a new one, mate. I'm gettin'... ah... fingers?'

'Magic Fingers?' said Harry, suddenly taking the woman seriously. 'Danny Myles? What's happened to him?'

'Lost, Harry,' said Richard. This was news to the Most Valued Member.

'Damn.'

''E says, don't think, feel... Does that make sense?'

To Richard, it did. He shut his eyes and in the dark inside his head sensed Danny, or something left behind by Danny. He stopped trying to work out which way the train was speeding, just let his body become aware of the movement, the rattle, the shifting. He had little thrills, like tugging hooks or pointing arrows.

'Spin me round,' he said.

'Like the party game?' asked Mrs Nickles.

He nodded. Big hands took him and spun him. He went up on the points of his shoes, remembering two weeks of ballet training, and revolved like a human top.

He came to a stop without falling.

He knew which way to charge and did so, opening his eyes on the way. He didn't even know which end of the carriage he was exiting from. He opened the communication door and plunged on, as if Mrs Sweet's gun were a divining rod.

The others followed.

VI.

Richard knew Danny was tied here, along with many others. Magic Fingers was fresh enough to have some independence, but soon he'd be sucked in and become another head of a collective pain-eating hydra. The Scotch Streak was home to a Bad Thing. Haunting a house, or a lonely road or public toilet or whatever, seldom meant more than floating sheets or clammy invisible touches. The worst haunters, the Bad Things, were monsters with ambition. They wanted to be free of the anchors that kept them earth-bound, not to ascend to a higher sphere or rest in peace or go into the light... but to wreak harm. Plague-and-Great-Fire-of-London harm. Japanese-Radioactive-Dinosaur-Movie harm. End-of-all-Things harm.

He was in a carriage he hadn't seen before but didn't doubt he was on the track of the Gecko.

There were no windows, not even black glass. Hunting trophies on shields – antlers and heads of antlered animals – stuck out of panelled walls, protruding as if bone were growing like wood, making the aisle as difficult to penetrate as a thick thorn forest. There were rhino-horns and elephant tusks, even what looked like a sabre-tooth tiger-head with still-angry eyes. Low-slung leather armchairs were spaced at intervals, between foot-high side-tables where dust-filled brandy snifter glasses were abandoned next to ashtrays with fat cigar grooves. Potent, manly musk stung Richard's nostrils.

'What's this?' he asked Arnold, appalled.

'The Club Car, sir. Reserved for friends of the Director, Lord Kilpartinger. It's not usually part of the rolling stock.'

In one chair slumped a whiskered skeleton wearing a bullet-bandolier, Sam Browne belt and puttees. It gripped a rifle-barrel with both hands, a loose toe-bone stuck in the trigger-guard, gun-mouth jammed between blasted-wide skull-jaws, the cranium exploded away.

'Any idea who that was?' asked Richard.

'He's in Catriona's pamphlet,' put in Harry. '"Basher" Moran, 1935. Some aged, leftover Victorian colonel. Big-game hunter and gambling fiend. Stalked anything and everything, put holes in it and dragged hide, head or horns home to stick on the wall. Mixed up in extensive crookery, according to Catriona, wriggled out of a hanging more than once. He's here because he won his final bet. One of his jolly old pals wagered he couldn't find anything in the world he hadn't shot before. He proved his friend wrong, there and then.'

An upturned pith-helmet several feet away contained bone and dum-dum fragments.

'Case closed.'

'Too true. They made a film about Moran and the train, *Terror By Night*.'

Richard advanced carefully, between trophies, tapping too-persistent horns out of the way with the gun-barrel.

'Could do with a machete,' he commented. 'Careful of barbs.'

The train took a series of snake-curve turns, swinging alarmingly from side to side. A narwhal horn dimpled Richard's velvet shoulder.

Richard heard Harry ouch as he speared himself on an antler-point.

'Just a scratch,' he reported. 'Doesn't hurt as much as my bloody hand.'

'Shouldn't ought to be allowed,' said Mrs Nickles. 'Shootin' poor animals as never did no one no harm.'

'I rather agree with you,' said Richard. 'Hunting should be saved for man-killers.'

Gingerly, they got through the club car without further casualties.

The next carriage was the dining car, again. Harry wanted to give up, but Richard pressed on.

'Table-settings here are the other way round,' he said. 'It's not the same.'

'There ain't no bleedin' great 'ole in the roof neither,' observed Mrs Nickles.

'That too.'

'We shall be pleased to serve a light breakfast after Inverdeith,' announced Arnold. 'For those who wish to arrive at Portnacreirann refreshed and invigorated.'

'Kippers later,' said Richard. 'After the world-saving.'

Beyond this dining car was first class. Richard led them past the sleeping compartments. Annette's door hung open: her night-gown was laid out on the counterpane, like a cast-off silk snakeskin. That was a thump to the heart.

The decoy couriers snored away. No need to bother them.

Another expedition was coming down the corridor towards them. Were they so turned around in time they were running into themselves? Or had evil duplicate ghost-finders emerged from the wrong-way-round dimension where knives and forks were right-to-left? No, there was a mirror at the end of the corridor. Score one for eliminating the impossible.

'Where's the connecting door?' Richard asked the conductor.

'There's no need for one, sir,' said Arnold. 'Beyond is only the coal tender, and the locomotive. Passengers may not pass beyond this point.'

The Gecko had managed, though.

One of the doors flapped, swinging open, banging back. Cold air streamed in, like water through a salmon's gills.

Richard pushed the door and leaned out of the carriage, keeping a firm grip on the frame.

Below, a gravel verge sped by. To the east, the scarlet rim of dawn outlined a black horizon. Up ahead, 3473-S rolled over the rails, pistons pumping, everything oiled and watered and fired.

An iron girder came up, horribly fast. Richard ducked back in.

'We're on the bridge,' he said.

Before anyone could object, if they were going to, he threw himself out of the door.

Clinging to the side of the carriage, it occurred to Richard that someone else might have volunteered to crawl – essentially one-handed, since shotguns don't have useful shoulder-slinging straps like field-rifles – along the side of a speeding steam train.

Harry had seniority and responsibility, but his injured hand disqualified him. Mrs Nickles was too hefty, overage, and a woman besides. And the conductor was not entirely of their party. The Gecko had fitted into him much too snugly. There was more mystery to Arnold – a streak of sneakiness, of evasion, of tragedy. Richard had noticed a spark in his mild eyes as Mrs Nickles was talking about the good old days of the LSIR, about the Shagging Scot and the Headless Fireman and the In-for-Death Run of '31.

So, the train-crawling was down to him.

Once he'd swung out on the door, he eased himself around so he was hanging outside the train, blasted by the air-rush, deafened by the roar. About eight feet of carriage was left before the coupling. That was a mystery – a compartment not accessible to the passengers. No, it wasn't a mystery – it was a toilet and washroom for the driver and the fireman, reachable by a wide, safe running-board along the side of the coal tender, with guard-rails and hand-holds he would just now have greatly appreciated on this carriage.

Above him, however, were loops of red chain – the communication cord. Richard grabbed a loop and held tight. The whistle shrilled over the din of the train. Cold chain bit into his palm. He should have put gloves on.

He dangled one-handed, trusting the chain to take his weight, back against the carriage, and saw glints on the dark waters of Loch Gaer several hundred feet below. Down there were the angry spirits of Jock McGaer's 'graysome' dinners, the drowned Inverdeith Witches and the cut-loose passengers of '31 – they must all be wrapped up in the Gecko too. Not to mention the "stoon o' fire spat out frae hell" of 1601. This had all started with that.

The flimsy-seeming bridge, he reminded himself, was the sturdy structure put up to replace the one that fell down. Girders flashed past, faster and faster. He used the stock of the gun to push himself along, and the barrel caught on a girder. The gun was wrenched out of his hand, twisted into a U-shape, and dropped into the loch. Mrs Sweet had made a special point of telling Arnold to look after her artillery. A stiff complaint would be made to British Rail in the next day or two, providing there was a next day or two.

With both hands free, it was easier to travel from loop to loop. He'd think about how to deal with the Gecko without a weapon when he got to it. A sound rap on the nose didn't seem likely to do the trick.

The door clanged shut behind him. Harry and Mrs Nickles hung out of the open window, fixed expressions of encouragement plastered on anxious faces.

He fought the harsh wind, cruel gravity, hot spits of steam and cinder, and his own clumsiness. Something shaped like a little girl had done this earlier, he knew. The Gecko could probably stick to the side of the train, like a real lizard.

Eight feet. A hard eight feet. The skirts of his frock coat lashed his thighs. He had no feeling in his hands, but blood dripped from weals across his palms. He reached out for the next loop, the last, and his fist closed on nothing, then locked. He had to force his hand open and look up, hooking nerveless, perhaps boneless fingers over the loop. He saw his grip, but couldn't feel it. He didn't want to let go of the hold he was sure of. But if he didn't, he was stuck. He reached out his leg, which didn't quite stretch enough to hook over the guardrail. His boot-sole scraped tarnished brass. His cuff was sodden with his own blood. With a prayer to higher powers, he let go the sure hold, put all his weight on the unsure one, and swung towards the platform.

He made it and found his feet on a veranda-like platform at the end of the carriage. He shook with fear and weakness and relief. Feeling came back, unwelcome, to his bloodied hand.

Between the carriage and the locomotive was the big, heavy coupling. Black iron thickened with soot and grease.

On the coupling squatted the Gecko. Only the braids and oily pyjamas even suggested this was still Vanessa. It was goblin filth on a poison toadstool, a gremlin dismantling an aero-engine in flight, the imp in Fuseli's *Nightmare* hovering over a sleeping maiden.

With stubby-fingered, black hands, it picked at the coupling.

The Gecko looked up, eyes round, nostrils like slits. It hissed at Richard.

Blasts of steam came, surrounding them both with scalding fog. The whistle shrieked again.

In the coal tender, nearly empty this close to the destination, rolled two bodies, the driver and the engineer. They were sooty, with red torn-out throats. No one was at the open throttle.

Richard shook hot water off his face, which began to sting. He'd be red as a cooked lobster.

He grabbed the Gecko by the shoulders. He held folds of Vanessa's pyjama top and pulled.

It gnawed his wrists.

Things hadn't all gone the monster's way. In 1931, it had unhooked the coupling at this point on the bridge. Now, it was using one little girl's hands rather than two experienced men's. The Gecko could give its hosts strengths, ignore their injuries, distort their faces... but it couldn't increase a handspan, or make tiny fingers work big catches.

The Gecko tried to take Richard and he shrugged it off.

They were more than halfway across the bridge.

'No room here,' he told it. 'No room anywhere for you. Why not quit?'

Vanessa slumped in his grip, hands relaxing on the coupling. Richard picked her up, pressed her face to his chest.

'Can't breathe,' she said, in her own voice.

This was too easy.

In the coal tender, two bodies sat up and began to crawl towards Richard and Vanessa. The Gecko had found experienced railwaymen's hands. This was where having a shotgun would have been useful – he doubted he could shoot Vanessa, even if he had smashed a plate in her face, but he'd have no compunction about blasting a couple of already-dead fellows.

The Gecko had no trouble working both corpses at the same time, which meant there was probably still some of it in the child. It had been hatched in the driver's cabin of 3473, and was at its strongest here.

The fireman threw a lump of coal, which broke against the carriage behind Richard's head. The driver clambered off the tender, down to the coupling platform. There was a lever there, its restraints undone.

The bridge might not come down, but at this speed and gradient the uncoupled carriages would concertina, come off the rails, break through the girders, fall into the loch.

There was a lot of dawnlight in the sky now.

Holding Vanessa close, he felt something in the hankie pocket of her pyjamas. He shifted her weight to his left shoulder, freeing his right hand to pluck out the Go-Codes.

He held the celluloid up in the rush of air, then let it go, snatched away, up and over the lake, sailing towards Inverdeith. One of the most closely guarded military secrets in the world was tossed into the wind.

'You should have committed the Go-Codes to memory,' he told the monster.

The Gecko's corpse puppets opened throats and yelled, like the whistle. Then, the whistle itself sounded. The Gecko wasn't only in the driver and the fireman. It clothed itself in the iron of the locomotive, the brass-trim and scabby purple paint. Its fury burned in the furnace. Its frustration built up a seam-splitting head of steam. Its hunger ate up the rails.

Richard thought he'd saved the world, but not himself.

'What's keeping you here?' he asked.

Dead hands reached the uncoupling lever. Richard slid his cut-throat razor out of his sleeve and flicked it open. He drew the edge swiftly, six or seven times, across greasy, blackened meat, cutting muscle-strings.

The corpse's hands hung useless, fingers flopping against the lever like sausages. The corpse was suddenly untenanted, and crumpled, falling over the coupling, arms dangling.

The Scotch Streak was safely across Inverdeith Bridge.

VIII.

The fireman lay dead, empty of the Gecko.

It was just in the train now. The Scotch Streak's lamps glowed a wicked red.

World War Three was off, unless the Gecko could somehow let the Soviets know NATO's trousers were down. But everyone on the train could still be killed.

At this speed, slamming into the buffers at Portnacreirann would mean a horrific pile-up. Or the Scotch Streak might plough through the station, and steam down Portnacreirann High Street and over a cliff. Like Colonel Moran, the Gecko was intent on spiteful suicide. It could carry them all with it, in fire and broken metal.

Richard knew Diogenes Club procedure. Solve the problem, no matter the cost. His father had told him from the first this was a life of service, of sacrifice. Every Member, every Talent, gave up something. Danny and Annette weren't the first to lose their lives.

It might be a fair trade.

'Are we nearly there?' Vanessa asked, laying her head on his shoulder. 'I'm very sleepy.'

He felt the weight of the child in his arms. He had to carry the fight through. For her. He only had a half-life, snatched from a void. He should have been dead many times over. There was a reason he'd survived his childhood. Maybe it was Vanessa. She had to be saved, not sacrificed.

'There's one thing left to do,' he told her. 'Have you ever wanted to drive a choo–choo train?'

She laughed at him. 'Only babies say "choo–choo"!'

'Chuff-chuff, then.'

Vanessa's giggle gave him the boost he needed, though he was still terrified. While facing demon-possessed zombies and nuclear holocaust, he'd misplaced his fear. Now, he was in charge of a runaway train, funk seeped back into his stomach. He found he was trembling.

He set the girl down safely and stepped over the dead driver, climbed the ladder to the coal tender, passed the dead fireman and got to the cabin. The furnace door clanked open. Levers and wheels swayed or rolled with the train's movement.

It occurred to him that he didn't know how to stop a train.

'Can I sound the whistle?' asked Vanessa. She had followed, monkeying over the coal tender, unfazed by dead folk. She found the whistle-pull, easily.

Richard absent-mindedly said she could and looked about for switches with useful labels like 'pull to slow down' or 'emergency brakes'. He heard the Gecko's chuckle in the roll of coal in the furnace. It knew exactly the pickle he was in.

Vanessa blew the whistle, three long bursts, three short bursts, three long bursts. What every schoolchild knew in Morse code. SOS. Save Our Souls. Help! Mayday. *M'aidez!* Richard wasn't sure she even understood it was a distress signal, it was likely the only Morse she knew.

The sun was almost up. The sky was the colour of blood.

Ahead, the rails curved across open space, towards Portnacreirann Station.

'I can see the sea,' shouted Vanessa, from her perch.

Richard muttered that they might be making rather too close acquaintance with the sea – rather, Loch Linnhe – in a minute or two.

'Here comes someone,' said Vanessa.

More trouble, no doubt! He looked back and couldn't see anything.

He was reluctant to leave the cabin, though he admitted he was useless at the throttle, but surrendered to an impulse. He was sensitive: he should trust his feelings while he had them. He made his way back past the tender.

The door to the staff toilet was open and Arnold stood with a fire-axe. He had smashed through the mirror. Mrs Nickles was behind him. And Harry Cutley. Richard kicked himself for not thinking of that, but hadn't known there was a door beyond the mirrored partition.

Arnold raised the axe and Richard knew the Gecko had its hook in him, had been reeling him in like trout. Mrs Nickles shouted something. They hadn't come in response to the SOS.

Now, in addition to the runaway train, he had an axe-wielding madman to deal with.

Richard dashed back to the cabin. Arnold leaped across the coupling, treading on his dead colleague, and followed.

The conductor was the full Gecko now. Richard had a razor against an axe.

He pulled the first lever that came to hand. Instinct paid off. A burst of steam pushed Arnold back, knocking him to his knees. Richard kicked at the axe-head and wrenched the weapon out of the conductor's hands. He took hold of the man's throat and held up his fist, enjoying the look of inhuman panic – the Gecko in terror! – in Arnold's eyes, then clipped him smartly, bang on the button. This time, fortune was with him. The Gecko's light went out. Arnold slumped in Richard's grip, blood creeping from his nose.

Mrs Nickles had followed Arnold. She clung to the hand-rail.

'It's Donald,' she shouted. 'Donald McRidley. I didn't recognise the blighter without 'is 'air. 'E were a ruddy woman about his blessed beautiful 'air when 'e were the Shaggin' Scot, an' now 'e's a bald-bonced old git.'

Arnold's – Donald's! – eyes fluttered open.

So, he wasn't a navvy. Or not any more. He was back on his train. Unable to get away, Richard supposed. No wonder.

'Driver,' he shouted. 'Bring in the Streak!'

'Passengers aren't allowed in this part of the train, sir,' he mumbled. 'It's against regulations. The company can't be held responsible for accidents.'

Richard saw the red glint, the Gecko creeping back. He slapped McRidley, hard. The eyes were clear for a moment.

'Time to stop the train,' he told the man. 'Do your duty, at last. Redeem your name.'

'Do it for Elsie, ducks,' said Mrs Nickles, cooing in McRidley's ear. 'Do it for poor Nick. For the LSI-bloody-R.'

McRidley broke free of the pair of them.

As if sleepwalking in a hurry, mind somewhere else, he pulled levers, rolled wheels, tapped gauges.

The station was dead ahead, sunlight flashing on its glass roof. Wheels screamed on rails. Vanessa tooted the whistle happily.

Harry was with them now, arm in a makeshift sling, hair awry. Every boy wanted to be in the cabin of a steam train.

They all had to hang onto something as McRidley braced himself.

Sparks showered the platform, startling an early-morning porter. The buffers loomed.

They did not crash. But there was a heavy jolt.

IX.

Donald McRidley, Arnold the conductor, was dead. When the train stopped, so did he – like grandfather and the clock in the song.

3473-S was decoupled now and shunted into a siding. The Gecko was still nestled in there, but its conduit to the train, to the passengers, was cut. Richard thought it might have been the communication cord, which had to be unhooked – but the monster had also been tied to the lifeline of the once-disgraced, now-redeemed driver.

''E were an 'andsome devil,' commented Mrs Nickles, putting her teeth back in. 'Loved 'is train more than any girl, though.'

Harry was on the telephone to Edwin Winthrop. He said the entity was in captivity, but Richard knew the Gecko was dying. As the fire went out in 3473's belly, the monster gasped its last. A bad beast, Danny had called it. The iron shell would just be a trophy. They should hang the cow-catcher in the Diogenes Club.

The decoy couriers were gone, off to the NATO base. Mrs Sweet was marching down to the baggage car, where a surprise awaited. The terrifying vicar looked even more ghastly in the light of day. Richard had brushed past the man several times, mind open for any ill-omen, to convince himself the Gecko wasn't sneaking off in this vessel to work its evil anew.

Police and ambulances were on their way. Edwin would have words in ears, to account for Danny, Annette and the crewmen, not to mention general damage. Richard found Annette rolled under a table, and carried her to her compartment, where he laid her out on her bed, over her night-gown, eyes closed.

A straight-backed American civilian, with teeth like Burt Lancaster and a chin-dent like Kirk Douglas, scouted along the platform.

'Buddy, have you seen a parcel?' he said. 'For Coates?'

Richard tried to answer, but no words came.

The American looked further, walking past Vanessa.

EPILOGUE: PORTNACREIRANN

The train finally came, as Richard finished telling the story.

They had been up all night. Cold Saturday dawn had broken.

Now, they sat in a carriage, not a compartment. Fred settled in, but Richard was restless.

'I used to love trains,' he said. 'Even after my Ghost Train ride. It was a nice way to travel. You had time and ease, to read or talk or look out the window. Now, it's all strikes and delays. This might as well be a motor-coach. She hates trains, you know. Mrs Thatcher. To her, anyone who travels on public transport is a failure, beneath contempt. She's going to bleed the railways. It'll be horrid. Like so much else.'

Fred still had questions.

'So, guv, who is Vanessa?'

Richard shrugged. 'Vanessa is Vanessa, Fred. Like me, she's no real memory of who she was, if she was anyone. In my case, there was a war, a decade of chaos. It was easy to get misplaced, left out of the records. With her... well, it shouldn't have been possible. Someone dropped her off at Euston with a label round her neck. A woman, she thought, but not her mother. Surely, she couldn't be a stray, she must belong to someone?'

'What about that Coates bloke? The Yank at Portnacreirann.'

'That wasn't "Lieutenant-Commander Alexander Coates, RN". That was a Colonel Christopher Conner, SAC. "Coates" wasn't an alias or a code – just a name on a label. Winthrop made enquiries. The only "Alexander Coates" even remotely in the Navy was a fourteen-year-old sea-scout. We looked into the system of couriering the Go-Codes. The Americans had only given us the cover story even when they'd wanted help, so we threw a bit of a sulk. They eventually admitted – and this is how strange defence policy is – that they had, as they said, "contracted out". Hired a private firm to make delivery, not telling them what was being carried. The firm turned out to be a phone in an empty room with six weeks' rent in arrears. Maybe some semi-crook was hauling kids out of orphanages and bundling them up to Scotland under official cover, then selling them on or disposing of them. We'll never know and, in the end, it was beside the point.'

'You adopted Vanessa?'

'No. No one adopted her, unless you count the Diogenes Club.'

'Does she have a surname?'

'Not really. Where it's absolutely necessary, it's "Kaye". Catriona took an interest, as she did in me. Without her, we'd be complete freaks.'

Fred kept quiet on that one.

'What about the Gecko? Harry Cutley?'

'The Gecko died, if it could be said to have lived. When 3473-S turned into cold scrap iron, it was gone. Puff. Harry poked around with his instruments before giving up. For a year or two, another old steamer pulled the Scotch Streak. Then it went diesel. Harry dropped out in 1967. Went to Nepal. And I became the Most Valued Member. There's a ceremony. Very arcane. Like the Masons. You know most of what's happened since.'

Fred thought it through.

He did know most of the stories, but not all. Despite ten years' involvement with the Diogenes Club, with Richard and Vanessa, there were mysteries. They could both still surprise him. Once, in a close, tense, unexpected moment, before Fred met Zarana, he and Vanessa had kissed, deeply and urgently. She said, 'You do know I'm a man,' and, for dizzying seconds, he had believed her. Then she giggled, they were back in danger, and anything further between them cut off.

After a decade, he still didn't know if Richard and Vanessa had ever been a couple. Everyone else assumed, but he didn't. Now, knowing about the Ghost Train, he saw how complex their entanglement was: a kinship of siblings, raised under the aegis of a unique institution, but also guardianship, as Richard brought Vanessa into the circle the way his adoptive father had brought him. The only thing he really knew now that had been mystifying before was how Vanessa had got her eyebrow scar. Richard had given it to her.

Lately, Vanessa had been absent a great deal. So had Fred, of course – with Zarana, or at the Yard. But Vanessa had been on missions, cases, sealed-knot and under-the-rose business. A change was coming in the Club. When Richard took a seat on the Cabal, as seemed inevitable, was Vanessa in line to become Most Valued Member? There was a woman Prime Minister, so no reason why a woman couldn't hold that title. If she wanted it – which, Fred realised, he didn't know she did.

For three months, there'd been no word. While Richard and Fred were tracking cornflakes cultists, she was somewhere else, unavailable. Fred could tell Richard was concerned, though confident in the woman. She'd survived a lot since throwing off the Gecko. Now, this summons.

...to Portnacreirann.

'It's not over, is it?' said Fred. 'It can't be coincidence that it's the same place.'

Richard gave a non-committal pfui.

'We're at Inverdeith,' he said. 'And that's a Portnacreirann train on the other side of the platform.'

They were off one train before it had completely stopped and on another already moving out.

And then Inverdeith Bridge. Sun glinted on the surface of Loch Gaer.

'This is where the Gecko was born,' said Richard. 'Between Nick Bowler and Donald McRidley and 3473-S. And that "stoon o' fire spat out frae hell", if I'm any judge – which I am. The stoon was an egg, waiting for the right circumstances to hatch. All the other bloody business around the loch was influenced by the unborn thing. Maybe it was an alien, not a demon. The stoon was what we'd now call a meteorite, after all. From outer space. Witch-drownings and human haggis kept the embryo on a drip-feed for centuries, but it awaited a vehicle – literally. The shell-shards might still be down there. Maybe it was a clutch of eggs.'

Fred looked at untroubled waters. This local train proceeded slowly over the bridge. He saw rust on the girders where paint had flaked away, missing rivets, spray-can 'Independent Scotland' graffiti, scratched swear-words.

'In-for-Death,' he said.

'Think calm thoughts, Frederick. And we'll be safe.'

This was where it had happened. With that thought, Fred had a chill. He didn't only mean this was where the Gecko was born and defeated, but this was where Richard and Vanessa had started. When Richard got on the Ghost Train, he'd been a kid himself. When he got off...

Past the bridge, with Portnacreirann in sight and passengers taking luggage down from overhead racks, Fred's insides went tight. They had been delayed. What if they were too late? What was so urgent anyway? He had learned to be ready for anything. But what kind of anything was there at Portnacreirann?

'Did you bring your elephant gun, guv?'

Richard snorted at that.

They got off the train, carrying their bags.

They walked along the platform and into the station. It was busier than Culler's Halt, but emptied quickly.

A centrepiece of the station was an old steam engine, restored and polished, with a plaque and a little fence around it.

Richard froze. It was 3473-S, the locomotive that had pulled the Scotch Streak, the Ghost Train, the favoured physical form of the Gecko. Now, it was just a relic. No danger at all. A youth in naval dress uniform was admiring it. He turned and saw them.

'Mr Jeperson, Mr Regent,' he said. 'Glad you made it in time. Cutting it close, but we'll get you to the base by breaking petty road-safety laws. Come on.'

The officer trotted out of the station. Fred and Richard followed, without further thought for 3473-S.

A jeep and driver waited on the forecourt. The officer helped them up. Fred had a pang at being treated as if he were elderly when he was only just used to thinking of himself as 'early middle aged'. It happened more and more lately.

'I'm Jim,' said the boy in uniform. 'Al's cousin. We're a navy family. Put down for ships at birth like some brats are for schools. In the sea-scouts as soon as we're teething. I hope your lady knows what she's getting into.'

Fred and Richard looked at each other, not saying anything.

'We all think she's rather super, you know. For her age.'

'We admire her qualities, too,' said Richard.

Fred had a brief fantasy of tossing Jim out of the jeep to watch him bounce on the road.

They travelled at speed down a winding lane. Three cyclists with beards and cagoules pedalling the other way wound up tangled in the verge, shaking fists as Jim blithely shouted out 'Sorry!' at them. 'Naval emergency,' he explained, though they couldn't hear.

Whatever trouble Vanessa was in, Fred was ready to fight.

The jeep roared through a checkpoint. The ratings on duty barely lifted the barrier in time. Jim waved a pass at them, redundantly.

They were on the base.

It had been a fishing village once, Fred saw – the rows of stone cottages were old and distinctive. Prefab services buildings fitted in around the original community. The submarine-launched 'independent deterrent' was a Royal Navy show now. NATO – i.e. the Yanks – preferred intercontinental ballistic missiles they could lob at the Soviets from their own backyards in Kansas, or bombs dropped from the planes that could be scrambled from the protestor-fringed base at Greenham Common. There would still be Go-Codes, though.

The base was on alert. Sailors with guns rushed about. There were rumours of trouble in the South Atlantic. Naval budget cuts had withdrawn forces from the region so suddenly that a South American country, say Argentina, could easily get the wrong idea. It might be time to send a gun-boat to remind potential invaders that the Falklands remained British. If there were any gun-boats left.

The jeep did a tight turn to a halt, scattering gravel in front of a small building. Once the village church, it was now the base chapel.

'Just in time,' said Jim, jumping down.

He opened the big door tactfully, so as not to disturb a service inside, and signalled for Fred and Richard to yomp in after him.

Fred remembered Richard leading him into a deconsecrated church at dead of midnight to stop a then-Cabinet minister intent on slitting the throat of a virgin choirboy in a ritual supposed to revive the British moulded plastics industry. The minister was resigned through ill-health and packed off to the House of Lords to do no further harm. The choirboy was now in the pop charts dressed as a pirate, singing as if his throat really had been cut. This wasn't like that, but a ritual was in progress.

No one in the congregation gave the newcomers a glance. Jim led Fred and Richard to places in a pew on the bride's side of the church. They found themselves sitting next to Catriona Kaye, and her nurse. All the others from her day – Edwin, Sir Giles – were gone. Barbara Corri was there too, in a cloud of ylang-ylang with her hair done like Lady Diana Spencer's. Even Inspector Price of the Yard, sporting a smart new mac. Fred looked around, knowing the other shoe would drop. Yes, Zarana, in some incredible dress, was at the front, clicking away with a spy camera lifted from Fred's stash of surveillance equipment.

'We got telegrams,' whispered Professor Corri, fingers around Richard's arm.

Vanessa stood at the altar, red hair pinned up under the veil, in a white dress with a train. Beside her stood a navy officer Fred had never seen before. He couldn't focus on the groom's face for the glare of his uniform. He even had the dress-sword on his belt and plumed helmet under his arm.

'How did this happen?' Fred asked, no one in particular.

'A loose end, long neglected,' whispered Catriona. 'Not that it explains anything…'

She dabbed a hankie to the corner of her eye.

Fred looked at Richard. The man was crying and Fred had absolutely no idea what he was feeling.

Fred looked at the altar, at the naval chaplain.

'Do you, Alexander Selkirk Coates take this woman, Vanessa, ah, No Surname Given, to be your lawfully wedded wife?'

Fred looked up at the vaulted ceiling, gob-smacked.

⇥⇥ SWELLHEAD ⇤⇤

ACT 1: 'ARNE SAKNUSSEMM, HIS SIGN'
1.

'Bloodybuggerinmixmaster…' said Richard Jeperson.

Detective Sergeant Stacy Cotterill looked across the troop compartment at the man from the Diogenes Club. Since take-off from the Air-Sea Rescue helipad, he'd been sitting quietly, secured by webbing which reminded her of a strait-jacket. He wore a dayglo orange oilskin poncho with reflective road-safety trim, folded newspaper hat that was actually a PVC sou'wester with a novelty design, padded plaid jumpsuit with multiple pockets and pouches, and lemon-yellow moon boots with chemical lights in the heels.

For his first enigmatic pronouncement in hours, Jeperson didn't seem to need to raise his voice. Stacy heard him clearly over the chopping whirr of rotors, through the big blue baffles everyone wore to protect their ears.

'…blong Jesus Christ,' Jeperson added, emphatically.

She wondered if, in addition to everything she'd been briefed on, the old man had Tourette's syndrome.

Onions ('O-nye-ons,' he had insisted, understandably) looked up, as if jolting awake inside his expensive parka. Stacy noticed he always kept half an eye on Jeperson, like a bear sharing a cave with a languid adder. Onions adjusted his baffles, exposing an ear.

She glanced around. None of the others were interested.

Mr Head munched a Lion bar, fixated on *Petesuchis*, a high-end crossword magazine. The little man, whose boiled-egg baldpate and wide watery eyes suggested something without bones, did not fill in a puzzle, just solved all the clues mentally, left the grid virginal, and proceeded to the next, more challenging page. Onions had told her *Petesuchis* scorned newsstand distribution. The publishers set an entrance exam for the subscription list, charging on a sliding scale, lower price for higher grades. Adam Onions paid a thousand pounds a year for thirteen slim numbers; Sewell Head got his for free.

Persephone Gill, the Droning of Skerra, wore tiny walkman earclips under her baffles, nodding serenely to something bland. Once she got past the notations in 'Percy' Gill's file ('twenty-one years old, inheritrice of the most unearned wealth in the United Kingdom, no educational qualifications'), Stacy was still venomously glad the girl had been voted out of the mansion at the first cull of Channel 4's *Posh Big Brother*.

Franklin Yoland, the tech guy, gripped his webbing, white-faced and praying for deliverance. He suffered from airsickness and flight terrors, perhaps not ideal qualities in an editor of *Jane's Book of Air-Launched Weapons*.

'I'd been trying to remember,' Jeperson explained to Stacy. 'You know what it's like when you have something in your head but can't fish it out. The name of a tune you hear in a fresh arrangement. The new capital city of a country that's changed its name. Whether Dante ranks virtuous pagans above or below Christian hypocrites in Hell. Pidgin English for "helicopter".'

Through a floor-set Plexiglas bubble that sealed a gunport, she saw the arrowheaded shadow of the Royal Navy Sea King Mk4 rushing across the Norwegian Sea at 100 knots. Crescents of sunglint flashed on roofslate-grey waters. Lieutenant de Maltby, the pilot, was flying them almost at wave-level, under radar.

'Bloodybuggerinmixmaster blong Jesus Christ.'

Jeperson nodded to himself, happy that his pidgin vocabulary was filed away neatly. In London, Chief Inspector Regent had told her Richard Jeperson knew more arcane facts than anyone alive, but that whole years were missing from his memory banks. Stacy supposed that if she lost her primary-school years or Thatcher's second term, she'd be as concerned as Jeperson with accessing what was left in her skull. Still, he wasn't someone she was comfortable around. She wondered again why she'd drawn this duty.

'What's that?' asked Onions, voice raised.

'Nothing important,' said Jeperson, dismissing the enquiry with a flutter of long fingers. 'Are we there yet?'

Jeperson perfectly mimicked the stereotypical whine of a bored child on a long car journey. His prog-rock moustache, coal-black but flashed white at the corners, twitched with amusement.

It took Onions long seconds to tumble that he was being spoofed. He looked at the plastic-wrapped chart in his mittened paws before he got the joke, then made a sour face.

'Very mature,' he commented.

Jeperson gave Stacy a private eyebrow-wiggle. She almost warmed to him.

Onions detached himself from the webbing and, unsteady as an astronaut going EVA, hauled himself down the compartment to confer with (i.e. nag) Lieutenant de Maltby.

'Cuppa char, sir?' asked Aircrewman Kydd, a cockney gnome. His duties obviously included keeping the passengers from distracting the driver while the bus was in motion.

Kydd held out a Thermos, face arranged into a feral smile.

Onions hung from hand-holds, unsure.

'I'd care for some tea, if that's all right,' said Jeperson. 'And maybe the ladies...'

Kydd, who knew a proper gent when he saw one, delivered

568

a real smile and a salute. He had different flasks for English breakfast, orange pekoe and lapsang souchong.

'Best not bother the Viscount,' Jeperson told Onions. 'He probably has a lot on his mind, what with avoiding diplomatic offence to our esteemed allies in Oslo or Reykjavik. Last thing we need is another Cod War.'

Lieutenant de Maltby was Viscount Henry de Maltby, somewhere in the mid-thirties in line of succession to the throne. He had the House of Windsor habit of being unable to string together a sentence without saying 'uhhhm'. It was not settled whether Debrett (or Dante) reckoned the Viscount more or less royal than the Droning of Skerra, but in this party of geniuses and idiots he was the one Stacy felt herself level with in the middling-cleverness bracket. Shame his Hapsburg lip was so developed that it resembled a facial foreskin.

With a wink, Kydd handed her a mug of English breakfast tea. It was a plastic beaker with a childproof top. She nodded thanks and drank.

The tea hit the spot.

'Perhaps you should look out your big orange suitcase,' Jeperson suggested to Onions. 'Check if your anemometers are all in order.'

After consideration, Onions got back to his seat. He was most particular about his kit, which indeed came in a big orange suitcase. Jeperson said it was full of ghost-hunting gear.

They shared the troop compartment with an all-terrain vehicle, weighted down by neatly stowed supplies and equipment. The ATV occasionally shifted on its tethers. If it got loose, it would crush them all.

The intercom crackled.

'Skerra up ahead,' said de Maltby, sounding uncannily like his great-great uncle abdicating from the throne. 'We should be aground in… uhhhm… about ten minutes.'

Yoland thanked the gods but had to gulp back his silent words. He waved away Kydd's tea.

'Exciting, isn't it?' Jeperson said to her. 'Venturing into unknown territory.'

She wasn't exactly sure how she felt.

'Look, sir, you can see the island.'

Kydd pointed out of a window. Jeperson casually turned to glance at Skerra. Onions lurched from his seat, again hanging apelike from strapholds, and peered at the seascape, searching for their destination.

'There,' said Jeperson. 'Such a tiny scrap of rock.'

The only thing this assignment had in common with regular police work was that Stacy had the usual feeling of coming in late and having to pick up story threads before she could make any progress.

If she was to cope with Skerra, she needed to catch up.

II.

Two days earlier, DS Cotterill learned she was to be despatched to the blue plaque jungle of London, SW3. In New Scotland Yard, DCI Frederick Regent ran off a list of who else had lived in Cheyne Walk, Chelsea.

'Isambard Kingdom Brunel, George Eliot, Turner, Mrs Gaskell, Whistler (of *'s Mother* fame), Dante Gabriel Rossetti, a bunch of other Pre-Raphs, Thomas Carnacki, Henry James. With Carlyle round the corner in Cheyne Row.'

Stacy said she'd heard of them all, except Carnacki.

'Carnacki the Ghost-Finder, Cotterill,' her guv'nor said. 'Secret history. Bone up on it.'

Easier said than done.

It struck her that the guv'nor either wished he was going

out on this call himself or was profoundly grateful seniority kept him snug in his office. Or both at the same time. Regent was a funny specimen of top cop. Higher-ups didn't often let him do telly interviews. Gossip at the Met was that he was the only senior officer ever to turn down a CBE, nearly get married to Diana Rigg and earn the honour of laying the wreath on Joey Grimaldi's grave at the annual Clowns' Service at Holy Trinity Church in Dalston.

Stacy didn't fully realise how out of the ordinary the errand was until Regent told her to take a chit to Sergeant Ellbee, who would scare her up a driver and car. That luxury was a first in her career.

Ellbee recognised the address and laughed.

'Haven't seen that one in an age, Stace,' said the sergeant, who had a London Welsh accent. 'Surprised Jeperson is still alive, what with all he went through. Put the guv'nor through, too. How do you think Fred Regent lost his hair?'

It wasn't something she'd ever considered.

'The famous Richard Jeperson,' clucked Ellbee. 'Name from the seventies. Sixties, even. Fab crazy gear, man. Austin Powers era. Watch out he doesn't try to shag you, baby.'

'Was he a copper?'

'Not with his haircut. Richard Jeperson was a private consultant. A spook. The spooks' spook, in fact. Ever hear of the Diogenes Club?'

She hadn't.

'Read your Sherlock Holmes, girl.'

She had the feeling everyone knew more than she did. Regent had given her the bare bones and a large brown-paper parcel tied with pink string.

'Diogenes wasn't a club, really,' continued Ellbee. 'It was a Department of Dead Ends. Like our old, pre-PC Bureau of Queer Complaints. That was nothing to do with policing Gay

Pride marches. Know why the CI's thrown you this scrap? Fred's had an eagle eye on you ever since the Maudsley murders.'

Stacy didn't think the case was her finest hour. It had seemed a simple, if gruesome triple homicide. A middle-aged man found in a fugue state in his own home, sitting amid the remains of three diced street kids. Evidence indicated that the vics, all well-known to the courts, had entered the premises with unlawful intent and received something very like just desserts. A history of ill-will existed between the district's druggies and the reclusive householder, Mantan 'Misery' Maudsley.

Before the likely perpetrator could be roused enough to understand the formal charge, Maudsley perished in his cell. Not just died, perished. Autopsy suggested he'd been dead for three weeks at the time of arrest. When Stacy had met Maudsley, he wasn't speaking much or smelling fresh but had been capable of walking about. The file was still open.

'Some plods go through a whole career without anything like Misery Maudsley,' said Ellbee. 'Others clock Scooby-Doo cases every week but never tumble to the way the world really works. You took it in, Stace. Adjusted to accept it. When he was with Diogenes and Richard Jeperson, that was Fred Regent's special knack. He thinks you've got something similar.'

She remembered the sick, clear atmosphere after the Maudsley case, the way station-mates treated her differently, the eagerness of her shift commander to get her onto something else quickly. It wasn't something she had enjoyed at all. She didn't relish the prospect of anything more in that line.

'Come off it, Ellbee,' she said. 'I happened to be in the office with a clearish desk when the guv'nor wanted a parcel delivered to Chelsea. End of story.'

'Mind how you tread in the dark, Stace.'

Somebody else who had lived in Cheyne Walk was Bram

Stoker. Stacy remembered the peasant pressing her crucifix on the young man on his way to Castle Dracula.

This wasn't how she usually thought of Sergeant Ellbee. She put his theory into practice and adjusted to accept it.

In the car on the way to Chelsea, the driver didn't speak to her.

The only thing Maudsley had said as she was bringing him in was, 'A cavern, far north.' She had thought it random sparking in a broken brain, not even addressed to her.

Now, she wondered if Misery had known about Skerra.

III.

At first sighting, the island was a greenish thumbnail barely sticking out of the sea. Then, as the helicopter neared, Skerra looked more like a sinking aircraft carrier: an oblong wedge rising steeply, sloping deck sliding into the ocean, barnacled stern lifted clear of the water.

They circled. Stacy got a good look at the place.

Skerra was a British Isle, but only for cartographers' convenience. Too far North to be a Shetland (let alone an Orkney), the outcrop lay alone and desolate in cold grey water between Iceland and the Norwegian coast. As much, or as little, Scandinavian as Scots, a case could be made for calling it the easternmost Faroe. In the reign of Macbeth (yes, that one), Skerra had been gifted to Scotland among the dowry of the Princess of Denmark. An agreed reciprocal tribute went unpaid, so the transfer of sovereignty was moot. If either crown had regarded it as a possession rather than a dependency, Skerra might have become a medieval Schleswig-Holstein Question. As it was, Dunsinane and Elsinore remained barely aware that such a place existed. The islanders looked to their own matrilineal monarchy.

The title of Droning still existed, but the Skerrans didn't.

The hardy, vicious flocks of goats that supported the local

economy and ecosystem (and fashion statements) declined over the centuries and were all but extinct by 1932, when the last remaining islanders were evacuated to unimaginable Southlands. This emergency measure led to the dumping of a knot of insular, Innsmouth-featured folk in a Glasgow slum. Their descendants were allegedly the city's most violent criminal gang. One of the few surviving words of the Skerran tongue was *dreep*, underworld slang for an especially horrific form of murder-by-torture.

Sir Piers Gill (né Paddy Kill) had bought Skerra from another private owner when Persephone was six, so his daughter could legitimately call herself a princess. This was the first time the Droning had come within five hundred miles of her island realm.

Stacy saw where waves washed the incline. Rising seas had swallowed the harbour decades ago. Choppy waters swirled around the few stone skeletons that remained of Skerra Landsby, the abandoned village.

'Look,' said Onions, 'the A-Boat.'

It was caught in among the shattered buildings, on its side, mostly underwater. If the hull hadn't been rust-red, the boat would have passed for a reef.

Onions whistled.

'How the hell did that happen?'

'Strange waters,' commented Richard Jeperson. 'Look at the whirlpools.'

There were three around the village end of Skerra, spinning like submarine Tasmanian devils, and a far larger maelstrom to the north.

'The Kjempestrupe,' said Jeperson. 'It's as if God pulled the plug.'

For the first time, Mr Head took an interest. He closed his *Petesuchis* and peered out the window.

The Kjempestrupe was a funnel in the sea. It seemed

bottomless, spiral walls of whirling water keeping open an impossible chasm.

'Any man who wants to marry you is supposed to brave that in a coracle,' Jeperson told Persephone. 'Otherwise he's not fit to be consort to the Droning of Skerra.'

Persephone looked as if she had heard the legend so many times it wasn't even worth commenting on.

Being a princess evidently wore thin.

'And any woman who wants to challenge for the iron crown has to face you in single combat,' Jeperson added.

'They're welcome to try.'

The Sea King circled the whirlpool, clockwise to its anticlockwise. It was too much for Yoland, who finally spewed. Aircrewman Kydd tactfully provided a paper bag.

'Does he have to?' asked Persephone, infinitely weary.

'Yes, love, he does,' said Kydd.

The Droning of Skerra didn't care to be addressed as 'love'. Kydd was too busy tidying up after Yoland to notice her moué of annoyance.

'Better out than in, sir,' said Kydd, with cheery deference.

Yoland nodded something like thanks.

The helicopter passed over the Kjempestrupe and approached the island. Skerra was a volcanic extrusion, originally expelled through a hernia in the planet's crust, bursting molten above the seas to solidify like an igneous loaf, then shaped and sculpted by unrelenting wind and water. When the satellite pictures had come in, the first theory was that the volcano was active again. Met Office wags nicknamed it 'McKrakatoa'.

The squared-off cliffside had been gouged out by millennia of brutally battering waves. A torrent poured into the vast cavemouth, and washed back out again as froth. The island was hollow, like a decayed tooth. It should eventually collapse on its caverns and become rocks strewn across the seabed, lamented by no one but map-maintainers and reduced-to-commoner female Gills.

The ridge of the cliff whizzed below.

There wasn't a tree on the island, though its upper slopes were infested with long, thick grass. Survivalist goats had persisted after the people left, the toughest specimens emerging from some cave-shelters to reclaim the surface. Their savage descendants looked to the sky as the helicopter passed overhead, but did not abandon tussock-chewing to run for cover. De Maltby and Kydd had been issued small arms, but Stacy fancied Skerran goats likely resistant to everything this side of depleted uranium shells. They were a prison population: faces smashed by head-butting horn-fights, flanks ripped by scars like tattoos, each lifer the perpetrator of a multiple rapes and *dreeps*.

As the Sea King descended, propwash whipped grass into crop circles. De Maltby searched for a likely landing spot.

Onions waved downwards, indicating to the pilot the urgency of making ground.

Even as they hovered, the island slipped out from under the Sea King. De Maltby had to fight strong winds to avoid dipping in the drink. An intermittent stone wall rimmed what had once been a field. De Maltby put the Sea King down by it. After the rotors stopped, there was still whirring – the wind, trying to wipe the island into the sea.

'I own this carbuncle,' said Persephone Gill. 'Any offers? I'd have to abdicate, but I think I could be persuaded by any convincing bid. A bean and a button?'

Stacy wasn't tempted. Even if owning Skerra meant being able to call herself a princess.

'Let's get out and make camp,' said Onions. 'It'll be dark soon.'

It wasn't quite lunch-time and night was about to fall.

No wonder Princess Percy wasn't surprised by the lack of potential buyers.

IV.

In Chelsea, Stacy had told her driver to wait in the car and searched for the address she'd been given. She had the brown-paper parcel under her arm.

The house didn't show a street-number. Inset in the front door, where neighbours had number-plates, was an art nouveau stained-glass panel with an Ancient Egyptian eye motif.

When Stacy thumbed the button, a bell jangled inside the house. Shadows shifted.

She noticed the milk – eight bottles – hadn't been taken in. A rain-eaten roll of free newspaper was rammed into the letter-slit, drooping like a fag from the mouth of a charlady in a 1970s ITV sitcom. Freesheets were the burglars' friend – you couldn't stop them when you went on holiday. From the looks of this place, the home-owner was never home. She wondered why DCI Regent thought she'd find him in.

The clear glass pupil of the Egyptian eye darkened. A real eye looked out at her: startling silver-flecked blue-grey iris trapped in veinous cobweb.

She held up her warrant card.

'Come on in,' boomed a voice. ''S'not locked.'

She took the handle and pushed the door, which resisted. A small avalanche of newspapers, pizza menus, minicab cards, AOL start-up discs, estate agent's brochures and letters from the council shifted, was ground under, then stopped the door dead at half-open.

Stacy turned sideways and slipped into the house.

She smelled incense, sweet and heavy. The long, narrow, crowded foyer rose three storeys to a murky glass roof. Potted plants exploded from tubs and grew up banisters, reaching tendrils toward the distant sun. Odd objects were piled at random: books of all formats and thicknesses, primitive masks, fancy-dress finery, dissected animals under glass domes, unsleeved vinyl records, unnameable musical instruments, ancient valve wirelesses in various states of dismantlement, obscure statuary. And multiple cats – which explained the milk. They roamed free, clambering and searching.

'You must be from Fred.'

Richard Jeperson stood before her: tall, thin and gaunt. He could have been any age, but working it out from the backstory – child in the War, career in the 1970s – Stacy knew he must be in his mid-sixties. When younger, he'd looked older; now, he just looked himself. Dramatic streaks ran through the Zapata moustache, but the long fall of tight curls was glossily black. He had the pale skin of someone who's stayed indoors for decades, deep-etched around those silver-flashing eyes but unslack under the chin, unspotted on the backs of his hands.

A Persian kitten peeped out of a pocket and a Siamese cat perched on his shoulder like Long John Silver's parrot. He wore suede winkle-picker shoes, pinstripe city-gent trousers, a turquoise kaftan tunic belted with a sash, and, as if to offset the Siamese, a gold-frogged green velvet greatcoat over his other shoulder, pocket unflapped so the kitten could breathe.

'You expected Howard Hughes fingernails and a Ben Gunn beard?'

He spoke like a theatrical knight, but his eyes were lively. She could imagine him headlining the Glastonbury Festival in 1972 or playing Don Quixote in a silent movie.

She introduced herself as DS Cotterill.

'Stacy,' he said, surprising her. 'Interesting career.'

She wouldn't have guessed that he kept up with New Scotland Yard.

'Teenage model, then policewoman. Why the change?'

Almost no one mentioned it any more. At Hendon Police College, she had done extreme things to blokes who thought it funny to go on about her after-school job. Jeperson had wrong-footed her, though he seemed genuinely interested rather than attempting a put-down.

'It's no life for a grown woman without an eating disorder,' she said, uncomfortable. 'And the agency dropped me when I refused to have my back-teeth pulled. It was supposed to make my face look thinner.'

He cocked his head to one side, then the other, considering her face.

'I bet they wanted to keep the teeth.'

'As a matter of fact, they did. All the girls' teeth. In jam-jars in a cupboard, individually labelled. In solutions of brine.'

'Better than a contract. You're well out of that.'

Jeperson looked at her face first and last. Which made him different from ninety-five per cent of men. That shouldn't be a surprise; everything about him was different. She found herself almost disarmed, then remembered he was mad.

'Come through to the study,' he said, dislodging the Siamese, who streaked squirrel-fast up branches to the second-floor landing. The plant was a spreading green apocalypse, a tree that became a vine when it suited. It was stapled to the wall in several crucial places.

'Would you believe this began as a cutting? From Yggdrasil, the Norse world-tree. A gift to the Diogenes Club from William Morris in the days of gaslight and pea-soup fogs. When Mycroft Holmes sat on the Ruling Cabal. Brother of the more famous. Charles Beauregard lived in this house then. You won't have heard of him, though some scholar has been struggling to research a biography for years. I met Beauregard once, when I was a little lad. Nearly a hundred, but kept au fait with the comings and goings. A very interesting Englishman. Unlike me. I'm foreign, you know. Non-specific, but foreign.'

He slipped back the cuff of his kaftan, to show a blue tattooed number.

'Adopted by an Englishman, adopted by the Club. Raised for the position, as it were. I'm a foundling of War. I must have had a name and a nationality before 1945, but the cylinders don't fire up here.'

He tapped his temple.

'Nothing before the Liberation. A few other gaps, sadly. It's been a crowded life, so I have had to forget things to make room. Wish I could have planned better. I remember a great many things it would make sense to forget. But not...'

He let the thought dangle and opened a door.

The white study was strip lit. Windowpanes were whitewashed to match the walls, ceiling and carpet. A large picture hung opposite, canvas as blankly white as the frame. A milk-white shelving unit contained books with white, featureless spines. Soft white plastic cubes formed a settee along one wall and chairs around the room. Hard white plastic boxes made a desk and tables. A perfect-bound magazine for the blind, glossy pages stamped with Braille, lay open on a low table. A towering sound system, white as a fridge, played 'Happiness is a Warm Gun'. The almost-invisible CD jewel-case on the floor reminded her the song was from the *White Album*.

'This is a visually sterile environment,' Jeperson explained. 'I need it sometimes. There is too much information out there to process comfortably. I have an open mind. That's my gift and curse.'

Jeperson sat, arms laid along the back of the settee, shrugging out of his coat, long legs crossed. He motioned her to make herself comfortable. She put her parcel on the low table, a violent intrusion of brown, and sat on a stool.

'Is that a present? For me?'

'CI Regent asked me to bring it to you.'

'Ah-ha. It's evidence, isn't it? This is a case. You know I'm retired? I don't consult or sleuth or intuit or adventure. Not my decision. Things changed. Certain elements among our rulers made judgements. The Diogenes Club closed its doors. I am given to understand that some quango took over our duties. You can probably reach them in a unit on an industrial estate in Wolverhampton. Whatever threatens the fabric of our reality will prove a nice change from playing solitaire with Rhine cards or theorising undetectable assassinations or whatever Adam Onions's little helpers do to justify their expenses claims.'

She waved him to a halt.

'This is too much for me, Mr Jeperson—'

'Richard, please.'

'This is too much for me, Richard. Until this morning, I'd never heard of you or the Diogenes Club and I'm really not up to speed. DCI Regent—'

'Fred.'

'CI Regent has requested that I work with you.'

'Very clever. Chuck the old dog a dolly-mixture and creep up with the muzzle.'

Hot-cheeked, she stood up.

'You resent that,' he said.

'They told me you were perceptive.'

He was standing too, close to her, hands around hers, radiating sincerity.

'I apologise. I forget myself. As I mentioned.'

She damped her momentary anger. But she wasn't ready to trust this dinosaur.

'Fred Regent wouldn't have sent you round if you were only blond. You collared Misery Maudsley, did you not? Fred must have fought hard to keep that little brouhaha out of Onions's remit. Tell me, it wasn't in any of the papers, but… when you slapped the cuffs on him, was Maudsley doing something with his eyes, something more than looking at you?'

She remembered. A squirming. Like REM dream-twitches, but with the eyes wide open.

'I thought so,' said Richard, wheeling across the room. 'Maggots. Little tiny maggots, hatched and hungry. An inconvenience, at the least. Always the problem with reanimation by force of will. Any qualified houngan cures the corpse before raising the zombie. Still, Maudsley got his job done. What happened to his books? Mislaid in the evidence room as usual?'

'Everything from the house went. There was no court case pending, so the coroner brought in an open verdict. Maudsley's stuff got tossed into a skip.'

Jeperson shook his head.

'So anyone could breeze along and filch the tomes? That's like tossing a sackful of loaded revolvers into a playgroup. Never have happened in my day.'

He was enthused for a moment. Then he stopped.

'But I'm out of it. As you'll have gathered.'

She said nothing. Jeperson wandered around his white room, touching things, looking away from her.

'It's all parapsychology now,' he said. 'Target figures and year-end reports and jolly-promising-results-minister. We had mysteries, Stacy. Riddles of the sphinx, conundrums of the incalculable. Not parapsychology, but parapsychedelia. Not phenomena, not anomalies, not quantum metaphysics, but magic… enchantment… deviltry!'

He stood by the table, fingers drumming on brown paper.

He looked at her, eyes piercing, looked at the package, bit the end of his moustache, looked at her again.

'What's in the parcel?'

'I thought you said you were out of it.'

'Minx! What's in the parcel?'

'You of all people should know what they say about cats and curiosity.'

Jeperson picked up the parcel, like a six-year-old with a present on Christmas Eve. He shook it, and held it to his ear.

'Very light for its size. Not a case of wine or an occasional table, then.'

He squeezed and crackled.

'Feels fabricky. Like a blanket. Or a party frock.'

He tweaked something through the paper.

'Brass buttons. It's a coat. I've guessed. I'm right, aren't I? A coat, found in evidence. Bullet-holes and bloodstains.'

His mood switched, from playful to serious. She felt a chill.

'I'm right about that, too,' he said, sober.

'Open it,' she urged.

'Very well,' he decided. 'For you. Because you told me about Maudsley's eyes. But no commitment. This is not going to be Richard Jeperson Rides Again.'

He slipped a tiny blade out of his sleeve and snipped the string. The paper fell away and he held a stiff, greyish green coat. There were bullet-holes in the left sleeve and the hip pocket. And old blood.

The sound system was playing 'Rocky Raccoon'.

Jeperson looked at the maker's label. He held the coat against himself, mouth open in astonishment.

'This is…'

'Yours. We traced it through your tailor. They had the record on a hand-written card in a box in the basement. You bought it in 1968, about the time this album came out.'

Jeperson shook his head. He was trembling, garment shaking in his grip. She thought he might have the beginnings of a seizure.

'It's the same cut as that one there,' she added, nodding at the settee.

The kitten had escaped from its pocket and was trying claws out on the silk lining.

'I don't own two of anything. This is that coat over there. Where was this found?'

'You'd better come with me to the Yard.'

Jeperson laid the coat down next to its identical twin.

'To help you with your enquiries,' he said, frowning hard. 'I think I better had. This, Stacy, is serious. This makes Misery Maudsley look like a purse-snatching in Safeway's car park. There isn't room in the world for two of this.'

'I have a car waiting,' she said.

He picked up his coat, the one she hadn't brought, dislodging the kitten. It nosed the doppelgarment, thought better of it, and dashed from the room. Jeperson slipped an arm into one sleeve, but needed her help with the other. His shoulder shook, almost spasming.

For a moment, he did look his age.

'You'd better bring that,' he said, finger aimed at the surplus coat. 'Wrap it up again. It should be sealed in lead, but sturdy brown paper will have to do.'

She knew she was not suggestible. But she no more wanted to touch the coat than the kitten had, or Jeperson did.

Still, she picked up the paper, using it like an oven-glove, and took hold of the coat, wrapping it tight against the possibility that its arms might come to life and throttle her.

At the doorstep, Jeperson hesitated.

'It's been a very long time,' he said, weakly. 'I don't know if I can...'

He seemed to flinch from daylight, from the outside world. Then he looked at her parcel.

'No choice,' he said, striding through the doorway.

They left the house. Jeperson did not lock up behind them.

V.

'It's your island, Miss Gill,' Jeperson said to Persephone. 'You be Neil Armstrong.'

Stacy noted Onions sulking whenever Jeperson acted as if he were in charge. The man from I-Psi-T needed to feel he was tour operator for this jaunt.

At Jeperson's nod, Kydd hauled the handle and swung open the door. The temperature in the back of the Sea King plunged.

'Best not,' said Onions.

Persephone had unstrapped herself. Ignoring Onions, she slid across the floor and out of the helicopter.

'Mind the goats,' Stacy advised.

Through the door, Stacy watched the Droning of Skerra stamp around, doing the hunting set version of t'ai chi – thumping the heels of her green wellies against grassy sod, flexing her back and thighs as if she were on horseback, and struggling against the wind to tie a Hermès scarf around her hair. She lost the scarf, which was sucked upwards by an invisible Kjempestrupe.

Nothing killed Persephone, so Stacy assumed it was all right to get out of the transport. She took off her ear-baffles and undid all the straps.

Jeperson made a 'ladies first' bow. Stacy dangled her legs out of the helicopter, then took the jump. She realised how stiff she'd become and uncrooked her back.

Wind slashed her face.

Onions thumped onto the turf beside her, and strode off purposefully. Kydd helped the others leave the Sea King. De

Maltby clambered down, snug in his flight-suit and helmet.

Yoland was on his knees, grateful for solid ground under him, grasping handfuls of Skerra.

'I wouldn't do that again in a hurry,' he said, smiling.

Stacy didn't point out that unless he wanted to become Persephone's sole subject he'd have to take the return trip.

'Should I get some grub up?' Kydd asked Jeperson.

'A very civilised notion.'

'No time for that,' said Onions, coming back. 'We need to find Captain Vernon. I don't mind saying I'm worried about the A-Boat.'

'Lost with all hands,' said Jeperson.

'You can't know that.'

'Quite right, Onions. I can't. But I do.'

'Vernon had a six-man team.'

'They're gone. Forget them.'

Onions frowned. Jeperson lost interest and drifted away, towards Sewell Head. The little man hadn't brought a hat, and was trying to protect his bald dome with his hands. Jeperson gave him a knit-cap he had spare. Head smiled weak thanks.

Stacy noticed Jeperson was the only one who could talk with Sewell Head. She worried that they shared more with each other than anyone else here.

'We should get to the village,' said Onions.

'The Blowhole, surely,' ventured Jeperson.

Onions ignored him and strode downslope, expecting to be followed. Jeperson gave Stacy a look, then shrugged and plodded carefully after the man from I-Psi-T. Stacy let the others get moving before taking up the rear.

De Maltby stayed with the Sea King, but Kydd came along.

A mean-eyed goat peered through a hole in the wall, cynically examining the newcomers. If war came, it'd be a toss-up who'd get eaten and who'd get to eat.

After only a few steps into merciless wind, down a field that inclined enough for a ski-slope, Stacy couldn't feel her face but was hobbled by pain in her ankles. She wished she had a city around her.

Onions paused to look at his flip-book.

A large blue bat attacked him, all spiny frame and enveloping membranes. He was wrapped in an instant, and spun off balance.

Sewell Head threw himself face-down in the dirt. Maltesers bled from his pockets.

Onions yelled from inside his blue cocoon.

'Shoot it! shoot it!'

Stacy jogged down, miraculously avoiding a twisted ankle. She joined Jeperson in hauling the 'bat' off Onions. It was a tent, trailing guy-ropes and skewers, poles snapped.

Kydd had drawn his revolver and assumed the stance. Now, with Onions free of the tent and sat on the ground, Kydd's gun was aimed at his head. He waved it aside, red-faced, hair stuck up in an undignified crown.

'You have been attacked by an item of rogue camping equipment,' said Jeperson.

He helped Onions stand up.

The wind caught the tent again. It hurtled off like a crooked kite, chasing after Persephone's scarf.

Onions patted his hair and twisted inside his anorak, realigning the hip-pockets with his hips.

'Vernon was supposed to set up camp,' he said.

Jeperson laid a hand on Onions's shoulder.

'Vernon is gone, Adam.'

'We have to look.'

Jeperson nodded and let Onions continue.

'Don't know what they're talking about half the time,' Persephone said to her.

Stacy thought that was a fair average.

Onions had been right about one thing. It was getting dark.

VI.

The briefing was not at the Yard, but in Whitehall. From the yellowed ceiling, Stacy guessed the panelled, windowless committee chamber had been one of the legendary 'smoke-filled rooms'. New Labour had taken out the ashtrays and put up 'thank you for not smoking' signs.

Notional chairperson was Morag Duff, Deputy Minister for Heritage and Sport, who didn't actually appear. A sound-activated minidisc recorder lay on her blotter at the head of the table. A tartan tam-o'-shanter perched on the back of a chair, suggesting that the Deputy Minister had been here but just popped out.

Stacy looked at the Walter Sickert on the wall – saved from Patricia Cornwell by public subscription – and wondered if Duff were behind it, peeking through hidden eyeholes. This was the apparatus of the secret state, and spooks loved these games.

Jeperson was a study in suppressed excitement, alert to the point of hypertension, given to chewing on a knuckle. He had been in deep thought during the drive over.

Now, he took in the room. Three men sat like wise monkeys.

'Adam,' Jeperson acknowledged the alpha ape, hear-no-evil.

'Richard Jeperson,' grunted the bearish man. 'We are calling out the reserves.'

Stacy pulled out a chair for Jeperson, who insisted she take it. She ended up sitting across from the big man. He looked like a rugby player five years into beery middle age, a slackening mountain in a baggy suit.

'This is Adam Onions,' said Jeperson.

'O-nye-ons,' he corrected. 'Nothing to do with the vegetable. A whole different etymology.'

'He is from the Institute of Something Trickology.'

'I–Psi–T. Pronounced "Eyesight". The Institute of Psi Tech. Director of same.'

Onions's eyes took in her chest. She didn't need to be psychic to know what he thought of her.

'I'm Stacy Cotterill. Detective Sergeant.'

Onions did a not-a-secretary-then take. She'd seen that before.

'I don't know these other fellows, I'm afraid,' said Jeperson.

'Call me Rory,' said see-no-evil, a chunky cardigan chap who reminded her of an eager young vicar she'd arrested for molesting elderly parishioners. 'I'm a civil servant, but don't hold it against me. I'm really a good bloke.'

Rory smiled, delivering what Stacy recognised from her modelling days as Benign Variant Two. She wondered if he was working from the book they'd had at her agency, *101 Expressions for All Occasions*.

'And this is Franklin Yoland…'

Say-no-evil put up his hand. He had a tan and lush lips.

'He's one of those weapons inspectors you hear so much about. Nothing he doesn't know about whizz-bangs, nerve gases and anthrax spores. Up on all the latest euphemisms. Made us laugh earlier – what was it, Frank? Yes, he was describing missiles as "delivery systems for" – how did you put it? – "geography parcels and history parcels"?'

Yoland shook his head. 'Physics packages, chemistry packages or biology packages.'

'In the long run, you're more right than you know,' Jeperson told Rory. 'It comes down to geography and history.'

'Very true. Take a pew.'

Jeperson walked round the room. He picked up the tam-o'-shanter and put it down again.

Yoland looked at the man from the Diogenes Club as if he might detonate.

At the opposite end of the table, a secretary sat with an open laptop, fingers poised over the keyboard. Jeperson smiled at her, acknowledging her presence with a little wave. She did not respond.

Jeperson found an odd little old man sat in the corner, away from the table, reading a book. A strange look arced between them.

'Don't mind him,' said Rory. 'That's Sewell Head.'

'Swellhead,' mumbled the little man.

Jeperson shook his hand, warmly.

Head was bald, with an odd, dome-shaped skull, no chin to speak of and flattish wet eyes. The sleeves of his shabby overcoat were too long for his childish hands. A knit scarf was wrapped several times around his neck, so his head nestled like an Easter egg in its presentation bow.

'He was Brain of Britain a while back,' said Rory.

Head gave a puzzling smile, one Stacy had never seen demonstrated in a photograph. Almost lipless, he had a lot of extra teeth. He had eaten chocolate recently.

'Mr Head is Adam's discovery,' said the civil servant.

'What's your IQ, Jeperson?' asked Onions. 'Off the scale? Next to Sewell Head, you're a cretin. So am I. Technically, he's the cleverest man in England. Top Five in the world.'

'Barred from pub trivia contests throughout the Home Counties,' put in Rory. 'You used to hustle, didn't you, old son? Guys, he would go in alone on quiz night, nurse a gin and it, then bungle a couple of easy ones. "Who won the World Cup in 1966?" "Was that perhaps Italy?" Big laughs. Then he'd get a bit tipsy. Apparently, tipsy. Come over all shirty, insist on a big money bet with Local Hero. You know the type, Captain Know-It-All, memorised his *Guinness Book of Uninteresting Facts*. Fifty, a hundred quid on the table. Side-bets with everyone in the bar to bump up the total stake. Quiz gets serious, one-on-one, make-your-mind-up time. Our Mr Head suddenly switches on like a toaster, goes from wondering if "I Should Be So Lucky" was a hit for Bananarama...'

Head's lips twitched, a downturn at one side, peculiar pain in his glassy eye.

'...to rattling off the fifth paragraph of Article Ten of the Treaty of Utrecht of 1713—'

'And Her Britannic Majesty,' said Sewell Head, conquering panic and rising to the occasion, 'at the request of the Catholic King, does consent and agree, that no leave shall be given under any pretence whatsoever, either to Jews or Moors, to reside or have their dwellings in the said town of Gibraltar; and that no refuge or shelter shall be allowed to any Moorish ships of war in the harbour of the said town, whereby the communication between Spain and Ceuta may be obstructed, or the coasts of Spain be infested by the excursions of the Moors.'

Rory laughed and pointed.

'I love this guy. Penny in the slot. He knows the answer. Anyway, by the end of the evening, Local Hero is bleeding from the arse, fallen faces all round the room. Our Mr Head is off with a fistful of notes. And that's another pub off the list. They call him the Triv Terminator.'

'It's not a memory trick,' said Onions, warming. 'He's not some autistic savant with a set of encyclopaedias. He's a puzzle-solver. We've never tested anything like him. He's a Talent. Off the scale.'

Head shrugged modestly.

'I like to think things through,' he said. 'Make everything neat and tidy.'

'Call him the zen master of quantum cleverness,' said Rory.

'Duke have offered the dean's left nut for a free run at him,' said Onions. 'The Tibetans have their antennae a-twitch. He could take the field up to the next level. Scientifically verifiable. None of your "feelings" and "intuitions", Jeperson. Cold, hard, steely data. And he can do it every time, under laboratory conditions.'

Jeperson looked down at the little man.

'He works in a sweet shop,' said Rory.

Onions gave a what-a-waste sigh.

'Nothing in the constitution says everyone should be ambitious,' continued Rory. 'We dug out his old report book from Coal Hill Secondary Modern. Min Inf keeps copies of those, you know. I burned mine. Forgotten what your netball teacher thought of you, Detective Sergeant? We could find out. Any guesses which phrase came up all the time in young Sewell Head's reports? All his teachers said it. Over and over.'

Jeperson stroked his moustaches. He nodded to Stacy.

"Could do better if he tried,"' she said, flatly.

Rory thumped the desk in delight.

'Spot bloody-on. Give Juliet Bravo a cuddly panda. Cripes, the brainpower in this room! Find a way to harness it, and we could light up Blackpool's Golden Mile.'

Jeperson gave Rory a penetrating look, then left Head in his corner.

He took off his coat and threw it on the table. It flopped over Morag Duff's minidisc recorder, and lay like the king's deer tossed dead onto Guy of Gisbourne's table by Robin Hood.

'Adam,' said Jeperson, seriously, 'tell me about the apport.'

Rory tried a 'now-we-come-to-brass-tacks' chuckle but it died.

Onions looked at the coat. Stacy unrolled the brown paper and let the other coat (the same coat?) lie next to the original (copy?).

Onions bit his lower lip.

'Yes,' said Jeperson, insistently, 'they're the same. Not in the way two peas in a pod are the same, but in the way one unique special never-to-be-repeated, once-in-a-lifetime pea is the same as itself.'

'What's an apport?' Stacy asked.

'A physical object manifested supernaturally,' said Sewell Head.

'Rabbit out of a hat,' footnoted Jeperson.

'At I-Psi-T, we've documented the phenomenon extensively,' said Onions. 'Apports are often household items. Inanimate. We have a collection. Hairbrushes, fireplace pokers, a clock with mangled guts. One theory is that they slip through wormholes, travel in time. Miss 1893 loses her garter and it pops up a hundred years later, to the bewilderment of all concerned. Others don't obviously come from the past or future but from somewhere else.'

'Dimension Xxxx,' said Jeperson in a hollow, echoey, radio-announcer voice.

'We discourage that sort of talk, but yes... some other continuum, where things are put together differently. That clock is interesting. Turned up in a bus station in Eastbourne. We have it on the surveillance camera. Not there one instant, there the next. Its insides are the bones of small animals we can't identify, fitted together with sticky gum we can't analyse, generating a small but quantifiable electric current. Because it didn't keep very good time, we thought it was something disguised as a clock. Then Mr Head worked out that it keeps perfect time, if hours were to ebb and flow like the tides, getting longer then shorter again. The cycle is beyond me but he says it makes perfect sense.'

Head nodded.

'So this is pretending to be your coat?' she asked Jeperson.

'No, this isn't like the clock. This is my coat. Messrs Drecker and Coote, Savile Row and Carnaby Street. Made to my order in

593

1968. And this is my coat too. It has just come here by a different route.'

'A rough route, by the looks of it,' said Rory. 'We DNA-tested the blood.'

'Some of it's yours,' said Onions, enjoying the thought.

'And the rest of it's mine,' put in Sewell Head.

VII.

Skerra Landsby barely qualified as a ruin. All the buildings were roofless, and most of the walls had fallen. A war memorial (Boer, 1914–1918) was a brass plaque, names unreadable, plinth aswarm with bubblewrap seaweed. Stacy remembered mindlessly happy childhood days at Southend-on-Sea, bursting the little brown bags between thumb and forefinger, jimmying whelks off rocks with her Swiss Army knife.

More collapsed tents flapped in the wind, tethered by skewers. Onions's torch was the only light.

There was supposed to be a Royal Navy assault team here, despatched under cover of a training exercise, kitted out with arms to last through a small war. Her understanding was that the boffins' security would be provided by Captain Vernon's mob, who had been here before and scoped out the potential dangers. That was out the window.

'What do you suppose happened?' Persephone asked her.

'Nothing good.'

The Droning of Skerra chewed that over. As the expedition's volunteer, she must be kicking herself. Really-a-Good-Bloke Rory had decided they ought to ask Persephone before camping out on her island. She'd given in to a whim, insisting she be taken along to check out her realm. Ascot was a wash this year, evidently.

Onions and Yoland climbed a wall which extended into the sea, and walked out across the waves. Onions shone his torch at the A-Boat, which was in a sorry state, hull shattered below the waterline.

'We should be below,' said Jeperson.

'Out of this bloody weather,' put in Persephone. 'Too right.'

Head skinned the wrapper from a Twix and bit off both biscuit fingers at once.

'My understanding,' said Jeperson, calling out to Onions, 'was that all the observed manifestations were in the caverns. Up here, it's just wind and goats.'

Yoland and Onions stuck out their arms like tightrope walkers and came back to shore, footing wobbly on none-too-secure stones. Yoland took a run at the last few feet and jumped onto dry land.

Onions made a show of coming to a decision.

'We should make our way to the Blowhole,' he said.

Jeperson refrained from pointing out that he had made that suggestion when it was still light.

'Lead on,' said Stacy.

Onions looked at his map and strode uphill.

Before his light got too far away, everyone fell in behind him.

VIII.

CI Regent had turned up at Euston to see the party off on the midnight sleeper for Edinburgh. While Really-a-Good-Bloke Rory issued 'non-optional suggestions' to the man from 'Pronounced "Eyesight"' and Sewell Head filled a carrier-bag with sweeties, Regent had a moment with Richard Jeperson. Stacy gathered they hadn't talked in over ten years. She hung back tactfully and wondered if she'd packed enough warm clothes. Before she boarded the train, her guv'nor took her aside, nodded at Jeperson, and said, 'He's special, take care of him.' She agreed he was and promised she would.

The first leg didn't even get them halfway to Skerra. At

Edinburgh Airport, they breakfasted and Persephone Gill joined the party, with luggage. A private jet, a luxurious waiting room with wings, flew them to Thurso, almost as far north on the mainland as John O'Groats. Stacy had never been to Scotland before. Edinburgh seemed essentially London with different accents. Only after flying over green glens and glinting thin lochs for tedious hours, did she have a real sense of being hideously off her patch.

If she'd been asked yesterday where Thurso was, she'd have ventured a guess at Antarctica; she wasn't sure now that she'd have been wrong. At home, whether in her flat or on duty, she knew how to get Tampax, small-arms ammunition or last Thursday's daily papers at three in the morning. Here, she wasn't even sure what to ask for when she needed directions to the Ladies.

In Thurso, mid-afternoon, they all had complete medical check-ups at the Air-Sea Rescue station clinic. She got a five-minute once-over and a nurse congratulated her on not being pregnant and having all her limbs. Jeperson was in with the woman for an hour and a half. Everyone else sat around a reception area. Sewell Head offered round Fisherman's Friends, and hers went tasteless during the wait. When let free, Jeperson shrugged an apology. He kissed the nurse's hand; she gave him a seal of approval that struck Stacy as a lot more personal than the one everyone else in the party had stamped on their file.

Then they were all put in a 'guest house', opened especially out of season. Before dinner, Viscount Henry de Maltby made himself known. He looked with disdain down Persephone's dress, said 'uhhhm' several times, then had a huddle with Adam Onions to go over charts and reports. Aircrewman Kydd was there, too, rubber-faced and cheery, Falklands and Gulf War I insignia on his jersey shoulder.

'Better get an early night,' suggested Onions.

That made Jeperson decide to stay up by the fire in the snug. Stacy's prime directive was to be his minder so she did too. Onions frowned a little, but plodded off up the wooden hill to Bedfordshire without complaint.

This was the first time she had been alone with her charge since leaving his house thirty hours previously.

She still didn't know what to make of him.

'And who might you be, my dear?' he asked.

The snug was warm, but the question chilled her.

'Ah,' said Jeperson. 'We've met. Pardon me.'

He shut his eyes and massaged his temples. Then, he clicked his fingers.

'All present and correct, Stacy. Fearfully sorry to give you a fright.'

The knot inside her relaxed. Jeperson was so spry and mercurial it was too easy to forget his fragilities.

He insisted on killing a bottle of thirty-year-old Scotch. After two busy days, a single tot made her head swim and she was seeing shapes in the fire. But he drank steadily without seeming more or less affected.

By firelight, his face was dramatic, almost pantomimish.

'CI Regent told me to catch up on my secret history,' she ventured.

'Sound advice.'

'But if it's secret...'

'I see your problem. Don't you have that welcomed-to-the-inner-circle feeling yet? Corridors of power, meetings with mandarins, transport laid on, Royals and Nobs, accommodation to order. It's very different from chasing villains and making court dates.'

'I still get the impression I've not been told anything.'

Jeperson chuckled. 'I've been in this game as long as I can

remember, and I mean literally, and I feel like that too. Of course, I'm supposed to be super-sensitive. I don't need to be told, because I have to keep on proving that I'm still sharp. I have to intuit, feel, scry…'

He waved his fingers.

'You and CI— You and Fred… used to work like this? In the seventies?'

'Not quite like this, though he also came to the Diogenes Club from the Met. Only just out of uniform. Shaved his head to go undercover with a bovver gang.'

So that was how he lost his hair!

'Diogenes was the philosopher who lived in the barrel,' she said, 'told Alexander to get out of his light.'

Jeperson raised an eyebrow.

'I've been on trivia teams too,' she said. 'But what is the Diogenes Club? Everyone goes on as if it were famous, but I'd never heard of it.'

'The original idea was to be obscure. It was a club for the unclubbable. Also, a trunk of our family tree of intelligence agencies. It was there for all the business the other plods weren't comfy with. Businesses like Misery Maudsley. That'd have been a Diogenes show in my day. Angel Down, Sussex. Tomorrow Town. The Seven Stars. Many other matters mysterious and malign. Few of which mean anything to the general public. Part of the game has always been protecting the Great British from knowledge deemed likely to send them off their collective nut.'

'In my experience, the general public can cope with a lot.'

'Maybe so,' he said, swivelling his eyes to peer at her, thinking. 'However, for more than a hundred years, the Diogenes Club was a court of last resort. The Ruling Cabal were the original "spooks". Before me, the Club harboured others with special interests. Mycroft Holmes, Charles Beauregard, Henry Merrivale.

Women, too: the Diogenes was the first gentleman's club to go co-ed. Katharine Reed, Catriona Kaye, Dion Fortune. My immediate sponsors were my adoptive father, Geoffrey Jeperson, and Beauregard's protégé, Edwin Winthrop. My intention was that Fred and… and another person, unknown to you… should succeed me. It didn't work out like that.'

'What happened?'

'Nothing dramatic. Drip-drip-drip of history. Some might blame Arthur Conan Doyle. He let Dr Watson put in print the observation that Mycroft Holmes not only worked for the British Government but "on some occasions, was the British Government". Naturally, that earned a black demerit in Whitehall. Steps were taken to ensure that those occasions never reoccaised. Winston Churchill spent years trying to set limits on the remit of the Diogenes Club. He was a man for fixations, hanging onto Hitler, standing up to India (pardon me, twixt and about) and curbing that blasted Club.'

Jeperson frowned and somehow made his face Churchillian. He laughed, breaking the illusion, and refilled his glass.

'When I was under Winthrop, adventuring with Fred, successive governments were fractious. This is what happens when you become Prime Minister, or used to anyway. Just after you've had tea with the Queen and been given the launch codes for the independent nuclear deterrent, the man from the Diogenes Club presents you with irrefutable evidence that there are more things in Heaven and Earth than came up on *Any Questions?* during the election campaign. If you're very polite, the Man tells you who Jack the Ripper was, what happened to the *Mary Celeste* and where that thing at Roswell the Yanks are so bloody sure is an alien spacecraft actually comes from. PMs shudder and stick their heads in the sand. The Diogenes Club is then left to get on with defending the realm from ghosties and ghoulies.'

She thought of pressing him on the identity of Jack the Ripper, but the moment passed.

'Winthrop did Wilson and Heath. Your darlin' Harold grumbled a bit but sat up straight when he was shown a genuine fifteenth-century manuscript describing the course late-twentieth-century history would take if British troops were committed to fight in Vietnam. Ted Heath got very enthusiastic and interested in curses and banes in the context of industrial relations, then bothered Winthrop with "suggestions". By the time Jim Callaghan took over, Winthrop was gone and I wound up with the thankless task. Actually, that's inaccurate. Callaghan said, "Thank you very much." I told him that the chicken entrails suggested it might be an idea to keep a gunboat or two near the Falklands, and he said right-o. Otherwise, he continued as if we didn't exist. Which was as it should be. Then, in 1979... I bet you can guess the rest.'

'Margaret Thatcher.'

Jeperson raised his glass in toast.

'Got it in one, Stacy. Margaret Hilda Roberts Boudicca Thatcher. Not so much a new broom as a new defoliant.'

'She refused to believe in anything?'

Jeperson smiled.

'Oh no. She knew it all beforehand. She had associations. The Club was never alone in its interests. It always had powerful rivals, and Mrs Empty... Mistress M. T.... was a sponsee of the worst of 'em. There was talk of privatisation, but in the end she went for dismantling us, tearing up the historic charter, boarding up the premises in Pall Mall. Those who could be pensioned off, were. Some others were kept out of it with the threat of prosecution or worse. Fred was seconded back to his original job and began his long slow climb at the Yard. I, ah, had several episodes which did me no credit. There is such a thing as feeling too deeply. Mrs

Empty, you'll gather, scrapped the South Atlantic gunboats too. You know how that played out.'

'Where does Onions come into it?'

'O-nye-ons? He's a scientist, you know. Not a crackpot. Well, just because the Diogenes Club was out of commission didn't mean that the vast and strange forces of the world slacked off. There were still ghosties and ghoulies. And some official response was required. "Pronounced 'Eyesight'" was a typical Thatcher body – not responsible to parliament, a huge drain on public money, and with barely a result to show for it. But it is scientific. It's a wonder they didn't try to sell shares. Onions publishes enough to keep tenure and submits reports on the practical applications of the paranormal. John Major's man originally, he's very New Labour now. The woman who left her cap at that meeting is covertly the Minister for All Things Weird. "Heritage and Sport" is a euphemism, of course. The last Big Idea was that economic blackspots were under ancient curses. Focus groups were quizzed as to how to lift the gloom. They came up with the Millennium Dome. One could be forgiven for weeping. The whole apparatus trundles along, most of the time. It has managed tolerably without me.'

'And you? You left it all behind?'

'Took my bat and ball and repaired to Cheyne Walk. It was a relief, really – not having to feel anything any more.'

He made her angry again. It was all very well to sneer at Onions and the government and the bloody dome. If he'd done anything in the last twenty-five years except stare at white walls and feed the cats, she might have been more inclined to sympathise.

'Good point,' he said.

He had picked up her thoughts. It was like ice-points in her heart.

'I'm sorry,' he said, genuinely. 'We're just in tune. Fred knew we would be. You haven't tumbled yet.'

'But I will?'

'Don't be peeved. It's not so terrible. What harm can I be? I'm a bitter old recluse, totally ineffectual and probably on drugs.'

She didn't want to laugh, but his boyish look of querying innocence tickled her.

'That's better. You were a smiler, not a pouter.'

It was true. She had always been photographed showing her teeth. She thought that was why the agency made a fuss about them.'

'Besides, I'm here, aren't I?' said Jeperson. 'I could have thrown a pillow over my head, but I'm on the way to Skerra like the rest of our merry band.'

'Have you been to the island before?'

'I don't know. Possibly.'

IX.

The Blowhole was the highest point on Skerra. It looked like a volcanic crater, but the file said it was man-made, a vertical shaft sunk from the levelled-off plateau abutting the cliff into the water-carved caverns below. Steps hewn into the rock wound around the hole, though a Post-it note on the page advised against attempting any descent without climbing gear.

Adam Onions, big orange suitcase fetched from the Sea King, stood at the lip of the Blowhole and pointed his torch down.

The 'steps' were a wet-looking groove around the shaft. However, a ladder – orange rope and silver treads – dangled, secured to the rock by pitons.

'"Arne Saknussemm, His Sign,"' quoted Jeperson.

'Beg your pardon?' said Onions.

'*Voyage au centre de la terre*, Jules Verne,' explained Sewell Head, the trivia champion, '1864, expanded 1867; translated, anonymously, into English as *Journey to the Centre of the Earth*, 1871.'

'Also a film with James Mason,' Kydd added.

'I'm so glad that's cleared up,' said Onions.

Head scrunched the wrapper from a large bar of Cadbury's Fruit and Nut, held it over the Blowhole, and dropped it. Weighted by silver foil, it spiralled downwards, then an underground gust caught it and disappeared. For a moment, Stacy didn't know why her spine prickled. Then she realised the chocolate wrapper had been sucked rather than blown.

It had started to rain. The wind was so fierce that pellets of water came at them horizontally, or even from below.

'We should get out of this weather,' said Persephone Gill. 'Seriously.'

'So speaks the classical Queen of the Underworld,' said Jeperson.

'Also known as "Proserpina",' footnoted Head.

'Our business is down there, Adam,' said Jeperson. 'It is why we're here.'

Onions made show of thinking it over.

'Until we find out what happened to Captain Vernon's team, I don't think we should risk—'

'We won't find out by standing up here catching our deaths,' said Jeperson. 'I deduce from this ladder that the estimable Captain and his hardy tars are quite likely down below.'

'They were ordered to stay—'

Jeperson silenced him with a look.

'In case you'd forgotten, we're the professionals in this field. We're the psychic detectives, the occult adventurers, the ghost-hunters. And this hole leads to a haunted place. It's where we should be.'

Jeperson bent to grasp the ladder and get his foot on a rung.

His moon boot slipped, and Kydd grabbed his arm.

'Thank you,' said Jeperson. 'Nearly a nasty accident.'

With Onions's torchlight on him, Jeperson made his way down the Blowhole. The reflective strips on his poncho shone red.

Kydd followed.

Onions reluctantly surrendered his torch to Stacy, which meant she'd have to go last. Before descending, Onions fastened a rope to his suitcase and lowered it to the temporary custody of Kydd. Once the others had touched bottom, Stacy dropped the torch, which Onions managed to catch.

By the time she was at the foot of the ladder, the others were arguing about underground breezes. Though shielded from the worst of the rain and wind, there was a definite air current.

Onions played torchlight across ancient rock.

For a moment, Stacy assumed Captain Vernon's initial report had been a complete wind-up. This was just a hole in an island.

Then Sewell Head coughed.

And the rock walls parted with a metallic clang.

Bright, artificial light struck them blind.

ACT II: HEAD OFFICE
I.

After the murderous wind and rain topside, the cavern was pleasantly temperate.

Though rusty on cutting-edge tech, Richard Jeperson had seen the inside of enough military-industrial complexes to recognise the installation under Skerra as private enterprise rather than government. It was designed first to impress visiting shareholders, then to be a work environment.

Once the party had stopped exclaiming and clattering, he heard the thrumm of big engines somewhere below.

'Just heating and lighting this must suck an enormous

wattage,' he mused. 'And we're well off the national grid. What d'you reckon, Yoland?'

The weapons inspector was thinking it through. 'Geothermal, from the volcanic fault? That'd be extremely high risk. Ask the Pompeiians. My gut says it's the sea.'

'Waves?'

'Could be. If they've found a way to harness the big whirlpool, that'd be something... exciting.'

Huge banks of Wembley floodlights hung under the bare rock roof.

The entrance doors had led them onto a railed-off metal platform that was also a lift.

'Don't touch any controls.'

Onions issued his order while on his knees. He was entering the code to open his suitcase. Yoland ignored the diktat and picked up a plastic handset at the end of a python of insulated wire. He thumped the big button with the down arrow. Smoothly, without a lurch, the platform began to descend.

The cavern was of a size that would suit a collector of fully inflated antique Zeppelins. Natural rock formations had been shaped to accommodate the base. The floor was levelled and metalled, marked off like a runway or a launch-pad. The place was littered with white mini-jeeps, uniformed bodies and hard-to-identify machines. Concrete bunkers and blockhouses surrounded the ruin of a large, rail-mounted device with a Jodrell Bank-sized circular array. There had been a major fire here – a thick layer of soot blackened a swathe of wall and roof, and half the big dish was burned through to the frame. A forklift truck had been driven into a gantry and brought the structure down.

Déjà-vu made Richard's knees and ankles weak.

He saw shadows flitting about the cavern-floor, from cover to cover. Distant alarums of machine-age battle sounded: klaxons, automatic weapons fire, warning bells and whistles, shouts of pain.

The others were immune to such phenomena. For now.

His coat had been found here, covered with his blood. Any déjà-vu could be down to the circumstance that he really had been here before. No, it would not wash. He was used to holes in his memory, but here there was a hole in everyone's memory. If he had been here before, it would have made the secret history books. Limiting the circulation of information on an eyes-only basis paradoxically means preserving it.

Richard gripped the guardrail for support. He missed his white room, the neutral calm. This trip had disturbed his carefully maintained equilibrium. He had been preserved in his home; exposed to open air, he worried the decay he had staved off would catch up with him.

Everything hurt.

A colophon appeared all over the place: a yellow capital H, bent in at the corners to fit a white oval shield. It was huge, if half-burned, on the face of the array, and in miniature on everything else. The oviform pommels on the guardrails were three-dimensional versions of the same logo.

'What's the H for?' asked Stacy. 'Hers?' she suggested, thumbing at the awestruck Miss Gill. 'Hellfire Club? Hugeness? Hidey-Hole?'

'H'egg?' suggested de Maltby.

'Head,' said Head, touching one of the egg-shapes.

The doors had opened at the sound of Sewell Head's cough. Had anyone else noticed that?

Yes. Head had. *Naturellement*.

Richard perceived he had not been entirely right about the immunity of the rest of the party. This place affected Head. Onions had spent far too little time thinking about the problem of Sewell Head.

If only it were easier to concentrate.

Onions had his suitcase open. Instruments nestled in foam-rubber padding. He took off his anorak to reveal a utility belt and braces, tailored to fit when he had been a stone or two lighter. He had home-bored a frayed extra buckle-hole to loosen a harness which still cut into his tummy. Expertly, the man from I-Psi-T transferred his precious gadgets from compartments in the case to holsters on the harness. A complex doodad, which resembled the universal remote for a multi-function entertainment system, strapped watchlike to his wrist. Onions entered a code on the keypad and the doodad beeped to life. Green, orange and red LEDs lit up.

'Prepared for the unknown, Adam?'

'It's only the as-yet unquantified.'

Richard looked out at the cavern.

The wrongness of it all was nauseating, an electric thrill. With his gadgets, Onions could doubtless measure the condition as an increase in ozone levels or ambient charge or some such jargon. Richard did not doubt the physical effects were quantifiable. He just thought figures did not really help.

As they neared the bottom, he saw bullet-pocks on rock and concrete.

'This was a battlefield,' he announced.

Under the thrumm of the generators and the grind of the lift-platform, he again heard ghost gunfire, shouts. An explosion, mid-air, very near.

Spectre shrapnel shot through his mind.

Stacy was at his side, holding him up. He was momentarily riddled with scraps of hot pain. Then it was gone.

'You felt something?' she asked.

'Is it all coming back?' demanded Onions.

'Not a memory,' Richard said. 'Ghosts. Everywhere, ghosts.'

The others could not feel anything yet.

'I don't have any readings,' said Onions, tapping his doodad. A lone light flashed red. 'Except that. Variation in atmospheric pressure. Entirely natural phenomenon in a cave this size.'

It was what Richard had expected.

Onions cooed over his gizmo. Richard had a flash of Professor Calculus in the Tintin books – swinging his plumb-bob and muttering, 'A little more to the west.' Of course, he turned out to be right.

Everyone else – except Head, who was chewing placidly on a cud of fudge – craned over the low guardrail and peered out at the cavern, looking for movement where there was none.

'What's that thing?' Stacy asked. 'The giant satellite dish?'

'A transmitter,' said Yoland. 'It was gimbal-mounted, and on those rails. A nice bit of workmanship, if obsolete. Now, nanotech is sexy. Next generation isn't worth gasping at unless it's tinier than the last. But once upon a time, your equipment had to be monumental to attract funding.'

'What did it transmit?' asked Stacy.

'Two-year-old episodes of sitcoms you didn't watch on their first run,' suggested Richard. 'Championship dwarf-tossing from Glamorgan? Those radio broadcasts that teach alien invaders to speak English with BBC accents?'

Yoland shook his head, but did not venture an opinion.

As they neared the cavern floor, the corpses were more obvious. Skeletons in white H-on-the-left-tit jumpsuits. H-logoed dome hard hats chin-strapped to clean skulls.

Kydd whistled. The aircrewman was the only one among them who had served in a shooting war.

'Those people have been dead for a long time,' said Stacy.

'Decades,' Richard agreed.

The skeletons had died clutching automatic weapons

with fold-out tube-frame H-stamped stocks and unfamiliar horizontal magazines.

'Did they turn on each other?' asked Stacy. 'I see only one type of uniform.'

Among the jumpsuits were a few dead people in lab coats, full-skirted like spaghetti Western dusters, and oversized peaked caps. Not officers, but technicians, scientists, supervisors.

'The other side took away their dead,' deduced Richard.

'The winners,' said Yoland.

'Not necessarily. Whatever happened here isn't finished. If it were, our presence wouldn't be required.'

'That's what I like about you, Jeperson,' said Onions. 'Always reasons to be cheerful.'

'If you think I like making ominous pronouncements—'

Onions's belt beeped an interruption. He examined himself to find the gadget that had sounded out of turn.

The lift platform was level with the cavern floor. The dish towered hundreds of feet above them, lights shining through holes where plates were missing. Fighting had been fierce around the lift-bed. Many skeletons were spilled about, dusty brown-black stains on their uniforms, obvious bullet-holes in skulls.

'It's a mess,' said Head, intently. 'It should be tidied.'

For Head, Richard realised, H stood for Home.

The lift sank below the floor. Yoland looked at the control handset and found nothing besides simple up and down buttons.

They descended several further levels.

Suddenly, it was dark. Then light again. As the lift sank, circuits connected. Overhead strip lights tried to come on. Some panels buzzed and flashed and died, others sparked dangerously. Whole sections lit up perfectly, as if installed yesterday.

Richard had a sense of corridors winding into successive layers of labyrinth. Admin offices, supply areas, living quarters, cafeterias, recreation facilities, laboratories, lecture halls, testing grounds, museums, toilet facilities, information storage. No bare rock, but metalled walls, rubberised floor, heating and ventilation ducts (note to infiltrators: suitable for crawling through). Framed pictures were designed to seem like windows, the sort of touch you only got after expensive consultation.

They were deep underground, deep under the sea. Below the sea-bed, probably. He had a sense of enormous weight pressing in.

Without so much as a judder, the platform stopped.

Here, it was more than warm. The atmosphere was humid, tropical. Richard doffed his sou'wester and poncho, then unzipped his flight suit, which came away in sections. Underneath, he wore thigh-flied scarlet buccaneer britches and a lemon-yellow bumfreezer jacket buttoned to the throat, with an explosive cravat of red lace. He plumped the black silk rose in his lapel.

'Fab threads,' said Stacy, satirically.

Others followed his example and took off their heavy-weather gear.

The Detective Sergeant wore brown corduroy trousers and a zip-up matching waistcoat.

'Very practical,' he commented.

She took an onion-seller's beret from a pocket and tucked her hair into it.

'This is my arresting outfit,' she said. 'Your average villain tends to leg it if a bloke with size-eleven boots gets within spitting distance, but he'll hang about like a prat if someone blond asks him the way to Acacia Avenue. Most bollockbrains still give out bullshit directions after they're cuffed and in the van.'

The guardrail automatically folded into the floor of the platform.

Ahead was a plate-glass barrier, studded with white star-shaped opacities. Beyond was a reception area and a corridor. With a hiss, the glass was withdrawn into the ceiling. No one wanted to step under it – the glass would make a very serviceable guillotine.

A concealed sound system began to tinkle, 'Aquarius' from *Hair* played in the style of Herb Alpert and the Tijuana Brass.

Miss Gill mewed surprise, then said, 'It's not exactly Chris de Burgh.'

'Why did Chris de Burgh cross the road?' asked Stacy. Miss Gill shook her head. 'To get to the middle. Boom-boom.'

Yoland and de Maltby laughed and Onions looked impatient. Miss Gill took the joke as a personal dig, which Richard assumed Stacy intended. Head, he noted, was puzzled. That was worth filing away.

It was Onions's place to press on. Richard waited for him.

The man from I–Psi–T was fazed, not eager to venture further. Richard heard susurrus under the muzak.

Ghosts.

Head made the first move and wandered off the lift-bed platform.

That jolted Onions out of his reverie. He nodded to de Maltby and followed Head.

Richard saw the pilot had his side-arm out.

'I'd put that away if I were you,' cautioned Richard. 'Someone'll only get hurt.'

'Uhhhhm,' said de Maltby, affecting not to hear the advice.

Richard shrugged. 'Just trying to help,' he told Stacy.

Yoland, Kydd and Miss Gill padded after the others.

Richard hung back, mind open, all receivers alert. The place was shrieking at him now. Stacy touched his shoulder, carefully.

'We'll be left behind,' she said, gently.

He looked into her face, glimpsing skull under skin. He saw for an X-ray instant the back-teeth she would not sacrifice for a career, sensed the sparking synapses of her admirable brain. Fred had not assigned his minder casually. He had a spasm of fear for her. This place was dangerous.

Between seconds, he had a flash – more than a vision, it came with sound, smell, temperature. The corridor was swept by a blossom of fire. The stutter of gunfire was tinnitus, cutting through his skull. His skin broiled, his hair crisped.

'Richard,' Stacy said, snapping her fingers under his nose, 'come out of it.'

He did. His face tingled, his ears rang. Otherwise, he was fine.

'Who am I?' she asked.

He knew who he was. He knew who she was. He knew where this was.

Though exposed, he was growing stronger again.

'You are an arresting woman,' he said, startling a smile out of her.

The sound system burbled 'Let the Sunshine In' scrambled with 'Spanish Flea'.

At least, she was starting to trust him. Refreshing as it was to be treated bluntly like a mad old relic, the tonic lost its effectiveness after a few doses.

'Flaming Nora!' screamed Miss Gill.

The others were out of sight, beyond a turn in the corridor.

'That's a call to investigate,' he told Stacy. 'A good many dramatic situations begin with screaming.'

'That's from *Barbarella*,' she said, making him feel younger. 'My dad's favourite film,' she added, rubbing it in that he was ancient.

Miss Gill's scream segued into a nails–down–a–blackboard laugh.

At a trot, they rounded the corner. The floor was lush as an executive suite, though the nap was moistly squishy, mouldy in patches. The carpet pattern consisted of tiny interlocking H symbols.

They found the others, gaping up as if at an art exhibit.

Miss Gill honked astonished laughter. You had to have unearned wealth to get away with a bray like that.

On a brushed steel plinth was an eight-foot tall marble egg, carved with Humpty Dumpty features.

It was a monumental bust of Sewell Head.

II.

'Someone's got some bloody explaining to do!' said Miss Gill, through snorts of aghast hilarity. 'I mean, whose island is this?'

Head looked up at his own face, curious. Richard could tell the little man wanted to touch the marble but was afraid to. He had chocolate on his fingers and did not want to spoil the surface.

'You're the pub quiz king, Head,' said Onions. 'Any answers?'

Head said nothing. Onions pointed his doodad at the sculpture and pressed buttons.

'He doesn't remember,' said Richard.

Onions wheeled on him, hostile.

'He doesn't want to remember. Like you, Jeperson.'

'Back off,' said Stacy, protective, eye on de Maltby's gun.

Onions, surprised, did. He wasn't handling this well.

'I don't remember,' admitted Richard. 'It's not a choice. It's a condition. There is more here than we see. More than you can quantify, Adam.'

Onions huffed. An old argument was in the offing.

Stacy had stepped in for him. He squeezed her arm as silent thanks. They had an understanding now.

With her strength, he wasn't so feeble.

Beyond the monumental bust was a sculpture garden, with AstroTurf for grass and subdued lighting. A path wound between a dozen pieces, all representing the same subject – Sewell Head.

Some were naturalistic, showing a younger man than the shuffling original, crudely attempting to convey dynamic presence; some were completely stylised, just H–stamped ovals; one was a mobile on which twenty or so transparent crystalline eggs were arranged to represent the atomic structure of an element unknown to science; another was a parody Easter Island head, eggskull elongated and eyes exaggerated.

'I should say somebody has a big head,' said Miss Gill, more pettish than amused now.

Sewell Head said nothing. Next to these three-dimensional images of himself, he seemed insubstantial, as if he were the third–generation copy and the artworks the original.

At the base of a Soviet–style statue of Head heroic in overalls and hard hat was the skeleton of a woman, laid out like a sacrifice. A long white evening dress clung to bones. At first, Richard assumed her head was miraculously intact, then he realised she had worn a wax mask. The doll–face was cracked across, pinned to the skull by a black–handled throwing-knife.

'I'd kill for those shoes,' said Miss Gill.

The spike heels were at least six inches. Gold filigree bands wound up almost to the knees; they curled slackly around unclad shinbones.

'Feel free,' said Head. 'They're your size.'

Miss Gill looked at the little man as if seeing him for the first time. He was past his insubstantial phase. The likenesses reflected back on the original, lending him a charisma that had gone unnoticed.

Richard knew Onions wasn't pointing his doodad in the right direction.

At the end of the path, doors opened.

Head passed through, followed by Miss Gill and de Maltby.

There had been an uneasy shift of authority within the group.

'Adam,' he said. 'Don't let this get away from you.'

Onions had been looking at the dead woman. He reacted to Richard as if slapped.

'I don't know what you mean, Jeperson. I am in complete control.'

Could have fooled me, thought Stacy.

'What are you smiling at?' snapped Onions.

Richard did not explain. There were so many voices in his head here that it was a delight that at least one was friendly.

Onions, grumpy, stamped off towards the open doors.

III.

The hallway was lined with heads, mounted on shields fixed to the walls. Some were skulls, ancient and cracked. Others were poorly preserved, features dripping like wax. A few were disturbingly lifelike.

Under each trophy, museum-plates gave details. Richard looked at the prize of the collection.

Australopithecine, Sterkfontein Caves, c.3m BC, *axe-bite.*

It was just a partial cranium, with a jagged gash. Most of the others were of far more recent vintage.

He considered the next trophy.

R. J. Tuomey-Rees, MA Cantab, 1953, six-inch nail embedded.

'Six-inch nail embedded,' said Miss Gill. 'It bloody is, too. Grue-some!'

Tuomey-Rees was one of the incompletes, flaps of dried meat over grey bone. A lot of goldwork in his teeth.

'"Could do better if he tried,"' said Sewell Head.

The little man looked into the empty eyesockets.

Everyone stared at Head.

'My Second Year form-master at Coal Hill Secondary Modern was called Tuomey-Rees,' Head explained.

'He didn't happen to disappear in 1953, did he?' asked Stacy.

'Not at all,' said Head, missing any accusation. 'He was still flapping about in his blessed mortar-board and gown in '57, when I left school. Tuomey-Rees was a most humorous fellow. "With your name, young Sewell, you should be, ahem, Head of the Class." He gave me my nickname. He would say, "Don't get a swellhead, Sewell Head!" Soon they were all calling me "Swellhead". Very amusing.'

It was the longest speech Richard had heard from Head.

'Happy days,' mused Head. 'The tuck shop, playground japes, Nurse dosing for nits. And "Whacker" Tuomey-Rees. That was his nickname, "Whacker".'

Head made a swishing motion, whipping an imaginary cane.

'The strange thing was that I was an obedient boy, got my homework in on time, never ran in the quad or talked out of turn. But, every few weeks, "Whacker" found reason to chastise me. "Six of the best, Swellhead, six of the best!" Looking back, I think he was one of those sad fellows who got pleasure from caning small boys. It wouldn't be allowed these days.'

The nail had been pounded into the skull in the centre of the forehead. Dents around the nailhead showed that a few hammer-blows had missed.

Richard looked from the Tuomey-Rees trophy to the others.

'Do any other names mean anything to you, Mr Head?'

Head scuttled down the hallway, examining plates.

Morris 'Basher' Cropshaw, Holly Nook Recreation Grounds, 1954, penknife in occipital hollow.

'There was a boy called Basher Something. Lived three doors down. Always hanging about on the corner when I was coming home from school. Very high-spirited, boisterous, got into scrapes. He took my satchel once and never gave it back. My homework was in it. Whacker striped my bottom for that.'

Head came to a trophy with fine red hair done up in a topknot with a big blue bow. The face was shrivelled.

'Here's another old friend,' said Head.

Melanie Potter, Holly Nook Youth Club,
1956, crushed hyoid.

'Pretty girl, but not very friendly. She danced with me once. To win a bet with Mavis Bryant. Oh, how funny!'

Mavis Bryant, 'Bryant the Tyrant', Holly Nook
Youth Club, 1956, multiple simple fractures.

'Have you noticed how that happens? You don't think of someone in nearly fifty years and then when you do their name comes up in some completely unconnected manner.'

Richard noticed stricken looks among the party. Even Onions was taken aback.

Sewell Head was getting excited by his nostalgia wallow. He came to a nearly preserved head wearing an army cap.

Sergeant Arthur Grimshaw, Walmington-on-Sea
Barracks, 1960, .303 bullet in cranium.

'When I did my National Service, there was a very loud sergeant called "Grimmy". Used to get into a lather about close-order drill. Said I had two left feet. Always had me peeling mountains of blessed spuds. You know, I think this really is Grimmy. He's still frowning, and red in the face.'

Stacy tugged Richard's sleeve.

'Richard,' she whispered, urgently, 'I went through the files on Head. School, family background, National Service, employment history, the lot. Boring as Bognor on a wet bank holiday. If his past were littered with headless corpses, it'd show up. Surely?'

After Grimshaw in 1960, the names meant less to Head.

'Professor Etienne Bolin, the particle physicist. I've heard of him, but who hasn't? Ken Dodd, the comedian. I always found him more irritating than funny. Scary clowns were a phobia of mine when I was little. And do you remember that ghastly pop song that was on everywhere you listened for months in 1965? "Tears for Souvenirs". Put me off *Top of the Pops* for life.'

Yoland gave a sympathetic 'ugh'.

Richard and Stacy looked at the preserved pop–eyed, crooked-teethed Ken Dodd trophy.

'Now *he's* not beheaded,' said Stacy. 'He was in that Kenneth Branagh *Hamlet* film.'

'This does look like him, circa 1965, though. As if he were cut off in his prime.'

'"Tears for Souvenirs". Can't say I've heard of it.'

'You haven't missed much.'

They were nearly at the end of the trophy hall.

'And this fellow means nothing to me,' announced Head.

Frederick Regent, the Diogenes Club, 1972,
decapitation via monofilament.

Richard heard the ghost of a scream.

His hands knotted into fists.

Time passed inside his mind.

He forced himself out of fugue, and realised everyone else had heard the scream, which still echoed.

No, not echoed – continued.

Another dramatic situation.

IV.

'It's in here,' said Onions, his LED readings flashing angry red.

The scream careened about the hallway like a pinball. There was an associated visual phenomenon, a ragged freeform shadow that darted in a zigzag. It caught Kydd out in the open and passed through him with a ripping sound. The aircrewman patted his chest.

'That wasn't half a funny feeling,' he said. 'Warm and wet.'

Richard was pressed against the wall, Stacy by him. He tried to follow the shadow, but it flickered too swiftly.

'Nothing to be afraid of,' announced Onions. 'It's an after-image. It's not happening now. It's long gone. Just a recording on the Stone Tape.'

The wall was trembling. Richard wondered how dormant that volcano was.

At the end of the hallway a door flapped open and a figure lurched into view, like a target at an army shooting range. A person of indeterminate sex in a white coat and hard hat, opaque white visor over the face, loose white polythene bootees and mittens tied over the extremities. It held one of the unfinished-looking guns that had been in the hands of the corpses in the cavern.

The apparition moved at half-speed and was silent.

Onions pointed his doodad at the white figure. Its edges blurred and Richard saw the knees kink as if the thing were a hologram projected on drifting mist.

'Now, that's a ghost,' said Stacy.

The figure's movements slowed. It was wheeling about,

bringing its gun to bear on the hallway. The outlines were smeared completely now, bleeding into the background. Even the gun was soft, barrel and magazine floppy.

Stacy made a gunfinger and popped her mouth.

A red wound flowered on the ghost's chest, unfolding like one of those pellets that become roses when dropped into water. It was knocked off its feet and floated upwards, legs trailing and dissipating.

Stacy, astonished, raised her finger and blew on the tip.

'Temperature is down ten degrees centigrade,' said Onions. 'It's sucking heat, converting it to matter.'

The ghost's phantom gun kicked. Black blobules coughed from the barrel and lobbed through space. Yoland bent out of their path, knocking Miss Gill down, covering her against the floor.

Sewell Head, fascinated, turned, watching ghost bullets pass by him. They left visible ripples in the air. Head prodded one of the wakes with a long finger, and twirled it into a nebula-shape.

Stacy drew both index fingers and popped like Wyatt Earp emptying his six-shooters into Old Man Clanton. The ghost jittered and staggered.

The blobules still swam through thick air.

De Maltby fired his real gun. The report was appallingly loud, but the shot did less to the ghost than Stacy's pretend bullets.

De Maltby stuck out a hand to steady himself as he took aim again. One of the blobules collided with his palm.

Everything sped up. The ghoststuff fell like rain, splashing the carpet in a splatter, leaving a Hiroshima blast shadow.

The single shot still resounded, an assault on the ears.

Another scream exploded, not ghostly.

De Maltby's left hand was a red ruin, fingers stiff and shaking, blood welling from a ragged black hole. He dropped his gun.

'Now that was bloody stupid,' said Richard.

The viscount gripped his wrist and fell, swallowing yelps of pain. He thrashed a little and swore a lot. The barracks vocabulary sat ill with his plummy accent. Kydd got to the pilot's side with a battlefield med-kit. Richard helped Stacy pin de Maltby down as the aircrewman prepared a syringe, drawing from an ampoule of morphine. Stacy skinned de Maltby's sleeve and held his arm steady so Kydd could get the shot in him.

Yoland had picked up de Maltby's dropped gun; he aimed at the doorway. Head still stood out in the open, puzzled. Miss Gill was in a crouch by Yoland, presenting a small target. Onions was flat against a wall, Ken Dodd gurning over his shoulder as he fiddled with his doodad.

De Maltby stopped kicking and Kydd got a proper tourniquet around his arm. The blobule hadn't gone through the pilot's hand, but dissipated on impact, turning to nasty black gunge. Kydd washed out the wound with bottled water and slapped on a pressure bandage.

'…Uhhhm… hurts,' said de Maltby, redundantly. He shook his head and gritted his teeth.

The pilot was in no shape to fly them off Skerra. Richard hadn't qualified on a helicopter in twenty-five years. Unless someone else in the party had hidden talents, they were stuck here until they could be rescued.

De Maltby relaxed, eyes fluttering shut.

If the viscount had shifted a bit more to the left, his lesser relations would have bumped up in the line of succession. The Royal Navy would have had to do some embarrassing explaining to the Royal Family.

Miss Gill got up and angrily aimed a finger at Onions.

'You said it was an after-image! You said it couldn't harm us!'

Onions tried to show her a read-out. She wasn't interested.

'Where are the proper experts who're supposed to protect us?'

she demanded. 'I was promised a crack team of up-for-anything sailors armed to the teeth and ready to throw up a ring of fire and steel around us. All I've got are useless old weirdos and a bloody meter maid. I didn't come here to be shot at.'

Stacy, the 'meter maid', cocked her gunfinger and pointed it at the back of Miss Gill's head. Richard gave her the nod and she put it away.

'It's extremely rare that a manifestation causes injury.'

'Tell him that.'

De Maltby was smiling now, morphine kicking in.

Miss Gill and Onions glared at each other.

'Listen to me,' announced Richard. 'This is a haunted house. Bigger than most, but still a haunted house. Adam's little gadgets are all well and good, but what is going on here isn't just an atmospheric phenomenon, like weather. It's reactive and it's directed. A show is being put on for us. But we aren't just an audience, we're targets. The place is inhabited, ensouled. Make no mistake, the stone tape isn't a medium of recording but of transmission. Whatever haunts here will try to affect us, to work on our weaknesses. It's already begun, subtly and, ah, not to subtly. From now on, be alert, open, on your guard. I needn't say we shouldn't go wandering off alone. Always know where everyone else is. Fix on that. It'll help you when there are others among us. Beware of circles – physical circles, mental circles. The place would like us to go round on its little rails. Haunted houses are traps and tests. The bad ones, that is, and this is certainly one of those. Adam, give a heads-up whenever your needles twitch. It'd help if we knew something was coming before it arrived. We've seen what can happen. Let's not let it happen again.'

Onions opened his mouth, as if he had a long, prepared answer.

'Let's move on,' said Richard, cutting him off.

Kydd relieved Yoland of de Maltby's side-arm with, 'I'd best look after that, sir.' The aircrewman helped the doped pilot stand, making sure he could walk without falling over himself.

Before leaving the hallway, Richard looked at the Fred trophy. It was the best-preserved of the modern collection, as if curing methods had improved between 1953 and 1972. It was a real severed head, very deathlike, and was somehow really Fred, hair close-cropped, mouth open. Fred as he had been as a young plod in 1972, not the top cop Richard had seen two days ago at Euston.

The eyes were blue, not hazel: they were taxidermist's glass, a detail mistaken by whoever prepared the head for display.

Staring into Fred's wrong eyes made Richard queasy.

But determined. Being shut up, inside himself, inside his home, had been a mistake.

If this was out here all along, he should have been in the world.

Skerra was his problem.

V.

They were in a control room.

Yoland whistled in astonished amusement.

'Vintage,' he declared.

Banks of computers were stacked against a wall – bulky cabinets wired together, each the size of a fridge-freezer, with exposed spools of tape and letterbox slots for punchcards and print-outs.

'Pre-silicon chip,' said Yoland, stroking a machine. 'Installed in the late 1960s, maybe early 1970s.'

Richard picked up a Pirelli calendar from a strew of papers on the floor. A naked woman snarled, holding a scary African mask next to her face. The photograph was manipulated to shade into a drawing at the extremities.

'Might I take a wild guess and suggest this facility was

abandoned sometime in February 1973?'

'That sounds about right,' said Yoland. 'What was happening then?'

'Oil crisis. Power cuts. Television shut down at half past ten. IRA bombing campaign.'

'All that never happened,' said Miss Gill, born 1983. 'He's getting the seventies confused with the War. People his age were all on drugs.'

Richard was more amused than offended.

Yoland twiddled some knobs on a console.

'Does it still work?' asked Stacy.

'Unlikely,' said the weapons inspector. 'These old jobs were as dicky as Christmas tree lights.'

One wall was given over to a grey and dead display screen, a stitching of bullet-holes across the glass.

There had been fighting in here. Some cabinets were overturned and ruptured, bleeding wires and circuit-boards.

'I told a lie,' said Yoland, holding up a component. 'This is a silicon chip. Or some sort of prehistoric ancestor. Ceramic, micro-printed. It's the size of my thumb, but it's definitely a chip. Whoever put this together was way ahead of the game.'

The tile floor was patchwork-quilted with spilled files, strews of punchcards and streamers of magnetic tape.

This, Richard knew, was where his coat had been found.

Head walked up to a black swivel chair on a dais. He sat in it and whirled around like a child, legs pointing out. As the chair revolved, gears clicked. The big screen hummed and warmed up. Behind spiderweb of cracks, static buzzed. Richard's attention was drawn to it for a moment, but he forced himself to look away. It was too easy to see shapes in static.

'Clock this,' said Stacy.

She picked up a cardboard file-folder, embossed with the

familiar H. Under the oval, in a retro-futurist typeface, were the words 'Sewell Head Industries'. Yoland took it and passed it around.

'You're a captain of industry, Swellhead?' said Miss Gill. 'I thought you worked in a sweet shop.'

Head found a control panel in the arm of his chair. The designer must have been a *Star Trek* fan. Head pressed a button: lights came on at the base of his dais and in a circle overhead, catching him in a shaft of brightness.

'This is all new to me,' he said.

'But you know where the light-switches are,' said Yoland.

'Which button opens the trapdoor to the alligator pits?' asked Miss Gill. 'Or do you prefer piranhas?'

Head was thoughtful. He stabbed another button.

A section of the floor flapped downwards. Richard was suddenly at the edge of a hole. A foul smell wafted up. Richard tottered but Stacy pulled him back from the brink. He slipped. A sharp stab of terror went through him as he felt Stacy going over too.

'Got you, miss,' said Kydd. He had stepped in to grab her around the waist.

It took some doing, but they were all restored to safety.

'I'm so sorry,' said Head. 'I didn't think.'

The bottom of the pit was dark and liquid. And inhabited.

'Best not fiddle with the toys any more,' said Richard.

'Quite right,' said Head, mildly.

He didn't get out of his chair, though. More and more, he looked comfortable.

'What is this place?' asked Miss Gill.

'Head Office,' said Head.

'Very clever,' said Richard. 'But you'd have to be clever, wouldn't you?'

Head sat, impassive.

'There is no Sewell Head Industries,' said Yoland. 'At least not off this island. Never has been.'

Head nodded.

'That's what puzzled us when Vernon's report came in,' said Onions. 'We found Mr Head very easily. He's in the phone book. There's only one of him.'

Richard wondered if that was strictly true.

'And we know, in exhaustive detail, what he's done with his life. There just isn't any gap in which he could have done this...'

Onions spread his hands, indicating everything in this complex.

'Some obsessive trivia quiz fan did all this for him?' said Miss Gill. 'I find that impossible to believe.'

Head's fingers hovered over buttons.

Kydd stood by the dais, de Maltby's gun tucked into his belt, at attention.

'What's it all for?' asked Stacy.

'That's an interesting question,' said Yoland, 'and I can make a range of guesses. But the big question is, "How's it all here?"'

The techie was in his element, getting up to speed.

'This couldn't have been built in secret,' said Yoland. 'It's a major construction project. Hundreds, maybe thousands of men would have had to work on it. Think of all the raw materials that must have been transported here, to an abandoned island. There'd have had to be a non-stop back-and-forth on the sea-lanes. Where are the ships' logs, flight-plans, invoices, bills of lading, pay-slips? This is a small underground city. Supplying must have been a mammoth operation. It would all have gone on in the public eye. Millions of pounds must have been spent. Multiples of millions. There may be no Sewell Head Industries, but something wealthier than most countries created this place.'

Richard remembered how he had felt when he saw the apported coat, how he had instinctively avoided touching it, how it had been an affront to his sense of the way the universe fitted together. He was feeling the same thing again, on a colossal scale.

This whole place was wrong.

VI.

They made camp three levels above the control room, in a block Richard guessed was accommodation for SHI executives. Spartan barracks and dormitories were provided for jumpsuit drones, but this sector offered rooms arranged like an American motel, in balconied tiers. Instead of sky, the central courtyard had naked rock. Garden furniture was scattered around, but there were no corpses.

Stacy and Kydd had gone topside, to fetch supplies from the Sea King.

De Maltby was in drugged sleep, but otherwise stable.

Richard checked the room he had staked for himself. It was anonymous Scandinavian moderne, with clown paintings in place of windows and piped-in dabba-dabba-dabba muzak. A duvet lay on the drum-tight fitted sheet of the single bed. At first, he thought the bedding a uniform grey, but his touch disturbed a thin layer of dust. The duvet cover and pillowcase were white, imprinted with the bright yellow H logo.

The door had an airtight seal. Ventilation and heat came through grilles in the walls. Besides clown paintings, decor extended to a framed photograph of a young, Kupperberg-suited Sewell Head with his arms around a couple of sweaty Americans who proved, on close examination, to be Richard Nixon and Elvis Presley. The Prezz and the King both looked up to Zen Master of Quantum Cleverness.

An en-suite bathroom offered a Plexiglas shower booth and

stainless-steel toilet and washstand. He ran the taps and got hot and cold water. After bursts of rusty-red, the flow ran clean. He tasted the cold and found it drinkable. He assumed there was a desalination plant somewhere in the complex, converting seawater. A bathroom cabinet contained a solidified tube of unbranded toothpaste, a blister-pack of contraceptive pills and a bottle of Breck shampoo. A H-logoed sampler kit contained syrettes, vials of powder marked 'heroin' and 'cocaine', and purple lozenges stamped 'Lovely Shining Dream'.

The muzak – José Feliciano playing the Doors' greatest hits – came through the speakers of a large telescreen inset into the wall opposite the bed. There were no on-off or channel controls, and no handset. Whoever lived here listened to and watched whatever the master programmer gave them.

A wardrobe contained three identical lab coats and dispenser-packs of disposable plastic bootees and mittens. A bedside table had unread paperbacks of *Valley of the Dolls* and *Airport* with early seventies covers. He also found the *2001* movie tie-in, and raised an eyebrow to see Ray Bradbury and Stanley Kubrick listed as co-authors. The first chapter began 'When Heywood Floyd was a boy in the Midwest he used to go out and look at the stars at night and wonder about them.' Reluctantly, he closed the book and slipped it into his pocket. A drawer that pulled out from under the bed had an array of gleaming silver-steel, H-stamped weapons – automatic pistols, clips of ammunition, combat knives, a samurai sword.

A fizzing cut through the muzak.

He looked at the telescreen. It had come to life, or at least static.

The swirls resolved into a blurry H logo, then the letter faded and the oval shield grew brighter. Richard fancied eyes and a smile.

He picked out one of the pistols, rammed a clip into the butt, slipped off the safety and shot the screen. The tube imploded with a cough of smoke. In the sparking wreckage, a necklike attachment craned – it ended in a blinking lens.

There was a sharp rap at his door.

'Come in, it's not locked.'

Onions, free of his gadget belt, tentatively looked round the door.

'I shot the screen, Adam. A pre-emptive strike. It was trying to get to me.'

Onions humoured him and pressed on.

'Meeting in the courtyard in five minutes, Jeperson. We need to hash out a schedule for the investigation.'

Onions withdrew.

Richard hefted the automatic pistol. As a rule, he disliked guns, but this had a satisfyingly heavy feel. It hadn't kicked when fired, and the noise – the thing he hated most about using firearms – had been damped somehow. His ears still rang from the shot de Maltby had fired in the trophy hall, but his own more recent discharge had wiped itself out. He turned the gun over in his hands, getting the heft of it.

Then he put it down and went to wash his hands.

He didn't even like using the water in this room, let alone the weaponry. The gun had been on its best behaviour, endeavouring to win his confidence, wheedling to get holster-close to his heart. He had no doubt that if he trusted the thing, it would turn traitor. Worse still was the *2001* paperback, which whispered, 'Read me, read me,' in his ear. He would happily burn the negatives of every movie Steven Spielberg ever directed to get into a screening of this *Space Odyssey*.

Somewhere under Skerra, there must be a cinema.

He killed the thought and looked at the mirrored cabinet.

Behind his old eyes, there were lacunae. Maybe Ray

Bradbury had written *2001*, and it had slipped his mind, liquid misinformation rushing in to fill the hole. Maybe Sewell Head had mounted Fred Regent's head on a board thirty years ago, and the decades Richard remembered were a protracted psychotic episode, born of guilt at being unable to keep his friend alive.

He took the vial of cocaine from the drugs kit and thought about it.

Circles, he realised. He was beginning to think in circles.

But there was something else. The sense of wrongness was still there, but other senses crowded in. He was thinking more clearly, with fewer of his memory lapses. He even felt better, long-settled aches lifting from his limbs. The air down here was good for him. He had not expected that.

Was this another trap?

He left the room, sealed it behind him, and walked along the balcony to a white filigree spiral staircase.

Assuming that Stacy and Kydd were not back and de Maltby excused, Richard was the last to make it to Onions's meeting.

They were assembled in a gazebo affair at the centre of the court, sitting on folding chairs around a wrought-iron table under a giant candy-striped umbrella. Yoland had a laptop computer fired up. Miss Gill had changed into a Skerra tartan designer skirt with matching sash. Onions had an agenda drawn up and was checking it over.

Sewell Head stood a few feet away, his back to the others, looking up.

'I was listing the types of phenomenon observed here,' said Onions. 'Spectral figures, ectoplasmic spores, hot spots, cold spots, cyclic apparitions, aural and visual manifestations…'

'Apports,' prompted Richard.

'Of course, apports.'

'Lots of 'em. Adam, who wrote *2001*?'

Onions frowned.

'I know that one,' said Miss Gill. 'George Orwell.'

Richard felt his mind crack again.

'No, that's *Nineteen Eighty-Four*,' put in Yoland. '*2001* is… it's on the tip of my tongue. Wait a minute, we've got the triviameister here. Swellhead, who wrote *2001*?'

'Arthur C. Clarke,' said Head, dully, not turning round.

The world settled again, and Richard nodded.

'That's decided then.'

'What are you on about, Jeperson? This is no time…'

Richard produced the book. Onions looked at it, puzzled. Then saw the names on the cover. He passed it to Yoland, whose instinct was to turn to the last page.

'How does it end?' Yoland asked Head.

'"For though he was master of the world, he was not quite sure what to do next,"' recited Head. '"But he would think of something."'

'Wrong-g-g-g!' said Yoland. '"Then, as the moon watched, the Star Child left the wilderness behind and walked into the town."'

Head turned, almost angry.

Richard realised the little man could not bear to be mistaken.

'Let me see that,' he said.

Yoland tossed him the book. He looked through it roughly, breaking the thirty-five-year-old spine.

'This isn't right,' he said.

He tore the book in half and threw the pages away.

Richard had a pang of loss and fury. Then he remembered the insinuating gun. The book was best out of reach. It had been a dangerous temptation.

There must be books in all the rooms. Maybe LP records.

Best not think of that.

'Nothing is right here,' said Richard. 'This is not a natural place.'

'If there's a prize for speaking the bloody obvious,' said Miss Gill, 'the old hippie just took it home.'

'Just because a thing is bloody obvious doesn't mean it shouldn't be spoken.'

'Could you please stop bickering,' said Onions. 'And pay attention.'

Onions slapped his agenda on the table.

'Now,' he said, 'observations, please.'

'This is treasure trove, right?' said Miss Gill. 'But on my land. So I own it.'

No one wanted to debate that. Yet.

'Yoland, can you give us your preliminary report?' said Onions. 'You've a different remit here.'

Richard had wondered about that. What did Morag Duff and Really-a-Good-Bloke Rory expect to get out of this expedition? People like them always thought of 'practical applications'. I-Psi-T was Min of Def-funded, too.

Yoland shut his computer. 'Too early to say, but I think there are things here of immense worth.'

Miss Gill clapped her hands and threatened to laugh again.

'Yes, monetary worth,' said Yoland. 'But more than that. Mr Jeperson, you asked about the power source. I've ferreted about a bit and it's definitely tidal. We have nothing like it. And the equipment we've seen is a paradox. A lot of it is bakelite and solder antique, but there are shortcuts I don't understand. This place is thirty years old, but whoever built it was forty or fifty years ahead of their time. Handicapped by the tools available, but spooky brilliant. My guess is that a handful of circuit-boards from the control room could yield patents that would bring in millions of euros a year. You know my field. Weapons. I've been tinkering with one of those machine-pistol jobbies, the things with funny magazines. It's not like any small arms I've ever seen. Recoilless, silenced, and fires pellets that expand in the air. And we haven't cracked the puzzle of the big dish. I reckon it does something interesting. Whoever ends up with ownership is going to be, ah, enormously at an advantage.'

'"Whoever?"' protested Miss Gill. 'Daddy paid good money for Skerra.'

'For the island, not for what's under it.'

'So, who else's is it? The Skerrans are all gone. And this isn't Britain. It's an independent country and I can make up my own laws.'

Richard saw Yoland and Miss Gill were being seduced. Knowledge, money, power, justification, intrigue. Even Onions, with quantifiable results that could not be dismissed, was half in love with the complex.

He wondered when Stacy and Kydd would get back. Of the party, they were the two he trusted most.

'You're forgetting something,' said Head.

'What?' asked Miss Gill and Yoland, together.

'Whose name is on everything here. Whose initial marks everything.'

Head thumped his chest. The place was getting to him too. It could be that he had the most to gain from it.

'We'll come to that in a minute,' said Onions.

'Can I be the one to talk about the impossible?' said Richard.

'I think that falls under the "bloody obvious" category, Jeperson,' said Onions. 'The impossible is our daily bread, remember? Even for the amateur dabblers of the Diogenes Club.'

'I don't mean the unexplained, the supernatural. Ghosties and ghoulies. I mean evidence of things we know did not happen. Fred Regent was not decapitated in 1972. Ray Bradbury did not write *2001*. Sewell Head did not broker the meet between Nixon and Elvis.'

'That photo's in your room too?' said Yoland.

'A corporation that has never existed did not build an underground complex on Skerra in the late sixties. A small war was not fought here in February 1973. Mr Head and I did not bleed all over my third-best coat in that control room.'

Head said nothing.

'I know you'll be thoroughly prepared,' said Richard. 'You'll have a record of everyone who has set foot on Skerra between the evacuation of '32 and our arrival this morning?'

Onions flinched, minutely. Yoland looked at his computer screen.

'I see that information is available.'

Richard pulled Yoland's laptop across the table.

'That's interesting,' he said. 'Miss Gill, when your father bought Skerra, did anyone tell him that Winston Churchill used it for anthrax experiments?'

Miss Gill was aghast. 'Bloody hell they did!'

'Those Skerran goats must be the hardiest creatures on Earth. They were supposed to have been wiped out by bio-warfare in 1944. The spores were active and deadly in '57, when a trawler off its course ran aground. There were deaths. The team from Porton Down who visit every ten years reported non-lethal traces in 1964 and no danger at all in 1974, 1984 and 1994. No danger from anthrax that is. In '84, there was a fatality due to goat attack. I suppose this jaunt is incidentally supposed to take the place of the scheduled check-up?'

Yoland nodded. 'It's perfectly safe now.'

Richard scrolled down.

'I see there was a naval exercise here in 1996. We must have been thinking of invading an island. No, it's the other way about.

There was a worry that Spain might take the presence of Israeli or Moroccan tourists on Gibraltar as violation of the fifth paragraph of Article Ten of the Treaty of Utrecht and pull a Galtieri. It seemed like a sensible idea to play out a "liberation scenario". You'll be relieved to learn we showed Johnny Spaniard he couldn't hold the Rock for long.'

'Shouldn't the Navy have asked me first?' protested the Droning of Skerra.

'You might have a case for invoking a UN sanction against the British Crown for invading your sovereign territory, but I doubt you'd get very far.'

'All this is still classified, Jeperson,' said Onions. 'You didn't need to know.'

Head stood erect, hands behind him. For a moment, he wavered.

Something was different about his eyes. As if the taxidermist had the wrong reference.

'Jeperson?' said Onions, irritated.

'Yes, where was I? History of Skerra visitations: 1944 to the present day. Got it? Now, you may be right in that we didn't need to know about the germ warfare or the relief of the Rock, but it is certainly relevant that, far from being an unvisited and forgotten protrusion in a far Northern sea, Skerra has been only marginally less congested than Piccadilly Circus at ten o'clock on a Saturday night. You'll have all the reports filed after the bio-weapons tests and the naval exercise?'

Yoland nodded.

'And what don't they say?'

Yoland frowned.

'Pardon me, that's a confusing question form. But I'll lay you a tenner in old money that no one who trod on Skerra before Captain Vernon's team – and I haven't forgotten them, Adam –

ever reported a dirty great underground complex in the caverns. Not that easy to miss. And don't tell me those thorough mad science wallahs or resourceful jack tars stayed topside and never so much as peeped down the Blowhole.'

'No,' said Onions.

'No, you won't tell me? Or no, they never peeped? See, now I'm confusing myself.'

'According to reports, this place wasn't here in 1974, 1984, 1994 or 1996.'

'Thank you for your directness, Mr Yoland.'

'The reports must be wrong,' said Onions. 'It's not impossible to suborn officials.'

'Indeed it isn't. But I'll bet you checked out the names on the papers. Did extensive re-interviews? With persuasive methods? I'm right again, aren't I? I could get used to this. Is it how you feel in quiz contests, Mr Head? When you know all the answers. So, to return to the impossible factor, what we have is a vast installation that evidence suggests has been here for at least thirty years but which can't have been here as recently as 1996? Do we agree?'

'Is this some sort of Omphalos argument, Jeperson?'

'The benefits of a classical education. Mr Head, could you expand on Adam's reference for those among us unfamiliar with the works of Philip Henry Gosse.'

Head was silent. He loomed, face craning forward.

His eyes were intense, wary, cunning. As if he had just awoken among strangers.

'Come on, Swellhead,' joshed Yoland. 'Penny in the slot.'

'The Omphalos argument,' began Head, tone unfamiliar – not a blank recital, but impassioned, 'was advanced in the nineteenth century by fundamentalist Christians in reaction to archaeological evidence that the world is older than the biblical date of 4004 BC. Gosse, among others, put forward the notion that God created the Earth complete with a fossil record of creatures that never existed just as He created Adam and Eve with belly-buttons – the word *omphalos* is classical Greek for navel – indicative of conventional birth.'

'You're saying that this place was whipped up in the last few years,' said Yoland. 'But faked to seem older? Pirelli calendar and all? It still doesn't solve my problem. No matter when the complex was built, it'd have been impossible to do it in secret.'

Head was smiling at Richard, nastily.

The man was remembering. Something trickled inside Richard's mind, trying to take shape.

'No, this isn't fake old,' said Richard. 'It was built in the 1960s and it wasn't here until this year. Both statements, irreconcilable as they are, hold water.'

'You're raving, Jeperson. And you're well off-topic. Next on the agenda—'

'Listen to me, Adam. It's important. This whole place is an apport!'

VII.

'As I said,' continued Onions, 'next on the agenda—'

Richard tried to appeal to the others.

'We're inside a big ghost. That's not a safe thing.'

Yoland and Miss Gill did not seem bothered. This was so outside their experience that it didn't sink in.

Head was thinking.

Richard really did not like that.

'I've drawn up a rota,' said Onions. 'To keep watch for phenomena. Each should be logged and categorised.'

'Phenomena!' shouted Richard. 'You're sitting on a phenomenon...' (he kicked the deckchair) '...under a phenomenon...' (he slapped the umbrella) '...inside the *fenomenoni di tutti fenomena*, this whole place!'

Richard's outburst echoed. He was breathing heavily.

Head walked towards the table, taking tiny steps.

He was craning, twisting his head from side to side as if trying to work a crick out of his neck. Or trying to get his skull to fit properly onto his spinal column.

'May I see that?' he asked, indicating Yoland's laptop.

He took the gadget and peered at it.

'Have we missed something?' asked Yoland. 'All the details of the visits to Skerra are in the memory. You can click on the reports and read what went into the secret files.'

Head was not scanning the information on the screen. He held the computer as if it was the first he had ever seen, turned it over to examine the ports in the case, brushed his fingers over the keyboard.

'Ingenious,' he smiled. 'Compact.'

'If we might press on,' said Onions.

'Silence,' said Head, firmly.

'I beg your pardon.'

Head struck Onions across the face with the laptop, cracking the casing, and knocking the man from I-Psi-T out of his chair.

Miss Gill's mouth gaped in an O of surprise.

Onions was astonished, and bleeding from the scalp.

Head gave Yoland back his computer.

'Mr Jeperson,' said Head, quietly, politely. 'Would you care to try to kill me now?'

Richard knew he should. It would cut the Gordian knot.

Sewell Head – Swellhead – opened his hands and tilted his head back. A tiny bulge in the frog-fold between his mouth and collar was his chin. A forceful blow struck below the bulge would crush his larynx and end everything.

Long seconds stretched.

Richard made no move. The ghost of the pub quiz champion who was content to work in a sweet shop was still before him, displaced by an apported personality but perhaps not lost for ever.

'I thought as much,' said Head, turning his back. 'You are weak. It is why you will not win this day.'

Swellhead was acting as if he owned the place, which – of course – he did.

'Not killing people on the off chance it'll solve a problem is just one of those habits,' Richard remarked. 'Maybe it's one of the things that makes me better than you.'

Head wheeled, eyes flashing fury.

'Yes, Mr Swellhead, I said better.'

'Is that a challenge?'

'If you choose to deem so.'

Head was tempted, but decided against it.

'You're a spent force, Mr Jeperson, a distraction. Momentous business is being conducted. Maybe we shall settle things later.'

Onions got himself together and crawled back to his chair.

Yoland and Miss Gill were lost.

Head raised a hand in a signal.

Other people emerged from around the courtyard. They wore white jumpsuits and faceguards, and carried H-logo weapons. They were not phantoms like the thing in the hallway, but substantial, physical beings.

Perhaps they perceived Richard and the others as ghosts?

Guns were pointed at them.

'The place has been run on a skeleton staff,' said Head. 'But that will change now.'

Miss Gill stood up and said, 'It's time you stopped playing silly buggers.'

Head walked over to her. She was inches taller, but could not look him in the eye.

'Who are all these people?' she demanded. 'And where have they been hiding?'

Head took her hand and kissed it, bowing at the waist.

'The Droning of Skerra,' he said. 'Miss Kill, you are my guest. Your every comfort will be seen to.'

He made a signal. One of his jumpsuited goons brought over an attaché case.

'This, my dear, is a gift,' said Head. 'From me to you.'

He held the case and thumbed the catches. It sprang open, with a slight hiss.

Miss Gill folded back some translucent paper and picked up a mask. It was wax and bore her own face.

Richard had seen the like before, on the corpse in the sculpture garden.

'Let me help you,' cooed Head, raising the mask to her face.

Miss Gill didn't struggle.

'It feels funny,' she said.

'Only for a moment.'

Head took his fingers away. The mask was fixed to Miss Gill's face. She touched it herself. The wax fitted perfectly around her eyes and mouth. She was disguised as herself, but without expression.

'There,' said Head. 'That's nice and tidy. You'll always be pretty now, Miss Kill. You'll always be a proper princess for this island.'

A giggle leaked through the mask, somehow terrifying.

'Oh, Swellhead,' said 'Miss Kill', girlish and imbecilic, 'you aren't half clever.'

Head stroked her stiff cheek.

Onions was still groggy, and thus more useless than usual. Richard wondered if he could count on Yoland. The weapons inspector showed signs of open-mindedness. He was quick enough to sense changes in the psychic temperature, and ought to be attuned to rapid reassessments of dangerous situations.

Head was busy making up to his Miss Kill, with an eye on Richard.

He was expecting trouble from Richard. He might not have considered Yoland. If nothing else, this was all the work of a monumental solipsist, someone who considers himself alone at the centre of the universe.

Yoland shifted, getting a good grip on his laptop, the only proven bludgeon to hand.

Onions blinked. Head saw.

Yoland launched himself from his seat with a war-cry. Nimbly, elegantly, Head was out of the way.

Miss Kill kicked Yoland in the face, pirouetting like a dancer.

Yoland grabbed his laptop and ran across the courtyard, dodging the lumbering figures in white.

Head was mildly irritated.

Yoland whirled up the spiral staircase and made it to the landing.

Then a door opened and a man came out. It was de Maltby, wearing a white jumpsuit and milk-white goggles, an elaborate silver glove over his injured hand.

The glove buzzed and passed into Yoland's chest.

The weapons inspector's eyes reddened.

De Maltby raised his arm, lifting Yoland off his feet. He dangled the twitching man over the edge of the balcony. Bloody rain pattered onto the courtyard, along with one of Yoland's shoes.

The pilot withdrew his gloved hand, which was lined with tiny whirring blades. Yoland slid off de Maltby's arm and fell, landing with a thump. His body leaked.

De Maltby produced a large monogrammed handkerchief and fastidiously wiped his mechanical hand.

'Now, honoured guests,' said Swellhead, addressing himself to Richard and Onions, 'let me give you some ground-rules for maintaining my even temper and not abusing my hospitality.'

Richard had heard him say that before.

Head smiled, and nodded at him.

'Yes, that's right,' he said. 'Here we go again.'

ACT III: A GAME OF TIN SOLDIERS
I.

When Stacy and Kydd got back to the Blowhole, things were changed.

Kydd had driven the all-terrain vehicle up from the landing site. Powerful searchlights, fitted on the roll-bar, lit up the area.

A rumbling, grinding noise came from the Blowhole.

Stacy peered into the cavity. Rings of jagged rock revolved at different speeds. The dangling rope ladder jounced around, shredded.

The Blowhole was working like a giant kitchen disposal device.

'A good thing that didn't start up while we were on the ladder.'

'Yes, miss,' agreed Kydd, as unsurprised by this turn as everything else. Either the aircrewman had been more fully briefed or he'd learned to accept literally anything. It could be something the Navy put in the tea.

Goats lurked in the dark, making low, threatening noises. She had no idea whether this was natural: she'd never seen a goat in the wild before, or even on a farm. It was about half past eight: she should either be two hours into a night shift or an evening in front of the telly. Maybe out at a film or a pub or club.

The searchlights made the grass a vivid yellow-green. Her breath frosted like steam. Beyond the light, everything was midnight dark. No sodium-orange street lamps, passing car beams, curtained but lit-up windows, twenty-four-hour supermarkets, electric signage. Cloud cover must be thick, because there were no stars.

This was not ideal.

She checked her mobile. No signal and nobody to call anyway.

Among the gear on the ATV was a communications centre: headsets for the whole party, so the team could remain in constant touch with each other. Onions should perhaps have distributed the equipment before venturing below. She'd mention it at the official inquiry.

'There must be another entrance,' she said.

Kydd didn't respond.

'I mean, the place is huge. The mysterious They can't just have used the Blowhole. There must be other ways in and out.'

Skerra Landsby was underwater. Any entrances there would be flooded.

That left the rock face.

Stacy climbed the ATV and directed the searchlights. White shaggy flanks were caught in beams. Goats hurried away. Kydd got into the driving seat and they bumped across a hundred yards of grass, halting a safe distance from crumbling cliff-edge.

She wasn't looking forward to this.

Hopping down from the vehicle, she was surprised to find the rumbling persisted. They were well away from the Blowhole. She knelt and put her hand on the ground, pressing. The long grass was wet, cold and irritatingly scratchy. The earth was warmer and vibrating. She felt it in her fillings. A thrumm, too low for human ears but still bone-rattling, goat-maddening. A big machine, she thought, buried deep.

Kydd unhooked the searchlights, which were on extensible flexes, and carried them to the cliff-edge. He whistled.

Stacy joined him and looked down.

'Christ on a bike!'

'Yes, miss.'

Hundreds – thousands? – of feet below, the sea churned white. Foam swirled around black rock chunks. Mad waves hammered into eroded caves and frothed out again. It looked like God's washing machine.

Kydd tried to play the light on the cliff itself.

It wasn't sheer rock face but battered and broken, with many obvious paths and handholds. It was impossible to tell which were reliable, and which dangerously loose.

'There, miss,' said Kydd, pointing.

It was a metal door, flush with the rock. Once it had led to a natural balcony, but most of that was broken off, leaving only a vestigial ledge. The door was fastened by a chain.

Kydd fetched a reel from the ATV and fed blue nylon rope over the cliff. At first, the rope was caught by the wind and blown almost out of his hands. He tied a three-litre plastic carton of milk to the end, threading the rope through the handle and confidently tying a seaman's knot. That gave enough weight. The carton bumped against rock as Kydd lowered the rope.

Stacy directed the lights, all too conscious that chunks of this cliff had been joining the seabed for millennia. Where she was standing would eventually fall, ten minutes or a hundred years from now.

The carton bounced against the door.

'Fifty-five feet,' said Kydd. The rope had red rings every five feet.

'No distance at all,' she said, not believing it.

Kydd gave Stacy the rope, then took the reel away, unspooling until he was back at the ATV. The reel fitted into a catch on the vehicle and fastened tight. The aircrewman cleated the rope to prevent further unspooling. He signalled and Stacy let the rope go. It twanged and bit into the cliff-edge, carving its own groove.

A big gust of wind came, staggering Stacy sideways. She heard an explosion.

Looking over, she saw the carton had burst. Milk splattered against the door, and dribbled in runnels. The rope caught in its groove, and whipped about.

'Never mind,' said Kydd. 'We'll weight it down.'

That wasn't a comfort. Stacy imagined a red splatter against the cliff.

'I'll go first, miss.'

'I'd rather you were up here keeping the rope secure,' she said.

'Fair enough.'

Kydd fetched bolt-cutters from the ATV. Stacy hooked them over her waistband.

She wished he'd argued more.

Ten feet below the edge of the cliff, she decided her gloves and boots weren't thick enough. The bolt-cutters shifted, pressing an ice-cold metal handle against her thigh.

Twenty feet below the edge of the cliff, she remembered the Blowhole's stone grinders and wondered if any sections of rock face were devices like that. She kept kicking at stones which fell.

Thirty feet below the edge of the cliff, she needed a rest and found a ledge. Rope wound around her arm, she leaned against wet rock. It was raining again. The wind aimed marble-sized drops at her eyes. Her beret was snatched away, which meant her face was now also lashed by her own wet hair. She'd liked that beret.

Forty feet below the edge of the cliff, with fifteen feet of rope flapping below the section pinched off between her boot-insteps, she remembered an old school exercise about judging height by counting seconds as something fell and multiplying by ten. She clawed a rock free, held it out, and dropped it. After six seconds (sixty feet?), it bounced off an outcrop. If it splashed down, she couldn't make out the individual noise amid the roar of surf. So she was no wiser.

Fifty feet below the edge of the cliff, with hands on fire and (she thought) ripped bloody inside her gloves, it occurred to her that the door might be locked as well as chained. With burglar tools it wasn't especially legal for a policewoman to carry, she could crack most household locks. They'd done a seminar on it at Hendon. However, one-handed, in darkness, lashed by wind and rain, clinging to a precipice and pretty bloody fed up, she wasn't confident that she could use what was in her pockets (tube of mints, some tissues, flat-keys, coral lipstick, mobile) to effect an entry.

Fifty-five feet below the edge of the cliff, she found she was still not level with the door. She didn't know how that was possible, but here she was – toes scraping the upper edge of the metal.

She tried shouting to Kydd, but couldn't hear herself.

Looking up, she saw his face peering over, waving encouragingly. From his angle, he might not be able to see her problem.

Off to the side, beyond the light, she had a sense of other faces looking over the cliff at her, white-bearded, evil-eyed and horned. She decided she really hated goats.

All she needed was for Kydd to uncleat the rope and give her five more feet.

She waited, hoping the penny would drop. No such luck.

Her choices were: a) climb all the way back up and ask politely for a longer rope, then hope the door didn't sneakily work its way down the cliff another five or ten feet; or b) go off-rope and make her own way down to the ledge, trusting her luck not to lose grip, rely unwisely on an unsafe hold or be plucked from the cliff by the elements and thoroughly battered against rock on her plunge to be sucked under whirling waves and marr–i–ed to a mer–my–id at the bottom of the deep blue sea. Neither appealed. Climbing down had been hard and, with no feeling at all in her hands, climbing up would be much harder. The thought of going untethered opened a cold wet anemone in the pit of her stomach which she recognised as stark terror.

She gave Kydd another wave, pointing down, shouting 'more rope'.

Kydd's face disappeared as he stood up.

She thanked a power higher than the Chief Constable that her message had been received. She wound herself around the rope, entwining it with both arms, gripping with thighs, knees and heels.

A little give came and she lurched downwards.

Her cheek pressed against metal.

She lurched down again, way too fast, and scraped over rock. Her feet scrabbled for perches. The cliff sloped out a little and she stopped falling. The rope was loose above her.

Had something happened to Kydd?

She tugged the rope. Yards of it came free.

If something had happened to Kydd, that something's attention would be on her next.

She relaxed her grip on the rope, still keeping it between her and the cliff, and experimentally reached upwards. Her hand crested a ledge – the door-ledge! – and she got a reasonable hold. She raised her other hand and let her whole weight hang from the ledge.

The bloody bolt-cutters shifted again, handle twisting her knickers, business-end pressed into her belly. She thought for a moment she was gutted and bleeding, but it was just the freezing metal against her soft tummy.

Her first attempt at lifting herself was pathetic. Her elbows wouldn't bend. She just succeeded in fraying pebbles from the ledge. She couldn't think of Kydd.

Ordering herself to do better, she hefted herself up, getting her torso over the ledge, then her bottom. She was sitting, looking out at the dark sea, getting another faceful of rain.

A dim white circle foamed on the waters. The Kjempestrupe. Never mind that, anyone who braved this cliff was a worthy consort for the Droning of Skerra. Not that she fancied Persephone Gill.

The rope was free. It whipped away, well out of reach.

She was on her own. The business of getting both feet firmly on the ledge was tricky enough, but then she had to stand up and turn around to face the door. She took a hold of the chain, which crumbled to rust-flakes and fell apart. Angrily, she extracted the bolt-cutters from her underwear, minded to toss the bloody tool into the sea.

Then, sense prevailed. She might need them as a bludgeon. Or nail-clippers.

The door had a handle, like an old-fashioned freezer. She expected it to come off in her grip, but it was firm. There was no keyhole, so even if she'd had a full set of picks they'd be no use. She wrenched the handle, feeling a catch go free, and pushed.

The door didn't move.

She pushed again and realised the door opened outwards. It wasn't a convenient set-up. In order to pull, she had to lean away from the cliff and risk the fall. In opening, the door swept the ledge she was standing on. She had to ease herself around it, dangling for horrible seconds. Hinges strained and complained. A blast of warm air shot out at her.

If the hinges broke, she was dead.

Clumsily and in a tangle, she managed it.

She wound up inside a dark place, looking out, with solid floor under her.

Peeling off her gloves, she found slight weals across her palms, but not the churning open wounds she expected. She pulled her shirt out of her waistband and bent to wipe rain out of her eyes. She ran her fingers through her hair, wiping runnels of cold water back across her skull and down her neck and spine.

She was inside, not exactly safe.

What about Kydd? She yelled his name.

No response.

Frustrated, she clanged on the metal door with the bolt-cutters, as if sounding a dinner gong.

She poked her head out and looked up.

All she got was wet again.

The fringe of light still shone, marking the cliff-edge. Then, it shut off.

There was no reason for Kydd to turn out the lights.

Angry, guilty and scared, she knew she had to go further into this dark place and find Jeperson and the others.

The prospect did not appeal.

II.

'Traditionally, I should explain everything to you,' said Swellhead. 'But I am not one of those inadequates who needs the respect of his enemies. I don't mind toiling in the dark. My achievements are their own satisfaction. I don't demand that the whole world recognise how clever I am. Indeed, in the end, no one will know what I've done. Possibly, when the story is rewritten I will myself be unaware of how much I have accomplished. That's still undetermined. Mr Jeperson, how's your memory? Giving you a headache?'

Swellhead was right.

It was increasingly hard to concentrate.

The gaps were filling in, but not comfortably. Now, Richard remembered…

…a briefing from Edwin Winthrop, in 1973, about the interest the Diogenes Club was being forced to take in Sewell Head Industries.

…a woman in a leotard and mask, leaping from the revolving restaurant of the Post Office Tower to a SHI advertising blimp, absconding with vital components of a communications satellite relay.

…a game of chess at a Surrey estate, played with real people and electrified board squares.

…Fred Regent's headless body dumped on Richard's Chelsea doorstep, with a note, 'He lost his head over a girl.'

…wearing a white jumpsuit and faceplate, mingling with minions.

…black-clad SAS men abseiling down the Blowhole.

…a firefight around the Big Dish.

…duels, deaths…

It was fragmentary and did not fit facts he was sure of. Fred Regent was not dead. The revolving restaurant shut down in 1971 after a bomb attack by the Angry Brigade. There had never been a Sewell Head Industries.

These were not his memories, but those of another Richard Jeperson.

Somewhen where Sewell Head was an industrial giant/ diabolical mastermind (not a counter clerk in a sweet shop), Richard had been responsible for undoing his colossal schemes. At great personal cost.

Scalpels of pain slid behind his eyes.

The overlaps and contradictions hurt. From remembering too little, he switched to remembering too much. He was not struck by memories from two lives, but dozens…

…the 'Horst Wessel Lied' played over and over as German athletes won gold medal after gold medal at a 1956 London Olympiad.

…tracking a psychic assassin through the crowds at the Glastonbury Festival in 1969, saving the life of a future prime minister.

…arguing through an interpreter with an Okhrana man about screening the guests at a Royal wedding in St Petersburg in 1972.

…an embassy siege in 1980, negotiating with vampire terrorists demanding Transylvania as a homeland.

…a kidnapped London mayor replaced by a perfidious impostor in 1999.

…under torture in 2001, compelled by arachnid overlords to betray a human resistance cell in Highgate.

…biplanes battling over a London of 2003, the city radiating out not from Buckingham Palace (which was missing) but from the Tower…

In all the lives he had led, that other Richard Jepersons had led, there were no memories before 1945. The blank that had been with him all his adult life was a constant.

'Come back, Mr Jeperson,' said Sewell Head, chuckling.

For a terrifying moment, he was not sure which Richard he was, which world this was…

'With concentration, I found I could compartmentalise continua. Of course, I have eighth-stage Asperger's. As syndromes go, it's one of the more useful ones. Your partial amnesia is not going to be an effective substitute.'

'What is all this nonsense?' demanded Onions, getting annoyed again. He had been in shock since Yoland's death, hankie blotting his messy scalp-wound, sulking about the turn his expedition had taken, warily eyeing the mask-faced Miss Kill. Now, he was ready to reassert himself.

'You're not part of the backstory, Onions,' said Swellhead, pronouncing the name like the vegetable.

'O-nye-ons,' corrected Onions, automatically.

'Do your feet suffer from bo-nye-ons?' snapped Swellhead. 'As anyone who's faced me in a pub quiz damn well understands, I know my onions!'

The little bald man was transformed. His forehead bulged, as if extra brains packed his cranial cavity. He still chewed, popping Belgian chocolates like a pep pill addict. He radiated the sort of confidence you get when you know fanatical devotees are on hand, prepared to murder at your whim or die to protect you.

Miss Kill and de Maltby were solid presences, as were some of the whitesuits – Vernon and his team? – but there were phantoms as well, coalescing, gaining substance. The complex was coming to life, each section getting noisier, busier as its inhabitants grew corporeal, purposeful. From Swellhead's swollen head flowed a conviction that gave his world hard edges.

'I'm not sure where you fit in,' Swellhead told Onions. 'But unless you give me reason to have you eliminated, it'll be interesting to find out. As the world rearranges, everyone in it will be affected. Maybe you'll fade, become one of the ghosts you've been chasing. That'd be an appreciable irony.'

Onions tried to stand, but Miss Kill laid a slim hand on his shoulder.

Richard could not see Persephone Gill any more. Just the woman in the mask whose fingers and feet were weapons as deadly as de Maltby's silver-knived hand attachment.

He remembered Miss Kill...

...thrown off balance by that revolving restaurant, he'd realised the thief hadn't trapped herself by fleeing to the top of the tower, that she had a prepared exit.

And, later...

…a struggle in the sculpture garden, taking blows to the chest and face, twisting on the AstroTurf to roll out of the way of a stabbing spike-heel aimed at his eye, an accurately thrown knife.

Did she remember? She would not leave that opening twice. And he was thirty years older, slower. Even a simple break-fall would probably throw out his back and leave him flapping like a fish, easy to skewer with a deliberate stab of a stiletto.

'Just for the record, Onions,' said Swellhead. 'There are no ghosts.'

The pain in Richard's head kinked, then shut off.

'That's not strictly true,' he said. 'This whole complex is a ghost, not of a person but a thought. An idea you had, Mr Head. Maybe you had it in another place, where you were an international mastermind with a cadre of loyalist goons at your command. Maybe you had it while you stood behind the confectionery counter, your wonderful brain switched onto another track by years of breathing in chocolate dust. Dreams can come true. That's what magic does. And you're not one of "Pronounced 'Eyesight'"'s Talents. You're a natural-born magician. Onions would say it was all down to chemicals in your brain. Others would give you a pointy hat and call you a wizard. We both know it doesn't matter what you are.'

Swellhead clapped, slowly.

'Quite right, Mr Jeperson. What matters is what I can do.'

'Which is?' demanded Onions.

Swellhead nibbled the corner of a bon-bon, almost flirtatiously. 'Ah, wouldn't you like to know?'

'Will you get someone to write you a theme song?' Richard asked. '"Swellhead, Swellhead, on sweeties fed, he'll leave you dead…" Or how about: "You should have stayed in bed, it's got to be said, you'll fear to tread, after… the man with the swollen head."'

'You know, that's not a bad idea. Miss Kill, who should I hire?

John Barry? Burt Bacharach? Stephen Sondheim?'

Swellhead took music seriously. Richard remembered Ken Dodd, slaughtered and mounted for hogging the number-one spot with a dreadful ballad.

'Percy is twenty-one years old,' he said. 'She'd want N'Sync or Robbie Williams or Eminem.'

Swellhead's brows contracted, then relaxed.

'Trivia Man, are you still in there?' Richard asked. 'Your Specialist Subject is Popular Music Since 1973...'

'Soon, all that will be forgotten. In my reality, we have proper music.'

'You can hear the lyrics and hum the tunes, eh?'

Swellhead looked almost offended. 'Yes, why not?'

'Don't ask me. I'm probably sixty-five. I haven't liked a chart-topper since Mary Hopkin. That's the point of pop music. It's irrelevant to us oldies, just as we're irrelevant to it. No matter what you do to the world, you won't change that.'

Swellhead was a little flustered.

De Maltby's silver hand began to whirr. Revolving needles protruded from the knuckles.

Swellhead calmed down and wagged a finger.

'Very clever, but you can't distract me.'

He snapped his fingers. The muzak billowed: 'These Boots Were Made for Walking'.

Miss Kill danced, mask making her seem like a robot.

She wound around the impassive Swellhead, then de Maltby, then took a solo spot. She was very good, had all the moves, and each air-kick had a force that could have broken bones. At the end of every chorus, she broke something: arm crushing through a wrought-iron table, heel battering a chair out of shape.

One of these days, these boots are gonna...

Richard's old wounds ached just to watch her.

…walk all over you!

She finished her routine. Swellhead applauded. So did de Maltby, very carefully.

Sincerely, Richard joined in.

'I think it's time to go up and visit the Big Dish,' said Swellhead. 'What do you think?'

Richard nodded.

End game. With people-pieces.

III.

The complex had changed while she was topside.

Now, it was fully operational. If Stacy touched the walls, she felt vibration. As she'd guessed, vast machines buried below Skerra were turning over. Energy thrummed throughout Head Office.

And there were staff.

She pressed into an alcove as white-suited soldiers jogged by. Ghosts? Or woken from deep-freeze?

She was in an area of the complex they hadn't toured earlier. Corridors curved but had no corners. Through glass doors, she saw illuminated rooms where scientific processes were being carried out. Most involved large, bubbling tanks of different-coloured liquids.

One room contained nothing but ghosts, row upon row of clothes-hangers draped with the white jumpsuits. She knuckle-punched a pad by the door, which opened noiselessly. She found a large suit and wriggled into it. A groin-to-throat seal had to be pressed closed with a toggle-zip affair of unfamiliar design. The garment bulged everywhere, but could be belted in. Plastic bootees went over her boots. She replaced her gloves with gauntlets that clipped easily to the sleeves. The helmet screwed into a collar-ring.

Though opaque from outside, the faceplate was transparent for the wearer.

Cool.

As the helmet locked, a red display lit up at the lower right of her vision. The H logo hatched, and figures she didn't understand scrolled.

All she needed was one of those machine gun things.

The weapons weren't stored here, though.

Returning to the corridor, she strode on, trying to project purposefulness.

She thought she was walking into a mirrored barrier. It was only an identically dressed figure coming the other way.

The ghost made a salute, a fist pressed to the forehead.

Inside her helmet, Stacy struggled not to laugh. On her manor, the gesture was slang for 'knob-head'.

She returned the salute, Harpo mirroring Groucho.

The other whitesuit stepped aside to let her pass.

Another jogging platoon passed. They all turned and gave her the knob-head salute, which she returned.

When they were out of sight, she stopped, bent over and grabbed her knees, painful spasms in her gut. She had to laugh. An odd out-of-body feeling suggested remotely that she was on the point of genuine hysterics.

Tears leaked down her face. She clanged a gauntlet against her faceplate trying to wipe them.

Her own barking laughs filled her helmet.

She realised she was shaking with terror.

IV.

The Big Dish was healed. Its H shone as if new-painted.

The soot-patches on the walls had shrunk. They were disappearing like condensation on a warm morning.

Richard was not surprised.

The dead bodies were all up and about, flesh on their bones. Some had dwindling red stains or contracting black holes in their jumpsuits. One passed by: a network of cracks in his faceplate disappearing as if the film were running backwards at double-speed.

As Swellhead stepped off the lift-platform, the white ghosts turned and thumped their foreheads in salute.

Respectfully, he returned the gesture.

Activity all around. Busy, busy ghosts. Technicians, lab coats flapping, ran silent diagnostic tests at banks of controls. White jeep-cum-golfcart vehicles trundled without colliding, like well-controlled model trains, some dragging trailers of white, H-logoed barrels. Mechanics with dark stains on their uniforms oiled the rails on which the Big Dish ran.

'All very satisfactory,' said Swellhead.

A pipeline burst across the floor, slithering like a serpent, coughing out thick black liquid. A clean-up crew descended automatically, spraying foam on the spill, tethering and repairing the line.

This crisis did not impinge on Swellhead's calm.

Richard looked up, towards the Blowhole...

...a hundred black figures rappelling down, firebursts in the air all around, the roar of attack choppers...

He could not count on that this time.

In the 1973 of his phantom memory, Edwin Winthrop was waiting at the Club, monitoring all frequencies. An SAS strike force was scrambled and at the ready in a secret base in Orkney. At Richard's signal, Swellhead's complex would be attacked, breached and overwhelmed.

Here and now, Really-a-Good-Bloke Rory was snug in bed waiting for a report about intellectual salvage rights that would win him bonus points with his minister. Morag Duff could no more authorise a military attack on Skerra than she could get reform of the Common Agricultural Policy through the EU.

Soon, the government would be irrelevant.

All governments. All churches. All beliefs. All aesthetics. Everything.

The whole world would be living inside Sewell Head's head.

V.

Stacy tried to imagine a cutaway diagram of Skerra, but found the mental map of the complex made her head hurt. It probably didn't add up anyway. She wasn't sure there was room under the island for all this.

She found herself back in the sculpture garden.

Something was missing.

By the Easter Island–look Sewell Head lay the elegant skeleton, black–handled blade stuck in its skull. The mask it had worn was missing.

Stacy plucked out the knife. It was about three inches long. Whisper-touching her thumb to the blade, she sliced open her gauntlet.

It wasn't a machine gun, but it was something.

She'd only had an afternoon of firearms training, anyway. A knife ought to be more use. She had taken, and now taught, an evening class in women's self-defence. To demonstrate the proper counter-move for knife-attack, twisting a wooden sticker out of a volunteer's grip, she'd picked up dirty-fighting skills. She usually had to cheat on the final exams, letting pupils take the sticker away from her when she knew she could easily get it against their throats.

Blade out, she entered the hallway of heads.

Stalking past, she tried to conquer the impression that the trophies were looking at her.

She was at the point of peering into the control room, when a bloody stare caught her attention.

There was a new trophy, crudely hacked and inexpertly mounted.

Aircrewman Victor Kydd, Skerra, 2003, machete.

She swore, furious and grief-shocked.

VI.

'But what's it for?' asked Onions. 'What does it do?'

Richard wondered if Swellhead would go back on his word and explain his grand design. Possibly, he was as trapped as all other players and had to act out the role of diabolical mastermind. That was a chink of hope – villains always lose.

'It'll make things neat and tidy,' said Swellhead.

'In your terms, it'll amplify his Talent,' Richard told Onions.

'Very perceptive,' said Swellhead.

'He's going to overwrite reality.'

'That's ridiculous.'

'Look around, Adam. It's been ridiculous all along, but here it is. In an infinite number of possibles, many of them will be extremely improbable. Is this that much stranger than regular reality?'

'Yes.'

'Then you haven't been paying attention.'

'I'm a scientist, not some cracked guru.'

'An old argument.'

As Richard and Onions squabbled, Swellhead beamed.

Richard tried to reserve part of his mind for thinking this through. There was still Stacy.

'Don't think I've forgotten Sergeant Cotterill,' said

Swellhead. 'I'm sure she'll pop up eventually. Miss Kill and Viscount de Maltby will see to her. She'll make a fine addition to my Head Room.'

Richard told himself it was not a mind-link, like the one he was forging with Stacy. Swellhead had a knack for following thought processes through deduction and inference.

The Big Dish moved. Ancient gimbals screamed.

Slowly, the array trundled on its railbed, dish angling upwards. The rails sloped down, into a tunnel under the sea-bed. A mini-jeep drove up, and Swellhead took the front passenger seat. De Maltby indicated that Richard and Onions should get up on the rear section, and prodded Onions with his inert hand to hurry him along. The man from I-Psi-T had a slight shock and hopped up on the trolley. Richard needed a hand to clamber up. His back and legs were giving him severe gyp.

After the exertion, he suffered from cold caresses and whisper kisses and was tempted just to drift away. It took several moments to get his mind back on track. When he was able to pay attention again, the mini-jeep was apace with the dish. Crews with big brooms swept the rails ahead of the array. Wire-strung whitesuits clambered monkey-like on the face of the dish, checking and cleaning. Trundling the vast device about a quarter of a mile, deeper into the Earth, was a major operation.

A whitesuit was caught in the machine, turned to a red smear. No one commented. Richard had flash-visions: slaves hauling pyramid blocks, worshippers ground under the juggernaut.

The deeper they went, the colder and wetter it was. Bare rock walls cascaded with water, which sluiced away through new-carved streams. Great crude wheels turned to keep the system flushing. Gusts of steam periodically escaped from a valve, with a dreadful whistling.

In addition to the grinding of the wheels on rails, a greater roaring filled the cavern. The air tasted of salt.

'We are directly under the Kjempestrupe,' announced Swellhead.

A goon handed out white, H–logoed sou'westers. Swellhead, Richard and Onions put them on.

Richard looked up at the rock ceiling. A hole appeared, water falling through, and then irised open.

He gasped, expecting a heavy gush as sea flooded in. The black hole expanded. Then Richard saw night sky. Above the dish was a big liquid funnel. The sea was kept from pouring through the hole by the mighty force of the whirlpool, augmented by Swellhead's mightier self-belief. Water fell, but no more than a heavy rainfall.

At Swellhead's command, banks of switches were thrown. The dish lit up.

Richard felt heat. Water on the face of the dish sizzled and evaporated. Then the fall stopped. Richard doffed the sou'wester.

'You've turned off the rain,' said Onions, awed.

'Merely bored a hole in the cloud cover,' explained Swellhead. 'A necessary preliminary.'

A shilling-bright full moon shone. A thousand points of starlight were caught and reflected in the revolving rings of the Kjempestrupe. Flashing marker buoys whizzed around on their swift courses, held by centrifugal force against the vertical surfaces.

'What are you using to rebroadcast?' Richard asked. 'A ring of satellites?'

'Another dish, on the moon. I've run a covert space programme to set up the installation.'

Onions snorted disbelief.

'Yes, without anyone noticing,' Swellhead answered the unasked question. 'Clever, isn't it?'

A technician came up, thumped his forehead, and gave a silent report.

'It will take some minutes to align our dish with the one on the moon,' said Swellhead. 'We should go to the control room. You'll find the next phase of the process fascinating.'

Richard looked up at the stars.

Then at the man he was afraid could change their alignments.

'He's a Talent,' Onions had said. 'Off the scale.'

VII.

She stood at a console in the control room and tried to look busy. It wasn't too difficult, since ghost activity consisted mostly of silently checking dials and read-outs.

The room had changed. The computers were all back in place, and working. Big reels whirred back and forth. Tickertape stuttered out of slots. Lights flashed and beeped.

The big screen was uncracked and showed a televised picture.

Stacy saw the dish hauled into position and the ceiling open. Tiny white figures watched. It looked like an outtake from *Thunderbirds*. An amazingly detailed miniature, imperfect because of the impossibility of scaling down water.

The screen split into quadrants: one showed the dish; two had postcard views of the White House and Number Ten Downing Street; and one was a complicated animated diagram showing the Big Dish, the Earth and moon, some sort of moon complex and a lot of dotted lines for trajectories. The White House was replaced by scrolling numbers, like logarithm tables. A giant H-egg logo appeared in the middle of the screen, expanding to overlay all four quadrants.

A digital clock flashed on at 15:00:00 and began to count down.

She looked around, hoping to see a plug she could pull.

Doors shushed open and Sewell Head walked in. No, someone who looked like Sewell Head walked in. This man had a different presence.

Jeperson and Onions were with him, and de Maltby and the Droning. The first two were prisoners, the latter guards. The Viscount had a strange shining mechanical glove. Persephone Gill wore a wax mask. They weren't completely changed (like Head), but they were different – redressed and redirected.

She didn't risk signalling Jeperson, but he looked directly at her.

She remembered he could sometimes tell what she was thinking.

What the…? she thought, hard.

Meet Swellhead, thought Jeperson, clearly in her mind. *And watch out for Miss Kill.*

Stacy had a panic stab that Persephone – Miss Kill! – was staring straight through her faceplate, but it passed.

Sewell Head – Swellhead – climbed into his favourite chair.

13:34:01.

Whatever was due to happen at 00:00:00 was unlikely to be good.

She had flashes of the possibilities: all the world's nuclear arsenals activated at once, space weapons searing every patch of arable land on the planet, the activation of super-anthrax engineered to wipe out all non H–logoed life forms, fomented tidal waves and cyclones washing over continents. War, famine, pestilence and death.

12:43:00.

Swellhead fisted his forehead.

All the drones returned the salute – de Maltby even raising his unwieldy prosthetic. Stacy was a moment out of sync, and mashed the rim of her faceplate painfully against her nut.

'Friends,' began Swellhead. 'We are on the brink of a great venture. In less than a quarter of an hour, the world will be neat and tidy. I should like you all to take a moment to pray...'

She wasn't surprised he turned out to be some species of religious crank.

'...to me.'

Good grief! she thought.

It's worse than that, came Jeperson's mind-voice.

The drones all took off their helmets and bowed their heads.

Stacy had no choice but to follow suit and hope not to be noticed. The unfamiliar helmet arrangement didn't unscrew easily. She made a comical bumble of the business of getting loose, then got her hair in her eyes.

The other whitesuits had colourless faces and hair. Ghosts.

'Detective Sergeant,' said Swellhead, 'so kind of you to join us. You are our final guest.'

11:50:01.

Hands, unghostly, gripped her arms.

Jeperson looked at her, with sympathy.

If you get a chance, he thought, *kill him.*

VIII.

If you can, Richard added, damping the thought so Stacy would not pick it up. It was horribly possible that Swellhead had such control over the situation that any holes in him would heal instantly.

11:34:00.

He felt something cold against his palm. No, he was feeling through Stacy, something cold against her palm.

A blade.

Such a small thing.

'Isn't this about the time when you call up the Prime Minister or the President of the United States or the Secret Ruling Council of the League of Pata-Nations to make your demands?'

'This isn't extortion, Mr Jeperson. This is inevitability.'

Richard was worried. The many memories that had plagued him earlier were like dreams, almost forgotten on waking, leaving only incoherent images and impressions. He had no idea what Fred Regent looked like as an older man.

The past was a blank.

Only this countdown was real.

The muzak began to play 'Welcome to My World', the Jim Reeves recording with psychedelia mixed in.

10:56:00.

'Listen, Head,' he said, trying to get through, 'even you aren't big enough to do this. I've no doubt you can rearrange all of us here, perhaps even all over the world, but you'll be spread too thin. Where you are, in your mind empire, it'll be a satisfying illusion, cartoonish but still convincing. But the further away from you, the sketchier the effect will be. No one can encompass the universe in his skull. You know a great deal in theory, but you can't really imagine, say, the life of a South American tribesman or a market-trader in Kuala Lumpur or a teenage girl in California. The vast bulk of humanity will be milling extras, barely templates, low-resolution, bad painted backdrops. Most of your world won't be real enough.'

09:34.00.

'I know best,' said Swellhead, almost benignly.

'Penny in the slot, Trivia Man,' said Richard. 'Alfonso the Wise, King of Castile—'

'1221–1284.'

'That's the fellow. Most famous saying of…?'

'"If I had been present at the Creation, I would have given some useful hints for the better arrangement of the Universe."'

'Alfonso wasn't being the Wise when he said that, he was

being the Funny. Alfonso the Wise-Cracker. It's supposed to be a joke, to expose hubris.'

'That's not fact, that's opinion. Too debatable for a quiz question.'

08:57:01.

'Not in nine minutes it won't be. There'll be only one Opinion. Do you really want to live in that world?'

'So long as it's the right Opinion.'

'Yours.'

'Absolutely.'

'You'll be on your own. Despite all these masks and ghosts and puppets, completely alone.'

A tiny glimpse of Sewell Head came through.

'I'm used to it,' he said.

08:02:01.

So much for Reason. His only back-up plan was Violence.

Stacy, he thought, loud enough for all the ghosts to hear, *now!*

IX.

07:54:01.

She pulled off her transparent gauntlet and gripped the knife.

As she shrugged, ghostfingers sank through her arms, giving her a bone-scraping tingle she hoped never to feel again.

She hadn't followed Jeperson's argument.

And she wasn't sold on being an assassin. That hadn't been what Fred Regent hauled her off shift for. She'd never signed up for that. Whenever it came up at the Police Federation, she voted against ordinary coppers carrying firearms or even stun-guns. That wasn't how she wanted the world to be.

But no one was listening to her now.

07:36:00.

She waded through ghosts. They moved slowly. Guns spat

floating, easily dodgeable blobules.

Then a regular-speed kick winded her.

Her knife skittered off on the floor.

She bent double, trying not to retch.

Miss Kill, the masked Persephone Gill, walked around her. She wore a long dress slit to the thighs, and the gold spike-heeled pumps modelled by a well-dressed skeleton. Above her mask, her hair was done in a topknot with a flowing tail.

Stacy tensed, anticipating the kick at her side.

Miss Kill looked to Swellhead. For applause?

Stacy braced both hands against the floor and swept-kicked Miss Kill's legs out from under her. A simple, textbook self-defence move.

The masked girl went up arse over tit.

In mid-air, she flipped, regained balance on her points. She wheeled round, ponytail whipping out.

Stacy was on her feet now.

A lot of her pupils expected *Crouching Tiger* business, which she always patiently explained required a team of effects experts and hidden wires – hardly practical when a yob shoves you against a wall by a cash machine.

Miss Kill might actually have been on wires. She tucked one foot against her knee and flew straight at Stacy's face like Peter Pan, arm stretched out, fingers pyramided into a killing point.

06:32:01.

Stacy ducked and thumped upwards at Miss Kill's silk-covered stomach. She couldn't get the leverage for a forceful blow, but had the satisfaction of connecting.

Miss Kill touched down and slapped Stacy, open-handed, contemptuous.

It smarted and kinked her head almost off her neck. She responded with rib-punches that had no effect.

The mask made it impossible to tell whether Miss Kill was hurt.

Stacy tasted her own blood.

She got close to Miss Kill, pressing her body against her opponent – it's hard to hit someone who's practically hugging you – and getting a hold on her hair, which she yanked hard. Any woman who remembered playground scraps knew how effective a solid hair-pull could be at disabling a trouble-maker. She always advised her pupils that it was better to be mugged by someone with crustylocks than a baldie (for skinheads, she recommended a nailfile across the scalp – those cuts bleed like fountains).

Miss Kill's head went back as Stacy pulled, but no scream came through the mask.

Pincer-grips came at Stacy's sides, long-nailed thumbs stabbing between ribs, vice-pressure fingertips digging into her back. She was lifted off her feet and held out at arms' length.

She tried battering Miss Kill's hands, but only bruised her own fists.

06:00:00.

She was sure Miss Kill's thumbs were knuckle-deep in her torso.

She looked down at the impassive pretty-doll face. Red and black blotches swarmed across her vision. Whatever happened at 00:00:00, she wouldn't be here to go through it.

Probably a mercy.

Miss Kill's stiff lips might have smiled.

Furious, using a move she only ever recommended with caution ('tends to hurt you as much as him'), she executed the classic Glasgow kiss, known in London as 'nutting'. She rammed her forehead against the bridge of Miss Kill's nose. The argument for this is that bony skull bests nose-cartilage as often as paper wraps stone. It might not apply to a mask.

An almighty *crack!* sounded through her head.

She was let go, and Miss Kill staggered back. Stacy had blood in her eyes, mostly her own.

Miss Kill held her mask to her face. It was split across.

'Percy,' shouted Jeperson.

The mask fell away. Persephone Gill looked as if she'd woken suddenly from a bad dream. Her bloody face wasn't a mask, but mobile with an incipient scream.

05:32:00.

'Congratulations,' said Jeperson. 'The iron crown is yours.'

Having defeated Persephone Gill in single combat, Stacy supposed she had the right, for the next five and a half minutes, to call herself the Droning of Skerra.

She didn't feel like a princess.

X.

05:31:01.

Though Swellhead looked unconcerned, Richard saw a crack.

De Maltby, silver fist whirring with knives, stepped past Miss Gill and squared up to Stacy.

Stand down, Richard thought.

Stacy – good girl! – held her empty hands out and backed off.

De Maltby lowered his deadly gauntlet.

Swellhead settled in his chair and tapped a series of buttons. He smiled serenely as a helmet descended from the ceiling on a thick rope of wires and settled around his dome. A rim of lights on the helmet began to flash.

04:52:01.

Richard gathered Swellhead was charging the machine. His brain was a key component. Anything powerful enough to will a moonbase into existence ought to be subject to the strictest international controls.

Whatever happened, Richard did not intend this apported apparatus, or this unmatched Talent, to be put at the disposal of Really-a-Good-Bloke Rory and the Deputy Minister for Heritage and Sport. Their overwhelming Opinion, shaped by focus groups and policy studies and target figures and budget assessments, would probably make for a worse world than the supervillain fantasy hatching inside Swellhead's egg-dome skull.

04:26.00.

Adam Onions had been close to boiling over for hours. Now, he stepped forward.

'Really, Mr Head, what do you think you're doing?'

Swellhead swivelled his chair to look at Onions, umbilical wires stretching.

'Sod this for a game of tin soldiers,' said the man from I-Psi-T, turning to leave the control room. 'I'm radioing in from the helicopter.'

Onions walked across the room.

Swellhead flipped a tiny switch.

The floor opened up under Onions. With a look of resigned irritation, he fell into the chasm. A splash, thrashing, screams.

'I enjoyed that,' said Swellhead.

03:46.01.

The hatch sprang closed.

Richard walked onto the trapdoor section of the floor.

'Stacy, if you'd help me,' he said. 'I need to sit down.'

She was by his side, holding his arm as he sank. His back spasmed and he felt his joints creak. She helped him to the floor.

'This will be tricky. I need to lotus.'

She pulled off his boots – he wore wasp-striped socks – and helped him tuck his feet into the crooks of his knees. He pressed his palms together and settled, trying to find a focus.

Swellhead observed all this, almost with interest.

02:55:00.

'What do you plan now, Mr Jeperson? Have you reached the stage of acceptance?'

Richard chuckled.

'No, I intend to out-think you.'

Richard sub-vocalised a mantra. Not very fashionable these days, but still effective.

He thought of a spiral, let it whirl around him.

Pains and aches faded, a pleasant side-effect. The whitesuits were wispier, more ghostly. He could tell which ones had Captain Vernon's team inside, and which were made up from whole cloth.

He gained a precise sense of where he was in relation to the complex, to the living and half-living things all around.

He had a Talent too.

02:02:01.

He was nothing compared to Swellhead, but at least he knew what he was doing. If the late Adam Onions had put the possibly late Sewell Head through the full battery of tests, or let the Americans or Tibetans have a crack at him, then Swellhead might have had even more control. As it was, Richard's earlier criticism held: the illusion didn't have enough detail.

Too many ghosts.

A comparatively weak lever can unseat a monument.

02:00:00.

But maybe not within two minutes.

He finished chanting.

Everything was clear.

'Sewell,' he asked, 'why did you choose to be a diabolical mastermind?'

Swellhead had no answer.

'Villains have more fun, I suppose?' ventured Richard. 'But you must have seen the flaw? Remember the coat? It's what brought us all here. Our blood was on it, and this place was a ruin. This happened before, and you were thwarted. Good word, that. "Thwarted". Has the old melodramatic tone. Like "foiled", "bested", "vanquished".'

01:39:01.

The faintest line of concern appeared between Swellhead's brows. His helmet-lights flashed faster, in more complex patterns.

'That was somewhen else,' Swellhead said.

He gestured.

De Maltby, deadly hand raised to swipe off Richard's head, stepped forward.

At the same time, just to make doubly sure, or perhaps through a split-second indecision, Swellhead flicked his switch.

A wasteful gesture. Counter-productive.

The floor opened. De Maltby tumbled into the darkness.

Cold wafted up, but Richard hung suspended in the air.

01:02:01.

'Didn't I mention I could do this?'

It was not easy. Richard felt a strain in his back-brain far worse than anything he had put his spine through.

He unlotused in mid-air, letting his legs dangle, extending his arms crucifashion.

Beneath him, there was a whirring and screeching. De Maltby's prosthetic killing arm outlived him by seconds, cutting through something from the inside, parting black slime, spilling knotty gut. The rising stench was dreadful.

Richard tried to make his pose seem effortless.

Actually, he had never levitated before.

He was siphoning Swellhead's Talent, the villain's belief in the worthiness of his foe. It was why Richard had actually felt stronger, sharper in the complex. Swellhead needed an antagonist who could put up a fight. This story needed a hero, and Richard was elected.

Given time, Swellhead would notice.

00:55:01.

But there was not much time.

00:55:00.

'You know how the story goes...' said Richard.

Klaxons were sounding.

'...the villain is always thwarted...'

00:50:00.

'...in the last minute.'

XI.

No one had told her Richard Jeperson could fly. All her doubts vanished: this was a man to follow into the jungle.

00:45:01.

She found her knife and threw it at Swellhead. It struck an invisible barrier feet away from him and bounced, falling into the trap along with Adam Onions and Viscount de Maltby.

00:40:00.

Jeperson floated upwards. She saw strain in his face. A trickle of black sweat ran beside his eye, slid down a groove in his cheek, dropped from his chin. The black, she realised, was hair dye.

00:35:01.

On the big screen, the dish transmitted a preliminary signal skywards, visible waves of radiant force emanating from its centre.

00:30:00.

'In the last minute,' Jeperson had said. Not 'at the last minute'. She'd instinctively grasped what the man from the Diogenes Club meant. Somehow, Sewell Head had cast himself in his own movie. She knew from experience that every neighbourhood drug peddler and receiver of stolen DVD players fancied himself as a Bond villain. Head just had the brain-juice to make it so.

But this could be a post-modern, ironic story. A despairing, millennial vision in which the baddie triumphs.

00:25:01.

Swellhead was radiant. His muzak was playing 'All You Need is Love', whale-songs, a football crowd version of 'You'll Never Walk Alone' and the '1812 Overture' all at once.

00:20:00.

'Trivia Man, what is transhumance?' asked Jeperson.

'A form of Swiss crop rotation,' he responded.

00:15:01.

You ask him one, Jeperson thought to her.

She didn't think that would work. Everything was in Head's head. Everything. History, geography, maths, physics, mythology, archaeology – the whole core syllabus.

'His specialist subject is Popular Music Since 1973…'

00:10:00

A beam rose from the dish, so intense that the video hook-up couldn't handle it. It whited across the screen. It was on its way to the moon, and then would come back to break against the whole world.

Head's lips twitched. She'd seen that before, in Really-a-Good-Bloke Rory's office. She recognised the look from hours of suspects lying to her, the 'tell' that meant she'd found a button she should press again.

00:05:01.

'Who had a hit with "I Should Be So Lucky"?' she asked, praying.

00:04:00.

No instant response.

00:03:01.

'Come on,' said Richard, 'even I know that! She was in *Moulin Rouge*!'

00:03:00.

'No clues,' shrieked Sewell Head, furious.

00:02:01.

The big picture fragmented and fell. A glimpse of Kylie Minogue's face appeared and disappeared in the white static.

00:01:01.

Only the numbers, now in black on white, remained. There was a rumbling in the earth, shaking the floor and the walls.

00:01:00.

Not in the last minute, the last second!

00:00:01.

Swellhead was stricken, Sewell Head looking through his eyes, under his Heath Robinson–Jack Kirby hair-dryer. She could tell he was aware of his own absurdity.

'Kylie,' she said, putting him out of his misery.

With a sad, should-have-known look, Head slumped. His head exploded in a shower of red fragments.

00:00:00.

Jeperson fell, landing on the edge of the trap, falling the right way, away from the hole.

00:00:00:00:00:00.

The zeroes were egg shapes.

Stacy looked for Persephone Gill, and found her dead, a dagger-wedge of Sewell Head's skullbone stuck in her eye, spearing into her brain.

The tremors were more sustained. The floor was bucking under her. She scrabbled to help Jeperson to his feet.

He was looking around, confused.

'It's all still here,' he said. 'I thought it'd just go pop and be gone.'

The computers kicked their spools, unreeling tape across the control room, and sparked showers that set many little fires.

The whitesuits were phantoms, coming apart and forgotten, or slumped corpses.

'It won't be here much longer,' she said.

Somewhere in the complex was an almighty crash. Everything shook, and there was a huge roaring.

A spout of saltwater rose gusherlike from the trapdoor, tossing remnants of Onions and de Maltby, along with sleek black toothy things, up against the ceiling of the control room, battering away asbestos tile to show bare rock. Water showered all around. Stacy had to fight to keep her footing and hold of Jeperson.

'The Kjempestrupe just poured in,' he said. 'Head was keeping it out through force of will.'

She dragged him from the control room, a wash of water around their feet, into the Head Room.

The trophies on the walls were fake now, moulting papier mâché.

The walls themselves slumped, running down in waves like a dropped curtain. Glistening rock showed through.

They had to get to the Blowhole.

XII.

Sewell Head was dead and Swellhead sucked back into the void from which he had come, but the Talent was still here. Breaking a pot doesn't make the jam disappear. The complex, the huge apport, was collapsing, resolving itself to its physical components – salt and water, mostly – but it would take time. Perhaps traces would remain for ever.

In a way, Richard hoped so.

Without Swellhead's belief, rigidly suppressed but devout, that every villain must be bested by an arch-nemesis, Richard felt again like a broken old man. He was sure bones had snapped inside him, but the soaking chilled him so much that he could not yet tell how badly he was hurt.

He was back in the world again.

Perhaps Fred was right and he never should have left. If he had stayed in the game, knocking heads with dolts like Onions, perhaps this would have been handled differently. Good people and bad might still be alive, including Adam Onions. There might have been a place for a Talent like Sewell Head, even if it was as the cleverest shop assistant in the universe.

His feet kept working as Stacy helped him through corridors. The lighting was uniformly dim and dying. The carpeting was sludge.

They made it to the lift-platform.

'If you can still fly, it'd be a useful back-up,' she said, hammering the up control.

He shook his head, too racked to explain.

The platform rose.

Stacy gasped.

Richard shifted – agonies shooting through him – to look.

Beyond the guardrail, he saw the great cavern. The big dish was bent out of shape like an origami structure trampled by Godzilla, and washed back up its tunnel by waters that still poured into the guts of Skerra. White shreds that might have been ghost-goons were whipped around inside the torrent. A mini-jeep was tossed out of the maelstrom like a dinky toy, smashing against the cave-wall.

Water got under the lift-platform and raised it higher.

Stacy yelled as if on a fairground ride.

The guardrails were like liquorice sticks pulled out of shape. The platform itself felt rubbery and melted in patches.

Richard took Stacy's hand and held fast.

He tried to believe again in Swellhead's world. Where a hero might survive something like this. Where the valiant were rewarded.

Not only was Stacy Droning of Skerra but she was also the new trivia champion. She had remembered, no, intuited, that Head hadn't known the answer to the easy pop-music question Really-a-Good-Bloke Rory had raised.

Of course, he could have been peeved enough to look it up in his *Guinness Book of Hit Singles* in the meantime. Then, things would have been different.

The Blowhole grew bigger as they were forced up at it.

He patted her hand, well done.

The platform threw them up into the open air.

They tumbled down the hillside, away from the water-spout that rose high as if geysered, demonstrating how the Blowhole got its name.

Jagged stone scraped his side. He heard Stacy swear.

It was not too late in the day to break his neck.

He came to rest in a tangle of limbs, wet clothes twisted, and looked up at pre-dawn sky. Dramatic clouds were incarnadine as red washed over his vision.

A bearded face, upside-down, obtruded into his eye line. And neighed rather nastily.

He shooed away the goat.

XIII.

After a bare five hours of morning, Skerra day was almost over.

The radio crackled, but neither Stacy nor Jeperson were inclined to climb back inside the Sea King to answer it.

A rescue chopper was on its way.

Soon, they would be lifted off this rock. She would abdicate, turn the iron crown over to the goats. Placating them with chocolate bars, which they ate wrappers and all, she had already come to a truce with her vicious subjects.

Jeperson was comfortable, not complaining of his injuries.

She supposed she was bruised and battered, too. Two of her fingers bent the wrong way and she couldn't feel them.

Stacy sat by the man from the Diogenes Club.

He handed her a Bounty. Sewell Head's back-up stash of sweets had been in the Sea King.

She ripped the paper and bit off a chunk. Chewing hurt. She thought she'd lost a filling – though not, Lord willing, any of her precious back teeth – while being knocked about.

'What's down there now?' she asked.

'A mess. And dead people. Mostly water, though. The apports haven't lasted in coherent form. Adam Onions missed his chance to study a unique set of phenomena.'

The rescue helicopter approached the island.

'It'll be good to be back,' she said.

'It is good,' he responded, eyes flashing bright silver.

⟶ GLOSSARY ⟸

NB: many of these notes were compiled for American publications where editors felt some Britishisms needed explanation. Sorry to British readers for whom these arcana are everyday knowledge.

⟶ The End Of The Pier Show ⟸

nark – Informer, snitch, grass, stoolie, squealer.

Peter Noone – Lead singer of the band Herman's Hermits.

bonce – Slang, head.

mug – Slang, face.

Docs – Doc Martens' boots, often called 'bovver boots' ('bother boots'). Form of footwear favoured in the 1970s by skinheads and others who thought they were 'hard'.

Fred Perry – The name comes from a tennis player.

mod – 1960s youth cult, opposed to 'rockers', occasionally revived. The Who were originally a 'mod' band.

skins – Skinheads.

grebos – 1970s evolution of 1960s rockers – greasy hair, leather jackets, too poor to own motorbikes and become bikers.

Pakis – Pakistanis, though people who use the derogatory term tend not to make fine distinctions among immigrants from the Indian subcontinent and use it to cover Indians and Bangladeshis also.

nicked – Stolen.

aggro – Aggravation, violent assault.

put the boot in – A distinctively skinhead form of aggro, which involves knocking a victim down and then kicking him with bovver boots.

DI – Detective Inspector.

Hendon – Hendon College. The leading UK police academy.

plastered – Intoxicated, drunk.

6d – Sixpence, in pre-decimal coinage. 2½p in today's money.

nutter – Violent lunatic.

Chu Chin Chow – *Arabian Nights*-themed musical drama, which opened in London in 1916, had a record-setting long run, and was frequently revived between the wars.

bints – Young girls – from the Arabic, imported into English via servicemen posted overseas.

'when chocolate was rationed' – From 1942 to 1953.

Gormless – Stupid.

Swan Vestas – A brand of matches.

Crystal Palace – Fred is too young to remember the original structure, built for the Great Exhibition in 1851, which burned down 1936. The name persists to denote the area in South London where it stood, as well as the local football team.

old pennies – As opposed to new pence. Twelve old pence (12d) made a shilling (1s), equivalent to five new pence (5p). In 1971 Britain adopted decimal coinage, but old money lingered in parallel for a few years before fading away completely.

flick-knife – A switchblade.

ARP – Air Raid Precautions, a civil defence unit of air-raid wardens active during World War Two.

New Scotland Yard – The original Scotland Yard, so-called because before the Union of the crowns of Scotland and England it was a London residence for the kings of Scotland, was headquarters of the Metropolitan Police from 1829 until 1890, when they moved to New Scotland Yard on Victoria Embankment. From 1967, the Met has been headquartered in a new New Scotland Yard, which is the place with the revolving sign out front.

Fu Manchu – Droopy moustache, named for the master-villain – who was clean-shaven in Sax Rohmer's books.

the King's Road – A fashionable thoroughfare in Chelsea.

Marks & Sparks – Nickname for Marks & Spencer, a chain of clothing and food stores.

mac – Mackintosh, raincoat. Old jokes' home. First man: 'Got a light, Mac?' Second man: 'No, but I've got a dark brown overcoat'.

'sign the Official Secrets Act' – A formality for civil servants dealing with secret information, who give a written pledge not to reveal same to outside parties. Actually, passing on secret information one happens to come across is illegal whether or not you've signed the Act.

HM Government – Her Majesty's Government.

topping – Excellent.

take a spin – Go for a drive.

Spirit of Ecstasy – The Rolls-Royce hood ornament.

panda cars – Police patrol vehicles.

Brooklands – Car racing track.

plods – Policemen. The expression comes from Mr Plod the Policeman, a character in Enid Blyton's children's books.

Pouf – Effeminate or sexually ambiguous fellow, which in 197— meant almost everyone with longish hair and a wardrobe. Closer to the Regency term 'dandy' than the homonym 'poof', which is a demeaning term – Australian in origin – for gay man.

Rupert scarf – Distinctive yellow check scarf, as worn by the comic-strip character Rupert Bear.

dolly-mixture – A brand of sweets (candy).

the Festival of Britain – 1951.

Jutland – Naval battle of 1916.

new bug – Novice.

panto – Pantomime – a Christmas theatrical tradition, not mime.

Vera Lynn – Popular British singer of World War Two. That's her singing 'We'll Meet Again', her signature hit, over the explosions at the end of *Dr Strangelove*.

ack-ack – Anti-aircraft fire.

a jiffy – A moment.

a rugby try – Equivalent to a touchdown in American football. 'Converting' is the rough equivalent to the American 'try'.

upped stumps – Died. The expression refers to the aftermath of a cricket match, when stumps are pulled up from the wicket.

the Common Market – The EEC (European Economic Community); since 1992, the European Union. Great Britain joined in 1973 (when it was called the European Community).

hot-pants – Short shorts.

Hire purchase – HP. Paying on the instalment plan – the pre-credit card version of 'live now, pay later'.

ITMA – A wartime radio comedy programme. The acronym stands for 'It's that man again'. 'That man' was Hitler.

tommies – British soldiers. The expression comes from 'Thomas Atkins', the name used in notices that showed how a form mandatory for all those entering military service should be filled in.

Post Office Tower – A London landmark, now the BT Tower. It briefly featured a revolving restaurant on the thirty-fourth floor but that was closed after a 1971 terrorist bombing perpetrated by the Angry Brigade.

Milton Keynes – A post-war 'new town'. Sarah Pinborough lives there.

inflatable chairs – Late 1960s/ early 1970s artefacts – very comfortable, but they were prone to leaks that had to be patched like bicycle tyres.

Sunday supplements – A UK publishing phenomenon of the 1960s, magazines included with Sunday newspapers. The pioneering rivals were the *Sunday Times* and the *Observer*.

Top of the Pops – BBC TV's weekly pop music programme from 1964 onwards.

fifty-pence pieces – Replaced the ten-shilling note.

Simon Dee – Radio disc jockey, then TV chat show host (*Dee Time*). Fell from favour overnight in the early 1970s.

Edward Heath – Conservative Prime Minister.

Germaine Greer – Feminist academic and media pundit, author of *The Female Eunuch*.

George Best – Irish-born football player, a star with Manchester United, then tabloid fodder for alcoholism-related incidents.

Cilla Black – Liverpudlian singer.

'White Horses' – A UK chart hit, it was the theme tune for a children's television programme.

Dan Dare – 'Pilot of the Future' in the *Eagle*.

Jet Morgan – Hero of the BBC's radio science fiction series *Journey Into Space*.

Lucian – Lucian of Samosata, author of *A True History*, the first lunar-voyage story.

Francis Godwin – Author of *The Man in the Moone, or a Discourse of a Voyage thither, by Domingo Gonsales*.

Cyrano de Bergerac – Author of *The Other World: The Comical History of the States and Empires of the Moon*.

Hans Pfaall – See Edgar Allan Poe's 'The Unparalleled Adventure of One Hans Pfaall'.

Baltimore Gun Club – See Jules Verne's *From Earth to the Moon*.

Hergé's Tintin – See *Destination: Moon* and *Explorers on the Moon*.

Heywood Floyd – Played by William Sylvester in *2001: A Space Odyssey*, and by Roy Scheider in *2010* – though it's hard to believe he's the same character.

Jonathan King – Something certainly was off about him, and he was jailed for sexual offences against minors.

John Peel – Britain's greatest disc jockey and pop savant. Many might think that the highlight of my career was doing a two-hour, two-handed radio programme with the late John Peel.

Patrick Moore – Broadcaster, astronomer, author of juvenile science fiction, presenter of the BBC's long-running *The Sky at Night*.

James Burke – Broadcaster, science journalist, television producer. Burke's magnum opus was *Connections* (1978), a ten-part, interdisciplinary documentary about conceptual breakthrough. Imagine any major TV channel these days giving prime-time airspace to the equivalent of *Wired* magazine.

Edwin Winthrop – See *Jago, The Bloody Red Baron, Secret Files of the Diogenes Club*.

the Wurzels – Somerset's greatest band. In 1969, they still retained the authenticity of 'Blackbird, I'll 'Ave 'Ee' and had not yet succumbed to the sell-out commercialism of 'I've Got a Brand New Combine Harvester'.

'Donald, Where's Yer Troosers?' – A 1961 novelty hit by Andy Stewart, which charted again in 1989. Rather surprisingly, sung to sinister effect by an evil robot from the future in an episode of *Terminator: The Sarah Connor Chronicles*.

The Simon Dee Show – A talk show on the BBC. Host Dee, a star on a level with Johnny Carson in the US, fell from grace in 1970 – with a suddenness and lack of explanation usually reserved for heads of the Politburo.

Rhine cards – Devised by Dr Karl Zener and J.B. Rhine at Duke University in the 1920s, used to test telepathy, clairvoyance or precognition. Each pack has twenty-five cards; each card shows one of five symbols (square, circle, wavy lines, star, cross).

EVA – Extra-Vehicular Activity, NASA-speak for 'going outside'.

Sky-Ray lollies – Space-themed iced treat.

I-Spy Guide – The I-Spy books – initially published by the *Daily Chronicle*, later by the *Daily Mail* and now by Michelin – are spotters' guides for children on various subjects (churches, railways, etc.), edited by bogus Native American 'Big Chief I-Spy' (actually, Arnold Cawthrow). They made long car journeys more bearable.

Wednesday Play – A BBC One drama slot. Among the most significant works broadcast under this rubric were *Cathy Come Home*, *Up the Junction* and Dennis Potter's Nigel Barton plays and *Son of Man*. Too many of these dramas were wiped.

Tizer – A uniquely British soft drink. Slightly less horrible than Vimto.

Nicholas Goodman – See 'Mildew Manor'. Or hear it, if you can track down the full-cast audio, which has mysteriously disappeared from the internet.

Swinging Blue Jeans – A popular beat combo, m'lud.

Ali Bongo – Magic advisor on the TV programme *Ace of Wands*.

Sooty – Puppet bear, conjurer – perhaps a soul-sucking mass murderer (see Eugene Byrne, Neil Gaiman and Kim Newman, 'Who Was Jack the Ripper?' in *Prince of Stories: The Many Worlds of Neil Gaiman*).

Tich and Quackers – A television show with a ventriloquist (Ray Alan) whose wooden friends were a schoolboy and a duck. I remember being very annoyed when the BBC replaced it with something as trivial as the Prime Minister talking about the budget.

New Scientist – UK weekly magazine.

a Cyberman – They tried to conquer the moon in 'The Moon Base'.

Skaro – Home planet of the Daleks.

⇒ You Don't Have to Be Mad ⇐

loud-hailer – Bullhorn, megaphone.

bubble car – Blanket term for those tiny, three-wheeler automobiles (technically, 'micro-cars'), like the BMW Isetta or the Messerschmitt Tiger.

'the policeman on the comedy record' – 'The Laughing Policeman' by Charles Penrose.

Lichtenstein – Roy Lichtenstein (1923–1997), the pop artist.

Reginald Bosanquet – ITV newsreader.

fizzog – Face, from 'physiognomy'.

glossy – Also known as an 'eight by ten glossy', a publicity photograph.

'Enery Cooper – Henry Cooper,

British Heavyweight boxer, better remembered for two of his fourteen defeats – two title bouts to Cassius Clay (one very dubious) and his particularly brutal 1971 final match to Joe Bugner – than his forty wins. In later life, Cooper did TV commercials for Brut aftershave.

barmy – Slang – slightly mad, daffy.

'Cor blimey!' – UK Expression of astonishment. Derived from 'God blind me' as in 'God blind me if I lie.'

FO – The Foreign Office.

bonkers – Slang – mad.

Dinky Toys – A line of model cars, introduced in 1934.

over-egging the pud – Overdoing something.

squaddies – Slang – soldiers, esp. privates.

Pan's People – Troupe of female dancers, regulars on BBC TV's *Top of the Pops*.

pre-fab – Pre-fabricated.

Miss Lark (Dr Myra Lark) – See 'Going to Series', *The Hallowe'en Sessions* and *The Ghost Train Doesn't Stop Here Any More*.

the Black Watch – The Royal Highland Regiment, first raised in 1725.

tannoy – Though a registered trademark of a specific brand, this is a UK colloquialism for any public-address system.

Zebedee – A puppet character from the children's television programme *The Magic Roundabout*; originally a French show called *Le Manège enchanté*, it became a cult in the UK partially thanks to wry narration by Eric Thompson (Emma's dad). There was a film spin-off, *Dougal and the Blue Cat* (1970), and a needless CGI update in 2005.

Ring-a-ring-a-rosy – A rhyme and a game, inspired by the Black Death.

blub – UK slang – cry.

the Gnomes of Cheltenham – GCHQ (Government Communications Headquarters), which is located in Cheltenham, is the department of British intelligence charged with gathering 'signals intelligence'.

Whitehall – General term for the British Civil Service, whose offices are in Whitehall, London.

⋙ Tomorrow Town ⋘

Since the Yeer [Year] Dot – Since time immemorial.

Wilson government – Harold Wilson was Labour Prime Minister of Great Britain from 1964 to 1970 and again from 1974 to 1976. A Maigret-like pipe-smoking, raincoated figure, he famously boasted of 'the white heat of technology' when summing up British contributions to futuristic projects like Concorde. At the time of this story, he had been succeeded by the Tory Edward Heath, a laughing yachtsman.

Raymond Baxter – Host in the 1960s of BBC TV's long-running *Tomorrow's World*, a magazine programme covering the worlds of invention and technology.

BBC Radiophonic Workshop – The corporation's sound effects department, responsible for Dalek voices and the *Doctor Who* theme. Their consultants included the Pink Floyd and Michael Moorcock.

The Crazy World of Arthur Brown – 'I am the God of Hell Fire,' rants Arthur on his single 'Fire', which was number one in the UK charts in 1968. An influence on Iron Maiden and other pioneer heavy metal groups, Arthur was also a devoted surrealist-cum-Satanist. He never had another hit, but is still gigging.

Auberon Waugh – Crusty conservative commentator, son of Evelyn Waugh, author of satirical novels. In the 1960s, his waspish journalism was most often found in *The Spectator* and the *Daily Telegraph*.

Varno Zhoule – British sf author, most prolific in the 1950s, when he published almost exclusively in American magazines. His only novel, *The Stars in Their Traces*, is a fix-up of stories first seen in *Astounding*. His 'Court Martian' was dramatised on the UK TV series *Out of the Unknown* in 1963.

Valerie Singleton – Presenter of the BBC TV children's magazine programme *Blue Peter*. Well-spoken and auntie-like, she famously showed kids how to make things out of household oddments without ever mentioning a brand-name (a co-host who once said 'biro' instead of 'ballpoint pen' was nearly fired).

Smarties – Chocolate discs inside shells of various colours, available from Rowntree & Company in cardboard tubes. Still a staple 'sweet' (i.e. candy) in the UK; similar to M&Ms.

Kit-Kat – A chocolate bar.

Tomorrow Town alphabet – Q and X are replaced by KW and KS; the vestigial C exists only in CH and is otherwise replaced by K or S. e.g. THE KWIK BROWN FOKS JUMPED OVER THE LAYZEE DOG.

The Man in the White Suit – Film directed by Alexander Mackendrick, starring Alec Guinness. An inventor develops a fabric that never wears out or gets dirty, and the clothing industry tries to keep it off the market.

'can't even beat as it sweeps as it cleans' – The UK slogan for Hoover vacuum cleaners in the 1970s was 'It beats as it sweeps as it cleans'.

Michelin Man – Cheery advertising mascot of the tyre company, he consists of white bloated tyres.

Schleswig-Holstein Question – Bane of any schoolboy studying O-level European history in 1975. It's a key plot point in George MacDonald Fraser's novel *Royal Flash*.

muggins – A sap, a patsy.

Kingstead Cemetery – Among the more famous dead people interred there is Lucy Westenra, Count Dracula's first British victim.

Curse of the Mummy's Tomb – A 1964 Hammer film. Not one of their best.

Derek Leech – See 'The Original Dr Shade', 'SQPR', 'Organ Donors', *The Quorum, Life's Lottery,* 'Seven Stars', *Where the Bodies Are Buried,* 'Going to Series', 'Another Fish Story', etc.

Daily Comet – The *Daily Comet,* a tabloid owned by media baron Derek Leech.

Bay City Rollers – 1970s boy band, very popular with the sisters of boys who hated them.

BOAC – British Overseas Airways Corporation. Merged with British European Airways in 1974 to form British Airways.

Drache – The architect. See 'Organ Donors', 'Going to Series', 'Another Fish Story'.

⇒ **Soho Golem** ⇐

John Galsworthy (1867–1933) – Author, of course, of *The Forsyte Saga.*

skiffle – Form of music popular (briefly) in the late 1950s, typified by the use of a washboard base and the mangling of nineteenth-century folk songs. Stuart Sutcliffe once demeaningly referred to the Beatles as 'John Lennon's skiffle group'.

Carnabetian – Coinage by Ray Davies of The Kinks, in 'Dedicated Follower of Fashion'.

A to Z – The London *A–Z* – a once-indispensable book of street-maps.

fuzz – Police.

tart – Girl of easy virtue, prostitute.

the filth – Police.

Black Marias – Police van, used for taking suspects into custody.

susses – Suspects. Verb – to suss, to

suspect or find out.

grasses – Police informants.

toerag – Person of inferior morals and status.

hawkshaw – Synonym for detective, originating in a character in the nineteenth-century melodrama *The Ticket-of-Leave Man.*

crim – Criminal.

nabbed – Arrested.

Dock Green – George Dixon. Introduced in the film *The Blue Lamp* (1950), PC George Dixon, played by Jack Warner, was the archetypal friendly British bobby. Though shot dead by wideboy Dirk Bogarde in the film, the character was revived for the TV series *Dixon of Dock Green* (1955–1976) – which in UK TV terms holds the status of being equivalent to both *Dragnet* and *The Andy Griffith*

Show, as police procedural and cosy vision of paternalistic law enforcement. The American urban legend of cops beating a suspect while whistling the theme to *The Andy Griffith Show* has a British equivalent involving the memorable *Dixon of Dock Green* theme. A memorable post-modern take on the character is the TV play *The Black and Blue Lamp* (1988).

giving Fred the shout – Keeping Fred abreast of the situation.

Glastonbury Tor – Site of alleged psychic importance in Somerset – a steep hill on which sits a medieval tower.

papaloi – Voodoo priest.

tetrodotoxin – Drug used to simulate death, essential in the recipe for enslaving folks as zombies.

trimmer – Lazy, morally lax type.

rozzer – Police.

guv'nor – Governor, superior.

given Richard a bell – Called Richard on the telephone.

lumme – Ancient cockney expletive – derived from 'God loves me'.

goin' spare – In a state of desperation.

blower – Telephone.

cuppa – A cup of tea, universal British salve.

Typhoo – A brand of tea.

two pound – Expensive now, exorbitant then.

'I'm Backing Britain' – A patriotic-but-trendy campaign ('Buy British') of the late 1960s – it revived the use of the Union Jack in design, but didn't exactly reverse the long-term decline of the UK manufacturing industry.

Jungle Jillian – Heroine of the serial *Perils of Jungle Jillian* (1938), played by Olympic swimmer Janey Wilde. See 'The Big Fish'.

glamour films – Silent, one-reel 8mm short subjects sold mostly through mail-order, essentially depicting strip-tease acts. The most prolific director of the genre was Harrison Marks, and his biggest star Pamela Green – who can be seen as the model in *Peeping Tom* (1960).

News of the World – Sunday tabloid, traditionally packed with crime and scandal stories. Bought up and closed down by Rupert Murdoch.

on the game – The practice of prostitution.

cove – Man, fellow, bloke, chap, guy.

mince pies – Rhyming slang: mince pies = eyes.

Crombie jacket – The sort of jacket you'd wear in 197— if you didn't want to be labelled a poof.

Bristols – breasts. Rhyming slang: Bristol City = titty. Bristol City is a football club.

chancer – Spiv, wideboy, petty grifter, opportunistic crook.

flash git – Showy bastard. 'Git' is from 'illegitimate'.

with-it – Stylish, up to the minute, in the know.

Smithfield's – London's premier meat-market.

the firm – Organised crime.

diamond – Outstanding.

St Trinian's – A notorious girls' school, first seen in cartoons by Ronald Searle, then a series of films starting with *The Belles of St Trinian's* (1954).

my patch – Territory, fiefdom.

the full frighteners – A menacing stare.

toodle-oo – Good-bye.

Carry On Cleo **(1964)** – The one with Amanda Barrie as Cleopatra.

Donovan hat – Large floppy headgear, popularised by the singer Donovan but mostly worn by women.

sta-presses – Smart jeans.

sarnie – Sandwich.

nosh – Food.

herbert – Fellow.

Shane jacket – Hideously out of fashion after Jon Voigt threw his away at the end of *Midnight Cowboy* (1969).

demobbed – Demobilised, just out of the armed forces.

knockin' shops – Brothels.

cigarette cards – UK equivalent of bubble-gum cards.

Teddy boy – A late-1950s youth phenomenon – roughs and layabouts who liked rock 'n' roll music but dressed in modified Edwardian gear – frock coats, tight trousers, greasy quiffs.

Variety Club of Great Britain – Showbusiness charity organisation which raises funds for underprivileged and disabled children (now called Variety, the Children's Charity).

quota quickies – Inexpensive British B-feature films, often with a faded American star, made to take advantage of a law that insisted a certain quota of films shown in British cinemas be British-made.

Diana Dors – Britain's biggest film star of the 1950s, famous for blond bombshell roles and probably more for her personality than any of her actual credits. The prison movie *Yield to the Night* (1956) was an unusually dramatic role for Dors, who was most often found in fluff like *An Alligator Named Daisy* (1955) or London noirs like *Passport to Shame* (1958). In later life and several dress sizes larger, she was a regular in 1970s horror and sex films – *Nothing But the Night* (1973), *Theatre of Blood* (1973), *Keep It Up Downstairs* (1976).

Shirley Anne Field – Star of *Beat Girl* (1960), *The Damned* (1962) and other British cult films.

Lew Grade – British cinema and TV tycoon, scuppered his empire by making *Raise the Titanic* (1980).

Royal Film Performance – An annual showbiz institution, whereby the Royal Family are shown a specially-selected-as-inoffensive film.

tom – Prostitute.

Gilbert O'Sullivan – Mysteriously popular 1970s crooner. Wore bigger Donovan hats than Donovan.

ponces – Men who live off the immoral earnings of women, pimps.

Special Patrol Group – More familiarly 'the SPG', controversial police unit of the 1970s – often accused of racism, excessive force and the like.

gob – Mouth.

Mrs Grundy – An unseen character in Thomas Morton's *Speed the Plough* (1798), who epitomises the prim, disapproving neighbour. 'What will Mrs

Grundy say?' was a mocking catch-phrase for decades, until Dame Grundy simply entered the language as a by-word for priggishness.

Dr Bowdler – In 1818, Thomas Bowdler published *The Family Shakspeare*, in which all material construed as offensive was omitted (e.g. the entire character of Doll Tearsheet from *Henry IV, Part II*); these cut texts were the default for fifty years. He lent his name to the verb 'to bowdlerise', meaning to dilute by censorship.

Kia-Ora – Brand of alleged orange-derived juice, endemic to cinema refreshment stalls in the UK.

plates – Rhyming slang: plates of meat = feet.

Screen International – UK film trade paper, along the lines of *Variety*. Now online as *Screen Daily*. I occasionally review for it.

pinta – Pint of milk. A 1960s slogan ran 'drinka pinta milka day'.

fladge – Flagellation.

s.b.g. – Stunningly beautiful girl.

clocked – Took notice of.

a right cow – Not a very nice woman.

Prince Prospero – The character played by Vincent Price in Roger Corman's 1964 film of Edgar Allan Poe's 'The Masque of the Red Death'.

Clean Air Act – The law, passed in 1956, that regulated coal-burning fires in London and put an end for ever to the famous pea-soup fog. Whenever you see a London fog in an American film set after 1956, it's a mistake.

⇒ The Serial Murders ⇐

BBC Two – At the time of this story, British television had only three channels. The BBC (British Broadcasting Corporation) channels BBC One and BBC Two were, and remain, free of commercial interruption, supported by the TV licence fee; BBC One is fairly populist, while BBC Two purportedly caters to more select interests. The third channel was ITV (Independent Television), not so much a network as a loose grid of franchise-holding local broadcasters (e.g. Thames Television in the South East, Westward in the South West) who carried a great deal of programming in common but with many regional variations. ITV shows might air on different days of the week and in different timeslots in diverse parts of the country. This author remembers manually retuning the family set to catch the blurry, distant signal of HTV Wales to watch Hammer films not being shown in our area.

Autons – Lesser-known alien villains from *Doctor Who*, introduced in 'Spearhead From Space' (1970). They returned in 'Terror of the Autons' (1971) and, after a long absence, 'Rose' (2005). Plastic entities resembling shop-window mannequins.

Ealing – A London borough

(postcodes W5 and W13). Associated with the now-defunct Ealing Studios, where many famous post-war British films – including the police drama *The Blue Lamp* (1950) – were shot. The police station is at 67–69 Uxbridge Road.

Holloway – A women's prison, located in North London.

bluebottle – Slang – police constable. The expression comes from the distinctive British police helmet, which also gives rise to ruder synonyms.

'get yer hair cut' – from 1945 onwards, the moaning battle cry of middle-aged, balding or short-back-and-sides conservatives at the sight of a man or especially youth with long or even long-ish hair. It has fallen into disuse since kids began to opt for shaven heads or elaborate but cropped hairstyles, but isolated incidences persist. As the generations who endured mandatory military haircuts die off, the shout – which tends to betoken a lack of basic manners on the part of the shouter rather than the usually unassuming shouted-at – will fade away completely.

briefs – Slang – lawyers.

Old Bailey – London's Central Criminal Court.

Broadmoor – Broadmoor Asylum for the Criminally Insane – now Broadmoor Hospital – in Berkshire. The largest secure psychiatric facility in the United Kingdom. Past and present inmates include Daniel M'Naghten, would-be assassin of Prime Minister Robert Peel, Richard Dadd, the artist, June and Jennifer Gibbons, 'the Silent Twins', and Peter Sutcliffe, the Yorkshire Ripper.

DS – Detective Sergeant.

primary school – Grade school.

Tube – London Underground Railway, i.e. subway or metro.

that documentary about the Queen eating cornflakes – *The Royal Family*, telecast on BBC One on June 21, 1969. Sixty-eight per cent of the British population watched the (excruciatingly dull) two-hour programme. There was much comment about the hitherto-unrevealed details of the Windsors' dietary habits.

Max Bygraves – Born 1922, popular crooner and comedian, top-liner of a string of ITV programmes, including *Singalongamax* and the quiz show *Family Fortunes*. Specialised in sentimental novelty songs, like 'You Need Hands' and 'Gilly, Gilly, Ossenfeffer, Katzenellen Bogen by the Sea'. Had UK hits with covers of 'Mister Sandman', 'The Ballad of Davy Crockett' and that monologue 'Deck of Cards'.

Albertine disparue – The sixth volume of Marcel Proust's *A la recherche du temps perdu*.

MI5 – The branch of the British Secret Service concerned with internal security, i.e. counter-intelligence, counter-terrorism.

Goodwood – A British race-course.

Grauniad – The *Guardian*, the UK newspaper, often chided for its misprints. The nickname comes from the satirical periodical *Private Eye*.

News of the Screws – Popular nickname for the *News of the World*.

slap – Make-up.

Brighouse and Rastrick Brass Band – Founded 1881, they had a chart success in 1977, holding the UK number two spot (Paul McCartney kept them from number one) with 'The Floral Dance'.

the Pink Floyd – Well-spoken people, like Richard Jeperson and Michael Moorcock, always use the definite article.

Shrewsbury – A women's college at Oxford University. Among Lady Damaris's contemporaries was the crime writer Harriet Vane.

Television Monograph – Published by the British Film Institute.

Crossroads – ITV soap opera, set in a motel outside Birmingham (and about as exciting as that sounds). It ran from 1964 to 1988, and was briefly revived as an afternoon show in the early 2000s.

Coronation Street – The UK's longest-running TV soap (*The Archers*, on the radio, has been going longer), first broadcast in 1960, set in the fictional Weatherfield, which seems a lot like the real Salford. The present author has never watched a single episode. Just minutes after finishing the story, I saw a story ('CORRIE CALL IN GHOST BUSTER') in the tabloid *Daily Star* about an alleged haunting on the set of the show which parallels the events of 'The Serial Murders'. Spooky.

ylang-ylang – Perfume derived from the flower of the cananga (or custard-apple) tree.

National Front – A far-right (oh, all right, fascist) British political party; in the 1970s, openly racist and noisy with it.

lose their deposit – To stand in a parliamentary election, a candidate must post a sum of money which is forfeit if they poll less than an eighth of the popular vote. From 1918 to 1985, the deposit was £150; now, it's £500. Though fringe parties of the right, left and satirical (e.g. The Monster Raving Loony Party) traditionally lose their deposits and aren't fussed about it, any candidate of a major party who suffers this fate is greatly humiliated.

Guy Fawkes Night – 5 November, aka Bonfire Night. So named for a Catholic plotter who tried to blow up the Houses of Parliament and is still burned in effigy ('the guy') on bonfires. Associated with fireworks displays. In Lewes, Sussex, they symbolically burn the Pope.

Eugène Sue – Author (1804–1857) of *Les Mystères de Paris* (*The Mysteries of Paris*, 1842–1843) and *Le Juif errant* (*The Wandering Jew*, 1845).

Whistler forced George Du Maurier to rewrite *Trilby* to take out some digs at him – The artist Joseph Whistler objected to a caricature of him as 'Joe Sibley' in the serial version of Du Maurier's novel – which he rewrote for book publication to omit the offending material. The original version has been restored in modern editions.

Clive James – Australian-born cultural commentator, long resident in Britain. He was the TV critic for the *Observer* from 1972 to 1982; his columns are collected in *Visions Before Midnight* and *The Crystal Bucket*.

rag trade – Garment industry.

Haslemere – Mid-sized town in Surrey.

Home Counties – The counties which border London: definitively Surrey, Kent, Middlesex, Essex; arguably, Berkshire, Hertfordshire and Buckinghamshire. The stereotypical haunt of the upper-middle classes. Conservative candidates rarely lose their deposits in Home Counties elections.

Home Service – One of three BBC radio channels – the others being the Light Programme and the Third Programme – from 1939 to 1970; it was replaced by Radio 4, which is still on the air.

Celia Johnson – Star of *Brief Encounter* (1945), famous for her clipped, 'cut-glass' English accent.

Dick Barton, Special Agent – BBC radio adventure serial on the Light Programme, from 1946 to 1951. At the height of its popularity, fifteen million listeners followed the adventures of ex-commando Dick and his pals Jock (a Scotsman) and Snowy (a cockney) as they defied foreign baddies. There were three Dick Barton films in the early 1950s.

Journey into Space – A series of BBC radio science fiction serials, broadcast on the Light Programme, beginning with 'Operation Luna' in 1953.

reptiles – Derogatory slang, yellow press reporters or paparazzi. The term is often used by people in the PR business.

ginormous – Large.

Financial Times – UK equivalent of the *Wall Street Journal*. Published on pink paper.

Cluedo – UK trade-name for the board-game known in the US as Clue.

Fortnum's – Posh department store. Formally, Fortnum and Mason's.

Round the Horne – BBC radio comedy programme, hosted by Kenneth Horne. The performers Kenneth Williams and Hugh Paddick played recurring characters, Julian and Sandy, who popularised camp patois ('polari') at a time when male homosexuality was technically a criminal offence. 'How bona to vada your eek,' means 'How nice to see your face.'

mangle-worzel – White turnip. The vegetable, hence the accent, is associated with the West Country (Somerset, Devon, Dorset, Cornwall).

Mummerset – Another term for a non-specific West Country accent, like that used by Robert Newton as Long John Silver (or, more often, people impersonating Robert Newton as Long John Silver) and, indeed, many screen pirates.

chits – Invoices.

full English – Cooked breakfast.

Norton – British make of motorbike.

three-piece suite – A sofa and two armchairs, inevitable in the parlours of lower-middle-class or upper-working-class families with aspirations to gentility.

looney bin – Insane asylum, bug-house, nut-hatch.

sides – Theatrical term for an actor's lines.

oiks – Low-class brutes.

Harold Steptoe – The long-suffering son, played by Harry H. Corbett, in the classic BBC TV sitcom *Steptoe and Son* (1962–75), which was Americanised as *Sanford and Son*.

Barclay's Bank – High street bank, much boycotted in the 1970s for its ties with apartheid-era South Africa.

Bradford – Town in Yorkshire.

vest – Undershirt, not a waistcoat.

'Penny for the Guy' – The cry of children soliciting coins for showing off their stuffed effigies of Guy Fawkes in the build-up to Guy Fawkes Night.

Peter Wyngarde – A 1970s icon in the shows *Department S* and *Jason King*, playing a dandyish fashion-plate mystery novelist turned detective. He's also in *The Innocents* as a ghost, *Night of the Eagle*, the 'Touch of Brimstone' episode of *The Avengers* and the remake of *Flash Gordon*.

Spotlight – The UK directory of actors.

War on Want – A charity campaign.

structuralists – Followers of a critical school, ascendant in Academe in the 1970s.

Frank Bough – UK TV sports commentator and news presenter, roughly equivalent to Howard Cosell in America.

we're on a sticky wicket, up against the ropes, down to the last man, and facing a penalty in injury time – Bad situations in cricket, boxing, cricket and soccer.

keys-in-a-bowl parties – A 1970s thing. You had to be there. Or maybe best not.

Steenbeck – A flatbed film editing machine.

TV Times – ITV's TV listings magazine.

goolies – Testicles.

the worst bits of James Herbert – Usually castration-anxiety fantasies with extra adjectives (cf. *The Rats, The Fog*). The word 'nasty', as applied to 'video nasties' in the 1980s, was devised to describe the brand of moist paperback horror of which Herbert was the pre-eminent 1970s practitioner, followed by the even more prolific Guy N. Smith (*Night of the Crabs, The Sucking Pit*).

Clarks tracker shoes – They had animal footprints on the soles, so you left tracks with them.

Triumph TR7 – Not the best car ever made in Great Britain.

titfer – Hat. Rhyming slang, tit fer tat = hat.

Dennis Potter – UK TV playwright – famous for, among others, *Pennies From Heaven* and *The Singing Detective*.

Alan Plater – UK TV writer, who debuted on the seminal cop

series *Z-Cars* and has scripted
many series and serials, like *The
Beiderbecke Affair*, *Flambards*
and *A Very British Coup*.
Farrah hair – A 'do popularised by
Farrah Fawcett.

Dad's Army – Classic BBC sitcom
set in World War Two, about the
Home Guard.
shove ha'penny – A pub game, which
involves competitively shoving
small coins across a board.

⇒ Cold Snap ⇐

dustbin – Ash-can.
Jean-Claude Killy – French ski
champion.
Bernard Levin – Journalist, author
and broadcaster – a very familiar
TV pundit in the 1960s and 1970s.
Late Night Line-Up – A BBC TV
show that ran on BBC Two from
1964 to 1972. Its original remit
was to publicise other programmes
on the then-new channel, but this
expanded to cover many cultural,
political and media topics.
Charles Shaar Murray – Journalist,
who specialises in pop music.
He was at *IT* between spells at
Oz and the *NME*. He wrote the
introduction to *In Dreams*, an
original anthology I edited with
Paul J. McAuley.
IT – The *International Times*, an
'underground' paper published
from 1966.
**Leo Dare, Isidore Persano,
Colonel Zenf** – Stories for
which the world is not ready,
but see 'A Drug on the Market'
for Dare and 'Sorcerer Conjurer
Wizard Witch' (*The Secret Files
of the Diogenes Club*) for Persano
and Zenf.
**Derek Leech had popped up
apparently out of nowhere in
1961** – In the first chapter of *The*

Quorum, actually.
Brian Epstein – The Beatles'
manager.
Enoch Powell – Politician of the
1950s–1980s, who left the
Conservatives to join the Ulster
Unionists. A controversial figure
(to put it mildly), he famously
espoused anti-immigration and
repatriation policies (as expressed
in his racially inflammatory
'rivers of blood' speech). Arthur
Wise's novel *Who Killed Enoch
Powell?* (1972) imagines his
assassination.
Mary Millington – The leading
British porn star of the 1970s.
She appeared in films (*Come
Play With Me*, *The Playbirds*),
stag reels and many magazine
and newspaper spreads. She
claimed to have had a one-night
stand with Harold Wilson, and
committed suicide at the age of
thirty-three in 1979.
Jimmy Saville – Disc jockey and
TV personality, host of the long-
running *Jim'll Fix It*, and known
in the 1970s for creepy road-
safety adverts ('clunk-click, every
trup') in which he smarmed over
children who'd been horribly
mangled in car accidents.
Posthumously revealed to be a

serial sexual abuser of monstrous proportions.

Wedgy Benn – Anthony Wedgwood Benn, Lord Stansgate – who gave up his title and spent decades trying to get the media to call him Tony Benn. A minister in the Wilson government of the 1960s, later a left-wing gadfly.

Billy Butlin – The founder of Butlins Holiday Camps.

Zenith the Albino – Anthony Zenith, dilettante master criminal, most active in the 1920s and 1930s, repeatedly clashing with the detective Sexton Blake. See *Monsieur Zenith the Albino* (1936) by Anthony Skene. Reported killed in the blitz, but we'll take the word of a Dr Shade over hearsay…

Albert Steptoe – The 'dirty old man' played by Wilfrid Brambell in the BBC TV sitcom *Steptoe and Son* (1962–75).

my O-level results – Or CSEs. O levels and Certificates of Secondary Education were exams taken in the 1970s by UK schoolchildren at about sixteen.

Brain of Britain – A radio quiz programme. It's still running.

Bertie Bassett – The mascot of the Bassett confectionery line, manufacturers of liquorice allsorts.

Gary Glitter – UK pop performer, prominent in the early 1970s 'glam rock' trend with hits like 'Rock and Roll, Parts 1 and 2' and 'I'm the Leader of the Gang (I Am)'. He is one of several 1970s entertainment figures now best known for being convicted of child sexual abuse. In current rhyming slang, 'the Gary' means 'rectum' (Gary Glitter = shitter).

Worm War, Wizard War – See 'Sorcerer Conjurer Wizard Witch' (*Secret Files of the Diogenes Club*).

Duel of the Seven Stars – See 'Seven Stars' (*Secret Files of the Diogenes Club*).

Janet and John – The UK equivalent of Dick and Jane – much better brought-up, they wouldn't dream of running after Spot but would walk politely after the dog.

the Great Edmondo – Robert Edmond Stone, see 'Sorcerer Conjurer Wizard Witch' (*Secret Files of the Diogenes Club*). Edmondo was the Conjurer.

Nigel and Joanne Karabatsos – See 'Mother Hen' (reprinted in *The Quorum*).

Kitten Kong – A well-remembered 1971 episode of the BBC TV series *The Goodies* features a giant cat which climbs the Post Office Tower.

⇒ The Man Who Got Off the Ghost Train ⇐

British Rail – The national railway service between the 1940s, when the UK's private rail companies were amalgamated under public ownership, and 1997, when the dying John Major government broke up the network and sold it off again. People used to complain about British Rail – but anyone who's tried to get from London to Manchester on one of Richard Branson's Virgin trains now looks back on that era with a rosy glow of nostalgia tinged with unforgiving resentment for the politicians who decided the railways should benefit stock-holders rather than passengers.

bin-men – Garbage collectors.

fag-end – Literally, a cigarette butt; colloquially, the remainder of anything that's been used up.

time-and-motion study – An efficiency survey.

funk – Panic.

ticked off – Irritated.

slam-door diesel – Type of train in use in the 1980s.

Benson & Hedges – Cigarette brand.

Bunty – Girls' comic.

The Lady – Uppercrust magazine.

Patrick Mower – UK actor, a familiar face in film (*The Devil Rides Out, Cry of the Banshee*) and on TV (*Callan, Target*).

Tit-Bits – A bland gossip magazine.

Robot Archie – A comic strip character.

Lion – A British weekly comic. Besides Archie, it ran the adventures of master criminal 'The Spider'.

Number Ten – No 10, Downing Street, the office and official residence of the Prime Minister.

LSE – London School of Economics.

Manchester Poly – Manchester Polytechnic.

RADA – Royal Academy of Dramatic Art.

All Souls – A college at Oxford University.

the Old Vic – A London theatre.

Larry Parnes – Promoter of Tommy Steele, Billy Fury, etc.

Health & Efficiency – The official magazine of the British naturist movement.

short back and sides – A severe haircut.

angry young men – Writers like Kingsley Amis and John Osborne, who later got older but didn't stop being angry.

Ronnie Scott's – Jazz club in Soho.

passed the conch to Catriona – Let Catriona speak. The expression comes from William Golding's *Lord of the Flies*.

Lady Lucinda Tregellis-d'Aulney – See 'Clubland Heroes' (*Secret Files of the Diogenes Club*).

the interregnum – The period between the execution of Charles I (1649) and the coronation of Charles II (1660).

a navvy – A 'navigator', one of the workmen who lay and maintain railway tracks.

Windmill Girl – One of the nude tableau performers at London's Windmill Theatre.

Elsie and Doris Waters – Variety artistes, known for their act as 'Gert and Daisy'.

Ribena – A diluted fruit drink.

Archie Andrews – Britain's answer to Charlie McCarthy, a ventriloquist's dummy popular on the radio with the long-running programme *Educating Archie*. Archie was worked by ventriloquist Peter Brough, who never chopped off his own fingers. Miss Kaye is probably thinking of Hugo, the nastier dummy operated by the tragic Maxwell Frere – whose personality disorder inspired numberless *Twilight Zone* episodes.

Aldermaston marches – CND protests, regularly held at Easter.

Borley Rectory – The most haunted house in Great Britain, allegedly.

cold spots – Patches of unnatural chill, often found in haunted places. Maybe not unconnected to the fact that haunted houses tend to be draughty.

a butchers – Rhyming slang: butcher's hook = look.

rag week – Period when students pull hilarious pranks and dress up in silly costumes to raise money for charity. It's stupid and irritating but, unlike equivalent American college traditions, doesn't involve torturing other students and at least notionally benefits good causes.

Biro – Ballpoint pen, so named for the inventors, Messrs Biró.

five one-pound notes – For decades, the standard fine for pulling the communication cord on a British train without good reason was five pounds. Eventually, that seemed like a small price to pay for just seeing what would happen.

Gene Krupa – A virtuoso jazz drummer.

Naked as Nature Intended – A nudist-camp film, starring Pamela Green. Directed by Harrison Marks.

a funny – A joke.

primary school – Grade school.

Sabrina – A UK pin-up and television personality of the 1950s.

snoek – Snake mackerel, a staple food during wartime shortages (often rumoured to be whale meat).

gyppy tummy – Upset stomach.

striding to the crease – Going in to bat at cricket.

Burton's – Menswear chain.

Escher space – Named after the artist M.C. Escher, who drew paradoxical pictures playing with perspective and gravity.

⇢ Swellhead ⇠

CI – Chief Inspector.

warrant card – British police ID.

Charles Beauregard – See *Anno Dracula*, *The Bloody Red Baron*, *Dracula Cha Cha Cha*, *Secret Files of the Diogenes Club*.

quango – Quasi non-governmental organisation – a publicly financed body, but (theoretically) independent of the government of the day.

wellies – Wellington boots.

Maltesers – UK confectionery – small spherical malt honeycombs coated with chocolate.

Patricia Cornwell – The US crime writer believes that the Victorian painter Walter Sickert was Jack the Ripper, and has been known to buy and dissect his works in pursuit of 'evidence'.

gin and it – A sweet Martini. The 'it'

is red vermouth.

Duke – Duke University, home of the Rhine Research Center Institute for Parapsychology.

sweet shop – Candy store.

Coal Hill Secondary Modern – See *Time and Relative*.

Juliet Bravo – A UK TV series about a policewoman; the title refers to the heroine's call-sign rather than her name, Jean Darblay.

Blackpool's Golden Mile – A string of seafront amusement arcades, tourist attractions, casinos and the like in the Northern resort town. Dick Barton and Adam Adamant both saved it from diabolical schemes.

Ascot – Royal Ascot, a major horse-racing meet, prominent in the English social calendar. Eliza Doolittle causes a stir there in *My Fair Lady*.

John O'Groats – The Northernmost spot on the British mainland.

Fisherman's Friend – A make of strong, semi-medicinal lozenge, created in Lancashire in 1865 and marketed to the men of the fishing fleet as a means of assuaging respiratory problems.

Angel Down, Sussex – See 'Angel Down, Sussex' (*Secret Files of the Diogenes Club*).

Seven Stars – See 'Seven Stars' (*Secret Files of the Diogenes Club*).

Henry Merrivale – Sir Henry Merrivale See *The Plague Court Murders* by Carter Dickson (John Dickson Carr), et seq.

Katharine Reed – See *Anno Dracula*, *The Bloody Red Baron*, *Dracula Cha Cha Cha*, *Secret Files of the Diogenes Club*, *Angels of Music*.

Catriona Kaye – See *Jago*, *Secret Files of the Diogenes Club*, *The Secrets of Drearcliff Grange School*, *An English Ghost Story*.

Dion Fortune – Born Violet Firth (1891–1946), English magician and author (*The Secrets of Dr Taverner*, etc.).

Any Questions? – Long-running BBC Radio topical debate programme. The television version is called *Question Time*.

Wembley – The English national football stadium, also used for other sports and large concerts.

Jodrell Bank – An observatory, home to the UK's vast array of radio telescopes.

bumfreezer jacket – A short jacket, obviously.

Flaming Nora! – An expletive of astonishment.

Cantab – A graduate of Cambridge University, abbr. for the pseudo-Latin term cantabrigiensis.

tuck shop – In-school sweet (candy) shop.

six of the best – Six strokes of the cane on the buttocks – traditionally, a significant corporal punishment.

Sergeant Arthur Grimshaw – See 'Teddy Bears' Picnic' in *Back in the USSA* (with Eugene Byrne). See also *Carry On Sergeant*, with William Hartnell.

National Service – Mandatory spell of military service, introduced in the UK in 1939 and extended by a parliamentary act of 1949 (which did not apply in Northern Ireland) until 1960. Young men over the age of eighteen were required to spend two years in the armed forces – or the Forestry Commission if they made an especial fuss about not wanting to shoot people – and remain on the reserves list for a further five years. Never as fiercely resisted, for obvious reasons, as the American draft of the Vietnam War, National Service produced a trickle of grumbling books (Leslie Thomas's *The Virgin Soldiers*) and plays (Arnold Wesker's *Chips With Everything*) about the inequities of the system.

Bognor – Especially dull seaside town in Sussex. After King George V visited in 1929, the place took to calling itself 'Bognor Regis' – though it was never given formal permission to add the royal honorific. Reputedly, the King's last words, upon being told he would soon recover enough to return to the town, were 'Bugger Bognor!' And no wonder.

'Tears for Souvenirs' – Truly horrible hit record. Don't let anyone tell you the charts in the 1960s were exclusively full of great music – Ken Dodd, perhaps most familiar to non-UK viewers as Yorick in Kenneth Branagh's *Hamlet*, was more successful in record sales in Britain than Jimi Hendrix.

Stone Tape – Expression coined by Nigel Kneale for the TV play *The Stone Tape* (1972), describing the theory that 'ghosts' are recordings that play back under certain circumstances.

meter maid – A uniformed traffic warden.

Pirelli calendar – Posh girlie calendar, sponsored by the tyre company.

Porton Down – The Defence Science and Technology Laboratory, where the United Kingdom carries out its (defensive) biological and chemical weapons research.

Angry Brigade – A British libertarian communist guerrilla movement, responsible for a string of bombings between 1970 and 1972. They did a lot of property damage, but only slightly hurt one person.

SAS – Special Air Service. UK equivalent of Navy SEALs or Special Forces.

Common Agricultural Policy – Controversial (i.e. unjust and unworkable) EU system of farm subsidies, much beloved by French farmers.

cash machine – ATM.

Heath Robinson – William Heath Robinson (1872–1944), a British illustrator who specialised in elaborate, ramshackle machines. The American Rube Goldberg is an exact equivalent.

~≈ AFTERWORD ≈~

Here's how these stories happened.

In the 1990s, Stephen Jones edited an anthology called *Dark Detectives: Adventures of the Supernatural Sleuths*, dedicated to the sub-category of weird tale in which detectives, in the traditions of Sherlock Holmes or Philip Marlowe, tackle cases which involve the supernatural or the strange. The book represented William Hope Hodgson's Carnacki the Ghost-Finder, Manly Wade Wellman's John Thunstone, Clive Barker's Harry D'Amour and Jay Russell's Marty Burns. Also in the magnifying-glass-and-wooden-stake business are Algernon Blackwood's John Silence, Anthony Boucher's Fergus O'Breen, Bram Stoker's (and Chris Roberson's – but not Stephen Sommers's) Van Helsing, *The X-Files'* Mulder and Scully, Jeff Rice's (and Dan Curtis's, Richard Matheson's, Darren McGavin's and David Case's) Carl Kolchak and a run of comic-book or -strip characters famous (Dr Strange, Batman in a certain mood), middling cult (the Phantom Stranger, Zatanna) or obscure (Cursitor Doom, anyone? Dr Thirteen?).

Steve asked me to contribute to the book. I'll let him describe what happened next. 'After I had explained to Kim that the book would be themed along a loosely assembled chronology, we came up with the concept (probably over glasses of wine and beer) that it would be fun to have one serial-like case which would be investigated across the centuries by many of the characters he had created in his earlier novels and stories. These episodes would then be interspersed amongst the contributions from other writers to the book.' Since part of the point of doing sleuth stories is that you can do a whole series – unless, like E. C. Bentley, you kick off with a book called *Trent's Last Case* – my plan was to have the serial that wound up being called 'Seven Stars' feature detectives I'd written about in earlier stories or novels. The Victorian section ('The Mummy's Heart') revisits adventurer Charles Beauregard and journalist Kate Reed, who were in *Anno Dracula*; a WWII-set Los Angeles interlude ('The Trouble With Barrymore') uses the anonymous narrator (plainly, a version of Raymond Chandler's Philip Marlowe) who'd been in a Lovecraft–Chandler pastiche called 'The Big Fish'; the 'contemporary' 1990s section ('Mimsy') is a semi-sequel to my novel *The Quorum*, featuring London private eye/single mum Sally Rhodes, etc.

'The only problem,' Steve says, 'was that Kim did not have a psychic investigator for the period covering the 1970s. Of course that was no problem for Kim, who simply went back to his very first efforts at fiction while still a schoolboy and revived the character of ostentatious amnesiac Richard Jeperson, along with his striking associate Vanessa and ex-police constable Fred Regent. Inspired by such TV characters as Jason King, the Avengers, Jon Pertwee's Doctor Who and the novels of Peter Saxon and Frank Lauria, Jeperson made his official debut with the novella "The End of the Pier Show" in my 1997 anthology *Dark of the Night: New Tales of Horror and the Supernatural*.' Since then, Jeperson has made further appearances in the stories collected here. Thanks and credit are due to Steve and other editors who have commissioned, edited and published (and republished) them. *The Man From the Diogenes Club* isn't quite the complete Richard Jeperson. I've omitted 'The Biafran Bank Manager', the episode of 'Seven Stars' he was revived for in the first place: it features significant moments in the history of the Diogenes Club (the death of Richard's mentor, Edwin Winthrop), but is too tied in with the overall story to work as a stand-alone. *Dark Detectives* has also been reissued, so it's easy enough to fill in the gap. Furthermore, continuing my habit of presenting alternate versions of my characters (blame Michael Moorcock for this, or else those DC Comics 'Imaginary Stories'), Richard and the Diogenes Club feature in alternate timelines in 'The Man on the Clapham Omnibus' in *The Second Time Out Book of London Short Stories*, edited by Nicholas Royle (reprinted as an extra in the Titan edition of *Jago*), and the Anno Dracula novel *Johnny Alucard*.

To backtrack, where did Richard Jeperson come from?

As Steve said, my very first efforts at fiction. In the 1970s, I was growing up – which is probably obvious from this book. As a schoolboy and later a university student, I wrote essays, plays, stories, attempted novels, pastiches, humour, sketches, long letters, scripts, comic strips, gossip, filmographies, book and film reviews, articles, fanzine filler, song lyrics, a pantomime, monologues, musicals, etc. Almost all this stuff was disposable, though I showed some of it to friends. By the early 1980s, I was getting plays performed and songs sung, even as I segued into more or less above-ground publication. None of this is unusual: you learn to write by writing, and you need to produce millions of words of rubbish before you get anywhere. I started early on my rubbish. You may not think much of me now, but – trust me – the juvenilia was much, much worse.

At the age of eleven, in 1970–71, I wrote 'plays' – cursory adaptations of Universal or Hammer horror films roughly put on in drama lessons at Dr Morgan's Grammar School. Don't be too hasty to sneer – Stephen King started out by handing round his 'novelisation' of Roger Corman's *Pit and the Pendulum* on his playground. Like Universal and Hammer, I got into sequels quickly: after a one-page *Dracula*, I followed up with *Dracula Returns*. This wasn't an adaptation, though originality was not a strong suit: the plot featured a honeymooning English couple menaced by Dracula (another long-running character in my work) in Transylvania. I described a certain castle as having 'turrets reeking of evil', which explains why I'm not reproducing any more of my teenage prose here. Our heroes were Richard Jeperson, occultist know-it-all, and his new wife, Vanessa. Watched by some classmates, I played Dracula, and Brian Smedley – who later wrote the music for some of my theatrical efforts, including *The Gold-Diggers of 1981* and the near-legendary 'Rock Rock Rock Rock Rock Rock Rock Rock Rock Rock Rock Rock Rock Rock Rock Rock Rock Rock Rock Rock Rock Rock Rock Rock Rock Rock Rock Rock Rock Rock Rock Rock Rock Rock' (with Eugene Byrne and Neil Gaiman) – was Richard Jeperson. Dr Morgan's was an all-boys' school, so it's no wonder the player cast as Vanessa didn't make enough of an impression for me to remember who he was.

In the early 1970s, I typed up a book's-worth of Richard Jeperson stories, in which he mixed with more vampires, mummies, a golem, a zombie in a bikini (I should get round to rewriting that one), a secret society, lost civilisations, etc. In these, he picked up some of the supporting cast who're still around – sidekick Fred Regent, gloomy Welsh Inspector Price, exotic Zarana (originally an Ancient Egyptian princess, though I like her more as a stripper) – and the idea that he was part of an extended 'family' of ghost-hunters. In 1973, I even wrote a novel, *The Amazing Dr Leon Theodore Karell*, in which he was a supporting character: the lead was a music-hall magician revived a hundred years on as a heroic vampire (I was mixing the premises of *Adam Adamant Lives!* and *Blacula*). The best thing to be said about this effort was that I finished it – I even sent it to a publisher (who sent it back). After that, I got on with other things. I doubt if I gave a moment's thought to Richard until *Dark Detectives* came up – though, now I come to think of it, Charles Beauregard, hero of the Anno Dracula books, was in the flashback sequences of *The Amazing Dr etc.*, so this stuff has been creeping back into my work through the years. The lesson is: never throw anything away.

Besides me being grown-up and less impressed by reeking turrets, things had changed for Richard between 1973 and 1997. I decided he and Vanessa weren't married, for a start: because I wanted them to have one of those Steed-and-Mrs Peel relationships. And I had a backer for his adventuring. In the Anno Dracula books and other odd stories (like 'Angel Down, Sussex'), I'd been working out a history for the Diogenes Club, sponsor of several generations of my investigative characters. This was especially useful for the 'pass the parcel' plot of 'Seven Stars'. The Club comes from Sir Arthur Conan Doyle's Sherlock Holmes stories (read 'The Greek Interpreter', if you want to check out its first appearance) but my version was specifically inspired by Billy Wilder and I. A.L. Diamond in *The Private Life of Sherlock Holmes*, where it's a covert, high-handed British secret service responsible for passing off an experimental submarine as the Loch Ness monster. Like Alan Moore in *League of Extraordinary Gentlemen*, I was influenced by Philip José Farmer's Tarzan and Doc Savage biographies, with their complex family tree of other people's fictional characters. There's less of that in these stories than in the Anno Dracula books – though score extra points for ticking off Carnacki, Flaxman Low, Sir Henry Merrivale and one or two others, not to mention knowing where in my work you can meet Myra Lark, General Skinner, Stacy Cotterill and Heather Wilding (some answers in the Glossary). Borrowed folk who pop in here and have been in other Newman (or Newman–Byrne) efforts include Colonel Moran and Sergeant Grimshaw.

When I created Richard, I gave no thought to him as a

'typical' character of the 1970s. This wasn't just because I was eleven: I didn't think of Sally Rhodes as a 1980s/1990s character when I created her, but the stories she appears in now seem to me rooted in those decades. When I went back to Richard, I saw that he was a very 1970s fellow, and I spotted all the influences Steve later pointed out, and made an effort to work in even more. A few remain well-enough known to need no further explanation: *The Avengers*, a 1960s show well remembered in the 1970s (and sequelised in *The New Avengers*), and various incarnations of the Sherlock Holmes, Doctor Who or James Bond franchises (even Scooby-Doo's Mystery, Inc.). But also in the mix that informs Jeperson and his world are less often-repeated UK TV series: psychic detective efforts like *Ace of Wands* (little Neil Gaiman's favourite – about a mystery-solving magician named Tarot and his owl Ozymandias) and *The Omega Factor* (ESP and spy stuff from 1979 – now out on DVD) and Victoriana like *The Rivals of Sherlock Holmes* (with Donald Pleasence in one episode as Carnacki) and Robert Muller's *Supernatural* (about a tale-tellers' institution, the Club of the Damned). While Columbo, McCloud, Kolchak, Rockford, et al., were busy in America, British television had 'tecs, cops and spies like Jason King (played by Peter Wyngarde in *Department S* and the sillier sequel series *Jason King*), Marker (Alfred Burke in *Public Eye*), Callan (Edward Woodward – Best Spy Show Ever, it's official!), Barlow and Watt (Stratford Johns and Frank Windsor, who started in realistic shows like *Z Cars* and *Softly, Softly*, then moved to poring over historical evidence about Jack the Ripper and Richard III), Paul Temple (Francis Matthews), The Incredible Robert Baldick (a terrific one-off by Terry Nation, starring Robert Hardy), Eddie Shoestring (Trevor Eve) and the Professionals.

Also, the racks at W. H. Smith's were loaded with 30p-a-throw paperbacks mingling mystery and the occult, often with a vaguely counterculture tinge and under 120 pages: Robert Lory's Dracula series (which began, like Richard Jeperson, with an instalment called *Dracula Returns*), Frank Lauria's books about Owen Orient (*Doctor Orient*, *Lady Sativa*), Philip José Farmer's racy *Image of the Beast* and *Blown*, Peter Saxon's 'Guardians' series (*The Haunting of Alan Mais*, *The Killing Bone*, etc.), Michael Avallone's 'Satan Sleuth' series (*The Werewolf Walks Tonight*, *Devil, Devil*), Richard Tate's lone 'Marcus Obadiah Mystery' *For the Dead Travel Fast*, anthologies edited by Michel Parry and Peter Haining, *Demons by Daylight* by Ramsey Campbell (who'd started writing when he wasn't much older than I was then – and was much better at it), and pulpy New English Library one-offs like *Night of the Vampire* or *Village of Blood*. These were the things I read in the 1970s, and which percolated – along with fashions, music, food, politics, jokes, interior design (we had inflatable chairs in our living room, which was papered with pictures clipped from Sunday supplements), attitudes, haircuts, scandals, slang – in my subconscious for the years I wasn't thinking of writing about Richard Jeperson. When I came to him again, all this stuff bubbled up, and filled out his world. Most of the stories started with me thinking about aspects of the 1970s or vintage occult mystery fiction I wanted to play with – left-over seaside arcades (I remember working dioramas exactly like the execution collection in 'End of the Pier Show') and the brand of hooliganism found in NEL books popular at my school (*Skinhead*, etc., by Richard Allen – author, under another name, of *Dracula and the Virgins of the Undead*), the changing tone of British smut, brainwashing camps in picturesque countryside retreats like in *The Prisoner*, something set on a train (a 1960s TV serial had Laurence Payne as Sexton Blake solving a mystery on a train), the huge underground installations blown up at the end of every Bond film, etc.

The 1970s were bright, but grim: glam rock and the three-day week, moon missions and Watergate, *The Man Who Fell to Earth* and *Star Wars*. I didn't 'get' a lot of it while it was going on, but I keep being pulled back there – I suspect everyone feels that way about the decade they spent between the ages of ten and twenty, but the 1970s really were an up-in-the-air era, between the openness of the Swinging Sixties and the oppression of the Iron Eighties.

Richard Jeperson was there. He knows what really happened. And now, so do you.

Kim Newman, London, 2005 (rev. 2017)

ACKNOWLEDGEMENTS

Thanks to the original editors of these stories: Chris Roberson, Bill Sheehan and William Schafer, Ellen Datlow and Stephen Jones.

ABOUT THE AUTHOR

Kim Newman is a novelist, critic and broadcaster. His fiction includes *The Night Mayor*, *Bad Dreams*, *Jago*, the Anno Dracula novels and stories, *The Quorum* and *Life's Lottery*, all currently being reissued by Titan Books, *Professor Moriarty: The Hound of the D'Urbervilles* published by Titan Books and *The Vampire Genevieve* and *Orgy of the Blood Parasites* as Jack Yeovil. The critically acclaimed *An English Ghost Story*, which was nominated for the inaugural James Herbert Award, and most recently, *Angels of Music*, are also published by Titan Books. His non-fiction books include the influential *Nightmare Movies* (recently reissued by Bloomsbury in an updated edition), *Ghastly Beyond Belief* (with Neil Gaiman), *Horror: 100 Best Books* (with Stephen Jones), *Wild West Movies*, *The BFI Companion to Horror*, *Millennium Movies*, *BFI Classics* studies of *Cat People* and *Doctor Who*, and *Video Dungeon*, a collection of his popular *Empire* magazine columns of the same name.

He is a contributing editor to *Sight & Sound* and *Empire* magazines, has written and broadcast widely on a range of topics, and scripted radio and television documentaries. His stories 'Week Woman' and 'Übermensch' have been adapted into an episode of the TV series *The Hunger* and an Australian short film; he has directed and written a tiny film, *Missing Girl*. Following his Radio 4 play 'Cry Babies', he wrote an episode ('Phish Phood') for Radio 7's series *The Man in Black*.

Follow him on Twitter @annodracula. His official website can be found at www.johnnyalucard.com.

For more fantastic fiction, author events, exclusive
excerpts, competitions, limited editions and more

VISIT OUR WEBSITE
titanbooks.com

LIKE US ON FACEBOOK
facebook.com/titanbooks

FOLLOW US ON TWITTER
@TitanBooks

EMAIL US
readerfeedback@titanemail.com